Destiny's Conflict

Janny Wurts

DESTINY'S CONFLICT

The Wars of Light and Shadow

VOLUME 10

SECOND BOOK OF THE
SWORD OF THE CANON

Harper*Voyager* an imprint of
HarperCollins*Publishers* Ltd
1 London Bridge Street
London SE1 9GF

www.harpercollins.co.uk

First published by HarperCollins*Publishers* 2017
1

A catalogue record for this book is available from the British Library

HB ISBN: 978-0-00-823002-9
TPB ISBN: 978-0-00-731391-4

Typeset in Palatino by Palimpsest Book Production Ltd, Falkirk, Stirlingshire

Printed and bound in the UK by CPI Group (UK) Ltd, Croydon, CR0 4YY

MIX
Paper from
responsible sources
FSC
www.fsc.org
FSC C007454

For my brother Jay Wurts
and Suzanne Niles

in memory of my first offshore voyage
on their yawl
Skywave

This story was aboard, all along

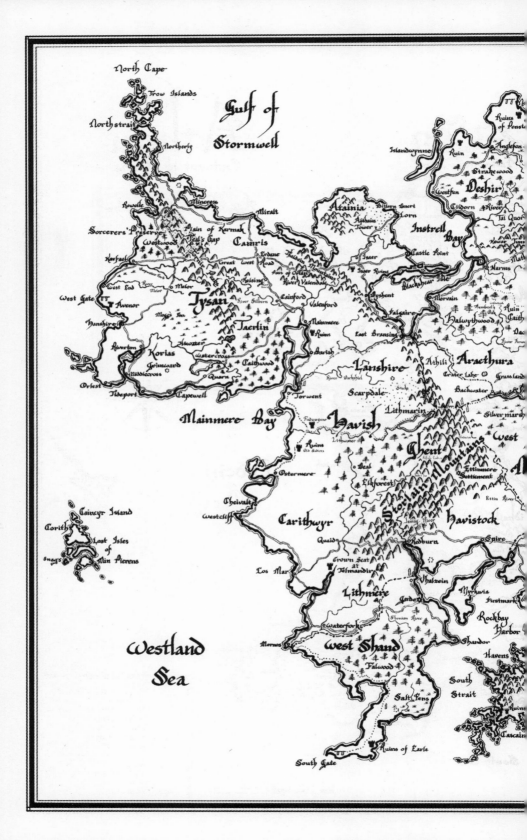

Athera
Continent of Paravia

Age of the Mistwraithe

N

Cildein
Ocean

Los Lier

South Sea

	Town		✿	Grimward
	Ancient Ruin			
	Unvanquished Town			
	Worldsend Gate			
	Paravian Marker			
	Kingdom Boundary			
	River			
	Forest			Preserve
	Marsh			
	Waste or Desert			
	Roads			
	Mountains			

0 10 25 50 100

© 1986 JANNY WURTS

North Ward
Brimwood
Fallowmere
East Ward
sin of Araithe
Werpoint
Perlorn
Crescent Isle
Etarra
Valleygap
Mountains
Ithilt
Minderl
Bay
thain
Furl Rocks
Karlien
Eastwall
Ramon
Shamon
Minderl Ruin
Minderl Strait
Mountains
Narrens
Valescarp
Saint's Point
East Gate
Athir Ruins
Caelst
Bay of
Eltair
Vaststrait
rockfell
Tharidor
Whitehold
Northstor
sport
Narsee
Eastfair
Varens
Tirans
Perdith
Atwood
Allain
East Halla
Tirans Ruins
idhalla
Mountains
Alestron
Kalesh
Adruin
Mirthlvain
Swamp
Orvandir
ttheisle
Durn
Methlas Lake
Ishlir
Ganish
Six Towers
Lissine
Shand
Atchaz
Alland
Telzen
River Ippash
Scimlade Tip
Merior
rthmark
Selkwood
Sickle Bay
Shaddorn
nnich
Desert of
Sanpashir
River
Southshir
Ruins
Sanshevas

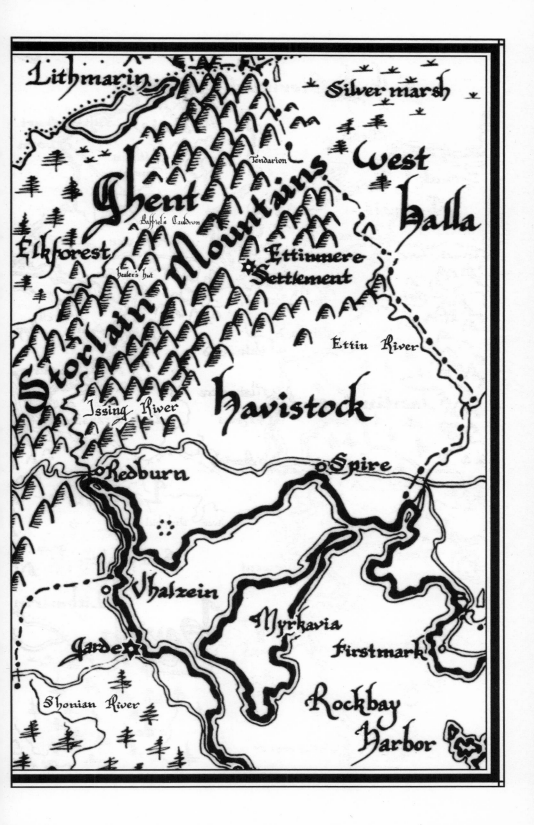

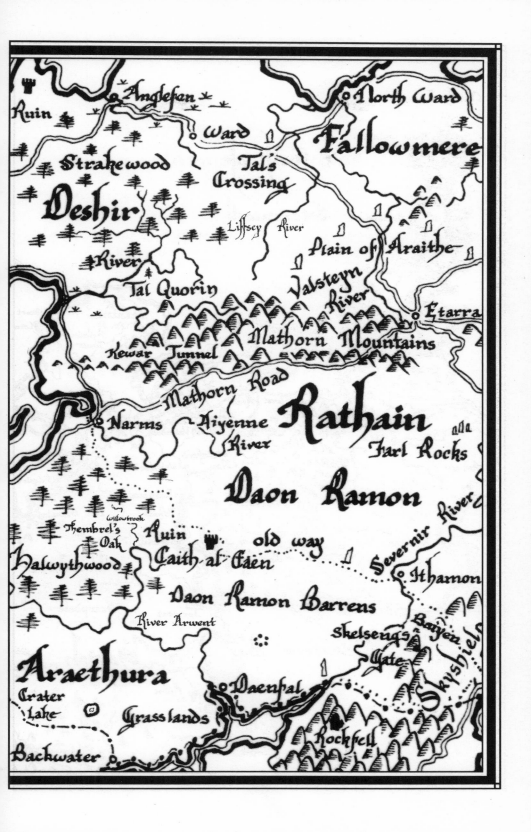

Acknowledgements

Thank you to the following individuals, whose generosity above and beyond the call, walked alongside me as support group and safety net. My thanks goes beyond words, for having my back:

Jeffrey Watson, Andrew Ginever, Giada Romano, Sandra Jacobs;
Robert and Sara Schwager;
Jean Marie Kelly and the heroic crew at
HarperCollins 360;
Editorial and art department,
Natasha Bardon, Lily Cooper, Dominic Forbes,
My agents,
Jonathan Matson, sadly missed;
Ben Camardie, superhero,
And my loving husband,
Don Maitz.

Contents

Sword of the Canon
Timeline with relevant dates

—5671/5672 A rash move: Dakar the Mad Prophet uses his Fellowship authority to attach Rathain's crown with an oath of debt to the Koriathain, enabling Elaira to make use of the sisterhood's knowledge to salvage Prince Arithon's life. While she does invoke her initiate training to recall Arithon's strayed spirit, she alters a very intricate ritual to create a Grand Confluence, making her healer's lore adhere to the Major Balance precepts taught by Ath's adepts. This change based on free will replicates an original, extremely ancient construct, historically stolen from the Biedar tribe by the Koriathain.

—The Biedar crone on Athera intervenes: through Elaira's alteration, she seizes a thread of the working, and when the subsequent conception of a child occurs, calls the spirit of one of her tribal ancients to be reincarnated as Arithon's daughter, born to Glendien at Althain Tower.

—Interim events following Stormed Fortress

—5672 Birth of Teylia to Glendien at Althain Tower.

—Elaira returns to the Koriathain under summons.

—5674 Arithon is betrayed and taken captive by the Koriathain, ignorant of Dakar's oath of debt to the crown, since all that occurred at Athir to save him was kept secret.

—Pressured by the Prime's threat to Elaira's life as leverage to break him, Arithon sequesters all of his memories of her, together with his perilous knowledge of Grey Kralovir necromancy, into the emerald signet ring of Rathain, which is protected under Fellowship auspices, and guarded by Elaira as his handfast beloved.

—5674 The Fellowship Sorcerers gamble with extreme risk: to prevent Arithon's immediate destruction at the hands of the Prime Matriarch, Kharadmon collapses the star wards that are holding back a mass invasion by Marak's free wraiths. Prime Selidie is forced to negotiate, or see the world become devoured, since only a Masterbard's art can ameliorate the threat.

—The Koriani Prime drives a harsh bargain: for a stay of execution, to last only until the last free wraith is settled, she demands that Sethvir surrender guardianship of Teylia to the sisterhood to seal the bargain.

—5676 Teylia is oathsworn as an initiate Koriathain. Her training to become the Prime's successor is a disaster, her untrained power so great that every crystal she touches shatters.

—5683 The Great Schism: Lysaer abandons the Religion of Light in Tysan and retires to the mayor's seat at Etarra. True Sect split of the faithful establishes a High Temple at Erdane.

—5688 Reform Years begin in Rathain: Lysaer's justice creates a treaty with High Earl Barach that establishes fair law and brings stable peace with the clans of Rathain.

—5691 *First Book of Canon Law* and True Sect law is established at Erdane by the True Sect priests.

—5867 Drake War fought to a standstill by Fellowship Sorcerers at Penstair.

—5902 Treaty signed between True Sect zealots in Tysan and the Crown of Havish establishes a tenuous accord, to expire upon the death of the reigning queen.

Initiate's Trial

—5922 Last free wraith from Marak is redeemed, and Arithon's stay of execution is forfeit. On that hour, Teylia arranges for his release, without any of his prior memories, which alters him enough that the Koriathain cannot track him.

—Asandir relinquishes charge of Arithon's fate back to the Prime Matriarch in a formal audience held at Whitehold, where he swears the Fellowship of Seven to a binding of nonintervention.

—The Prime Matriarch's death spell to destroy Arithon through a blood binding backfires and claims Teylia's life in his stead, leaving Arithon as a fugitive on his own devices.

—Arithon takes refuge with Tarens and his family on a croft near Kelsing in Tysan.

—5922 Dakar is summarily discharged as a Fellowship apprentice and evicted from Althain Tower.

—Elaira sets off to seek the Biedar crone and becomes bearer of a flint knife with arcane properties.

—Asandir swears Daliana sen Evend to Lysaer's service to curb the effects of the Mistwraith's curse.

—5922-5923 True Sect priests raid the crofters' home under suspicion they harbour a heretic, and Tarens kills the examiner. He and Arithon take flight under close-pressed pursuit into Caithwood.

—5923 Arithon wakens the wardings of Caithwood to evade an invasion by hostile pursuit, blending ancient knowledge of the Paravians, the Fellowship Sorcerers, and his bard's arts.

—A resonant intersection in time/space allows High Earl Jieret to bequeath his memories to Tarens.

—A plot by Koriathain and True Sect priests triggers the Mistwraith's curse, causing Lysaer to abdicate the mayor's seat at Etarra, join the True Sect cause, and lead the Light's invasion of Havish.

—A bold move by three clan children: Siantra s'Idir, Khadrien, and Esfand s'Valerient steal the sword Alithiel and set off to seek Prince Arithon.

—Tarens falls out with Arithon after a narrow escape from the True Sect at Torwent. The pair part company, Tarens to escort a band of refugees to safe haven with the High King of Havish at Fiaduwynne, and Arithon to take flight eastward, where he hides in plain sight as a healer in the True Sect war host.

—The great drake, Seshkrozchiel, goes into hibernation, and Luhaine, the Fellowship colleague who is still discorporate and therefore able to survive, assumes the burden of Davien's bargain.

—Battle of Lithmarin: The Hatchet's campaign to defeat the crown of Havish and seize Arithon sweeps across Lanshire, pinning Arithon against the shores of Lithmarin. A heroic stand by Havish's war band wins the opening for Arithon's escape, but the activation of the Crown Jewels and the land's attuned power come at the tragic price of High King Gestry's death.

—An impulsive move: Siantra, Esfand, and Khadrien are under Tarens's escort home when Khadrien tries to borrow Asandir's horse to deliver the sword Alithiel to Prince Arithon, who is in flight. The boy gets separated from his companions on the battle-field, and is ignominiously thrown, leaving him unhurt but on foot.

—The loose horse is subsequently caught by Arithon, and the sword it carries is recovered while he flees over the border of Melhalla.

—Dakar and Daliana remove Lysaer from the field at Lithmarin while the war host is still dazed and spirit him away into the barrens of Scarpdale.

Destiny's Conflict

The season is spring in Third Age Year 5923

Late Spring 5923

Stone as my impartial witness, behold!
The Terms of the Fellowship's stay of execution for
Arithon Teir's'Ffalenn are withdrawn.
Crown debt to Rathain, sworn at Athir, is confirmed.
Koriathain are freed to determine his Grace's fate,
henceforward.
—Asandir's oath of nonintervention
witnessed in stone at Whitehold Third Age Year 5922

I. Duress

Lysaer awoke, groggy, his nostrils clogged with the parched taint of volcanic rocks and blown sulphur. His reflexive cough raised an aching complaint from cramped limbs. He lay bound hand and foot. His stubbled cheek rested against the rough boards of a wagon-bed, splotched by old blood-stains and sliced by the shadows cast by a sturdy, spoked wheel. Dizzy and sick, left with the disjointed recall of a battle, Lysaer squinted through glare and identified the transport the surgeons' corps sent to move the Light's wounded.

Which made no sense. He had sustained no injury. Lashed in discomfort, he stirred, annoyed, then lifted his head, furious enough to lambaste the healer who had miscalled his condition. But the wagon loomed empty. No other casualties sprawled, strapped into splints or field bandages. His confused survey met only burlap sacks of provisions, two barrels of ale seared with Cainford tax brands, and a crate of bottled brandy, then the knotted leads fixed to five head of horseflesh, hitched to the cargo rings meant to lash field tents.

Evidently, the dray was not hauling the surgeon's gear in the baggage train. Lysaer heard no chatter, no gossiping wash-women. The baked air was not clouded with dust from the lance companies' ranks or popped by the whip-cracks of the war host's outriders. The vehicle was parked in full sun, in a desert without habitation.

Lysaer gritted his teeth. He tried to roll over, jerked against tight restraint. Whoever bound him also had trussed his frame in oiled canvas. Which extreme measure suggested the horror of madness inflicted by Desh-thiere's curse, and far worse: the recall of a shameful act, fraught with pain sufficient to break him.

He had killed again, wantonly mass murdered innocents in an act beyond human conscience.

The coward in him preferred not to bear what could never be reconciled. Thousands of times, over hundreds of years, the voice of self-censure condemned him: better he died than survive to fall prey to the next wretched bout of insanity. Logic destroyed the weakness of delusion, that he ever had owned the brute will to defeat the forces that rode him.

Lysaer tested his bonds with a useless tug. Strap leather and rope reinforced with wrapped wire redoubled his crushing despair. Someone's pitiless foresight already had thwarted the pitch of his desperation. Conjured light could not singe him free. Not without crippling damage to both hands and feet, or risk of igniting the oil-soaked tarp bundled over him. Without recourse, he breathed, while the midday sun scorched the air into ripples. Only pride stifled his frustrated groan.

Lysaer raised his chin. Plagued by a throbbing headache, he surveyed his surroundings to see whose mishandling imposed the ignominy.

Nothing met his eye past the wagon's edge. Just barren ground: an unbroken flatland of parched lava and gravel. The stabbing flash of flecked mica melted seamlessly into the shimmer of heat-waves. Yet he was not alone. Two of his captors locked horns, beyond view, with a grainy voice Lysaer recognized as Dakar's shouting over the other's obstinate protest. "No. That would get us fricassied for betrayal the instant he starts to wake up!"

Dread retreated a fraction. Perhaps his nightmare fear was a phantom. Lysaer eavesdropped, hopeful the dispute haggled over the terms for a ransom by Elkforest's barbarians.

"I won't shoulder that risk!" Dakar ranted on. "Yes, I lack the main strength. No ranging ward I might weave can subdue an elemental mastery of light. Be patient for another few days. At least until I've ascertained we're clear of Arithon's fatal proximity."

Which callous mention of that accursed name triggered Desh-thiere's geas. Whiplashed by the assault, Lysaer shuddered in agony. The vicious drive to embrace wholesale ruin set his wits under siege. He battled for reason, as always. Clung to the rags of free choice: not to blast everything within reach with a levin bolt charged to melt stone into magma. He suffered in recoil. While the primal torrent surged to consume him, the gall of repeated past failures made a mockery of his resistance.

Torment wrung a gasp from him.

The sound stopped the ongoing argument. Gravel grated. Someone's scuffed tread approached.

Lysaer twisted for confrontation. Any frail stay to distract him from the drive of the curse.

Glare stabbed his eyes like needles to the brain. Squinting against the white dazzle of sky, he made out the loom of volcanic formations grotesquely weathered and eroded with crumbling arches. Then a shadow flicked over him. A clownish face eclipsed his view, raffishly bearded and wisped with grey hair, streaked by faded chestnut. Cheeks and snub nose wore a peeled scald of sunburn on a countenance stripped of forbearance.

Dakar snapped, "Don't think to put on your statesman's mask, Lysaer! I'll stand for no pretence. Are you able to govern your natural mind? Or speak with frank honesty? Then defend your case. Convince me that you didn't kill her."

Which test of trustworthiness needed no name. Viciously personal, the accusation frayed the last thread of sane balance. Lysaer bridled. He sucked an offended breath through clenched teeth. Whether to plead or to scream became moot: as if human language existed to stem the cascade towards disaster.

The idiot spellbinder lectured, oblivious. "This is not Sithaer, but a place in the Scarpdale Waste called the Stacks. Before you cry foul, accept your lot, held under my charge in good faith."

Lysaer's temper ignited. His lethal retort in pure light tipped towards destructive release.

Dakar yelped. Eyes widened, he scrambled too late for a stop-gap intervention. Yet what murderous damage might have ensued, his unseen companion's blow, swung from behind, clipped Lysaer's nape like Dharkaron's vengeance.

He dropped limp, hurled back into black-out unconsciousness.

Saved, but not sanguine, Dakar rebounded from shock and glared at his slighter accomplice. "That's thanks for the killing strike I didn't field?" he shouted in caustic astonishment. "Best hope your crude remedy didn't crack his Lordship's thick skull."

Daliana hurled aside her makeshift bludgeon: a chunk of fire-wood, padded at need with a grimy Sunwheel surcoat. The billet thudded into the wagon-bed next to Lysaer's slack form. "Necessity," she stated, crisp. Stripped to a squire's shirt and torn hose, she scrambled over the tail-board and knelt to examine her prostrate victim.

Blond and royal-born, chiselled to a statuesque fitness made to bring sculptors to rapture, Lysaer looked, every inch, like the downfallen avatar worshipped by the Light's faithful. Unwashed, dishevelled in his soiled white tunic, he sprawled with an unconscious majesty designed to wreak female havoc. A stone heart could but melt at the sight of such helplessness, trussed ankle and wrist in looted strap leather.

Daliana's features already softened as she explored Lysaer's goose-egg bruise. "This wants ice." Flushed by shameless regret, she leaned on Dakar's scant sympathy. "Might you fashion a construct to freeze a piggin of water?"

"My sleep spell wouldn't have dunted his noggin," Dakar grumbled with reproach.

"No." Daliana unfurled the surcoat from the billet and wadded a pillow for

3

her liege's bashed head. "But your callous comment left his Lordship no civilized course to salve his wounded pride. Someone had to do that for him."

When Dakar said nothing, she straightened, contrite, a tanned, slender minx with tawny eyes fierce enough to outface a tigress. She brushed back chocolate hair that a fortnight in barren country had tangled for want of a comb. "Your sack of wound remedies includes poppy? Then perhaps a tisane for headache could be added to his next dose of valerian."

But when her concession to further drugged sleep failed to lift the fat spellbinder's frown, Daliana lost patience. "You claimed Asandir had swept Lanshire clear of The Hatchet's war host under Fellowship mandate!"

"He has." Dakar's pouched eyes blinked with injury. "My scrying shows the last companies of rear-guard have withdrawn past Havish's northern border."

"Since when?" Her irritable gesture encompassed the spires of lava, pocked in between with ash pits and hot springs rimed with bilious mineral deposits, plumed geysers, and steaming mud pots. "Why are we still skulking like rats in a place fit only for scorpions and lizards?"

Dakar deflated. Careless of splinters, he perched on the dray, which was flat, without shade for relief since an awning increased visibility. "The orderly troops have departed. But I cannot trace every straggler or the criminal bands of deserters." He cut her off. "Oh, yes! There are rogues holed up in the Storlain foot-hills. They'll be making their furtive way on the sly. Hungry enough to slaughter our draft team or kill for the theft of a horse." He need not broach rape. Not after Daliana had braved the peril of the Light's war camp. Alone, without a stitch of protection beyond several daggers and a lance squire's dress, she must acknowledge her personal vulnerability.

Since Arithon's recent escape from Lithmarin ruled out travelling south, the inhospitable terrain to the east provided a brutal haven. The reduced chance that Lysaer might be seen forestalled the armed rescue that would come in force if word of his presence alerted the True Sect fanatics.

Daliana tossed back the damp braid pasted against her neck. "Stop lying, then. You don't need to buy time to perfect any ward ring. You haven't the means to fashion a shield against elemental light in the first place!"

Dakar side-stepped. "You can't know that for certain."

Which evasion sparked Daliana's mercurial laughter. "I wear Asandir's mark, or did you forget? At Morvain, tossed into the holocaust of Lysaer's curse-driven fire-storm, even your former master's ward wasn't infallible."

Trickling sweat, Dakar warned, "Be most careful. It's a deadly folly to presume with regard to the actions of Fellowship Sorcerers. The power they wield was bestowed by the dragons. They can do the unimaginable, and without limit. Never ever forget the more dangerous list of what actions they might be withholding under some abstruse ethical preference."

But reckless as Dakar had been in the past, Daliana shrugged off the gravity of semantics. "Whether or not a sure safe-guard exists against Lysaer's gift, why not admit the truth? You're past your depth. We're here because there's minimal brush and nothing in range that's combustible!"

Dakar deflated, stung by the irony that had landed him on the flip side of his own argument: Lysaer could not be drugged unconscious, indefinitely. The palliative use of medicinal draughts tore away what remained of a spirit already shattered by a cursed compulsion.

"Why not stand off and allow me to handle him?" Daliana pleaded. "Could I do any worse? Your blunders have done little else but inflame the wound in his self-respect."

Mightily worn by his shortfalls in the arena of subtle relationships, Dakar lashed back. "I should abet your impetuous ruin? What happens the next time your liege goes insane and fries the ground where you stand? Don't tempt fate! You haven't the strength to constrain him each time he loses his grip."

"Then think beyond the use of brute force!" Before the spellbinder shouted her down, Daliana admonished, "After hundreds of diligent years of apprenticeship, surely you've learned other options!"

The spellbinder stared, moon-calf features slackened as though the heat had broiled his wits.

Daliana reached for her billet, galled enough to hammer him senseless.

She lost the chance.

From stunned windless to owlishly rapt, Dakar reversed. "I've got an idea." He surged erect, slapped his forehead, and chortled. "Oh, indeed, yes. My dear! The notion is genius!"

Daliana glowered in suspicion. "What now?"

The Mad Prophet's smile sparkled with teeth. "You've asked all along to stay at Lysaer's side, a death sentence waiting to happen. But not if I stand that prospect upside down."

The method was brilliant. Once, Asandir had done the same: wrought a punitive stay that bound Dakar to Arithon's company with the persistence of a malediction. More, Luhaine had fashioned a similar spell, years later, an obdurate constraint on Fionn Areth's rebellion, weaving him under protections within the spellbinder's close proximity. Both approaches opened intriguing possibilities when combined with the homing ciphers stitched into the aura of Asandir's stallion. Dakar flexed his fingers, empowered by enough sundry knowledge to rig an inventively nasty variation.

"What in Dharkaron's name are you thinking?" Daliana broke in.

"Bless you, sweetling!" crowed Dakar. "I'm going to tie Lysaer's presence to you! Give him a leash that extends for three leagues, you can duck beyond range of his rages. He might slip your guard at the whim of his curse, but not bolt out of reach without your complicity." The spellbinder hitched up his pot-belly with venomous satisfaction. "Ath above, I can't wait. We can leave this forsaken place, soonest. Just nip off a thread from your clothing and loan me a knife to prick his little finger."

"No." Daliana uncoiled from nursing her invalid. "I can't sanction this plan."

Dakar shrugged. "Then I'll seal the craft-work without you." Undeterred by the scorch of her rage, the spellbinder bore in, "How many more temple war hosts will wreck the peace for your pride? Canon Law will purge more clanbred families, and for what good end, Daliana?"

She did not stand down. Small, scuffed with dirt, and rabidly furious, the minx defended her ground. "Dakar, you can't. This is not a solution. Your proposal does nothing to bolster my liege's besieged integrity. Compulsion can't mend his raw self-esteem! You'll do naught but destroy the last shred of true spirit if you rope down a man already ridden beyond mercy."

Dakar slid off the wagon. "Athera cannot afford your squeamish instinct to coddle Lysaer's cursed madness. You don't fully grasp the scope of the stakes. Stick now over principle, or hang up on your infatuation, I will the more ruthlessly clip the man's wings." The snatched move to unsheathe her belt knife raised only the spiteful slap of his indifference. "Don't imagine bloodshed will stop my interference."

"Should I worry?" Daliana retorted. "The moon will fall out of the sky on a wish before my liege grants you permission."

The spellbinder's crafty smile stretched wider. "A grand gift, for sure, he's tossed out of the compact, and also that I've been dumped from the upright graces of Fellowship auspice."

"You daren't stoop to coercive extortion! That verges upon dark practice!" But as the Mad Prophet braced to take action, Daliana promised, "Try, and I will not rest until I find means to prevent you. I don't care how many innocents you believe you'll be saving! The back-lash you cause will strip Lysaer of his humanity and leave us with a monster."

A man less resolved should have quailed from her smoking glare on him, except the leeway for debate was exhausted. A muffled groan from the wagon-bed warned that their charge recovered his senses.

Dakar eyed the tousled blond head sheltered by such untoward sentiment. "You wanted an ice pack to ease his bashed skull? Then strike me a fire to heat a fresh tisane. We need that valerian infusion, right quick."

"We? No." Daliana leaped down from the tail-board, as determined a bundle of feminine rage as ever set off to thwart destiny. "Do the scut work yourself since you fear to burn!"

Forthwith, she claimed a pair of saddle packs and began to stockpile provisions. "I'll be taking two horses and Lysaer. You can test the mettle of Asandir's mark and try to stop me at your peril."

Dakar turned his back. However brave, Daliana's resolve would not upset his decision. Neither did he revel in her misery, or cave in to the tears she swiped off her grimed cheeks as she tacked and loaded the pick of the available string. Stressed as she was by rough living, the spellbinder weighed what had to be done with a cold heart and ironclad purpose.

Forget the fair fight. Past service to Arithon s'Ffalenn gave him the long view and the scars of unpleasant experience: a sharp adversary corrupted by Desh-thiere's geas never spurned dirty tactics. First chance, Lysaer would snatch the advantage against any fool who volunteered as his chaperone.

"Pack the valerian as you wish," Dakar said. "Or leave me a horse and a share of the stores and drive off with the wagon."

When Daliana spurned his effort to ease her lot, the spellbinder hunched stoic shoulders and stumped off into the dazzle of heat-waves. Discomfort compounded his sullen mood. The flint rock burned through his boot soles. Insects whirred aloft upon glassine wings from the desiccate cracks in the boulders. Through the scrape of his stumbling strides, he deafened himself to the ring of shod hooves, receding. Onwards, he plunged from the glare of midday into the abyss of shade beneath the high arch that buttressed the nearest rock stack.

The bounce of a kicked stone cracked an echo that died. Dakar sucked a vexed breath, pulled up short while his eyesight adjusted. He required a flat surface, less reactive to flux charge, to lay down meticulous boundaries. Care must be taken with a work not in form: no chance influence should warp his intent.

"Did you believe your twisted bumbling wasn't noisy enough to draw notice?" admonished a voice from the desert silence.

Brought face-to-face with the tall shadow that detached from the gloom, Dakar discerned the faint emanation flared off of uncanny embroidery. The impression of a gaunt face, framed in a streaked tumble of shoulder-length hair crossed the keyhole behind, and punch-cut the figure into silhouette.

"Davien!" the spellbinder yelped. "Did Sethvir send you as my keeper or have you come to champion Daliana's appeal?"

The Sorcerer also known as the Betrayer took pause, a stalking lynx against the parched vista behind him. "I happened to be afoot in the vicinity."

Dakar swallowed back his panicked consternation. Recall surfaced too late, that the dragon Seshkrozchiel had denned up in the volcanic spur of the Storlains to hibernate. The nonchalance behind Davien's phrase distilled into visceral dread.

Lately released from the thrall of the drake, the most untrustworthy of the Fellowship Sorcerers meddled here as a radical free agent.

Amused, Davien rested his foot on a boulder, crossed his arms on his thigh, and leaned forward. "I'm not ready to answer Sethvir's cry for peace. Here's the pot and the kettle, both sooted black. You seem hell-bent to grant Althain's Warden due grounds to ban you from the compact."

Dakar forced his lungs to inflate. "After my choices killed High King Gestry, does another transgression even signify?"

"Perhaps." Davien straightened. Not impervious, his person showed the frayed snags and cinder burns from mean travel through Scarpdale's rough country. "Your first course of action salvaged Arithon's life and threw no one to grief against their will. Don't overplay your importance, besides. The strengthened potency of the flux lines was far more to blame for Gestry's untimely demise."

"No one else could have pressured that wild-card play," Dakar insisted. "Since I wasn't condemned for up-ending Asandir's standing orders in Havish, I have reason to dread my murky call may spark the next round of catastrophe."

"Are you trying to win my agreement?" Davien chuckled. "Or is this an attempt to stiffen your nerve?"

"Why else are you here?" Dakar snapped. "Except maybe to gloat at the on-going expense of your overtaxed colleagues."

"I am not crowing!" Davien contradicted. The fixated glitter of black eyes and white teeth like the stoat, he slashed for the jugular. "In fact, my courtesy call is a precaution. Don't waste your effort or your good name. Because if you proceed, I will stop you."

"Who are you saving?" Dakar cracked, annoyed. Though his nape puckered up into gooseflesh, he pressed, "Daliana? Or Lysaer? Don't pretend you stirred a finger to spare me. After your handling of the Teir's'Ffalenn against the grey cult at Etarra, I'd kill myself laughing."

Davien grinned. "You forget. The mist-bound entities locked down in Rockfell Pit are not free wraiths. If you compromise Lysaer to serve Arithon's survival, our means to curb Desh-thiere might go down in flames."

Dakar sighed. "Don't play me for a gullible idiot, that you have any loyalty left to the Fellowship."

The Sorcerer's figure stayed dangerously still, more silent than the primordial boulder under his foot.

Soaked in run sweat, Dakar cleared his throat. "Pray, have you a better solution in mind?"

"Maybe." Davien shrugged. "If so, the option relies upon Daliana's cooperation."

Dakar sat on a nearby outcrop, ribs clutched against wheezing laughter. "If your counsel will move her, by all means, try! Kharadmon failed to cool her devotion. Not even the True Sect war host, with its cohort of priests and diviners, kept her from returning to her liege's side!"

"She has the brute courage to hammer through bed-rock," Davien agreed. "Who says I intend to dissuade her?" Before Dakar pushed erect and rushed back towards the wagon, he added, "Don't bestir your protective instincts to warn her against the hazards of hearing my offer."

The spellbinder wilted. Chary of the chit's knack with a billet, he said, hopeful, "Daliana's already loaded her liege and gone on her way." Bone-tired, he knuckled his inflamed eyes. "Asandir should have told you I've been outfaced since the day of my birth."

When Dakar looked up, the span of the archway stood empty. Davien had gone. A glance over his shoulder confirmed: the tacked horses with Daliana were already diminished to blots in the dazzle of heat-waves. Since the spell-binder was too pudgy to give chase, he opted to bury his misery and take an oblivious nap in the shade.

Lysaer roused again to a furred mouth, vile with the after-taste of a drugged syrup. His fuddled awareness added a pounding head to the inflamed discomfort of sunburn. Hurting, he stirred, gouged by crushed pumice and tufts of razor-edged grasses. His limbs were cut loose. The breeze that stung his abraded flesh wore the chill of on-coming twilight. Another day waned in the unknown span of his prolonged captivity. If his keepers had not let him soil himself, the affront to his dignity chafed even through the haze of turned senses.

Sundown burnished the snow-capped peaks, their crumpled flanks folded into cobalt shadow, except where spewed smoke from a volcanic vent smudged the horizon. Lava sand gritted between his teeth and invaded his soiled clothing. His stubbled chin itched, and his tangled hair hung rank as the thatch on a bogman's hovel. Propped halfway erect, Lysaer surveyed the view. Nothing moved. Only the breeze riffled the clumps of stunt thorn, their crabbed twigs darned with tattered foliage.

Lysaer dared not assume Dakar's watch had abandoned him. Irked to have lost the civilized service of his valet, he examined his wrists, dye-stained where the straps had dug into his flesh. His hose had matching marks at the ankles.

Given freedom of movement, innate caution distrusted the impression of autonomous solitude.

"Forget Dakar's spectacular failure," the voice of the woman he thought he had murdered declared from behind him. "The setting's my choice, and this isn't my reckoning for your catastrophic behaviour at Morvain."

Lysaer spun around, terrified. But the diminutive female who faced him in squire's dress was not an apparition. The pert face with too-bright, tawny eyes raked him over. Her dark brown braid was no longer luxurious but roped into a wisped knot and pinned up with a hazel stick. The worse for him, she witnessed his panic: shock destroyed his prized poise as a statesman. Her intact, living presence slammed through heart and mind, a visceral blow that also hit below the belt.

While Lysaer gaped, paralysed, she attacked first. "I did not burn by your hand, as you see, and nothing between us is finished, yet."

Lysaer twisted his vulnerable features away. Not fast enough: twice shamed as the force of his anguish unmanned him, he had no way to silence her or any word to fend off her analysis of his weaknesses.

"At least you should know why you failed," Daliana pursued. "The rage that turned Desh-thiere's curse against me was no fault of your character. Your demise was set up. In fact, you fell prey to the tricks of the Koriathain."

But excuses were empty. Nothing relieved the responsible ethic demanded of his royal upbringing. His short-falls and his privacy were subject to no one's ruthless dissection, far less any female bent on interference. Once laid open by Talith, and after the inexcusable pretence of his political marriage to Ellaine, Lysaer s'Ilessid brooked no exception. The merciful woman would withdraw as a kindness; likewise, the stout-hearted one plunged beyond her depth.

But this brazen creature respected no boundaries. Her courage possessed too much gall to salve his beleaguered spirit. The locked pause extended. Coarse with the whisper of breeze through the brush, the grey mantle of nightfall continued to leach the last colour out of the world.

Yet falling darkness lent cover, at least. Lysaer torqued his facade back into the semblance of equilibrium. His voice was ice, and his nerves, armoured steel, before he tried speech. "I want you gone."

Her calm contained the strength to eviscerate. "I won't oblige. Leave on your own merits."

She would not enable a coward's retreat. Or else she understood him too well and refused the reprieve in his plea for rejection.

"Hold out in vain, then." Lysaer gathered himself to arise, shocked by the quiver of atrophied muscle and sun-poisoned nausea. How long had he languished in drugged oblivion at the whim of his self-righteous guardians? Bitter, he wondered if he also suffered withdrawal from an addiction. Dakar knew his herbals. Given a wagon equipped to haul casualties, the slippery spellbinder could have plied him with a war-time stockpile of narcotic remedies.

Daliana addressed that transparent suspicion, aware that he sorted his appalling infirmity for evidence of further treachery. "You were not dosed with poppy."

She extended a hand to him.

Lysaer stifled a fury that clenched his jaw, brought to his knees by sapped vitality and cruel despair. Pride refused to yield. He hoarded his right to unfettered autonomy and spurned her care though he scrabbled like a dog to buy distance.

Darkness hid his agony, while the vertigo ebbed. When in due time he commanded himself and used a boulder to claw himself upright, Daliana did not mock or step in to brace up his wracked balance. Instead, she silently offered the bridle of one of her two saddled mounts.

"If you go, the choice becomes yours alone." Golden eyes pinned him, direct beyond quarter, though her grasp on the reins trembled with distress. "I will not leave. No matter if you succumb to the curse, or how brutal the provocation, nothing you do, alive in this world, can make me abandon you."

Which lashed him to fury and cut him in places too harrowed to bleed in her sight.

Destroyed, the last shred of control he possessed: Lysaer strove to drive such innocence past the hazard of reckless endangerment. Proximity to him would see her dead, and far worse, unravel the dregs of his self-control that chose not to sully his last, tattered remnant of decency. Once, he had yielded himself to affection, only to endure heart-break great enough to demolish his principles. Never again would he divide his autonomy under the sway of feminine influence. He had cast off both women pledged to him in marriage, turned from them and denounced their memory. The Mistwraith's fell madness blighted his future, too murderous an affliction for him to sustain.

Of all the mis-steps with power to wound him, he had lost control: nearly scorched alive the tender innocent pleading to save him. Lysaer rejected the unthinkable liability. He owned no sane means to protect Daliana or spare her from the fate that had destroyed Ellaine and Talith before her.

Lysaer fought venomous self-revulsion, too choked up for words, even had sickness not wrung him wretched.

He staggered forward, snatched the reins without touching her. Disability forced him to lean on the hack to stay upright but did not weaken his besieged defences. He clawed himself astride. Shaky and soaked in febrile sweat, he searched the gloaming for Dakar's campsite. Though no fire burned to draw unfriendly eyes, he picked out the angular bulk of the dray, with the unhitched team tethered nearby. Lysaer turned his mount's head in the other direction. Then he dug in his heels and set off at a break-neck gallop without a glance backwards.

Night swallowed him, sultry with the steam vented off the simmering hot springs. He did not slacken pace or guide the horse under him. Reckless, he let his mount's keener instincts pick the path through treacherous country. Lysaer scarcely cared if he broke his neck. He drove the animal at clattering speed through the craters of hardened caldera, leaped over seams where the rills of old lava flows yawned underfoot. He coughed on the fumes belched from the mud pots, and taunted fate, where the pressurized gush of the geysers seethed in the obsidian shadows. Alone, he need not wrestle to mask the misery of total despair . . .

Under the ice-chip glitter of stars, her heart crushed, Daliana sank to her knees. Tears fell for the fracture she could not mend. But she did not sob aloud. Failure preferred the night's silence since Dakar's vindictive lecture surely would finish her. How many would come to die in the future lay out of her hands, nor might any measure of sore regret lift the gravity of tonight's miscalculation. Done was done. She had acted as her intuition directed. No matter how dimmed the hope of Lysaer's long-term healing, she had turned him loose with his spirit intact.

Numb to the bite of the volcanic gravel, she bore the disastrous hurt. She renounced self-pity, straightened, and rose, and gathered the reins of the gelding left to her. Unable to face the Mad Prophet just yet, she laid her wet cheek against the animal's shoulder.

Lysaer's cause would not be forsaken. For more than a sealed oath under

Asandir's auspices, she would search the breadth of the five kingdoms for a remedy. "Until I've found some way to redeem my liege, before Ath, I will not rest his case."

"You are worth ten of him," a dismissive voice snapped from the darkness.

Startlement whirled Daliana volte-face and dislodged the hazel twig pinned through her hair. Half-blinded, she clapped a hand to her belt-knife and braced for a defensive throw.

But the speaker's stark stillness smothered her impulsive attack.

"Whatever you say, I promised my liege. Nothing else matters." She drew herself up though the presence before her radiated the might of a Fellowship Sorcerer. "Kharadmon already forewarned that I pursued Lysaer's better nature in vain."

Her visitor strode forward. Angular and tall, he wore a belted tunic and simple hose. The lean face, brushed in starlight, was graven by absolute confidence; or else smelted by the flame of an arrogance that brooked no impertinent questioning.

Daliana regarded the dangerous creature last seen in the company of a dragon. The edge had not left him. His attention still blazed like a brand, even cloaked under nightfall.

Davien said, "I am not here to part you from your desire but to offer you means to pursue it."

Her bitterness echoed off the naked rocks. "How? Lysaer distrusts women! Worse than that, he views affection as a fatal weakness. He won't abide his deepest dread, that he might fall prey to his vulnerability."

"Intimacy could bring him down, wide open to enemy leverage." Davien capped her list, razored with irony. "The greater his love, the more fear of loss, added to the horror he can't stand the guilt if his cursed nature drives him to murder."

Daliana leaned on the horse, all the brazen starch shaken out of her. "The honest spirit should panic, in fact."

The Sorcerer stepped closer. "You're weak at the knees?" Presumptuously bold, he prised her fisted grip off the bridle reins. "My dear, let go. If the horse strays, I will summon it back for you."

Escorted aside, nostrils filled with the sulphurous taint ingrained in his clothing, Daliana permitted the steering touch that perched her on a nearby boulder. "How can I possibly keep my sworn charge if my liege allows no one near him?"

"Ah!" Davien straightened. "Is that strictly true?"

Daliana regarded the face notched out of the deep sky above her and conceded the point. "Well, he does have his retinue." Galled by her defeat, she raised a nervous hand, yanked out the skewed twig, and let her crimped braid tumble over her shoulder. Rewinding the hair to steady herself, and through the stick clamped in her teeth, she carried her share of a dialogue that led nowhere. "My liege will bear no one's familiarity. He isolates himself through his station. I know he has no one he consults for wise counsel though history records that my forebear Sulfin Evend relied on the steadfast allegiance of his Lordship's personal valet."

"A male lackey is invisible in that regard," Davien agreed, too complacent.

Daliana jammed the hazel shim through her tucked plait and glowered at his insolence. "Yes, I played the lance squire. But not directly for Lysaer, and only at a safe distance. The disguise worked in the crowded confusion of the True Sect's campaign. I got by, always by feigning to be the malingering servant of somebody else!" Amid the massed host, one face more or less risked little notice, and lazy boys everywhere contrived devious ways to shirk duty.

Davien said nothing. But one booted foot tapped in impatience.

Which cue emptied her chest in bolt-struck epiphany. Daliana shoved straight so hard, the pumice against her braced seat ripped sound cloth, and her braid came unmoored from its fastening. "You couldn't!"

"Could I not?" The Sorcerer laughed outright. "Ask Dakar. In fact, more than once, your spellbinder stymied himself against my skilled touch for concealment. Although strictly speaking, a masking spell won't fully address your straits. Illusion can't blindside a necromancer, or evade the trained Sight of the True Sect's diviners." Head cocked, Davien peered down with an intensity to drill through pretence. "How strong are you, really?"

Daliana crossed her arms over her breast, while her heart raced, and dread lanced her viscera.

Once before this, Dakar had warned, "Don't let him cozen you," while the ceiling of an inn cellar became ignited by drakefire over their heads.

This Sorcerer's bargains never were wont to tread the straightforward path. Flesh and blood, breathing, he was not mortal: the air in his company still crackled, unseen, with the volatile flame of a dragon's live dreaming.

Daliana's question ground through her tight throat. "What moonstruck scheme are you proposing?"

Davien bent, plucked a thorn cane barehanded, and gave it a vigorous shake. Sparks flew, as though flint had struck steel, and the whisper of fallen leaves pattered his boots. He extended his offering. The stripped stem was not as it had been: a fine lacquered hairpin glistened under the starlight. "Forms can be changed."

Daliana accepted the perilous gift, finger-tips tracing the refigured wood through the Sorcerer's resumed explanation.

"You don't behold trickery, or a disguise. The thorn has not forsaken its nature. The core substance is not shape-shifted. Only the outer surface has been remade."

Stunned as though hurled into the abyss, Daliana dropped the polished stick.

Davien picked it up, laid it flat on the boulder. His stride kept the grace of a predator as he paced before her, still speaking. "Lysaer does not confide in his servants. However, with time, the ones who are faithful do earn a measure of trust. They handle his person. Come and go when he sleeps. How strong are you, lady? Have you the fibre to lurk in the background, watch his struggles, his failures, and even, the ghastly course of his short-falls? Could you wait, hold your tongue, keep to the shadows behind his affairs and bide without snapping? Can you live for the day that unforeseen destiny might grant you the perilous opening?"

As she measured herself, wrung by trepidation, the Sorcerer stopped before her. Features in shadow, his regard could be felt, searing as coals on her skin. "You would be alone as never before. None would know your identity. On the days you suffer in pain and despair, no one's kindly word will support you. While you watch aggrieved, your beloved may destroy himself. His worst hour might break him. Can you survive? Is the purity of your love deep enough?"

Daliana swallowed. "Didn't Dakar just warn that my decision to let him go would murder untold thousands of innocents?"

The Sorcerer regarded her, bleak. "But you were not blind to the danger inherent in the fool's intervention the spellbinder proposed."

A knifing breath, snatched into seized lungs. "Then we agree? Lysaer is a good man, yes, with human flaws that have been unconscionably pressured and twisted!" Daliana swallowed again. "Somebody has to stand by his character. Else watch the last fragment of his true grace fall to wrack and ruin." A second justification, no steadier, "Asandir sent me into the breach already aware I was overfaced. So Kharadmon informed me, too late."

Davien's teeth flashed, not a smile. The line of his shoulders reflected no humour but only the indomitable steel that bore the weight of two ages. "Asandir did as he must. The options he had were most likely fatal. Lady, most brave, do not miscalculate the purpose that drives the Fellowship! Mankind on Athera walks the razor's edge. All the more as the True Sect gains sway, humanity's long-term survival is threatened. Against that disaster, you are hope itself. Or else the frail straw cast into the breach to buy a brief margin of time. Never doubt, Daliana, we Seven are ruthless."

She shivered. "I accepted Sulfin Evend's oath, willing."

In whip-crack retort, Davien's pacing resurged. "Did you know the bad odds? The best years of your natural life could be lost!" He spun and regarded her. "I will not lie. Nothing can guarantee the victory you seek."

Daliana took up the hairpin. Defiant courage reached up, determined, and restored her braid into a coil. "You would make me appear as a man?" Despite iron will, her hands trembled. "Would I be so, in fact?"

Davien raised his eyebrows. "Enough to pass close up scrutiny, and not as a figment for show. You would need to shave, or the lack would raise questions. More, your aura must withstand the Sighted scrutiny of even the True Sect's most gifted diviners. To alter your signature presence that deeply means, yes, you would have to bear a measure of masculine responsiveness."

The idea made her choke. "Then what if—"

While her blush heated scarlet, Davien chuckled. "The young women need not be a problem, I think. As you wish, I could fashion a form that makes you seem older in years."

Daliana reeled under suffocating apprehension. "Would I even know myself?"

"You will hold your self-image, but only in Name. And only the fullness of that true identity could sunder the binding. Few but the most wise own the vision to sound your true essence. No man alive, beyond Athera's Masterbard, or through a human love great enough to surpass the awareness of flesh and blood. I would not leave you helpless. The means to free yourself will remain under your command, always."

Daliana skewered the braid, wound too painfully tight as gooseflesh prickled her nape. She scrubbed her hands over her face, rattled by atavistic reservations. Sensible caution knew her experience was inadequate to plumb the enigma Davien represented. His motive could not be read in the hands casually hooked at his belt, with the sparkle of citrine set in his ring a captive spark under starlight. Unable to fathom his greater purpose, and hag-ridden: since only one choice upheld Asandir's charge, Daliana picked at the flaw in the Sorcerer's terrifying proposition.

"How many years would I have before death? Would the effect of your glamour shorten my lifetime? Lysaer does not age as a natural man."

Davien's snapped fingers dismissed the concern. "This point can be redressed without consequence." Shown disbelief, his peaked eyebrows rose. "Ah! You'd have proof? Dakar never informed you? My hand engineered the Five Centuries' Fountain that crafted your liege's longevity."

Rocked by that admission, Daliana leaped to mad impulse and bargained, "Then you'll match that advantage since I gave my heart-felt promise to Lysaer that I would never desert him."

"With your due permission?" Davien yanked a black thread from the embroidery stitched through his cuff. The strand flickered bright as contained lightning as he knotted it into an intricate bracelet. "Lady, push back your sleeve and give me your left wrist."

Her arm quaked, despite her hard-set resolve. The Sorcerer cradled her hand, his touch tenderly brisk as he slid his enchanted cincture over her skin. A quick movement noosed the weave firmly in place: nothing more, after all, than a frayed linen thread, except for a pattern that defied sight and sense to discern.

"Most brave," Davien challenged, "you are quite certain?"

She dared not pause. Second thoughts would destroy her: love's question, unanswered, would haunt her the worse if she failed to rise to this test. "Yes."

Consent melted the construct into her flesh. A wave of heat followed. Then a flush like high fever, while her ears rang through a barrage of dizziness.

Deft support rescued Daliana's reeling balance as the firm bounds of her body seemed to dissolve.

Dimly, she realized the Sorcerer's handling laid her down gently onto firm ground. His words echoed across a chasm of distance and chased her fall into reeling black-out, "You will waken refreshed. Spend enough time alone as you need to adjust. I will leave you with more than sufficient provisions to supply your journey from here. When you wish to restore your true form, the change back will become irreversible. Simply grip your left wrist. Repeat your birth name three times, and break the circlet as it resurfaces."

Pitfall

The country rose steeply beyond the pebbled moraine that lined the lake-shore of Lithmarin. Here, where a great fault-line bisected the continent, the Storlain foot-hills shattered into slopes of slab-sided rock. Stunted trees knuckled into the cracks, crabbed branches yawed over the shadowed gorges. A region riddled with bolt-holes aplenty for a hunted fugitive, including the desperate bands of deserters who fled the True Sect ranks from the warfront. A man alone set upon by such brigands survived by the sword, else, mage-gifted, slipped through the rugged vales undetected.

Such stalker's cunning let Arithon move swiftly. He slept lightly by day. Travelled by night to elude the two-legged predators, who would cut a sleeper's throat for his boots or be drawn by the glimmer of fire-light to steal a scrap of charred meat. Criminals under crown justice in Havish, the worst of them fled across the north range towards the backwater towns in Melhalla.

Arithon bent his solitary course due south, into the western spur of the ranges.

The desolate land climbed under his furtive steps, sap-green tangles of scrub oak replaced by black fir and interlaced balsam. Thinner air wore the perfume of pitch pine, lent the mineral tang of wet stone where the springs welled over the flanks of the gulches. Alert for human voices, Arithon re-entered the bounds of Havish. He climbed the baked ramparts, reared upwards into serried ridges where the snow-toothed peaks carded the summer clouds into ice-crystal wisps. Under the jagged spine of the Storlains, he sought a particular small cabin tucked into a sheltered vale. The site where the stuttering pulse of the flux lines still whispered the imprint of a woman's presence.

With his journey's end a short league as the crow flew, Arithon forged ahead as though drawn by a beacon. He ached to restore his memory of her, no matter how tenuous the fragment.

He crested a ridge-top lightly as wind. Breeze from the far side slapped his face like wet felt, stiffened with storm scent. He breasted the buffet, a cut silhouette punched against a wracked sky that spat lightning in actinic bursts. The descent plunged him back into pine forest that shuddered and tossed overhead. Snapped off needles smacked into his leathers. Such seasonal squall lines broke over the Storlains with tumultuous ferocity. Too far to bolt for the cabin's dry roof, Arithon pushed to seek shelter before the deluge unleashed and stymied his subtle senses.

He could not trace *her* through the lane currents while the elements snarled in rampage. Better to wait than to wander astray and plunge off the brink of a gulch.

That moment, he heard a woman's scream through the roar of the inbound gale.

Arithon altered his course toward the cry, odd though it seemed, that a Sunwheel deserter might push this far south. Few town-bred rogues owned the woodwise skills to outstrip his pace through these wilds.

Which puzzle must wait. A second cry sheared through the wind-tangled greenery. Even raised to hair-trigger alert, a mage's tuned senses could not measure the danger he faced. Already, the storm charged the flux into tumultuous static. Arithon slipped his sheathed sword off his shoulder. Hand on the hilt, he ducked through the stunt trees. He heard a man's grunt of exertion. Through the tossed boughs, veiled in gloom, someone's curse guided him towards a scuffle screened by the undergrowth.

Slowed to quiet his step, pelted by icy raindrops, Arithon peered through the thrashed branches. Lightning flickered. Flash-lit to grey upon mercury, the hollow beyond held the grappling form of a man. Crushed underneath, struggling with pinned wrists, the woman he forced fought him, weeping.

Arithon drew the sword, tensed by expectation: but the star-song within the black steel stayed quiescent. The gleam of the Paravian runes failed to ignite the sound-and-light chord of enchantment imbued at its forging. Without time to question, Arithon moved. He grabbed the man's shoulder and hauled his bulk off the violated woman. While he angled the weapon as a deterrent threat, the compromised female jerked her pinioned wrists free.

She thrust her attacker away and rolled clear, a blur of pale limbs in the gathering dark. Terrified as a wild thing sprung from a trap, she scrambled and fled, clutching her rifled clothing.

Arithon let her go. Wary, he faced her assailant, who did not bellow, or rally in response to her surprise ally. Instead, the lusty fellow writhed on the ground. Lightning flared again and illuminated the blued flash of metal sunk to the hilt into flesh.

The game little vixen had stuck him with a skinning knife.

Arithon rebounded from startled shock. He sheathed the sword, bent, and bore down to constrain the man's agonized thrashing. His explorative touch marked a forester's dress: a sturdy leather jack, belted overtop of a town-woven jerkin sodden and warm with let blood. Guided by mage-sight, he assayed the dagger protruding between neck and shoulder. The artery had been severed deep down, where no skilled pressure might stem the gushing spurt. Life fled, catastrophically. Under flux patterns storm-charged to uproar, scant seconds remained to interpret the man's fast-expiring matrix.

Arithon cradled the dying man's frame. While the sky opened up into torrents, and thunder slammed earth and sky, the tempest scattered his refined senses. He could not plumb the imprint of the ruffian's Name. Helpless, except to lend human comfort, he offered what gentle condolence he could to ease and hasten release.

The stricken man battled the throes of extremis. The erratic flicker of storm-light recorded the wracked struggle of his last, urgent effort to speak. Wide eyes stared, imploring. The corded throat worked. But the dagger had gashed the dying man's windpipe. Convulsed, rendered helpless, he passed without requite. His desperate message perished along with him though the stranger who kept vigil through his gurgled, last breath stayed until his contorted hands loosened.

The tormented spirit crossed over at length.

Arithon laid the lolled head to rest. Rocked back on his heels in the thrash of the downpour, skin-soaked and shivering, he closed the slack eyelids against the rain. As he straightened the contorted limbs, he noted the snares looped at the man's hip. The pulled knife, wiped clean, had the curved edge to dress pelts, suggesting a trapper's livelihood. With nothing else to be done to lend succour, Arithon abandoned the corpse and shoved off to find the distraught victim still living.

Flight had turned her eastward, spurred by a panic that left a swathe of snapped twigs and thrashed greenery. Arithon traced her through the crack and slam of the storm, while rainfall sheeted the pocks of her footsteps and puddled them silver. His arcane talent stayed unreliable, though fitful bursts of her graphic distress pierced through the chaotic flux. He followed with deliberate care, first not to lose her tenuous trail and also to let her traumatized nerves settle at least enough to withstand the approach of a kindly stranger.

Something had changed since the storm struck at nightfall. Elaira scrubbed at the gooseflesh that puckered her nape, anxious to unriddle the source. With the trade-road through Orvandir's flats windswept and open, and the cross-roads at Durn teeming with the encampments of the silk trade's northbound summer caravans, even the late hour thwarted her need to find solitude. The bad call had to be faced without flinching: that distance from the dense, brawling noise increased the grave risk of interference by the Koriathain.

Since the sisterhood's seat at Whitehold wielded a very long arm, the peril of isolation outstripped the town-based threat to trained talent posed by the Sunwheel fanatics. Scarcely a wise refuge to practise her arts, Elaira currently knelt on the scuffed flagstone floor in a wayside inn's fusty wine-cellar. Silence and dust weighted the stifled air, encased by walls of dense brick. Sunk deep into earth, the site naturally muffled the rambunctious emotion that stewed in the jammed upstairs tap-room. But not the flaring unease arisen from Arithon's sharp change of course.

Enroute to the cabin that once housed her herbalist's work in the Storlain ranges, he veered west: not chased in pursuit but lured. Elaira shivered again, her hands shaking. The pitch-darkness lent her no ease and no clarity. Determined, afraid, she laid out the bowl, then the corked flask and the candle stub filched from an unoccupied room. She worked quickly while her beloved's changed straits threw her fitful impressions: of wet skin and harsh gusts, icy rain and rife urgency, fragmented by static disturbance where the flux stream crackled over the fault line.

The region posed her a scryer's worst nightmare. Even without the tempestuous squall, natural interference disrupted the electromagnetic currents. The same jagged bursts once utilized to advantage to balk her order's invidious prying also upset the innate gestalt of her emotional link with Prince Arithon.

Perturbed enough to chase her apprehension, no matter the risk, Elaira unstoppered the flask and filled the brass bowl, listening against the boisterous noise from the tap-room: for the tread of the serving maids, coming and going to fetch and carry for customers, and for the noisier boots of the cheerful lad who tapped beer kegs. She dreaded disclosure, despite the cobwebs that curtained the arched brick vault, where grain spirits and wine aged in casks.

However removed, the niche was not safe. Caught at arcane practice, Elaira might suffer a branding, or worse, be dragged off in irons for the priests and the scaffold at Durn.

The upstairs door opened. Warm light sliced the gloom, followed by the boom of clogs on the stair. Starred beams from a candle lamp jittered and swayed, while grumbling over a cranky patron, the bar's ham-fisted wench collected a wheel of cheese and retreated.

Elaira expelled her stopped breath. Masked in the dark, she laid a half-consumed crust of bread to one side of the bowl, a thin effort to disguise the arcane array illumined as she sparked the candle. Misconstrued as a vagrant, she might be tossed out, or perhaps be made to wash pots with the scullions in recompense for illicit shelter.

But no such innocuous pretence might excuse the black-and-gold hawk's quill she smoothed in the tremulous glow of the flame. Stone floor, for earth, the vessel of water, the taper for fire, and feather for air: she dedicated the ritual with a whispered cantrip. Then she palmed the emerald signet of Rathain, wrought of white gold and imbued with the live charge of Arithon's past amid its layered tapestry of ancient history. Elaira passed the band over the flame, whisked it under the feather, then touched it to the surface of the brim-full bowl and asked earth to complete the connection.

Last, she cupped the set gemstone between her palms, invoked Arithon's Name, and awaited the vision engaged by the energized construct. When the connection flowered, her sight of the candle melted away. The surface of the water darkened to night and unveiled the storm broken over the Storlains with unsated ferocity . . .

Wild gusts thrashed the tree limbs, while the deluge pelted the ground to frothed run-off. The huddled woman did not hear Arithon's step through the crash of tossed branches. Forlorn stranger, to him, she could not know the silence of his movement, guided by his attuned sensitivity. Her first warning of his approach became the drummed punch of the rainfall, interrupted by the flick of spread cloth as he cast his hide jacket over her shivering frame.

She recoiled in terror. Sobbing from the after-shock of another man's violence, she surged to her feet, a wary creature lent panicked strength to take flight.

Whatever Arithon said to disarm her drowned under the drum of the rainfall. But lightning revealed the trapper's knife, reversed handle first, and extended toward her.

The traumatized woman snatched up the peace offering. She brandished the blade and lunged to fend him off, while he melted back, his palms raised. Although he remained armed, the black blade, Alithiel, stayed sheathed and secured at his shoulder. Small, chilled as she, and quite as miserable as his shirt soaked through, Arithon posed her no threat.

This, the woman before him would see: as initiate master, he knew how to infuse his presence with genuine calm . . .

Which emotional balm poured through the scryer's construct intact. While Elaira suffered the wrench of separation, a close lightning stroke in the Storlain wilds hammered the crest of the ridge and excited the flux currents. Electromagnetic chaos unravelled her established connection to Arithon.

Shaken, the enchantress closed her fist over the emerald ring and fought welling tears. Closed in the dim cellar, plagued by formless anxiety, she waited for her wheeling senses to settle, while the rushed blood pulsed through her veins, and her quickened breaths stirred dust from the casks.

Fleeting as the contact had been, the flash-point awareness cut with aching clarity: Arithon was hungry and cold to the bone. Hunted by enemies for far too long, he was tired and altogether distraught, unexpectedly saddled with helpless company against his marked preference for solitude.

Blood bound to compassion, he could not turn away. Even for self-preservation he would not ignore an abused woman's need for comfort and shelter.

Elaira had no cruelty in her nature. Her healer's instinct understood trauma. The battered person just rescued from rape was too wretchedly hurt to be left to fend for herself. Whatever motive had prompted a town-bred female to brave the Storlain wilds alone, the victimized wound to her spirit was real.

Elaira swore softly. Too well, her dread measured the vulnerable entanglement. Arithon's forthright ethic left no one in need, even when hounded by covert enemies. Though caution ought to question why such a forlorn innocent crossed his path, Rathain's prince answered to empathy first. He would smother the cry of his heart and take the destitute creature in tow.

An hour passed, two, while the squall raged apace in the Storlains. Elaira sought to restore her smashed contact as serving-maids came and went on the stair, and the electromagnetic chaos of weather smote the reactive lane currents.

Through the hours, she netted glimpses of vision: of Arithon, working beyond his safe limits, picking a tenuous path through the turbulent elements. She felt his slipped steps on slicked rocks and roots, while the sodden trees thrashed in the wind, and the woman shivered in her ripped skirt and borrowed jacket, blinded by rain in the relentless dark and reliant upon his talent-based lead.

She followed, dependent, while his guidance led down a rock-cliff and through the ravine, infallibly drawn by the whisper of a love that tormented him for its absence. Guiding flame to his yearning, Elaira shared the piercing desire by which Arithon extended his overstrung faculties. He followed the remnant trace of herself, as lightning gashed the sky overhead, and the downpour sapped his vitality. The toll of exposure forgave no mistakes. Survival relied on the abandoned cabin tucked in the lee of the ridge.

Midnight came and went within the dry cellar. Elaira stayed wakeful in the musty gloom, while the drudges swept the tap-room overhead and the boy rousted out the stupefied drunks. The stout landlord made his final rounds and closed up. He extinguished the lamp at the stair-head, then shut and locked the strapped door to the wine-vault.

Secure from interruption at last, Elaira bundled up in her mantle and catnapped. Fitful Sight wracked her sleep: of Arithon's spare words of encouragement, pitched to lift beaten morale when the woman's strength faltered. Inched across a slippery deadfall, he saw her safely over the swollen spate, raced to froth in the sunken ravine.

The little cabin perched on the far side, up a steep path shored with cut logs, puddled under the forest canopy. Above dripping firs, the angry clouds shredded to patched indigo scattered with stars.

Wakeful in the calm aftermath, Elaira shared the intimate flare of anticipation as Arithon mounted the cabin's plank stair. His thrill when he lifted the latch banished weariness, then dissolved into pain as he flung wide the door and discovered the place had been ransacked.

Nothing of value remained. The floor wore a mat of soaked leaves. Oiled-hide windows chewed through by mice had tattered from prolonged neglect.

Elaira suppressed the hot prickle of tears. Her beloved would find no meaningful trace of her. The possessions that mattered had long since gone with her, light enough to be carried. On departure, she had picked everything clean: scoured the cracks and swept all the crannies, then burned every last stick of furnishing. By such rigorous measures she had foiled the Koriathain, who would have seized the ruthless use of her leavings to anchor their divination.

"Come in," Arithon urged the fraught woman, who shrank into the shadows behind. "If there are no comforts, the roof appears sound. I can kindle a fire, close up the shutters, and get ourselves warm and dry."

Banal talk to steady the female stranger: but Elaira's tender perception sensed his suppressed note of desolation. Unable to bear his forlorn disappointment, the enchantress flung off her mantle and paced the wine-vault like a caged beast. Her steps riffled the cobwebs in the cramped space, while the slow hours unreeled towards dawn, and the stutter of the Storlain flux patterns smoothed enough to refigure her scryer's array . . .

. . . the bowl's image cleared to show Arithon, seated on the floor, with his arms tucked over his drawn-up knees. His drenched hair, rinsed clean, was neatly tied back, and his damp shirt half-unlaced in the carmine fire-light. Belt and baldric had been stripped off to dry where the heat would not crack the leather. The black sword, unsheathed, leaned against the board wall beyond reach, a firm statement of neutral disarmament.

The woman huddled nearest the hearth, her dishevelled bodice still swathed in his jacket. The dead man's blood stained the blouse underneath, and her muddied skirt clung to scraped ankles. Trapped in cramped quarters, shame and misery exposed, she feared to turn her back, even to mend her frayed laces. Her fixed regard blazed with distrust, while his gaze in turn read every nuance of her hostile rage and discomfort.

Arithon asked gently, patient enough to overlook her antagonism, "What is your name?"

Hoarsely, she answered. "Vivet." A shudder raked through her. Eyes blue as a glaze on fine porcelain glinted back through tear-swollen lids. Then she ducked her head, her heart-shaped face veiled behind tangles of red-gold hair. Bruises on her wrists marred creamy skin, delicate in the grain as veined marble. Her alto tone coloured by a mountain dialect, she added, defensive, "I was on my way home."

"Alone?" Arithon asked, his Masterbard's timbre velvet with calm.

Her shoulders moved, a shrug of stiff impatience. "I was born in the region. These peaks have been native soil to my family for generations."

She pinched her lips, terrified. The strangled pause stretched.

Endowed with a healer's tactful restraint, Arithon displayed no inclination to pry . . .

But the surge of his unspoken compassion raised a piercing ripple of pure emotion. The water in the scryer's bowl shivered, while Elaira reeled in wrenching empathy.

Ath on earth, how she missed his testy company!

The fact Arithon was free in the world, and untouchable, threatened to break her in pieces. Relief came, ridden by desolation as the unstable flux sawed through the clear linkage and cut off rapport like a mercy stroke. The scried image winked out. The puff as Elaira released her seized breath extinguished the fluttering candle.

Plunged back into fusty dark, she blotted the emerald ring dry, then restored the band to the chain hung from her neck. Trembling, distraught, she sheathed the hawk's quill in her sleeve. Then, wrung ragged, she leaned against the stacked casks. Face shuttered, she released the pent storm of sheer longing and helpless resentment. The Biedar crone's warning given at Sanpashir haunted her: *"Can you let Arithon go beyond your control? Do you love enough to keep faith in him, even afflicted by your own loss? For he will seek his fate. If he can invent a fresh course by his wits, he will try to resolve his own happiness. Stand or fall, his life's path will be forged in this world. The gifts of his birthright will claim their full due. He will find himself, with or without you."*

Elaira firmed her shaken discipline. She packed up the tools of her practice. Sorely as she wished otherwise, she dared not forsake love's inviolate trust. Arithon must be left to rely on his instincts. If she wavered and intervened without cause, her selfish weakness would come to destroy him.

His state of ignorance shielded them both.

For as long as Arithon did not know her whereabouts, and while the sequestered recall of her identity stayed lost to him, Koriathain could not use her as the weapon to smash his defiant free will.

Whether Vivet's straits engaged his heart-felt sympathy, the Prince of Rathain would be safest from the reach of his enemies left upon his own merits.

Cold daybreak brought in the next squall line. A rampaging tower of anvilheads with gale-force winds broke over the Storlain Mountains. Vivet slept in a corner, outworn by exhaustion, curled beneath her torn cloak. The soaked fabric had dried. Her snarled chestnut hair curtained her cheek. The arms folded over her breasts lay relaxed, fingertips with broken nails flushed pink as a child's. She did not stir, even when thunder and driven rain rattled the cabin's rickety shutters.

The coals in the fire-place warmed off the dank chill. Since nothing else could be done for her comfort without the intrusion of touching her, Arithon left her undisturbed.

More, he welcomed the peace. Taxed to the edge of endurance himself, and still wracked by the bound and start of stressed faculties, rest escaped him. Given calm reprieve from the young woman's strident terror of his male presence, he snatched the chance to act for himself.

The driving blaze of his preference resurged: to relentlessly quarter the cabin and seek the lost memory of his beloved. Vivet's trauma curtailed a tranced assay through *tienelle*. The herb's heightened expansion would mire his wits and sweep him into the magnified pain of her wounded emotions.

Arithon reclaimed his discarded jacket. He replenished the fire, lit a brand, and under the juddering light, pondered his limited options. No trace remained to suggest where his heart's partner had slept. The soot-stained chimney showed nothing, not even a pot-hook, to define the character of her inhabitancy. In a dwelling stripped unremittingly bare, the weathered timbers themselves presented his only available sounding-board.

Patterns pervaded the flux currents. Over time, repeated events, or an individual's unique traits combed the structures of stone and wood into sympathetic alignment. Listen deeply enough, and the sensitivity of his Masterbard's ear might capture the ephemeral imprints. Latent impressions of his beloved should linger even after an extended absence.

Arithon wedged his torch in the cracked mantel shelf. He proceeded, no matter how exhaustively tired. His search must be done promptly. Before the delicate presence of her abraded under the stamp of recent experience, and Vivet's reactive turmoil clouded the near-faded trace.

Wood's vibration best amplified harmonic nuance, where mineral's retentive record endured. Arithon began with the fieldstone hearth. Eyelids half-shut, he stilled into a receptive state and stroked his finger-tips over the masonry.

Fire spoke to his inner ear first, the pungent vitality of fir logs just burned for lifesaving heat. Below the sibilant shriek of live flame, beneath the drummed rampage of weather, he heard rain-song: a wind-driven sluice ringing yet with shrill overtones wrought by the winds of high altitude.

Arithon sounded deeper. Underneath surface noise, he touched a faint pang of desolate sorrow. Loss and regret wove in poignant refrain, beneath which should lie the strata of her more significant presence. But as he reached into the tenuous veil, seeking, a vehement blast of *Fire!* and sage smoke razed through, a deliberate scour unleashed for the purpose of annihilation.

A ritual cleansing had swept this place clean!

Adamant, thorough, the measure had unravelled the residual record. Gone, the patterns that would have charted the cherished inflections of her personality.

Wrung blank by the purge, Arithon shuddered in recoil. Nothing more remained to be read. With all resonance of her prior tenancy erased, *she* had fled this dwelling with no ties and no plan to return. Cast adrift where he sorely hoped to find answers, and crushed by desolation, Arithon opened his eyes.

Plunged back into the framework of natural sight, he caught a pinprick flash of reflection: something shiny, wedged into a crack between floor-boards.

Before thought, he seized on the hope a small leaving of hers may have been overlooked. Not glass, he discovered upon closer survey. A tiny, broken sliver of crystal surfaced under his effort.

Crouched with held breath, spurred by careless persistence, he fingered the shard, intently listening. The rush of awareness took him by storm, a leap of revelation that crushed expectation and shattered his incomplete recall with terrible truths: *that she was a sworn sister of the Koriathain, trained in the usage of sigils amplified through a quartz matrix. The very same vicious knowledge once had been engaged to seal his long-term confinement. More than poisoned bait, she had made her love the willing tool of her superiors. Attached to his affairs by her Prime's directive, she had abetted his downfall, her person the infallible leverage behind the capitulation that saw him ensnared.*

Facts damned, by stark honesty. The impressions distilled in the fragment of crystal did not lie: he knew her well enough to sting under the bitterness of her heart's yearning, shackled in oath-tied subservience. She had been a weapon beyond all compare: a danger to him above death itself, her magnetic allure a force fit to level all of his core defences. Even wounded, he ached with irrational yearning. Peerless proof of her secret duplicity did not destroy the fatal attraction. Arithon wept, unable to reconcile his instinctive, flawed trust with the voice of her very self.

He flung the crystal chip into the hearth. He could not bear the message, far less assimilate the black agony that stranded him in separation.

Since rain and cold, and the violent storm matched the bias of his temper, he stumbled erect, yanked open the door, and barged outside to quench his bleak fury.

Practical measures steered his direction. Any anchor to dull a raw hurt that no remedy could assuage. Over the ridge, the corpse of a knifed trapper awaited a burial. More, survival relied upon setting game traps for sustenance. He could manage the insignificant chores. Fix his attention upon mindless work, before the crippling blow ground his spirit under the weight of stark sorrow.

Arithon ran. Downpour soaked him, and lightning flared, silver-white in the grey dawn. But the cruel severance could not be escaped, unequivocally framed in betrayal.

Personation

The breezes stirring midsummer's brass heat still carried the tang of defeat out of Havish. Rampant talk sown by Sunwheel deserters spread vivid accounts, embellished by the disaffected anxiety still building apace since the past spring's explosive flux surge. Few townsfolk doubted an outbreak of sorcerous Shadow had broken the True Sect invasion. If rumour claimed the Light's avatar also had vanished from the field in the after-shock, as dust settled in The Hatchet's retreat, port towns along Instrell Bay moved more reliable news in sealed dispatches. These confirmed the Master of Shadow's escape. Fewer, kept secret, traced Lysaer s'Ilessid's reappearance in anonymous seclusion at East Bransing.

While Sethvir at Althain Tower strained errant hearsay from truth, news of the war trickled eastward across the continent, hampered where Athili's bounds and the haunted pass through Lithmarin thinned the hectic flow of town trade across the Storlain ranges, and stalled altogether where the merchant guilds' influence languished at Backwater. Itinerant tinkers crept word of mouth northward. Morbid fears and suspicion spread from Daenfal Lake gradually through Araethura's back-country herders, where Iyat-thos Tarens and his youthful clan companions traversed the open steppe.

Footbound for weeks in an isolate vista of grassland and quicksilver streams thatched with briar, the party had been run off by vicious dogs. Where the goats grazed, unfenced, they were stoned on sight by furtive boys wielding hide slings.

Distance from the settlements added rank distrust. Appointed as spokesman for his friendly smile and crofter's accent, Tarens found his most polite knock met by a screech from the cottage matron who answered her door. His honest request to trade for a waxed cheese was put off by a meat skewer, the uproar unpleasantly quick to draw riled kin from the byre brandishing hay-forks.

"You'd think I'm a sorcerer in league with Shadow!" he vented, chased to breathless flight. Returned to find that morning's campsite stripped down, and no sign of his furtive companions, he required a clan tracker's skills to ferret out their direction.

Tarens caught up with Siantra at midmorning, soaked to the neck and flushed after crossing the swift-running creeks that furrowed a landscape riddled by narrow ravines. "Slinking weasel!" he accused. "You knew my reception was going to cause mayhem."

Sidir's willowy descendant fingered her strung bow and shrugged. Seal-dark hair and the fey glint in pale eyes accented the wolfish cast to her cheek-bones. "Why the injured surprise?" Daughter of her lineage, she evaded with truth. "You look like a ruffian inclined to steal eggs."

In fact, thieving was the most likely aim of a townsman this far off the beaten track: a large stranger scarred by a broken nose and armed with knife and sword posed a threat great enough to inspire hostility. Perhaps shamed she had played that advantage and bolted, Siantra flicked her sly glance askance. "You swam to throw off pursuit? That's foolhardy."

More than wet clothes prickled Tarens to chills. Warned he ruffled more than the young woman's poise, he bristled with incredulity. "This near the Arwent Gorge? Brazen sneak! Don't mock me with the belated concern that I might have drowned in the current!"

The vixen blushed. "If you're all that wise to the lay of the land, why risk your life?"

"Because I don't trust the pair of you out of my sight." The glib request to restock supplies in hindsight should have been questioned. "Esfand's gone ahead," the frank crofter accused, doubly annoyed to have fallen for the transparent deception.

"I stayed." Guilty, Siantra defended, "You can't fault us! Esfand rightfully should report first as his sire's heir apparent."

"More than my own sensibilities would argue," Tarens flared back.

"You can't overtake him," Siantra protested, hot on the crofter's heels as he passed her. "I held back only to stop you! If you manage to find the way down to the gorge, Esfand's alert will have warned the patrol scouts."

But Tarens possessed in full measure the past memories of Jieret, once *caithdein* to Rathain and High Earl of the North. He required no guide. Unless two hundred and fifty years of weather had crumbled the gap through the notch, he knew the hidden access into Halwythwood better than any.

Tailed by Siantra's dismayed footsteps, Tarens glanced backwards and spat in the dirt. "That, for cold-blooded murder! Your choice."

Then he sprinted. Shocked, nearly tearful, Siantra could not check a grown man twice her weight, short of taking him down with an arrow. Which the forest scouts' vigilance might well do anyway, denied their due chance to verify the outlandish twist: that this affable stranger who spoke in town dialect was not the bumpkin he appeared but a feal liegeman to Prince Arithon of Rathain.

Siantra shouted, distraught. "Esfand went to break the news that the clan relay through Halwythwood may be overfaced. And he's right! We can't grasp how deeply the True Sect's defeat has gutted treaty law, or what oppressive policy's arisen since Lysaer abdicated the mayor's seat at Etarra to Canon Law."

The recent lane shift unleashed hard against the disastrous campaign to fight Shadow had recoiled into fanatical hysteria. Distrust fed the Light's cause, while the volatile terror stirred by the heightened flux incited still more widespread purges. Old blood-lines were pursued under bounty again as True Sect doctrine inflamed the south. Irruptive outbreaks of latent talent at Backwater unleashed the renewed predation of trackers with dogs, funded in force by the head-hunters' leagues and the temple's coffers. Hounded under blood-letting unrest, the free wilds' scouts would be primed to kill any outsider on sight.

When Iyat-thos refused to wait upon reason, Siantra shed her cumbersome pack roll and raced in scared desperation to flank him.

The snare dropped with barely a slither of warning. Twine mesh weighted with stones netted Tarens halfway down the notched path, zigzagged through the cliff where Araethura's plateau dropped off sheer at the central fault-line. The cleft where he tumbled swooped a hundred yards downwards, straight for the rocky ravine that channelled the snaked froth of the Arwent. Banged and cut as he fell, unable to save himself, he slid at frightening speed towards the precipice.

A spindly, stunt fir snagged him short of fatality. Subject to a rough rescue, spluttering the spray inhaled from the white water boiling down the river-course, he swore vengeance in outraged Paravian. Siantra's shouts, more than his fluent insults, forestalled the scouts' ready swords. Murderous still, unimpressed by his grasp of old language, the clan patrol guarding the fringes of Halwythwood preferred distrust over lenient caution.

They trussed his hands, no surprise, given such callous handling deserved the honest retort of his fists. The gag that followed imposed an indecency Tarens fought tooth and nail.

The scouts jerked the knots brutally tight, while Siantra sniped from the side-lines. "Well, what did you expect? You've trespassed without leave, and not only that, crossed the honour of Esfand's ancestral name."

Which provocation Tarens already had acknowledged in unvarnished words. Restraints alone forestalled his scathing redress: Jieret's outrage demanded due reckoning. Dharkaron Avenger's Black Spear take the hour he should face High Earl Cosach s'Valerient: a blood chieftain, a father, and unconscionably terrifying, an invested *caithdein* whose cowardice had let three youngsters hare off after the realm's rightful duty to Rathain's crown prince.

That dangerous trek into enemy territory had led onto the red field of war and entangled their fates, with one feckless boy's life lost untimely.

Where Esfand's rebellious impulse had strained the leash of adult interference, not every rigorous standard had slipped since the day of Earl Jieret's authority. The patrol scouts that Tarens had thrashed to singed rage still reacted apace to unsanctioned intrusion.

They hauled his bulk upright. Efficient and quick, they disarmed him, then prodded his person at weapons' point down the precarious, switched-back trail into the ravine. Met at the river's edge by Esfand, and spoken for over the thundering rapids by Siantra's passionate argument, he found himself blindfolded and hoisted on a sling across the white race of the Arwent. Forced, stumbling, over the slippery rocks on the far bank, then from chilly shade into sunlight, he smelled grass, ears deafened by the shrilling of summer cicadas in the parched scrub underfoot. He endured more brisk handling. Another tussle, that ended with him in duress, lashed by a stout rope on horseback. By then, his captors' exasperated forbearance suggested his fight, or Siantra's insistent appeal, had been heard.

"Rest easy, fellow!" the scout captain snapped. "You're under our escort for a clan hearing."

If Jieret's inherited wisdom approved of the ruthless precautions, Tarens endured a pace that blistered his knees, painful sacrifice for the blessing of speed. His imperative charge to reach Halwythwood's council scalded his nerves to unease. Each passing hour since the past evening, the gut wrench of his instincts screamed warning. Wherever Arithon fared in the Storlains, whatever his current activity, Tarens sensed that a crucial dynamic had turned for the worse.

Family ties, before Sighted urgency, shaped the High Earl of the North's explosive response to the news of the prodigal children's return. The message relay that sent word by notched arrows flagged him down where he stood in tense conference. Cosach ran out on the council's debate over the True Sect hazard brewing at Etarra.

Burst into the lodge where his fair-haired wife nursed their four-month-old infant, he grinned ear to ear through his wiry beard and lunged for his weapons. "Esfand's back at last!" Aware of her tears as she surged to arise, he kissed her forehead and resettled her before the babe lost its suckle and howled. "I'm going myself." Busy with buckles, he answered her thought. "Laithen's heard. She's already away. When you've done with the wean, take over the reins and talk common sense to the chieftains. A few flaming maniacs think we can repel the Canon's blood purge with a war band."

The door flap slapped to his vigorous exit, through Jalienne's bemused rejoinder, "I'm not the best choice to keep order in there. Ask me, our warmongering dolts should be cooled like a dog scrap with pails of flung water."

"If only that worked," Rathain's *caithdein* lamented over his shoulder. A scrambled thud of hooves saw him mounted and gone, swiftly enough to meet the inbound scouts enroute from their post by the Arwent.

As usual, Laithen s'Idir's stringent sense outpaced everyone else. Her advance dispatch saw a hide tent pitched in wait, tucked under the dappled shade at the southern fringe of Halwythwood.

Late-afternoon sunlight seeped through the tied-back entry when Cosach stalked in. He found pine torches staked in place, but unlit, beside a plank trestle surrounded with grass-stuffed hassocks. Surprised to raised eyebrows by the banner of Rathain, hung behind, his glance met the whipcord-tough woman who emerged from the shadows. "I've received state visitors with much less fuss. My son won't be cowed. Are you trying to wake the fear of Dharkaron's vengeance in your only daughter?"

"As if anyone could," Laithen said, too blunt for his blustering. "Our youngsters may come in hungry and tired. Let's welcome them home and hear their report. In formal quiet, before they are mobbed for details by a raucous audience."

"Well." Cosach gestured askance at the curtain strung to provide private quarters. "Jalienne will skin me alive if I stall our boy overnight."

Laithen's mouth quirked. Slender in restraint as a planted spear, she countered the feint. "They aren't children, no matter they've not come of age. After this, you don't think they deserve the respect of an adult reception?"

Cosach snorted. "Maybe." He fumed, bunched broad shoulders, and swore with bad grace, then shucked his sword and filled the cramped tent with his restless anticipation. Ever the model of cool sobriety, Laithen leaned on a support pole to quell her impulse to pace.

A woodpecker's tap pocked the stillness from the humid depths of the forest: no bird's industrious foraging but a signal from a concealed sentry. Cosach froze between steps, while Laithen let go and shoved forward. Muscular High Earl and mercurial woman barely avoided collision as the outriders reined up lathered mounts in the glen. Both anxious parents poised with stopped breath until the boisterous commotion sorted itself out, and the dismounted pack of scouts swirled and parted.

The son whose rash exploits had sent him too dangerously far afield emerged first. Esfand was no longer the unfinished stripling, all elbows and knees with the gawky neck of adolescence. Taller, fleshed out, he advanced with confidence, his seal-dark clan braid secured with grass twine, and his leathers the worse for hard wear. Intent hazel, his eyes locked on the father poised at the tent's entry.

Then mature poise shattered. Esfand surged forward in naked relief and burst out, agonized, "Khadrien—"

Cosach swept the lad into a bear hug. Gruff with pride for the young man in his clasp, he said, "Never mind. Later. We already know. Your mother's well, and you have a new sister to welcome. Cordaya."

Hard at Esfand's heels came Siantra. Grown as well, but fretted rail thin, her coltish frame still moved with incongruous grace, but no more in impetuous innocence: under charcoal brows bunched into a frown, her enormous, pale eyes held an unearthly light. Met by her diminutive mother, she burst out, "I'm sorry! The black sword, Alithiel—"

"We're aware of that, also." Laithen embraced her daughter, tearful and smiling. "Khadrien's exploits can be discussed later." Overjoyed though she was by reunion, the fair-skinned outsider the scout guards hauled in blind-folded had not escaped her. "That won't be his Grace. Who else have you brought us?"

Cosach scowled at the bound stranger, which prompted the patrol to present the unplanned arrival forthwith. "Inside," he snapped, then, "You, as well," to the son just reassessed at arm's length. "Sit with us. I'll hear your report once this trespasser's case is settled to my satisfaction."

Siantra and Esfand exchanged a tense glance, not canny enough to duck Laithen's quicksilver intelligence. "Not now!" The jerk of her chin towards the tent implored them to retire without argument.

Commanded to the side-lines, the youngsters watched, silent, as the scouts dragged Tarens from horseback and hauled him to the tent for summary judgement. Laithen settled at the end of the trestle, overshadowed by Cosach, who stalked in and retrieved his sword. The baldric hung in place at his shoulder when the stranger's person was manhandled before him and shoved onto his knees in the dirt.

"He's unarmed?" Cosach cracked. "Then cut the wretch free. I would see a man's face while he's questioned." Through the bustle as the scout escort wrestled their trussed prisoner back upright, the High Earl repeated Laithen's clipped inquiry. "What have you brought us?"

Siantra's swift assessment, called out of turn, "An ally who knows Prince Arithon better than we do!" entangled with Esfand's appeal, "Let the fellow speak for himself."

"Ally!" Surprise never softened High Earl Cosach to leniency. He kicked a stuffed hassock towards the armed scouts. "Sit the trespasser down." Arms braced on the board at his back, he watched slit-eyed, while the scouts prodded their charge as directed, spring-wound to strike at the least provocation. They severed the knots at the intruder's roped wrists, then whisked off the cloth bundled over his head.

Blond hair in need of a trim pasted the fellow's flushed features: a visage moulded by country-bred honesty, handsome before the welted scar that disfigured his broken nose. Weathered to creases by sunburn, blue eyes blinked in the dazzle of sunlight shafted through the open tent flap.

A poised threat recessed into gloom, Cosach sized up the scouts' catch at stilled leisure. His own stance stayed hackled as he found himself as directly surveyed in turn. The captive did little but chafe his cramped hands, an innocuous gesture that also lent space for his unmasked senses to reorient. Plain as a shout, his incensed silence protested his uncivil treatment.

"Rough times have returned," Cosach allowed softly. "Town-born strays are apt to be head-hunters' spies. Best give us your reason for slinking into the free wilds."

The stranger's response cut past Siantra's protest. "I would have your name before I confide." Head tipped upwards in dangerous inquiry, he laced his limbered fingers.

The realm's *caithdein* showed teeth and responded with all of his titles. Then, mocking, he inclined his head and acknowledged the witness of Laithen s'Idir.

"Ah!" Wheaten eyebrows rose with brazen amusement. "By all means, I'll endorse Sidir's lineage for probity. Provided, of course, the lady serves also as unimpeachable oversight for my case in turn." Clasped fists hardened, the rogue leaned aggressively forward. "I am known by Iyat-thos Tarens." In flawless Paravian, he repeated Cosach's state titles, added Laithen's full name with deference, then declared, "Mind your impeccable tradition since I will deliver the tidings I bring on my feet!"

He shoved erect then, palpably angered as the armed guard behind slapped a hostile grip on their weapons.

Cosach's barked order defused the attack. Equally matched in height and broad stature, he had not misread the capable stamp of the farmer. Yet the balanced stance wearing the guise of a crofter pitched more than his scouts onto prickling edge. Cosach acknowledged the fighting trim on a man whose business screamed primal danger.

Tarens invoked clanbred etiquette, crossed his wrists at the heart, and continued. "I bring word of your own. Be it known to s'Valerient kin that my best effort could not avert tragedy. Your boy, Khadrien, crossed the Wheel in Scarpdale in the brave service of Rathain's prince."

Laithen made a sound, hands pressed to her mouth, while Cosach's chopped signal enforced her silence. "Town-whelped upstart! How dare you presume."

"To your shame, on the contrary," Tarens replied. "Explain why three youngsters not grown to majority left the safety of Halwythwood to shoulder a perilous cause for the realm. The answer you give better satisfy, obligated as I have been by the shade of your titled ancestor, Jieret s'Valerient. His outraged memory as a clan chieftain demands a reckoning in full."

Cosach purpled.

"He's telling the truth!" Siantra pealed, desperate.

Which shocking breach impelled Laithen to break protocol. A diminutive brown sparrow swooped in to scold at an eagle's threat to the nest, she flung herself between the insolent stranger and Rathain's incensed *caithdein*. "Sit down, both of you!" Her open palm slapped Cosach's barrel chest, while she spun in chastisement on Tarens. "Don't condemn the harsh choice you know nothing about. Ath above! If your claim of connection is genuine, then find the civilized reason to air both sides of the matter before you cause bloodshed."

When Tarens folded back onto the hassock, face masked behind shuttered hands, she pealed over his shoulder to one of the scouts. "End this cruel falsehood. Now! I will not abide! You're sent. Yes, at once! He's assigned at the horse picket."

Yet the person she summoned required no messenger: a sheepish cough and a crack in the privacy flap disclosed the eavesdropping presence of a gangling scamp in trail leathers, the carroty wisp of yesterday's clan braid gnawed between nervous teeth. "I'm here, actually," confessed Khadrien, singed red for the prank played on his aghast companions. "Sorry about that. But who could resist? Since you thought I was dead, you deserved the comeuppance for leaving me." He managed no more, overturned with a yelp as Siantra and Esfand pounced both at once, knocked him flat, and pounded him breathless.

Amid bemused commotion, Laithen transferred her repressive scowl from Cosach. Sympathy moved her to grip Tarens's wrist as she realized his shaken clasp masked relieved tears.

She said quickly, "We had word from a Sorcerer, yes, within days. The youngsters should have been informed straightaway. Since our miscreant carelessly lost the heirloom sword and the horse, the Fellowship decided he had no further business mucking about in the Kingdom of Havish. Asandir dispatched Khadri home from the focus circle at Fiaduwynne. As you see, he has suffered less than he deserved. I'm so sorry! No one meant to be callous. We had no idea that you'd shouldered a harrowing trip and misplaced anguish in our behalf."

Cosach recoiled and roared at Laithen, "Dharkaron's grief, woman! What insanity prompts your trust in an outsider whose outrageous claim is not verified?"

Laithen paused. Rod thin, she glared upwards at her chieftain: who backed off a step, hiked one hip on the trestle, and perched in stonewalled confrontation.

Laithen's whiplash grin followed. "Likely I've seen the same thing as my daughter. This man shares your lineage in truth. You're not convinced yet? Let me show you proof."

She bent once more to the town-born on the hassock, stunned yet in mortified after-shock. "Here's the filthy secret to dealing with Khadrien. If his exploits bother your conscience again, understand that fecklessness runs in his blood. As our High Earl's family descends from Barach, here's the flip side of history: Khadri's branch springs from the sister, who wed Sevrand s'Brydion."

Tarens lowered his hands. *"You say Jeynsa married the bullheaded nephew of Alestron's warmongering duke?"* Through an unembarrassed sheen of stalled tears, his expression showed genuine horror. "The minx! Was she mad to breed with that clutch of rife trouble?" He winced. "Though fiends plague the hindmost, nobody else owned the cast-iron bollocks to deal with her spitfire nature."

All at once, he succumbed to the irony, threw back his blond head, and laughed.

When finally Iyat-thos recovered his breath, he bypassed the shield of Laithen's acceptance and tackled Cosach's recalcitrance directly. "I've been endowed with Jieret's memories and the full measure of his trained skills. Not to supplant your sworn charge as *caithdein*, but to grant Arithon a reliable ally to access his forgotten past."

Cosach fielded the remarkable statement, prepared to seek disposition. "This is an appeal?"

"Perhaps," Tarens ventured. "I came to help your effort to contact his Grace and restore his connection with Rathain's feal clans. As a friend, I entreat your council to weigh my attributes in good faith. My background bought your youngsters safe passage through Backwater." Through the distraction of Khadrien's glib talk, and Siantra and Esfand's recounted experience, the outsider offered, "A town-bred crofter might move freely where clansfolk would face deadly risk."

Granted his own shrewd angle of insight, Cosach spun and accosted the youngsters in cahoots by the curtained alcove. "I'll have your opinion before your report! Do I rely on this fellow to keep the integrity of our affairs?"

As observer, Laithen interpreted two boys' crest-fallen consternation, then lost her breath, chilled by the uncanny depth in her daughter's regard. "Surely we must." She brushed off her chieftain's disgruntled surprise. "Well, how else can we hope to thwart these three miscreants from trying their next lame-brained escapade?"

But Cosach's assessment of the errant trio belied her dismissive remark. The stunning expansion of Siantra's talent, offset by Esfand's obdurate commitment and Khadrien's hot-headed impulses, suggested that the three together posed something greater than their individual destinies.

"Ath wept!" muttered Cosach, jellied by a fore-running tremor of prescience. He folded onto the nearest hassock and dismissed the scouts' guard from the tent. His capitulation called upon Laithen to scrounge someone's brandy and a suitable vessel.

"Iyat-thos!" he concluded in outright demand. "You're prepared to swear a guest's oath of amity?"

Shown the man's unreserved acquiescence, Cosach's broad gesture invited the townsman to claim a proper seat at the trestle. "Let's hear your story. Leave nothing out! You say our dead ancestry has seen fit to provide living guidance from beyond the veil? Then I'll have the facts on the matter straight up! What under Athera's mysteries are Rathain's liege folk being stiffened to face?"

Realignments

Called onto the carpet before the High Priest at Erdane, the Light's First Commander, known as The Hatchet, accepts the new orders for his beaten troops; and while eyes chill as ice chips flick down the lines, his clamped lips flex into a predator's grin, that his proposal to harden morale has been endorsed to his satisfaction . . .

Amid the rainy streets of East Bransing, a charitable, blond aristocrat halts his retinue for a destitute elder who pleads to black his boots for a penny; and when the fellow's deft expertise brings up the reason for his unemployment, the tale of a master's demise in the war prompts a kind invitation to serve in his Lordship's household . . .

Briefly returned to Althain Tower from the High Queen of Havish's late coronation, Asandir sees his black stallion stabled, then all but collides with Sethvir, caught descending the stairwell in agitation: "The Prime," he admits. "Her next move's set in motion, a play of deceitful exploitation far worse than anything she's tried before . . ."

II. Entanglement

The swift onset of evening in the high Storlains welled a breath of dire cold off the glaciers, even in summer. Arithon shivered, chilled since the cloud-bank that rolled over the peaks had shrouded the sunlight. Caught in the gloaming with clothing and hair still damp from his wash in a freshet, he secured his gleaned bundle of rushes. Then he turned his dispirited steps towards the cabin in the ravine.

Night's gloom deepened his cankered malaise. He skirted the feathered boughs of stunt firs, unmoved by the primal thrill of a wolf pack howling beyond the ridge. The vigorous rustles of nocturnal creatures failed to shake off his low spirits. Though a night and full day of hard labour had laid Vivet's knifed attacker to rest, the nameless man's violent passage left a nagging sense of unease.

No record remained to decipher the final words left unsaid. Arithon's sensitive talent had failed to sift meaningful clues from the roiled cascade of the regional flux lines.

That arcane endeavour, and the back-breaking chore of hauling loose stone for a grave cairn, yielded an exhaustion without numb relief. Subsequent pursuit of wild herbals fell short as a peaceful distraction. Scraped hands and the ache of spent muscle could not blunt the appalling wound to his spirit.

Arithon had never grappled the scope of such pain. The brute history packed into a sliver of crystal seared his heart-strings to anguish and unreeled a desolate future.

Last place on Athera he wished to revisit, the cabin offered the nearest shelter. He needed the immediate warmth to dry off and sleep before he moved on.

The rose tint of the afterglow bled from the ranges as he retraced his path down the remnant track, cut by the harness mule that had once hauled an ice cutter's sledges. Spent, he crossed the streamlet and mounted the log stair, zigzagged upwards from the deep ravine. His arrival at the derelict shack found no one inside. The unlatched door swung open to fastened shutters and quiet.

Except yesterday's velvet-thick darkness had changed. No longer musty, the air wore the spiked fragrance of balsam. The boards underfoot were swept clean of debris. Once his fumbling, chilled hands lit a spill, he took stock of Vivet's industrious tenancy: a bed of cut pine boughs arranged in one corner; also a table fashioned from the salvaged wreck of a muleteer's sleigh. Logs hewn from a deadfall served as makeshift seats, with birch kindling stacked by the hearth.

The axe wielded to split the stockpiled fuel seemed nowhere in evidence.

Arithon ignited the woodchips in the grate. The quickened flame melted the shadows and confirmed: the tiny cabin lay empty around him, with Vivet gone off on her own.

The small blaze burned fast. Arithon added more logs. Then he shed the cross-strap of his baldric, unslung his sheathed sword, and settled to rest by the fireside with the black blade propped against his bent knees. He soaked in the heat, grateful for privacy. Later was soon enough to assist Vivet's busy intent to claim residence. Since noose traps for game were best set before daybreak, he catnapped, forehead braced on the crooked forearm that cradled his weapon.

If the exquisite enchantments forged into the weapon spun him uncanny dreams, he was not given solitude to plumb their content. The scrape of the door, then the icy draught wafted over the threshold signalled Vivet's return.

Snapped awake, Arithon surged erect in apology. "I shall leave at once for your peace of mind."

But if his presence seemed cause for dismay, the woman did not shrink from the surprise encounter. The knot torch in her hand revealed tidied hair, russet coils pinned at her nape with a hazel sprig still jewelled with peridot leaves. She carried two woodcocks strung up by the legs. Also a resourceful haul of wild berries, tubers, and greens, bundled up in her mended overskirt. Pale cream, marked with bruises, her oval face turned. Wide-eyed, she regarded him.

"Please stay. I don't fear you." The hatchet looped through her sash lent teeth to a statement at odds with her tremulous grip on the brand.

Moved under the whispered flutter of flame, Vivet spilled her bounty upon the crude table.

"I brought food for two. In case you came back." She nodded towards the evergreen bed, where the brightened light showed a cache of muddied belongings. "My things tumbled down-slope in the scuffle last evening. I saw your work during my search to recover them. You need not have shouldered my troubles to start with, far less stayed on to give decent burial to a criminal stranger's remains. A meal's the least you deserve for the kindness."

Pain hitched her hesitant step. The livid bruises on her throat and neck strained her voice husky with swelling. Defiantly able to fend for herself, she jammed the knife used to dispatch her assailant into the boards, then attacked the gruesome task of dressing game.

Her presumptive gesture of repayment galled. Arithon shook off a stab of pique. Tired past sense, he recovered his misplaced courtesy. "At least allow me my fair share of the plucking."

"I require no help!" Vivet's quaver banished him to a safe distance.

Arithon tried conversation to soothe her jagged aggression. "You mentioned before you were on your way home?"

Vivet's pinched mouth jerked. "Why not say what you think?" Knife brandished to lop off the birds' heads, she sighed. "Surely you'd say these rugged mountains are no place for a woman alone."

Which venomous bitterness attacked first in assumption: that men believed female vulnerability invited the opportune assault of a predator. Masterbard, healer, Arithon let her stung denouncement flounder in silence.

For a while, only the torch-flame whickered in dialogue with the drawing blaze in the fire-place.

Vivet presently dropped the halfway-gutted bird and banged down her fists. "Damn you!" Outrage pointed enough to drill flint turned her battered face towards him. "You act as though naught in the world has gone wrong!"

But the purple contusions on her flesh shouted testament to the contrary.

To stand with a sword, even sheathed, posed a threat. Arithon tucked up and sat by the hearth. He laid the shining, obsidian blade flat, deferent to the axe she kept within reach. "Should I forget? You knifed your attacker." Arms folded atop his bent knees, he added, "I've witnessed your courage. Therefore, I'm able to bow to your fears without prejudice." His grave regard was an initiate sorcerer's, grounded in the self-knowledge to bear the most vicious hatred, unflinching.

Vivet spun away. The gleam on her hair like warm carnelian, she raised her blood-smeared wrist to her cheek to blot her ashamed tears.

Arithon's patient remonstrance pursued her. "A past act of abuse can't vanquish the strength of the survivor I see before me." He petitioned for truce. "Tonight's calm is equally real. And without pretence, despite the after-shock of an unspeakable trauma."

Vivet quivered. Fragile poise undone at a stroke, she snatched the knife from the trestle and bolted. Her tempestuous exit slammed the plank door, forceful enough to shake cobwebs down from the rafters.

She could not be gone long. Without a wool mantle, the relentless cold must outface her emotional storm. Arithon slid the black sword out of sight behind the stacked firewood. Then he took charge of the half-prepared meal, goaded by the ruthless irony: that his platitude consoled nothing. Within and without, his presence was emptied by desolation. The core of his heart had been just as savaged as Vivet's used body. Naught existed in the wide world to salve the anguish encountered within these four walls. His own needled urge to take flight found no respite in the rote plucking of carcasses.

Yet a master's awareness viewed the hard road ahead without quarter. All pain must be measured, and met, and finally conquered. Life demanded resilience. Or else the mired spirit would languish, forlorn, crippled under self-indulgent regret.

Arithon stuffed the split birds with wild onion, then wrapped them in herb leaves for flavour. Spitted, they roasted over the coals, while his makeshift oven contrived with flat rocks baked the tubers inside their scrubbed skins.

Vivet returned to that savoury aroma, her downcast eyes puffed, and her arms burdened with additional evergreen. Not to seem useless, she dropped the fresh boughs for his bed in the opposite corner.

"I'm sorry." Her strained limp brought her back towards the trestle. "I've given poor thanks for your civil forbearance."

Arithon shifted at once to restore space between them.

"Stay," Vivet objected, singed red with shame. "Don't freeze yourself on the floor for my sake."

The first torch had burned down. She kindled another and wedged the stake upright before perching in rigid defiance across the table.

His own raw emotion battened in shadow, Arithon studied her. Up close, underneath the patched bruises, her skin was too young for crow's-feet. Barely into her twenties, she had a sparrow's pert grace, a firm chin, apple cheeks, and an expressive dimple beneath coral lips. Her independence carried the cracked fragility of fine porcelain, savagely used but not ruined, though her shadowed glance had forever lost the care-free sparkle of innocence.

"I was returning to Ettinmere Settlement," she admitted, a brazen effort to forge trust in good faith. Sooty circles beneath downcast lashes wore the pouches of recurrent weeping. Trembling unmasked her false confidence as she added, "I have family there. A father, now passed. Three brothers. Two married sisters. My mother fell ill. I heard through a fur trader. But no word since then to know if she's living."

Vivet's lids flicked up, her bloodshot eyes the vivid blue of a fair-weather lake. "My people are proud of their insular ways. They'll say, perhaps rightly, I should not have run off on a feckless adventure to Deal."

The moment filled with the sibilant crackle of flames, while wind off the peaks swooped over the roof shakes, and prised a complaint from a squeaky shutter. Arithon studied Vivet's clenched hands, without obvious marks of a gainful profession. Distress obscured her true personality. Left to his musician's gift, he sifted the overtones of her remark and answered her plaintive uncertainty. "You'd have had good reason to seek your own way. One just as important as the resolve that drives your contrite return."

Vivet's breath hitched. "More than anything, I wanted the learning to read and write." More tears might have spilled, had she not been wrung dry. Her loosened hair hazed under flame-light, she huddled like a storm-battered bird, fluffed after a cruel drenching. Her panicky outburst escaped before thought, "Fatemaster's mercy, I daren't be seen by my people like this!"

And that sharp, fateful phrase struck the sensitive ear of the Masterbard. Arithon sounded the unpremeditated truth and mapped Vivet's untenable conflict. Beneath fear, under desperate, trapped rage and stunned hurt in the aftermath of violation, her mangled spirit required the unpressured solitude to recoup and heal. There, vital need floundered into the pit of her frantic anxiety. Wing-broken, her shattered confidence quickened the terror of being alone.

Arithon committed himself without thought. Rootless after his own love's betrayal, the ashes of his desire embraced Vivet's agonized need, uncontested.

Distraught incentive cared very little how long her predicament shackled him. Since his ancestral compassion abandoned no wounded spirit to languish, the man sanctioned as the Crown Prince of Rathain plucked the spit off the hearth in deferent anonymity.

"Your brace of woodcock appear to be roasted." Pain masked by the trivial matter of supper, he set the unwarranted seal on his future. "You need go nowhere before you are ready. I'll keep watch at the door while you sleep. When you're comfortable travelling, and if you wish, I'll guard your way back to your kinfolk in Ettinmere."

Vivet's tension unburdened in flooding relief. Arithon rode the impulse of his generosity, salved by his power to offer redress, where his personal hurt found no solace. No farsighted glimpse of dire complication ruffled his sensitive instincts.

Instead, as the evening deepened, the quiet camaraderie shaped by the meal wove a web of frail magic. Meat knifed off the bone and eaten with fingers wore down reserved self-consciousness. His teasing remark about duelling with straws to determine who washed up, without pots and plates, almost raised Vivet's shy smile. The fleeting flicker of forgotten joy touched the moment she thought he looked elsewhere.

Eased by a beauty that transformed her marked face, Arithon conceded her path to recovery was not entirely one-sided. Though a prolonged stay at the cabin did nothing for his pierced heart, his earnest offer of escort to Ettinmere perhaps posed an unforeseen advantage. Vivet's grateful family might give him shelter. If not to over-winter in safety, at least he might bargain for warmer clothing and needful supplies. The settlement was remote. Its insular society, hidebound in tradition, shunned outsiders and distrusted Sunwheel priests. As a passing haven, the site could thwart the deadly reach of his enemies.

The present meanwhile rested on the ordinary. While Vivet attended her necessities outside, Arithon tossed their leftovers through the window to fatten the scavenging mice. He secured the loose shutter, replaced the spent torch with a rushlight, and banked the embers in the fire-place. After Vivet's return, he took up his sword and moved the piled evergreen boughs for his bed to the threshold. Then he sat with his back against the shut door. Tired himself, he honoured his word: burned reckless resource to keep wakeful vigil until the woman settled her nerves and rest overcame her anxiety.

The rushlight burned low. Melted into shadow, the swept boards smelled of damp. Long fled, the sweet fragrance of the bundled herbs once hung to dry in the rafters. No ephemeral trace of the healer's presence remained to chafe Arithon's overkeyed senses.

Aching, bereft, he watched Vivet fight the stir of incipient nightmares. Reflection sparked a fitful gleam in her opened eyes until the reed ember winked out. She did not toss and turn but lay in taut stillness into the deeps of the night. Chafed by her turbulent tension, and haunted by other ghosts from his gapped memory, Arithon yearned for the balm of his talent on the lyranthe. The cabin's too-personal history made the silence ring loud on his ear. Each breath offended his nostrils with the stinging pungency of balsam: a strong scent, not *her*, and a signal wrongness that frayed every natural instinct.

Fretted past sense, Arithon shouldered the watch through another wearisome hour. The thud of his heart-beat yearned for another woman's secretive thoughts. He felt more alone than ever before in his years of extended life.

The onerous minutes crept by. The risen moon silvered the cracks in the shutter. Naught stirred the fir boughs outside but the breeze, while the shuttlecock flight of an owl chased mice come to gorge upon the scrapped bones.

Until Vivet broke the unbearable quiet with a tremulous whisper, "I'm sorry. I never asked for your name."

"Call me by Arin," said the Prince of Rathain, disinclined to share his identity. That mistake had harmed the crofters in Kelsing, whose fortunes had turned for the worse by his presence. Better to consign Vivet's well-being to her family and depart without leaving a trace.

Time came at long last when the body's exhaustion surmounted distress and the throbbing complaint of fresh injuries. Vivet's tortured breathing deepened and quieted. Beyond weary himself, Arithon fashioned a simple cantrip to awaken himself before sunrise. Then he retired the sword and snugged down his mantle. His depleted awareness let go at once. Alert for too long, reserves utterly spent, he welcomed oblivion and plunged without care into dreamless sleep. But not as he wished, until dawn.

Pulled from the drugged syrup of black-out exhaustion, Arithon stirred to the blissful, bold heat of a woman's hands on him: fingers that teased through his parted clothes and caressed him with intimate urgency. Her touch trembled, shameless, arousing as fire, intoxicate with the fierce promise of release. The assault on his undone defences caught his breath, then drove the wind from him, branding his skin with desire that rushed him senseless.

He roused, consumed. Vital, alive, hazed by animal lust after repressive years of cruel abstinence, his flesh screamed. The air he fought into punched lungs wrung him dizzy. Clinging as velvet, musked in piquant smoke, the scent of exotic perfume unmoored him. He need only surrender himself. Falling into the abyss of raw pleasure, he plunged heedless towards blind conflagration. Past reason, the urgent clamour of male ecstasy trampled his desolate hurt.

Confusion welcomed the storm wind of passion, a forceful antidote for the heart-break that stranded him in bleak solitude. A longing too vast to contain might be drowned, if only for one fleeting moment.

If he dreamed, here was surcease. Veiled in a silken fall of warm hair, raised to heightened torment by blind need, Arithon groaned. Thought fled as her fecund weight straddled him.

Reflex took over. Yearning drove the leap of his being: but no answering spiral surged in response. No rarefied synergy kindled delight. The lightning bolt of her counterpoint harmony did not rise to balance him. If ever he had shared such exquisite joy, or flown, bedazzled, into the glory of a matched consummation, no such seamless experience unfolded. His spirit encountered no flowering grandeur but launched into nothing, unpartnered. No piercing tenderness thrilled his raced pulse with the grace of a mirrored response.

The hands gripping his shoulders were none that he knew: and in the burgeoning blaze where emotion *should have* melted him into cascading completion, Arithon slammed, bewildered, against an implacable separation.

In fact, the glad shimmer of physical pleasure *on her part* was utterly absent.

This frenetic bid to possess him was not carefree eagerness but the desperation of dread, overwritten by calculation. His shaken faculties curdled. Pain of the flesh and anguish of mind violated his initiate's integrity.

Arithon recoiled as though struck in the gut. He broke the chokehold of her embrace. Wrenched free of her naked weight in revulsion that tore the eyelets of his unstrung laces out of his rifled clothing. Slammed backward against the cabin's latched door, he cried out. The jolt to his frame scarcely registered. Cold to the bone, breached desire quenched utterly, he stared reeling into the dark, blistered to mage-sighted outrage.

The waif's face he confronted wore bruises.

"Vivet!" he shouted, aghast. "Ath's greater mercy!" Moved again, jackknifed upright, Arithon snapped off his shredded shirt. He flung her the garment with a hoarse plea to cover her nakedness. "What are you about? Grace above, you can't want this! Not from me, tonight, surely not from any man!"

"Believe it." She crumpled, shivering, the mangled cloth crammed beneath her soaked cheek. Damaged in body and spirit, she languished in artless prostration amid the scattered balsam. "More than life, I crave your affection."

Which was an outright lie. The note of her falsehood jarred his musician's ear and splashed ugly echoes across his rogue far-sight.

Arithon jerked away lest she debase herself further. Yanked up his smallclothes and breeches, even as she stretched and clasped his ankles in entreaty.

Offended, he shoved her off. "What do you want of me, Vivet?" Furious, he pressured her frigid intent. "Comfort? Favour? Security? Do you wish a house, a mate, or just a randy champion to cosset your injuries on a pedestal? Is it children you want to salve loneliness? Or do you seek a stranger's infatuated sympathy to bury your sorrows? Take care how you answer! I am no puppet to be yanked on the strings of a craven manipulation."

"I want nothing!" she retorted. "Only to win back a measure of happiness."

Which indignant denial made Arithon feel soiled. "Stop cheating yourself." The heated air gagged him, smoke-thick, floral sweet, and cloying enough to blanket his senses. "Tell me the truth before I walk out!"

She hung her head. Tangled hair, fallen, muffled her plea, "Is your offer to guard me so easily shaken?"

Sickened, wrung dizzy by his raced pulse and the mangle of grief left by his own ravaged hope, Arithon side-stepped and flung open the shutter. He needed the shock of cold air in his lungs. Anything to quench the rife scald of his temper, before he vented his outrage and struck her.

Whatever forsaken sentiment drove her, Vivet rejected all instinct for self-preservation. "Why spurn my thanks for your generosity?"

Arithon met her pandering question with sarcasm. "Should I succumb? A strumpet requires less attention. How long, before you also demand my loyalty and my confidence? Poppet, enlighten me. Is wanton sport in my bed worth so much?"

But his cruel bid to win solitude failed to shake her tawdry masquerade. "The choice, of course, is still yours to make."

Arithon's smile bared teeth in the moonlight. "And if I am ruthless? Would you balk at vice? Or protest if my habits don't suit your fancy?"

"I trust you," she insisted. "Give my favour a chance."

"Blindly?" he shot back, the more vicious as his rocked equilibrium resettled.

"Even so." She swallowed, her bruised features ribboned with tears. Piteous under his blistering scorn, she wrestled down sobs to finish. "Yes. Blindly."

"Then you debase yourself like a dock-side whore! Why throw me your charms without self-respect? That's a dangerous folly. *Because I could take you, Vivet, on those libertine terms*. Hard and fast, with no pang of remorse, because to do otherwise mocks integrity."

The revilement that ought to have shaken her only clenched her obstinate fingers in his rucked shirt. "Even so. I offer."

His response mocked. *"You offer me what?"*

Moonlight mottled her mussed hair and shadowed her eyes too deeply to read what he sought: the least trace of the honest, misplaced feelings she denied for who knew what reckless purpose.

Restored to command by the bite of the draught, Arithon tried again to rend the pretence driving her to self-destruction. "Then who will drink the cup of pain that remains when I have deserted you?" He gripped the sill. Presented his back, whipped to a shiver that taxed his chilled frame. Masterbard, trained to interpret emotional nuance, he braced himself against flinching mercy and pitched his revulsion to break her. "For you would waken alone, my hot strumpet, because the passion you tender with such persistence is none of my making!"

Her riposte stung with anger. "Then go ahead and abandon me now since I'm ruined for life in the eyes of my kinfolk!"

Surprise caught him short. Arithon's mage-sighted faculties slipped as her admission smashed his expectation. While he doused the blindsided scald of his temperament, sorting the puzzle of altered dynamics, Vivet hung shieldless and vulnerable through a silence that lasted too long. Shattered, she lunged upright. Faster than thought, she plucked out the trapper's knife left impaled in the table-top. Steel flashed in self-determined aggression. Not against him, but angled inwards to pierce her own heart.

Arithon moved then. Shoved off the sill, he gripped her forearm with bone-crushing force. The blade tumbled free and clattered to the floor. The metallic clang too loud in his ears, he crushed Vivet's balked agony into submission against his bare chest.

The contact unravelled his barriers again, spun him off centre, and ripped him wide open.

He reeled, fighting to ground his unhinged perception. Trained reflex escaped him. The exotic fragrance of Vivet's perfume sucked his subtle awareness headlong into her fevered passion. Enveloped by frightening, intimate empathy, he drowned in the heat off her skin.

Her naked desire stormed his reserve. Thrown under redoubled assault and wrestling his besieged intellect, Arithon fought to breathe. The tainted air whirled him giddy and sapped his will to stay upright. Carnal instinct this time found no sheet-anchor. Nothing to stay his innate male response to her female bid for possessive conquest.

Dimly, he realized something was wrong. *This prepotent beguilement could not be natural.* In fact, his adamant outrage spoke true: a narcotic herb, unknown to his training, swirled through the trapped smoke in the cabin.

Disgust restored reason. Arithon shed Vivet's clinging embrace. Plunged back to the window, he sucked a clean breath. Then he bent and retrieved the loose knife. Moved on, revolted, he dodged Vivet's lunge and snapped the axe out of her reach. One stroke smashed the latched shutter opposite. He thrust the helve through, hurled the weapon into the ravine, beyond recovery until morning.

Arithon secured his abandoned sword next. Chest bursting, he surged to the hearth, where he hooked the hot iron damper with the quillon and reopened the draw of the flue. His kick scattered the poisonous coals. Tainted smoke swirled. He backed in retreat. Braced at the gapped window, he leashed his fired nerves. Inhaled the fresh air, again and again, while the restored draught cleared the fumes of Vivet's potent aphrodisiac.

Streamed sweat and reaction by then made him shiver. Bitterly chilled, Arithon waited until his mage-trained reflex threw off the intoxication. In sharp command, fully guarded at last, he turned back and regarded the pitiful woman huddled in distraught collapse.

She would be freezing, unclad as she was. Arithon stirred to locate her shucked cloak. Minded as well to recover his jacket, he kept knife and black sword in hand, as much to shave tinder and rebuild the fire as to foil another attempted suicide.

Vivet flinched from his step. Weeping, she shouted, "I meant you no harm!"

Arithon granted her histrionics no sympathy. "Don't prevaricate!" He hooked up the mantle from her rumpled bed. "I know my butchery better than that." The cloth he shook out flicked over her shoulders, without human contact. "Why, Vivet? How could a planned seduction mend a rift with your family?"

He extended no hand to raise her up. No touch assuaged her limp pathos.

While the icy breeze leached the warmth from the cabin, Arithon retrieved his profaned shirt. Distasteful of the narcotic residue ingrained in the fabric, he proceeded with riveted patience to lay a fresh fire with kindling and birch. "I will listen," he said, "when you've regained composure. Let's discuss your problem with adult sense, or else forfeit my pledge to assist a safe return to your kinfolk."

Althain Tower blazed with light from top floor to sallyport, a rare sight in the misty dark, where little but wind whipped the lichened rocks, gusts moaning a constant dirge through the stunt scrub and briar. Travellers seldom paused on Atainia's bleak heath, bald hills heaped against the desolate Bittern, once laid to waste in a Second Age battle. Yet this night's observer was not mortal.

Discorporate Sorcerer, summoned in haste, Kharadmon viewed with alarm the glow smeared through the fog from the library's unshuttered arrow-slits. Sethvir's normal, daft habit neglected the sconces, unless crisis threatened. Kharadmon reassessed the scale of the trouble behind this display, come already enraged by a train of events that defied credibility.

A cold gust embedded in summer's northern chill, the Sorcerer's vexed passage snarled the brush like jerked knit. His shade entered the tower with a gale-force shriek that rattled the panes in the casements.

Sethvir, Warden of Althain, peered up from his vigil, the black onyx table under his spidery hands cleared of pen nibs and clutter. Without his bastion of books and loose parchments, pocked with uncorked ink-wells and tea-mugs, he looked lost. The neglected beard tufted as a mouse nest overpowered his wizened features. But not his pale eyes, which tracked Kharadmon's entry with piercing focus.

Keen as steel unsheathed, he did not prevaricate. "Don't start, with Davien! We have worse afoot than his capricious obstinacy."

"The Betrayer can jump with his eyes crossed and hang himself!" Kharadmon's gusty essence prowled the chamber, candleflames guttering in his wake. "Was Luhaine stark crazy? Why should he shoulder the crass bargain with Seshkrozchiel to spare the Betrayer's restored skin from decay? Am I meant to applaud him for back-handed genius? The wind-bag stickler is exquisitely fit to bore a great drake out of its skull, *if* the fool's move had not seen him entombed for as long as that dragon's sequestered in hibernation!"

Harangued to whipped elf-locks, Sethvir straightened to interrupt the tirade.

"Ah, no," Kharadmon ranted, "you're too cleverly glib! Don't try again to excuse Davien's back-stabbing games or brush off his baggage of vengeful neglect. Isn't the criminal practice of the Koriani Matriarch busting our bollocks enough? That's if our Fellowship has got a virile pair left intact between us!"

While the Warden of Althain stared, owlish, Kharadmon delivered his blistering grievance. "Well, you must have seen how that web-spinning crone's blindsided Elaira's perception."

Sethvir did not flinch, which spoke volumes. "Do you think," he lamented, "that current awareness of Arithon's straits could do aught but destroy her last peace of mind?"

The wind devil seethed up by Kharadmon's ire spiked hoar-frost across polished stone. "She would be free to act if her sight were not compromised!"

Althain's warden blinked. "Free? At the risk of breaking her crown prince's trust?"

Which unmalleable point *should have* reined a more sensible colleague's rant up short: for Arithon's need to secure Elaira's safety, the enchantress who loved him had sworn she would keep his past liaison with her under a seal of secrecy.

But no appeal to moral nuance tamed Kharadmon's agonized tirade. "Just what is Prime Selidie masking from view?"

Sethvir blinked again, and doggedly side-stepped. "You're needed elsewhere. Traithe must be escorted away from Rathain. Yes, with all speed! He's at dreadful risk. Twice, he's been hounded by True Sect diviners since he challenged the trial for witchcraft as Daliana's advocate."

Which bitter heroic had failed, in the end, to prevent the True Sect usurpation of Lysaer's governance of Etarra. Kharadmon stilled his arctic tantrum to object.

"No! Forget Asandir." Sethvir shoved erect. "He's posted back to Havish directly to finish the High Queen's instruction." Past argument, the risk of King Gestry's tragic sacrifice must not be repeated. "If the next ill turn calls a crowned sovereign to rise to the kingdom's defence, we don't *have* another grown s'Lornmein heir strong enough to bear the succession!"

"But Havish lies under no threat, tonight!" Kharadmon blasted in rejoinder. "And if, in fact, Traithe was in serious jeopardy, you'd have dispatched me there directly without this hopscotch summons through Althain Tower."

Sethvir crumpled and sat, his eyes glacial turquoise. "You can't break charter law. Or kite off to beard the Prime Matriarch without touching off a mass catastrophe."

Kharadmon snorted with freezing contempt. "Thwarted by your shell game of diversion? I might wish instead Davien's treasonous anarchy would smash Asandir's unholy pact with the sisterhood at a stroke! Someone should obliterate that nest of harpies."

"I know." Sethvir foresaw *all* the bleak probabilities. The Seven's hamstrung resource could scarcely stem the bleeding breach as Selidie's plots pitched their guardianship of Athera to shambles. Tough as nails amid building disaster, he folded veined knuckles and temporized. "The short-term defeat may not lose us the war. And I lit up the tower on the outside chance Davien might take notice. A token show of his support at this pass might give the Prime wary pause."

But even provoked a third time, Kharadmon never swerved. "What rankling ploy is that she-spider hatching?"

"Today? Another manipulation against us." Sethvir picked a loose thread from his sleeve and sighed. "Her mission is desperate. Either she must snare a talented candidate strong enough to survive the succession, or she has to defeat the compact and fall back on her order's cache of proscribed secrets. For one cause, or both, she's playing a puppet initiate from Deal as the woebegone victim of rape."

"And?" Kharadmon prompted, while the anguished pause stretched to the whicker of candleflame.

Sethvir glanced up, desolate. "The chit's being used as the baited trap to exploit the glaring flaw in Prince Arithon's character."

The discorporate Sorcerer recoiled, aghast. "To acquire his blood-line?"

"Or break him," Sethvir said, unflinching. "Either convenient happenstance suits the sisterhood's cause."

The worrisome scene tracked by the Althain's Warden unfolded in the Storlains, well into the nadir of night. The old ice-cutter's cabin by then was snug, even cozy under latched shutters. Lit rushes spilled softer light over the makeshift trestle, littered with wintergreen sprigs shorn of berries to compound a liniment.

Vivet refused the astringent paste, mashed to soothe her livid bruises. "I'll not touch the rank stuff!" She puffed a vexed breath. "It stings, and the smell makes me queasy."

Seated opposite, his bowl of spurned remedy a strained declaration of tension between them, the Crown Prince of Rathain measured her sullen regard, too canny to rise to the bait. A woman scorned, Vivet well might try rejection as her next inveigling weapon. Braced by the tingling scent of crushed herbals, he matched her complaint with cool silence and did not volunteer to poultice her injuries.

Vivet slapped down her comb. Reclothed, erect in the tatters of her dignity, she began with crisp yanks to rebraid her hair. Arithon watched, careful to dampen the outrage smouldering beneath his leashed temper. As deeply betrayed by another woman, even yet beloved beyond measure, he dared not lose his grip on the embedded hurt that clouded his mage-sighted discipline. Vivet's pique perhaps stemmed from misdirected pain and not venal manipulation.

Mindful of his thoughtless power to wound, Arithon waited for accurate insight, while she eyed him sidewise, unchastened. Empathy forgave her contrary behaviour, given how little he knew of the crisis she battled. Trauma alone would not drive an intelligent young woman to fling herself on him, try suicide, then irrationally neglect the physical marks of abuse.

Initiate restraint must outlast moody tumult. Tidied himself, reclad in his marred shirt, and in charge of both knife and his shoulder-slung sword, Arithon perched on the makeshift log seat.

He could do nothing else.

Althain's Warden witnessed, in full, the invidious thread of Prime Selidie's design. An innocent female, cast as victimized pawn, paired with the damning, implied falsehood sown by an incomplete record left planted crystal, had skewed Arithon's internal boundaries. The mix spelled disaster. Vivet's straits grappled his vulnerability, abrasive as slivered glass on torn nerves in the confines of the remote cabin.

The blood-bound tenets of Rathain's crown heritage disallowed comfort, or distance. S'Ahelas foresight stayed silent, as well, while Arithon's recoil sought the blind solace of an outside distraction: easier for him to redress Vivet's woes than to bear his own desolation.

Sethvir's flash-point acuity plumbed the abyss of uncertainty caused by the prince's blocked memory. Stripped of Tarens's steadfast loyalty, Arithon's purposful character lost firm direction. Where safety and solitude would have granted space for mage training to master the impasse, Arithon endured in resigned suspension, his innate faculties entrained on another's behalf.

The battered victim in front of him trembled, too damaged to function. Sent as she was on a mission to ensnare him through her human weakness, Vivet leaned, and commanded his strength.

"What if my future is ruined?" she confided in jagged distress.

Arithon measured her lustrous hair, the blemished symmetry of temple and cheek, then the expressive eyelashes and pert chin. Against her dispirited anguish, he said, "You are individual as a melody sung once, then lost in a storm. Calm will refound the cadence again. Beauty survives, and healing demands a fallow time for renewal." His tender entreaty insistent, he added, "I promise you this. The harm you have suffered is an affront to all that is right in the world. You will find the joy that eludes you tonight. But only if you gather your courage, stay the course, and live in the present."

Vivet convulsed with sobs. He did not gather her misery close or smooth back the hair slicked to her swollen cheeks. And yet, though his intimate trust remained shaken, he did not disown her suffering.

"Your affection is not a gift to be squandered over a night's inflamed passion." The bitter edge underneath his straight speech eluded her wounded perception. "Entanglement now would upset better choices. Do you understand, Vivet? Your worth is greater than any male stranger's thankless, quick toss in the sheets."

Blinking through tears, she fastened on his promise of requite. "You'll still see me home?"

"Better," said Arithon. "I'll make sure of your welcome. If your kin cast you out for what happened, we'll leave them. Your fortune will thrive in a different place, among kindly folk who deserve, and appreciate, the unique grace of your company."

Vivet mopped her face, encouraged to venture a tentative smile. "Then you don't spurn belief in chance-met fate?"

"That upsets don't happen by accident?" Arithon shrugged. "I'm too tired to hazard the question." Slight as shadow itself, green eyes lowered, he stirred to retire.

Reluctant to release him, Vivet blurted, "My mother told futures. She taught me the art. What will happen is marked in the lines of your palm." Flushed slightly, she seized his right wrist, poised on the trestle between them. Arithon curbed his recoil. He suffered the touch to appease her and let her uncurl his long fingers.

Shiny white, the old knot of scar tissue exposed to the rush-light. Apologetic, Arithon freed her shocked grasp. "I've no past and no future where you are concerned. Wiser for you to remember that."

Yet the gathered probabilities of Sethvir's earth-sense foreshadowed no simple release from his tacit engagement and no turning away. Bred to heal fractious conflict in whatever form, and royally gifted with the insight to forge unity between Mankind's wayward factions and the mystical presence of Athera's Paravians, Arithon could not resist his born nature or callously force disentanglement.

A snarling blast of frigid wind yanked the Warden's distanced awareness back to Althain Tower.

"The hussy is pregnant!" Kharadmon snapped. Two shelved books toppled and smacked into the floor, while precipitate moisture crackled and froze under his ferocious outburst. "Not by Arithon, either, mark that!"

Sethvir caught the whip-cracked ends of his beard and peered through the gyre of snowflakes. "Two days ago, yes. I observed the conception. The woman is bearing the dead trapper's get."

"Our prince can't ascertain that!" Kharadmon fumed.

Which nailed the strategic quandary behind Vivet's attempted seduction. Sethvir kept his own counsel. Nothing could be salvaged. The Prime's aimed directive ascertained the by-blow's paternity would stay blurred until the misfortunate birth.

More, the discorporate tempest of Kharadmon's rage already vaulted beyond that festering obstacle. "You suggest the Prime's long-term desire seeks to breed the latent talent from Dari s'Ahelas's line of descent? Then why hasn't Selidie fashioned a second campaign aimed at Lysaer s'Ilessid?"

"I can't say that she won't; although at the moment, Lysaer's better guarded." Quick to divert Kharadmon's inquisitive prodding, Sethvir pounced with the gambit. "You have Davien's unlicensed genius to thank since the bold masquerade he staged for Daliana just made Selidie's prospects immeasurably more difficult."

Predictably nettled, and roundly upstaged, the discorporate Sorcerer abandoned debate, blew out the latched shutter, and blustered away on his assigned errand.

Machinations

The three-storey merchant's house Lysaer rented for residence in East Bransing fronted the bustle of Broad Street, where the port town raised by Mankind encroached upon the Second Age sea-wall, and the crescent breakwater erected by Paravian masons once protected the delicate, moored boats of Sunchildren. No ruin remained of the rope ferry that had crossed the river at the harbour's inlet. The present-day view from the upstairs casements showed a jumble of sandstone and brick shops stacked against the grade of a cobbled street. The eaves of the tenements notched pleated silhouettes against the tarred rigging that cross-hatched the quay-side. Square built of grim, Blackshear granite, the mansion lacked filigree rails and tiled galleries. Only plain cornices brightened with whitewash inflected its genteel elegance.

Inside, the décor was antique and restrained, the comforts of the gentleman's chambers served by fusty staff corridors and backstairs with scuffed treads.

Servants came with the house. The master's privacy was guarded by a tyrannical steward, which stymied a newcomer without proper references, attached from the street at his Lordship's whim.

Called by Dace Marley, the elderly fellow was viewed askance as an opportune pilferer. Tasked with the kitchen staff under the sharp-eyed cook, Dace endured the smirks that implied no upright valet ever dirtied his hands. Decency should drive off a true man of quality before he stooped to sweating buckets, or lugging the butcher's cuts for the spit.

Since the Fellowship's mandate left no slack for snobbery, Dace rose to his wretched lot, swearing.

"His nibs wants you run out, mark my word," the cook confided with smug hypocrisy. Given a diligent worker in place of the indolent lad, Quince, just unsuitably promoted to the gentleman's chamber, the man swiped his greasy hands on his apron, and added, "My fuel bin's low. Get me split hardwood, mind! None of that rubbish pine kindling for cheap. A pitch fire in the stove chimney could burn down the house."

Dace stifled comment and shouldered the sling. Such mean errands let him survey the town and sift through gossip in the market. A servant in livery might tally the numbers of armoured dedicates in their white surcoats unnoticed, or spy upon True Sect diviners and priests.

Buffeted in the raucous midday street, through the hawkers and seamen on shore leave, Dace also took soiled linens daily to be laundered, then packed the sopped load back in baskets to be dried and pressed by the maid. Jostled by tradesmen and chandlers, snubbed by the factors' lackeys, he lugged wicker cages of hens from the market to slaughter, then collected them, headless and dripping. Homeward bound, stung by pebbles shied by the dock rats who loafed and cut purses, he ducked into shelter behind the customs shed.

His frustration did not signify against the stakes if he failed. By luck or through infighting, he must raise his station before fate's stacked hand, or The Hatchet, fomented another disaster.

Yet patience cost dearly. His tiresome days began before dawn, first trip to the well made amid the racketing drays hauling cargo downhill to the docks. Toil finished late, the last buckets drawn for the master's bath lugged under the guttering lamps, through the raucous drunks' laughter. Shouts pierced the dark as the harbour watch cracked belligerent heads, and the town's rag and salvage men scurried for patsy's pence, paid to finger the malcontents ousted from the shoreside taverns.

The lot were tossed in the gaol and fined, or else handed off to an out-bound ship, one silver for the comatose and upwards to ten for the most obstreperous.

While the water-front's seamy rambunctiousness tried nerves that no one had cause to suspect, Dace continued to black Lysaer's boots. Even that lowly service inflamed the steward's ambitious distrust.

Pouched eyes slitted, the cook volunteered, "Mark me, one slip will see you washing the pots alongside my gutter-snipe scullions."

Dace doused his resentment. As the vindictive bone caught between rivals, he stood his ground, forced to watch the back postern and guard his Lordship's interests from belowstairs.

Lysaer liked his pressed shirts stored in camphor, with collar and sleeve points unlaced. He eschewed scented candles. His fastidious taste preferred sheets without starch and the luxury of warmed towels. Royal bearing rebuffed intimacy. He received both petitioners and guests upon formal terms, summoning them from the front foyer for audience in the vaulted sitting-room.

Which rigid etiquette exposed the muffled stranger, slipped in through the pre-dawn fog by way of the servants' door. The house steward stalked like a furtive crow from the unlit pantry. He dismissed the scullion slicing the bacon and chased off the harried maid eating her breakfast. A murmured exchange saw the unannounced visitor ushered upstairs. Yet the fellow bore no parcel sent from the tailor's; no evident reason for intimate business conducted in the master's chambers.

Unnoticed behind the loom of the wash-tub, Dace shed his emptied yoke buckets and snatched wax and rub rag from the broom closet. He dodged the cheeky scullion who snitched and nipped up the backstairs on the pretence of buffing his Lordship's boots.

This hour, the dressing-room should be empty, street-side curtains drawn before sunrise. Yet light flickered through the cracked-open door from a sconce on the marble-topped mantel. Past the master's stuffed chairs, the wardrobe's lacquered doors were flung wide, the fine clothing apparently under inspection. Prone to sea-side mildew, the velvets were often brushed out and aired, though usually under the afternoon sun, and never before the mist lifted. The steward himself hovered by his Lordship's closed study. Dour features pinched into a thunderbolt frown, he eavesdropped, while Quince's coarse handling set creases into the master's best jacket.

Dace suppressed Daliana's madcap grin. Threatened with demotion to the scullery anyway, he lost little by kicking the hornet's nest. Rag and tinned wax abandoned, he barged in, and grabbed the boy by a jug-handle ear.

Quince squealed in surprise.

The steward gestured with bilious dismay, frantic to forestall a disruption of the private dialogue on-going inside his Lordship's shut chamber.

"Bumbling fool!" Dace let fly, oblivious. "What do you think you are doing?"

While the idiot boy squirmed, coarse fists wringing the disputed velvet, Dace rebuked, "Have you no care for costly fabric?"

The thwarted steward bristled, "Get out! Straightaway. Await me in the kitchen!"

Dace rebelled, snatched the jacket, and indignantly whisked at the furrowed nap. "A shameful disgrace, to assign an oaf to tend his Lordship's garments."

Which noisy effrontery brutalized protocol. The door to the study banged open. Lysaer filled the entry, from brushed-gold hair to fawn breeches radiating mortified affront. "Take your servant's quarrel elsewhere."

The steward temporized, "They'll both go, milord. I'll just tidy this mess."

"You'll all leave as you're told!" Lysaer snapped, indifferent to his debased clothing.

Discomposed as a vulture chased off a carcass, the steward had no choice but to scuttle along with his chastened underlings.

Dace feared more than the haughty man's enmity, stoked to avenge the shameful embarrassment. Instinct had not erred. His impetuous glimpse through the study door showed the stranger's doffed cloak, draped over a chair. Unveiled, the gilt braid and white vestments that had been concealed underneath. Badges differentiated the Sunwheel priests. Lysaer's secretive visitor likely came as an inside informant, positioned amid the ranked hierarchy of the True Sect Temple.

Disadvantaged, disgraced, Dace jockeyed to outpace the punitive speed of event. He elbowed past the grumbling Quince, reached the kitchen ahead of the irate steward, and reclaimed his discarded yoke buckets. Luck deserted him as the blindsided cook hounded him in reprisal.

"Larking off, were you? D'you think I'm a fool? Mooners who squat over-long in the privy cut no slack with me. I've sent Manda after the water. You'll fetch her dust-bin and shovel, forthwith. On with you, then! Clean out the grate in the sitting-room fire-place."

Dace tossed the implements into the ash bucket and bolted, before the steward burst in and sacked him on the spot without pay.

The sitting-room's drawn curtains plunged the room's marquetry furnishings into airless stillness and gloom. Spared in brief reprieve, Dace crossed the vacant carpet to the mantel and knelt in despair on the marble apron.

Davien had warned that his course would be harsh. A moment's impatience may have wrecked his best chance to temper Lysaer's cursed nature. Bent to a scullion's task, Dace shovelled up cinders and swore. "Ath above, what I'd give to uncover the report delivered by that slinking spy!"

An intrusive movement flickered in the shadow behind. Dace started, head turned, fearful he had been followed. Yet he encountered no flesh-and-blood presence. Only the fugitive impression of Kharadmon, dapper in lace cuffs and velvet, a sardonic finger touched to his lips.

The room still loomed empty. Frowning, returned to the ash in his dust-bin, Dace beheld a perfect red rose, there and gone in an eyeblink. Two such apparitions were not prompted by nerves. Stilled in thought, Dace picked up the faint sound of voices funnelled through the flue from the master suite's upstairs fire-place.

In hindsight, the cook's remedial punishment suggested the sly meddling of a Fellowship shade.

Poised, Dace listened in as Lysaer demanded, "You insist you have proof?"

". . . beyond question," the temple informant responded. "Confirmation by direct pigeon, the High Priesthood endorses the cleanse. Most agree that a sweep to root out clan blood-lines is long overdue."

Lysaer's murmured answer at tensioned pitch, then, "Oh, yes. The sealed order's already mustered the war host's remnant companies. The Hatchet's busy as the weasel tossed into the hen coop. Defeat by the High King of Havish has badly scorched his towering pride. He'll enforce the mandate to kill, and damn all to the wave of red slaughter unleashed upon folk who may never have been in collusion with Shadow."

The pause hung. Breath stopped, his grip on the dust-bin white-knuckled, Dace strained to fathom the tenor of Lysaer's suspended opinion.

The mask of the statesman must have prevailed, for after a moment, the Sunwheel agent resumed, "You're keen for the list?"

Lysaer's stiff annoyance could almost be felt.

"Here's the copy, then, with the active roster." A brief lag, while a document changed hands. "Straight off the pen of my man in the copyist's chamber at Erdane."

To a friend, Lysaer's suave response sounded frayed, "This selection was made by a damned astute eye!"

"You have no idea." The stranger chuckled. "Diviners selected the most faithful. They picked for strong stomachs and unquestioned zeal to enforce Canon Law without qualms. His Hallowed Eminence, the Light's Priest Supreme expounded upon needful slaughter. With reason, or hadn't you heard? The clanblood condemned among Torwent's crofters escaped from their execution by fire. The captain in charge was stripped of his insignia and flogged a fortnight ago."

Lysaer's murmur broke in.

"Guilty? Beyond doubt." The stranger's contempt echoed down through the chimney. "His own sergeant attested to his craven weakness. More, the men who failed to secure the Light's prisoners were put to death under evidence. Trackers with hounds confirmed someone helped the heretics break out of the barn that confined them."

Lysaer paused in stark disbelief. "I was told that all of the able young men were killed outright on the field."

"So they were," verified the temple informant. "Shut in for the pyre were their women and babes. Telling fact, the nailed doors failed to hold them."

This statement also raised a poisoned silence. Dace could picture Lysaer's composure, a chipped-stone facade that armoured the gut wrench of horror beneath. The dawning awareness about froze his blood: this exchange must be the covert report garnered from a secret network high in the ranks of the True Sect temple.

Dace dared not presume he was the sole witness to the sensitive meeting upstairs. The flue in the sitting-room also connected to the bread oven's stove-pipe, a convenient conduit during the summer, when the day's baking was done before dawn.

Above, a deliberate tread indicated that Lysaer strode to the casement. Not for an innocuous breath of fresh air. Grey daylight would punch-cut his features like sculpture, a trick he often used to harden the appearance of invulnerability. Distance from the hearth obscured his next words.

"But they have dared to extend their reach beyond Tysan," the temple informant contradicted. "While the whirlwind campaign razes the clan enclave at Orlan, the companies fragmented by casualties will be re-formed and drilled back to fitness. Mid-season, they'll be dispatched to Rathain for the next course of brisk action."

58

"The priesthood's bid to consolidate True Sect rule at Etarra by force of arms?" Lysaer's acid surprise framed rebuttal. "There's an arrogant trespass not to be borne."

"Temple gold's been allotted for staging." Perhaps the priest smiled before he resumed. "You'll soon hear more than rumours. Galleys are being chartered for the troops' passage across Instrell Bay. The campaign under The Hatchet will take Rathain's shore before the autumn storms disrupt his supply."

Lysaer's oath inflected sheer disbelief.

"The invasion's no feint," the visitor insisted. "Our Lord Highest Examiner claims to hold evidence that Fellowship interests cannot intervene. You'll have to choose which advance to endorse. Blessed Lord, I suggest that you favour Etarra. Because Erdane's foray into the Thaldeins confronts the most pernicious of the clan outposts, that thrust will involve the leagues' finest trackers and the most gifted True Sect diviners."

Lysaer's diction bit. "You insist the temple's sealed orders will target children and babes without quarter?"

"No question," the visitor snapped, and killed hope. "The command calls for a sweeping extermination, backed up by the resource to route every hidden survivor."

Lysaer's venomous stillness this time carried a palpable force that unsettled the sen Evend ancestral instinct. Dace shivered, raked by the visceral certainty his liege's disastrous sentiment showed. Lysaer was human and fallible. A True Sect devotee beguiled by the dangerous myth he was god-sent perhaps beheld a crack in the immortal facade.

If the avatar's closing phrase was too low to discern, the brisk rap of his informant's step in departure suggested an ominous quittance.

Dace bottled his helpless fear and applied himself, shovelling. The reek of carbon seemed chillingly apt. The True Sect High Priesthood would move with alacrity to defend temple interests if today's visitor played his avatar false. Worse, atop pending calamity, the door-latch clicked open before Dace contrived any plan to amend his gross breach of etiquette. The scullion poked in with a freckle-faced sneer. "Not done, yet? Lazy sod. I'm sent to finish. The cook needed Dolcie to strain the new cheese, and you're tasked to fetch him more water."

Dace arose, hoping the steward was preoccupied.

Hag's luck prevailed: the gaunt stick still lurked by the servant's stair, engrossed in a whispered discourse with the stranger, who was cloaked and hooded for his anonymous exit. Interrupted untimely again, both parties stiffened.

"You!" barked the steward. "Still slinking about? I'll have your severance forthwith!"

The turncoat priest coughed. "I'll be about my business." He breezed toward the back door on the pretext he had lingered for casual gossip.

No chance to expose the curtailed encounter as a collusion: the steward squared off like a blood-letting weasel for Dace's immediate quittance.

Except that a sturdy obstruction blocked egress through the kitchen. "If you're tossing my help out, that's stinking spite." The cook's bull-dog jaws gnashed the carved-ivory shim he kept for picking his teeth. "Manda's moping in the privy, and I can't be hauling the water myself. Not with these feet! My bunions would hobble me in a chair with a hot brick for a fortnight."

The steward sniffed in rapacious disgust. "Send Quince."

"I would." The cook smirked. "The brat's scarpered. I'd waste the morning chasing his hide to no purpose."

Dace seized the desperate initiative and braved the cross chop of argument. "I'll finish the errand, if I can get past."

"Hurry on," the cook groused. "I'll be needing eight trips with the buckets at least."

"Work up a sweat all you like in the street." The balked steward glared above his starched collar. "Just don't expect to be let inside if you show the gall to come back."

Dace barged past. "The master," he said, "will allow me a hearing before I'm excused." To the obstreperous cook, he remarked, "You want your filled cauldron? Then appeal to his Lordship for his final word on my case."

"The master won't trouble himself!" the supercilious steward insisted. "Or weigh an upstart's claim above mine."

"Wouldn't he?" The cook chomped on his toothpick and grinned, pleased to hackle his rival.

Dace seized the impasse. Slim as a mackerel and quick on his feet, he accepted the corpulent cook as his shield and retreated into the kitchen. Two steps ahead of the thwarted steward, he snatched the buckets and fled.

But his narrow escape only drove his vengeful antagonist to act on the sly. Seven round trips to the well occurred without any counter-move. The eighth and the last forced a detour to duck some carousing sailhands on shore leave. Hawkers with hand-carts and the mobs by the trinket sellers drove Dace the long way around the money-lender's walled mansion. Collar stuck to his neck and chafed shoulders aching, he gulped air reeking of fish offal and jetsam stranded by the ebb-tide. Shoreside, the overseers barked at their stevedores, while the sun-baked heat off the docks sweltered into the breezeless shimmer of midday.

Dace pushed on. Braced for the steward's revenge, and dazzled as he stepped from the shaded lane back into the street, he received no warning as an on-coming body crashed into him. Encumbered by the yoke, he swore murder, while the pails slopped and drenched his shoes.

"Give over the buckets. Right now! To me!" snapped the reckless female who clutched at his jacket.

Irritable, astonished, Dace recognized the plain-faced scullion who snitched. "The steward's sent you to replace me?"

"No!" The raw-boned girl mopped a forehead plastered with dingy bangs.

"Cook's whim chose to spare you. Hurry! The constable's sent the armed guard. Under the steward's sworn accusation, they bear a sealed writ for your arrest."

Dace floundered to grapple the malicious riposte. "On what charge?"

"Sneak thief. He's claimed you lifted property." The scullion rolled her eyes, impatient. "Hand off those buckets! Don't let the watch catch that evidence on you."

"They give a rat's arse for a brace of old pails?" Dace shrugged off the yoke, scared to reeling.

"Are you daft?" The scullion's lip curled. "Mail shirts would issue a warrant to nab you for carrying fleas at a twopenny bribe."

Dace scarcely believed the girl routed a strategy aimed to ruin him. "You must hate the steward past measure," he said.

The drudge muscled his burden, her dish-water eyes bright with hatred. "That devious creep only makes my life miserable. But flouting cook's orders gets me a beating." She turned her cheek, already puffed by the weal that drove her compliance. "Go! Run. I'll hurt worse if the guard sees you with me."

Spurred by the tramp of hobnailed boots rounding the bend by the harbour-master's, Dace darted down the noisome alley behind the fishmonger's. He shucked his jacket, turned the livery lining side out, and shoved back into the hurly-burly press of the main street.

Reprieve would not last, with the house barred against him. East Bransing sold indigents to the galleys, and the thieves' gangs extorted whoever sought refuge in the warrens beneath the board-walk.

Dace had until dusk to clear his disgraced name, against stakes more sinister than any snob servant's enmity. If he were to languish in lock-up, then be dispatched to sea on a false arraignment, Lord Lysaer would remain at the mercy of a possible temple conspiracy.

The steward might be complicit, with the gentleman's house near the water-front perhaps too conveniently rented. More than staff might possess the keys, which left Lysaer's back lethally vulnerable.

Dace rubbed the thread concealed in his left wrist. Features too old for his natural years, he rued the day he had given consent to the affairs of Fellowship Sorcerers. His true form as a woman might side-step the town watch, even assume a street child's garb and join the loud-mouthed ragamuffins who played stickball on the doorsteps of the wealthy. At least as an urchin, he could watch the door. The forfeit advantage of Davien's disguise scarcely mattered if his liege fell to a predatory conspiracy.

Undecided which way to turn, Dace fretted, while the pooled midday shadows lengthened towards afternoon.

Summer 5923

Undercurrents

The steward rushed into the lord's private study seconds after the tinkle of glass disrupted the household quiet. He noted the smashed casement rondel first. Then, in sepia shadow, the master himself, seated across from the sparkle of fragmented glass. Lysaer s'Ilessid had turned his stuffed chair from the desk, the medallion carpet scuffed where the lions' paw feet had furrowed the pile. On the papers behind, the inked quill just laid down suggested the day's correspondence, rudely interrupted.

"Light preserve!" gasped the steward, breathless from his sprint. "You're unhurt?" His solicitous fuss met rebuff although the gentleman said nothing. A fair man informally clad, cuffs turned back and his collar unlaced in the heat, should not possess such a magisterial bearing.

To mask his inquisitive interest, the steward temporized stiffly, "Does my lord have enemies?"

Arctic blue, Lysaer's eyes, in a face chiselled clean of expression. Unlike other pedigree lordlings, he never unbent under chatty sympathy. A faint sparkle of glass sequinned the wrist he raised from the chair arm. His clenched fingers, uncurled, served his stinging reply: nestled into his palm, the pried chunk of cobble-stone a vandal had tossed from the street.

"Children!" The steward huffed in disgust. "Poor-quarter ruffians at their careless games. Rest assured, I'll summon the watch. They'll haul the insolent wretches into custody straightaway."

Lysaer's mild response struck the note green ambassadors always mistook for agreement. "What befalls young offenders when they're declared guilty?"

"If they can't pay the fine for disruptive behaviour and punitive repairs?" The steward took the liberty to inspect the damage, then clucked over the crack found in one of the casement mullions. "The urchins are sent to the docks, where forced labourers pick apart worn ropes for oakum. They serve a month for every silver sentenced in recompense."

The brisk move as Lysaer shoved upright stirred the air like the first hint of storm. "Get Dace up here to polish my boots. I'll be off to the magistrate inside the hour."

The steward bowed. "Your Lordship, my word is sufficient to seal the conviction. No need to address this low grievance in person."

Lysaer's fixed regard never wavered, clear as a mineral pool before the geyser's eruption. "I have no complaint to press charges. None whatsoever. My purse will settle the landlord. And the fine, if your accusation is not proven spurious. Now send Dace!"

"The boy Quince will tend your footwear," said the steward, his arch condescension routine to coddle a flighty lord's fancy.

Lysaer's firm response still raised no flag of warning. "Dace is off on an errand? I'll await his return."

The steward rubbed his hook-nose, discommoded. "Then your boots will be polished by my own hand, while the matter of finding a glazier awaits on your vanity."

Where another aristocrat might have deferred, Lysaer's silken inquiry pressed, "Where is Dace?"

The steward prevaricated. "Milord, such unpleasantness is beneath your attention." Given no leave to dismiss the question, he squared his tapered shoulders. "If you insist, regretfully, I've just dismissed Dace for thievery."

Lysaer said nothing with such elegance, the steward cleared his dry throat. "I don't know what the wretch stole, milord." Deceit flowed off his oily tongue. "That would be the cook's grievance."

"My business alone!" Lysaer rebuked. "Dace is part of *my* retinue, fellow, and no lackey attached to this house. If the resident staff is displeased with his conduct, I expect the malfeasance brought to me directly. I will not be deferred. Fetch Dace back. I want him retrieved from the street before sundown unless you prefer your own trip to the magistrate to save him from a vagrancy charge!"

"You're too generous with petty dishonesty, milord," the steward chided. "By far too forgiving as well. The man's of dubious background. Scarcely quality, and I would further suggest, unworthy of your noble stature."

Lysaer smiled with corrosive contempt. "I'm not forgiving, or overly generous. Cross me, and the fine for this case will be docked from your payshare."

The steward blanched, stiffly bowed, and departed. Sweat moistened his nape as he clicked the door shut. Not from the afternoon's stifling heat but sprung from the dreadful, sudden awareness he had tweaked the tail of a sleeping tiger.

Alone once again, Lysaer strode to his desk and sat down. He unclenched his right fist, smoothed the rag held wadded inside, and reviewed its message in crudely stained writing. Then he took up fresh paper and quill and composed a cryptic response.

"Spend this for a private room at the Galley-men's Rest, and above all, avoid being seen. Stay until I come myself."

Lysaer sanded the ink. He folded the note around a ten-royal silver piece, then sealed it with wax and a torn scrap of cloth: a distinctive fawn linen, torn from the lined jacket of one of his liveried servants. His mouth a clamped line that made state envoys cringe, he lobbed the packet through the broken pane. Then he polished his own boots with grim intent to impose upon East Bransing's magistrate, then proceed with a meeting of greater importance.

The Galley-men's Rest straddled the breakwater, a concoction of plank walls and shake roof propped upright on gangling stilts. Renovated from a pierside fish-shack, the structure looked ready to slide with a tired splash into the harbour. A rope-slung gangway bridged the canal sloshed by the incoming tide. The propped-open door-panels sported matched port-holes, salvaged off a scuttled shrimp-boat.

Arrived in the blued shadow that silted the entry, Dace Marley paused and surveyed the tap-room throng: a garrulous stew of crews from the mackerel skiffs and shirtless stevedores come straight off the docks. Gin sold at a tuppence the tot, which a slogan scrawled over the bar claimed to sprout curly hair on a virgin's tits.

Dace breathed a fust of alcohol fumes thick enough to fuel the bull's-eye lamps. Several sawn off oar-handles leaned by the tap, ready bludgeons to quell drunken riots.

The lowbrow dive was a sly choice: inconceivable, that the Light's avatar would rub shoulders with such unsavoury company. Dace waded into the raucous heave. He by-passed a dice game, ducked a contest at darts, and two meaty fellows locked in an arm wrestle, circled by bettors screaming encouragement. Grotesquely displaced, Dace was greeted with mockery.

"Lost your way, fella?"

"Come in slumming for a two-minute trick?"

And from the one-eyed smith in the corner, picking his teeth with a meat skewer, "How much d'ye charge to lick a man's todger to a spit polish?"

Dace grinned. He had worked the rough bars in Etarra as a pretty young woman, unfazed. "How much would it take to watch you do the same for everyone's wide-eyed amusement?"

Through the startled laughter provoked by his cheek, Dace inquired after a private room.

Whiskered in wool almost to the eyebrows, the landlord weighed the request. "Would that be for a bed with one doxie or two?"

Dace raised open palms. "No wenches." Before the onlookers made sport, he retorted, "I've two soft hands, after all. They're clean, I know where they've been, and better, their service is free."

The obscene roar of approval rattled the rafters, while the floor-boards shuddered to the tidal chop that slopped against the slimed pylons. Dace ignored the next round of chaffing and offered up Lysaer's ten piece.

The landlord claimed the coin with a moist fist. "Ah! *That* particular room, reserved for the gentleman, is it? The fee doesn't budge." A deft move whisked the bribe out of sight and bestowed upon Dace a grimed key. "Under the stairs and out the back door. Take a stroll down the dock. The quarters for blueblood whoring are under the copper cupola."

Dace acquiesced to the landlord's extortion and made his way through the rear exit.

The annex reserved for private dalliance was a gazebo, enclosed in weathered clapboard and roofed in the verdigris scrap of old sheathing torn off of derelict hulls. Dace approached, touched by a sudden qualm, as if an incipient warning of danger crossed the straight grain of Lysaer's orders. Yet he had to earn the unquestioned trust his true purpose required.

Dace poised at the door-sill under the glare of full sunlight. Nothing seemed untoward. Wavelets lapped and sucked at the pilings. The strident gulls mobbing the fish pier sliced the bustle of late-day commerce eclipsed by the board wall of the Galley-men's Rest.

Dace slotted the grimed key and turned the lock, jumpy as a dropped cat as the panel swung inward. With reason: the gloom beyond held two hooded fellows of muscular build, shod in hobnailed boots out of place on the docks. With them, ghostly white, two more figures wore the robes of Sunwheel priests. Neither of their startled faces belonged to that morning's temple informant. Dace recoiled, too late. A hard blow slammed into his nape from behind.

As he folded, someone's mailed grip crammed an astringent, damp cloth over his nose and mouth. A second punch in the belly drove the air from his lungs. Reflex forced him to inhale the drugged fumes. He succumbed to nauseous, wheeling dizziness and sagged into a faint.

Dace woke to a fire-ball searing his skull, and a dry mouth that tasted like ashes. The malaise of the narcotic and the bludgeon just used to fell him, or so he supposed, until his muddled senses picked out the pressure of moist hands clasped at his temples. The intrusive hold sourced the unbearable headache, and more, he felt as though a cincture of hot wire scorched his left wrist under the skin.

Laboured awareness attached that discomfort to the enchanted thread that knotted Davien's wrought disguise. By the ripe oaths puffed in onion-breath over his head, the Sorcerer's conjury did more than shape-change his gender.

" . . . be damned to the nadir of Dark, I cannot read into this wretch! His simple mind's empty of purpose as wiped slate. Anyone but a moron would be pissing his breeches by now from the morbid echoes of primal terror."

A blurred shimmer of white betrayed the proximity of a temple priest. Dace shuddered, aghast. Now aware his discomfort stemmed from the active probe of a True Sect examiner, he thrashed weakly and retched.

The temple-trained talent released his entrained grip. "At best, anyway, a lackey's experience offers us questionable value. Slit his throat, I say, before he wakes up. We can't have our faces remembered."

"No," snapped another gruff voice. "Bind the wretch first. We don't know why Lysaer sent him ahead, and he may prove more useful alive."

"He's only a footman," the examiner scoffed. "The Light's avatar will never be swayed by low-class human sentiment."

"Perhaps not," the speaker agreed. "But deliberation does not discard an advantage, and patience ensures that we'll finish our day's business quietly."

More grumbling ensued, while one of the cloaked men-at-arms was convinced to step out for a length of stout rope. Dace sprawled on his back, miserable under the after-shock, and reeled by the scents of stale sweat and whore's musk that cloyed the air like a stain.

Another heavy-set tread creaked the floor-boards nearby. A stranger's cowled face hovered above, pale as a bloated fish. Dace grasped the distorted impression of watery-blue eyes, thick-lidded beneath sandy lashes. Then a slippered toe shoved him onto his side.

Through his gasping discomfort, his laconic captor observed, "Better test him again, before your dedicate captain returns. I'd rather ascertain beyond any doubt Lysaer doesn't suspect we know anything."

The examiner's protest that naught would be gained became overridden by nervous authority. "And you'd swear by the Canon such stupidity's innocent?"

"The ethic of my office forbids me to speculate." The temple's arcane inquisitor sniffed. "I've reported as much as my talent can see. Another probe is a waste, more than likely to injure the subject."

"This affray goes beyond paltry harm to a servant! How much damage can the True Sect doctrine withstand, subjected to a debate over policy spear-headed by the fallen avatar? Have you better means to find out why the Light of his godhead forsook the war against Shadow in Lanshire?"

The examiner yielded on that point, discomposed. A whiff of almond soap and sweet incense breathed out of his clothes as he bent, pudgy hands cupped at Dace's sore temples to resume his frustrated inquest.

"I'll need more help," he complained to the muscular dedicate poised by the door. "Bear down and restrain this fellow before he goes into frothing convulsions."

Dace moaned, still unstrung in a muddled haze. The men overcame his pitiful struggle as though they pinioned a rag doll. Stretched against a rug rank with mildew, he braced for the excruciate pain as the examiner pried into his mind.

No such dreadful horror occurred. The redoubled assault instead triggered a sharp flare from the buried thread that sustained Davien's working. The examiner grunted. A powerful talent, he sharpened his effort, determined to tear through the unexpected resistance. Whether his next thrust aimed to smash Dace's psyche at the cost of crippling insanity, the Sorcerer's construct lodged in Dace's left wrist blazed into conflagration. The tingling, electrical burst combed through flesh and spirit. The effect doused the examiner's Sighted incursion as thoroughly as a wet blanket.

For Dace, the burst triggered a flash-point gestalt that exposed his tormentor's double-blind plot. After the Master of Shadow escaped the field at Lithmarin, and since the True Sect war host's decisive defeat by a sanctioned High King's crowned power, Erdane's high priesthood suspected Lysaer s'Ilessid's lapse into heresy at the Great Schism had progressed to incorrigible corruption. The examiner sought proof the Light's avatar had become suborned beyond salvage.

Dace had blundered into a True Sect ambush, arranged under the pretence of a covert meeting. The temple cabal's interrogation for lapsed divinity was meant to occur here in secret, masked by darkness and the rowdy debauchery of seamen on shore leave. After they exposed Lysaer's wilful course as a threat to the True Sect cause, none would notice the splash of a naked corpse, sunk off the pier for the crabs. A decomposed body stirred up by the tide might raise some desultory questions. But never for long in the stews of East Bransing, where knifed casualties were the routine victims of drunken disputes.

Dace shuddered and raged. He could not save himself, far less disarm a deadly conspiracy poised for his liege's destruction.

Already the structure beneath him thumped to an inbound tread.

"Here's our man with the rope," the temple authority mused with self-righteous confidence.

"Check to make sure," snapped the Sunwheel dedicate, crouched over the servant's pinned wrists. "Let's have no more pesky surprises upsetting our mission."

Dace reacted first and bellowed in agony.

A hand muffled his mouth. But not before the incomer's reaction delivered the ring of drawn steel. The locked door banged, kicked open to admit a shattering flare of daylight. Gloom and shadow fled, pierced by a blade poised for bloodshed.

Dace twisted his head. Dazzled, he picked out distinctive gold hair: Lysaer s'Ilessid, come early to hear the account of the lackey whose flung stone had delivered a warning of treachery.

Shock froze the tableau, while Lysaer's freezing gaze met the servant drugged and held in duress.

The compromised examiner shoved off his knees and spluttered excuses. "My exalted lord! Forgive us, we had to be certain of your man's loyalty."

As quick, the cowled priest in authority oiled over the awkward disruption. "Lord Exalted, put up your blade! Naturally, your sacrosanct safety demands our diligent oversight."

"I found nothing, besides. The fellow is earnest," the examiner hastened to add. Brazenly indignant, and quite unaware that Davien's agency had exposed his murderous duplicity, he gushed, "He's quite unhurt! We gave him a posset to ease his discomfort under our examination."

Dace held his tongue through the unctuous display. To show more than a commoner's ignorance would destroy credibility, if not damn him as a minion of Shadow. Yet if his liege shut the door and stood down, the temple cabal might try to recoup their upset initiative.

He had to respond. Dizzy and nauseous, near incapacity as Lysaer's outraged order freed his cramped limbs, he let the sick after-shock fold him double. With luck, he might spew on the traitorous examiner, or render the air in the stifling shack too disgusting to breathe.

But his retching heaved nothing from an empty stomach. Up-ended by vertigo, limp as slaughtered meat, Dace heard his liege's rebuke through the whirlpool as consciousness fled. "I will sanction no such cavalier handling or excuse a worthy servant's abuse. Bear the fellow up. Now! I'll attend him myself. A harlot's bed is no place for a sick man, no matter his humble station."

Counter-currents

Awake in the comfort of clean sheets, Dace hears his liege's contrite confirmation: that the steward's connection had exposed the temple informant's duplicity; and asked what reward he desires for an act of selfless, true service, he requests the grant of position as his Lordship's personal valet . . .

Engrossed over tactical maps in a tent, surrounded by his ranked captains, The Hatchet stabs a thick finger into the notch at the Pass of Orlan, and declares, "Like slinking rats, the clans have denned up where the terrain is riddled with bolt-holes. The High Priesthood wants them flushed out before winter. Let's hear your proposals to meet that directive . . ."

Gathered in Halwythwood's lodge to select the party sent after the Prince of Rathain, Iyat-thos Tarens squares off against Cosach like the boulder pitched against granite: "No one besides me knows his Grace's history at first hand, and none of your scouts has the town-born background to travel the open roads with impunity . . ."

III. Fissure

The hidden approach to Ettinmere Settlement devolved to a terraced footpath, ancient and weathered. Arithon followed Vivet's lead with care, often required to leap crumbled gaps or surmount wheeling vertigo where the way narrowed. The precarious track notched a near-vertical slope, edged by sun-beaten rock crocheted in the cracks with the roots of crabbed firs. The dizzying view opened up over air, the milky haze of midday filmed over the gashed chasm below. Hawks soared like flecks of nicked gold, with the indigo sky overhead a stretched drum between snow-capped peaks.

In an open vista that extended for miles, the trail behind snaked like unreeled cord through the contorted vales. Any unfriendly movement could not be concealed. Yet Arithon could not shake the persistent impression of watching eyes.

"We're not far." Paused to sip from one of the spring-fed falls that splashed over the brink and frayed into mist, Vivet tipped her chin skywards. Her flushed, freckled skin was no longer yellowed by fading bruises. Two patient fortnights at the cabin, and more time on the trail had settled her nerves. Or else the familiar ground eased the tension that rode her like a whipped horse.

Arithon looked up at her prompt. A vulture spiralled on the thermals, distanced to a taut pen-stroke. Common enough in the Storlains, where wolves and mountain cats hunted, carrion birds circled in tireless search of gnawed carcasses: except that something shiny winked through the feathers on the raptor's breast. "Yon creature is tame?"

71

"Not exactly. Our shamans link with them as observers." Vivet qualified without artifice, "That one's tracking our presence."

"And Ettinmere doesn't like trespassers." Annoyance gouged Arithon back to his feet. "I hope you'll be more forthcoming about how your folk receive strangers."

"My people kill suspected rapists on sight," Vivet answered, wilted. "That's why we waited to leave. I dared not risk misplaced blame for my shameful condition."

Arithon measured her belated sincerity, flicked to guarded distrust. "I have gone far enough. As one of their own, such arcane protection should see you the rest of the way without harm."

Vivet exclaimed, "Please! You can't go." Alarmed, she expounded, "We have rigid customs concerning outsiders. If you turn away without proper leave, you'll forfeit your place as my guest. My people must know who you are, first. If you don't face them honestly, they will shoot you down. I can make things right!" she hastened to amend. "I promise you'll be welcomed warmly once the formalities are satisfied."

Arithon weighed his choices, pinned in discomfort as noonday sun smote the clear air and baked the rocks like a furnace. His sword was no use against concealed archers. Conjured shadow turned upon folk without any cause for hostility risked a notoriety that might draw his enemies. Better, he judged, to earn amity and let Ettinmere's vigilant suspicion of strangers guard his back as a windfall advantage.

"Lead on," he told Vivet.

"I cannot," she added with chagrined regret. "By our ways, I must take you in, blindfolded."

That protocol nettled him. Nonetheless, he endured with iron forbearance while she tore the dusty hem from her chemise. His bent head concealed his distaste as she bound his eyes and knotted the cloth at his nape. Her seductive scent and her touch offended his person. Yet indignity scarcely merited a fight, not when he was tired at heart and disinclined to provoke cultural friction.

"They will come for us," Vivet said at a rushed whisper. "Do as they say and stay quiet."

The sentries arrived fast, two on foot from behind, their step almost sound-less, while two more unreeled from above, the creak of stressed rope occluded by the bounce and crack of dislodged pebbles. They asked no questions of Vivet but took brusque hold of Arithon. Because they did not attempt to disarm him, he allowed them the blistering liberty.

They bound his wrists. Roughly, as though they handled a criminal, he was noosed by the neck with a slip knot. Then he found himself prodded ahead, the man in front and the one at his heels his sole guidance on the narrow path.

Their intention was plain: if he resisted, a shove off the rim would hang him outright. Arithon broke into a sweat. On the whim of a woman he had no grounds to trust, his life lay at the mercy of eccentric strangers. Whether the Ettinfolk tested his courage, or tried his mettle to measure his earnesty, he had no recourse except to rise to the uncivil challenge.

Unrelenting, the Ettinmen were, but not cruel. They paused for rest when the ascent left him winded, and quenched his thirst from their unstoppered waterskins.

Yet the imposed conditions upon him overspent kindness or courtesy. Chilled after dusk, while the glacial gusts buffeted through his thin shirt, Arithon checked his temper, fed up by the relentless silence. Yet before he rejected Vivet's advice, the footing beneath his nose-led step opened up in descent. The rock ledge broadened to packed gravel and mud, grooved by the passage of cart-wheels. Then the rutted track gave way to pasture, fragrant with alpine flowers. Through muffling cloth, Arithon scented the redolence of penned livestock. Breeze moaned through a nearby wind-break, embellished with the tinkle of goat bells and fragmented chatter: a woman's chirped laugh, and the treble excitement of children, underscored by male voices and downhill, barking dogs, perhaps kept for herding.

Yet Arithon's keepers did not turn towards the settlement in the valley. Blindfolded still, tugged by their rope, he was shepherded into a timber enclosure. The tight space cramped even his slight build, and soaked up sound without echo. Head ducked beneath the low, raftered ceiling, he sucked in the rancid aroma of a smoke-house recently used to cure butchered meat.

The door creaked shut, followed by a rasp and thunk as someone outside shot a timber bar stout enough to thwart bears.

Then urgent hands pushed and shoved till he sat on the packed-earth floor. The stale strip of rag was yanked from his face. Mage-sense plumbed a darkness frowsty as cut felt, with two of his escort huddled beside him.

Then one sparked a tallow dip. Painted by the yellow ripple of flame, Arithon studied the Ettinmen.

Each wore a peaked felt cap, with rolled brims and wool bands stuck with feathers or knot-woven oat straw. Fair-skinned and sunburned, they had cropped, sandy hair, and eyes pale as coin silver. Narrow, refined features bespoke insular blood and inimical lack of expression. Long-boned, with slender hands, they were as alike as fledged hawks with their thin, high-bridged noses and feral attentiveness.

Among their kind, Arithon was the crow tossed into a harrier's nest.

The extravagant detail of their dress began with embroidered shirts, chamois vests, and elk-hide leggings stippled with indigo ink. Belts and boots were adorned with braided furs, or stitched quills, or the flayed bones of small birds. Each man wore a curved dagger, the handles inlaid with lapis and gold and topped with varnished knots at the pommels.

No move was made to free Arithon's wrists or remove the looped rope from his neck. If he was a prisoner, no one yet asked him to forfeit his weapons.

When loaded stares failed to pressure him to speak first, the fellow with eyes like steel grommets and the hatband with a cock pheasant's crest snapped off a statement in his native dialect.

Arithon did not understand. Given his clammed silence, one of the pair at length ventured a stilted translation. "Vivet Daldari claims you as her guest. We wait with you here while Ettinmere's elders hear her petition in your behalf."

But Arithon had firmed his own course: to smile and be gracious, and smartly move on once he had established his harmless credentials. "No matter the outcome of Vivet's appeal, I expect to fare eastward directly."

The speaker bared wolfish teeth. "Stranger, our custom says otherwise. If the elders reject you in Vivet's behalf, you will not leave here alive."

Arithon controlled the spark of his anger. Conversational, uncompliant, he said, "You would seize rogue authority and condemn a blameless traveller subject to crown justice?"

The spokesman returned a bold ultimatum. "The blameless man does not venture here, and we answer to no other law beyond Ettin."

Arithon kept his own counsel concerning the sovereignty of charter law. Rather than argue, he showed them contempt and settled back for a catnap. Mage-trained and in sharp command of his nerves, he slept, perhaps for an hour. Until inbound tension like a plucked string stirred the dead air and roused him.

Incomprehensible voices in dialect approached the barred door. A Masterbard's sensitivity picked out the discordant notes of outraged surprise, fast tempered by someone's authority. Whatever the unforeseen hitch, the Ettinmen with him surged to their feet. The bilingual fellow, eyes gleaming, explained in his stilted accent, "Vivet is brought here. You are permitted to speak with her alone. None will disturb you although our guard stays until the elders request your word on the matter."

Prickled at his nape, Arithon probed with delicate courtesy, "What business of mine concerns Ettinmere's council?"

The man smiled, eyebrows raised. "If the business in question is yours," he began, then snorted back sudden laughter, and grinned. "Ah, by Teaah's sacred pink tits! You don't know, then? Well, laddie, bequeathed by my breath to your ears: our shaman's confirmed that Vivet Daldari is pregnant."

The news punched Arithon windless. Stone-faced, he watched the door open and shut behind the spokesman's departure. The tallow dip fluttered to the influx of draught, then steadied and streamed again as the panel flung inward. The young woman entered, whose artless deceit had contrived this benighted embarrassment.

She had bathed and changed. Hair twined with primroses cascaded in splendour, reddish strands glinting over a draw-string gown that exposed the freckled, cream skin of her shoulders. Her scent pervaded the windowless gloom as she knelt at his feet, a scared doe in poised entreaty.

Her upturned face and the imposed view of her cleavage raised a stab of visceral hatred. Stung as though whipped, Arithon moved back, annoyed that his mindless male instinct still stirred to her flaunted attributes.

"I told my elders the quickened child was yours," she confessed, scalded scarlet. "What choice did I have? Its life would become forfeit without a willing sire's grant of child-right."

"Your dishonest seduction was an attempt to establish paternity?" Arithon accused, stunned incredulous. Her claim was unconscionable, that one bungled tryst might pin her luckless conception on him. "The chance is slight, Vivet. Birth is likely to prove I am not the babe's father."

"Although you could be!" She clung, head bowed, and disclosed in agony, "Outsider, you don't understand. If my people find out I've been used, unwilling, they'll say my womb's been cursed. A forced woman brings sour luck. If no man claims the burden as ward, her offspring henceforward are shunned as ill-fated."

"Without my protection, you claim to be ruined?" Brittle with sarcasm, Arithon snapped. "That's bathos!" Her glass-beaded necklace shivered as she shrank. The glint against her trembling flesh did not stir him, and the tawdry effort to dress for appeal offended his natural intelligence. "Just leave. Why stay for this piteous drama, Vivet? Anywhere else, you'd live free. Why not marry for love, without stigma?"

"I prayed to Sky and Earth that my courses would come," the woman gushed on, woe forced through a choked throat. "I wasn't beyond a fortnight overdue!"

"Then why rush things into a public scene?" Arithon asked, furious the issue had been broached before strangers without his prior awareness.

Vivet lifted a face streaked with tears, delicate as the glaze upon an heirloom porcelain. Fragile enough to shatter at a touch, she reached for his hand, and the constraint of s'Ffalenn compassion entangled his personal need to pull back.

"A woman's moon time is not private, here!" Vivet hastened to explain. "By Ettin tradition, females who travel abroad are questioned upon their return. The shaman condemns those who answer him false. Could I forsake my last pretence of virtue? Of course I told the truth! Roaco's divination ascertains I will bear a male child in the spring."

Arithon engaged his mage-sight straightaway, loath to rely on an Ettinman's word. For self-integrity, he confirmed the ephemeral gleam of the quickened seed in her belly.

Yet Vivet refused to have her get's rightful paternity deferred until birth. "What proof will matter, then, whose babe draws breath? Here, offspring of rape are killed without quarter! Exposed on the mountain side and left to die, unless someone of character agrees to foster them."

Arithon's fury exploded past restraint. "Murder in cold blood! Your people execute blameless newborns for the lack of a paternal *name*?"

JANNY WURTS

Vivet flinched. "Ettinmere raises no half-orphaned children. More, as the mother abandoned, I would be outcast. Fit only to serve others, and never to be *chia*, cherished as a wife. A woman in pregnancy must have a provider to pledge surety for her welfare and the babe's upbringing."

Wisdom in this case spoke for mature strength. "A liaison gained by manipulation won't give you that happiness."

"Did I ask to be forced?" Sobbing, Vivet clutched his legs and poured out the dregs of her misery. "This is my home, with my ties to family thrown into jeopardy by an ill turn. Ettin's way embraces *tuoram*, a code of responsibility that assigns privilege through honour."

"I should walk away." Arithon wrenched free in disgust. "Your people's tradition is nothing but vicious barbarity."

Yet in the dense distance between them, the unspoken, slim chance: her babe *might* in fact bear his lineage. And if the innocent get of a stranger, his choice to sacrifice that unborn life laid an infanticide at his feet. S'Ffalenn prince to the core, his blood heritage chained him to Vivet's needy plight.

"What of the child?" Arithon pressed. "Could a luckless bastard find any joy amid this rigid culture?"

Crest-fallen, Vivet exclaimed, "But you sorely mistake us!" She flooded him with eager reassurances. "Outsider blood is highly prized! We may be an unworldly folk, hidebound by obligation and kin ties, but our lines are in need of fresh vigour. Your charge as a foster parent won't last for life. The community holds our children as equals after they celebrate puberty. Mine would be sought as a coveted mate if, by your grace, he survives."

Tallow-fed flame dipped the moment in gold, the flush on the woman's over-bred skin transparent with hope, and the slim man before her armoured in retreat, his stubbled jaw clenched and his eyes chipped emerald. Twelve years of freedom, balanced against a blameless, new life: forced to capitulate through compassion, Arithon Teir's'Ffalenn yielded to the bitter price that silenced the outcry of his royal conscience.

The static that deranged the flux through the Storlains allowed only erratic glimpses of Arithon's straits. The bursts of connection brushed over Elaira where she camped under stars in the flatlands beyond the outskirts of Shipsport. The air smelled of dust and paper-dry grass, muddied by a south breeze fecund with marsh taint off the river delta. A squall line formed over the Cildein deeps riffled her skin to the distanced flicker of heat lightning.

The mainland would be sodden by dawn. Therefore, her blankets stayed laced in cerecloth, stuffed under her neck as a pillow. Her journey tomorrow would breast flaying wind and cold rain like the snap of a wet rag in her face.

But not yet. Poised as an indrawn breath before change, the electromagnetic currents in the high Storlains surged into a lucid stream.

The connected touch of her distant beloved raised Elaira to flash-point

76

gestalt. The tumultuous wave of Arithon's recent past and the burden of his entangled present threw her a jumble of impressions, the charge of emotional turmoil a surprise punch to the gut. Rapt mastery alone let her anchor until the morass settled into cohesion.

The impact of Vivet's pregnancy surfaced first, her dread fear and vulnerability warped into a selfish demand for protection. The result wove a snare to bind the tenets of any s'Ffalenn born true to his lineage. The price wrung Elaira to empathic tears. "Don't," she gasped, helpless. "Arithon, don't give way."

Yet he would, he must: even as once before he had staked his life to spare Fionn Areth.

Elaira knew his true heart, as no other. She grasped the deep-set revulsion that savaged his dignity: the bitter trial laid on his spirit, suppressed under pressure through forty-eight days since the storm had compelled him to share the decency of charitable shelter. Woman herself and healer-trained, the enchantress stripped the false tissue from Vivet's clinging need and exposed the manipulation behind the beguilement that fuelled this moment's trapped anger.

The unstable flux in the Storlains rang to Arithon's stifled revolt as he bent to appease his inflexible heritage. The sorrow driving his resignation stamped the crux like a granite engraving: *what gave an extended life its self-worth? Where could a man go to find peace of mind, relentlessly hounded by enemies? What better priority ruled him if he could not commit a mere dozen years to salvage an innocent life?*

Elaira shuddered, wrung in the crushed turbulence of his emotion as her beloved divested himself of his blades and stepped from the smoke-house in surrender. *His own, or hers, the sense of suffocation and bleak foreboding?* The hour felt lidded in darkness, each movement sealed in jet glass. Again blindfolded by Vivet's possessive touch, Arithon resigned himself to the escort of four Ettinmen, three padding a wolf's pack tread at his heels, with his bound wrists leashed to one in the lead. Their route skirted the nearby settlement, chased by snarling dogs and breezes sooted with woodsmoke from an open-air spit.

No offered meal assuaged Arithon's hunger. Beyond water, no comfort had eased him. Tired, light-headed, discomposed, and ungroomed, he stumbled over a rootlet.

The cascade of connection wavered and broke. Dissipated, the thread of rapport frayed away in the thrash of the Storlain flux currents . . .

Elaira surfaced, enraged. Discipline shredded, she pounded the dusty ground with her fists. "Fight them!" she gasped. "Sweet man, for your own sake, and mine, lose your temper and damn that brazen hussy to the fruits of her own devices!"

Yet Arithon would not. Torbrand's legacy bound him to wretched silence. Elaira bowed her head, overcome. "Don't fall to the flaw that killed King

Kamridian," she pleaded, undone by enforced separation. Arithon would not hear: had in his past hour of desperate peril cut off his recall of her steadfast partnership. Lost at this terrible crux, the counterbalance that once shielded him from the inborn flaws of his character.

Elaira plumbed the bleak pain that stifled his innate perception. She knew, oh, she knew! the ache was sourced in the agony of her absence. Heart and spirit, she raged at her helplessness. For female instinct screamed warning that the hidden cost might impact far more than a child survivor and a vain woman's dishonour.

That same night in the deeps of Halwythwood, the clan seeress retired, worn after three days spent in trance. Her arduous effort had unearthed no meaningful insight to suggest Prince Arithon's whereabouts. Talented resource stayed stymied, while blood-letting change whetted the Canon doctrine for death, and choked Etarra with dedicate troops.

The danger of inaction chafed tempers, with the Earl of the North and Iyat-thos Tarens faced off like male wyverns, scales bristled in territorial challenge.

Big men, too well matched to cross steel without the risk of crippling injury, they hammered out their contention with practice sticks, each bout fought to a ferocious draw. Both were left wincing and mottled with bruises. Yet Cosach's imperative question was satisfied, that Jieret's skilled legacy left Tarens no weakness in training at arms. Measured through Jieret's perspective, in turn, the realm's current *caithdein* lacked the ruthless years of survival under persecution. Battered to welts, Tarens allowed the brute strength of the man's constitution was not deficient.

Other arenas stayed open to challenge. The scouts' dismissive regard for all town-born sparked the latest: a test of the upstart guest's mettle through a knock-down contest at drink. Cosach pranced over his wife's objections. To blindside his impressionable heir, and side-step her complaint that the boisterous noise would aggravate their teething infant, he sited the affray on the grassy knoll carved out by the meandering Willowbrook. There, where the summer crowns of the oaks wore tiaras of constellations, Rathain's *caithdein* and his fettlesome rival took opposite seats at a massive table, hewn from a fallen tree ancient enough to be known by Name to the lost centaur guardians.

Between chieftain and guest, clumped like rain-sprouted fungus, spread the hoarded stash turned out of bunks, chests, and blanket rolls. In casks, corked bottles, and heirloom flasks, a liquid banquet for inebriation: beer, cider, honey mead, and cherry brandy, and worse, the evil, colourless poison that generations of hung-over misery had dubbed Dharkaron's Redress. The raucous scouts crowded the stream-bank as witnesses. They tousled Tarens's cropped hair while the merry fellow appointed as arbiter presented two ram's horn flagons.

The antique rims were embossed with silver. Ornamental knobs at the pointed ends spurned the practicality of a flat base. The curved vessels might be rested upside down, but only if they were emptied.

"All right, listen up, hear the rules!" The gleeful speaker addressed the contestants. "The contest opens with beer. You'll match drinks with your rival, flagon for flagon. Once you get sodden and can't hold your piss, first penalty switches your refill to honey mead. The second time you void your bladder, you'll step up to brandy. White spirits, third round, if you haven't puked. Whoever heaves up his guts first or falls senseless becomes the loser." Enthusiastic, he walloped the townsman's back. "Accepted, Iyat-thos? Then cross wrists in a double handshake with Earl Cosach to seal your sober agreement."

"Might we have an arbiter who's not staggering soused?" To hooted laughter, Tarens shared a farmer's ham-handed grip with the *caithdein*'s nutcracker fists. He hefted the cavernous flagon pressed on him, surrounded by ribald advice and reproof. A petite female scout wearing an acorn strung on a hoop earring tapped the selected cask, to the chink of coin placed on last-minute wagers.

"You're all barking mad," Tarens mused, while a prankster poured beer till the head foamed over his wrist. "This is how a rag-sop *caithdein* steers the kingdom's affairs during royalty's absence?"

But upright duty cut no bait with Cosach. "Case in point, swear that your unnatural memory doesn't play devil's advocate. In his time, Earl Jieret dumped the realm's woes on his captain, Sidir. This occurred more than once, even while the clans were beset. Claim my ancestor didn't chase Arithon's shirttails *and* drag his Grace by the scruff out of fatal trouble."

"Your cantankerous forebear succeeded," said Tarens, and licked off his dripping fingers. "By his proven experience, I'm better equipped to shake your prince back to his senses."

Provided, forbye, that anyone could. The impasse that dead-locked the quarrel was that nobody knew where to look. The search for a desperately hunted man, damned to fire and sword by the Canon, could not light off for the hinterlands without direction. Given the seeress had scried herself blank, theory argued his Grace had holed up in the most forbidding terrain on the continent.

"If Prince Arithon's gone to ground in the Storlains, he won't be found till he shows himself." Cosach flourished his brimming horn. "Dharkaron avenge and Sithaer take the hindmost!" Flint eyes level, he blew off a splatter of froth, then chugged down the contents. "Jieret," he declared as he clapped the drained cup bottoms up on the trestle, "never tested his skills in that benighted country." A back-handed swipe of his soaked moustache bared the gleam of pearl teeth. "The place is a botched mess of radical currents. Our talent hunters can't track wounded game through the griped flux in those ranges."

"That may well be," Tarens allowed, and drained his own vessel as smartly. Knowledge derived from the past chieftain's identity validated Cosach's objection. "Yet I say you've never brangled with Rathain's royal blood-line in person. Kiss yon rabbit's foot on the hilt of your eating knife. If you wear that for luck, you're going to need it."

Cosach belched behind a clamped fist. "The fuzzy token's a gift from my sister. I wear the toy because she's a shrew. Apt to notch the man's ears who tries to dine with a war blade at her table. And did I hear you wrong? You've dared suggest I'm no match for a runt who stands barely chest high to a stripling?"

"Yes," Tarens said, straight-faced.

"Then you're mushy as pudding!" Cosach waved to hasten the refill, while to Iyat-thos, he demurred, "Caught in a scrap with his Grace, I'd whack his sovereign head with a stick and drag him senseless by the heels. Which question begs asking. Why didn't you?"

"Because," Tarens snapped, "just like you're doing now, I stopped my ears with the bone-brained notion I knew better than Jieret's instincts. You won't blindside his Grace by brute force. He'll foul your plan while you go for your club and be elsewhere before you can swing."

As the side-lines chorus devolved to a chant for more drink, and a grizzled brute with a badger-pelt jerkin moved to oblige, Tarens stabbed back, "Who's grown soft, besides? Under Jieret's hard wisdom, you should burn down your lodge. Do away with the comfort of cabins, before the Light's campaign to scour Halwythwood makes your people a sitting target."

"Dismantle the outpost?" Cosach pounded the boards. "Only after I'm senseless! Defeat me, and by rights, you might pitch that besotted idea to our council. I'd have to be laid out unconscious, first. Else while you're flensed for the barbaric sentiment, Jalienne would eviscerate me."

"Fall quick, then," quipped Tarens. "I don't fear your wife."

"Merciful Ath! The more fool you, fellow." Cosach beckoned the cup-bearer on, while a mirthful companion, gleaming with knives, hefted the beer cask and poured.

Tarens held no illusions. *Something* uncanny bothered his instincts: unease prickled his skin as he raised the next round. Whether for an unknown threat to his liege, or if the boisterous horse-play at hand masked untoward animosity, Jieret's heritage as a Sight-sensitive talent lent no edge in the present arena. The legendary past chieftain had not been a hard drinker. No secret, apparently, since the on-going odds stacked fast in Cosach's favour. Tarens prayed for his brother Efflin's bone head, while dread worm-holed his gut at the unlucky prospect of failure.

To best his rival before he succumbed, he would cheat for bald-faced necessity.

The raptor's gleam in Cosach's eyes suggested he angled to muscle the victory, himself. Surrounded by wolves, Tarens needled, "The fatal flaw lies with the inbred drive of Rathain's crown lineage." He demolished his portion and banged down his horn. "Your prince can't escape his compassionate empathy."

Cosach belted off his share in turn. "That's your lame excuse for the fact he shed your escort straight off?"

"Acknowledge the weakness," Tarens attacked. "If not, you leave his Grace's back exposed to his enemies."

The grin Cosach returned showed contempt. "I'd correct your limited grasp of royal history. In this very glen, Arithon Teir's'Ffalenn once built a gentle stay for his woman that required Fellowship might to unravel. He'll protect his own interests if he has a mind."

Tarens bucked the High Earl's opinion in earnest, while the flagons were topped for the third time. "Before Arithon regains his full memory and recoups the informed mastery to raise such a warding, someone's human frailty will flush him from cover."

"That's why we're drinking," Cosach declaimed. Yet the breath he drew for rejoinder stalled as he fumbled his grasp on his cup.

Splattered by spilled beer, Tarens gained only that instant of warning before vertigo up-ended his balance also. His awareness unravelled: no dizzy rush from inebriation. The surrounding forest appeared etched in light just before the night split under what felt like the shock of a thunderbolt. He sensed fear in the bystanders' dumbfounded shouts. Then the stretched cloth of his cognizance burst. He plunged, wheeling, into the throes of tranced Sight, envisioned through Arithon's experience . . .

. . . in a closed space heated by a cedar fire, rough hands snatched off the blindfold. Blinking, annoyed, he stood amid expectant quiet in a round log building. Facing him, a row of inimical elders perched like mushrooms on squat hide hassocks. Men and old women, each wore a ceremonial mantle stitched with feathers. Greased hair dangled from conical hats, the felt brims pinned with wheat cockades. A wizened shaman at the centre presided. Thin and unkempt as knotted string, his shaved head wore a crust of dun-coloured clay. Bird-black eyes glared from rims of eldritch red paint, and his shoulders were draped with a cape that stylized a mountain raptor.

Magic coiled here, uncanny and sere as an icicle shot through a hot spring.

Trapped in an amber-tinged moment of dream, Tarens felt *Arithon Teir's'Ffalenn* draw in a wary, taxed breath. Leashed rage burned as, before those uncanny witnesses, he swore a binding oath that seared his spirit to inward revolt . . .

. . . Sighted unconsciousness rippled. Tarens resurfaced to open air, seized in shocked silence. Flat on damp earth, bathed in sweat and trembling, he breathed in the musk scent of Halwythwood's summer oaks and strove to steady his senses. Sobered faces bent over him. No longer ribald, the sturdy scout who had shouldered the cask knelt in shaken concern.

"Are you with us, Iyat-thos?"

"What happened?" Tarens demanded, confused. "That wasn't the after-effects of strong drink."

"An event woke the mysteries and tore through the veil," murmured someone in tremulous awe.

Before explanation, a bullish intrusion elbowed the stunned onlookers aside.

"You received a tranced vision?" Earl Cosach accosted. "What did you see?"

Propped up by earnest hands, Tarens came back to his wits before the chieftain's glowering presence. "Why did his Grace raise the wardings over this glen?" When no one answered, he pressed, "Earl Jieret was mage-bound to our liege. Whatever just happened, if the ripple twisting the flux cast an echo, I need to know the connection!"

Cosach folded his arms and reluctantly qualified. "Here, long ago, his Grace was said to lie with his beloved. The union begun was the first, and not consummate. Yet legend and our historical record confirm the couple's twined passion awakened the mysteries. The linked spirits of the crown prince and his mate excited the land's electromagnetics and unleashed a grand confluence. The upshift in resonance retuned the octaves this side of the veil. All reactive connections since then are more volatile. Possibly the event you experienced was provoked by a harmonic connection."

"I dreaded as much." Tarens covered his face, his anguish muffled through tensioned fingers. "But the fragmented view I received hasn't disclosed the meaningful impact."

"What did you observe?" Cosach repeated more gently. "I sensed that his Grace was held in duress. But the impression arose without context."

Tarens shuddered and bared his flushed features. "If I saw true, Arithon Teir's'Ffalenn has just willingly sworn a binding oath under an arcane power." Burdened with grief, the crofter described the outlandish scene in detail.

Mention of the shaman in black scalded Cosach to swearing alarm. "Ath preserve, those wily creatures are Ettinmen! A tribal culture tucked up in the Storlains, ferocious as rabid weasels and inbred to the verge of stark madness. Their sentries use buzzards for scout's eyes, did you know? Besides the unsavoury fact that they murder strangers on sight, they serve their retribution by ritual butchery. They could be holding our prince for a barbaric rite of execution!"

"No," Tarens assured. "I gathered our liege is not under threat." Muddled with drink and fretful unease, he sought the comfort of back-handed assets. "If the Ettin society is defensively insular, they're unlikely to sell his Grace out to enemies, or welcome a dedicate invasion sent into their midst by the True Sect priests."

"They'd skewer our peaceful emissary as readily." Cosach fingered the dagger struck through his belt. "Don't think you'd fare any better as town-born. Those savages desecrate their human kills. String the flayed carcasses over the cliffs for their pet vultures to feed on the carrion."

Tarens offered a hand to the Halwythwood chieftain, grateful this once for the aggressive strength that steadied him onto his feet. "Then we have little choice but to fashion a plan to draw Arithon away."

Legs braced to offset the surfeit of beer, Cosach shut his eyes in morose forbearance. "I would sooner dig my own grave with bare hands! But in fact, we need help from that gormless worm of a traitor."

"Dakar?" quipped one of the by-standing scouts. "You want the raunch wastrel shaken down?"

Cosach grimaced. "First we have to find him. Much as the prospect pains me, that spellbinder's the only spirit we have who might know what caused tonight's rip in the veil. More, if we have to twist his fat arms and spit him over a bonfire, he'll serve us with the arcane tricks to blindside the hexed birds that keep watch for the Ettinmen."

In cold-sober fact, the Mad Prophet would fight tooth and nail before crossing his path with Arithon Teir's'Ffalenn. Although a slow death by roasting seemed preferable did not mean fate granted him a blind eye. Always, his fickle penchant for augury upset his bone-deep cowardice. Where other seers lost their faculties in the static clouding the Storlain flux stream, the discredited master spellbinder sprawled in the gutter, naked and helplessly wrestling to stifle the torrent of unwanted vision.

Ratted out by a doxie, brow-beaten with threats, he cringed at the feet of a furious pimp outside the whore-house in Backwater. "Be off!" The ignoramus tossed Dakar's shucked clothing after him. "I won't peddle my girls to dark-mongering devils! Or risk them to the horrors of death rituals and evil practice!"

The spellbinder rolled clear of a puddle of horse-piss. Draped in flung cloth like a ragman, and pinked by the gravel paving, he cradled his splitting headache and winced. Since the region as yet had no temple faction frothing to burn suspect talent, he gave injured tongue in retort. "Crazy jape! Look past the ripe nuggets plucked out of your arse! I have nothing to do with black arts or necromancy."

"Eternal Light burn your spirit, I'll hear no more lies!" The bawdy-house rooster slammed his door with a boom that cracked echoes down the lake-front alley. In final retort from a top-storey window, the dainty hands lately prised off Dakar's pleased flesh jettisoned his orphaned boots. The scuffed footwear plummeted, streaming the tongues of his hose, and thwacked into his hunched shoulders.

Which abuse failed to stem his Sighted view of the disaster unfolding in the high Storlains. Dakar cursed the spiteful doxie with a venom she scarcely deserved. She had not disparaged his prowess in bed, at least until his outburst in actualized Paravian ignited the mattress beneath them. The shocking disruption had done little good: his barrage of Sighted talent continued apace. Better the footwear had knocked him unconscious than to bear further witness to Arithon's straits.

Dakar unhooked the small-clothes snagged on his ear. Spitting out the taste of horse-urine and sour nausea, he stood and jammed on his trousers. He refused to suffer the ghastly mistake; could not bear watching Rathain's prince swear child-right at Ettinmere by the Prime Matriarch's dastardly scheming. Without looking, the Mad Prophet knew how a crystal shard had been imprinted to spring Arithon's downfall: how not, tricked into falsified belief that *his cherished enchantress had betrayed him, with his steadfast love wielded as a tool by a dutiful Koriathain.*

No recourse, for the misery: the record was true. A past Prime's directive once *had* sought to turn Elaira's affection against him. But the partial view had shaped a tactical deceit, deliberately planted for Arithon's search of her cabin. The impact shook the deep bulwark of a trust yet held flawless between them. But only the uncut perspective of the complete incident could refute the invidious fragment of evidence.

Dakar ground his teeth, ridden by the benighted vision of Arithon's reciting his oath before the Ettinmere elders. No recall of his Masterbard's knowledge of law had served the gravity of due warning. To his Grace, bludgeoned into numbed bitterness, the sacrificed years while a child matured seemed a meaningless pittance, where by a more callous measure, the stakes should have hurled Vivet's venal dilemma off the nearest cliff.

"Once in your life, just this *once*, Arithon!" Dakar fumed. "Be the natural bastard, scrap ethics and fly into a rage! Don't indulge every damned self-righteous idiot who tweaks your bleeding heart! Lash out! Dharkaron Avenger wept, don't shoulder the load for a wanton git who's been gaffed by Selidie's filthy directive!"

Yet Arithon checked his prickly temper and let himself become shackled.

Dakar winced, as the ceremony of child-right concluded. Stuffed back into his shirt, uncaring the garment was inside out, he ploughed into the marshy breeze off the lake and sought the first lit casement. Shoved into the rowdiest waterman's dive, he perched like a glum toadstool and ordered a jug of cheap gin. He popped the cork. Swallowing down the raw liquid, he begged sorry fate for the grace to pass out before prescience disclosed the outcome.

Yet even Backwater's rot-gut gin failed to grant him oblivion fast enough.

Dakar felt the visceral, glass edge of pain as Arithon stepped from the timbered building. Vivet met him on the plank stair, crowned by a wreath of flowers. Pulled forward and pounded on the back by her jubilant relatives, he found himself prodded by too many hands, then seized and kissed by chattering sisters. Revolted, in leashed fury, he endured the embrace of her brothers and cousins, gathered into the circle of family.

Prophet, accursed with true Sight, Dakar caught the wretched reaction twofold: as the fickle flux in the Storlains surged clear, and Elaira suffered the intimate view through Arithon's dumbfounded eyes. She echoed the recoil of his clubbed surprise. Wept, while the noisy, exuberant crowd received him as one of their own.

Child-right, in Ettinmere, involved more than the rearing of offspring. The horror dawned late, that his earnest consent saddled him with a nuptial celebration. The happy crowd hazed him and plucked at his clothes. Crude laughter and jokes herded him towards a hut to bed Vivet as though joined in marriage.

Dakar recognized the set to Arithon's shoulders. The Teir's'Ffalenn met his unwanted bride like the chained dog jerked towards the kennel.

Then the evil belt of the gin did its work; or else static noise broke Elaira's empathic connection. Cognizant vision dissolved like dashed foam off a breaker.

Dakar crumpled into a slovenly heap, the plunge into drunken unconsciousness welcomed. While his awareness dimmed, alone in Atainia, a last witness followed the turbulent thread of event closed at Ettinmere Settlement.

Warden of Althain, immersed in broad-scale earth-sense, Sethvir beheld Arithon's vehement rejection of Vivet's possessive embrace.

"Would you shame her in public?" a shocked celebrant cried, alike enough to be a sibling.

Arithon returned a vitriol glare. "Your customs," he cracked, "have the delicacy of rats baked into a wedding cake. I've accepted guardianship for the child. After that, who sleeps under your kinswoman's roof is not my affair. Or your business."

"And if her brat's yours?" the fellow pursued.

"No difference. Her babe *is* mine until he reaches puberty," Arithon blistered in correction. "Sworn to my name by your council of elders and sealed before the eyes of your shaman. Best you Ettinfolk never forget that!"

The flare sprung off the vehement statement struck Sethvir as a spark touched to flame. If Vivet and her kin believed Arithon's spirit could be leashed, they soon would find their net snagged on the thorn in the blossom of Torbrand's descent. The Sorcerer winced. *Almost*, he pitied the Ettin elders, subject to the wicked explosion their repressive culture deserved.

Indeed, the bleak hour had come, forecast over two hundred and fifty years ago: the dimming of Arithon's psyche, engineered by Koriathain through the tactical severance of Elaira's influence. Once, on a damp tide-flat by a drift-wood fire, Traithe had served the enchantress due warning: *". . . for good or ill, you're the one spirit alive in this world who will come to know Arithon best. Should your Master of Shadow fail you, or you fail him, the outcome will call down disaster . . ."*

Sethvir bowed his head. Tangled hair like shaved ice in the moonlight streamed through the library casement, he listened with every hair prickled erect.

No whisper arose from the absent colleague whose silence stayed adamant: Davien ventured no overture towards a contrite return to his colleagues. Yet

Althain's Warden sensed the first whisper of avalanche. That dire wave of fore-running impetus, set off and gathering force, that could see the riven Fellowship of Seven restored back to unity at their full strength. Or else tonight's consequence tripped their downfall. If destiny's card came to shatter their covenant, entropy must not be allowed to unravel the harmonic that bridged the arc of Athera's mysteries.

Provocations

The Hatchet thumped down his mallet fist hard enough to displace the stones weighting his tactical maps. Correspondence and lists exploded in flurries from the stacks on the trestle in front of him. "Say again!"

Officers summoned for his revised orders quailed, while the mousy scribe startled out of dictation squeaked and splayed his best pen nib.

Few dared to bait The Hatchet's ill temper. Not since the momentous disaster that routed his invasion of Havish, and never under the redoubled fury incited by unforeseen set-backs.

"My summer campaign plan's bedevilled, thick as pests in plague-ridden batches." Up to his nose in the scent of hot horseflesh steamed off the latest courier, the Light's supreme commander fumed on, "Speak up, boy! Spit out whatever foul news has blown in here with the squall."

"The galley-man you hired for transport from East Bransing has defaulted on your signed contract." The pimpled adolescent dripping on the carpet braced rattled nerves and yanked off the sling hanging his dispatch case. "Best read the details, Lord. The vessel in question's already sailed."

"This happened *yesterday*?" The Hatchet hopped in livid distemper. "Light scorch her venal master and broil his skanking carcass! Show me the merchant captain alive who won't duck a war-bond requisition for a bribe!"

"Not for coin, and not for apostasy this time," the browbeaten courier dared to insist, too exhausted to cower, as The Hatchet's cobra-quick snatch ripped the packet away from him.

The senior staff waited, trapped in the storm's eye. Tension crackled the pause. The guttering lamps distorted the shadows of the command tent's grisly, stuffed-animal trophies, while the gusts outside battered the torrential rain, and leaks through the canvas pavilion pattered The Hatchet's volcanic annoyance.

He cut the soaked fastenings with his knife, ranting onwards in his bass growl, "The two companies I just force-marched into Dyshent are stalled at the dock without shelter because of your tardy disclosure."

The courier wrung his gloves in petrified silence. His desperate urgency had lamed two mounts, and brought a rider to grief on the road. The dispatches delivered at such cost in flesh became slapped on the table. Unrolled, the official wax seals and gold ribbon should have curbed the most arrogant displeasure.

Yet the panoply of High-Temple authority failed to quench The Hatchet's vexation. He read, lips clamped, his fuming breaths marked by the flutter and tap as moths blundered into the lamp panes. Soon enough, the gist raised his stentorian bellow. "Did you know the contents of this before you darkened my threshold?"

The courier unlocked his chattering teeth. "Rumour's flying like bale-fire. Has your hired galley in fact been pre-empted on the pretext of divine authority?"

"Pirated, rather!" The Hatchet punched a stub finger into the salient line: '. . . her captain forced to cast off in duress, or watch his vessel burn to the waterline with all hands . . .'

When the next leaf disclosed the run-amok avatar's motive, The Hatchet's complexion turned purple: '. . . the s'Ilessid scion's heretical pursuits have not abated . . . his movements were contained until he slipped the over-confident grasp of our Examiner at East Bransing . . . now believed to be moving to thwart your advance to eradicate unreformed clansmen . . .'

"Lysaer? Coming here?" The Hatchet stiffened. "Light's havoc! No way I'll suffer the next dose of ruin sown by that dandy's rank cowardice!" His meaty fist banged again. Parchments encrusted with seals bounced and settled, while the stacked notes that directed supply collapsed in a slithered cascade. "The mincing flit abandoned the field when the battle turned sour at Lithmarin! I'll hang the daisy by his curly short hairs before he befouls my tactics again!" A gesture spurned the offensive documents, while tactical diagrams and requisition slips sighed to rest in the shavings spread underfoot to sop up the puddles. "Yon High Priest's blustering drivel is useless. We've no facts to plot a sound strategy, besides, thanks to that lame-brained examiner. Which way will the avatar jump, plying havoc? Back towards Rathain, or will he muck into my campaign in north Tysan?"

The nervous courier disclosed the development too sensitive to be penned under seal. "The latest informants' reports favour Tysan. The co-opted galley weathered the storm in a cove down the coast, which suggests her course lies to the west."

"Flimsy guess-work!" The Hatchet scraped at the stubble on his bull-dog jaw. "No one can say with authority what that whey-faced wastrel intends. He might have been out-bound for Falgaire or Morvain before heavy seas forced him to snug down." Squat as an armoured battering ram, the Light's first commander shoved his chair back. Kicked papers fluttered like birds in his wake as he belaboured his officers. "I want that galley overtaken and searched. Cuff every living deck-hand aboard and shake them down by rough questioning!"

Tasked with what seemed a suicidal assignment, a dismayed staffer denounced, "You believe the avatar's elsewhere?"

"I like my targets kept tidy," The Hatchet cracked in earnest. "If the detail you send gets scalded alive, we're hell-bound to know, like the weathercock, which way Lysaer's pointed for certain."

The pavilion headquarters seethed into motion, the dismissed officers treading over the papers jettisoned under changed orders.

"I'll have the veteran divisions split into skirmish groups. Equip the best to cross the mountains towards Valenford, then swing them north to engage the rest of my battle plan soonest. The second wave will fan out behind and muster beneath the western foot-hills."

"Supply's caught short-handed," a rattled voice protested. "Rearrangements on that scale are going to take days!"

"Then improvise, quick!" retorted The Hatchet. "Hungry men can forage at need during summer. *This post will be stripped.* Lean troops on the march are better off than a batch of post-sitting, burned skeletons, paralysed by ineptitude!"

Against scoured silence, The Hatchet plunged on. "I'm saving our finest! Do you understand? March them out before dawn. Take what food they can carry. No wagons. No tents! I want speed. The heavy equipment left here must maintain the illusion we haven't dispersed."

Cooks and camp-followers were to wear surcoats and helms, while the raw recruits stayed on to keep staging drills in the practice field.

"Our dregs will form up tomorrow for Erdane to defend the High Temple against the rogue avatar."

Another captain gasped. "They're sheep herded to slaughter!"

"Maybe." The Hatchet glared at his detracting officers. "Tell me, which bunch would you sacrifice?"

Only the next in command dared a protest. "Our strongest would hold that line and not break."

"Yes, and die to a man for no purpose!" The Hatchet waved off his underlings' outrage. "If the demoralized companies and green recruits run, weakness favours their chance of survival. Maybe the mad avatar will lack the stomach to murder a pack of puking tenderfeet." His bark chased the stunned officers crammed at the exit. "Get on, directly! My orders won't wait."

Barged after them into the black pelt of rain, The Hatchet yelled for his messengers, some to ride straightaway to alert the towns and the Light's stationed garrisons. Others would carry his notes of requisition and summary records to placate the priests.

Urgency cut no slack for the midsummer gale churning the coastal road into soup. The Hatchet returned, breathless and soaked, and lit into the scribe caught resharpening his nibs. "Sit up and take my dictation!" Given the extensive planning that Lysaer's surprise move overturned, neither the Light's lord commander or his master of letters saw rest.

Cloudy dawn pierced the gloom when at last The Hatchet stood up. The campaign trestle before him was swept clean of the last revised dispatches. Smoke gritted the air, with the newest campaign plans burned to doused ash inside a commandeered chamber-pot. No evidence remained to disclose his rapid redeployment. Outside, the thinned encampment kept the boisterous semblance of an unchanged routine: troops engaged in practice bouts with enough blundering racket to maintain the appearance of numbers. A shrewd eye might discern the reduced strings of horses hitched to the messenger's picket line; or notice that the cauldrons under the cook shack's sagged awning served less than yesterday's head count.

Short bones aching, The Hatchet knuckled his eyes, too restless to retire. Gadded by nature, he moved to inspect the night's progress before his swift raid overtook the renegade vessel. Met by another obstruction, his bulled stride all but mowed down an inbound equerry.

"Messenger, sir! Bearing a High-Temple mandate, arrived under Hanshire's banner."

"Get the fellow in here double-quick." The Hatchet lurched back and dropped into his chair like a sackload of bricks.

A voice murmured without, while another's light tread squelched over the sodden ground. The figure that darkened his entry came alone: no man, but a slender, imperious female in a purple cloak banded with scarlet.

The Hatchet shoved erect as if pinked. "I've more pressing priorities."

Yet evasion did not stem the woman's impertinence. "If your urgency concerns the delinquent galley shipped out of Falgaire, my business might speed your endeavour."

The Hatchet shrugged. "At what ruinous price?" But the witch had forestalled him. Caught at close quarters, he stared upward with blistered hostility. "I might rather know the Master of Shadow's current activity. Ah, no! Not again," he chided. "Don't trouble me with a replacement for your last shady talisman. Or didn't you mean to add spin to the failures that botched my invasion of Havish?"

"No. Our mutual aim was subverted as well. Seek due revenge upon Arithon Teir's'Ffalenn." The Koriathain advanced with cool equanimity and placed a cedar box on the trestle. "Our token today is sent in good faith."

Since The Hatchet failed to snatch up her gambit, the enchantress flipped the catch and raised the fitted lid. Nestled inside, a steel crossbolt quarrel scribed a bright line in cold daylight. The notched end for the cable had razor-edged fins instead of plumed fletching. When her gloved fingers eased the coffer closed, the metal's suspect sheen imposed the after-image evoked by a latent enchantment.

The Hatchet grinned without delicacy. "You seek an assassin to slaughter a god? Find a more gullible fool. One who doesn't mind dying in martyred flames, condemned for collusion with Shadow."

"Soon enough, your High Priests will revise their priorities." Shown caustic contempt, the Koriani witch returned a feline smile. "The veracity of the True Sect Canon can't withstand the word of a living avatar. Lysaer s'Ilessid poses a liability to the purity of their creed. Unless, of course, his divine status becomes discredited. He is mortal, in fact. Fellowship sorcery grants his longevity. Wound him in public, and his divinity will be exposed as a sham."

"I have other priorities," The Hatchet repeated, annoyed enough to shoulder aside her insinuations.

"Do you truly?" she challenged, a post in his path. "Why not accept help? I might spare you the waste of resources, even by-pass a squalid day's search for a commandeered ship."

But her blandishment misfired. The Hatchet clenched his jaw as though he chewed marbles and ploughed on with insane disregard.

"Brute!" gasped the enchantress. Spurned by the rough shove that displaced her, she dropped civilized discourse for spellcraft.

For one breath-stopped instant the air seemed to burn. The Hatchet blinked, staggered backwards. By the time vision cleared and his balance recovered, the pavilion lay empty. No sign remained of the nosy enchantress beyond the latched box left behind on the trestle.

The uncanny artifact was far too dangerous to leave at large in the war camp.

The Hatchet spat a ferocious oath. Forced to secure the damnable construct under lock and key, he pursued his disrupted course of inspection in a viciously poisoned mood. Throughout, the anxiety haunted: *had* his late campaign in Havish been sabotaged, with a victory snatched from his grasp? Who knew *what* twisted wickedness motivated the Koriathain.

To be wrangled again by their wiles mocked his competence. Worse, fumed The Hatchet, the bedevilling shrew played on his fierce desire to see Lysaer s'Ilessid deposed after the shame of defeat. Hooked bait on that weakness galled his thorny temper.

"Damn your meddling Prime, I will seize my reckoning," he snarled, then shouted outside and summoned his equerry at a frazzled sprint.

Repercussions touched off by the upset in Dyshent flared more than The Hatchet's distemper. Across the continent, surrounded by packing crates as the Senior Circle of the Koriathain uprooted itself from their entrenched lair at Whitehold, the Matriarch vented annoyance. "The cagey snake has rejected my overture!"

"Your morning's work was scarcely in vain," soothed the attendant, hovering Senior. The spelled crossbolt had stayed in The Hatchet's possession, a temptation planted in fertile ground. "The game is young. The Light's prickly commander will surely succumb, if only to upstage the avatar."

But Selidie's displeasure rejected optimism. "The overblown martinet lacks respect for our order." How *dared* he threaten a reigning Prime with his pipsqueak talk of retribution! She needed the man to react on his merits, not haltered in spells as a puppet.

Her bit players must all be engaged by free will. Anything less circumvented her cause to wrest the sisterhood clear of the Fellowship's compact. But the very tools to pressure the Sorcerers carried a double-edged price: where The Hatchet's directive to eradicate clanblood weakened the historic guardianship of the free wilds, such butchery also reduced the available pool of heritable talent. Fewer gifted candidates would survive to be inducted and replenish the order's strength. Koriathain wrestled other perverse inconveniences: Selidie dared not risk a passage by galley to leash the Light's mongrel commander herself. The might just restored by recovery of the Great Waystone made the amethyst too precious to hazard at sea.

Her choice to relocate to Daon Ramon imposed an inconvenient journey by land. Hence this invasion of boxes, up-ending her household just as fractious events approached a critical crux.

Lysaer's double-blind play was exposed: The Hatchet's over-zealous detail would shortly board a galley held under storm anchorage. When the challenge at the sterncastle door went unanswered, the lock would be smashed by war-bond authority.

Selidie knew, seated amid the echoing chaos of her windowed gallery at Whitehold: the frantic search would find an empty cabin. The Light's delinquent avatar and his personal servant were not aboard.

On the sore subject of Lord Lysaer's activity, her own stellar resource fell short. Repeated auguries by Koriani talent sank into murk.

Selidie chewed over her thwarted frustration, irritated by back-ground chatter, and the scrape of filled trunks dragged aside for the porters. Since the scryers tagged the Mad Prophet's presence well to her west, today's obfuscation most likely involved a Fellowship Sorcerer's mark.

Asandir's ward of guard upon Daliana might be clouding Prime Selidie's reach. The pesky chit had vanished after her collusion with the Mad Prophet had engineered Lysaer's abduction from the carnage at Lithmarin. Separated from the spellbinder's protection in Scarpdale, the inconvenient young woman had never resurfaced, even under an exhaustive search backed by the order's Great Waystone. Therefore, another bold finger had meddled. Only one other power in reach owned the main strength and audacity.

Selidie called her attendant Seniors to active duty despite the convulsive disarray. "I require an immediate circle of twelve, a cleared room, and the chest that contains the Great Waystone for the purpose of engaging Davien."

The announcement reeled the room to shocked silence. None dared flout the Prime, no matter the peril inherent in crossing the Fellowship Sorcerers; and of the Seven, the Betrayer was unspeakably dangerous. The most experienced Seniors recalled: last time their Matriarch had wielded the might of the Waystone against him, the affray had seared her to a stub-fingered cripple.

On the moment the Prime Matriarch firmed her resolve, the renegade Fellowship Sorcerer in question stood on a rock slope in the Mathorns, red-and-white hair like a stallion's mane tumbled over his taut shoulders. Above, like a massive stilled pendulum, a boulder half the size of a house creaked in a sling, cranked vertical by a match-stick brace of fir logs. The stone overweighted its groaning support, suspension maintained by permission and sorcery mighty enough to unravel the mountain beneath.

Being Davien, no such carelessness happened, though from an earth-linked vantage at Althain Tower, Sethvir winced for the timing as Kharadmon swooped in, bristling to level the ancient score of his grievances.

Arctic draught at the nape his first warning, Davien flexed his interlaced fingers in an artistic stretch. "What, no flowering nightshade? No hellebore? Not even the toxic flamboyance of the tiger-lily? Provocative orange would suit us both, if you still style yourself in that obnoxious green cloak."

Clad himself in autumnal russet and brown, the coarse outdoor wool paired with calfskin boots and cordovan leathers, Davien perched on the pile of casks and provender, stored under tarps in the open. The refuge at Kewar engineered for a shade now required renovation to suit his incarnate release from the dragon's service. The old entry, drilled out, underwent the critical step of receiving a guardian cap-stone: finicky spells and physical effort interlaced in fraught measure with fatal danger.

Insolent necessity, Davien snatched the interruption to eat. His usual satirical mockery absent, he peeled the wax from a cheese, cracked a loaf of dark bread, and with a thoughtful expression, dug in.

Kharadmon commanded the wind for his voice. The question became, not how many, but which mothballed fight he picked first.

While the shade coalesced for the opening salvo, Davien raised an eyebrow and busily chewed as the tirade unleashed. "Not mentioning your colossal mistakes that saddled us with the rebellion, or the brutal inventiveness that destroyed King Kamridian, sunk in your criminal culpability, what excuse grants you the license to fling Asandir's gift of survival into our teeth? Also Luhaine's sacrifice in your behalf! How deadly the irony, that his butchered flesh once paid for your mess at Telmandir, only to lend you the undeserved grace to salvage your reincarnation."

The Betrayer said nothing. He did not belabour the pertinent truth: that Kharadmon's culpable action had upset Asandir's intervention, which would have disarmed Shehane Althain's sprung defences on the historical hour that he became fatally savaged.

Yet Davien's weighted silence failed to stem his discorporate colleague's furious accusations.

"By your passionate claim, our use of clan blood-lines to treat with the Paravians created the schism between town-born and talent. Who's the yapping hypocrite, now? Your accomplishment's driven a zealot religion into the bleeding breach. If you're not shamed by the Light's slaughter of talent, and while you sat idle as three of us cleaned up the carnage after a *drake war*, I demand to hear from your lips: by our sworn covenant to protect the Paravians, why have you not stirred to explore what's befallen the guardian at Northgate? Restored to flesh and bone, can't you lessen the burden on Asandir? Explain now, in full! By Dharkaron Avenger, why not pursue the reason for Chaimistarizog's absence?"

Davien straightened and jettisoned his bread-crust. "Sethvir likely knows. And if not, only Asandir has earned the right to inquire."

Air shrieked to Kharadmon's incensed recoil. The blast creaked the ropes, and whitened the plies a hairbreadth from flash-freezing the fibres. "Enough cagey evasions. I'll have answers no matter the threat to your self-centred independence."

"Some other day," Davien dismissed.

Behind him, the guardian stone slung on its precarious ropes emitted a crack like the snap of a whip. The gryphon his artistry had yet to carve glowed briefly inside the unstructured granite, while the orb to become the watchful eye suddenly flared livid red. The precursor spell seating its protective enchantments scribed a ring of white fire around Davien's planted stance and also encompassed the indignant swirl of Kharadmon's indignant essence.

"What outrageous bombast!" The discorporate Sorcerer's temper cracked before incredulity. "We're not under attack."

"We are, in fact." Etched in the sharp sunlight and shade of high altitude, Davien flaunted an insolent grin. "Try a surprise visitation steered by the Prime Matriarch. She's trying the might of the Waystone against us, backed by twelve circled Seniors."

"You'll have staged that charade," Kharadmon huffed.

"Do you *truly* think?" The Betrayer measured the Fellowship entity pinched in the malicious breach. "If you can't believe me, at least curb your pique. We're stuck together for the duration. Unless, of course, you snatch your safe exit and flit?"

Kharadmon snorted. "What, turn tail and run from Prime Selidie's wiles? Try my patience again!"

Davien laughed. "Then stay at your peril. Her sally to test me isn't a feint."

No toothless threat: wielded by a Prime at full strength, the amethyst focus packed force enough to endanger a discorporate Sorcerer. Particularly if the Matriarch drained her subordinates to leverage the contest.

Kharadmon's presence snuffed out, condensed to a frosty vacuum.

Then Prime Selidie's concerted blast struck and shattered the rudimentary wards laid into the unfinished cap-stone. Spelled ropes and unpolished granite exploded. Shards flew like knives. Planted inside the nexus with folded arms, Davien seemed unfazed as though he outfaced a social embarrassment. Yet the actualized spells that wrested the lethal missiles aside and crashed them impotently at his feet broke a sweat on his forehead.

He mocked, "A stone-throwing tantrum's the best you can do?"

Reckless strategy, to taunt a powerful rival maimed under his past round of trickery: bolt lightning stabbed downwards out of clear air. Harm deflected just shy of electrocution, Davien held fast, caged in branched forks that scribbled scorched channels of carbon around him. Through smears of wisped smoke, he needled again, "You won't have your way using pique for diplomacy."

Yet his challenge just missed the dismissal of sarcasm. His straits were dire. Yield one step, and the entrance to his library would lie open to rifling trespass. Too many dark secrets were cached within: volumes of knowledge too dreadful to be shelved with the Paravian archives at Althain Tower.

Selidie had rancorous bones aplenty to pick with the Seven and a vengeful personal score outstanding against Davien for centuries. Which ferocious awareness scarcely prepared him for her next scalding strike. Dazzled nearly blind and hammered to his knees, Davien seized the moment to palm a flake of stone from the wreckage. The fragment yet retained the grant of permission to stand ward and guard for him in free partnership.

Also, within, the eidetic stamp of the violence that had snapped the harmonic working asunder. Davien tapped the mineral's matrix and grasped the aggressive thrust of the Prime's motivation: a fury that echoed from her past failure to best Sulfin Evend. Thwarted plots to separate Lysaer from his steadfast war-captain's moral influence had balked her order's intentions. Again poised with the True Sect priesthood as agent under her thumb, Selidie raged to find a new obstruction guarding Lysaer's vulnerability. Hell-bent, the Prime sought the secret that sheltered the sen Evend heir, Daliana.

Davien sorted his counter-moves, appalled by the stakes. Barraged under the lightning shimmer and crack of the Prime's hostile charge, he seized the split second and sounded the chip for the remnant of his burst ward. Since mineral forgot *nothing*, the imprint remained, a plan configured to perfection well before the disruptive attack.

But set-back dealt him an unforeseen shock: the founded circle had included no safe passage for crossing, and *Kharadmon's wise retreat had never occurred.* The discorporate's choice to take cover in hindsight posed a drastic mistake.

Davien dared not risk that appalling disclosure with his resource taxed under fire. Pitched on the defensive with the Prime unaware of his colleague's collateral peril, he stared down disaster and pressed the end game.

The stone fragment held the template of the wardspells already designed to withstand a hostile assault. Davien wielded the pattern. A further split second's reckless intent engaged *other* forces that no Fellowship Sorcerer before this had been hardened to bear.

His hands flared into unnatural fire: a shimmer azure as gas-flame, and reactive beyond all imagining. Naked flesh and blood, Davien's finger-tips unfurled the prepotent aura possessed by Athera's great drakes.

The phenomenon, until now kept shrouded, exposed how profoundly Dragonkind's dreaming had changed him. The volatile power sparked to his will and ripped the air with an ozone-spiked crack. The elements screamed. The staid cliff-face before him ignited to the might of his focused desire and restored the pulverized statue. Reshaped in completed manifestation, the sentinel gryphon gargoyle engaged its guardian spells at one stroke.

Prime Selidie's thrust tangled in the matrix.

White fire met blue with a shriek that cracked bed-rock. The ground rumbled and shook, while the elements bled light, a wild coruscation that fountained aloft and unfurled the shimmer of an aurora.

Prime Selidie's lightnings snuffed instantaneously.

Socked by the earthquake punch of the recoil, Davien wrestled, hands locked, and vised his thoughts still. Crouched with singed hair, seared clothes smoking, he regarded the blackened ash dusting his skin.

"I'd rather the meddling Prime was not privy," he gasped, while a land-slide of stones ploughed into the vale with a thundering roar. "Insolent shade! *Were* you endangered?"

"The question is moot!" Kharadmon's presence unfurled with a whoosh. "If the Prime was desperate before, you've just torched the core of her insecurity." The shade added, thoughtful, through a chattering storm of loose gravel and carbon, "I had not expected that move to protect me. If this force-majeure bequest of Seshkrozchiel's is behind your feckless delinquency, consider my grievance reproved. Your absence from the crisis at Northgate was justified."

"Do you think?" gasped Davien, unable to muzzle a vicious onset of the shakes. Kharadmon's damnable perception was true. He had not stabilized even wayward control of his untoward legacy. Until he mastered himself, a drake conflict was the last conceivable place Althain's Warden would wish to dispatch him.

Diversion

While The Hatchet's elite dedicates seized the rogue galley and ransacked an empty cabin, their absent quarry braved the gale's aftermath aboard a lugger festooned with nets. Another soaked fisherman swathed in stained oilskins withstood the search in plain sight. No one glanced sidewards at men seining cod. Particularly one whose chapped chin itched with several days' stubble.

Few ever beheld the Light's avatar without the groomed panoply of his state dress. Yet true human dignity owned no such pride. Lysaer fielded the grimy discomfort with astonishing equilibrium. Instrell Bay tossed to a moil of cross chop, the hazard of a gentleman's razor apt to risk a slit throat. Vanity cheerfully balked at testing a new valet's expertise: particularly one curled up in green misery, seasick and suffering the back-lash from a True Sect examiner's invasive probe.

Dace groaned in a berth, too ill to do aught but heave up his guts in a basin.

The Light's avatar was not wont to fraternize. Court etiquette instilled by his royal birth maintained a cool distance from the mean lives of his servants. Yet a buried facet of his character emerged under the anonymity of borrowed oilskins.

Stripped of his state status, Lysaer sat on the drenched deck, learning to mend a frayed halyard from the youngest sailhand, aged nine. Two bent heads and two sets of hands, the smaller pair correcting, spliced the hemp plies to thread the masthead sheave without binding. Lysaer's care-free laugh floated back on the wind. The boy's flush reflected no awe. His eagerness guided an aristocrat's fingers, unfamiliarly shorn of seal ring and jewels under the dousing spray.

The storm eased at dusk. Breeze slackened, and night fell dense as spilled ink. Crammed below with the off-watch crew, Lysaer ate rough fare from a common pot. Dace peered at his liege by the reeling swing of the lamp, braced for patronizing indifference. Instead, blue eyes lifted, Lysaer noticed his servant's wakeful regard.

"Has the headache eased? Then you need to eat something. Perhaps a bit of broth will stay down?" The hand that offered the bowl lost no elegance, raw with blisters and slivers of rope.

Dace always had grasped the quality that once earned Sulfin Evend's relentless loyalty. Not before this had he seen the humility behind tonight's earnest solicitude.

He could not refuse the gruel and spoon, regardless of his queasy stomach. His liege tucked him under the blankets again when the bland nourishment failed to settle. Dace recuperated, excused from his duties, while the fishing lugger ploughed up Instrell Bay, rounded Atainia, and smashed westward into the frigid waters wreathed in pale fog and afloat with the summer's calved icebergs. Here, where the perilous reefs met the current of the polar ocean, Lysaer tended the nets, glued in fish-stinking sweat alongside the hard-working crew.

Yet shared labour never led him to confide. Whatever purpose took him to north Tysan stayed shrouded in self-contained silence.

A servant dared not presume to venture an inquiry. Though his unsettled awareness suggested the avatar courted disaster, Dace lacked the effrontery to broach the perils of an unknown decision. Close enough to touch intimate flesh, and prized only for quiet efficiency, the steadfast valet must watch what unfolded and hone his perception to compensate.

The lugger meantime tacked her wallowing course off the desolate coast of Atainia. She plied her nets. Shrouded in mist, she dropped her anchor at last off Miralt Head in the grey hour past sunrise. There, gently rolling, she awaited the breeze, while the settled calm sheened the swell salmon pink and mercury as a polished mirror.

Dace worked on deck in the half-light. Supplied with a heated bucket and soap, he took a razor to his liege's neglected grooming. The rigid jaw being scraped exposed his liege's clamped tension. Yet Lysaer withheld criticism or encouragement. Dispatched along with his scruff of blond beard, the care-free banter with the lugger's crew: again the aristocrat, he endured his subordinate's handling in withdrawn reserve.

Dace fretted, hoping the rude setting excused his inexperience; while under fog, a port only know at second hand through its history came awake at the water-front.

High and sweet, the temple bells sounded carillons, stitched by the cries of hawkers and gulls, female laughter, and swearing stevedores. Staccato clacks spoke of board shutters being thrown back on the wharf-side trinket stalls. Miralt had been settled since the early Third Age. Its wide crescent harbour cut into the Camris headland, ice-bound through the winter. The seasonal bloom of brisk trade swarmed over the bones of what had been, for centuries, a back-country settlement: until the Light's avatar first disclosed his divine mission in the open street.

A riot sparked off by a captured assassin had been quelled, and a ravening mob stunned into an awed retreat. Yet the spectacular display of Light unleashed then did not explain Lysaer's reticence. His brooding more likely stemmed from the time of the Great Schism recorded in True Sect scripture.

The brutal, eye-witness memoir penned in Sulfin Evend's personal journals provided perspective. The liegeman who had stood his adamant ground for Lysaer's sanity became a contentious target after the fall of Alestron. The fighting man's rankled script described his battle-worn troops, denied victory spoils to shoulder the refugee crisis incited by the wrathful dragon that unleashed a fire-storm on Avenor. Amid the smoking ruin, Sulfin Evend's account sketched the priesthood's seditious influence. Gouged pen-strokes reflected his efforts to blunt the influence of Desh-thiere's curse: and which prevailed. Lysaer's sensible policy had backed Fellowship edict and jilted the priesthood's demand to rebuild Avenor's slagged ruin.

But the triumph had incurred an unthinkable price.

Then and now, gadded by the Mistwraith's directive, Lysaer wrestled to curb a fanatically entrenched religion. Again, his pursuit of responsible justice might tip zealotry over the brink.

Once, Sulfin Evend's command of armed force had contained the volatile storm like a lightning-rod. His muscular will had transplanted the High Temple's disputed authority to Erdane. Statecraft and political acumen tempered the Light's runaway creed, until his heroic, relentless support became undermined by filthy rumours. The jackal pack of his rivals had scented blood in the cries of apostasy from the priests, until charges of collaboration with Fellowship sorcery named him the Heretic Betrayer.

Dace laid aside the razor and shivered. The perils bequeathed by that past had grown teeth, with centuries of Canon doctrine given a deadlier reach. The battle about to be joined held no quarter if, under the fresh threat of curse-born madness, Lysaer resumed his brash fight to disband the religion.

Dace reached for the towel, awake to the fury that hardened the shaved jaw-line he blotted dry. The sen Evend descendant could only mourn the ancestral courage that once had foiled the repeated forays of hired assassins. The terrible price spoke yet on the page where Sulfin Evend's firm grasp on the pen was cut off, reft by the poisoned cup that the priests' machinations arranged for his downfall.

Etarran history recorded the aftermath, stripped of the desolate grief: of the beleaguered flight out of Tysan, while Sulfin Evend lay comatose, undone by the near-fatal attack, which left him blinded and crippled with palsy.

The cryptic summary resumed months later, the fallen champion's slurred words recorded by a punctilious scribe. Compiled for posterity, that piercing entry shouldered the blame for the mis-step that cost Lysaer his control over the Light's dedicate troops.

No chronicle spoke of the intimate strain, or the fear, as Lysaer had defied the swords of the temple war host to salvage the life of his helpless friend. True Sect scripture enshrined only the poisoned account of the Heretic Betrayer's corrupted influence. Canon history of the Great Schism insisted that Lysaer s'Ilessid had turned apostate to the Light's cause.

By unadorned truth, the withdrawal from Erdane had been triggered by ambush, and the harried retreat across Camris, a feat to save Sulfin Evend, condemned by a Sunwheel decree and at risk of being savaged by a zealot mob. Lysaer had been forced to wield light against his deluded pursuit. When the galley he seized escaped to sea out of Miralt, she had rowed into the gales of late autumn, while the handful of trustworthy officers forestalled her pursuit at the dock.

Of the bravest and best, none had survived to reach haven under the governor's law at Etarra.

Oppressed by that history, Dace oiled the razor, and heaved the bucket of suds over the lee-side rail. No surprise, that his liege's expression stayed wooden. For Lysaer, the clangour of temple bells and the northcoast combers breaking like slivered glass bespoke the ghosts of his sacrificed dead.

On this day, ruthlessly living, the faithful had multiplied a thousandfold. The True Sect Canon ruled Miralt, the established order emerged into view as the early mist lifted.

The dazzle of gold winkled first, where slant sunlight polished the egg-shell domes gilded over by temple revenue. Visible next, the milk outlines of buildings, block towers, and the spindled rails of the galleries crowning the headland in many-tiered splendour. Dull trade port no longer, the Light's worship had repaved the town in palatial opulence, a necklace that shimmered like opal along the wide curve of the harbour. Shrines and sanctuaries and hostels overlooked the bleached wharves, where, in summer, the galleys of the Sunwheel priesthood rocked gently, their pencilled spars varnished citrine and amber, and rigging strung with white pennants streamed gold fringe like the glister of sparkling wine.

A fair vista, nested with coiled adders, and an insane prospect for a covert venture.

Breeze shivered the dew from the lines. Through the spangle of droplets, a skiff drawn up alongside delivered the pilot to steer the squat lugger to her paid dockage.

"I'll be changing clothes," Lysaer informed his servant. "Brush up a doublet and trousers tailored in plain cloth of respectable quality. Afterward, if you please, have my luggage strapped up and brought topside for landing."

* * *

Lysaer's choice to enter Miralt without artifice made tactical sense to his valet. The jewels sold off to hire his passage left coin enough for a respectable boarding-house lodging. Discarded also, the pretext of station, where glittering ornament would have attracted undue envy and curiosity. Yet modest trappings and impeccable manners allowed an unknown young man of good looks into the upper-crust practice hall. Lysaer was admitted to the stylish baths frequented by the unmarried dedicates and the idle rich.

Dace observed the seamless acceptance, primly composed, from the side-lines. A proper clean towel draped on his arm and his master's kit parked at his feet, he was skirted like furniture by the more stylish servants. Many an impoverished aristocrat visited Miralt for holy penance, attended by faithful old serving-men.

But even plain cambric and linen could not reduce Lysaer to anonymity. His skill with the sword sparked whispered comments. Dace adhered to propriety. He disclosed nothing to sate the curious bystanders though ragged nerves made him sweat when an off-hand remark likened his master's fair grace to the beauty of the divine avatar. Since Lysaer never mentioned his background, his admirers speculated on their own.

"Likely he's from a family with too many sons and limited prospects," suggested the whiskered fellow who managed the idlers' wagers.

Heads nodded. Many an ambitious sprig came to Miralt chasing his youthful dreams. Scholarly hopefuls applied to the Light's priests at the temple. The fiery idealists who craved adventure flaunted their prowess at arms, where their mettle might earn them a dedicate captaincy.

"That one needn't lather himself in the ranks," a wistful bravo observed.

His stout companion added a smirk. "Handsome enough to break hearts as he is? The right bed or marriage could better his station without risking his pretty neck."

"Do you think?" another gallant remarked. "Those lovely blue eyes might string the ladies along. That heiress from Erdane whose father dropped buckets of gold as a temple offering? Well, she tried to plaster herself to his side. Got her charms refused with sweet words and no interest."

Dace fretted, distressed by more than feminine overtures. Within two days, as the hall's avid sportsmen learned not to waste silver on Lysaer's opponents, the Sunwheel officers jockeyed to cultivate him as a recruit.

Their target smiled with disarming candour. Folded into their circle, he consented to spar with the elite dedicates in their company.

Ever discreet, Dace brought dry towels as bidden. He fetched water, not amused by the performance of youthful innocence. Lysaer risked lethal stakes, blindsiding Miralt's most devout professionals. How long before veteran sword-play sussed out the experienced ripostes Lysaer withheld from his side of the practice match?

A week passed without incident. Too personable to seem devious, Lysaer masqueraded a talent too raw to clinch a decisive bout. Dace watched male vanity played without shame to side-step social restraints. A hired valet must support the brash act, while the back-slapping, over-confident victors swept their glum loser along to the bath.

There, hot water eased battered muscles, and more: amid rosy intimacy and veiling steam, Lysaer's guile gave teeth to the statesman's weapon of neutral silence. Loosened conversation echoed into the dressing-room where, meekly waxing his master's boots, Dace watched the ploy of green innocence inveigle the dedicates' confidence.

". . .be fighting aplenty, lad. Not only against unbelievers, but the worst breeding enclaves of black practice. Opportunity's ripe! The move against clanblood opens up a rare chance for early promotion."

A mumbled answer, then somebody's laugh, punched through by a derisive comment, "Well, who said an engagement with free-wilds barbarians gilds a man's prowess with honour?"

Through splashes, a gravel voice added, "A campaign led by head-hunters? No detail for faint hearts. It's like stalking beasts at perilous risk, rife with horrors and gutless wickedness."

"Ah, lad, don't be cozened," a risen tenor cut through. "D'you suppose we'd give warning in jest? The pestilent creatures lay traps that can butcher an armed man like a noosed animal."

Another's grumble capped that salacious comment, ". . .not unjustified . . . the High Temple's order dispatched The Hatchet to slaughter them to their last woman and child."

Metallic chinks from across the dressing-room betrayed the sullen mood of the temple novices assigned to polish the dedicates' harness. They clumped like inquisitive ferrets, adolescent heads shaved and toothpick limbs clothed in white tunics. Most had been sworn to the Light since their birth. Others were street orphans, inducted as penance for thievery. Past question, their strict sensibilities disapproved of the gossip bandied between their superiors.

Dace played blind and deaf. He reinspected his morning's handiwork. The packed kit at his feet was immaculate, the brushed clothing hung, with fresh towels readied for the moment his liege emerged from the communal pool. Yet Dace could not shake a sharp onset of chills, or dismiss the overt reproach the acolytes nursed at his back.

A servant could not bridle his master's audacity, while the northland days passed one by one and assumed the cadence of habit.

The master arose before dawn. Shaved and dressed, he sat for his breakfast, then left on his own, clad informally. Chores left Dace no recourse to track what transpired in the misty streets. He tidied the bed, dropped yesterday's clothes at the laundress, fetched those cleaned, and made purchases at the market. Back by daybreak to attend daily practice at arms, he carried his liege's light armour and sword. After the Light's officers dispersed to their duties, Lysaer ordered a meal at one of the wine-shops frequented by the idle rich. A servant was privy to their casual talk though he was forbidden to sit at table. Dismissed to lug his master's kit back to the boarding-house, Dace fetched water, cleaned harness, and freshened the clothes chests, wash-basin, and towels.

His liege retired in the early afternoon, closeted with his correspondence. The letters were never left at large, unsealed. Lysaer hired the couriers himself. The wax for his cover sheets was frugal brown, impressed with a flourished initial, but use of the red wax tucked in the drawer suggested a second seal, nested inside, the weightiest dispatches signed under the Lord Governor's cartouche. Those would be destined for recipients linked into the network allied to Etarra. Exiled under alias at Miralt Head, Lysaer kept in touch with his informants elsewhere.

Dace never rifled the missives or pried in his master's absence. The exemplary servant knew trust must be earned.

Meanwhile, the dread wracked him, deep in the night and through the agonized days while the sun baked the roof-tiles outside the dormer. His facade masked the turmoil of uncertain thought and strained ears constantly listening. To the pulse of temple processions and prayer bells, Dace memorized the back alleys and by-lanes, and tracked the overheard talk within the walled court-yards. Under noon heat, and the limp flap of the Sunwheel banners, he walked wary, past the hypnotic chants of the priests. He observed idlers, striped azure in afternoon's shade, where dicers and craftsmen mingled over beer for the latest news from the port.

His hours of solitude could have dragged, awaiting his master's whim. But Dace seized the chance to polish his expertise. He thoroughly knew how to maintain a wardrobe but redressed his inability to barber hair. A seamstress taught him to turn hems like a tailor. He practised the poise of a genteel valet, then callused his hands buffing buttons and boots until the temple's burnished-gold spires dimmed against the citrine sunset. Lysaer always returned when the bell towers shivered the air with the evening carillons.

His Lordship expected his bath and a change of wardrobe. Immersed in the finicky details, Dace saw his master dressed in style for Miralt's elite society. Whether his liege stalked the ball-rooms, or pursued the High-Temple's secre-tive policy amid the crush of the aristocrats' wine parlours, the servant who botched his personal appointments would receive short shrift and dismissal.

Grateful the close air masked his sweating nerves, Dace laced and tied off silken-cord points and blessed the simplicity of summer attire. Dagged sleeves, starched cuffs, and velvet doublets were not fashionable until autumn. Left at leisure, he could eat his frugal meal, then wash before he emptied the bath.

"You needn't wait up," Lysaer always said, arisen to leave in the shadow of dusk.

"My lord is too gracious." Ever deferent, Dace clicked the door shut after his liege's departure.

Yet he never retired to his cot in the closet under the eaves. Dace sat wakeful by the open casement and lit the lamp when his master's tread mounted the outside stair. Silent as Lysaer undressed, he received and hung the used clothes, gleaning sparse clues from the fabric: often the musk of temple incense, combined with the dampness of tensioned sweat, or the whiff of acrid smoke ingrained from the taverns. Watchfulness gauged his master's mood, and accounted the hours of restless sleep from Lysaer's crumpled sheets come the morning.

The frisson of Dace's instincts led to clenched teeth to keep his own counsel. He smothered the impulse to flinch when the pigeons winged aloft, bearing temple messages over distance.

Lysaer s'Ilessid refused to confide. A spirit bent on a vengeful mission, he acted, implacably fuelled by royal justice, and shame, haunted guilt, and the pattern of inward self-loathing. The grievance of Sulfin Evend's demise would be driving his deep-set recrimination. To stir the poison would undermine hope and destroy what must be a precarious bid for requital.

Summer's height brought the shimmering heat of a glass furnace, and no crack in the shield of propriety. The master pursued his pitched course, while the servant recorded the creeping change: slight differences, adequate cause for alarm as Lysaer altered his style on the practice floor, extending himself just enough to decisively win a few matches. Dace observed the most astute veterans shift their outlook, snapped short by an unforeseen depth of experience. Fair-haired and serene, Lysaer fielded their surprise. He smoothed over the stinging transition from arrogant superiority with cool wit, while a stunned hush fell over the officers' bath, and the faces of the attendant novices resharpened to salacious suspicion.

There came the late night under candlelight when Dace found a mark scorched by Light on his master's linen cuff. Somewhere, tonight, a select few in Miralt shared the dangerous secret of Lysaer's identity. The only reason would be to spear-head an inside conspiracy. Frozen by dread, Dace hung the singed garment. He poured the warmed wash-water, hoping his trembling would pass unremarked in the flow of routine.

"Ath above, you're drained white!" Lysaer lowered his hands, wet from rinsing his face in the basin.

"A man comes to care," murmured Dace without blinking. "Should that cause astonishment?"

Lysaer regarded him, blue eyes level with frightening honesty. "No. As well as I, you must be aware I've been courting the leap to disaster."

Dace proffered the towel. "What use to speak out of turn?" A single mis-step could upset the game, either through a zealot's public exposure or by the swift back-stab of righteous betrayal.

"A man comes to care," Lysaer shot back, shoved erect without taking the offering. Blank as a cameo, he added, "By every honourable code, I ought to dismiss you for your own safety."

Dace's heart-beat slammed under his ribs. "You would have to use force."

Lysaer bridled. Paced to a nearby stuffed chair, dangerous as a spread cobra, he matched his valet's spaniel loyalty with fury. "I expect a betrayal! Have invited the prospect. Why set yourself up as a pawn in the path of near-certain destruction?"

"Because," Dace demurred, moved by deferent steps to resume his lapsed duties. Instinct prompted him to risk everything. "After the spying of East Bransing's priests, I'm convinced the servant behind you cannot be a stranger."

Under his applied towel, Lysaer's alarmed start verified every foreboding. Dace blotted his master's chin fast enough to stifle an argument. S'Ilessid justice demanded the uncompromised move in redress: against reason, against odds, his liege planned to challenge the might that enforced the True Sect Canon.

Against desperate stakes, Dace seized the initiative. "All I ask is sufficient notice and coin for the quiet purchase of two decent horses." Which meek request floundered into a strained silence.

When Lysaer retired and the lamp had been snuffed, Dace sought his cot in the darkness, terrified he had overstepped.

Then only, his liege relented. "You'll have five days. A week at the most, before my rogue dedicates defy the High-Temple and march against Erdane. I'll give you the silver for adequate mounts in the morning."

Vicissitudes

Having thwarted Rathain's clan trackers by boarding the Daenfal ferry before dusk, the Mad Prophet slips into a tavern, where, cornered, he delivers his ultimatum to Tarens, "No! I won't safeguard your foray to Ettin. Not before I've contacted his Grace's handfasted enchantress, Elaira. Tell Cosach and his henchmen the same, or burn in Sithaer and suffer the consequence . . ."

At Telmandir, under Fellowship guidance, High Queen Ceftwinn of Havish prepares to access the crown jewels' heritage for the first time: "Will I meet the same end as my brother?" she asks, aggrieved for the irony, that Gestry had seemed transported by the attunement; and Asandir's iron integrity cannot in honesty ease her concern . . .

On the hour The Hatchet's primary assault draws blood to scour the clan presence entrenched in the Thaldeins, a messenger pigeon flown across Camris breaks the explosive news: the rogue avatar marches from Miralt with a company of suborned dedicates, intent on upsetting the High Temple's decree and denouncing the True Sect Canon . . .

IV. Debacle

The scout runner who carried word of the catastrophe reached the outpost in the Thaldeins, reeling on exhausted feet. Winded beyond speech, he choked on stirred dust, forced to shoulder a path through the chaos that met his arrival.

Wailing children, foot-sore women seated upon bulky bundles, and dazed-looking elderly men crammed the inner bailey from wall to wall. The messenger cut through their heaving misery, toned in ochre and shade, with the fallow gold of full sunlight stamped against the black loom of the portal to the inner sanctuary. The noisy sprawl of refugee families choked every available cranny: still living, still safe, the heart-core of the ancient clan lineages, though immediate threat to Tysan's blood heritage was more urgent than anyone realized.

The messenger dodged a crying toddler, clinging to a tow-headed brother's grubby hand. The flashed recall resurged: of another child grotesquely gutted, alongside a sister no older than three. Nauseated, the scout runner pushed past, nostrils clogged still by the stench of the recently slaughtered. His anxious survey swept the moil for one angular form.

Even through turbid haze and the seethe of uprooted humanity, Saroic s'Gannley stood out. Too thin for his height, his gangling form was crowned by flaxen hair the day's crisis left no time to braid. A young man to be charged with the outpost's main garrison, his preferred reticence a lost indulgence, he towered, shouting for someone to unsnarl the activity jammed around the supplies.

Movement shuddered and heaved, shifting the stacked barrels and clearing the jumble of wagons and hand-carts, while another crisp order detailed the caverns to be cleared for communal shelter. Just acceded as *caithdein* of the realm, and yet unaware of the burden, he turned his head at the runner's approach.

"News?" he demanded, one hand raised to defer a healer's concern for the risk of disease under crowding.

The scout slid to his knees at Saroic's feet. He gulped the thin air. Spoke, though his hoarse voice scarcely pierced the racket stewed inside the fortified ravine.

"My Lord Steward, ill tidings!" which phrase broached the first word of an appalling disaster. "Your grandfather's fallen. The war band at his back is lost also, killed outright defending Orlan. Both pickets on the banks of the Valendale crumpled under a surprise attack. They failed to mislead a concerted advance, never had the numbers at hand to hold out for reinforcements. A dedicate war host pours up-country, unchecked. The enemy's on us as never before, guided by diviners and head-hunter trackers. They have swept the deep vale. Our outlying settlements are destroyed without quarter, the food stores for winter put to the torch."

"Survivors?" rasped an elder at Saroic's back.

The scout bowed his head. "The women, the children, and babes—all were butchered by arrows or ridden down and razed by the sword as they fled. We're facing a scour by a True Sect mandate, organized for extermination."

Like the splash of a stone in a pool spreading ripples, horrified outbursts settled into aghast silence. Shock reigned, and stark disbelief at the vicious speed of the disaster. A furtive advance by Sunwheel troops into free-wilds territory had called the most vulnerable folk into sanctuary. But no one foresaw a merciless cleanse unleashed on a scale such as this.

Saroic s'Gannley fought shattered composure. Too stressed to question why their seers' heightened prescience had failed to forecast the ferocity of the assault, he shouted to stem the imminent threat to clanblood survival.

"Round up every straggler still on the trail to the outpost. Hurry them in. Then shut the front gates. Archers! Break out lint and oil! Station yourselves with torch shafts on the battlements. You'll fire the forest outside."

Someone shouted a panicky protest. "That's against charter law!"

"Yes!" Saroic rebutted, bloodlessly pale. "But the flames can't spread far against a south wind. The blaze will die out at the timberline." Did no one see? The ruin of Orlan vale was the only tactical choice to wrest a margin for escape. "While the deep ravine burns, no Sunwheel troops can storm these defences. We have that long to lead our people out. To me, the armed garrison! Conscript every adult who's fit to bear weapons. Assign them in squads. They'll clump the refugees into groups and funnel them single file through the tunnel connecting the natural grottoes under the stores vaults."

Saroic tasked the field scouts to manage the exodus, then hand-picked the best twenty-five from the war band. "You're to cave in the passage after the last group. Then, if you can, collapse the archway to the galleries before the enemy breaches our gates. Should they break through beforetime, delay their advance. If luck favours, and you fight your way free, harry the dedicate troops at the rear-guard with traps and diversions."

A shadow raked over the distraught messenger. Weathered oak, with someone's strayed infant crooked in one muscled arm, the war captain of the Thaldein outpost reached Saroic's side. Kin resemblance was unmistakable, hewn into a middle-aged profile hardened by experience.

"You will leave through the tunnels and stay with the families," Saroic commanded the uncle displaced from succession. "I charge you to keep them safe! If I don't live to rejoin you, then serve the s'Gannley lineage and stand shadow for Tysan's crown after me."

"Not the Sorcerer's will, or a shrewd use of resource." Ice calm, the scarred campaigner handed the baby off to the anxious mother arrived at his heels.

"You will do what is best for the realm!" Saroic snapped, strained.

"Exactly." Authority spoke. The uncle snapped callused fingers. Five veterans poised for his signal closed in. A moment's demeaning, adamant scuffle saw Saroic s'Gannley hurled flat on his back in restraint.

"Truss him!" Tears moistened the stony cheeks of the man who betrayed his young nephew. "You'll run with the families as Asandir wished. I stay to fight. No, by Ath's witness! Don't gainsay sound sense! You know me, Saroic! I'd give rein to fury. Turn back and fight, when wisdom demands swift retreat for survival. Let my band shoulder the final stand, and don't sacrifice the better use of your canny leadership."

Saroic spat a mouthful of grit. "But your wife and children—"

The winded scout turned his head, sick with sorrow. "Dead," he gasped, brutal. "They were in the low country, remember? For your cousin Saieda's coming of age."

Saieda, who had loved roasted chestnuts and somehow acquired indigo ribbons for her oldest sister's wedding. Tysan's pinioned *caithdein* raged in bludgeoned grief. "Damn the murdering True Sect, and thrice curse the Fatemaster's cruelty!" To his insurgent uncle, he shouted, "No! I won't sanction suicide. Our people need you as never before!"

Yet the stricken husband and father stayed deaf. "Go on, you daisies! Gather the children. Get these people out! I'll see the withdrawal through as rear-guard. For those who object, call my bootless conduct down later!"

Against Saroic's furious protests, he thundered, "Try me for treason if I outlive the day! No contest, I will take up arms here and now. Yes! And cut down all comers who won't back your dutiful place as Tysan's *caithdein*!"

Lysaer s'Ilessid marched southward across Camris with the martial glitter of steel at his back. Requisitioned under his direct authority, the white-and-gold panoply of Sunwheel standards paraded before an elite mounted troop of

Miralt Temple's dedicates. They went armed for war beneath blazoned surcoats. The divine ultimatum thrust on their truculent priests had silenced indignant objections. Lysaer claimed his prerogative as their hallowed avatar: either the religion shouldered his bidding to redress The Hatchet's mandated massacre, or the temple and its lofty sanctuaries would burn, levelled by the Light of his wrathful hand.

Dace followed in the stirred dust of the baggage-train. Assigned to mind the wagon with Lysaer's effects and the loan of an upstaged officer's canvas pavilion, he travelled astride a dappled grey gelding of mild temperament. If he no longer tumbled from the saddle when horses shied underneath him, his plodding mount did not stem his anxiety as the cavalcade crossed the bleak grasslands of Karmak. Drought had baked the soil to flour. The wind bore the scent of crisped sedge and an ominous taint of distant smoke.

Yet no carmine glare stained the horizon. Insects clicked, while the sunlit dazzle of mica glanced reflections off the bleached rocks. Rushed by the ripple of displaced senses and another ephemeral whiff of torched pine, Dace battled distress: the clanbred traits of his ancestry sensed slaughter, stamped into the flux. While no fallen bled on the earth in this place, and no wildfires burned, Lysaer's challenge of True Sect authority came too late for the temple's campaign. Eastward, the swords swung by Canon decree already reaped barbarian lives.

Nauseated, Dace let the sensible gelding keep pace. He dared not pull up. Too many hooded eyes watched. Not only the ranks of the dedicate faithful, but two vested priests and a True Sect diviner marched with the column from Miralt. Though he remained shielded by Davien's conjury, an upsurge of Sight might be miscalled as madness or worse, an aspect of unsanctified talent.

The priests nursed their creeping suspicion that a corrupt influence acted on Lysaer. Night and day they sought for the signs of foul practice at large in his company.

After dark, crossing the scrub between camp fires, Dace heard the furtive whispers. He watched the uneasy glances exchanged. As he lugged his liege's warmed wash-water from the cook-shack, he drew scrutiny along with his tarnished master. If the dedicate guard conspired in disloyalty, Dace feared above all the stealthy blade of an assassin by night. His liege would be betrayed by the faith: not if, but when, as the road to Erdane steadily shortened, and the messenger pigeons flew daily from the priests' wicker cages, winging updated word across Camris.

Yet mornings came and went without incident. The company re-formed and tramped onwards through its ochre cloud of stirred dust. No underhanded attack disrupted their southbound march. White and glittering gold, the conscripted men snaked in columns across the taupe barrens. Dace was not reassured. When a horn blast from the vanguard brought the baggage-train to an unscheduled halt, he jabbed his heels into the grey and reined out of line to identify the obstruction.

The willing horse leaped the dry gulch at the verge and cantered through the open broom. Dace disregarded an officer's inquiry. Accusations shouted in his wake failed to turn him aside. Whipped frantic by need, he flanked the stopped squares of ranked men, climbed the hill-crest, and seized a clear vantage.

The bristling line of another war host occupied the country ahead, a daunting show of superior numbers to challenge Lysaer's bid for passage. Foot ranks and horse, their formation meant business. Dace sized up the banners, dismayed.

The moment was lost to try a deterrent. Before the poised muscle nerved up for the charge, the Light's proclaimed avatar spurred forward alone. A toy figure on a white horse, caparisons aflash with gold bullion, he left his escort, bare-headed and weaponless. The gesture outstripped human mortality. Godlike, Lysaer claimed his authority bald-faced. He would wrest the True Sect High Priesthood to heel through a blustering arrogance that caught the breath in the throat.

Dace knew the man behind the facade. Perhaps only he grasped the act's drastic courage, or foresaw the hideous price if the bluff went awry. Stakes that *in fact* might see another trained host razed to ruin, with naught left beyond winnowed carbon.

If The Hatchet understood the ploy was no game, but a duel waged with blunt nerve at lethal risk, no party came forward to parley under a flag of truce. Without even a token attempt to negotiate, an officer's bugle sent movement through the massed lines.

"No!" Dace exclaimed.

But like the cresting foam of a breaker, archers stepped to the fore. There, they poised with strung bows and nocked arrows, readied for the order to loose.

Dace shivered. Warning jabbed him to clap desperate heels into his horse and careen down-slope at a foolhardy gallop. Distance was the enemy: a windswept expanse of bleached grass spread between the unstoppable, unfolding tableau. Oblivious to the servant's belaboured approach, the lone horseman in dazzling splendour opposed the pale flash of drawn yew. Naked majesty faced the steel teeth of the war host aimed on a headlong course towards grief and tragedy.

Lysaer must shoulder the terrible crux. Defied, he could sensibly turn in retreat: but only if he granted the True Sect's murderous cause his endorsement. Back his stance with force, and he jeopardized three thousand lives. The humane statesman might treat for the greater good: yield in the hope that rabid, blind faith could be cajoled into a compromise. Hope and sanity died if inflamed zeal spurned reason and The Hatchet refused to stand down. Once the archers unleashed their staged volley, the blood-bath would be joined. The temple must answer the insolent threat served on the Canon by its tarnished avatar.

Apostate defiance had to be crushed, no matter whether the man on the horse wielded the direct might of an elemental power.

Dace charged his gelding over rough ground in a race that stared down futility. The heritage of s'Ilessid sprang from the royal fibre to treat with the Paravians, never to compromise inborn principle. The Hatchet's companies *should have* quailed, set at brash risk of the intractable fires and fell fury that had broken their comrades at Lanshire.

Martial orders ought not to smother survival before such a threat.

Yet not a man in the hostile host cracked. The ranks held, enthralled dedicates headed for sanctimonious martyrdom.

The grey galloped, reckless strides thudded against the baked earth, to the rake of green thorn in the tinder-dry brush. Dace lashed the reins and drove the animal's pace faster. Chaff and winnowed dust raised a plume at his back, while ahead, the lucent view etched a confrontation too distant to curb.

Dace groaned for the heart-ache. He could not arrest the spin of Fate's Wheel; could not belabour more speed from his mount. Through sight whipped by wind, then blurred through tears, he watched the glittering, gold-embroidered glove as his liege dropped his grasp on his destrier's rein. Hurtled towards the breach, too late to matter, the faithful valet saw the fingers close into a fore-warning fist.

Sunlight limned the vista like nicked brass, as though cast in the relief of a monument. Lysaer, on the horse, raised his arm overhead.

As one, the ranked archers nocked arrows. Their varnished shafts winked like needles as they bent their bows to full draw.

Dace's oblique approach, still bearing down, sighted the single odd movement amid the massed war host that did not fit: across the sweltering shimmer of air, a tin-toy, squat figure upright in a war chariot lifted a cocked crossbow and took aim from the shoulder.

Lysaer s'Ilessid had no cause to fear. Placed at front and centre, always, his gift of light had flash-charred hostile arrows and steel into carbon and dust. Upon this same heath, two hundred and eleven years ago, a barbarian marksman had sought his death. The levin bolt that sowed his claim to divinity had reduced that killer's shaft in mid-flight. For two centuries since, command of the wild elements had dispatched volleys en masse without casualties.

Yet history seemed poised to overturn this time. Warning tingled from the Sorcerer's mark on Dace's breast, then that caustic sensation joined the uncanny pressure where a hidden, spelled bracelet circled his wrist.

Another yard closer, almost near enough, Dace unclenched his grip on the grey's mane. He flinched as the bow-strings released, cringing under the deadly whine of the arrows as he launched his fly-weight in midstride from the saddle. Whether he meant to drop Lysaer out of harm's way, or if he offered his body as shield, none who beheld ever knew.

The flat whap of The Hatchet's poised weapon launched the quarrel beyond intervention.

The light-bolt crackled off Lysaer's poised fist. Air screamed under the volatile blast as feathered shafts and their lethal freight of forged broadheads winnowed to ash. Except for one missile, sped onwards amid the sheen of an uncanny counter ward. The deadly spin of a sigil sliced through the applied might of the elements. That fateful quarrel sheared onwards, not flared to a smoke-puff of carbon, but untouched on its whistling passage through the gusty recoil of white-heated air.

Impact struck the avatar in the right eye, a split second before the next levin bolt kindled, and just as Dace's flung weight cannoned into his stricken liege.

Collision knocked the breath from them both. Entangled, servant and master crashed to the ground.

Dace coughed on live sparks, wind-borne where the back-flash had kindled a grass fire. The nearby crackle of flame scarcely registered. Under his hands, back arched and mouth gaped, Lysaer thrashed in wounded agony. Dace fought his convulsions.

"My liege, be still!"

Lysaer turned his head. Amid his mauled face, the good eye shone sky-tinted blue. Dace flinched, wrenched by horror. Though revolted, he managed the strength to endure the ghastly sight of his liege's dawning awareness. Lysaer caught his breath, shuddered. One moment, he stared down the abyss of his irretrievable failure. Then his iris dilated with shock. Dace heard the slurred murmur, perhaps the desolate outcry of apology before his liege's consciousness faded.

Tears striped the smudged ash on the servant's cheeks. Smoke billowed, where the surrounding heath blazed in patches. Lysaer's slack torso pinned his folded knees. Dace glanced behind, struck in the teeth by an earth clod as the riderless white destrier took flight. His own trustworthy grey was nowhere in sight. Overburdened, he clung to a man mortally injured, who surely ought not to be moved.

Courage impelled him to survey the crossbolt, embedded down to the razored-steel fletching. Blood welled from the ruined socket, and wicked the blond hair sticky scarlet. Soaked in gore to the wrists, Lysaer's head in his lap, Dace fought not to gag. The fist he clenched in his liege's splashed surcoat ascertained a stricken body fighting for survival. The chest underneath rose and fell, and pulse throbbed in the vein above Lysaer's collar. Traumatic damage might not cost his life, granted the prepotent ward of longevity imposed by Davien's Five Centuries Fountain.

The grass fire ignored, Dace tore a strip from his cuff. He wrapped the nub of the shaft and applied careful pressure to stem the worst gush of the bleeding. The bolt had struck at an angle. As if, at the crux, Lysaer had averted his face in reflexive avoidance. The move saved little. The eye was destroyed. But the quarrel had lodged into bone with the flange protruding. A skilled healer might withdraw the sunk point from the brain without breaching the skull or slicing through additional tissue.

"I won't leave you, liege." Dace held on, against the rise of his gorge. People arrived: Miralt's dedicates, or Erdane's, which side scarcely mattered. No choice of his steered the outcome. Nearby, an officer's shouts detailed men to quench flames, while more booted feet crowded around the fallen avatar.

Numbed by fear and grief, and soaked in the stench of a dire trauma's incontinence, Dace shouted, "For mercy, summon trained help!"

"He's alive?" An authority in a High Priest's regalia advanced, his glittering hem fastidiously lifted clear of the splashed effluent. "Then no healer's required."

Dace's appalled protest fell on deaf ears.

"This is not a secular matter!" the priest dismissed with self-righteous admonishment. "No question pertaining to mortal flesh but a trial of divine veracity."

"You expect my liege to stand and walk from the field?" Dace attacked with savage impertinence. "The shaft of the crossbolt ought to be drawn. Straightaway, while your blessed lord is unconscious. Kindness would spare the pain of needless suffering."

"In due time," snapped the priest. "The Canon demands unassailable proof. Mortality will arbitrate an imposter's case. If Lord Lysaer recovers his health, his claim to spring from the Light of the godhead will be ascertained before witnesses."

Dace begged, beyond pride. "Then call for a litter. I'll find hands to carry him. Someone must care for my liege. Life or death, I ask leave to attend him."

Movement jostled through the gathered onlookers. Dust blew, and a nervous horse snorted. Then the rumble of wheels parted the pack, and the harness team drawing a war chariot reined up, stamping hooves to the jingle of harness. The Hatchet himself leaped down from the platform. Energetic, short-strided, he stalked in, helmet plumes jaunted sidewards in the stiff breeze as he took vengeful stock of his marksmanship.

Then, "Grant the servant his wish!" he barked at the hovering clerics.

The affronted fanatic bristled and glared. "Lord Commander, you overstep. How dare you entrust our sacred mission to a lowly stranger?"

"Why not?" Square teeth flashed in contempt beneath the war commander's lowered visor. "That fellow tried to take the fall in his master's place." The Hatchet shrugged, plate armour rasping under his emblazoned surcoat. "Base courage deserves recognition, if only to stand the death-watch for a coward who abandoned the field at Lithmarin. I won't let my officers stoop to the task, or dishonour themselves with disposal of any deserter's maimed carcass!"

Stung red, the upstaged priest bridled. "This is no commonplace issue of troop discipline!" Fuming through pinched nostrils, he pressed his superior rank. "For undue interference, by the blessed Light, you will allocate your troop's surgeon at once, along with two stalwarts fit to bear a litter."

The crested helm cocked upwards. "Your faith is miraculous!" Spun on his heel in contemptuous irony, The Hatchet dismissed, "I've seen more than my share of red carnage. A bolt in the eye socket's certain to pitch even a god into fatal extremis."

Arrived in ragged haste from Telmandir, Asandir scaled the dim stairwell at Althain Tower to the melancholy echoes of Sethvir's singing. The rasp that mangled the tune's minor pitch redoubled the field Sorcerer's distress. He sprinted the last flight, too rushed to light sconces, and rounded the spiral bend to encounter his colleague seated in the dark.

Knees tucked up beneath his rumpled robe, Sethvir perched on the steps at the fifth-floor landing, his white hair raked up into rooster tails.

Asandir whisked past in one stride. More than the fresh corona of charge from his transit through the dungeon focus, his clothes shed a storm-lightning crackle of static as he slammed his back against the locked door.

"How bad is it?" Surely no breaking disaster should warrant broaching the stilled power that coiled, barred in the spelled silence inside.

Drifty as a poet, Althain's Warden ceased his sorrowful maundering. He peered upwards. Reflected, the cruel toll of untimely deaths, as his earth-sense recorded the on-going slaughter of clansfolk in Camris. And yet, eyes turquoise as a dawn sky also gleamed with mutinous humour. "The occasion does not warrant laughter," Sethvir temporized. "Nonetheless, I think you'll enjoy the back-handed reason to celebrate."

Asandir shuddered, not a whit deceived. "Show me."

The Warden's flicked wrist scribed a circle in air. Colour and light bloomed amid the drear dark. An image resolved of an opulent chamber gilt-panelled in the temple's Sunwheel motif. Asandir identified the palace wing that housed the highest of Erdane's priests.

There, installed on an immaculate bed with gilt tassels, Lysaer s'Ilessid languished. A spotless bandage swathed his forehead and one eye. Stilled marble, his hands lay folded on his breast with the posed formality of a corpse lying in state, except for the pink tinge at nostrils and earlobes.

A blot of servant's brown broadcloth, Dace Marley huddled in vigilant watch, perched on a chair to the side. Where mortal regard discerned little encouragement, a Fellowship Sorcerer saw past surface appearances. Lysaer was not dying. Rainbow flares stitched through his aura revealed the restorative spells spun by the Five Centuries Fountain, stabilizing spirit and flesh, and stemming the ebb of vitality.

"That's not what I meant!" Asandir cracked, annoyed to be side-tracked. Davien's functional grasp of human physiology always had been nigh unto infallible, even before the hair-raising centuries of his discorporate adventure with Seshkrozchiel.

Althain's Warden sighed like a hound dragged off a bone. "Do you truly wish to behold the reactive impact of that accursed crossbolt?" He tapped his cheek, rolled a bothered glance skywards, then delivered a precise imitation of Prime Selidie's incensed shriek, "*How under sky has this bollux happened?*"

Asandir stifled his thrice-needled temper. Too wary of the iron-strapped door secured by his flattened hands, he chased the abstruse prompt behind the Matriarch's outburst. "Dace!"

Sethvir returned an enraptured smile. "The Prime missed the s'Gannley presence, in fact, and failed to account for an ally's true service when she hatched her nasty plot with the crossbolt."

"Not on the shielding of my mark alone!" Asandir weighed the virtues of his own construct, annoyed. "Ath's blinding glory!"

For presumption on his part had masked the change, where a consummate meddler had neatly altered his original cipher. The harmonic seal to strengthen the young woman's natural aura now displayed the glass-fine tracery of a realignment. "That crafty tinkering bears Davien's signature!"

"His subversive touch," Sethvir confirmed, smug.

Asandir's eyebrows lifted in astonishment. "He's crafted the quadrangle runes to draw chaos into Daliana's shape-change? But that's the same frequency Selidie's—!"

Sethvir's chuckle cut the rant short. "Oh yes." Indeed, like must attract like. The effect will upstage a hostile sigil like the vengeful clap of a thunderbolt." Swept along by resonant synchronicity, the True Sect priests never noticed that their contrary choice to keep Dace had been influenced. Neither would the insidious pressure end there.

"No wonder Selidie's uprooting her hair." Asandir snorted. "I should think twice about stirring the pot with that dab bit of mischief afoot. Dace is also protected from harm, given that volatile trigger in his proximity?"

"With immaculate conjury, of course." Sethvir laced innocuous fingers atop his draped knees. "Should you pause to wonder?"

"Yes!" Asandir snapped. "Saddled by Davien's genius, we're the minnows darting for morsels between the shark's teeth."

Any hostile move to wreak havoc with Lysaer *would* spin out of control, a disastrous set-back to the puppet-string spells that infused the steel crossbolt that felled him.

The beleaguered Fellowship must bless the audacious artistry binding a lock between master and servant. The reactive effects would defend Lysaer, too, while master and servant stayed in partnership. Koriathain dared not interfere without ruffling their manipulative alliance with the True Sect priests.

Asandir gripped his ribs, stern face split, while Sethvir dispelled the image and scrambled erect.

The field Sorcerer recouped his keen sobriety, still backed against the locked door. "Why dawdle to sing dirges here of all places?"

"Luhaine liked to complain that wind through a holed bucket whistled a less plaintive melody." Sethvir blinked, his evasive step sidewards balked as his colleague braced a booted foot against the newel-post.

"Don't claim you were feigning despair to deflect me! Or deny that Prime Selidie's actions suggest the frightening chance she's unstable."

Sethvir laid an ink-stained finger across his lips. Eyes ignited to turbulent fury, he vaulted over his colleague's obstruction: not to spurn sense, but to access the stairs. Asandir followed, forced to chase the breeze in the wake of his colleague's distress.

The forlorn response echoed downwards through the tower's obdurate gloom. "Because you insist upon sharing the grief, we'll sit down with tea in the library."

Slant sunlight glared through the western casements, yet the afternoon heat trapped beneath the slate roof never oppressed Althain Tower's top floor. Chased by the wind off the Bittern Waste, northward, the fragrance of the citrus peel Sethvir used to spice tea sweetened the pervasive must of old parchment. Asandir inhaled the soothing aroma, his boots crossed at the ankles atop a pre-empted pile of books. Between gusts, the acrid stench of scorched velvet caused by his rushed transfer by lane force offended his frugal character: field leathers better suited his lifestyle, the virtue of toughness preferred over comfort.

Across the obsidian table-top, the loose leaves of an ancient manuscript fluttered, pinned under fieldstone weights. Sethvir sipped from his mug, tucked up like a pixie, busy threading the waxed thread to restitch the folios. Calfskin and horse glue to replace the cracked binding displaced his usual clutter of quill pens.

Asandir felt the prickle of wards, raised by a potent cipher to repel rot and silver-fish from the original First Age chronicle: death histories preserved in the Books of Lost Spirits, illumined by the Athlien Paravians. He did not avert his glance quickly enough, the lyric, inscribed Names by themselves fit to wring tears of sorrow, no matter the beauty of the departed had been lost to the world over seventeen thousand years in the past.

Yet the Warden's haunted lament on the fifth-floor landing did not arise from those bygone elegies.

Asandir bided, while fading day shafted carmine motes through the casements.

Sethvir spoke at length, eyes downcast as if a grim pattern arose in the chiaroscuro drift of swirled steam. "How can the living Paravians bear the refrain, if the unchecked crises provoked by Mankind continue to flare beyond salvage?"

Asandir sat forward, rapt. "We're not facing that predicament yet! Why should you despair for the outcome?"

Althain's Warden sighed, unable to make a beginning.

"Let's continue with Lysaer," Asandir suggested. "I saw where the crossbolt struck. Given the neurological damage, is Dace prepared for the impact?"

"I've sent Kharadmon." Sethvir jabbed his hair into fraught tufts. "Mettlesome shade!"

"Kharadmon made free with sharp language regarding the Sunwheel elite?" Asandir snorted. "I expect you forbade him to shatter the faith of the dedicate guards posted at Lysaer's threshold?"

"Lest the poor, devout brutes should get burned for apostate heresy? Yes." Sethvir stuck no words in the meat of the problem: that likely Dace Marley would suffer the blame if the Sorcerer toyed with the feckless temptation.

Althain's Warden side-lined the sheaves of manuscript, dipped a forefinger into his tea, and inscribed a circle on the table-top. "You might as well bear living witness, since Kharadmon's about to fulfil his appointed errand . . ."

The room was a decorated prison, fit to overawe the most jaded state visitor. But for Dace, the gilt moulding with mother-of-pearl inlay and curtain pulls tipped with gold counter-weights did not merit a sideward glance.

Not while Lysaer s'Ilessid thrashed in the throes of another convulsion. Dace braced his liege's head with down pillows to cushion the wound and keep the healer's fresh bandages intact, while four muscled dedicates wrestled to pin their injured avatar flat on the bed. Back arched, the man's unconscious contortions tried even their trained strength. Jostled, the washstand basin upset. Porcelain shattered. Spilled water flooded the costly white rug.

The dedicates skidded in their hobnailed boots. One lost his grip on a flailing wrist. Dace ducked a punch, reduced to pleas that did nothing to settle the demented fit.

Lysaer collapsed in due time, reduced to limp flesh amid the wracked bed-clothes. The chafed bruises of rough handling purpled both his wrists and ankles. The dressing on his wrecked socket survived, though the reopened wound seeped a fresh stain in the linen.

Dace stepped back, while the irritable dedicates were displaced by staff, who whisked into the chamber like gad-flies, clucking and tidying. One sent for a mop to swab the mushy carpet. Another grumbled and righted the upset chair. Dace caught hold of the furnishing and sat, frayed to rags amid purposeful bustle.

Soon enough, the solicitous staff had Lysaer laid out beneath freshened silk. They left him impeccably groomed as a doll, his combed hair nestled on a plumped pillow.

He had not recovered his senses after the crossbolt had struck him down. Perhaps never would, although a parade of physicians attended his hurts with bandages and unguents. Plied with infusions for wound fever, momentarily peaceful, his damaged body kept breathing. Dace did the nurse's stoic chores and kept his liege clean when he voided. Wakeful through the anguished hours, he waited for the next bout of convulsions. Guarded by dedicates, surrounded by priests, and immured in the True Sect High Temple, he lived in stark dread, his covert role under constant threat of disclosure.

Fixated on Lysaer's motionless form, Dace shivered, chilled despite the heat trapped behind the barred casements. An unnatural cold rode an influx of draught that flattened the flame behind the paned lamp-shade.

"How staunch are you?" a voice inquired from the shadow behind.

Dace recoiled and spun, confronted by no Sunwheel priest.

Kharadmon's image bowed at his pleasure, regaled in an extravagance of velvet and silk. An emerald pin gleamed in the lace at his throat, striking match for his forest-green doublet.

Shot bolt upright in panic, Dace braced for the alarmed outcry from the armoured guards by the door.

None came.

The dedicates stood still at their posts, unresponsive as a pair of wax statues.

Kharadmon dismissed their presence with airy charm. "Relax. They're unharmed. If you wish, you might hang your cap on their halberds. They'll arouse after our conversation." His raised finger admonished. "By then, listen closely, you'll be on your own. Unless I might convince you to leave without Lysaer?"

Dace bridled and thrust to his feet. "Press that insulting argument further, I'll shout down the stairs for a banishment."

"Well, you match your master's rank stubbornness right well." Not amused, the discorporate Sorcerer expounded with a turbulent huff. "I can't salvage your liege from this fire, my dear, outcast as he is from the compact. The inquisitive priests are a serious problem, and delay will draw dangerous questions."

Kharadmon drifted closer. His interested survey noted the dark rings printed on the servant's lined features. The eyes were Daliana's: charged by the same reckless adamance that had fuelled her ancestor's tenacious self-sacrifice. The discorporate Sorcerer's brusque manner softened to pity as he acknowledged the ferocious depth of her inherited s'Gannley loyalty. "You weren't aware your liege would survive? That with time he will recover his sight if the eye is kept clean and bandaged?"

Dace's knees dissolved to jelly. He sat. "No. I wasn't. At least, not for certain." Overcome, he ran on, voice muffled by relief. "Lysaer has not reawakened. He suffers from fits since the crossbolt was drawn. The healers insist the injury to the brain is past hope. Apparently, I'm keeping a death-watch until his body quits breathing."

Kharadmon snorted. "Those claptrap fools know nothing at all. The Five Centuries Fountain's virtues won't fail! However, even lent Davien's enchantment, the severity of Lysaer's condition will demand a harrowing convalescence."

Dace lifted his head, hands limp in his lap. "How long?"

The reek from the bed-linens wadded in the basket declared the raw indelicacies left unsaid.

Kharadmon had no kindly words. "I'm sorry. A full recovery is bound to take years. If you stay the course, your task will be difficult."

Dace denounced the challenge. "What blighted fate could be worse than the traumas I've already shouldered?"

"Oh, my dear! You have no idea." The shade's dapper image flicked out. Where flesh might weep, he could express nothing, nor lend any ease to the benighted spirit beyond the icy wind of a cruel prognosis.

"Left the template of health that Davien provided, nerve tissue regenerates slowly. You've endured the convulsions. These will continue until muscle control is restored. Vivid dreams will resurge as the drive of the emotions start to reconnect without full awareness. Nightmares may sow raving madness while Lysaer suffers the hallucinations of his fragmented past. You must steady him through the morass. He will become cognizant. Until then, he won't understand who he is, or why he is trapped in this dreadful existence. Are you strong enough to teach him, all over again, how to walk and talk? To look after him as a half-wit? Because at first, he'll be malleable as a puppet, unable to separate friend from enemy."

Dace stared, appalled. "Surely the True Sect priesthood will exploit such vulnerability!"

"Yes." Merciless, Kharadmon added, "More than the religion, Koriathain aim to use him for gain. The crossbolt that felled him was riddled with spells! Nothing that Davien's long-term working can't stem, but an extended recovery opens the gates to subversive manipulation. Your presence alone thwarts the prospect. Should the Prime strike again, the Sorcerers' wards on your person offer your liege's only protection."

"Then no way under sky will I leave him!" Dace retorted. "I don't give ground for conniving witches. Or abandon my friends. In his right mind, my liege would rather be dead than permit the True Sect's creed to suborn him."

Kharadmon's image unfurled to a crack of wind that riffled the crests on the dedicates' helms. He bowed. "Your free choice must be honoured. I entreat you, stand strong! For if you should falter or fail in your charge, our Fellowship will be forced to act for the sake of Paravian survival . . ."

Back at Althain Tower, the earth-linked connection dissolved. Sethvir's gaze remained fixed on the obsidian table: as though stone still spoke, or the courage of Daliana sen Evend still sang through the library's book-scented quiet. Perhaps scalded by the far-ranging ripple of probabilities, he seized on his waxed thread with a fury and whip-stitched the repair on the ancient folios until Asandir probed the question left dangling.

"Do you think we are seeing a crack in the Koriani Matriarch's facade?" The possessed initiate's subdued spirit survived yet. "If the girl's original, smothered identity has pilfered a working knowledge of Prime power while in duress, she could rebel against her repression."

A vexed frown pinched the wrinkles on Sethvir's brow. "Perhaps. The issue's clouded, with Morriel's tortuous cleverness playing us for the diversion. In Lysaer's case, I expect she hoped for a puppet-string avatar to spear-head religious upheaval. War on the grand scale to harry our resource and flush Arithon into flight."

Rare anger bristled the field Sorcerer's response. "If so, she's delivered Lysaer to the vicious torment of his past."

Which fragmented mire of unfinished guilt posed a trial more brutal than Davien's enspelled passage through Kewar. Where the maze's mirror of self framed an unbiased challenge for release and amelioration, Lysaer embarked upon his fraught course entangled in distorted prejudice. Worse, he lacked the rigorous advantage of any initiate discipline.

Desh-thiere's curse warped the s'Ilessid penchant for justice to raging insanity, with Dace the frail stay in the breach: a servant's brave will, like the fly sealed in amber, trapped alone in the bastion of temple authority.

Early Autumn 5923

Stonewall

The flung dagger sheared through leaves and air, snicked a hank of white-and-chestnut hair, and struck with a *thunk* in a tree trunk a finger's width from impaling the Mad Prophet's ear. The napping spellbinder startled awake and recoiled against the blade's edge. Palm pressed to his tender, nicked flesh, Dakar howled.

"Cosach!" Scrambled erect, he added epithets fit to scorch hide at ten paces.

The heckler his language reviled slid from the autumn-blushed thicket. Past patience, he reached over Dakar's shoulder and snatched his quivering steel from the oak before the hackled victim turned the weapon against him.

"You were meant to be guarding the trail to the cove!" Cosach sheathed the knife in disgust. "An ill wind over your grave-site and to Sithaer with your useless slacking. The whole world could have slipped off to sea while you snoozed. How dare you run my scouts ragged while you nod off at your post!"

"I didn't." Dakar dusted damp leaves off his backside and glared with long-suffering injury. Weeks spent tracking their elusive quarry had left him as sunburned as any Halwythwood clansman. Yet the flush that coloured his dimpled cheeks exposed his sheepish embarrassment: in delinquent fact, he had not been scrying to disclose Elaira's activity.

Cosach exploded. "How under sky can that snip of a woman blindside my sentries for weeks? We should have picked her up straightaway. Nipped her in flight the moment she poked her nose into free-wilds territory."

"She doesn't want to be found," Dakar snapped. And no wonder: caught in the wrong hands, the Koriathain's reprisal could condemn Elaira to a fate far worse than death.

A third voice butted in with a flattened town accent. "Elaira hasn't been

122

seen because she's expertly trained not to ripple the flux currents." Silent as anyone forest-bred, Iyat-thos Tarens eased from the foliage behind, which rash approach nearly saw him impaled upon hot-tempered steel for rank trespass.

"Damn you, man!" Cosach sheathed his cleared sword, shoulders bunched. "Sneak up like that, and you're likely to bleed! Why can't you signal like everyone else?"

"Because I don't cheep like a wren." Tarens shrugged. "At least my attempt couldn't satisfy your cranky huntsman." The broad-shouldered crofter leaned on the oak, thumbs hooked in his belt and his broken face split by an insolent grin. "His fellows threatened to spit me, as well. Said not to pucker my bungling lips, or I'd get myself flensed as a Sunwheel spy. Why are you lot testy as stoats? Be grateful! If Arithon's woman can fend for herself, weigh the blessing against the rife score of his enemies."

"She's Koriathain, which makes her exceedingly dangerous! Jieret never met her. Isn't that so?" The *caithdein* bared contentious teeth. "Well, there you are. I'd stake my right arm: my blood ancestor would have slit his own throat before he trusted her compromised loyalties." That issue quashed thoroughly as a stomped rat, Cosach belaboured Dakar again. "If I discover you're playing us false, I'll punch your dough-face through your skull and scrape your brains off my knuckles."

Dakar cringed, his kicked-spaniel demeanour spoiled by a furtive glance sidewards. Cosach missed the deceit, distracted by an inbound scout's covert signal: too shrill for a song-bird, even to Tarens's stone ear.

The breezeless air wore a welded silence until the flustered runner shoved out of the scrub, sweating under his buckskins. "She's slipped past us."

"Again! Dharkaron Avenger clobber the hindmost!" Cosach fumed. "She couldn't have!"

"I suggested she might." Dakar rammed forward, jostling Tarens's riveted interest. "If you hadn't dismissed my pointed counsel, Elaira's not merely woodwise. She studied her craft to initiate mastery under Whitehaven's adepts."

"You're a slippery eel," groused Cosach, then spat. "Be careful. You'll face the rough score. The bay shore's scarcely four leagues away. Smell the salt taint? Likely your quarry is swimming already, the scheming witch!" He bulled past, waved the winded scout to his side, and slipped into the gloom beneath Halwythwood's primordial canopy. "Speak up! Be quick. I'll hear your report on the move."

But such juggernaut haste went nowhere fast. Cosach walloped into a tree-bole head first. He swayed. Yellow leaves spiralled down as his knees buckled. Then he keeled over and measured his length, his proud clan braid crushed beneath his slack cheek.

The scout swore, awed, and knelt to examine the goose-egg bruise on his chieftain's brow. "Daelion Fatemaster's witness! Our High Earl's belted himself unconscious."

"Has he?" Iyat-thos Tarens studied Dakar, poised a half-step behind, his expression cheerfully innocent. "You didn't!" he scolded.

"Tweak the flux current? Yes." The Mad Prophet ambled ahead. Wall-eyed and wary, he dodged the riled scout, then stepped over the hulk of the *caithdein* his sneaky prank had knocked prostrate. "Well, you have to agree the brute was insulting. Worse, his pesky distrust of my motives is a constant thorn in the arse!"

Tasked by two appalled glares, the plump spellbinder scowled. "Come along. Or stay, though I daresay a coddling touch isn't warranted. His nibs is unharmed. He'll recover his senses sore as a flipped snake. Kindly put, you may wish to be elsewhere."

"Are you kidding?" The scout runner shot erect as though bitten. "Cosach's already stirring. I say the fat prophet's a dead man, and belike any mother's son caught within reach will get skinned to relieve the embarrassment."

No such sorry fool, the scout runner bolted, leaving Iyat-thos Tarens to shepherd Dakar's escape.

Which ill-turned charge blazed a trail of bent boughs, chopped tracks, and thrashed brambles. Dakar's stumpy strides slowed to a puffing walk in less than a bungled bowshot.

Tarens shortened step also, sensibly concerned for the injured rage left at their backs. Before the culprit sidled into the forest, the crofter snagged the spellbinder's collar and yanked.

The Mad Prophet windmilled and sat in the mulch with a grunt.

Before he recovered, Tarens attacked. "You're toying with Cosach! That's extremely unwise. Beneath the tough crust, he's kind-hearted and honest, and privately fearful he might fail his crown prince. Why scald the sore of his conflicted duty to safeguard his threatened people?"

No need to belabour the danger. The scout pickets patrolled on nervous alert, while hostility sparked by the True Sect at Etarra pitched the head-hunters' leagues in full cry after bounties.

Dakar stalled, tugging down his ruckled shirt. "Rathain's *caithdein* is a suitable match for the realm's problems, I'm sure." Sullen cheek bulged, he tongued the tender, nipped flesh on the inside and nursed his martyred muddle of grievance.

Tarens lost his temper. "You don't corner an intelligent man who's terrified scalpers could slaughter his children! All the more, if Cosach suspects that your antics are whiplashing him for avoidance."

The spellbinder tugged his mussed forelock and clapped. "Bravo! How refreshing you know more than everyone else, including the Fellowship Sorcerers." Pinned by the crofter's abrasive silence, he bent his paunched gut, sat down, and picked burrs from his boot cuffs. But thick-skinned nonchalance won him no ground. "By all means, keep arguing until Cosach rams into the fight, stinging angry."

"Not yet!" Tarens impatiently gestured behind. "The crickets yonder have restarted their song, which means no one's shouldered the chase, yet. Ward our presence! Tweak a bend in the flux. You've just proven the adept ability!"

"I could slam you into a tree just as easily." Dakar gathered short legs. Clownish rump hiked to shove himself upright, he was never the laughable dupe he appeared but a devious weasel at ducking.

Tarens struck below the belt first. "Level with me. You're scared witless of Arithon! This stage play's about your reluctance to find him, and not any crisis concerning Elaira at all."

The spellbinder froze. Undignified, caught four-square like a dog, he sucked in a breath like the gust fore-running a thunder-clap. "Oh, past question, Elaira's in trouble! Worse than she knows. Your crown prince is being obstructively hazed by a glamour wrought by the Matriarch's influence."

"What!" Tarens stared, aghast.

"Oh, yes, hear the brunt, if you'll stand it." Prickled to injury, Dakar scrubbed dead leaves off his backside and qualified. "Arithon's being baited by an enthrallment attached to a woman Prime Selidie sent to waylay him. The binding is subtle enough to be troublesome. It enhances selective female traits, rifled intact from Elaira. While his Grace is annoyed, he'll fight the attraction. But if his active resistance stays wounded by a loss he can't fathom, he might fall prey to the temptation."

Speechless, the blindsided crofter scrambled to measure the complications. While he sorted his own recollections from Earl Jieret's inherited outrage, the sly spellbinder shifted to saunter away.

"Ah, no!" Tarens snatched hold of the Mad Prophet's doublet. "Your timing's too pat. We don't need Elaira! Why not warn his Grace and disarm the problem directly from Ettinmere Settlement?"

Dakar deflated. "That's just what I can't do!" He squinted against the sunlight speared down through the leaves, at last distraught beyond artifice. "His Grace can't remember Elaira, you see."

Genuine misery released Tarens's fist. "Don't burden the issue with melo-drama. Not against my knowledge his Grace's stripped recall will heal in due time."

"Mostly, that's true." Dakar averted his gaze, humbled by sorrow. "Arithon will regain his identity. But he can't access any aspect of his prior relationship."

Hush clothed the pause. A stray cloud muffled the sun, then passed, rekin-dling the motes that danced like fey gold in the burlap carpet of leaf mould. Bird-song resumed, but the crickets no longer chorused amid the underbrush. Oblivious, Tarens reined in his rage. "This was done for the sake of Prime Selidie's vengeance to punish Elaira's transgressions?"

"No." Dakar swallowed and parked his bulk on a deadfall. "The harsh tactic was Arithon's, seized under duress to shear the Prime's coercive hold on him. He renounced all he knew of Elaira's love, even her name, to spare her from becoming the fatal tool to suborn him."

Sethvir's archive at Althain Tower preserved the unsparing account of the tragedy. Dakar cringed, beyond language to express the appalling lengths taken to withstand an unconditional submission. How, captured by Koriathain, Arithon had grappled the reckoning and ruthlessly dispatched his deepest vulnerability.

Shamed, the Mad Prophet related the terrible crux. "Arithon would not suffer the fate of becoming the cause of his handfast beloved's torment. And Elaira agreed, aware she was the Matriarch's most merciless weapon against him."

If Tarens ached, the lens of a *caithdein*'s past insight exposed the core of Dakar's dilemma. "Arithon cut himself off beyond recourse, and for pride, you can't bear facing him to restore his integrity?"

"I could not if I wished." Dakar agonized, "Those precious memories were not destroyed but transferred into Rathain's signet, and sealed under Elaira's sole provenance."

Tarens withheld interruption while Dakar detailed the bitter quandary. "The Prime's current plot for seduction rides upon Arithon's broken recall. He has been fed the gross misdirection that his true beloved sold him out to the sister-hood under her oath-bound duty. The evidence used to deceive him was real, a fragment drawn from Elaira's experience, damningly stripped out of context. The impact was meant to drive him to despair. His Grace won't know that her trust is steadfast. Caught defenceless in isolation, Arithon may be emotionally unbalanced enough to succumb."

Dakar finished, wrung hoarse with misery. "Elaira herself remains unaware that her natural rapport with his Grace is afflicted. She can't scry his presence clearly enough to grasp the malicious distortion. Informed, she could snap the signature energy and dispel the falsified trace of herself from the decoy groomed for his Grace's entrapment."

Tarens straightened up in disgust. "You could set things right. Seems the least you could do, mage-trained as a master, and answerable for the grief set in motion by your wretched mis-step at Athir."

"I can't!" Dakar stood, shattered bloodlessly white. "Not without tearing asunder the shield of forgetfulness that guarantees Elaira's protection."

The fidgety spellbinder would have fled from the furious glint that was Jieret's, ignited in Tarens's blue eyes. Except that his craven half step backed him into the point of Cosach's broadsword.

Crept up from behind, Rathain's double-crossed High Earl glared daggers from under a livid swelling. "You're a dead man, right here, unless you agree to safeguard my access to Ettinmere."

Dakar spun, palms upraised. "But Elaira's turned north of us."

"To Sithaer she has!" Cosach advanced. His weapon flashed once. The button he snicked off the Mad Prophet's doublet arced into the undergrowth. "Odds on, she's already crossed Instrell Bay. No more gad-fly excuses for running in circles! I'll have his Grace under a proper clan guard! Not wasting his loins on a proxy who's string-tied to the Koriathain! Therefore, you'll fashion that talisman, *now*, to blindside the Ettinmere shamans."

Tarens sprang for an intervention, while the Mad Prophet stiffened to object.

Yet whether the spellbinder owned the raw power to gainsay cold steel, no man knew. His eyes rolled suddenly back in his head. He toppled in a tranced faint, caught by Tarens before he crashed flat from a prophetic fit. The vision's intensity seared the wild flux: with Iyat-thos and Cosach both gifted talents, caught by the resonant echo . . .

. . . *the stray in the Sunwheel surcoat stood out through the drizzle that dimmed the flame-colours of autumn. Noisy as well, he smashed through the wet foliage, calling for his companions.*

"Lost," mused the sentinel scout who poised with the clan squad, observing. "Likely attached to the march out of Morvain until he stepped off the road to relieve himself."

But even alone, the dedicate trespasser wore byrnie and blade, primed for bloodshed. Halwythwood's defenders took stringent precautions. Stalking bowmen fanned out, preternaturally silent. Trained and talent-born to the hunter's gift, they took no chances.

"Pin him down. Alive." Scout to scout, hand signals passed through the twilight gloom, bidding for restraint unless threatened. A dedicate separated from his armed company might have fellows nearby: zealot recruits, not confused or disoriented, eager to kill for religion. No clansman wished to provoke needless death. Not with the standing garrison at Etarra ruled by Canon law, under True Sect priests.

Like wolves, the scout pack closed on their prey. No ripple from the flux warned their instincts; no glancing wink of bared steel pierced the drizzle. They moved, unaware, as they crossed a set ward. The barrage of enemy quarrels ambushed them from deep cover. The marksmen targeted their grisly spoils, each worth a coin weight's gold bounty. Then they claimed their clanblood casualties, knives busy before the fallen had thrashed through their final agony amid the soaked leaves . . .

Cosach aroused from the prescient vision, enraged. "Sithaer's black death! Those savages are league head-hunters, backed up by the murderous craft of a Sunwheel diviner!"

He recalled the broadsword clenched in his fist. Steel flashed under sunlight as he swung towards Dakar, hunched like a rumpled sack on his knees, eyes shut, and hands clutched to his middle.

Tarens knelt in support. Dizzy himself, with his sweat-tarnished hair pasted to his temples, he spoke quickly to curb the High Earl's thrust. "Stand down, Cosach! The trees in that vision were turned brown! Which means, for some weeks, today's Sighted fatalities have yet to occur!"

"Haven't," Dakar croaked. "I know where to search for Elaira," he added, then heaved and rendered his gorge.

Cosach's fury remained unappeased. "We have drawn down our assigned sentries for this! But no more." He bent, seized the Mad Prophet's collar, and hauled him upright. "How far along the Mathorn road? I'll have the war band on the move straightaway to secure Halwythwood from this predation."

The spellbinder grunted, beyond incapable. Protest was futile in any event. Cosach rammed his weapon back into the sheath and walked off to forsake the search for Elaira forthwith.

Tarens tensed, braced to fell Dakar by force to forestall a renewed confrontation. With clan lives and a free-wilds invasion at stake, the *caithdein* might kill the bumbling fool who obstructed his duty.

Yet Dakar did not struggle. In miraculous recovery, his spasms ceased. He swiped his mouth with his sleeve and inquired, "Is his Lordship stomped off in a lather?"

The moment hung, pregnant, as Tarens realized no puddle of vomit fouled the ground.

"Blinding glory!" he gasped. "You couldn't have faked that display as a ruse?"

Dakar shrugged. His jaundiced glance verified Cosach's retreat. Then he waited, expectant for the astonished inquiry from the first scout to encounter his battered chieftain.

Soon enough, the woodland quiet erupted.

"Damn the fool mis-step that dunted my face!" Cosach's blistering salvo called for swift runners to pull back the picket. "Gather the band. We march north at speed to cut down a marauding pack of league head-hunters invading our turf from the trade-road."

The Mad Prophet's curved features flushed with relief.

"We'll follow, apace?" Tarens surmised. "In fact," he amended in awestruck surprise, "you planned as much from the outset?"

Dakar smothered a chuckle and confided, "Elaira's cut past us on the Old Way towards Narms. Shut your mouth. You'll trap flies. Had you any better way to win that snorting bullock's co-operation?"

"No, in fact." Tarens laughed. "But Dharkaron's Black Chariot and Spear save your hide if your crack-brained stunt gets discovered."

"No stunt, not entirely." Cold-bloodedly bitter, Dakar admitted, "That posited ambush is coming, and surely will happen without intervention." Inhumanly calm, he revealed the vicious extent of his scheming. "I had to steer Cosach until we knew for certain that Arithon's enchantress had evaded the scouts."

The Mad Prophet brushed the caught twigs from his hose. Unfazed by Tarens's hard stare at his back, he ambled ahead, jaws clamped with distemper at the grim prospect of crossing rough country apace.

Circumventions

Elaira might have reached up and touched the tooled-leather scabbard of the clan scout whose stealthy patrol brought him a finger's width from her tucked frame in the thicket. Wards alone kept her hidden. Burrowed beneath drifted leaves near the northern bounds of Halwythwood, the enchantress surveyed her predicament. Though the man's ruddy features suggested a temperament inclined towards impudent jokes, he had a scarred wrist and eyes chiselled by ruthless experience. No idle threat, his rapt stance disclosed refined senses, attuned to the flux with a stalker's focus.

No chance-met sentry, he might be leading the Mad Prophet's witch-hunt straight to her. Or else the young bravo had pulled the short lot on the watch list, dispatched to assess the league trackers' foray from Narms. The same murderous bunch had dogged her for six days: no routine squad of head-hunters hot to bag bounties, but a dedicate mission to exterminate old blood talent in the free wilds. The fanatics were guided by a skilled Sunwheel diviner. They also coursed a pack of mute hounds, dauntless enough to be worrisome.

At heavy risk, ringed by passive wards, Elaira breathed in the fust of half-rotted leaves, sweating in apprehension. If the clan sentry so much as *moved*, he would expose her position. Long since, the damp ground had chilled her to the bone. Exhausted and scraped, she projected *calm* and *peaceful quiet* to push the man on his way without incident.

Luck forsook her. The scout lingered, his gifted instincts perversely snagged by the heightened imprint of privacy woven to shield her. Lulled by that false security, the pragmatic fellow snatched the chance to unlace his points and relieve himself. Elaira cringed as his bent elbow grazed the spelled interface and unravelled her cipher of stasis. The coronal discharge from the breach hurled the hapless clansman off his feet.

"Fiends plague!" he yelped, tossed on his rump with his breeches undone.

Elaira ignored his red-faced distress. Flushed into the open, she kicked the placed stone, left engineered against mishap. The rock ricocheted through leafless saplings and dry bracken, miming the zigzags of a startled rabbit. The rustle masked her footfalls, sufficient to mislead the northbound scouts' picket: though not the flustered sentry thrown on his arse in plain sight.

That one scrambled erect, yanking clothing to rights and annoyed enough to retaliate.

He would not be alone: a set-spell the size of a rabbit would never fool the Mad Prophet's initiate awareness, or deflect the Sight of the Sunwheel diviner. Worse, the scout in pursuit blazed a wake through the flux fit to flag down a rutting bull.

"Wait, lady!" he pleaded. "Have faith, I beg you! Dakar offers news with your interests in mind, and Rathain's liegemen are not your enemies!"

Elaira had no breath to warn that his promised amnesty lured the deadlier noose of the True Sect's trespass to purge talent.

Prepared to run that gauntlet alone, she clawed a second stone from her pocket, infused with neat spells laced over the hair of a deer. That baited construct, shied to her left, unfurled the rattle of an autumn buck, raking antlers in courtship rut against a tree.

The scout laughed at her effort, fit and determined as a cocky predator steadily closing her lead. "My colleagues have twigged to the fact you're no deer! Why not trust our friendly intentions?"

Elaira gritted her teeth in frustration. Thin from privation and tiring fast, she used unfair tactics and seeded the ground with an ill-aspected sigil. *Ath forbid!* She empowered the bane, aware the upshifted, free-wilds flux must re-calibrate the response. The scout racing flat out behind in due course hooked his toe on a log and crashed flat. Fortune favoured her, this time: for her act of reckless endangerment, his pithy outburst decried a split shin and not the disaster of a broken neck.

Elaira reeled away, folded over with nausea. However minor, the transgression also branded her as a sorceress. The True Sect diviner would redouble his quest, hell-bent to seize her for dark conjury. Cornered, but not beyond recourse, she risked that encumbrance before entangling the misguided scout: Cosach's incoming war band had yet to grapple the vicious extent of the Sunwheel incursion. The vales southward of Narms swarmed with enemy trackers, directed by the temple's arcane talent and backed with dedicate force. The cat's paw behind which thrust was Prime Selidie, poised to take her pick of the seized prizes.

Elaira clawed through a deadfall and stumbled into a muddy gulch, footprints planting fresh scent in moist ground for the dogs. Dakar *must* cede his personal chase under the heat of an armed invasion. Surely, if she played the opportune decoy, Cosach's strong arm could make the spineless prophet grant Arithon his due support.

Whether the scapegrace spellbinder agreed to blindside the Ettinmere shamans, redress for her beloved's plight must bide in the hands of his loyal allies. Targeted by Prime Selidie's vengeance, Elaira sought to reach Althain Tower and beg for an audience with Sethvir.

She ran, lacerated by the bleak counsel once bestowed by the Biedar tribe's elder under last summer's stars at Sanpashir: *"Can you let Arithon go beyond your control? Do you love him enough to keep faith in him, even afflicted by your own loss?"* The power graven into those words overwrote dying leaves with the scent of parched sand. *"The gifts of his birthright will claim their full due. He will find himself, with or without you."*

Elaira threaded through a stand of young birch, gouged by bare twigs. She must stay the rough course. Committed by the tribe's heirloom knife, her fate had entangled with an ancient purpose only a fool dared gainsay.

Already, a tracker's hound crashed down her back trail. She spurred her lagged pace, the full pack seething after her, directed past doubt by the skill of the temple diviner. Against worsening odds, she ducked leftwards and splashed into a mossy ravine. The dogs checked and circled, near enough to overhear the handler's rank curses through the wheeze of her breath. Elaira plunged waist deep through a trout pool and breasted the icy sluice where a rock ledge spilled into a riffle. Scraped and banged in slithering descent, she ducked behind the rush of a falls and crouched, shivering.

The hounds overshot her chill refuge, confused. Veiled behind the curtain of spray, Elaira huddled against clammy stone and peered outward through the lens of the waterfall. Distorted shadows moved on both banks: trackers and men, arrived in force to cut off her safe egress. Immersed in her natural element, she could turn the properties of running water to her advantage if she acted before the cold impaired her faculties.

Elaira plunged her hands in the foaming current. Jaw clenched against chattering teeth, she engaged a light trance to align herself with the flow of the freshet. But the instant she opened to sympathy, a pulse of heightened energy lanced through her subtle awareness. The bore of the flux burned like oil-fed flame into her unshielded focus.

She flinched in dizzied recoil, struck by an unforeseen set-back. The energetic landscape had changed. Whether the natural resonance had intensified a latent channel, or if, like the aftermath of other ancient cataclysms, the recent upshift unleashed from Kathtairr had deflected the established lanes, the streamlet no longer coursed over innocuous ground. The localized electromagnetics had surged to the potency of a major flux line. Amplified by the diurnal tides, the noon crest *already* broadcast her presence.

Elaira shoved through the falls to escape the hyper-charged watercourse, and met with disaster: the white-robed diviner poised on the outcrop above, avid features triumphantly flushed.

"There's the witch! Take her!" His escort of dedicate archers loosed on her from the northern bank.

Elaira dodged their hail of arrows. Her panicked dive into the basin rebounded off a mossy boulder and tumbled her into the buffeting rapids beyond. Threshed head over heels, she twisted her ankle and felt the sickening shock as the bone snapped. The fragmented ends shoved through muscle and skin, and wrenched her to helpless agony.

She choked on inhaled water. Crippled, she fought onward in desperation. The legacies entrusted to her possession must not fall into enemy hands. Elaira clawed for the knotted thong looping the Biedar knife at her neck, hampered as her numbed fingers entangled in her laced shirt. Time ran against her, to hook the artifact free. While she struggled, four dedicates leaped into the shallows and splashed in pursuit.

Spun downstream, wrung stupid with shock, Elaira grasped Arithon's emerald seal ring with intent to twist the band off her finger. If no hope existed, Rathain's crown legacy was better off sunk beyond the priesthood's meddling reach.

Her firmed grip slammed a surprise jolt of power like a thunder-clap through her disabled flesh. Flung into split vision, Elaira beheld two simultaneous scenes: one showed her dire straits, with the dedicates advancing to take her. Overlaid was a second view like etched glass: the uncanny sight of a diminutive, robed figure in a darkened vault. A pearlescent shimmer haloed his presence, fracturing the gloom into rainbows. Unmistakable, the might of a Fellowship Sorcerer, even when encountered through a long-distanced projection.

Elaira recognized the sender's signature. "Sethvir?"

"Reach, my dear!" Althain's Warden extended an urgent hand, cuffed in ink-stained maroon wool. "For the sake of the talisman that you carry, I beg you, don't surrender yourself to the Sunwheel priests!"

Elaira lunged under the gauntlets of the dedicates reaching to seize her. Heart and spirit, she snatched the long shot opportunity and grasped the warm strength of the Sorcerer's clasp. Light blazed and surrounded her. The sensation of icy immersion spun away into vertigo, pervaded by a harmonic chord, deep and rich as the toll of a bell. An explosive force hurtled Elaira into a storm's eye of calm. The thwarted shouts of her pursuers fell away like the distanced cries of squabbling gulls.

Then the weightless void shattered. Elaira arrived, soaked, enveloped by the mild fragrance of candle wax, parchment, and sweet herbs, and folded like a storm-thrashed bird in Sethvir's angular embrace. She glimpsed the fading coils of energy, down-stepped from brilliant white, to electric turquoise, then subsiding through indigo into the invisible whisper of lane force purled through a Paravian focus.

Sethvir spoke before she wept in stunned gratitude. "Hush! Be still. No matter how brave, we can't dance for joy with that ankle unfit to bear weight."

Skin wet, Elaira could have laughed through her agony. But the vaulted ceiling wheeled in dizzied circles, then dropped like felt batting over her head.

In true form for a Fellowship Sorcerer, Sethvir left no untidy loose ends to inflame the True Sect's trespass of Halwythwood. Where the falls splashed necklaces of pearl foam across the stone basin, four dripping dedicates reported their fruitless search to the fuming diviner who paced on the bank. Since the cresting flux charging the free-wilds streamlet afflicted his talent with phantom illusions, he grudgingly stopped battling his flawed perception and called off the chase, empty-handed.

The expansive discharge from Sethvir's transfer nullified other ephemeral ties spun for scrying, the flash-point recoil clipping the most troublesome one straightaway. Dakar yelped, dropped like a heap of old rags into momentary unconsciousness.

"Rot take doings of Fellowship Sorcerers!" he grumbled the moment his vision returned.

Dazzled by the afternoon light punch-cut through the autumn canopy, the Mad Prophet sat up. Queasy and skin-tight with undischarged power, he wrestled to ground his deranged senses when Cosach arrived and worried his shoulder hard enough to rattle his teeth. At risk of a bitten tongue, he confessed, "I'm sorry. I've lost her. This time, for good." He added, before the badgering chieftain decided to garrotte him, "Elaira's beyond the clutches of any Sunwheel diviner. Sethvir has snatched her by a direct transfer to Althain Tower."

Though how the Warden had finessed the feat, or accessed the prodigious outlay of power defied imagining, given that an engagement of Rathain's flux lines by way of Arithon's seal ring remained proscribed under Asandir's oath. Dakar refused the temptation to pry. Cosach bedamned, only a fool crossed the will of a Fellowship Sorcerer.

A hunched raptor with slate-coloured eyes, the High Earl of the North checked his ornery temper only until the fat prophet recovered his feet. Then he said, triumphant, "Collect Tarens. Now we can turn south for Ettinmere, leaving my war band free to hunt scalpers."

The Mad Prophet bridled.

"Ah, no, not again! I won't stand for excuses." Cosach exploded in nettled suspicion, "Don't claim Althain's Warden cannot be trusted to act in the woman's best interest!"

"Fiends plague!" Dakar raised open palms before the clan chieftain drew his ready sword. "Strike me dead all you like, that won't flip the bad odds. Silver to toadstools, Elaira can't overturn the lure the Prime Matriarch's foisted on Arithon anytime soon. Not against Asandir's oath of noninterference, and twice never while Sethvir's dissembling delay lends the Fellowship's long-term cause an advantage."

"What?" Cosach stared, inimical, while a cat's-paw of prescience riffled chills down Dakar's cowardly spine.

"You cannot see why?" The Mad Prophet shivered, his mop of greying chestnut hair swagged over his slumped shoulders. "If Arithon succumbs to Vivet's lush charms, the Seven acquire their coveted chance of an heir for Rathain's crown blood-line."

Cosach weaned his fist off his weapon and clapped Dakar's back with a gut peal of laughter. "So, why the glum face? Ath bless! A wee royal by-blow's no moping tragedy."

To that, the Mad Prophet found no pat reply, engrossed as he was in brown thoughts surrounding a joyless encounter with Tarens.

"Can't make the Ettinmere plateau before the winter gales block the passes," Cosach ran on with testy practicality. "Are you coming? Bedamned if I'll twiddle my thumbs while you dither. Forbye, you deserve to be horsewhipped for the bother, chasing yon foxy enchantress for naught the full breadth of the territory."

"I owed Elaira the gesture of courtesy," the Mad Prophet retorted, if only for the unconscionable blow he had once dealt to her dignity. He turned up his collar and stumbled ahead, cheeks still flamed with remorse for a mis-step over two centuries unforgiven. Daelion, Master of Fate, pity him on the day he came to face Arithon. The wretch caught in that cross-fire might wish for one decent act for the mark of grace in his favour.

Legend and folk-tales agreed: the visitor who entered Althain Tower as the guest of a Fellowship Sorcerer never survived the encounter unchanged. The alternative being worse, Elaira drifted back into awareness, secured within stonewalls warded by ancient perils beyond her imagining.

Yet no whisper of such primal power pressured her subtle senses. Eyes shut, she listened, tucked like a jewel in a treasure-box, and surrounded by a rapt silence profound as the ages. The transient present spanned those quiescent depths, thin as slicked oil and defined by the gad-fly whicker of flame. A candle nearby was infused by the fragrance of rose extract.

Impossible, that she did not feel diminished, where the grandiloquent sorrows of Paravian history overshadowed humanity's busyness. She pondered that marvel and encountered instead its diametrical opposite: the tender care by which her mortal needs had been cosseted. Sethvir did not dispense impersonal comfort, but tended his guests with an intimate touch fit to pierce the heart and unstring her defences.

Through the swift well of tears, Elaira surveyed the exquisite appointments that furnished her south-facing chamber. A slit window framed the indigo mantle of evening above the wax taper, socketed in the mouth of a bronze dragon coiled with spread wings on the nightstand. Towel rack, ewer, and an embossed clothes-chest with trinket drawers occupied the shadowed corner, softened by antique tapestries patterned in idyllic foliage, and a waterfall cascading into a forest pool.

Which imagery prompted her alarmed recall of the disaster behind her shattered ankle. Elaira took immediate stock of her responsibilities. Rathain's seal ring was safe on her finger. The Biedar knife yet hung, sheathed, from the thong looped over her neck. She reclined against mismatched pillows, nestled upon the counterpane coverlet of a four-poster bed. Still clothed, she sensed the aftermath tingle of spellcraft that had left her tidy and dry. Such finesse had not humoured her injured leg. Skilled hands, and not talent, had removed her boot, snipped off the stocking beneath, then slit the calf of her leathers knee high.

The broken bone had been set in splints and the ragged flesh wound, expertly dressed: but without arcane artifice. Beyond the expected twinge, when she stirred, no thread stitches bound muscle or skin. Her mage-taught senses revealed only a supported alignment of the damaged tissue. Her injury would mend on its own, given rest, a stout crutch, and the tedium of convalescence.

Set against the specious regard for her modesty, Althain's Warden was disinclined to hasten her back onto her feet. Elaira could heal a clean break herself through the order's forced sigils of regeneration.

"But not here." From beyond the open arch of the doorway, the unnoticed arrival rebuked her irritable impatience. "That style of practice would place you at hazard, since Shehane Althain's guardian spirit must take exception." The Warden crossed into the light at the threshold. A tray piled with cups, bowls, and plates wafted enticing aromas, topped by a head of mussed hair like a cotton bole, and a wizened face sliced by a grin. "Might I come in?"

Elaira laughed, charmed by the chagrin in the Sorcerer's turquoise eyes. "On sufferance, naturally, for the unfair advantage."

For of course, as a famished invalid she was unable to fend for herself. Sethvir stepped inside, sprightly as a pixie despite his burden. The awkward reach to span her lap should have strained his frail frame, but did not: his offering hove to rest without clinking the pauper's collection of mismatched plates and tin cutlery.

Elaira regarded the tempting spread, salivating. The fragrance of hot muffins and jam, tea with cream, a steaming platter of herb-seasoned eggs, roasted apples, and honey cakes sprinkled with nuts demolished her wary resistance.

Sethvir chuckled at her crest-fallen sigh. "If you're anything like Asandir, you'll be deathly tired of trail fare." Sixth of his Fellowship colleagues to greet her, aside from distanced encounters through scrying, he pulled up a chair and sat with the toes of his frumpy buskins tucked behind the lower rung. Up close, he resembled a doddering grandsire. Absent was the *presence* of Asandir's might, gloved in peril as the sheathed sword-blade. Elaira sensed nothing of

Davien's mercurial intelligence. Sethvir's rumpled maroon robe was clean, if worn shiny and eaten with moth holes. Snagged threads fuzzed his cuffs, blotched with the faded, scrubbed spatters of oil and lamp-black left ingrained by the mixing of ink.

Elaira caught herself staring and blushed.

Sethvir winked back. Aimless as a fey creature woven from thistle-down, he softened into reverie, most pleased to encourage her dissecting interest.

A rank fool would believe that disarming facade. She had no shield at all, and no shred of privacy to outface the ferocious reach of his earth-sense.

Sethvir ventured nothing. Only blinked with an injury that suggested the most deafening complaint in the room was her meal's getting cold.

Elaira flushed deeper, shamed to have implied any Fellowship Sorcerer would violate her free will. She drowned her contrite embarrassment in the enjoyment of excellent food.

Left at length with scraped plates and two crockery mugs, Elaira slipped the cozy off the tea-pot and poured, then pushed one cup across the tray towards Sethvir. Since Fellowship Sorcerers were not wont to speak first, she steeled her nerves. "A Masterbard's song can unfurl the subtle light to stitch broken bone into wholeness. No splints are required. I daresay the spirit of Shehane Althain would revel in the experience."

Sethvir sipped his tea, waiting, eyes suddenly focused to an alarming intensity.

"I *gave* myself into your active protection!" Elaira snapped. "Why not fuse a snapped ankle? Or was my need answered only because you protected your crown prince's seal ring?"

"Ah. Is that what you believe?" The Sorcerer glanced upwards and surveyed the ceiling beams.

Which maddening obfuscation at last yanked her short, doused her temper, and forced her to think. "You could not act in behalf of Rathain's crown. Asandir's terms of settlement to the Order of the Koriathain forbade you?"

The answering twitch of his smile was bitter-sweet, wreathed in white tangles of beard. "Alas." The Sorcerer raised his mug to his lips. His shut eyes, overtop of the rim, evinced nothing more than savoury enjoyment.

Cued to reason aloud, Elaira continued. "I was on my way to seek your counsel. My case was not forbidden?" And the import dawned, quickly. "My charge to unriddle the Biedar mystery! The purpose behind their stone knife was the cause that enabled your hospitality?"

"But of course." Mildly vexed, Sethvir studied his tea. "The Rei-yaj Seeress possesses uniquely piercing vision."

Which remark shocked Elaira into a sweat. "Ath! Then you did act to spare the Biedar's artifact!"

Sethvir reached for the tin spoon and drizzled more honey into his mug. "The crone's request was urgently persuasive. You have arrived here by her grace."

"But not intact." Elaira regarded the crude splints and winced. Use of the clean precepts learned from Ath's adepts would not raise Shehane Althain to umbrage. However, with broken bone at the joint, she might hasten recovery by only a fortnight. She seethed with frustration like a bull-terrier. "Why hold me bedridden? Or is this an underhand bid to waylay me?" For winter would choke the high passes to Ettinmere before she could regain the hardihood for rough travel.

The Sorcerer flicked the spoon dry and balanced the shaft on one finger. "I might ask, instead, why you avoided Dakar. His hands are not tied by Asandir's oath. He seemed rather desperate to reorder your personal priorities."

Elaira's frown exposed the heart-felt wrench of deep conflict. She ducked her head before the tears welled. "Because I already know the stakes in play at Ettinmere." She added, unsteady, "You need not delay me here with a gimp leg. I could, anytime, from anonymous distance, destroy the glamour the Prime's spun over Vivet to snag Arithon's male fascination."

Salt thrown into her sore distress, Sethvir said, "Then, if you could free him, why haven't you?"

Stunned, Elaira looked up. Eyes the delicate tint of dawn sky met the Sorcerer's, that mirrored her anguish, redoubled.

Surprised to a strained silence, she paused through a moment as frail as cracked glass, set to shatter under the challenge posed by his question. Her intaken breath shook, while she groped for the abstruse thread of logic. "Because I have leave to use the Biedar knife only once in my own behalf. Never Arithon's. And because, am I wrong? I both shaped *and* witnessed Dakar's oath to the Order of the Koriathain at Athir. *He invoked the debt to the Crown of Rathain.* Kharadmon's statement to me revealed Asandir's sworn release, made at Whitehold, to discharge the obligation. I've never touched the engraved slab he created to verify his sealed intentions. But your cautious admission today confirms Rathain's seal ring falls outside the reach of the Seven's protection. Therefore, I must be correct to place absolute trust that your colleague's commitment has been kept in form?"

Althain's Warden stilled like a statue, while wafted steam sieved through his beard, and misted a stare fixed by suspended terror.

Elaira swallowed, shaken. "I dared not act first until I made sure." Past prevarication, she outlined the ghastly conclusion behind the Sorcerer's mute tongue. "Debt falls to the crown. If Vivet conceives to your acknowledged prince, if she bears an heir fit for the royal succession, then as long as that child breathes in this world, Arithon's fate would be freed from your Fellowship's absolute terms."

Sethvir's relieved smile dawned like the sunrise, achingly bright, while double-edged sorrow sluiced tears like thrown diamonds down his seamed cheeks. "If Vivet births a *son* for the lineage, in fact. Asandir's exact words bound *'his Grace'*, the obvious male pronoun nuanced to invite the leap of assumption. Though, Ath wept, at this jointure with Vivet, we cannot be certain your Prime did not grasp that stickling loop-hole at the outset." He added, distressed, "You'll forgive this?"

"For Prince Arithon's *life?*" Elaira broke down, anguished to contemplate a newborn child tossed out in cold blood as a bargaining chip: even one birthed through deception under the order's wicked design. Despite the weak character of the potential mother, the babe would be Arithon's! The posited impact *on him* scraped nerves already stripped raw. "No! I beg you, Sethvir, don't say any more! Never tell me how the outcome from Athir plays through, or infer that your Fellowship might ever sanction an infant sacrifice, even to salvage the compact."

"Never against the Law of the Major Balance! Nor can the question of Arithon's issue bear weight anytime before spring." For of course, the birth of the bastard came first. Without reassurance, Sethvir's misty eyes veiled the past, and also today's possible range of intangible futures: if in truth any cheat card existed to defeat the Prime's vicious settlement.

Rather than dwell upon that unpleasantness, Althain's Warden refreshed the tea, content to sit in companionable quiet while the candle burned down, and stars glimmered through the glazed arrow-slit. Elaira reclined in the pillows, still restless. The dangerous mystery behind her errand too piquant to let her settle, she unslung the artifact hung from her neck.

"Selidie Prime has hounded my trail across the breadth of the continent. Is this knife behind the reason? Since the Biedar crone appointed me as the interim bearer, I'd like to know why, along with anything else your greater wisdom permits."

Althain's Warden laid his beverage aside. Erect, his drilling, direct gaze upon her, he extended his palm. "May I?"

Hesitant, Elaira measured the knife. The desperate wear of her guardianship showed, the white goatskin sheath grimed from travel, with beads torn from the eldritch, whorled patterns of copper, turquoise, and red glass, and the rainbow glimmer of freshwater pearl.

"Your heirloom came here from another world," Sethvir added, apologetic. "My earth-linked awareness encompasses only what originates on Athera. Except for the hide, which belonged to a doe, I am blind to its making unless it is handled. I would not be the first outside the Biedar birthright. Once, Enithen Tuer minded its legacy. She passed the blade on to protect Sulfin Evend, who entrusted it for a short while to Lysaer s'Ilessid."

"In defence of what threat? Do you know?" asked Elaira.

"Yes." Althain's Warden inclined his head. "The talisman was loaned to thwart the black arts of the Grey Kralovir." Shown Elaira's sudden, rattled alarm, he appended, "Thankfully, due to Arithon's courage, that particular cult and its wicked practice have been expunged from Athera."

She surrendered the knife after that, as though further delay might raise blisters.

Sethvir tucked his feet cross-legged on the chair seat. Leaned back with closed eyes, the cow-licked fur of his buskins poked through the frayed edge of his hem, his artless disregard for decorum belied his vast depth of experience. Fleeting distaste flexed his mouth. Then a quick movement unsheathed what seemed a primitive blade. The Sorcerer stroked his fingers down the crude flint, reciting as though the voices of the Biedar ancestry whispered through his questing touch.

"This knife was knapped as a cry of lament, in redress for the shame that stemmed from a young woman's triumph. Called by Jessian, she was an outsider granted the exceptional privilege to witness the power of the tribal mysteries at first hand. She died for that knowledge, pressured by ambitious oppressors who coveted all forms of arcane practice. Though she kept her vow and never revealed the Biedar's secrets, her adamant silence under interrogation provoked a concerted search for disclosure. Those who authorized her execution for non-compliance did not rest, but pursued what was hidden. In their relentless arrogance, they extorted the tribes, seized the vital heart of the Biedar heritage, and proceeded to pervert its integrity."

"The Biedar crone told me that Jessian was Koriathain," Elaira admitted, worrying her linen napkin.

Sethvir opened his lids and surveyed her with unnerving sympathy. "The order is ancient beyond your imagining. This knife, created for Jessian's requital, predates Athera's Second Age."

Which striking statement implied that the Biedar artifact had been passed down for nigh on to twenty thousand years. Althain's Warden stroked the leather-wrapped handle, and resumed, "Jessian was the most infamous name from the early annals of your sisterhood. Your spirit, and hers, shine with similar light. She rebelled for the same reasons you have. More, I warrant the Biedar crone already has appointed her champion. Whether that choice sprang from the foresight of her desert prophets, or through your self-determined character, you've inherited a role in the charge of redeeming the great wrong inflicted through Jessian's legacy."

Elaira folded her arms against a ranging chill. "Ath's mercy on me, that you can't interfere!" Her instructions from the revered elder had not been to fulfil that legacy herself but to pass the tribe's relic on to Arithon when she saw fit.

Surely as troubled as she by the import, Sethvir snapped the blade home in its beaded sheath and handed it back with a cryptic precaution. "You carry an extremely powerful talisman, consecrated in part for the purpose of breaking the ritual workings of necromancy."

Elaira's heart-beat sped in the oppressive quiet. For the Sorcerer did not arise to close the audience when she tucked the Biedar heirloom away. Instead, he retrieved his neglected mug, spooned more honey, and replenished his tea.

Against every sensible fear, Elaira weighed that subtle encouragement.

Fellowship Sorcerers honoured free will. They gave nothing unless they were asked. *Sethvir had not healed her ankle, and yet his authority sheltered her.* He acted in her behalf, by admission, under the Biedar crone's wishes. Which contrary tangle suggested his hands were not tied, at least where tribal lines had been drawn to oppose Koriani affairs.

Elaira fished those perilous waters with delicacy. "Where you can't help, perhaps you may not resist my intent to seek personal knowledge. Surely I might pursue more information if I delve on my own initiative?"

The devious glint rekindled beneath the Sorcerer's lashes though his abstracted gaze never left his gnarled grip on the crockery. "Althain Tower houses the Paravian records. Also what appertains to Mankind under the concord defined by the Compact. The uglier aspects of human affairs, and the black grimoires of deviant rites, are not stored under this roof."

Thrown that provocative lead, Elaira said, "Kharadmon once told me the Biedar negotiated with the Paravians directly for their residency on Athera. May I have access to that chapter of history?"

"I don't see why not." Sethvir's daft smile cast sunlight through the cloudy fleece of his beard. "As your host during a long convalescence, I'd be remiss not to encourage reading."

Elaira nestled into the pillows, if not eased, at least given direction. "Later, perhaps, I'll pay a call on Davien at his mountain sanctuary."

Sethvir's teeth gleamed with sharp satisfaction. "Beware of Prime Selidie's wrath if you do." For of course, Prince Arithon's unsavoury study of necromancy had been rejected, first, in the library sequestered at Kewar.

Cross-currents

Pen back in hand, busy with scribing records, Althain's Warden reprimands the impertinent shade just breezed in through the open casement, "Elaira's asleep, Kharadmon, too exhausted to suffer your needling visitation, and no, given Selidie's spite, I did not reveal our bit of damaging history behind Jessian's legacy and that Biedar knife . . . !"

Informed that the bungled recapture of Elaira lands her in sanctuary at Althain Tower, Selidie Prime dismisses the set-back with chilling equanimity: "No matter. We're now granted free rein for a just consolation. While our entrained plan proceeds without interference at Ettinmere, Arithon cannot shirk his obligation to Vivet once the winter sets in . . ."

As the True Sect campaign of slaughter harrows clanblood in Tysan, Saroic s'Gannley looks backwards in flight for an uncle who never returns, while The Hatchet reassigns Miralt's suborned dedicates to Etarra to bolster the town garrison ordered to cleanse the free-wilds forests in Rathain . . .

V. Misfit

While The Hatchet's stream of dispatches armoured the marrow and sinew of war to extend broad-scale slaughter into Rathain, farther south, Ettinmere Settlement's lock-jawed council wrestled the undigestible morsel wedged into their teeth by Vivet's prodigal return. The shamed relatives tasked to collar Arin for his scheduled arraignment searched most of the day, empty-handed. Blind to their peril, callously broaching a near-to-desperately defended solitude, they cornered their quarry at last in the notch atop the north ridge.

The fey little outlander sat with his back turned, against the vista of scudded cloud, where the naked rocks combed the wind to a shriek. Shouts directed upslope went unheard. Forced to scramble like goats, balance yanked askew as their cloaks cracked and bellied like sails, the delegation to fetch him ascended, angry enough to rope him to heel by force if he raised an objection.

Tanuay and his brothers, grim as matched spears, brought the familial stamp of gaunt cheek-bones scattered with freckles. A pace behind panted their flaxen-haired cousins, their bony, hawk faces unsmiling. Grey eyes pinned their prey, granite hard, while more kinsmen trailed them, swaggers alike as birth siblings, but not: the indigo patterns that stippled their leggings identified a different marriage-house: which consanguinity justified curbing the outlander's mulish defiance. Ettinmere Settlement required fresh blood, above the scorching embarrassment that marred Vivet's status in the community.

If obstinacy caught Arin alone and outnumbered, his pursuit closed in with reluctance, their awkward confrontation thrust onto uneven ground.

The man should have heard nothing against the thunderous gusts. Nonetheless, he arose, a scarecrow too disarmingly mild to suggest warning spite. Until he turned around, and the wood shavings lofted out of his breeches pelted into the party below. The leaders swore and gouged watering eyes, while those sheltered behind craned their necks to berate their uncooperative target.

The outlander sheathed his whittling knife. Storm-crow hair tousled and green eyes intent, he regarded the visitation's approach with corrosive nonchalance.

Feet shuffled. Cloaks flapped. Nobody cared to speak first, harmless though he seemed for the fact he went swordless. No one knew where his blade was sequestered. He declined to grant Vivet his confidence. More, his self-effacing manner antagonized. The pack dispatched to confront his delinquency bunched up in bristled unease.

"You have been summoned to audience," Tanuay ventured at length.

The amused riposte would have hackled a stoic. "What pesky fault have you come to pick this time?"

"Not our complaint," Tanuay snapped. Beak-nose nipped white, he elbowed back his incensed youngest brother. "We've cautioned you plenty! Now formal charges are levelled against you for Vivet's discontent."

The outlander raised his eyebrows, beyond words: had their household elders not tested his probity? Their exhaustive requirements had been answered, each count, until what skills he possessed had declared him a fit provider. That Vivet languished without his conjugal service was the stickling burr jammed behind his contempt.

Tanuay gave that testy resistance no quarter. "To our shame, this matter has gone beyond family. You're called to task before Ettinmere's council."

"I see." Arin's smile bit frost to the bone. "Let's not keep them waiting." He leaped off his high perch, startled a gap in the ranks of his escort, and bestowed a wrapped bundle into the trailing cousin's surprised grasp. "Deliver these gifts, if you please, with my compliments?"

The contents laid bare were stout wooden spoons, sized for the communal cauldrons. Sturdy implements, and useful, had satirical whimsy not carved the handles into caricatures of the matrons, eyes pinched in droll malice, and oversized mouths with salacious tongues wagging.

Someone barked an astonished laugh, while another gasped, awed, "By mayhem, I'll stake my best shirt that Bektisha tramples Hanatha flat in the scuffle to stick a meat fork in yon foreigner, first!"

The council's bid to quash the outlander's insolence tweaked more than the familial tail-feathers. Upon Arin's presentation for reckoning at the round council hall, the plank door yanked open by Tanuay's stung pride let into disquieting gloom. An unsettled glance backwards forewarned his kinsmen. Arin watched with interest as the collective mood of vengeful authority dissolved.

"Teeah's virgin blood," someone murmured, afraid. "Here's trouble."

Tanuay's clamped grip shoved his sister's delinquent provider inside. Then the door whispered closed, the latch muffled behind a cousin's uneasy hand.

No cedar fire burned to cut the bleak chill, and no candle-lamp brightened the chamber. Seated figures lurked on the darkened dais, present and waiting since dawn: the mews reek of owl filled the shuttered room. Night-bird to the vultures sent aloft by day, the disgruntled creature swivelled its head and fixed orange eyes on the disturbance. The jewel strung at its breast flashed coal red, as the baleful relatives prodded their offender towards his overdue judgement.

A bird-bearing shaman did not bode him well. More, eight of the twelve council elders sat in ceremony, a battery row of stern silhouettes swathed in the doused brilliance of their feathered mantles.

"From the sun's fire into the pit," remarked Arin. "I've seen more cheerful funerals."

Tanuay's sharp tug underscored his frantic whisper. "All summary judgements occur without light! Maldoers are not shown the faces of those who declare retribution for standing grievances."

Arin twisted his wrist from the peremptory effort to steer him. "Accusation condemns a man without hearing?"

"You may speak as you wish." The speech was not Tanuay's but the gravel bass of the shaman. "Though bear in mind, our wasted time will weight your case with disfavour."

A reedy voice qualified. "Excuses won't waive just redress. Arcana was needful to quell the disharmony visited by your household upon our settlement."

"My household?" Annoyed to sarcasm, Arin ripped back, "Tell me, how does a bearing woman and her unborn child incite widespread mischief?"

Hassock leather squeaked. Disturbed clothing rustled through the ranks of the scandalized elders.

An old woman's waspish quaver attacked, "Arin, you have no cause for mockery. Vivet's unhappiness has drawn *iyats* to plague us! A shaman had to leave the night-watch to quell them before they caused malicious damage."

The foreigner refused to be cowed. "That's *all*?"

His upstart contempt cracked tempers and tolerance. "Do you not comprehend the potential for harm? Restitution for the exposure to risk shall dock you the worth of twelve cured hides, best quality; a pair of prime goats; a grown pig; and six sacks of millet. More, for depleting the watch, and as recompense for a shamanic intervention, you're assigned a stint of punitive labour."

"I'll pay nothing!" snapped Arin. "Not against losses that never materialized. I might have repelled the rank nuisance myself. Could have done so, had anyone troubled to ask me."

The shaman's incensed hiss sliced across the reprimand from the head-man. "We'll not waive this infraction for an empty boast."

The old woman preferred to deflate his arrogance. "This liar's bluff must be called!"

"Very well," the scofflaw agreed. "Do recall, you insisted."

He whistled the piercing threnody a gifted bard practised for fiend bane. The owl shrieked and bated to a rampage of wings. Seated elders clapped hands over their stinging ears, while the unprepared kinsfolk caught nearest buckled onto their knees. Before their sandbagged senses recovered, Arin barged past, kicked open the door, and walked out.

The shaman was quickest to recoup his poise. He soothed his riled bird, swivelled his painted face, and directed a venomous glare towards the vacated entry. He had underestimated the outland stranger: quite failed to imagine that such evasions covered more than pigheaded ignorance. The line of rebellion had been redrawn, with Ettin's authority dangerously upstaged. Too late, the shaman grappled the problem posed by an outsider who wielded true power. "How has a trained talent evaded our notice?"

Someone's shaken hand lit a spill, while Vivet's wilted kinfolk stumbled upright and talked over themselves to explain. "Arin told us he was a free singer but never presented us with any proof. Vivet admitted he carried no instrument. His claim was dismissed as a blow-hard's remark, once we verified his skilled archery. Bards don't, as a rule, strike a handkerchief target from two hundred paces."

The fact this one *could* raised importunate questions. While the kindled flame chased the gloom and brightened the stretched hides with their patterned charms of ward and guard, the council members blinked, fidgety as broody hens discomposed by a weasel slipped into their coop.

The eldest stabbed an irascible finger at the shaman. "This problem belongs to your eldritch peers. Let them break this foreigner's cavalier ways through menial service. New blood with the potential for talent is too rare to be squandered! Arin will share Vivet's bed and fulfil his duty to increase her household."

While the council fumed over the sentence, their unregenerate target sweated in dread, the threat to cage his wayward spirit too bitterly real. Huddled at the crest of a windy hill-top, Arin shivered like a wild creature shoved into a leg trap.

Below him, the settlement folded into the vale, the peaked roofs shingled with weathered cedar jumbled like dice between ragged black spruce. Rail-fences snaked across the sere meadows and edged the frayed burlap of fallow fields with their fringes of golden aspens. Industry hazed the idyllic scene in winnowed smoke from the shacks, curing meat. A dog barked, and a smith's hammer pounded out barrel staves. Children's laughter wove through the shrieks of a teething infant, clipped by the arrhythmic axe blows of men splitting logs into kindling.

At least one Ettinman side-stepped the diligent preparation for winter: the bard's tuned ear picked up vindictive footsteps, bearing down from behind.

Then Tanuay's nettlesome comment sawed into his preference for solitude. "The council has ruled upon Vivet's complaint and declared your term of bound labour. You're assigned, dawn to dusk, at the shamans' compound."

Which fatuous crow floundered into an initiate master's walled silence. Denied a reaction, Vivet's brother attacked. "Does a limp-cock dupe like you understand what's required to sustain an established household?"

Arin stared back in wide-lashed contempt. "By recitation in verse, or sung a capella?" For a Masterbard's trained tradition demanded a nuanced grasp of regional customs. Ettin law was communal: work shares determined the portion a man would receive from the harvest.

But Tanuay's entrenched grievance trampled ahead. "You'll know the misery of the winter hunt, Arin. While we crack nuts and drink beer by the fire, you'll have to trap for trade green hides to fill your scant larder."

Yet ridicule failed. Back-country hardship perversely gave Arin the vital prospect of privacy, once he contrived a plausible ploy to distance the nettled shamans. Until then, his assigned service offered a cat-and-mouse play for back-handed advantage. Let into Roaco's viper's nest, a trained master's inquisitive Sight might pry into the secrets the Ettin cabal clenched to its breast.

Alarmed as well as entranced by the prospect, the Teir's'Ffalenn masquerading as Arin smothered ironic laughter and whistled.

His spritely mood rattled Tanuay's affront. "D'you think to blindside our shamans, wee fool? You'll become the sap-head who reached to scruff a bagged hare and bloodied his mitt in the gob of a wolverine."

Arin's lilted melody paused. "Someone should warn Vivet?" Eyebrows raised, he sprang backwards as Tanuay roared and swung a fist.

He escaped the black eye he deserved only because Ettin's alderman puffed uphill to deliver the council's decree of punishment. The man's hickory cane sent Tanuay's rage packing but failed to douse Arin's amusement. Which provocation caused the piqued official to march the foreign upstart to meet his penance forthwith.

Their path soon merged with the terraced road, the buttressed turf chopped by the recent passage of the settlement's high-wheeled wagons. The switched-back curves accessed a higher plateau clustered with the toadstool rings of thatched huts that comprised the shamans' compound.

A fence of black-thorn and willow surrounded the dismal, squat roofs, their rough construction at odds with a stout central hall built of half-timbered stone, and other permanent structures sited in a natural hollow inside the earth-walled perimeter. A notch bisecting the mound of an overlook fashioned the gate, shored up with rammed timbers that, to mage-trained senses, harboured no eldritch protections. The crude eyes carved into the upright posts perhaps aimed to scare meddlesome children rather than repel a malign invasion. More effective, the two burly sentries, strapped into breastplates embossed with grotesque horned beasts. Their scowls were capped by steel helms lined with sheepskin, the die-stamped resemblance of in-breeding distinguished by beards, braided with ward charms and amulets. Distrust being Ettin's popular sport, they scowled down at the black-haired foreigner with abrasive prejudice.

Arin's slighter stature barely topped their embellished chests. While his cocky stare measured their rigid poise, a robed woman fleshed like a barracks laundress strode from the slat shack tucked in shadow behind. Her jaundiced glance skewered the penitent like vermin, then flicked to his bothered escort. "Why wasn't I warned?"

"The council's just bound him over for a month of remedial service." The alderman added, smug, "Burden him with unpleasant chores till the disrespect is knocked out of him."

"Too bad the latrines have been cleaned for the day." The woman sized up her charge, unimpressed. "That leaves mucking the mews, provided the runt has even a stripling's work in him."

She waved towards several small, whitewashed buildings in a row by the edge of the compound. "There you go." Her brisk dismissal instructed Arin to report directly to the head falconer.

Dispatched in advance of the council-hall shaman's informed precaution, the outlander went where he was bidden.

A gnarled oldster with string hair and milk cataracts left his sunlit bench and shuffled forward to meet him. "Detailed here for chores?" His tactile survey with a blind man's stick sized up what seemed a beardless stripling. "Young pest, eh?" Disgusted, he warned in a toothless lisp, "Bother my birds, and I'll have you flensed and staked out on the ledge for the buzzards."

Arin grinned in disingenuous silence. Sweet chance had enabled his keen curiosity to study the collared raptors up close. He permitted the falconer's prod, collected the basket and rake, and dug into the noisome, ammoniac reek of droppings and soiled straw. Those perches not vacant in day-time held hooded owls, jessed in fluffed repose until nightfall. Cheerfully whistling, Arin shouldered his assigned labour until twilight shadowed the vale.

Since lamp-light increased the hazard of fire, his grumpy taskmaster dismissed him. "Dump the muck on the heap, boy! Hang the rake and skulk for home, quick. If you get underfoot at the watch change, be sure you'll find yourself rendered for gizzard bait."

Arin tidied the tools. He nipped off, long gone by the time the nocturnal sentries reported for duty.

Darkness covered his furtive return to Vivet's cabin in the settlement. By then, he faced an emptied pot if he paused to wash the guano reek off his person. Famished beyond that civilized nicety, Arin by-passed the well. Perverse windfall, Vivet's distaste for the stench forestalled the council's mandate to sleep under her roof.

First light the next morning saw him crammed, shivering, into yesterday's damp garments. His pace brisk to offset the nip in the air, he reported back to the hidden vale for his second day's labour. The armed guards admitted him, woodenly unmoved by the madcap greeting he flipped into their teeth. Arin passed the rammed-earth defile, eyes gleaming with suspect anticipation, only to find his way blocked by a shaman.

Regaled in rumpled felt stitched with feathers, and indignantly rattling under strings of bone fetishes, the fellow's screwed features were suffused with blood and ingrained clay paint.

"The vultures!" he spluttered, spade jaw jutted with fury. "They're too sulky to eat. The mere sight of their handlers drives them wild. Our falconer's declared them unfit to be flown!" His tirade stalled, upstaged as another tempestuous ruckus funnelled through the entrance behind.

Arin nipped clear. Bemused by the flailing thunder of wing-beats and staccato outbursts of invective, he watched the owl handlers from the night-long vigil spill their agitation into the compound. The birds on their fists flailed in manic hysteria, fighting the jesses. The commotion shredded the morning quiet, encountered the shaman, and seethed to a halt.

Chilled from volcanic ire to ice, that fixed presence surveyed the uproar and winced as another bird bated. "The owls are distressed?"

The pale sentry in front bobbed with scared deference. "None would settle. Nothing calms them. As you see, they've been unmanageable throughout the patrol."

The shaman in authority asked nothing more. "Carry on as you were. Leave the problem to me."

The unnerved handlers sagged to a man with relief. While they crowded past, wrestling their disgruntled charges, the shaman glared daggers at Arin.

"Perchance have you meddled? I know Madraega's ignorance yesterday assigned you to clean out the mews. Our gullible falconer said he heard you whistling." The shaman stabbed the pertinent inquiry through the retreating avian clamour. "Has a talent fine-tuned enough to sing *iyat* banes cast an affliction over our birds?"

"I made song for the pleasure of being alive," Arin allowed without heat. "Why?" Smiling like velvet dipped into poison, he jabbed, "Have you come with a request for my services?"

"Never!" Jaws clamped, the stymied shaman breathed fire. Yet the damage was done: one thoughtless word touched off by s'Ffalenn temper had unmasked the pitfall that yawned unfathomably dangerous and deep. The shaman's cold gaze reassessed the insouciant prankster, whose effusive joy was not innocent. For his sly provocation keyed to well-being *had* sparked revolt: all the brooding rage of an enforced captivity turned back against the birds' abusive masters. That truth danced, unmasked, behind merry green eyes. The jewels that collared Ettinmere's raptors in fact steered them by spellbound coercion.

Where the fool might crow over the naked embarrassment, the initiate master took warning: two wary adversaries acknowledged their antipathy. The shaman struck back, aggressively fast, sharp and sure as a blade in the hand of a surgeon.

His thrust did not catch Rathain's prince defenceless, or best the reflex honed by Rauven's training. But diversion must supplant the sure parry in form, lest the innocent pose of dissembling humour come unravelled at a single stroke.

Arin feinted with a startled glance sidewards, then staggered as though something else had upset his artless equilibrium. His stumble evaded the stiffened forefinger punched at his chest and barely foiled the disastrous contact.

The opponent decked in primal fetishes was no idiot but a focused talent with dangerous strength. He would re-engage to seize the upper hand. Mis-step this fraught dance, break from plausible ignorance, and Arin risked catastrophic exposure.

Not only the stamp of his initiate mastery, his aura bore two adamant seals bestowed by Fellowship sorcery: Davien's unnatural longevity from the Five Centuries Fountain and Asandir's mark of crown sanction. Teir's'Ffalenn, he required a refuge to heal the broken links to his past. But Ettinmere's isolation could not shelter the impact of his royal heritage. Nor could a pack of bird sentries and crack archers harbour his fugitive identity as Master of Shadow.

Arin scrambled, entangled, his covert chance lost to map the pursuit ranged against him. Buffoonery as his last, innocuous shield from a power not to be trifled with, he staged a hooked heel and tripped in the path of his lunging opponent. Skulls collided with a tooth-rattling grunt. Concentration snapped, the shaman hissed, bowled into a clownish embrace. Jammed at elbows and knees, he could not shed the outlander's ham-fisted snatch amid toppling balance.

Clawed handfuls of arcane paraphernalia saved nothing. The shaman shared Arin's bumbling fall, garrotted by his raiment.

His bulk hit the ground, gargling. Cloth ripped, shedding feathers. Parted twine loosed a shower of bone talismans. Pelted by the fall-out, the red-faced shaman wheezed in a starved breath, while the idiot foreigner gasped an effusive apology, clutching his ribs. Choked by the pulverized cloud of clay pigments gusted off the shaman's clothes, or else snorting back laughter, Arin recovered himself, stood up, and extended a helpful hand gritted with dirt.

The shaman batted the courtesy aside. Purple with fury, he rasped his revised orders before the scapegrace sauntered away. "Not the mews, fellow! You've been reassigned."

The gate guards seized Arin. Their muscled force frog-marched him as far as possible from Ettin's cosseted familiars.

If the shaman crouched on hands and knees in the dust, rooting for baubles and beads, the stand down was no victory. The prickling itch between Arithon's shoulder-blades served him with perilous warning: on both sides, the exchange of antipathy remained unappeased.

* * *

The small, dark-haired foreigner found himself delivered forthwith to the compound's warehouse for tasking. Smudged by fresh mud, his shoulders squared, he faced the harried clerk who directed the yearly autumn exodus from a trestle stationed by the entry.

"Arin, you say?" A stooped figure topped with greasy grey hair reared behind the stacks of his meticulous ledgers. Features as crumpled as unfired clay peered over a moth-eaten quill. "Just what I need! An outland jape who can't read the tags. Bad omen, as well, since Teeah's wisdom knows a crow's malign colouring invites the death raven's curse." A fishy stare finished with a grumpy sigh. "What use, if you can't sort bottled poisons from tinctures for tonics and dyestuff? I suppose," the clerk mumbled, bent sideways to rummage, "you can handle a bucket and swab without careless mishap?"

The scrounged implements were thrust upon Arin with orders to mop the accumulated mouse scat and dust off the shelves detailed for inventory. "Be off, now, and make certain you don't disrupt the tally in progress."

Stepped through the door into velvet gloom, Arin sized up a maze of rack shelves, burdened by the lumpish loom of piled sacks, mismatched boxes, and casks. The glow of paned lanterns sliced through the fusty air, distorted by wheeling shadows where the compound's learned scribes sorted through the collection and packed select items in crates for transport. The cavernous space between groups invited unsupervised mischief. Too tempting in fact, likely posed as an entrapment. If Ettinmere's shamans tested him to reveal his esoteric knowledge, Arin embraced the challenge with the artless intent to pry, first.

He poked into the stores with inquisitive fingers. Where tacit tingles riffled his mage-sense, he hummed under his breath and sounded the patterns of crafted energies by harmonic resonance. The keys that fired the flux in response exposed the structure of the active enchantments. Most constructs were trifling: charms to sweeten unpleasant smells, delay rot, or ward away mishap, the lot easily fashioned by a green apprentice. Nothing approached the honed force of the probe lately launched against his defences. Whatever source buttressed the shamans' authority, not every working he sounded was clean. Informed by-play staged here potentially could stir far worse than raised hackles; wanton ignorance might inflict harm. Unsurprisingly, also, Arin noted his furtive activity had been observed.

Chased him down from behind, scolded to keep his malingering hands to himself, Arin snapped his clogged rag and pestered his watch-dog with tiresome questions. Shouted down as a nuisance, he staged an injured retreat that upset a tin of lead spheres.

The surprise bout of reliving struck then, amid the enclosed darkness. The sudden, clangorous noise sheared through his awareness and triggered a vivid surge of past memory. Arin swayed, abruptly unmoored as flashback recall hurtled his conscious reach backwards into a shadowed stone armoury. A place also crammed with laden, tiered shelves, rowed beneath massive ceiling beams where, in ghostly monologue, an unseen protester whined through a liar's protestations of innocence. The sly timber of that disingenuous voice woke a chain-lightning cache of associate memories.

Under his true Name as Arithon, he had been drawn into murderous peril: set up on the pretext of honest business for a vicious betrayal. The very same, unidentified charlatan had double-crossed him as Rathain's royal fugitive, in fact more than once, and for lethal stakes.

Arin gripped the nearest upright post, wrung by an onslaught of vertigo amid the ping and crack of lead balls tumbling helter-skelter. Caught under scrutiny by unfriendly eyes, he hid the appalling cause of his weakness by letting go. Fainting, he collapsed headlong into a flat iron. Strategically stunned, he flailed and upset a hamper from the lowest shelf. The wicker lid burst. A nestled collection of stoppered flasks clinked, hurtled air-borne, and smashed into the floor-boards. The debris loosed a noxious cloud of ground pigments, to ricocheted shrieks of dismay.

Belaboured by two angry boys bearing brooms, Arin curled in a ball to subdue giddy laughter. Netted in dangerous chaos, he still wrestled with his fractured grip on the present. Ungrounded and reeling, he careened onward by desperate invention and tipped a poke stuffed with puff-balls into a sheaf of goose quills. Displaced feathers kited, and dried fungi shredded. An evil explosion of spores winnowed outward, a choking blight that strangled the bystanders and folded them, helplessly coughing.

Their croaked outcries raised the head clerk from his desk. That bilious worthy stormed into the fray, screeching through the fingers pinching his nose, "Who let this idiot run at large?" Then, to the unregenerate outlander, crouched in faked illness that masked an ungoverned onslaught of flashback recollection, "Arin? Are you *trying* to get yourself shunned for stupidity?"

The outlander stayed doubled over in paroxysms that mangled his speech.

"Flaming glory! Vivet's kinfolk are fools. Anyone else would see your wretched get strangled for dog-meat at birth." Disgusted, the clerk hailed two brawny assistants. "Drag this man out. Let the wagon crew use him for loading."

Authoritative hands seized Arin's elbows. Hauled upright, he was dragged stumbling through the tiered shelves on expedient course towards the doorway. Dust swirled in his wake. The exasperated clerk sniffed, and sneezed, then hunched in a hacking fit alongside of the stricken underlings appointed for oversight.

The stout crates for travel were built to withstand mishap, nailed shut with their precious contents cushioned in straw. Those holding the most sensitive paraphernalia also bore copper talismans, enabled with marks of ward and guard. Steadied by daylight and open air, Arin recognized those straightaway, their latent powers striking his initiate awareness with subliminal, warbling dissonance. Prickled to gooseflesh, he sucked a hitched breath and suppressed a curdled rush of nausea. He dared not show distress, far less risk shielding his traumatized faculties after the disastrous mishap in the shed. The least sign of his advanced mastery would spring the disaster of a close inquiry.

"You there!" Bare-chested and broad as a ploughman, the brute with the squint who managed the loading let fly. "Shove off your runt backside and work! Break idle wind on my watch, I'll mince your carcass for pig swill!"

Some temptations could be too sweet. Prodded to shift the pile of crates into the nearest wagon, Arithon obliged with aimed malice and hefted the box with the most ferocious stays of protection.

"Not that one, pudding-head!"

The alarm saved nothing. The punitive lash of the ward hurled Arithon sideways. Viciously pleased in the throes of discomfort, he dropped the crate, staggered, caught his toe, and crashed flat. Dizzied under the virulent backlash, he mustered enough dazed presence to sit, knuckles pressed to his temples. Rushed footsteps converged. Through the pound of his pulse, shouts of imprecation shrilled above him like flustered gulls.

Blissfully retching, Arin gathered his blunder had shattered three vials of sunflower oil, and worse, tainted the blank copper beads that the Ettinmere shamans kept purified for the spells that enabled their charms.

Which bumbling might have seen him kicked to a pulp had a spindle-shanked elder not tottered into the moil. Combatants recoiled. Clamoured insults fell silent. A pair of bare feet yellowed with callus shuffled to a halt, attached to knobbed shanks kilted in a blanket fastened with a rusted pin.

Egg-shell frail under his thistle-down hair, and sexless as weathered bone, the ancient declared in a reedy quaver, "The outlander will not be killed out of hand. Not while he's likely to be healer-trained, and suited for medicinal foraging."

Arin's injured retort broke the hush. "Why speak for my vaunted skills now, when my word on the matter was suspect?"

The crinkled face swung in its cowl of wool, gashed lips and underslung jaw crimped beneath the baleful glimmer of rheumy eyes. "You have our wisest matron to thank that you're not breaking rock in the quarry."

Caustic grin unrepentant, Arin remarked, "Someone noticed I didn't trample the pennyroyal when the hamper upset in the shed?"

The eldritch ancient hissed through toothless gums. "Who taught you, fellow?" His question slapped like a blow, bladed by a lightning burst of deft conjury.

The assault pierced through Arin's froth of evasion. Speech strangled, he found his harrowed awareness darkened as though sucked into a vacuum. Scarcely able to breathe, a whisked moth in a gale towards black-out oblivion, he subdued his trained reflex *just barely in time*. Though his pretence of sickly distress stayed intact, that thin cover hid very little. This seasoned adept understood beyond question that a tender nerve had been struck. The pause stretched, polarized by the sharp recognition shared between joined antagonists: this war of locked wills would be run to the end with relentless persistence.

"Prove yourself!" snapped the elder. Senior in rank, and wary of a challenge to his rigid authority, he deferred the public pursuit of full closure in favour of stalking his prey from a distance. "Forage alone in the forest until sundown on the seventh day, and be judged by the value of what your knowledge delivers."

Urgent need to save his threatened privacy drove Arithon into the heights, where the steep vales wore black spruce in speared ranks, and icy streamlets gushed down-slope in silver floss tangles that swirled bubbles across the glass panes of the trout pools. The stand-off interval brought him little relief, even where the bracing gusts off the glaciers wore the perfumes of resin and scoured ice. Neither did the buttressed strength of Storlain bed-rock ground the fraught pitch of his nerves.

Danger still flanked him. The Ettinmere cabal's invasive interest blazed like a coal at his back. A persistent buzzard circling above kept his activity tightly watched. The entanglement posed him a deadly liability, far beyond the inconvenience of the child-right binding him to the settlement. For a babe very likely not his own get, he tossed dice with antagonists endowed with the vicious potential to ruin him.

Act he must, and decisively, for vital stakes. Sound sense advocated for flight. The plight of Vivet's unborn child by due right should be relinquished to Havish's justice. There, logic collided with s'Ffalenn compassion. Perish the hour he saved his own skin at the expense of an innocent's fate.

Paused at a rock-spring to splash his face, Arithon measured his unsteady hands. Any concerted assault on his faculties whetted his straits to a razor's edge. Overreact, and Ettin's sentinel archers would drop him under orders to kill. Respond too gently, and the shamans' persistence might provoke a disastrously vigorous defence. The spurious bouts of reliving imposed by his damaged memory undermined all cautious strategy. If he snapped, his volatile past could be ransacked at whim by a murky faction driven by *who knew what* secretive purpose. Past question their meddling must be repulsed without hazard to his autonomy.

How to rattle the hornets' nest and disarm the sting after seven days' trial faced him with the reckoning?

Where resonant magecraft likely would run him afoul of Ettinmere's extant protections, mastery of shadow left almost no signature, spun directly from the element. The whisper of impact would leave a trace too refined to deflect the Storlains' disturbed flux.

"Field this and choke," he murmured, then grinned. His subtle working unfurled on a thought and muffled the jewel collared to the ensorcelled raptor.

The freed bird flapped straightaway and veered off station. Arithon seized the moment. While his morsel of darkness impaired the shamans' augmented sight, he slipped past the sealed border that enforced Ettinmere's isolation.

The shamans' feathered spy banked northward and soared parallel to the ridge. Once it settled on a ripe carcass, its handler ought to be hassled to Sithaer reclaiming its fixed attention. But Arithon's gratified chuckle was brief, tainted by the farsighted ripple of a catastrophic upset, sown elsewhere . . .

The shrill scream resounded like a tortured animal's, caged within close, whitewashed walls stripped as barren as a dungeon cell. Draughts from the gusty weather outside never fluttered the single candle. The dead air entombed a tormented figure convulsed in restraints on the bed. Sodden, fair hair clung to the damp pillow and pasted the slice of pale forehead not swathed in bandages. Strapped amid snarled sheets, a spirit severed from human identity thrashed in a bestial distress at odds with the chamber's lavish appointments.

Candlelight gleamed on white silk and chased the glitter of bullion embroidery. Incense sweetened the miasma of sickness, and costly rose-oil anointed the wooden stool, currently occupied by an elderly servant who strove to lend comfort where none could be found.

"Lysaer?" The attendant gripped his charge's contorted shoulders. "Liege! You are safe. The nightmare's not real! This is Dace, a friend at your side, even in this wretched place!"

The cracked burr as Lysaer's outcry lost wind brought no surcease. At next breath, his eerie howls continued, charged by the sudden, actinic flicker that fore-ran an eruption of elemental light. The vicious drive of Desh-thiere's curse would outmatch all steadfast kindness and reason. Dace grasped the dread stakes. At risk of his life, he stayed at his post. "There's no threat here! No Shadow, I promise. Be still, I am with you. The restraints are only to keep you from tearing at your damaged eye."

Steps approached the shut door. One of the sentries bellowed an anxious inquiry from without.

The loyal servant never glanced sidewards. "My liege! This distress is not yours but arises from Desh-thiere's malice. Fight back, I beg you. Hear my voice and reclaim your compromised will from possession."

The dedicate exhorted the avatar's valet, "Shut him up, damn you! By Darkness, keep on, and he'll bring the Light's High Examiner for another bout of interrogation."

The presssured servant entreated, "Hush! Lysaer, please." While desperation wadded the pillow-case to muffle the noise, Dace pleaded onwards to stem the insanity raving beneath him. "Don't grant the True Sect their due cause to unleash The Hatchet's war host for slaughter!"

Whether the threat of armed conflict struck home, Lysaer's half-smothered shrieking changed pitch, cranked into shrill terror.

The latch tripped, and the dedicate sentry poked his crested helm through the cracked panel. "My watch officer's bolted to fetch the priests. Duty won't let me shield you. Once they arrive, I'm outranked."

Dace snapped without turning. "A healer's required, not prayer! More, if that examiner butts in, we'll all be destroyed!"

When the doubtful man hesitated, Dace exploded. "Somewhere, the Spinner of Darkness is active! My liege can't say where! Grace above, he's beyond incoherent! If anyone pushes him in this state, the mistake will provoke a disaster!"

Still, the guardsman demurred.

Dace released his fraught grip. His liege's chilling, feral wail drove him from the bedside to fly into the face of the sentry's inaction. "Stay out! Are you daft? Your avatar's frenzied beyond sense already. Crowd him, and the floor where we stand will run molten. Ruin will be your last sight of glory before divine Light burns us both to a cinder!"

Flummoxed as the boulder battered by a moth, the armoured dedicate recoiled. Dace seized the moment and banged the gapped panel shut.

Wafted air snuffed the candle. Darkness clapped down, while Lysaer's outcry pealed into raw fury. Dace spun back, spurred by fear, groping blind for the flint and striker. He snapped off a spark and rekindled the smoking wick before Lysaer lashed out, ruled utterly by curse-born hatred.

"My liege, settle back, here is light. We are safe!" Still speaking, Dace tore off his livery waistcoat. He snatched up the candle, shielded the flame with his palm, and hastened back to the doorway. Under peril of Lysaer's instability, he jammed the crumpled cloth into the latch with no second to spare.

Heavy footfalls approached. Erdane's High Priest barged through the outside guard's protest, unswerved. "Evil itself has infected our avatar. I will have the examiner here to put him to the question until we disclose where the Spinner of Darkness dens up. The Hatchet's orders will go out by pigeon and march the faithful to rout Shadow's scourge from Athera!"

The latch twitched. Dace torched his placed rag with a panicked shout. "Stay back! Blessed Light, be mindful of Lord Lysaer's wrath! Or his divine Light will see everyone burn!"

The set blaze caught. A daunting burst of smoke and cinders shot through the keyhole, to a yelp from outside. The priest recoiled, his forced entry forestalled as he sucked on his scorched finger-tips . . .

In the far-off heights above Ettin, a heart-beat before Lysaer s'Ilessid succumbed to ungoverned violence, the s'Ffalenn half brother dispelled his conjured wisp of darkness. Relief came in time: the Mistwraith's cursed insanity burned no one alive in the distanced recoil at Erdane.

But the price of remission cost Arithon the tenuous stay that thwarted the shamans' spy. The strayed vulture soon would veer back into range, enslaved again by the spelled jewel's directive. The Prince of Rathain languished on his knees, senses still spun by rogue far-sight. Cold wind and bleak stone failed to ground his awareness and stem the cascade of raw prescience.

Threshed in the slipstream, Arithon beheld blood and horror: *as the raving of the True Sect's avatar precipitated a blood-bath under the Sunwheel standard. Galleys loaded for war scudded across Instrell Bay's winter spindrift. White against dirtied snow, gilded under the pale sun at solstice, dedicate companies debarked at strength in Rathain's coastal wilds. Trees fell to the axe, erected as palings to fortify their encampments. Ox trains and sledges toiled from Narms supply until spring thawed the roads from Etarra. More than an aggressive invasion, Halwythwood's clans faced extermination in their stand to defend the sanctity of the mysteries.*

No Fellowship Sorcerer answered the crisis. While temple bounties whipped the head-hunters' leagues to frenzied slaughter, the current of augury showed Asandir crossing the bogs of Angelfen. A more urgent priority sent him to Northgate on the summer night a True Sect ambush targeted Rathain's war band. With Halwythwood's defences laid open, the reiving attackers poured into the heart-wood settlement.

Massacre followed, horrific as the historic affray at Tal Quorin, a relentless onslaught that saw the hacked corpses of families sprawled in the smouldering ash of the chieftains' council hall.

Arrived in the grim aftermath, Tarens tempered the High Earl's young successor with Jieret's hardened experience. "Esfand, bear up! You suffer what no stripling's inexperience should endure, just as other caithdeinen *have before you! Duty remains. The outlying sentries may survive still, and Laithen's shade is owed redress for Siantra, who sacrificed everything dear to send warning."*

A young woman of such dauntless strength, the imprint of her vision resounded across time with crystalline clarity. Arithon's threshed faculties received her appeal: not as the futile cry of a shade, but as a warning portent stamped through the flux by a spirit yet living . . .

Crouched on the peaks above Ettinmere, Arithon Teir's'Ffalenn beheld the young sender: *a grave, dark-haired girl with Sidir's flint eyes, awake to his presence through the driving spark of her uncanny talent. On this day, Siantra s'Idir had not met her death. More, her clarion call had never been aimed to alert the clans' slaughtered war band.*

Her summons instead begged for an intercession from the Prince of Rathain: "Help us! You are needed! Support your people, that this dreadful hour never sees daylight."

Her plea to his crown obligation brooked no refusal against a campaign to be written in the wholesale murder of innocents. *A last image seared through in graphic detail: of a matron with fair hair tangled with filth, speared while defending her infant, both corpses left flayed to the skull by the bountymen's knives.*

Vision shattered. Released to his natural senses with a wrench fit to render his gorge, Arithon swore. He anchored his displaced focus, shattered under the distraught awareness: the shackles imposed by Ettinmere's council could not be abided. Vivet's child was not the sole victim set at risk, if Halwythwood succumbed to a broad-scale campaign of eradication in his absence.

A frigid, changed wind sheered off the glacier. Clouds hazed the lowering sun, promise of an icy drizzle. Worse than the bad weather, the shamans' infernal bird had returned to circle overhead.

Arithon weighed his strategic choices. Shield himself, and he could mask a limited working of Shadow on his own person without upsetting Lysaer's cursed instincts. But even that basic use of trained mastery would alert Ettinmere's shamans. Which left only brazen intimidation to thwart their insidious prying.

Arithon shoved to his feet and glanced up. Another carrion bird joined the first. Annoyed by their surveillance, he wished merry hell on their two-legged handlers. "Let your overlords cross my free will at their peril." Done musing, he cut a dead sapling for a staff. Then, black head tousled by the risen gusts, the Masterbard of Athera engaged his artful talent and sang.

Choice

The temple novices who set the chamber to rights replaced the scorched bed-linen and wracked pillows without question, by now resigned to their avatar's rampaging fits. Dace tucked his blistered hand out of sight until the doors closed behind them. In private, he finished the intimate tasks that saw his maimed liege resettled and fed.

By servant's protocol, the valet ate his own supper afterward. The rhythm of restored routine brought a kitchen drudge to remove the meal trays, Lysaer's with its gilt spoon and bullion plate on lace doilies smeared with spilled gravy.

Dace snatched the interval to change the clothes singed and despoiled by spattered broth. The cross-grained priest appointed as chamber steward grumbled over the excessive laundry, yet his fussy management begrudged nothing else in support of the avatar's upkeep. The clean livery provided to Lysaer's valet was tailored from quality silk. The True Sect's high chamberlain also had offered the expertise of a healer, along with a day-and-night roster of staff for relief. Dace Marley rejected the additional help. Though his liege's helpless condition confined him, he carried the burden despite the monotony.

Little outside light brightened Lysaer's curtained cell as the seasonal dance of autumn gave way to winter. Sealed within hallowed isolation, behind the bulwarks of Erdane's High Temple, the days passed to the whispered drone of the throngs come to worship. The acolytes' chants smeared sibilant echoes through the labyrinthine stone corridors, a tidal surge from dawn to dusk's ebb, pricked by the clangour of cymbals and the sonorous toll of the bells. Near at hand, muffled by the strapped door, the tramp of hobnailed boots marked the watch change. Incense wafted in from the anteroom trailed the priests who observed their eightfold devotions at the niche altar, outside.

Dace minded the room's single candle throughout. He trimmed the wick before the flame sputtered and drowned in pooled wax. Lysaer s'Ilessid slept badly in darkness. Even while blessed with prime health and clear faculties, he had preferred light in his chamber past sunset. The habit became a necessity in the painful aftermath of his injury, when he was not lucid enough to escape the quagmires of nightmare. The erratic reflex as brain tissue mended scrambled his sensory stimulus into hallucinations.

The candleflame sometimes kept terror at bay, until the horrific dreams took hold in the fallen stillness past nightfall. Dace watched Lysaer's supine form without rest, perched on a footstool at the bedside.

When the first restive flicker twitched the invalid's eyelids, he applied a compress infused with lavender oil and chamomile. The mild soporifics eased very little. Narcotics to induce sleep were too strong. The temple healer's experience claimed that a drugged stupor aggravated a comatose head injury.

Dace persisted, no matter how inadequate his available remedies. While spoken words were not understood, he murmured as though to ease a whipped animal, while Lysaer's fitful distress progressed to sped pulse and shuddering breaths. The eleventh hour sometimes brought respite. Lysaer's thrashing subsided beneath silken sheets. His fevered skin chilled to moist marble. Dace seized the interval to freshen the bandages, braced for the dreadful moment the fragile calm tore away. No sand-glass was needed. Lysaer's tormented screams resurged when the lane tide crested at midnight.

The ghastly descent always wrenched the heart. Dace used soft ties to restrain the onset of convulsions, then wept for pity, devoted beyond peace. Naught else would spare his liege from taking harm under the relentless seizures.

No measure of mercy eased the harrowing trial through the black hours before dawn. When the marriage of spirit and flesh became tenuous, and the veil of the mysteries thinned, Lysaer's deranged ferocity forced Dace to take refuge under the bed. Cowering, he had to beat out errant flames, as flares of incipient light ran amok and levin bolts seared across the stone floor, and every taut second became a hard-won triumph of victory.

Dace spoke gently, no matter that words never curbed the violent outbursts. Aware provocation would worsen the coming trauma, he stroked the tangles from sodden blond hair and waited, alert for the first sign of danger.

Yet no such explosive eruption ensued. Only a whispered finger of draught ruffled his skin into gooseflesh. Then a nosegay of late-season wildflowers kited out of thin air and fluttered into his lap.

"I thought you might pine for the glory of autumn," a gusty voice remarked with amusement, then added, "My dear, no need for alarm! Go ahead, blaspheme the Light's doctrine and laugh. The pious donkeys posted at your door will stay deaf. They haven't two thoughts in their bone heads, besides, fed on the spout of the True Sect Canon."

"Kharadmon!" exclaimed Dace, jangled to pleased astonishment.

"At your service, of course." The Sorcerer's breathy snort conveyed irony. "Luhaine is thankfully bound to a dragon, which spares you from his moping gloom and boorish advice."

"I'd take a dull visitor as a relief," Dace responded, despite his apprehension flushed pink by the fragrance whisked in with the posy.

"You've enchanted Sethvir with your dazzling wit." Kharadmon's breezy sarcasm turned thoughtful. "Delightful to find your spirit still shines in this pit. You know you've confounded these pompous, frocked sheep? The Sunwheel priesthood's afraid to a man to face your mad avatar's presence."

"Perhaps they're sensibly anxious, today. But who's fooled?" A flim-flam ploy with a rag and a candle would scarcely withstand the righteous might of their doctrine. "How long before we're all martyred in flames for salvation? What I've noticed," Dace jabbed back, unappeased, "is that you Sorcerers don't have the resource to spare for dalliance and flattery."

Kharadmon unfurled an image, his emerald velvet accented with orange-silk ribbon and dapper lace. "You should have suitors lined up for a league." He clasped her wrist with an ephemeral touch and bowed over her scalded palm. "Do grant an unworthy admirer permission?" His insubstantial, mimed kiss quelled the sting and knitted her weeping blisters. "Regrettably, yes, I do bring hard news. Unrest troubles the dragons past Northgate. An outbreak from there could threaten Athera beyond any determined mayhem the True Sect stirs up against the clan lineages."

"Fiends plague!" Dace exclaimed, jolted. "You're serious?" Great-grandparents recalled when the northern sky had been lit incandescent by drakefire. The mighty retort of the Fellowship's defence, and cold wardings, had staved off wrack and ruin beyond imagining. "Are you facing another outbreak of drake war?"

"Not yet!" Kharadmon said in swift reassurance. "But not every dragon sided with the Eldest who ceded Athera to the Paravians. Quite a few opposed the Second Age treaty that stabilized this world's existence. Some of the great wyrms beyond Northgate disagree still. Their rash young, matured since, agitate to upset the ancient Accord. Our Fellowship is not reft of drake allies, not yet. The present upheaval attends a succession, while Chaimistarizog weakens as Gatekeeper. He has twice been forced to fight youthful claimants. While some dragons yet remain on Athera to forestall an invasion by their own kind, those guardians lie in deep hibernation. To wake any one of them now would place fractious humanity in mortal danger. Seshkrozchiel's bargain with Davien's consciousness has seeded a witch's brew of novel concepts. Elder dragons crave original experience. The exciting allure of a meddling encounter could shake the established priorities."

Dace weighed Kharadmon's words against the dilemma sprawled limp on the bed: the murderous peril of Desh-thiere's curse gloved in burnished hair and a one-sided profile handsome enough to shred sense. He said, a bit hot, "That explains why Davien's made himself scarce. But if Lysaer's wont to torch us to ruin at any outbreak of Shadow, the grim bent of your news is no boon to my predicament."

"My dear, I'm not here to fuel your worries. Only to convey Asandir's earnest warning: the Seven may not be available to salvage a crisis or rake you from the ashes a second time. While Lysaer's immured here, his name will be played to wage bloody war for the True Sect cause." The harrowing stare of the Sorcerer's image stabbed through the pause. "An armed assault against Halwythwood's clans must force the hand of Rathain's crown prince. Past quarter, your pledge to temper your liege's insanity presents a challenge of epic proportions."

"I'm not leaving!" Dace snapped. "Since Lysaer has no better voice to speak in his behalf, suggest something else to assist his case."

Kharadmon's image snuffed out to his restive impatience. "Well, you had to ask! By Ath's grace, did you know that? I thought for a bit you'd plant mulish feet and stay stiff-necked as the Teir's'Ffalenn's benighted woman."

Dace received that pearl of gossip, unmoved. "His Grace of Rathain is not cast from the compact. Presumably, he's of sound mind and able to appeal to your Fellowship directly?"

The discorporate Sorcerer chuckled, breezy as wind through dense pines. "Athera's royal progenitors were not selected for compliant dependency. A quality Luhaine laments at length, in tiresome monologue. You realize we confront certain limits? Indeed. You cannot petition us Seven to avert the True Sect's spree of slaughter in Halwythwood. Not from here, by the terms of town law, and nowhere under the chartered grant of Tysan's crown sovereignty."

Dace blinked. "I'm Lysaer's valet. Not a stickling lawyer."

The circular breeze winnowed to frosty stillness. "Then, as the person entrusted with his bodily care, whose well-being *may* lie within my purview to remedy, precisely what do you imagine you might require?"

Dace blotted damp palms on his trousers. He regarded his liege. Settled candleflame toned the milk purity of a face half-swathed under bandages. The wounded eye underneath still seeped moisture. By the healer's prognosis, scarred tissue blocked the tear-duct draining through the sinuses. Pity clamped Dace's throat and mangled his answer. "What's the implied riddle? Since you can't lift a finger in Lysaer's behalf, you suggest I must act on my own initiative?"

"The very gist," Kharadmon affirmed.

Dace sucked a taxed breath. "All right. Lysaer's moods are drastically volatile. He's unbalanced by even slight usage of Shadow because he cannot curb his primal response. He can't battle the curse without mindful reason to blunt his reflexive hatred. The Mistwraith's directive will wreak violence upon anyone who tries him with restraint. I must break that impasse. If not to calm him, then at least to redirect his attention. Some way to manage the geas that brands me in the crux as the enemy."

A puffed exhalation winnowed the candle. "I might teach you the rudimentary knowledge to cast a simple glamour." Innate humour banished, Kharadmon qualified with grave reluctance, "The working involved is not clean, do you follow? While Lysaer is incapable, to meddle in his behalf infringes upon his free will. Such action denies the due grace of his conscious permission."

Dace swallowed, anguished. "Don't I know! Lysaer will be furious. Nobody dares to cross his prickly autonomy."

Kharadmon demolished the wry dismissal. "To blind another is to bind yourself!" To his refined sight, the figure before him was not an aged man but a young woman subjected to cruel isolation. In other ways tenderly innocent, even her dauntless spirit might shrink from the consequence. "*Do you* realize the degree of accountability such a choice might invoke?"

"I can guess what happens if I stand aside!" Dace sighed. "Could I live with the slaughter? More, how will Lysaer? Can he be responsible in this state, stripped of his basic awareness as a civilized human being? And what is my oath to Asandir worth? I vowed under a Fellowship seal to stand as my liege's shadow! I promised to be the voice of his conscience. And more, love in his case cannot step aside, or abandon him with no compass. He will blame himself for the Mistwraith's designs: revile his faults and condemn the mistakes inflicted by this vital wounding. For every armed foray made in his name, he'll rake his conscience over the coals and brand himself for inadequacy. Tell me true," Dace addressed the nexus of cold that anchored Kharadmon's presence, "does the inborn gift of justice lend my liege any footing for self-forgiveness?"

"The royal endowments are not absolute." Kharadmon picked his words like silk thread unreeled through a thorny morass. "The trait does not direct choice by itself but plays in concert with personal character. Your liege must find his requital himself. I have no pat answers or platitudes to ease the rocky course of his fate. Only the cautionary advice: a glamour may stymie the drive of the curse by transference of Lysaer's fixed focus. But once he recovers empowered awareness, that false stay is destined to shred. Desh-thiere's geas is altogether too powerful. Your liege will break through any one-sided working the moment his wilful alignment embraces disaster."

Dace's sharp, expelled breath streamed the candleflame. Wax dammed at the wick dribbled like a widow's tears congealed in midfall, while outside, muffled by stonewalls, the temple bells in the Sunwheel towers tolled the hour above Erdane's rooftops.

Against faltering nerves, Dace reinflated his hollow chest. "If I do nothing, the cost will be writ in more than the blood of mass slaughter. My liege may survive to heal in the body, only to condemn himself by self-loathing." Courage shouldered the cause. "Someone must protect for Lysaer's integrity. While he cannot commit for himself, right or wrong, the friend at his side would never allow the atrocities driven by Desh-thiere's curse. Not to further the True Sect Canon, and never to feed a campaign of massacre visited upon innocents."

Erect on the stool, Dace set his jaw. "Grant me the knowledge. I'll proceed on hope. When the day dawns, and Lysaer regains his right mind, he *may* forgive my transgression tonight. Perhaps, if my faith in his goodness prevails, he'll agree to extend the stay by permission, and in conscious partnership we might continue to thwart the Mistwraith's directive."

Kharadmon's image unfurled and bowed to her. "You have more than upheld your sworn oath as *caithdein*. Under the law of the Major Balance, this burden you've taken as yours was never our Fellowship's, even to ask. A glamour is a binding enchantment, regardless of whether the act is done selflessly in Lysaer's behalf. You had to assume the willing responsibility. The outcome you strive for may never resolve. Or it could, and your purest intention may fail."

"Then Daelion Fatemaster must balance the debt after death, mine or Lysaer's," Dace determined. "Abandonment would be the greater betrayal."

Had Kharadmon still possessed the warm flesh to give comfort, he would have embraced Lysaer's guardian and eased his stressed trembling. As a shade, he had naught to bestow. Only a moment's inviolate safety, as he granted the layman's knowledge to enact the blood binding that anchored a stay spell.

"You're quite sure?" he said at the crux.

Dace took up the penknife kept to trim the candle wick, and without hesitation enacted the configured circle of containment. Kharadmon noted his grip did not shake as he let the requisite droplets from a pricked finger. The words that consecrated the ritual followed with level conviction. Amid the silence of a sealed tomb, Dace twined the subservient ties of enchantment and brought the invocation to closure.

The working locked with flawless care, each line of ephemeral energy finished with precision. "Treat with your liege's fate wisely, my dear," Kharadmon whispered in gentle farewell.

"Wait!" Dace pleaded quickly. "Please, I have one last request."

A breeze that recoiled and eddied the candle, Kharadmon paused with acerbic forbearance. "As long as I don't have to murder a priest!"

Dace managed a tremulous grin. "Will you accept my word of permission under Fellowship auspices? I request the privilege of your due warning, if I should stray from a *caithdein*'s true purpose. I would not cause harm. If I ever held my liege entrained past the point of conscientious restraint, would your greater wisdom advise me, by Dharkaron's witness?"

"That much can be done in good faith," though Kharadmon added the tart observation, "Let us acknowledge the stickling caveat. You never have yielded to anyone's effort to bestow due precaution before. Fellowship power can't stay your destruction. You shall proceed as your free will determines, by your innate strengths or your weaknesses. Can a principle bend your fixed loyalty enough to shift your personal stake in the outcome?"

"I don't know," Dace allowed. "At least, come the dark hour, I would beg not to stumble through blindness."

Kharadmon's devilish humour could almost be felt. "Your liege has won himself a staunch advocate. Let me add that your ancestor, Sulfin Evend, did not check the course of catastrophe through self-effacing humility either."

While Dace blinked in startlement, the Fellowship Sorcerer vanished and left him.

Alone in Lysaer's cell, nicked flesh stinging like vengeance, Dace leaned on the bedside and started to shake. Tears followed, a torrent of grief for the straits that imposed such a bitter decision upon him. "Ath above, lend me foresight! Let me wield the power of this perilous gift with awareness beyond my experience."

For the man who languished in tonight's wounded majesty one day would regain his unimpaired cognizance. Release Lysaer's natural focus too soon, and Desh-thiere's curse would ride him to cataclysmic destruction. Dally too long, and the tenets of royal character would recoil in righteous rage.

Dace found himself saddled with the dread reckoning Dakar had proposed in the flint stacks of Lanshire, that gut instinct had shied to embrace. Love spoken then with untrammelled clarity now trod a rough passage through murky waters. Denied self-reliance, Lysaer's spirit relied on a crutch, no matter how well-intentioned. He might not fall to the fatal mistake. But steered by another, neither could his mature growth evolve the blistering courage needed to heal.

Price for undue interference, Dace risked every footing for credible trust, precariously built up between them.

The deeps of the night at length wore away. The watch changed, and the distanced bells clanged the dawn carillons. Yet the nightmares that warped Lysaer's peaceful sleep, for a merciful first, never came.

Early Winter 5923

Trump

Days passed without the dark-haired outsider's return to Ettinmere Settlement. His defiance of the shamans' ultimatum sparked vehement criticism and gossip. The disapproval and pity directed towards Vivet suggested her man ran an honourless household, or worse, named him a callous dupe.

Her oldest brother met the slights with cold silence, then cornered his sister's misery in private. Unwelcome as nettle-rash, he darkened her door, while she, with rolled sleeves, plied the washboard two-handed, drubbing a hireling's collection of clothes in a borrowed wash-tub.

Tanuay's assumption of misbehaviour raised matters not even her sisters dared broach. "You've been the bone in Arin's craw, all along. Never mind he's planted his brat in your belly! You will never be *chia* to him, or to anyone else, now the skulking *faechaa* has gone. He's dumped his used goods and bolted down-country the moment he slunk past our patrols. End the family embarrassment, bend your stiff neck, and redress your sorry abandonment."

Vivet glared, eyes bright. "For our Daldari pride, my child's condemned?" She snatched the next soiled garment from her basket, shoved it under the sloshed water, and punched out the pocketed air. "What would I become, thrown to wretchedness as the lowliest of our kindred?"

Her brother reddened, shamed to acknowledge that a left woman, unmarried, must serve the wives of the extended family. Still determined, he crossed the threshold and banged his fist on the puddled trestle. "What are you now, stooped to washing your neighbours' soiled linens for a pittance?"

Vivet blushed. She slapped down the sopped garment and scrubbed, up and down, until spattered suds flecked the wisped hair at her temples. "You know nothing of Arin! Or his intentions."

166

Her brother, no fool, sensed her knot of deep fear. But not the dreadful secret coiled behind her trapped straits. His insular experience could not grasp the greater penalty riding her fate if she failed. Strict Ettin custom drove his disgust, his parting words as vicious as flung knives. "The family's disgraced, and you are a wanton to hang your future on a lying foreigner. Don't weep over your choice to ignore my last warning! By tonight, your plight will be sealed by the shamans."

Yet Vivet persisted with her independence. She hung the sopped clothes, ironed and folded them, dried from the line, and under the lengthened shadow of sundown, collected the coin for her work when the basket was emptied. At the last, nigh onto the hour of forfeit, the delinquent returned for his reckoning.

The watchers' birds spied Arin's approach, cresting the northern ridge bold as brass. As though their scouring searches had never lost track of him, he descended the stepped stone without hurry, while his belated arrival stirred Vivet's relatives to gather in force. Interest also attracted the curious. Granddames doddered in, elbows hung with satchels of darning. A gnarled grandfather propping a hay-fork stood amid a half dozen cronies, grizzled jaws jutted with talk. Craftsmen in leather aprons and goat-herds paused as they sauntered homeward, while children frisked in oblivious play and rambunctious dogs yapped on the fringes.

Since the Daldari kinfolk had been denied their requital for Arin's defection, the pack came for the thrill of witnessing the altercation.

The foreigner's transgressions defied more than a council decree: his evasion of Ettinmere's sentries had breached the integrity of the border. Twelve archers summoned from the mountain watch formed a line with strung bows: no empty threat, with their shafts tipped in bodkin points for an execution.

The penalty for flouting security was death. Arin's position appeared past reprieve when the council's ranked shaman and four bearers in masks came to mete out their summary justice. Roaco's presence itself inspired dread, his feather-cloaked figure furled like a bat enthroned on a lacquered sedan chair. The vulture plume fans on the posts rattled in the stiffening gusts, while the last daylight leached from the world and drained the colour out of the land-scape. His cabal of attendants unburdened their load. They lit torches staked upright into the ground, flames streamed under the afterglow blush that stained the surrounding peaks. The wait stretched, while twilight shadowed the vales, and the last notes of bird-song dwindled to quiet.

Arin's final approach raised the coarse scrape of wood grating over bare stone through the whisk of the breeze. A whistled melody followed, snatched to breathless gaps by exertion. When at length he emerged from the lace scrim of the evergreens, flame-light picked out the canvas of a cape-shouldered trapper's coat he had not owned on his departure. Besides that proof of barter with outside woodsmen, the scapegrace towed the laden hulk of a handmade sledge. The shapeless bundles strapped to the frame overtaxed his bent figure, leaned into the straps.

Then his merry tune ceased. The outlander straightened, confronted by Vivet's inimical kinfolk, and surely dismayed to find himself marked by the squad of archers.

He discarded the burdensome harness of tow-lines. Hands wrapped in cloth to ease blisters flexed once before his peaceable gesture linked them behind his waist. Then he spoke, a crisp statement addressed to the shrivelled elder upon the sedan chair. "Is this justice, when by your design I was set up to fail?"

The silence intensified. No rebuttal was possible: any versant herbalist knew that seasonal dormancy gripped the plants at high altitude. Frost had withered the seer's weed, and the brittle tassels of seed were already wind-stripped. Gum sap in the balsams withdrew to the roots, while above the timberline, the hardiest lichens useful for dyestuff lay buried beneath ice and snow until spring.

"An earnest trial demanded a trip across the north ridge." Unrepentant, Arin finished his case. "My obligation to support Vivet's household involved setting traps on the way. I've brought the requisite sack full of herbs. Also quality pelts and fresh meat for the smoke-house, collected upon my return."

Roaco thumped his staff. "You interfered with the sentries and flouted our established boundary. No matter how glib your excuse, the behaviour's a killing offence."

Impatient amid the thickening darkness, the outlander pressed, "I swore your oath of child-right in good faith! To deny my liberty is to hold me captive and enslaved." Undaunted, he challenged, "Accept my penance, or else risk unleashing your bowmen. Don't expect me to run for your wicked convenience. I won't brook the sacrifice, or abandon my pledge to a blameless infant, not to salve rankled community pride by an act of cold-blooded murder."

"Offspring sired by an untrustworthy parent are better off staked for the vultures! Your carcass also will be thrown to the scavengers by our lawful custom." Roaco lifted a slender black wand. Plumed tip brandished at the offender, he decreed in a rusty quaver, "We do not reprieve foreigners who flout our ways! Neither will a pittance of meat and pelts buy our leniency. Instead, for your arrogance, the offering becomes your widow's impoverished legacy."

The poised wand swept downward. Its death-whisper flutter of feathers brought tensioned gasps from the onlookers. Signalled, the archers drew their nocked shafts. Since no kinsman pleaded for the condemned, the villagers closed ranks and presented their backs. Twelve bow-strings twanged in release and let fly.

The outsider did not panic as the hail of arrows converged. Dusk obscured his expression. The clasped hands at his back never moved. Wary, the mage-sighted shamans detected no tell-tale, sly work of defence engaged through initiate mastery.

Yet the dozen shafts aimed at the devilsome foreigner glanced awry, scattered on harmless tangents into the forest behind. Against the staccato rattle of impacts, the wand in the Roaco's grip cracked in twain as an insolent, last retort.

Amid the stunned impasse, the sentenced man temporized, "I count the welfare of Vivet's child above your sentries' humiliation." Unfazed by the surge as the flustered attendants flocked to shield their spurned elder, the outlander capped his denouncement. "The bard's title I carry is a living record that interprets the nuance of law. Justice in Havish does not call a life forfeit for behaviour that has brought no harm!"

Roaco levelled a quivering finger. "The crown has no case and no standing, here! Not when you've threatened our people's security!"

"I have not!" Arin's exasperated rebuttal stirred the unsettled bystanders, and backed Roaco's bearers into an unnerved retreat. "The north vale has no pass to invite an invasion. What few hardy woodsmen fare up-country from Silvermarsh name you an inhospitable people, dangerously quick to draw blood. They take fearful care to steer clear of your territory, a habit my foray has not overturned. Further, I'll manage my own destiny through the encumbrance of Vivet's pregnancy. Be sure I'll rejoice to be quit of your claim when the infant I've sponsored reaches maturity."

The shaman's lackeys exchanged alarmed glances, while their master flipped back his cowl and shoved erect in his midnight mantle. Formidable despite egg-shell bones and frail balance, Roaco stepped from his sedan chair. The back-drop stir of the Ettinfolk quieted. Stillness gripped even the wind off the heights as the iconic figure of authority opened a line of arcane incantation.

"Don't!" the black-haired outsider warned. He never moved. Yet his stance in the thickening dark acquired the latent charge of a storm front.

Then, obscured from villagers' view, the broken wand cast at the feet of the shaman quivered and shuddered upright. The tassel of feathers lifted erect in defiance of gravity.

The initiate bearers exclaimed in shock.

"Save us!"

"He's accursed!"

"We've sheltered a fiend-bringer!"

"Execute the offender at once," the fourth one shouted, distraught. "He must die where he stands as an abomination!"

But Roaco deferred a public contest of strength. While the bystanders cowered in dread, he rebuked, "Past question, unbridled, you are a danger!"

The foreigner inclined his head, poised enough to stay reasonable. "As you say, I could be the rife thorn in your side. Choose wisely. You don't have to cross me."

While the left-handed bearer fumbled after a bane charm, the outlander whistled the threnody for fiendbane, pitched to a piercing crescendo. Screened from the curious villagers by the bulwark of the sedan chair, the upright stick with its bristling feathers toppled flat on the ground.

Which harmless overture foundered against a charged wall of cutthroat hostility. Roaco's filmed gaze raked Arin's person with a glare fit to freeze living flesh. Beyond negotiation, Ettinmere's master conjurer launched a probe aimed to drive the offensive bard to his knees.

Arin staggered. "Don't be a fool!" he snapped, his skilled voice pitched for the party bunched beside the sedan chair. Braced on planted feet, he did not counter Roaco's attack. Only moved: an innocuous gesture first perceived as a shrug brought his unclasped hands to the fore. He had stripped the wrapped cloth. Unveiled in the deepening night, the glimmering threat held all along in reserve: each exposed finger was gloved with an uncanny shimmer of blue-violet light.

Roaco smothered his conjured assault as though choked.

"Teaah's Breasts!" someone swore.

While a riled underling hissed through clenched teeth, the outlander gently listed his demands. "You must restore my liberty, and without question, unless you're still in doubt of your straits? I could make you a laughing-stock, and to no purpose, since I've no provocation as yet to upset your guarded existence."

Roaco received this, inwardly seething as pressurized magma clapped under a pot-lid.

For the deadlock presented a stark ultimatum: a thousand *iyats*, released on a thought, *would* evoke chaos enough to inundate his cabal's resources. The charms for fiendbane they carried were inadequate for a mass onslaught, and delay while they brought reinforcement would see the village savaged by the horde. Given the bard's whistle might effect a banishment straightaway, the Ettin shamans risked the loss of the people's respect, and the forfeit of their unquestioned standing.

Roaco's stymied fury quivered the coal plumage stitched to his mantle. "Do you think to survive as a larking fool with our hostile knives at your back?" Nonetheless, his clipped gesture dismissed the poised archers.

Arin ended the stand-off forthwith. He doused the glittering peril worn like jewellery under his cloak, then side-stepped his thwarted antagonists. The puzzled onlookers watched him stride past without a backwards glance.

Which uncivil retreat plucked the cranked string of a perilous, unresolved tension. Arin might actually command the ability to thrash Roaco and his colleagues in a contest of arcane strength; or else he went, clothed in bluster, daring them to call his bluff. This night's withdrawal was no truce, but a brittle suspension of overt hostilities. The laden sledge bearing the proof of his measure stayed at large: a careless sop for presumptive authority to claim in his wake.

Roaco spurned the lot outright, snatched his broken wand from the grip of a flummoxed underling, then settled into his sedan chair and snapped his imperious fingers. The archers formed ranks. His attendants scrambled as bidden to shoulder the poles and lift him aloft. They bore their aged shaman into the night without the flourish of a last pronouncement.

The stunned Ettinfolk inherited an emptied stage. They milled, uncertain, while bafflement erupted to indignation: the outsider's outrageous insolence had escaped both chastisement and just execution. Fists shook and talk circled, until the winter gusts numbed feet and pried through bundled clothing. Massed fury eroded as mothers cornered their fretful children and turned their dissatisfied husbands toward home. The Daldari kinfolk also broke away. Forced to take charge of the laden sledge before wild scavengers spoiled the contents, they shouldered the chore of salting and hanging the parcelled meat in the smoke-house.

Accounting of Vivet's household share fell to the Daldari grandfather, who assessed the raw furs with experienced hands. "These animals were deftly noosed and not punctured. None thrashed or suffered, besides. I find no chafed bald spots or tears from poor skinning. The pelts are first quality. Yon fellow's minded his duty, no matter we've no cause to like him."

The relatives gave over their grudging acceptance. If some were inclined towards lenience concerning their kinswoman's plight, none were mollified: for the maddening outsider had quit the scene and left them no ready target.

Vivet was alone when at length her provider reappeared at her cottage. Since doorways in Ettin were latched against nothing but storms and foraging mice, she spun to the soft, inbound step at her threshold, caught off guard as the panel creaked open.

Skirts flapped by the blast of cold air, she let fly in testy reaction. "Teeah's sweet mercy, you've wrung my nerves inside out and shown my family no courtesy."

"I have made my peace," said Arin, unruffled. "Your brothers saw fit to withdraw their threat to dissolve your household." Tangled hair as untamed as the night, he pinned his acute stare upon her and waited. The tallow dips fluttered and streamed greasy smoke: demonic lighting that exposed, unabashed, the purpose behind his arrival.

Fastidious, always, he had stripped to wash; was in fact dripping beneath his outlandish trapper's cloak. His white knuckles clenched a collection of straps: the doffed belt and sheathed knives slung over his shoulder. Where the briar-scraped leathers draped on his forearm had been brushed clean of mud, dried offal and blood stains fouled his breeches, small-clothes, and the shirt bunched under his opposite forearm. Nakedly shivering, he addressed her twice. Through her shocked paralysis, he tripled his request to make use of her iron cauldron.

Vivet remembered to breathe. He wanted to boil his rank clothing, of course. Her consent was required, his need to stay civilized the first break that his iron pride ceded to her advantage.

"Come in, then! Shut the door." Flustered to chills, Vivet blunted her unnatural surge of apprehension. He had no clue that her compromised future hinged on his domestic acceptance, or that she owed her primary allegiance against his interests. She arose from her spinning. Hoped he would overlook the mauled yarn, when she stepped to the hob and tipped the water pail into the pot. His wary regard like a knife at her back, she stirred up the coals and hung the filled vessel to heat.

Shortly, the hinge squeaked and the bitter draught ceased. Relief as the latch clinked galled her to scold, "You could have bathed under my roof in comfort." The brutal cold was a misery even for his stubborn spirit.

Arin denied her stab at sympathy and shed his belt, blades, and leathers into a heap a half step from the door-jamb. There, he poised, while the frail pause stretched like liquid glass drawn to its snapping point. She yielded first, and withdrew beyond reach. Barefoot, numbed bloodless by the chill, he still eschewed intimacy when he advanced. The bulky canvas coat obscured his slight frame as he seized the wooden paddle and immersed his soiled garments.

Vivet hoped he might soften enough to perch on her stool by the fireside.

But the prideful man skirted the braided rug and claimed the bare floor beside his wretched possessions. Tucked there, cross-legged, he mined the caped coat's flap pocket for a bone awl and a length of greased sinew. In relentless silence, he mended a tear in his trail-battered leathers.

Vivet stole furtive glances, praying the shadows would hide the untoward heat flaming her skin. Arin did not acknowledge her. Head bent, he stayed immersed in his work, while fire-light sharpened his angled cheek-bones and clean-shaved jaw, the toll of his alienation told over in sallow skin and lean flesh.

Which extreme independence overran sense. Vivet risked twisting the tail of the tiger. "You must be hungry. At least let me offer you something to eat."

His eyes flicked up, a spiked glint of sheared tourmaline. "With strings or without?"

"You'll need someone's shelter!" Vivet retorted. "Your high fettle won't stay upright on prickles for long, if you drive yourself to skin and bones. It's unfair to whet your annoyance on me. I never prompted my kinfolks' ill will, or set Roaco's disfavour against you."

His scorn slapped back like a ricochet. "Didn't you! In fact?" While she reeled, stung breathless, he added, "Which is the butterfly drawn to the flower, and which, the poised hand on the net? No!" he snapped as she filled her crushed chest. "Don't trouble to speak." His roughshod contempt trampled protest. "My trust is given, not steered. Someday, perhaps, your child may earn the right to ask for my confidence."

"Not if you succumb to malnourishment, first." Self-conscious of her ripening belly, Vivet slung the smaller pot onto the chain. Flame-light streaked gilt through her tumbled hair as she straightened, knuckles gouged into her

172

cramped lower back. "You don't want me beholden to Tanuay and my cousins? Then accept the need to keep yourself fit."

Arin jerked a tight stitch, broke his twine, and swore. "Debt to your relatives would strap me with the less tiresome complication." Yet this time, the jab reflected annoyance. Hostility quelled, he repaired his burst seam, while Vivet chopped onions and carrots on tenterhooks, and shredded a portion of salt meat. The meal simmered amid an armed quiet, while the droughts through the chinks breathed the scents of lye soap, steamed victuals, and the fust of the carded fleece readied for her drop spindle. Once the food had warmed through, better sense prevailed. Arin unbent and accepted a bowl and spoon from his helpmeet's hand.

But not enough to quell his recoil from her most casual touch. The enthrallment set on her spurred Vivet *to seek contact.* This near, the insatiable pressure woke urgency: to slide her hands under the obstructive canvas and caress his vulnerable, taut flesh. Knees weakened, she yearned to kiss his lips, until her pent-back, driven desire stripped her grip on restraint.

Just as desperately primed for evasion, Arin recoiled from her as though scalded.

"You hate me," she accused.

He glared back, exasperated. "Honestly? I prefer to feel nothing at all."

"That's not humanly possible." Vivet eyed the bowl he raised like a shield. In fact he was not as unmoved as he seemed. The spelled hook had set, well and deep in the viscera. Stymied under the force of the ensorcelled allure, she let balked passion fuel her argument. "No creature born into flesh lacks desire. Or heart. What makes you think you are different?"

His stare caught the sulphur flare of the coals. "Your shamans seem hellbound to argue the case."

"Well, you gave them a reason!" Vivet tossed back her chestnut hair, wrung to a sensuous gasp as his sight raked across the bare skin above her laced bodice. She reined in frayed composure, fought the relentless glamour enough to resume conversation. "Why make a display of your arcane talent if not for provocation?"

That snagged his unpleasant, riveted focus, as though sight alone could trace her inner thoughts and interpret her covert deceit. "You were not with the crowd to denounce me."

Vivet back-stepped, palms defensively raised. "A neighbour brought word. After all, your actions bear on my well-being. Tell me, what dire threat unnerved Roaco?"

Arin's twisted smile showed teeth. For the unadorned hands in plain view were quite ordinary: sculpted bone clothed in unremarkable flesh, chapped raw from exposure. "Are you still hot to bear my uncanny get?"

Her pinched lips went white, and her instinctive clasp laced her ripening belly. "The trapper's virile seed's the more likely. You know that."

The goad of his suppressed laugh stung too deep to choke back her embittered retort. "Damn all to my happiness, how you must detest me!"

"No." His quicksilver grin momentarily resurged. "But at least there's one point of agreement between us." He ate the meal, ravenous. Tousled head bowed over the food, he resembled a starveling waif. How easily forgotten the steel will that battled his entangled fate, no matter the sinister strategy aimed to noose him to a cause without quarter.

Vivet's anguished loneliness must have betrayed her. For his knitted brows rose, guileless with a surprise that curdled to irony. "Did you actually think I could relish the pinch of the oath your condition's laid on me?"

Vivet gave at the knees and claimed the vacant stool. "I daresay you've left little slack for debate." In need of a rescue, she snatched up the knife, rummaged for the soap cake, and carved off a generous dollop. Then she laid claim to the paddle, stirred up the suds, and began to pound the ingrained soil out of his laundry. "You mock even the pretence of goodwill when you insult blameless strangers. Why should you flaunt your contempt of our matrons?"

"Ah!" His expression settled, though not his keen survey, which bored through the puffed steam that polished her fecund bloom under exertion. "By all means, let's belabour the obvious. Your culture's coercion has secured my guardianship for the sake of your threatened child. I'll grant that the babe is entitled to live. But no Ettin custom, and no lustful indulgence on your part can trade on a newborn's survival for my affection."

Yet his reserve has been challenged: the instant before he returned to his meal, his gaze lingered upon the luxurious mass of her auburn hair. Desperation, more than indifference, armoured his adamant reserve. Close quarters over the winter would build up the pressure of intimate contact. Vivet meant to pry through his defenses, no matter the means or the cost. Though not tonight, with his temper glass-brittle with fight and exhaustion. Since he had breached her threshold at last, she granted what solace she might at safe distance.

When he scraped his bowl, she retired to her spinning, which enticed him to cross the room for a second portion. Food left him replete, enough to venture a trip to the hearth to add a log to the fire. Heat infused the small cabin. Likely warm for the first time in weeks, Arin succumbed to drowsiness. In time, his head nodded. Black hair curtained the curve of shut eyelids before Vivet dared to retrieve his used crockery.

When Arin failed to arouse, she stole the liberty to ease the spoon from his slackened grasp. Then she rinsed his clothes and hung them to dry. Lest he react to the further effrontery of covering him with a blanket, she left him wrapped in his disreputable coat.

Sleep allowed what his waking awareness rejected: her undisturbed survey measured his skinned knuckles and scrapes, and the squint lines etched by the glare of the snow-fields. His fingers seemed too fine for their office, nipped raw by the cold, with the hang-nail on his thumb altogether too poignantly human. Nothing suggested the inexplicable power that had stood down Roaco's ultimatum.

Vivet's allure *was* the tailored entrapment to snare this unlikely foreigner. Whether her mission brought ruin, or unravelled her worldly peace, the play for his spirit was joined. Since the attempted seduction begun in the woodland cabin, Vivet's aching desire built momentum. Release was impossible while the engaged imprint imposed upon her inflamed them both.

An unannounced rap at the door broke Vivet's reverie. Irritable, she cursed the intrusion. But the man in her charge did not stir when her impudent cousin cracked the shut panel.

"Brought something sent by the family. Came off the sledge. Since no one's laid claim, uncle's said this belongs here with Arin." The message ended with a resonant bump, as the boy propped a bundle that housed something wooden and hollow beside the entry. "I'm also to say that your tally is met. You'll have two shares of millet from the common harvest. If your man brings a second haul in before solstice, you'll merit a draw from the stores. Also a wagon to haul your household belongings down country to the lower vale."

Reprieved from indenture, Vivet dismissed the boy and snuffed the candles. Rather than risk awakening Arin, she left the delivery where it lay. After brushing her hair, she conceded defeat, banked the fire, and retired to bed.

She woke once in the night, alone in the sheets. Arin's dried clothing was gone, and the floor by the door-jamb lay vacant. A barefoot foray across the cold cabin confirmed that the covered object had been collected. Arin had left without leaving a trace. Or so Vivet thought, as she huddled in her blanket and opened a shutter to the windy dark.

The gusts tossing the firs also winnowed the sprightly notes of a lyranthe. Her breath stopped. Captivated by the musician's artistry, she listened, astonished, as carousing voices joined the plucked measures and belted into a raucous chorus. Vivet shivered, exiled from the convivial circle while the bard who disowned the grace of her womanhood claimed his place with the settlement's people.

Implications

Immersed in the reactive stream of the flux in the fast safety of Althain Tower, Elaira lies wakeful and weeps, aware of the desolation behind the bard's rollicking performance; worse, her heart aches for the spellbound attraction to Vivet, which impels Arithon's resolve to leave Ettinmere in the bitter hours before dawn . . .

"The glamour on the woman might be excessive," the scryer suggests, her temerity scorned when the Prime Matriarch laughs: "Quite the contrary! If the changeling imprint taken from Elaira fails to conceive a child suitable for my succession, Arithon's avoidance of Vivet's charms will seek solace in solitude and increase our chance to destroy him . . ."

Fey eyes distant with vision, Siantra shudders with the echoed after-shock seeded by Vivet's unnatural lust, and in a frightened conference with Tarens admits, "I know why she matters. The glamour frames an insidious trap, unimaginably dangerous! In spite of the storms that mire the passes, you must risk taking immediate action on Arithon's behalf . . ."

VI. Interval

The black chill before dawn seized the world with a cruelty to suck marrow from bone and curdle moist breath into steam, which pale plume flagged the outlander's presence behind the smoke-house. Doubly annoyed and almost too late, Tanuay Daldari kindled a torch and collared his evasive target, whose furtive activity centred upon his reclaimed drag sledge.

"You meant to sneak off with no one the wiser," Vivet's brother accosted, braced for a caustic retort.

Drenched in sulphurous light as the oiled rags flared, the disreputable canvas coat flapped to its owner's shrug. "The tame ass upbraiding the obstinate donkey? Don't think I'll be haltered to braying conformity." Bare head a blot of spilled ink where he knelt, Arin blew on his fingers and secured the ties holding a parcel bundled in blankets: the lyranthe acquired on his venture outside since no sober household had use for the frivolous instrument. Rightfully, he refused to entrust his frail possession to the winter exodus, jumbled among Vivet's kettles and furnishings.

Tanuay's resentment poisoned the air without any further word spoken.

His irritant target refused to cringe but finished the knots and straightened up with unhurried forbearance. "Ah, don't bother to bristle! The badgering thrust to your chin says your hate's large enough to rub shoulders with a pariah. Why tinker with truce on the pretence?"

"The elders sent me." Tanuay squared off, hostile eyes gimlet-bright. "I'm meant to suggest they may have misappraised your intent to shirk Vivet's upkeep."

The outlander returned stare for stare, his sardonic expectancy self-contained as a provocation. "You look stiff as the nipple on Teeah's divine tits. The brute reflex of chill, not the blush of seduction. Tell me, what flings a hypocrite's mealy-mouthed peace at the feet of the unregenerate?"

The blasphemy sparked a brief, vicious pause, while Tanuay gripped rowelled nerves in rank bitterness. "Your champion is the Daldari granddame, who suggested that highly skilled music is not the pursuit of a layabout. She's also acknowledged you could contribute to the common weal through your trapping. For the family's benefit, therefore, I've brought you some fur boots, and hide mittens lined with knit wool."

"After all, I can't serve Vivet's needy child if I'm crippled from frost-bite?" But the scorched bite of satire was eased by a smile of gratitude.

The genuine reverse threw Tanuay aback. "What perversity rides you? Why should your cavalier treatment of my sister mock even the pretence of affection?" Chiselled with reflection, the brother's hawk glare awaited an honest reaction. When his polite question earned no response, Tanuay gouged for the viscera. "If her child is not your regrettable by-blow, what do you gain? Did Vivet never warn you? Any standing she once had became forfeit when she left for her feckless adventure down country."

"If she held my esteem, and if her offspring owns even a wishful tie to my name, be certain if I'd known your ways in advance, I'd have counselled her to forsake your people. What sort of family treats daughters like chattel? Or exposes a naked newborn to die? *I have no shame?*" The outlander's wide-lashed regard showed astonishment. "Dare to say again that your sister deserves contempt, and I will turn my back on this festering place. Vivet may stay on as she chooses. But for kindness, I will take her child away to be raised in free air without prejudice."

Tanuay bridled. "Roaco will never—"

Retort sheared his protest. "Dharkaron's black vengeance strike your vile shamans! And any man here who cages strangers and justifies the slaughter of blameless infants. Don't try the mistake. I will draw blood without remorse and pitch the murderous lot unrepentant to Sithaer."

As though the vitriolic boast was not madness, the outlander sat on the sledge. He removed his inadequate, patched summer boots, then donned the greased sheepskin replacements one foot at a time, just like any man. The shadows cast by the torch carved his slender build into a child's, vulnerable under his cross-belted knife and the bulky, rag-market coat.

"Don't tangle further with Roaco," Tanuay blurted, wrenched to unwonted pity.

Animosity could not dismiss, quite, those exquisite hands, coarsely muffled in mittens. The foreigner had raised no unjust complaint: clearly he had proved his claim to an honourable livelihood. Ettinmere's virtues dismissed refined music. The Daldari elders lacked the background to grasp the gifts of the minstrel thrust into their midst. Until tonight's performance exposed that mistake, the slighted voice of an astonishing talent made Tanuay cringe with embarrassment.

Which pinprick of conscience found no relief, except to break the frozen silence. "The shamans' power is unspeakably dangerous. You have earned their undying fury by crossing them. Flaunt your contempt, and they have no other recourse except to destroy you."

The outlander fastened the wrist loops on the mittens before he responded. "I've found them overbearing, disrespectful of anything outside their stultified briar patch."

"We are not insular without reason. At your peril, continue to mock us as bumbling fools." Tanuay recoiled upon surly dignity, his hatchet nose fogged by a huffed breath. "The shamans' tradition protects an ancient secret with dangerous roots. Wisest for you not to trifle with matters outside your experience."

Restored to combative humour, the outlander's retort shamed the weasel. "I care for nothing beyond the survival of Vivet's infant. Since I won't endorse murder, beware of the thicket and thorn. If Roaco's familiars and everyone else honours my obligation, nobody needs to end up licking wounds." Coarsely gloved, the deceptive foreigner gathered the sledge straps and harnessed them crosswise over his shoulders. "Please pass along my regard to your granddame. Tell her in nice language I'll return before the last wagon is packed for the exodus, and by all means, go on and keep blinding yourself, post-sitting that useless torch."

Finished with discourse, the outlander went, his huge coat swallowed into the tar-pit of night. Tanuay frowned, flummoxed, until the gad-fly sting behind Arin's last rejoinder struck home: the crude sledge had no socket to secure a cresset. Whoever the man had been, whatever background he came from, his mockery implied the uncanny vision possessed by initiate mages. Whether his brazen hint was made for intimidation or the cock-sure warning of frightening strength, he ventured the hazards of the mountain wilds without need to carry a light.

Elaira aroused to Sethvir's warm clasp on her shoulder. Fallen into tranced vision beside the snuffed candle, her cheek pillowed on an open book, she refocused under the Sorcerer's touch, her wandered spirit eased back into breathing flesh. The pre-dawn chill in the Storlains receded, the pitch tang of balsam replaced by the fust of antique parchment and ink. Althain Tower's mighty defences embraced her, cased in the shelved silence of historical record and the bulwarked endurance of centaur masonry. The stone tower constantly whispered and rang, singing to the tide of the flux under starlight, and the charged pulse of Paravian wards.

"The hearth-fire's burned out," Althain's Warden said gently. His will sparked the dribbled candle stub back into wavering flame. "I suggest a warmer setting downstairs might ease the ache in your ankle?"

"Thank you." Mending bone twinged as the enchantress arose. She winced, braced against the obsidian table. "Another storm is sweeping off the north heath?"

Sethvir's glance was lucent as dawn sky. "More than one." But the earth-sensed perception behind that oblique comment stayed vague as he offered his hand.

Elaira accepted the gallantry, dumb-struck again by the strength self-contained behind his bird-boned frailty. She walked in the presence of quiescent peril. Framed in frangible flesh, the vast reach of an ageless spirit *almost* appeared tamed: until the moment that harmless, human warmth felt like staring unblinkered into the sun. "How dangerous are the Ettinmere shamans?"

Sethvir peered down his long nose. "Did you know," he remarked in congenial obfuscation, "that after Kharadmon became discorporate, research posed him an obdurate nuisance?"

"That spirit doesn't deflate his annoyances," Elaira agreed with a grin. "What happened?"

"Chaos." Sethvir's sidewise glance sparkled with glee. "He laid a wee cantrip onto the library, an animate working responsive to thought. The invocation summoned the volumes he required without any need to search for them by hand. We had books scuttling hither and yon like singed cats, until Luhaine's miffed complaints over damages called for a stay of restraint." The Warden paused, nonplussed as a book toppled from the upper shelf and smacked onto the floor, pages riffling.

Sethvir peered down at the windfall, and mused, "Apparently under certain, particular circumstance, the feckless construct still functions."

Elaira eyed the wayward volume with alarm. "What's changed? Does Asandir's oath of nonintervention no longer apply to Prince Arithon's fate?"

"Assuredly, your Prime's restriction still hobbles our Fellowship's choice in full force." Sethvir shrugged, his sly gaze direct. "But the walls here are shielded by Paravian wards, under the command of a spirit that's dangerously sentient. The binding that marshals the books in this case was engaged by Shehane Althain. If the Koriani Matriarch wishes to challenge this tower's primary guardian? Purely for the mayhem, I'd escort her over the threshold myself."

Reassured by the Sorcerer's daft humour, Elaira pounced on the gift and translated the faded ink of the chapter's caption. "A list of hostels maintained by Ath's Adepts, circa Third Age 1450. That's curious."

Sethvir's triangular smile peeped through the cumulus cloud of his beard. "Isn't it?" His chuckle echoed through the hiss of oiled hinges as he flung open the iron-bound postern. "Mind the hazard, my dear. Plagued by Kharadmon's erratic phenomenon, you don't want to trip."

Elaira yelped in delight, marked the page with her finger, and gimped at the Sorcerer's heels down the draughty stairwell.

The chapter contained an entry for Ettinmere, by then established for a thousand years as a White Brotherhood hostel. Training as a Koriani healer at Forthmark gave Elaira a first-hand appreciation of the reactive power endowed in such sites, even though the adepts had abandoned their tenancy. A prepotent resonance lingered in the stones that enhanced spellcraft long after the rituals sealed off the portals to access the mysteries from their inner sanctuaries.

Elaira parked the leather-bound tome in her lap, cold despite the guest suite's exquisite coverlet. A severance by the white brotherhood was never made without exigent forethought: *always* they disabled the ephemeral forces entrained by their arts before they departed.

Yet, what if Ettinmere proved the exception?

Her stay at Whitehaven had revealed the huge reservoir held under a brotherhood enclave's command. She had crossed the guarded threshold and experienced the volatile intersection of living potential and individual consciousness. The instantaneously translated response, where mortal thoughts quickened virgin energy had personified wilful intent with ruthless precision. Nurtured under the farsighted wisdom of the adepts' active stewardship, those hostels in current use contained uncanny pathways through the half-world of dreams. They cultivated whole existences spun from the banked flame of pooled power, called down from the purity of the prime source, then held in latent potential.

The mere possibility Ettinmere's hostel may have been wrested from the Brotherhood's vigilance upset her peace of mind and murdered the prospect of sleep. Elaira shoved off the blankets and pulled on chilled clothes. Past the slit window, the light-print on snow cast from an illumined arrow-slit above suggested Althain's Warden remained wakeful over who knew what greater conundrum. Elaira sparked the candle on the pricket. She left the guest suite and mounted the icy, dark stair, while the moan of the draughts frayed the flame sheltered behind her cupped palm.

Six floors above, she combed the catalogued archives for entries referenced to Ettinmere. If no volume fell at her feet, two drawers that indexed the Third Age at the turn of the fifth millennium, and another, three thousand years earlier, flopped open to cogent suggestions. She thanked Shehane Althain under her breath, refreshed her taper, and repaired to the upstairs stacks for the prompted titles.

When dawn brightened the chunk glass leaded into the arrow-slit, Elaira confronted the evidence that the Ettin hostel of Ath's adepts indeed had revoked the precepts of their tradition.

She stewed over the reason until the next day, when an aumbry door unlatched by itself and creaked open. A book thumped out, barely missing her wrist as she ransacked Sethvir's untidy baskets for heavy waxed thread. The open page scribed in Paravian runes bespoke the pen of a centaur guardian. Ripped leathers forgotten, Elaira sat. Light filtered through the eider-down snow on the sill exposed her crestfallen frustration.

The archaic writing was beyond her knowledge to translate.

"Deathless havoc!" she swore. "Where under sky can I garner the resource?"

The shout echoed off stone. Brushed by an inchoate shudder of dread, Elaira prickled with the dreadful suspicion she was no longer alone. Too late, primal fear screamed in warning of a wakened power beyond her imagining.

Then a diamantine blast of fire exploded across her awareness. Dazzled out of her senses, all but deaf and blind, she glimpsed the impression of a massive, antlered form looming over her. The unknowable presence blurred, wrapped in radiance and sound pure enough to pulverize flesh. The resonance tapped bone and burst mortal heart-strings. Smashed like glass by the chime of ecstatic joy, Elaira reeled as a lifetime's discipline shredded away. She did not hear Sethvir arrive at a run, or feel his arms catch her fall. Subsumed by the mighty surfeit of grace, she plunged into black-out unconsciousness.

Elaira awakened, harrowed by amplified senses. The roaring hiss of a nearby candleflame deafened her with the force of a gale-wind, and the weave of the bed-linens branded her skin with the imprint of every loomed thread. Bewildered sight shimmered, with everyday objects rainbowed by dazzling haloes.

Her alarmed outcry raised hurtful echoes, until someone's masterful word quelled the storm. Peace wrapped her. A Sorcerer's ephemeral touch stroked her lids closed, then cupped her cheek tenderly as a moth's wing until her overcharged nerves settled out of revolt.

"What happened?" she asked, and winced at the thunder of her own voice.

"*Be still. All is well.*" Sethvir's response disturbed nothing, silent as a trans-mitted thought. "*You are not sick or damaged. Only ridden by a natural back-lash from being touched by the tower's guardian spirit.*"

"Shehane Althain?" Her whisper reverberated like a dropped cymbal. "I transgressed?"

"*Certainly not!*" Sethvir's reassurance soothed her with amusement. "*Your spontaneous craving for knowledge was answered. Though just now, the result may not feel like a gift. You'll need time to adjust.*"

Elaira shifted, her limbs unwieldy as lichened granite.

"*Sleep will speed your recovery,*" Sethvir advised. "*Might you allow me?*"

Her grateful assent melted her into a dreamless rest.

Hunger roused her. Elaira opened her eyes to bright sunlight, reflected off snowfall and sliced keen as a knife-cut across the counterpane. Althain Tower's guest suite surrounded her, its antique tapestries woven with trees, and Narms carpet patterned in aqua and gold spread across the slate floor. A birch fire burned in the hearth, and a tray on the brass-cornered chest at the bedside held cream, an unlikely bowl of summer blackberries, and fragrant tea, buttered honey, and toast.

The commingled barrage of fragrances transported her senses.

Elaira ate, astonished first by her steady hands, then startled to delight. Food had never tasted so glorious, the flavours enhanced to marvellous complexity. An enriched perception remade everything with the zest of a renewed experience. She attacked her meal, famished, then lay back on the pillows, replete.

Inevitably, then, her reverie turned inward. Cognizance encountered the scope of the knowledge delivered by Shehane Althain. Nor was she alone when the impact of epiphany broke her illusion of peace.

Althain's Warden sat by the hearth, arrived like an uncanny secret. He had lurked without notice for quite some time: one of her stockings lay draped on his knee, the frayed knit seamlessly darned.

"Mending your clothes is a poor consolation," he remarked with apology. Clad in maroon wool with black-velvet interlace at cuffs and shoulders, Sethvir looked tired, eyes of faded turquoise couched in deep lines by two ages of tribulation.

Before Elaira shoved upright, he objected. "Be still!"

Flattened by vertigo, Elaira let fly, "I feel like my skull's been turned to tapped glass and shaken to splitting. How do you live here without going mad?"

Sethvir's features crinkled with laughter. "Luhaine always claimed I've been moonstruck." Paused, his head tipped askance, his mild regard became piercing. "Shehane Althain never reacts without purpose." The Sorcerer's survey peeled through her uncertainty and finished with an arched eyebrow. "If my preference mattered, I would count your comfort above everything else."

Which tacit confidence confirmed that the stone-graven oath at Whitehold hobbled his might. Brutal stakes attended the burden laid on Elaira. Sethvir waited with riveted patience, while she weighed the appalling degree of Arithon's peril, subject to Ettinmere's shamans.

For history's tap-root ran deeper than the records of the Third Age. The rogue enclave had not revoked their White Brotherhood's precepts at whim. Long before the original hostel's foundation, the volatile flux in the Storlains had been imbalanced by a drake war. Stabilized since by Athera's Paravians, Sunchildren and centaur guardians, both, had mitigated the stress that collided at the intersection of the continent's major fault-lines. When the old races faded, Ettin's adepts had to choose whether to uphold the passive tenet of their order or to shoulder the worldly burden. If no steadfast power acted, the unmanaged release of tectonic forces might shatter the backbone of the five kingdoms.

Brows tucked, the enchantress voiced her concern. "Arithon must realize the arcana those shamans wield is no trifle." Though rapport could not inform him directly through Elaira's experience, mage-sighted awareness should recognize a power not sourced by Athera's flux. Surely that detail ought to make him chary. "Unless he exposes their cabal's secret, he likely can't guess the reservoir hoarded by the ancients is limited."

"Don't misjudge Torbrand's temper," Sethvir warned. "Caution won't curb his Grace's fury against them. Under a crown prince's ethic, he can't, if the shamans should cross the grain of the s'Ffalenn royal gift."

Elaira grasped that appalling peril. "If Arithon's provoked into an open contest, or if he stumbles through their protections and encounters the site of the original hostel, you believe they'll defend their ground at the cost of his life?"

For the derelict sanctuary had been sealed off by the brotherhood's adepts to preserve the sanctity of their network from the rogue faction. The severance of the etheric portals had doomed the fair works of millennia to attrition, a thunder-clap echo that yet resounded through Sethvir's presentday earth-sense.

"My dear," the Sorcerer allowed with regret, "the choice to leave your beloved at risk must rest in your hands alone."

"Perhaps," said Elaira. "But the Ettinfolk don't realize whom they shelter."

Sethvir answered without reassurance. "The heirloom sword his Grace bears would be recognized, should the weapon fall under scrutiny." Constraint forbade him from the disclosure of royal identity's advantage or detriment. "Should your prince come to grips, if he isn't killed outright, he would assuredly rattle far worse than the branch that harbours their hornets' nest."

Elaira weighed the oblique implications, pinned under Sethvir's expressionless regard in the ice-fall of light through the casement. "And if Ettin fails?" She skirted the precipice, "If the shamans' remnant legacy breaks under Arithon's will, you infer the subsequent, untamed release may cause both major fault-lines to rupture?"

Sethvir disclaimed nothing. Could not, where no margin existed. His Fellowship must destroy Rathain's prince before such a disaster threatened Athera's integrity. Else forsake the bound charge of the dragons, which secured Paravian survival above all else.

The cruel conclusion fell to Elaira. "The life of my beloved, balanced against humanity's continued existence?"

The Warden of Althain bowed his head, aggrieved. "Our choice is proscribed, should Mankind's rambunctious ignorance tip the balance. This continent nurtures the heart of Athera. The etheric web that upholds the mysteries cannot withstand the shock of another grand cataclysm."

Distress wrung Elaira to pallor. "Another?"

"Oh yes." Sethvir's sigh ruffled his beard. "Thrice, the weal of the world has been fractured. Always by dragons, though Grace of Ath, just once in our time, and thankfully never in the Third Age under the compact's constraint." His dread simmered unspoken, concerning the dire unrest of the exiled drakes beyond Northgate. "Prime Selidie's aware of the harrowing crux. The plot she's spear-headed through Vivet has many threads, all of them woven through Arithon's fate to our calamitous detriment."

Elaira drew a vexed breath. "Is this a plea to break Arithon's trust? Are you urging me to resolve the sealed memories I guard to deny the Koriathain the unscrupulous leverage of our relationship?"

"I ask nothing," Sethvir declared in discomfort, his eyes lucent with pity. "You required to know, given your vision has been unsealed by Shehane Althain's directive. Whether as a boon or for warning, I am not at liberty to say. But how you keep faith with your handfast prince steers the precarious outcome."

Elaira punched the mattress and swore, until smothered laughter crinkled Sethvir's face and caught her short. The fragmented memory resurfaced, of a lonely night on a foggy shingle at Narms. There, Traithe had offered her kindly advice across a drift-wood fire. "If I should fail my beloved," she recited, "or should Arithon fail me, the result will call down disaster."

"Quite." Sethvir's levity died. He stood up in closure and poked up the spent logs that glimmered in the hearth. "Though you'll find you can't hurry your convalescence. If you hoped to bolt for Davien's den at Kewar, by evening, winter will close the north harbours." A desperate, last respite from the True Sect sword, for the hounded clan survivors put to flight under Saroic s'Gannley's protection: but the saving, mailed ice that choked passage across Instrell Bay would cage Elaira at Althain Tower until spring.

The storm presaged by Sethvir's earth-sense howled in with a fury that choked Tysan's sunset in sackcloth cloud and muffled the fells of Atainia in cotton drifts. Raging, the blizzard raked Rathain's free wilds and rampaged unspent against the cragged Mathorns. Its aftermath cracked trees and smothered both trade-road and river-course, and left the great firs and massive oaks bowed beneath crusted hoods. Hush battened the vales, while relentless cold halted the True Sect's eastern campaign in Halwythwood.

Chased by starvation, The Hatchet marched his frost-bitten companies from the field and quartered them to nurse their chilblains in shelter at Morvain, Narms, and Etarra.

For Arithon Teir's'Ffalenn, enmeshed in the Prime Matriarch's cat-and-mouse game-play at Ettin, the winter danced him through the artful steps of guarded avoidance. While his threat of rogue *iyats* forced the shamans' enmity to a stand-off, trapping for Vivet's upkeep required extended trips into the high country. The brutal cold and remote terrain at least granted him the needful solitude to redress his fragmented memory. Or so he believed, camped under the stars in the quiet between blizzards. He doused his wood fire, determined to tap his deep self-awareness through mage-trained discipline.

But the visions that flowered revealed Sunwheel war hosts and the horrors of battle-fields heaped with windrows of dead. Either the vistas had resurged from his past experience, or if they portrayed a glimpse of an unwritten future, Arithon lacked any means to discern. The initial effort left him dizzy and heaving. The after-shock felt like a violation. As though he had been stalked and covertly ambushed amid an etheric trance. He sounded the flux currents lightly. If no night-spying owl flew within range, the suspicion persisted that something stealthy watched still, just beyond his ephemeral awareness.

Unease stole his sleep. The fierce impulse to unsheathe the black sword he wore only outside the bounds of the village raised gooseflesh. He minded the warning. A blade whose defences raised ancient enchantments would attract more than quaint curiosity. Best to avoid such untoward attention until he mapped the source of the shamans' empowerment.

Daybreak failed to lift Arithon's apprehension. Arisen at first light, he turned out his pack, then reinspected his meagre belongings. He found the attached talisman wired onto the struts bracing the runner of his drag sleigh. He left the unclean construct alone; spent a day at the timberline constructing another sled with gut sinew and pegs. Then he stashed the compromised gear with his pelts in a cave, and moved on with the replacement.

And still, he snapped awake in the night, brushed by the uncanny awareness a watcher defiled his dreams.

A more rigorous search flagged the subtle spell inlaid in a button sewn onto a shirt that Vivet had mended. Tempted as he was to bury the token under a pile of offal, tracking charms were a fell craft, never to be treated lightly. Rather than endanger a blameless scavenger, or reveal his schooled knowledge, Arithon contrived a clumsy spill on his sleeve, and under the pretence of cleanliness, boiled the construct in an infusion of cedar bark.

Alhough he hung the sopped cloth to dry for two days, scoured in wind and sunlight, the itch of cat's nerves still dogged him. Arithon minded his workaday business, beyond careful to guard his steps. His ruffled faculties proved to be warranted: returned in disquiet, he discovered the ensorcelled hook in the button had failed to dissolve. Which pernicious integrity fed his reluctance to fathom its nature. Sounding the unknown pattern might lend its maker the opening to read him. He discarded the obvious counter-measure. If he neutralized the button in the poke of raw salt brought to field-cure his skins, his thwarted antagonists were hell-bound to try a more devious invocation.

Presumed ignorant, he could wear his unfriendly pursuit to cross-eyed boredom, then shed the offensive button into running water through a careless scrape while crossing a streamlet. The need for such obstructive restraint cramped far more than his spirit. He had not foreseen the inflexible threat, or imagined the brutal patience required to shield his anonymity. While the cold-blooded ploys to disarm his opponents compromised his free movement, Arithon faced the gravity of his mistake. The delicate game of appeasement to comply with the settlement's hidebound laws now entangled him in the murky practice of Ettinmere's shamans.

Ettinvale, where Vivet's folk wintered over, nestled into a gorge that snaked down to the basin of a thermal crater. Steam vents and geysers belched plumes of mist, puffed and coiled and clumped into wool bats that lidded the snow-clad peaks. The mizzle of cloud pocketed the hothouse humidity, and spilled moisture like floss down the flanks of the slopes. Year-round, the peat soil at the valley floor wore the velvet of greensward. Grazed milch cows gleamed, sleeked with buttery fat, and speckled trout leaped in the rain-fed pools, plentiful and quick to strike.

Solstice released the austere custom of contemplation and silence imposed throughout the long nights. The children's exuberance scattered echoes amid the nasal honks of the flocking geese. Like an emerald jewel bezelled in ice, the haven tamed the harsh weather in comfort, while piled drifts mantled and corniced the Storlains, and ferocious cold drove the creatures in the high wilds to dormancy.

The season did not abate quietly, even as the air freshened towards spring. Equinox brewed the most fickle storms, when the overburdened snowpack posed the lethal danger of avalanche. Forays up-country to trap became stalled.

For Elaira, hardened to the bitter ennui that gripped winter's end in the Storlains, the gales that smothered the peaks were no match for the slow suffocation of her unnatural estrangement. Disquiet rode her helpless vigil, until her secure haven at Althain Tower enfolded her like a tissue of dream. No toppled books shed light on the qualities imbued in the Biedar knife. Whether the artifact might stem the tempest brewed by the Prime Matriarch's meddling, Sethvir provided no counsel. Not with Arithon's fate snagged on the prong of the shamans' fixated interest.

The Teir's'Ffalenn bided, alert and inscrutable. Music allowed him to spend his nights wakeful, badgered by company eager to teach him Ettin's traditional roundelays. By day, laughing, he joined the rambunctious pursuits of the young: the manic feats contrived with goat-drawn sledges, the hurley games played at strenuous speed on black ice, and the cutthroat bets over archery contests that fleeced the inept. For a while, rough sport released his pent frustration and glazed the rapt eyes of the shamans.

But sunlight returned and dissolved the sulphurous fog. Blue sky ushered in the melt-song of thaws and burst the iced rungs of the freshets. Overnight, the frozen lace froth of the falls exploded into roaring cataracts. As early spring bird-song resurged with the snowdrops, Arithon confronted the trial of Vivet's confinement. By Ettin tradition, a birth was not private but regaled in communal ceremony.

When the expectant mother's time neared, the sire who claimed child-right became ousted from his warm bed by his rowdy male peers. Carried or dragged, then tossed from hand to hand, he would be pummelled into mock submission, to ribald advice and teasing laughter. The villagers relished their celebration of apprehensive, new fatherhood.

Yet Arithon was not to be taken off guard, or found naked in the marital sheets. Snatched while fully clothed, seated for a late supper, he suffered for the evasive affront dealt out to his Daldari relations. Sly kicks and punches landed in the scuffle, masked under the shadows cast by the streamed torches. If his hecklers trounced him without obvious damage, Arithon's ribs were bruised underneath sturdy clothing stressed to frayed seams. The hitched winces, however bravely suppressed, made even the toothless grand-uncles snigger.

No one looked askance at hard feelings. The waylaid victim was expected to mope. Evicted without shelter, his home quarters crammed with the expectant mother's relations, the young man was meant to bond with the community and earn the mercy of his companions.

Headstrong s'Ffalenn pride instead staked out the turf to do battle.

At Althain Tower, Elaira howled, forewarned by that signature flare of will. "Give in, you rank fool! Make your token show of surrender and let them embrace you in brotherhood."

But no such temperance restrained Arithon, dislocated from his preferred lifestyle and exiled in bleak isolation.

He carved a bone needle and mended his abused clothes. If his odd, sail-hand's whip-stitch raised tittering scorn, the outcome passed muster. Badgered in form to shoulder the chores that his woman relinquished for her lying-in, Rathain's prince spent a fortnight peeling potatoes and boiling hides. At female behest, he fetched water and washed reeking clouts for bawling Daldari infants.

No scatheful ribbing spurred him to complaint. He did all that was asked. But compliant resistance just stiffened the matrons, who saddled him with the unsavoury task of cleaning hog casings for sausage. He bent his back sweating over a boiling salt bath in a kettle, while around him, chattering, large women with reddened hands minced the cold pork with fat and spiced the congealed mix in iced buckets. The quips flew, denouncing his stature, with smirks at his reserved manhood sufficient to scald a flush on a deaf-mute.

"Did you hear the whispers?" the boldest one ventured, since their scorn failed to bait him. "That even when sober, the foreigner's member is limp as his tongue? For sure, to enliven the breeding, Vivet must have laced his broth with raw mussels."

Which comment scorched a bit too near the bone for Arithon's nettled indifference. Like the stalking cat sprung, he attacked, "Why tarnish the incentive? Your remarks are quick to imply Vivet's charm is ill-favoured. Forgetting all self-respect, could you value the mate who'd rut with a dog to prove his prowess?"

The gossip monger paused with her flensing knife lifted. "Do tell. Own up. Vivet's get is not yours?"

Arithon stared her malice full in the face. "Oh, yes, the coming child is mine!" Circled by smouldering silence, he smiled. "Why else should I abide this noisome task, or field spite from closed minds of low character?"

The curdled atmosphere failed to erupt, only because a runner arrived with the breathless news Vivet's birth water had broken. Natural sire, or claimant by child-right, the outlander bowed to the summons. The grumbling matrons took over his work, in no haste to bestow their attendance. Labour with a firstborn extended for hours. Given his scalding cheek, and the spurning of kinfolk, the settlement's new father might as well suffer his miserable vigil alone with the family.

Yet the prospect of a prolonged obligation posed Arithon's least thorny difficulty. More than apprehension mired his step down the muddy path through the settlement. Also raked over the coals of his turmoil, Elaira fumbled her tea-cup in the distant sanctary of Althain Tower.

The crash of dropped porcelain shattered her nerves.

She picked the fragments from her soaked hem, knowing: her Teir's'Ffalenn would never choose the wise course and forsake the child claimed by his compassion. He went, harrowed by the redoubled danger that birthings at Ettin commanded a shaman's presence.

The shack his low station afforded was small, an oblong box built of logs, the sloped roof of stringers and slats sealed with bog turf. Steam off the mineral springs sagged the timbers, splotched with a patina of lichen. The warped front stair jammed the swing of the door, wedged open to admit fresh air. Arithon's wary approach salvaged nothing. Every female relation not squeezed inside had gathered without, a gamut that seemed to include every matron not currently rendering pork. Met by pursed lips, he expected no quarter: not since the brutal ferocity used to defend his mauled privacy.

The packed bodies enveloped him at the threshold. Inside, every available bench, chair, and cranny was occupied. Glow from the hearth burnished flesh in relief and swathed the corners in shadow. Beyond escape, Arithon seized the challenge and with a Masterbard's grace, greeted the Daldari matriarch.

She rebuffed him with silence. Estranged beneath his own roof, with fine irony, he breasted an atmosphere of antipathy thick enough to cut with a knife. The breathed air cloyed his lungs. The hot-iron tang of the kettle and the bite of astringent herbs turned his senses as he forged into the press. Arrived at the bedchamber, he steeled himself and went in.

Darkness and heat smothered him like a blanket, fecund with the scents of birthing and sweat, and the pungent offerings burned by the shamans. Vivet reclined, a sister at hand with a compress to blot her flushed forehead. Red hair clung to her damp skin in strings.

Tripped by empathy, Arithon missed his astute step. The smile that brightened her strained face tore his heart. Momentarily, he failed to address the piercing regard of the shaman.

Then Vivet's winsome joy appealed from the pillow, "I scarcely believed you would come."

His reflexive compassion punctured self-possession. Where the lost recall of his true beloved would have unmasked her staged appeal, Elaira honoured her secret promise to stay out of jeopardy. Unchecked, the phantom imprint of her stolen signature set hooks in the trap that besieged his integrity.

She could but weep. In private, Arithon might repel the heightened draw of Vivet's allure. But decency before her relatives begged his considerate kindness while she lay in childbed as his dependent. He bore up. Clasped her hand, as he must, braced to salvage appearances throughout the distasteful contact.

At Althain Tower, Elaira cried out, aware of the pitfall sprung by his sympathy.

The mistake opened the gate to disaster under the scrutiny of a shaman. While Vivet clung, the insidious glamour on her person shocked uncanny desire through Arithon's defences.

Annoyed as his cheeks flamed, stung worse by her family's salacious interest, he covered Vivet's fingers, and with desperate embarrassment, hid the brute leverage that prised her grip free.

And again, the gesture of gallantry back-lashed: every concession in Vivet's behalf redoubled the binding glamour. While Arithon wrestled his rocked equilibrium, the shaman attacked.

Elaira reeled in linked empathy as the ambush smashed Arithon's guard. He staggered, dizzied by a star-burst of pain. Crashed to his knees beside Vivet's mattress, he fought dissolution, while the startled matrons exclaimed. He felt their hands prop his frame in support. Heard their amused laughter, and worldly remarks over men who fell faint at the sight of a woman in childbed.

Then cognizance wavered. The overheated room frayed away, sensation sheared off as the brutal assault milled him under. Elaira's connection unravelled as well, sundered by a fissure of darkness.

Spring 5924

Precipice

The severance jolted Elaira erect amid the fast stillness of Althain Tower. If the antique tea-cup broken at her feet had unsettled Sethvir, the wakened defences laced through warded stone would be tolling alarm through his earth-sense. He could not intervene. Would not, constrained to stand back while the shaman's assault threatened Rathain's crown prince. Whatever his greater vision perceived, the crafted protections that shielded Elaira from hostile exposure also doused her personal faculties. Thrown on her own merits, shaken and blind, she mustered her rattled discipline. Despite her panicked impression of ruthless invulnerability, the brutal strike must be parried. After she calmed and centred herself, she sought access to Arithon's plight through her heart's connection.

Yet no effort availed her. The tower's mighty enchantments shredded her entrained concentration. The uncanny vibrations surged through flesh and bone, until the air drawn into her lungs crackled with overcharged power.

"Plague take the curse of cosseting safety!" At least alone in the wilds, Elaira had been able to risk the endangerment without hindrance.

Stranded instead before a carved table heaped with the dusty wisdom of opened books, she clawed under her collar and hooked the chain necklace that strung the signet of Rathain. She tapped into the ring's emerald setting at speed, then launched her urgent appeal to reach Arithon as the designate guardian of a sanctioned crown prince's heritage.

Whether for Athera's need or love's affinity, her frantic effort won through . . .

Arithon did not remain stranded beyond consciousness past the initial attack. Schooled reflexes conquered disorientation and recouped the first glimmer of self-awareness. He resurfaced into a landscape of dream, his naked skin mottled by the dappled shade of an ancient forest plucked out of his fragmented recall. He confronted a towering archway of oak. Perilous hush attended the moment where his due permission, commanded in form, had once granted his rightful access.

Yet the seductive impulse to retread that past step touched off an inchoate dread. Unease hackled his nape. A steadfast companion should stand at his shoulder: yet a search for the requisite, strapping young liegeman found no one backing his quest. Arithon frowned. A sinister sense of violation infused the frame of his private experience.

The suspicion raised gooseflesh, followed by an uncanny, fierce jab of compulsion. Not alone after all: some unseen entity riding him sought to harry him across the threshold to breach the veiled mystery beyond.

Initiate mastery rejected the pressure. Arithon blanked his mind and dispersed his cohesive awareness into a featureless void. That skilled reflex should have dislodged the invasion as the restructured memory collapsed. Divested of any internal foothold, the subversive presence ought to fade away.

Except the ephemeral vista did not dissolve into nothingness. The vision persisted, a frightening sign that the outside antagonist exploited the construct. Perception and thought remained embodied still, while the abdicate course of his counter-move buckled him at the knees. Snared captive inside of a stolen memory, Arithon sprawled helpless, unable to stir. An ominous wind swept the guardian oaks and rattled the branches above. The internal template he had relinquished in an unwitting surrender remained viable, while the enemy that stalked him as prey from the shadows uncoiled to lay claim, unopposed.

Peril struck, with Elaira snagged in the breach as the unforeseen eavesdropper, given mandated access through Rathain's seal ring. She extended her consciousness from deep trance to contest the disastrous theft of Arithon's experience. An aspect of her living will, self-contained and invisible, held the line before the gateway of arched oaks. The arcane web that sustained the uncanny projection was not unfamiliar: Elaira had once ventured into the Whitehaven sanctuary, sourced by the exemplary practice of Ath's adepts. She knew the reactive existence was real, volatile energy structured by the imprint of Arithon's emotional memory.

Yet this manifestation was not consecrated by the benign auspices of the White Brotherhood. Elaira broached a confrontation ruled by their rogue faction, sundered in exile. Ettinmere's enclave commandeered the arena, first to expose Arithon's core identity, then to ransack his guarded integrity.

The key to wrest dominance over him loomed ripe for the plucking inside the sentinel circle of oaks that defended the King's Glade in Selkwood. There, Arithon Teir's'Ffalenn had engaged with Athera's mysteries to heal the fatal flaw sown by Desh-thiere's curse. Courageously vulnerable, in naked trust, he had given over his Name in surrender to the wisdom of Athera's Paravians.

Exposed, that moment of unconditional disclosure would enable the abusive gamut of usage by Ettinmere's shamans.

Their thrust to break Arithon's autonomous will permitted no grace to prepare. The bolt-lightning charge they deployed outmatched Elaira's resource. A direct challenge *would* invoke deadly force. The profligate might that had seized hallowed turf as a battle-field owned the main strength to destroy her at whim. Worse, Arithon's compromised fate still required the secrecy of their relationship.

Elaira flung down the gauntlet, her bluff against desperate stakes reliant on bald-faced surprise.

"You shall not sow your havoc upon proscribed ground!" she denounced with ringing authority. "Defile this man's free spirit at your peril, against my fair warning: I know who you are and from whence you came! Desist, or suffer in reprisal."

Her startled antagonist recoiled, enraged. "How bold, to meddle in sequestered affairs beyond your rightful purview! Whoever you are, do you grasp the full scope of what lies at stake?"

Through a terrified pause, Elaira returned an impenetrable silence.

Unable to fathom the blank face of the obstructive opponent, the shaman flung back with blazing impatience. "If your claim carries weight, you'll know why this foreigner cannot be permitted to flout our traditions! He will be curbed before his wilful prowess disrupts the balance maintained by our covenant."

For the vast resource required to stabilize the buckling pressure of two major fault-lines was finite. Elaira held only that flimsy card against Arithon's ruin: the fact Ettin's shamans lacked any means to replenish their reserve posed their only weakness.

Elaira risked all in one blazing challenge. "What is your aim, truly? Are you the steadfast guardians of Ettinmere's legacy or venal practitioners, corrupted by self-importance and fallen to shady practice?" She withdrew, fast and clean, leaving the echo of the accusation like rolling thunder behind, inventively flourished by the colouration of Shehane Althain's imperative warding.

Elaira roused from trance shaken, the clammy palm clenched around Rathain's signet ring gouged by her terrified grip. Nor was she alone.

Sethvir sat across the heaped table, white hair nested with tangles and his eyes owlishly fixed. "My dear, whatever happens, your brave masquerade was pure genius."

Elaira shivered. "The shamans have stood down?"

"Perhaps," Sethvir allowed. "We'll know very soon." For of course, the breadth of his earth-sense still tracked the on-going reaction of Ettinmere's enclave.

Elaira held on, bolt upright and afraid to breathe. No hope saved the fact her veiled innuendo was a fallacy, the teeth behind compact law hobbled since the moment the shamans compromised Arithon's outer defences.

Sethvir disagreed. "Brave lady, your ploy was impeccably founded. Roaco's unlikely to sanction a foray stacked with the potential to drain his cabal's hoarded strength." The Sorcerer leaned forward, scavenged the forlorn shards of her cup from the floor, and spoke in actualized Paravian. As though the restoration of pulverized porcelain was ordinary, he refreshed the tea gone cold in the pot, poured, and passed her the steaming restorative.

Elaira accepted the courtesy, fraught over the prospect a rogue faction might grasp how thoroughly Prime Selidie's settlement tied the Fellowship's hand. "They can threaten a royal lineage without hindrance. Nothing stands in their path if they choose to destroy my beloved or damage his spirit."

"Not today," Althain's Warden made haste to confirm. "You have secured a reprieve in the moment. The tide's turned. The enclave is cautious by nature. Roaco won't rush to confront the unknown or engage while his footing is tenuous."

But hesitation was the sole stay in restraint. Elaira could not rest on the Warden's dissembling complacency. "Ettinmere's shamans will only regroup. They'll pry at Arithon's temperamental resistance until they seize their satisfaction."

"Then better your prince should remain running scared!" Sethvir snapped, perhaps gadded by her restive fear as the immediate crisis lost impetus. "Count your mixed blessing. His Grace has stayed unaware of whose help just rescued him from the pitfall. Recovery will find him scatheless in fact though he won't know for certain his being has not become compromised."

No other palliative existed, where the probable futures converged without recourse. Under siege as Arithon was from all quarters, his movement was going to stay hounded.

Elaira watched the Sorcerer rise, undeceived as the tension quarried into his face softened into his usual daft air of reverie. When he left, the leaden quiet of Althain Tower's protections gave her no peace. Tea-cup shoved aside, the enchantress firmed her resolve and engaged her own resource once more.

Sethvir's counsel had not misled her. Arithon still rested before the oak portal. But the oppressive gloom of the storm front had lifted. Sunlight winked through the crowns of the trees as the outside influence bled away. Elaira maintained her vigilant watch until dissolution leached through form and colour, and the half-world plumbed from Arithon's recall faded back into the void.

Arithon roused back to embodied awareness, collapsed onto his knees with his shoulder propped against Vivet's bedside. He retained nothing. No recollection of what had occurred since his defensive retreat caused a black-out faint. He wrestled a galvanic surge of self-doubt, unsure whether the hostile attack had downed him in defeat.

Assessment suggested he suffered no injury. By the cramped complaint of his folded legs, he had been unresponsive for hours. The thick reek of blood and the drone of mingled voices informed him Vivet's labour meantime had

birthed a live infant. Someone with a fist like a maul cuffed him in congratu-
lation. A jubilant matron shrieked in his ear. Through a shocking clangour of
cymbals and drums, he gathered the babe delivered to his household was a
healthy son.

Arin struggled erect. He managed the aplomb to stay upright, despite
sucking vertigo and a skull that felt packed with cotton. A wave of fresh nausea
wrung him to pallor. He swayed, to an outburst of female laughter. Rocked
by additional, boisterous back-slaps, he gritted his teeth, while the facetious
comments of Vivet's kinfolk belittled his squeamish male nerves.

Like a coal burning holes in his back, the shaman's glare measured his
artless distress.

"Buck up, young man!" An aunt, or close cousin grappled his arm, her
inbred Daldari features too nearly alike for his swimming perception. She dealt
his woozy frame a rousing shake. "Moment's come for the blessing. Do you
understand?"

Tugged forward, he confronted Vivet's achievement. The chapped hands of
a smiling midwife presented a squirming mite, nakedly wrinkled and glistening
wet and howling with indignant fury. Tiny heels lashed the air, shocked by
the transition into tumultuous life.

The shaman shoved to the fore, hostile as an ill wind as he whispered, "Do
you know what you ceded to us in the dark?" Then, by Ettin's custom, he
raised a smeared finger and streaked Arithon's cheeks with the birthing blood.
"The babe's life is sacrosanct by your oath. He is yours to name, outlander,
though take due care. The life granted rides upon your integrity."

The warning ran chills down Arithon's spine. The Ettin enclave clawed for
leverage against him, whether Vivet's child was his natural get, or an unknown
stranger's.

The infant's appearance did not settle the question. He had a newborn's
unfocused blue eyes, his smudged hair a whorl that would dry to wheaten
fluff. His bruised features were too undeveloped to reveal the traits to emerge
with maturity.

"Say his name and be quick, before bad spirits enter!" snapped the Daldari
matron.

"Let him be called Valien," declared Arithon, sick at heart and worried in
fact, that the shaman's hovering spite might afflict the lad's future. He recom-
mitted his given word of protection, stumbling as the women prodded him
backwards and shooed him out. This was not the moment to sort his unease
or test whether the sanctity of his autonomy had been breached by the enemy
while he was slumped senseless.

Culprit

The Mad Prophet lost his last, lame excuse to defer travel to Ettinmere when spring's thaw mired the trade-roads. As the shrunken rime of the drifts sprouted jade shoots of fodder, he dragged his heels with dazzling invention. Clan sentries collared him when he sidled away to desert. Dragged back under protest, he promptly fell sick. Griped and bemoaning digestive disorder, he raised havoc until the camp herbalist suspected self-poisoning and tossed out his stash of emetics. Cosach and Tarens put an end to his stalling, strapped him, protesting, onto a horse, and prodded the laden beast over the Arwent before the melt-waters frothed the ravine to an impassable spate.

Progress only blistered Cosach's impatience. Once the bogs dried and the grass greened in earnest, The Hatchet would muster his idle troops, parade them on gleaming display for the faithful, then march them out, duly blessed by the priests for a campaign of red slaughter. Every lost hour jeopardized lives, further delayed as the perils of Athili swung their route into the open plateau.

Moving by night, they freed the gelding to fend for itself. While a south wind pelted rain in their faces, they slept in their cloaks and hunted the winter-thin bucks, and ate roasts barely seared over frugal fires. Dakar's choppy stride laboured to keep pace across the matt burlap downs. Lag behind, and by the *caithdein*'s decree, he forewent his dinner and suffered from shortened sleep.

Which draconian measure lasted until they approached the shore of Daenfal Lake, where Tarens's preference to visit Backwater's market for news and provisions locked horns with the *caithdein*'s wary distrust.

"Better for clanblood to pilfer a boat, then row like the furies by dark." Anxious over the bottle-neck crossing, Cosach argued with venom until he noticed Dakar's furtive disappearance. "Slinking weasel's scarpered into the country-side."

Tarens chuckled. "More likely he's nestled in Backwater's stews, tight on beer and burrowed like a tick in a brothel." He yanked the last haunch of hare off the spit, tossed the portion to the fuming *caithdein*, then licked his blistered fingers. "Go on, find your boat. Fight the wind at the oars. I'll rest here and do you the favour of flushing the spellbinder out in the morning."

The chieftain tore a savage bite off the bone, eyebrows arched in the glare of the cookfire. "You'll try that wearing a clansman's leathers?"

"Not quite. Certain risks can be measured." Prudent enough to douse his amusement, Tarens tucked into his mantle and slept.

Awake before daybreak, he set off alone. A clammy breeze that fore-promised drizzle swept the bog taint off Silvermarsh, tinged by the tannin of oak logs burned in the outlying smoke shacks. The scent guided Tarens to a muddy trail, chopped by goats, which he followed until sunrise unveiled Backwater's blocky silhouette, stepped against the pewter sheen of the lake.

Once before, out-bound from Lithmarin, he had restocked at the trader's market. The giant guard with the rumbling laugh still minded the gate. Tarens answered his challenge and shared a lewd joke in a bumpkin's drawl. Bespattered with mud, his oiled-wool mantle and stag-hide boots indistinguishable from a farmer's, he entered the town's central thoroughfare.

His ruddy complexion and unkempt, fair hair turned no heads as he dodged the wheeled drays and rattling hand-carts. Above him, Backwater's lichened, square houses reared three storeys high, gabled and shingled with slate. Tarens strode through the fragrance of birch fires and hot buns, wafted from the tea vendors. The river-stone cobbles were swept. Painted eaves sheltered the zigzag board walkways, humped with the railed bridges that funnelled pedestrians past the snug craft shops that spun finished yarns and cured the pelts purchased raw from the trappers. Araethura's silky-haired goats, and the expertise of the furriers loaded the mule trains bound over the Skyshiels to the deepwater harbour at Jaelot.

Yet even a prosperous town had its stews. Tarens ducked into an alley and rambled into the twisty narrows of Backwater's lanes. Here, boiled steam off the vats soaked the air with the ammoniac reek of the tanneries, and the mouth-watering aroma of spiced grease from the grills of the sausage sellers. He dodged rib-thin curs, and the huckstering girls who peddled clove pomanders and goose balm, but encountered no sly, rotund figure. Nor did the brothel madams he bribed yield a client of Dakar's description.

Tarens's balked search at midmorning perused the rowdy, packed fug of the beer-shops. No tipsy prophet wedged into the press, where the idle trappers at winter's end flattened their purses on drink. The fat layabout was not with the shiftless crowds, yelling in rings around tipped-over trestles, where hucksters smuggled live chickens in sacks and took shady wagers for cock-fights.

Since rumours abounded where loiterers received a halfpenny to piss in the barrels that supplied the fullers and dyers, Tarens swallowed a pitcher of water and stalled through an hour of chat. Tuppence richer, he gleaned word of a stout fellow's interest in an unusual anecdote.

"Oh, yes! A deceased free singer's lyranthe was sold to pay off his burial," related the street peddler, hung with strings of noisome amulets. "The tale intrigues you, too? Well, a lovesick trapper bought the instrument for his courtship, but ham-fists and a frightful tin ear couldn't rub two notes together that didn't yowl like fighting tomcats. In debt for a royal, and desperate for relief, he shed the lyranthe for some ermine pelts offered by a scruffy Ettinman."

Tarens shelled out both of his pennies. "The fat man you spoke of, where did he go?"

"Him? Left last night." The vendor stowed the coins in a purse clinking with tin charms for *iyat* bane. "Trotted out the town gate astraddle a mangy mule." Amused by the listener's crest-fallen face, the shyster winked. "Never fret. Your bloke's unlikely to get past Daenfal. His animal was a dupe's buy, hereabout, since the ferry over the Arwent doesn't board infested livestock."

"Fiends alive!" Tarens shoved off, his plan for provisions abandoned in favour of urgent pursuit. Cures for mange posed no obstacle to a master spellbinder, and the conjured illusion of silver would bribe passage from any obstructive officials.

Well beyond town, Tarens sheltered in a willow copse. Curtained by yellow streamers, newly leafed out, he picked a seat where tangled roots laced the lake-shore like gnarled braid. He hoped Backwater hosted no True Sect diviner able enough to bear the regional flux currents. The volatile mysteries ran perilously strong near the southern verge of Athili, channelled by the old Paravian way and stabilized by two ancient marker stones that grounded the tidal bore: an unwise site to invite the back-lash of an arcane exposure. Tarens fumed for the feckless risk, left without a better option. Settled against a tree trunk, he tapped the clan hunter's knowledge bequeathed by Earl Jieret's legacy.

The light-track skeins of the game trails should reveal where Cosach had lifted his boat. Yet no tell-tale ripple disrupted the flow since daybreak refired the lane tides. Crouched on his heels, Tarens cursed the shiftless behaviour of loony prophets and clansmen.

The stealthy hand that latched onto his shoulder startled him almost out of his skin. He stayed his knife hand, just barely, aware of whose features loomed over him.

"I bagged that wretched spellbinder in the night!" Cosach carped. "Took you long enough to find out he'd scampered east on the back of a mule."

Tarens shoved erect and batted away a necklace of willow fronds. "You've left the slippery wretch unattended?"

Cosach snorted, beard split to bared teeth. "Come and see."

* * *

The Mad Prophet remained lodged in a thornbrake, bound hand and foot to his lop-eared mount, which was still tethered by dint of a rope noosed around the dumpling folds of his neck. The knot had not minded his unbinding spell: as much because he was reeling drunk, as the fact the cheap amulets sold by the coot at the privy proofed the bearer against *iyats* and commonplace mishap.

Tarens stifled an unkind snort of laughter. "Don't claim he left Backwater gutful of beer!"

"No," Cosach admitted. "But he had a gin flask stowed to celebrate later." Which spirits had been ingested by force, after the Mad Prophet fell to the rock the *caithdein* pitched to waylay him.

Dakar swivelled bloodshot eyes towards his captor. "You didn't have to sneak up from behind," he accused with slurred injury. "Then or now. What's the point, if this animal shies and I swing?"

"I hedge my bad bets," Cosach agreed, redressing his vindictive handiwork. "Should I cry if a traitor meets his demise? Eriegal died on a loyal man's blade for your tricks! Surely his unquiet shade won't rest until you get your reckoning from your crown prince. No, don't spin me another sad tale that you only slunk off for supplies. Not when I caught your weathercock nose poked into the breeze from Daenfal."

"The windfall still benefits," Dakar grumbled, sulky, "since you haven't pitched my saddle packs into the lake."

Tarens brightened. "He's packing victuals?"

Cosach's sharkish grin widened. "Hard biscuit and salt meat, dry beans, rice, and corn. Yon lard-sack's steadfast in concern for his belly."

"The blight on the mule's a back-handed gift." For of course an animal disbarred from the ferry lent them plausible cause to proceed through the wilds. They could round Daenfal Lake in the open since the only passable ford crossed the outlet that flowed from the southern shore above Silvermarsh.

"Time's wasting!" Cosach stowed the coiled rope and tugged the mule's head-stall onwards with the miserable spellbinder still bound astride. "Try bolting again, and as Rathain's *caithdein*, I'll declare you a threat to my sanctioned crown prince. That's lawful cause under kingdom charter to drop you flat with an arrow."

"I've already survived one shaft in the back on his Grace's behalf," Dakar snapped, which truth brought the slanging match to a stand-off.

The patchworked farmland thinned west of Backwater. Crofters dreaded the roiling borders of Athili, and the haunts that lurked like gleaming floss near the old way discouraged the most hardy woodsmen. Spring damp made the nights a bone-chilling misery, except for one spent in a ruin abandoned by charcoal-burners. The caved roof beams wore the holed remnants of thatch, which shed the sullen downpour in streams. Cosach maintained his testy watch well into the Storlain foot-hills, where, habitation fallen behind, Dakar's itchy feet found no civilized sanctuary. Tarens loosed the mule before it lost flesh and divided the load to continue on foot.

Up-country by equinox, the party ascended on a scarce-trodden trail, snaking through the ravines and notched passes where the deep vales yawned in ink shadow, and the sunlit heights shimmered under snow. Mornings came etched in hoar-frost, melted by noon to melodious trickles that fed the spring cataracts, swollen to thunder that shuddered the ground. The green firs wore gilt in the harsh blaze of day, tinted in blue and white and pale violet by receding drifts under an azure sky: a vista so vast, all of Mankind's endeavour seemed an insectile intrusion. Only one wayfarer shared the remote path: a solitary trapper turned crazy, who cared not a whit that the ermines' pale coats had shed to dull brown.

But Tarens's patience eventually thawed the saturnine fellow's tongue. "The uncanny singer? Oh, aye! I've kent him. Walks the sheer rim atop Thunder Ridge. You'll know when you hear him. The sound's belike to drive any wrong-doing man to religion."

Extricated with delicacy, the three travellers distanced themselves from the trapper's eccentric company.

"Do you know this place, Thunder Ridge?" Cosach asked, craning over a dwarf stand of firs, pruned by avalanche on the far side.

Puffing, Dakar laboured to answer. "The same scarp the Paravians called the Tiendarion? Yes. The spur parallels the backbone of the Storlains, buckled to chaos where subduction pressure rams into the plain of West Halla. If Arithon's there, the approach will be troublesome."

The chieftain's response was a half-drawn sword, resheathed with a warning clash. "Don't try that excuse to hare off again!"

"You think I'm suicidal?" the spellbinder grumbled. "The terrain will pump a man's lungs like a bellows and dash out his brains on a mis-step."

A fortnight later, wheezing alike in the thin, frigid air, the three searchers huddled around a spluttering campfire under the rock face of the Tiendarion. The razor-edged rampart carved an obsidian rip across the night sky, dusted above with silver veils of cirrus and stars like sequins in shot silk. Ettinmere Settlement lay twenty leagues southward and west as the crow flew, within the range of a Sighted shaman, even where the eddied flux currents disrupted scrying. Dakar took no chances. He fashioned individual constructs of lead, inset with black tourmaline, pyrite, and hematite.

"For grounding energy," he explained, then enhanced the mineral amulets with charms against Cosach's corrosive derision. "Would you have the Ettinmen blinded or not? Stay angry, and no subtle working can mask you. You'll pose a ripe target for *iyats*, besides."

Honest warning, since electromagnetic flares always drew fiends like a magnet. The same instability scrambled Cosach's talent bent for the hunt. Pinched cross by the dearth of meat for the spit, the clan chieftain kept the spellbinder under his thumb and resolved to greet his liege by himself.

"That could be a mistake," Tarens cautioned, ahead of the Mad Prophet's pounce to seize the vindictive advantage. "His Grace hates the onus of titled formality."

"Well, too bad. Tradition says crown princes bend their stiff knees to acknowledge their liegemen's fealty. If his Grace balks, for the risk to my people, I'll challenge his delinquent pride, throw him over and thrash him." The *caithdein* jabbed his stick at the coals with contempt. "You've said yourself he's a dainty wee snip. More nerve than brains, if he thumbs his nose at the man with the heftier sword-arm!"

"Do you think?" Tarens slapped off the stirred sparks flurried into his mantle. "Pithless as Arithon seems at first glance, he has brute will enough to wreck mountains."

Dakar sighed, hunched into his cowled cloak like a browbeaten turtle. "You want a royal ally, Lord Cosach? Be well-advised. Curb your resentment and listen, or turn tail and keep your bowels intact."

"I should play the craven and help you slink off?" The High Earl of the North dug in his heels, rowelled by Dakar's overweening advice.

Tarens kept his own counsel and turned into his blankets. Sleepless, he tossed, chafed by Earl Jieret's remembrance: of Arithon's feral nerves in the aftermath of a prolonged chase through Daon Ramon. The past *caithdein's* experience fore-promised a temperament dicey as a cornered adder's. Cosach's bullish over-confidence would trample diplomacy. Add the blistering catalyst of the Mad Prophet's guilt-fed anxiety, and the volatile outcome surpassed imagining. Before Tarens relinquished the mission to folly, he arose in stealth and took the path up to Thunder Ridge on his own.

Dawn found the former crofter cresting the sheer, pleated ridge that gouged the world's roof like a curtain wall. Ruddied by the glow of new morning, he was closest when Athera's titled Masterbard made his appearance and started to sing.

A slight, tousled figure against livid sky, Arithon walked the jagged rock rim, shaping his art as he went. The crystalline purity of his voice awoke a primal restlessness in all things living. The fierce urge seized hold: to follow his lead and dance to his paean of exultation. With joyful abandon to quicken the blood, the bard wove desire to pique the voracious interest of Athera's energy sprites.

And the fiends came, irresistibly drawn, darting unseen from cleft rock and frisking through the crabbed tangle of firs. They spun out of the wind as small eddies and errant breezes. Impulsive wisps flocked to his lure, their pocked shimmers kited into a gyrating halo that tousled his hair and tweaked at his clothing. Tethered by rapt fascination, they became pared down and netted in shadow, their chaotic exuberance snugged into slender bands fitted onto his fingers.

Tarens tracked the bard at short distance, shielded from notice by Dakar's amulet. The oblivious singer continued. As though naught existed beyond sky and mountains, his sustained summons bound the thralled *iyats* until both hands gleamed with the uncanny fruit of his gathering.

Then the thrust of his enchantment changed key. Face tipped back, Arithon added the exquisite cadence of Paravian. His lyric shaped yearning, a cry beyond the human surcease of tears.

To witness a man's heart-strings laid bare became a violation. Tarens braced as though to deliver a death-blow, and stirred to interrupt.

Arithon's melody checked in midphrase. He spun, alarmed. Sight of the crofter woke shocked recognition, changed to distress as he clawed at his shirt to rip something offensive away.

"Stop!" Tarens exclaimed. "No harm's done!" Thrust forward by Jieret's uncanny perception, he caged Arithon's wrist before what seemed a plain copper button tore free.

"Rest easy! The Ettinmere shamans are blinded." Staggered a step by a murderous tussle, Tarens kept talking. "My safety's secure. If not, you'd have noticed my presence before this."

Yet Arithon resisted with dauntless ferocity. "Show me proof!"

Tarens let go. Palms empty, he opened his collar and hooked out the knotted string with Dakar's talisman. The frigid wind seared his exposed throat, while Arithon surveyed the construct.

"Who led you to find me?" Then, brusque as an interrogation, "What did you promise to buy a signature line of protection?"

Which ugly disclosure punched Tarens off balance. "Signature?"

Arithon looked exasperated. "Your Name is wound into that working! Count on the fact you won't keep any secrets away from whoever created it."

Which attack was a feint. Steadied by Jieret's infallible insight, Tarens answered the evasive panic directly. "You're not alone! I know why you can't leave. The enemies who test your defences are dangerous, and I've come to help heal the rifts in your memory."

Not disarmed, Arithon returned the viciousness of the caged tiger. "Who else has taken a prying interest?"

Lies would not serve. Before Tarens mustered the poise to confess, Cosach trampled in, loud-mouthed, from the access path.

"The *Caithdein* of Rathain, first of all!" Breathless from his ascent, the High Earl arrived on the ridge-top aflame with self-righteous reproach. "Should we need to chase after your coat-tails, your Grace? While you dawdle amid these benighted wilds, our realm confronts the horror of a True Sect purge. The Hatchet commands a veteran war host, the same one that sacrificed Havish's finest to win you free with your life. Shall your own people die under the forfeit of your oathsworn legacy?"

If Arithon had seemed strained before, his demeanour hardened, implacable. "You seek the entitlement for wholesale slaughter?" He added, "The benighted fools raised to arms against you will leave behind orphans who grow up to continue the next cycle of vengeful reprisal. You can't sow a legacy of meaningful joy while you widow their mothers and sisters to suppress a misguided canon."

"We are speaking of clan survival!" snapped Cosach, his tousled belligerence blossomed to rage.

"Is there any difference?" Arithon cracked. "What is any war, after all, but the abject surrender of hope? A craven rejection of human grace, with righteous mass murder ennobled in place of inspired imagination!" Against scorching rebuttal, he mocked, "The stubborn mind never looks for alternatives. Let's drop the cat-and-mouse rhetoric since you've come only to drag the chained bear to the mastiff's pit."

"Singed fur's bound to fly, anyway." Jabbed beyond sense, Cosach challenged, "Let's rip for the jugular and see who gets flayed."

Arithon's lip curled. "Perhaps I prefer to skulk like the cur before strutting your puppet's parade in the royal arena." Inimical green eyes raked back over the onlooking crofter. "Were you the eager conspirator or the sadly duped gambit?"

Caught out, Iyat-thos Tarens squared off. "I know you prefer to spare others from the hazard that dogs your company. But your liegeman's fate is not detached, and I came only for friendship."

The jet eyebrows rose beneath tangled black hair. "Ath wept! Did Earl Jieret not share the vicious brutality of his death? No! A sane man would gag before repeating that hag's brew of fatal sentiment."

But the choice to back down stayed squarely thwarted by Cosach's armed bulk in the breach.

"The agog audience, amazed by disgust for the freak?" Arithon's brutal regard swept the stalwart s'Valerient descendant, dismissed the bristle of weapons, the scraped leathers, and even the weariness of harsh travel stamped into a countenance weathered lifelong. "I prefer obscurity," declared the Teir's'Ffalenn.

Cosach shredded the flummery. "Well, this isn't a puppet-show drama. The plight of the kingdom can't spare you the luxury!"

The second that followed stretched beyond silence. Stymied where record and hearsay fell short, the *caithdein* found his ironclad duty no match for the royal heir in the flesh.

Head tipped back, his loosened shirt unadorned as an Ettinman without an upright claim to property, Rathain's titled crown prince returned, full bore, his unsettling interest. "As the latest chip off a rock-headed lineage, don't tumble for the romantic idea I'll sit for a coronation."

Cosach anchored his sword-belt with a hooked thumb and glared downwards with blood in his eye. "The Fellowship Sorcerers might flinch given the mob of armed factions clambering over themselves for your head."

"Bow to the pressure, or else stand up and slaughter a starry-eyed horde of fanatics?" Arithon rejected equivocation. "No. My refusal to Asandir stays in force."

Cosach bristled. "My office could declare you unfit!"

"Disown me?" quipped Arithon in fierce delight. "A pity I'm still the last of my lineage." Maddening as the gad-fly, he stung, "An accursed thorn in the craw since you're here, trusty steel at the ready! Or why haven't the Seven bestirred themselves to snatch my infant ward from the insular bosom of Ettinmere settlement?"

Tarens roared first. "Don't take the bait, Cosach! Your liege snaps worst when he's pinned by his short hairs. Always, his viciousness is a bluff to defend his bare-arsed embarrassment." Then, quick as balm on a wound, he addressed Arithon's anguish point-blank. "Creative invention did not fall short! They all survived, the women and children you spared from the True Sect's execution by fire at Torwent. I accompanied the dispossessed to Fiaduwynne, and saw them to safety under their High King's protection."

Arithon glanced away, not quite fast enough, as he wrestled emotion to find speech for Tarens. "You had earned my regard far and long before this." But the stiff reproach was capitulation. Fist to heart, Rathain's sanctioned crown prince acknowledged his *caithdein* at last though not yet by a formal acceptance of fealty. "Given your effort to find me, Lord Cosach, the courtesy's owed. I am listening."

There, hard-won truce met strategic disaster: a dislodged rock clattered down the cliff as another arrival, masked by furtive spellcraft, scaled the ridge-top behind Arithon's back.

The outflanked prince did not spin to denounce the latest unwelcome intrusion. Fixated on Cosach instead, Arithon caught the brazen lack of surprise, contrasted by Tarens's spontaneous gasp at the appearance of his rear-guard stalker.

The Mad Prophet had taken desperate steps: razed his unkempt frizzle of hair and beard, the fish-belly hue of his crudely shorn skin nicked everywhere with oozing scabs. Exposed beyond quarter, his shrinking advance trod a pitfall scaffolded with egg-shells.

But the thunder-clap of Arithon's recognition did not break the electrified stillness. His caustic temperament failed to explode into damnably just accusations, but leap-frogged courtesy without a peripheral glance. "You would be the spellbinder who crafted the wardings to foil the Ettinmere shamans?"

Dakar shuffled his feet. "The working is mine." Sweating through jellied nerves, denied sighted acknowledgement, he admitted, "We all carry a talisman. Need I broach the necessity? We have you surrounded to veil this encounter from a more perilous adversary. You must be aware. Your doings draw fatal attention from worse than Ettinmere's watchers."

"By all means, let's not forget the Koriathain." Arithon's front-facing expression stayed bland, without nuance to sort true equanimity from the subtle poison of satire. "I'm meant to trust your honeyed promise of a full restoration of memory? Then let's have surety. Deliver the name of the woman whose love sold me out to the sisterhood."

Dakar choked, his moon-calf features drained white. "I can't." Suicidally terrified, nonetheless he sealed his courageous refusal. "To tell you would overturn your given word. And break the secrecy of a sacred covenant, once sworn between the two of you."

Whatever Arithon expected to hear, *that* smashed his impervious poise.

Tarens thrust forward and quashed Cosach's bid to wring the upset for advantage. "Your Grace, if you daren't rely upon anyone else, you might lean on the one friend you know, verified by the sterling assurance of High Earl Jieret's intentions."

A straw-hope appeal, as sanguinity broke to the gut punch of horror. Arithon spun at last and beheld the fat spellbinder: whose traitorous countenance mirrored the moment's shared desolation of grief. No grace salved the aghast remembrance of sedition, inflicted under the pitiless sun of yet another spring morning . . .

. . . when, in the saffron light of new day, the Mad Prophet and the Crown Prince of Rathain had stepped off the grand pattern of the Paravian focus at Caith-al-Caen, still tipsy with vertigo from the after-shock of an arcane transfer. Arithon, laughing, had snapped off a lewd joke, incandescent with joy at the prospect of playing to celebrate Jeynsa's wedding to Sevrand s'Brydion.

Bald and self-effacing, Eriegal came forward to meet them, not in welcome, but with the bile of childhood losses crystallized into furious vengeance. The Companion had brought at his back a circle of twelve Koriathain, joined by the Prime Matriarch's hostile directive. Their laid spells to trap the Teir's'Ffalenn alive closed in at shocking strength.

Arithon unsheathed the black sword, Alithiel. Yet the might of a just cause abandoned him. No exalted chord sounded in his defence. The blade's arcane wardings remained latent as he shouted in anguish to Dakar, "Step back! Escape is still possible if you re-energize the Paravian focus at once!" For where a Masterbard's artistry might raise the lane force to pitch through the slow, artful resonance of music, the Fellowship spellbinder held the immediate keys the Sorcerers used to fire the power to peak.

Yet Dakar did nothing. By demand of the senior Koriathain, instead, he gave over to Prime Selidie's use the Prince of Rathain's free grant of permission, once entrusted to him for intervention under direst need.

"Why?" Arithon shouted, slammed to his knees in a hopelessly undermined fight. "Why, Dakar?" he pleaded, betrayed into captivity without explanation as the spellbinder wrested out of his hands Elshian's lyranthe, then the heirloom Paravian sword with its star-spell inexplicably silent. Rathain's crown prince fell into darkness, undone by the secret, back-handed bargain that sealed an arch-enemy's claim on his person . . .

Across two yards of air, too portly to run, and hedged right and left by a thousand-span drop-off, Dakar regarded the friend he had condemned to bear a fate beyond imagining. His lips had stayed sealed, then. The more bitterly guarded, here, while against good faith and justice, he withheld two critical confidences from Arithon's knowledge. One, the name of the beloved enchantress handfast as Princess of Rathain; and the other, that Cosach as *caithdein* must never find means to expose: of the intractable crisis at Athir two and a half centuries' past, when at the crux, Dakar had sworn an oath of debt against Rathain's crown under Fellowship auspice to salvage Prince Arithon's life. Not even Elaira knew of the girl-child born to Glendien at Althain Tower, then taken hostage by Prime Selidie in the desperate bargain struck in the aftermath: when Kharadmon had unleashed the free wraiths from the star wards to leverage the historic stay on the Teir's'Ffalenn's execution.

Dakar bit his tongue until the blood ran.

He suffered the whipping-post fury in silence, while Arithon accused with the venomous scald of his aghast recognition, "You are poison in the vein, more cruel than back-stabbing steel, and a living blight on my spirit. Your friends are not mine! Tell them to leave until we are finished."

Whether Arithon's surge forward meant harm, or if he only moved to demand an honest accounting, Cosach reacted first. His deft blow to the nape, from behind, felled the Teir's'Ffalenn in a senseless sprawl on the barren stone.

"Tarens, stand down!" Dakar shouted, appalled. "Don't make this travesty any worse."

Stopped short by the point of the *caithdein*'s sword at his breast, the blond crofter curbed his outrage a hairbreadth from bloodshed and tragedy. When he managed words, his fury was Jieret's. "That I have lived to witness the day a crown prince was laid low by the hand of a Teir's'Valerient! Cosach! As Shadow behind the Throne, you're forsworn. His Grace was owed your steadfast protection, even as all others failed him."

"On the contrary, this hour's work is well done," the High Earl rebutted. "Yon weasel-faced spellbinder has finally clarified my grasp of the realm's priorities. He'll confirm the necessity. Now that Arithon's alienated in Havish, the Fellowship Sorcerers are freed for the task of upholding Rathain's defence."

Partings

Wakened to a sore head and the after-taste of another betrayal, Arithon discovers Dakar's cryptic note, folded around select fragments of mineral and left tucked into his sleeve: "You have sufficient observant knowledge of wards to fashion yourself a clean talisman. For integrity's sake, Tarens acted alone, and the fullest access to your heritage lies with the desert tribes in Sanpashir . . ."

Though wise enough to absent himself from his liege's wounded recovery, Tarens rejects Cosach's choice to withdraw in support of Rathain's protection, and instead parts company to seek summer work as a farm-hand at Backwater until autumn, when the trapping season resumes . . .

The senior lane watcher's summary report to her Prime lists three movements of urgent interest: Elaira's leave-taking from Althain Tower, east-bound for the Mathorn Mountains; The Hatchet's order by carrier pigeon to unleash the campaign troops kennelled at Morvain and Narms; and Asandir's haste to reach Northgate side-lined by a summons from Kharadmon . . .

VII. Sidesteps

Elaira's covert plan to fare east from Atainia unravelled under the shock of rapport, as Arithon's betrayal on Thunder Ridge spiked an echo she could not suppress. The volatile flare caught her en route to Lorn on the lonely verge of the waste.

Deftly as she noosed sympathetic emotion and stabilized her composure, she could not restore the untenanted stamp of the regional flux pattern. Useless even to try to bind a glamour wide enough to mirror the natural stillness of the heath: her presence would already be marked. The graphic imprint of her response would have flagged the Sighted vigilance of the Koriathain. An informant rushed to Prime Selidie's ear surely revealed her departure from the impregnable sanctuary of Althain Tower: news that might extend the scope of disaster well beyond beleaguered Rathain.

Panic saved nothing. The damage was done. Elaira plonked on a boulder to regroup, while the gusts whined through the desolate brush, and swallows swirled in exuberant gyres through the bowl of blue sky overhead.

Her options to salvage the mis-step were few on a route sparsely travelled. Alone, she could do little but sow a broad-scale spell of gross misdirection. Elaira engaged her connection to water as conduit, then splashed the magnified echo of her distress the full length of the northern trade-road. With luck, the sisterhood's scryers would waste themselves, sifting for her presence among the ramshackle taverns packed with Lorn's dour fisherfolk.

Next, she masked her close signature under wards toned to mimic lichened granite and stunted thorn. The effort drained her to exhaustion by nightfall.

She slept, then turned south across country in the saffron glow of new morning. Her passage as light as a field-mouse, she crept with the rustling swoop of the breeze through the wild. While the buttercups nodded their vacuous heads, she swore in ripe language to kick Cosach senseless, then string Dakar up by his cowardly neck. No callous justification excused their denouncement of Rathain's crown prince.

Trouble would follow, surely as storm. She knew the Teir's'Ffalenn's temper. He was not going to bide, suffocated by Ettinmere's culture and the barbed poison of Vivet's allure. No surprise, when her next cautious scrying by night failed to draw his shuttered spirit. Instead, the tension linked to his name delivered a view of the Mad Prophet, his shaved scalp rouged by fire-light as he jerked straight from his sullen slouch. "*What* did you say?"

A hulk picked out by the carmine gleam of the coals, Rathain's *caithdein* repeated his sour remark. "That you can quit your theatrical sulk. Our timely severance surely has spared the s'Ffalenn lineage from extinction. His Grace is better off past the reach of The Hatchet's vicious campaign."

Dakar gaped, licked dry lips, and shivered as though Dharkaron's Black Spear had just skewered his vitals. "Ath wept. You blind dolt! You've learned nothing? Your sovereign prince won't abandon Rathain. Or you, no matter the harrowing surety that now, the Fellowship Sorcerers are bound to support the kingdom's defence."

Cosach shrugged to an irked creak of his sword-belt. "You claim to grasp Arithon's measure yourself? Then do me the favour. Prove your high-handed forecast and share the bent of his unlikely plans." Disbelief edged his contempt as he added, "Roped firmly to heel by Ettinmere's shamans, what under sky can the little man do?"

"I don't know!" Dakar chewed his moustache. "That's the problem. Guessing his Grace's next move has bedevilled me to white hair and hounded the Seven halfway to doomsday. For centuries, he's saddled everyone with a white-knuckled crisis of management."

As though cued, an intransigent gust raked the campfire. Cosach cursed, pelted by flurried sparks. Busy slapping out errant cinders, he failed to interpret the spellbinder's cringing, dough pallor.

"Daelion's mark on the hindmost!" Dakar shoved bolt upright in the hellish glare. "We're roped by the bollocks and already flayed."

"Kharadmon, without pleasure!" The Sorcerer's intrusive shade forwent mercy and blasted into a stinging whirlwind of agitation, "Since your blow-hard folly saw fit to dispense with a Fellowship-sanctioned Crown Prince, you're appointed! Charged in full to bear the responsible brunt for Rathain in his Grace's absence."

Dakar quaked down to his scuffed boot soles. "Ath forfend!" Jaws working like a beached fish, he yelped, "*Everything?*"

Kharadmon's ire bit deep as frost. "Did you think Asandir has the resource to spare?"

Silence fell as though shrouded in grave cloth. Dakar mopped his brow. While Cosach gawped, thunderstruck, at the side-lines, the Sorcerer's sarcastic tirade resumed.

"*Everything*, butty? You flatter yourself! Since I've no patience left to nurse-maid the incapable, another will be entrusted to guard the well-heads of the mysteries. Meanwhile, no free-wilds forest will get hacked down to fuel a True Sect invasion. You are tasked with Halwythwood's outlying protection to the limit of your abilities."

Dismissed like furniture, Cosach bridled. "Are trees worth more than the lives of my people?" Too outraged to heed Dakar's frantic gesture, and blinded by two centuries of stable peace, he ploughed on, "Is Sethvir ungrateful that Rathain's prince—"

"Ungrateful! We Seven?" Kharadmon's whiplash rebuke froze debate. "The clan families have always shouldered the burden of their blood heritage on our sufferance! Mankind's tenancy here is not entitled, and by Asandir's author-itative word, your successor is already measured and marked."

Dakar moved fast enough: kicked the clan chieftain silent, less afraid of a knife-thrust in retaliation than of watching the ruin unfolding before him.

Appeasement came too late. Kharadmon delivered his scathing retort with the speed of a wrathful kraken. "Cosach s'Valerient, his Grace of Rathain is no longer your concern." That single phrase stripped away rank and title without space for appeal. The discorporate Sorcerer departed forthwith. The vacuum imposed by his sudden exit ripped the air and boxed ears to a thunder-clap inrush of wind.

Dakar reeled, distraught, as the disowned clan chieftain bowed his head, face shuttered in shame. No words existed to ease a proud man, dispossessed and cut off from his family. For in fact the foundation of crown obligation relied on far more than the preservation of the old-blood families in the free wilds. Cosach had never encountered a Paravian. Sheltered lifelong under the justice by which Lysaer had curbed Etarran excess, the chieftain lacked the experience to grasp the full scope of his s'Valerient heritage.

Which tragic oversight hurt all the worse, when the pealing cry through the flux served due warning that Fellowship wardings had raised the ancient defences in Halwythwood against the on-coming True Sect campaign.

Dakar railed through his teeth at the maladroit blows of Dame Fortune. "You'd think I'd have learned there's no profit in crossing the doings of Fellowship Sorcerers." But his recrimination floundered and died, smothered beneath Cosach's stricken silence.

Elaira shivered, too pressured to mourn the botched plight of Rathain's rebuked retainers. Her own straits were precarious, embarked on a daunting, long journey, with every post stable and traveller's inn crammed past capacity with Sunwheel troops. A sparrow among cats, sought by the Prime Matriarch, she walked, every step, in fraught peril. Night became her inadequate cover. She stole like the trackless imprint of moonlight past the volatile nexus at Isaer and slept lighter than the kiss of spring sun, her breaths meshed with the breeze through the budded brush. Any purposeful haste would distinguish her from the foraging animals. Fear of discovery dogged her, each moment, while her tuned mage-sense listened for threats.

Yet her heightened awareness discerned nothing beyond the marching clamour of The Hatchet's host.

She reached the cross-roads as wary as any small prey sought after by predators. The way to Castle Point was choked with dusty columns of troops. Mounted officers in blazoned surcoats, and priests, and the white-liveried temple messengers claimed the right of way, coming and going from Erdane and Etarra. Trade caravans were displaced by gravid supply trains, toiling with commandeered crofters' drays. A lone woman abroad in the turmoil of war watched her back. Since passage by galley across Instrell Bay increased the risk of entrapment, Elaira melted into the workaday traffic and continued southward, the long way, by land.

Weary, and itching for want of a bath, she sought news in the crowded tap-room of a public post-house. She picked a dim corner, her rapt interest in the surrounding talk obscured by a haughty dowager with two horse-faced attendants. Past her braying demands, an officer's complaint rose over the rattle of crockery.

". . . saying the campaign's accursed with bad luck. Storms flatten the tents. Streams flood, and the fords wash out underfoot, no matter how often the priests mouth their sanctimonious prayers to the Light."

From the trestle behind, a grain merchant with basset-hound eyes bewailed his lost profits to hailstorms that flattened a season's crops. As though a sick miasma poisoned the flux, a drover weighed in, "Two mules lamed from stones after casting shoes on the highway, and a linch-pin sheared at the cost of six shattered wheel-spokes? That much bad luck is unnatural. Ask any man eastbound on the Great Road. Evil's abroad, and blight rides the haulage forced on us by temple decree."

"Be silent!" The Sunwheel officer hammered a gauntleted fist on the trestle. "I'll have no loose talk. Not while my lancers bear arms against Darkness."

Elaira's heart skipped a beat in recoil from the resonant flare that surged off the tavern's slate floor. Mage-sense grasped the spelled pattern that magnified dissent into harmonic sympathy. Likely the Mad Prophet's patent touch, selectively sharpened by the receptivity of common minerals. Every stone, brick, and sand-grain around her imprinted the carping of hagridden travellers. The massive transfer of troops, and their cumulative roil of angst framed the source that skewed the course of event. Folk bemoaned their ill luck, unaware their distress augmented the rip-tide of mishaps.

While the officer ranted away, the merchant grumbled behind his lace cuff to the sallow clerk seated adjacent, "If Erdane's examiners don't fathom the cause, the assault in Rathain may founder before The Hatchet's companies are positioned to cull the forest barbarians."

Elaira lost her taste for the inn's bitter ale, sobered as she weighed the upcoming recoil of righteous back-lash. Added scrutiny by Sunwheel priests redoubled her chance of exposure, a fresh thorn in the quandary given her need to obfuscate the Prime's scryers. She made herself finish her savourless meal, left the boisterous tap-room, and forwent her comfort to push south. Against drastic risk, she must hazard the distance and reach Davien's protection at Kewar.

Since a healer's trade would draw notice, Elaira bought an awl, heavy needles, harness tacks, and wax thread from a tinker. Mending and saddlery peddled on the road provided an innocuous upkeep. Burdened with only a satchel, she pressed ahead into the storm.

The long days dawned under pale summer haze stilled to stifling heat, shimmering through the ochre pall churned up by the ox-drawn drays. Evenings she spent with her fellow travellers, stitching harness or clothing by fire-light. Gleaned conversation provided her only awareness of current events. From caravan traders out-bound from Dyshent, she learned that The Hatchet's invasion fleet had stranded itself at the fringes of Halwythwood. A foray of lancers became disoriented in Daon Ramon, while supply trains were plundered and wrecked by furtive clan raiders. Against the ill wind of hysterical rumour, the True Sect priests unleashed their diviners. The witch-hunt swept down from Erdane like a grass fire, with all suspect talent condemned to burn, and the hapless populace wont to be stopped for inquisition by Sunwheel examiners.

Elaira kept her head down and sewed, in dread of the prickling chills that bespoke the prying scrutiny of fanatics, or worse, the scrying interest of Koriathain: but none came. That puzzling absence nagged her to concern, stretched over days into worry the sisterhood's exclusive focus might have prioritized Arithon. Beyond the occasional, startling grue, Elaira's innate rapport with his Grace remained silent. The withdrawal had extended for far too long. Yet she dared not jeopardize his precarious safety or threaten her own to pursue his activity.

Not while caught in the paranoid fervour stirred up by a True Sect purge.

The zeal to stamp out Shadow continued, spread with the billows of dust that choked the summer trade-road. Sunwheel couriers out-bound from Erdane galloped through, flinging mud clods, while the commonplace traffic scrambled and parted. Carts slewed into the ditches and mired, and an elderly shepherd was thrown from the saddle and trampled when his upset flock scattered. Just another victim mowed down by an armed company on a forced march. Elaira carried no simples to help. She stanched and bound the stricken man's injuries, then stayed by him to soothe his shocked trauma.

"How many won't live to come home?" he asked, while the final rank passed them by, and the young dreamers with more bravado than sense chased the rear-guard to enlist, boastful and eager for the Light's glory. Too many had straw in their hair from tying the shocks of cut barley. As disturbingly ominous, the must of spoiled grain wafted off the fields, where unharvested crops were abandoned to rot.

Elaira had no happy answer but urged the shaken herder not to sell his flighty mare.

"Heed the drovers, they'll say the same." Reliable mules were scarce, and horseflesh for harness nowhere to be found. With so many animals taken in tithe by the temple, two stalwart smiths stopped for rest vented their bitter opinion, unasked.

"The cartwrights' shops are overburdened," said one. "Worked day and night without pay to keep up with the war host's allotment."

The other spat out a chewed grass stem and carped, "We've forged shoes and pounded new wheel-rims till our backs ache, no matter the post-houses are stripped of stock. Sound horses broken to saddle or draught are scant on the market at any price."

"Our hostler's stuck harnessing swaybacks and plough mules," chorused a liveried groom, bent by the wayside to buff his caked boots, while a subordinate watered the lathered team for the public coach en route to Falgaire.

Everywhere, from tavern tap-rooms to the smoky fires where sunburned women brewed tea for the caravans, travellers bemoaned the short-falls inflicted by stalemated war.

Elaira stitched worn leathers and broken straps, listening, her eyes etched with crow's-feet by the summer glare as her snail's-pace progress hugged the coast. Flushed in the sweltering heat, she approached the choke point at the southern border, where old law customs still governed the segment of road that looped briefly through Havish. Traffic stopped. Folk clumped by the roadside, sweating through the hindrance. Their unease was justified: Tysan's soil hosted a troop of white dedicates, kept armed in fractious readiness. Across the dusty scar of the road, more slit-eyed watch-dogs in Havish's crown blazon all but breathed the same air, stewed jumpy by boredom.

Nerves stretched to short tempers, while the indigo shadow of East Bransing's walls swathed the disputed landscape each morning. Bay-side, the port seethed with True Sect steel, on guard and overkeyed with anxiety.

There, footsore under the parched blaze of noon, Elaira encountered a Koriani hospice pavilion pitched outside the brick arch of the landward gate. This far removed from the battle front, a sisterhood presence would not be tending the wounded. The town had been sealed, with all passing traffic subject to tightened scrutiny.

Elaira stalled at the verge. Palms clammy, she surveyed the hubbub, noisy with restive animals and the curses of nettled carters. Somewhere nearby, corpses had been burned: either Daelion's toll of corrupted dead or condemned flesh cut down from the gibbet.

If the latter, a busy Sunwheel examiner also pinned the region under the Light of the Canon. Elaira joined a cluster of country matrons, pink and moist as hams, as they rested through the inconvenience. She broke out hard cheese and bread and chewed, deep in circumspect thought. Soon enough, the idle conversation around her revealed that a True Sect mandate had closed the east-bound road.

"The way's unsafe, uncanny and haunted," explained a chipper granddame swathed in a shawl. Still vigorous despite her shortened breath, she accompanied a plump younger relative in a tired calico dress. Wilted under the burden of a cherubic babe in a basket, the woman abandoned her harassed effort to calm the whiny toddler tagging her skirts. But the smile turned towards Elaira was friendly. "Given the malfeasance of Shadow's abroad? The Light's soldiers are vigilant. No one's permitted to pass without challenge."

"And the affliction here?" Elaira offered a morsel of cheese to mollify the fretful child. "Is the town pestilent with fever as well?"

The elder wheezed derisively through yellowed teeth. "The town's teeming, truly, but not beset. Stranded folk have the dock-side quarter packed full. The rich leave by galley, while the rest fight the mob for an open deck passage. No one in residence has succumbed yet. Only the Light's dedicates, sent back from Rathain. They say Halwythwood's poisoned. Accursed by Shadow, goes word from the priests. Men encamped by the forest come out laid low, tainted by black arts and illness."

Elaira's surprise was miscalled as fear.

"The temple's examiners have stepped up the burnings," the matron was quick to qualify. As her child subsided to sniffles, she added, "Mostly to clap a lid on the panic. Gives some terrified folk reassurance to witness the purges."

Elaira gestured to ward off evil, an acceptable pretence much safer than truth: in fact the malaise of the men surely stemmed from their own disaffection. The Hatchet's intrusion brought town-bred ignorance. Taken into the heightened flux of the free wilds, where cause to consequence quickened, the confluence of their aggression would sow unsettled dreams, then unlucky accidents and cumulative outbreaks of raving and sickness. The resonant shock gathered force with exposure, perhaps tweaked for the worse by Dakar's subtle tinkering, or the ripple effect of Asandir's warding.

Hope withered, that Elaira might slip through unremarked, then abandon the road for safe passage across the fast deeps of Halwythwood. Daunted by the hurdle she faced at the border, she repacked her satchel and mustered the brazen nerve to move on.

Hoof-beats and the purposeful jingle of steel hushed the female chatter around her. Elaira glanced up, doused by sudden shadow as a half dozen dedicate lancers reined in. They were armed. The wolfish fellow at the fore barked an order that lowered their pennoned weapons. Then he tipped back his helm. Older than his cock-sure manner suggested, he surveyed the cluster of women detained by his grinning subordinates. A flicked glance dismissed the asthmatic granddame. His interest passed over the children, then measured the rest as though sizing up beef.

"That one!" His decisive nod ear-marked the sturdy matron.

"You've no right! I won't go." The basket with the infant clamped to her breast, the woman stood firm and clutched her bewildered toddler. "Who'll look after my children?"

"The weans have their granny." The officer signalled his right-hand man to dismount and hand off his horse. "Must we prise your offspring away by main force?"

"Whoremongering snake!" The woman spat. "I'll be warming no beds! Not though you promise the Light of salvation."

Ribbed by amused comments from his comrades in arms, the lead rider curbed his restive gelding. "Dame, shut your yap! We're upright husbands, not lechers. Nobody's hunting for trollops, besides. Our troop captain's sent us recruiting because we require a laundress. You're fit for the post. Now take leave of those bairns and get packing!"

The hefty woman dug in her heels. As her panicky children started to wail, the footbound lancer reached for the scruff of the toddler latched to her side.

Elaira thrust herself in between. "I'll go instead."

The challenged man recoiled in testy surprise. "Will you so?" His contemptuous stare raked her. "Woman, you're scrawnier than a plucked hen!"

Elaira returned the glare of a trained Koriathain, which ruthlessly analysed everything. "Besides washing, I can stitch cloth and mend harness. A skill that's deficient in your slackers' camp. A sharp superior might forgive your frayed seams, but the lot of you ought to be whipped for the untended wear on the straps of your armour."

Which tart critique raised the dedicate's eyebrows. "And you're not a rag-tag beggar yourself, besides lacking the muscle to wring out a dandy's silk shirt?"

"Irregular meals haven't helped," snapped Elaira. "You want proof? I carry trade tools in my satchel."

The lead rider shrugged, unimpressed. A clipped gesture remanded his lancer. "Carry on."

Elaira moved first and grabbed the nearest man's levelled spear. Braced hard, she yanked with a vengeance. The dumbfounded brute gripping the pole weapon tumbled out of the saddle and measured his length. His startled horse bolted. Amid shouting confusion, Elaira jumped on his kidneys and yelled at the matron, "Go! Get away. Take your children and run!"

Before the pinned rider's outrage dislodged her, she received the back-handed brunt of the captain's gauntlet. The blow hammered her down from behind and up-ended her into nothingness.

* * *

Awareness returned to ringing ears and the throb of a battering headache. "Light above, you're lucky I'm not tending a corpse." The speaker's calm hands bathed the clotted bruise beneath Elaira's hair with tepid water.

"Sadly not." The enchantress groaned. "My skull's split."

Swimming vision dazzled her with a taupe view of overhead sun through seamed canvas. The lidded air smelled of greased leather, mildew, and pungent sweat. Miserably nauseous, she tried to roll over.

"Be still!" The chiding female was not without sympathy. "What brainless folly led you to brangle with mounted Sunwheel recruiters?"

Elaira let jellied weakness defeat her effort to sit up. Outside, someone's cheerful whistling broke off to a surly order. A horn-call, muffled with distance, suggested the industry of the Light's war camp, shortly confirmed by the brisk rattle of steel, male complaint, and the unison thunder of drums that accompanied a phalanx of marching feet. Elaira's queasy focus returned to measure her care-taker. Surprised, she said, "Why didn't you run?"

The mother from the roadside paused, blew her nose, then tossed her cloth compress with a vehement splash into a nearby bucket. "Where could I have gone chased down by armed riders? Before you ask, yes, my wee ones are safe. I left them with their granddame."

"I'm sorry." Elaira shut her eyelids against the pound of rushed blood through her brain. She pulled a deep breath, which did nothing for the torment that savaged her temples. Her wrists were not bound. The hand she raised to explore her bashed nape was caught short by the matron.

"You have a bruise like a hen's egg, but no cracked skull, if the troop surgeon here knows his business."

"He should, though no thanks to the clumsy muscle wielded by the Sunwheel rank and file." Though the fact she recovered on an officer's field cot meant the lancer's assault had not aimed to kill. Dogged, Elaira pursued, "They wanted you for service as a laundress. After the press-gang, we're not in chains. Perhaps the captain's not lacking all decency?"

Encouraged, her fellow conscript talked freely. "The fellow admired your provocative spirit. Said you'll be kept as his personal drudge if you've the gumption to shoulder the labour." She added, "The wax thread and tools in your satchel also confirmed you pursued an honest trade."

Elaira snatched in alarm for the less obvious valuables hung from her neck. The fast move clenched her stomach. Curled, miserably retching, she fought panic, while the matron's kindness reassured her. "The Light's dedicates are not undisciplined rogues. They searched your belongings but left your coin. None of them rifled your person. Your dignity was respected the moment they saw the Sunwheel token."

Elaira stilled, breathless. "What?"

"The disk you now wear was my mother's," the woman explained. "She reached your side before anyone else. Her sly gift went unnoticed, she made

217

sure of that by the ruckus she threw when you fell. She even kicked the shins of the lancers ordered to pull her away."

Elaira lay back, bathed in unquiet sweat. Her shaking touch fingered the brass amulet pinned at her breast. "Why?" she whispered, touched. "How under sky did the goodwoman guess I wasn't a follower?"

The matron swiped moisture off her damp cheeks, her generous heart apparent despite the pouched eyes of raw grief. "Well, you stood up for my family, when no one of faith protested the Light's authority. The True Sect devout sometimes kill unbelievers. Likely, she wanted no blood on an upright man's hands for our sake."

Elaira swallowed. "I owe her a debt I can never repay." For her straits in the enemy camp were not desperate, employed as an officer's servant. She might evade notice, masked by bumpkin stupidity, as long as she kept to herself and ducked the boisterous men on the prowl for a wench in the blankets.

The troubled eyes of both women locked through a moment of sober assessment. "You wanted to be here?" the matron said, shocked.

"Maybe," allowed Elaira. "Fortune's cards might be turned to play in my favour." A camp-follower in The Hatchet's armed troop could find a legitimate passage across Instrell Bay to Rathain. "Whatever befalls, I will watch your back, if you'd have the friendship of a chance-met stranger."

"One who doesn't embrace the Sunwheel Canon?" But the matron's shrewd comment belied any threat. "I'm called Liess, and my mother's token stays with you for as long as you need it."

Past solstice and into the stifling days of late summer, all of the north seethed under the impact of the True Sect war. Fires blazed across Tysan. The Plain of Karmak brooded, dappled in smoke, where Sunwheel companies kindled the heath to drive Orlan's displaced clan enclaves into the open. By turns the chased fox and the blood-letting weasel, Saroic s'Gannley harried their lines, his genius for evasive retreat and covert strikes become legend. Where the temple expounded on virtuous good in reward for relentless trials and set-back, The Hatchet's pragmatic strategy applied steady pressure to keep his elusive antagonist on the run.

"The clan's fighting strength was well broken when we gutted the warren entrenched at the Pass of Orlan." A dismissive glower, a shrug, then the side-long gleam of bared teeth. "What's left to mop up but the fugitive dregs? They'll have no chance to stockpile provisions. Keep them hopping, and next winter's privation will finish them off with minimal losses."

Which laconic efficiency brought the Light's best strength to bear on the greater clan presence entrenched in Rathain. The towns used for staging suffered the scars, with the croft-lands at Narms and Morvain gridded with encampments, and commerce choked under troops and supply the length and breadth of Rathain.

Into a landscape seething with upheaval, bloodied by the carnage inflicted by spring traps and ambush, the Prime Matriarch transplanted her Senior enchantresses from their established residence at Whitehold. The move wrung the hands of the sisterhouse bursar, whose treasury coffers bore the extortionate cost of galley passage to Jaelot, then caravan transport on mule-back over the notches and slot narrows of the Skyshiel pass. A month's toil brought the frayed entourage to disgruntled settlement in an open encampment in Daon Ramon.

Only Lirenda raised no complaint. A dumb beast in thralled service, and lately reduced to muscling strapped trunks and split wood for the cookfires, she no longer agonized over the crow's-feet stamped into her lily complexion. She could sink no lower. After hauling ashes from fire pits and emptying chamber-pots, nothing in the wide world could make her degraded lot any worse.

Or so she imagined, until the morning Prime Selidie commanded her presence in the central pavilion. The attendant Seniors were already excused when she entered the private, partitioned enclosure, cloaked in gloom and rancidly tinged by the flame of a single taper. Lirenda performed her obeisance, suffocated by the moth-poison taint of wool hangings barely aired out from inclement travel.

Her tawny eyes as she rose were the stalking tiger's, thirsty for blood.

The Matriarch was installed in a carved chair across a low table. A muffled hand cuffed in velvet and pearls indicated the only available seat: a divan cushioned with ancient embroidery, the legs chiselled into heraldic swans with spread wings. The birds' necks were contorted like coupling snakes, shortly veiled by Lirenda's drab skirt.

Mute, but not patient, she waited, inscrutable.

The usurper wearing Selidie's flesh eventually must find herself compromised. Secretive plans that spiralled into ever-more-convolute activity suggested her omnipotent grip may have slipped since the shock of Davien's back-handed rebuff. Whoever looked out of the Matriarch's eyes, crone or coerced green initiate, the fixated pursuit of Prince Arithon's person invited contempt. Yet no Senior dared to question the circuitous chess-game in motion at Ettin. Lirenda's intent focus perceived no cracks under the gloss of imperial grooming.

Cold aquamarine eyes regarded her back. Half-shuttered lids iridescent with powdered mother of pearl revealed no flicker of weakness. Immaculate, fair hair braided through a gold-wire diadem glittered with rubies and amethyst.

On the table, the instruments of repression, unveiled like cut glass on black velvet: three initiates' personal quartz crystals rested in a surgical row. Lirenda recognized the first as her own, bestowed at the testing that followed her oath. Apprehensive, she marked the second, linked to Elaira. The last, caged in wound copper and thread, belonged to a first level junior initiate. A pair of silk gloves, and another ominous bundle secured by ritual knots lay in readiness, also.

"Properly unveil the shrouded effigy," the Matriarch opened. "I want it renewed with a fresh infusion." The prompt of a crippled hand swathed in gauze indicated the third subject's crystal. "There's your template."

Lirenda tugged on the gloves. Palms clammy inside the thin silk, she bared the cloth doll, wound with white ribbons once stripped from the sleeves of the specified novice. The opening of the ritual disclosed the sister marked for manipulation. As much the bound handmaiden to the Prime's will, Lirenda engaged the copper-wound quartz point and imposed the ciphers that stabilized Vivet Daldari's etheric imprint.

"You'll recline for completion of my directive." Prime Selidie's intent regard caught the flare of Lirenda's internal rebellion. "The yoke galls, does it not? Though for you, this particular case is not contrived as a back-handed punishment. The subduction of your identity through Vivet furthers our order's creed to advance the greater good of humanity."

Initiates died for the mission, the terms of their service made absolute since the inaugural matriarch had founded their secret society. Pity granted no stay of exception. Lirenda settled herself on the divan, skewered by dread, and unable to protest. The ordeal fore-promised much worse than the deep immersion invoked for screening the order's new applicants. For Vivet's fractured existence was a shaped tool, live puppetry fashioned by ruthless design to sweep a royal obstruction off the Prime's game-board.

Lirenda languished, while her superior loosened gauze ties with her teeth and fumbled her welted hands free. Anxiety choked thought, given the unpleasant ways a personal crystal might be put to use, combined with Elaira's. The scrape of the raised chair, the lisp of slippered steps on the dais stair, then the predatory sweep of full skirts rounding the table: Lirenda endured, unable to quail, as the Prime's icy touch traced the master sigil on her forehead. Closure kindled a flash of dry heat. Then implacable forces sucked away the stream of her consciousness. . .

. . . the senses returned to her were another's: raised from the well of oblivion into an alienated frame of awareness, Lirenda emerged into a tumult of sunlit colour and noise. An infant in a rug sling chafed at her shoulder. Overheated, and laced into a country-style bodice and homespun skirt, she sweated amid a buffeting crowd, crammed in between the pegged canvas stalls of a tinkers' itinerant market. The Prime's purpose had not subsumed her entirely. Folded into a borrowed identity, Lirenda became the unseen liaison, implanted as a live sounding-board and as a passive observer. She could influence nothing. Only partake as the hapless instrument immersed into Vivet Daldari's experience.

The subject herself blinked, swept by a surge of inexplicable dizziness. "Forgive me," Vivet interrupted the spiel of the stick-puppet vendor. "I'm a touch overcome, most likely from the crush and the heat." She shifted her squirming infant, startled afresh at the sudden firm grip, arrived in support at her elbow.

"Best you rest in the shade, then," suggested the callow, young cousin who steered her. He threaded her unsteady steps past the clumped wares and stacked baskets, propped bolts of dyed cloth, and strings of glass beads. Beyond the bazaar, a cluster of log benches under an oak gave the settlement's matrons a restful place to ease their feet. Vivet perched on the last vacant seat. Studied by a solemn boy chewing his fingers and scoured by reproachful glances from the married women, her face flamed. How embarrassing, that her weakness had required solicitude from a male relative.

"Thanks for the kindness, I'll do." When her escort kept hovering, she untied her points and loosened her bodice. "Valien's going to feed, or start fussing, enough reason for me to stay put."

The youngster fled, while a mother exclaimed and scooped her thumb-sucking daughter out of his path. No smiles acquitted the boy's self-conscious haste. Neither did the women fold Vivet into their circle. Though her infant was an asset to the community, her irregular household continued to set her apart. Murmured conversation resumed around her, over the clicked spools of an elder's lace tatting, and the hiss of bleached linen and carded wool being spun on drop spindles.

Vivet sighed. She ruffled the springing, dark curls of the babe fathered on her by a misfortunate woodsman whose oath of debt to Koriathain had claimed his life. She could do nothing else as a lowly novice immersed in a covert assignment, even if the stigma also afflicted her blameless son.

For already the settlement's toddlers took after their parents. The boldest directed their rough-house play elsewhere, squeals subdued when their ball rolled under her feet. The ostracism would have stung less if not for Arin's long absences. His seasonal livelihood kept her hearth lonely, even in summer, when the demand for an herbalist's skills sent him foraging for weeks on end.

"Well, pumpkin, I'm sorry. We're in this together." Vivet captured Valien's batting fists and worked his wriggling energy out of the sling. Sworn to the Order of the Koriathain, she upheld her duty: her fate, and the child's, bound Arin's interests under the Prime's directive.

Vivet hefted her son to her breast, lip caught in her teeth to stifle a wince as he clamped on her nipple. Fortune might shift her lot. The guarded insularity of Ettinmere offered the best haven to raise a gifted family, given her mission successfully conceived her next-born by Arin. Blood offspring of his would possess wild talent, liability enough to get such a youngster culled outright by the True Sect purges.

For Canon doctrine inflamed the northern kingdoms to war, with unbelievers and clanborn put to the sword by temple decree. Settlement folk hungry for outside news plied the merchants' drovers with beer, where they idled in boredom alongside the picketed draught teams. Vivet caught their outspoken opinion, the quickened tempo of argument evident through Valien's guzzling.

"Oh, I'd say for a fact there's been uncanny practice!" A man's passionate finger stabbed emphasis between the hulked oxen, switching at flies.

". . . that The Hatchet's scouts fingered a hidden encampment. Mark this! The report listed women and bairns, tucked as tightly as termites in rot under tents in the greenwood. But when the dedicates closed on the site, they found nothing, no sign of anyone there."

Someone interrupted, gruff with disbelief.

"I tell you that unlucky company died to a man," the original speaker insisted. "Fell with clean swords in a wave of red slaughter, lured into a baited trap!"

"Claptrap nonsense!" the cynic responded. "Even the Spinner of Darkness can't conjure the living semblance of women and children."

The scoffer met a nervous rebuttal. "What limit, given he's evil incarnate? The dedicates might have seen anything fell, even conjury that animates corpses."

"Fact's been witnessed already," another voice insisted. "The uncanny creature vanished clean off the field at Lithmarin. Melted into thin air. Faithful survivors swear he left no trace for the head-hunters' trackers."

The wizened man mending the mule whip spat. "Well, the surgeon who worked with the east-flank troops encountered the Master of Shadow up close. He insists the slinking devil's no paragon. Just a small, black-haired fellow, unassuming and shy, no more sinister than a mountebank with a knack for impersonation."

A slight man with dark colouring, though nothing like Arin, Vivet mused to herself. Her designate quarry was not retiring, given his insolent temper shoved burrs under everyone's skin. She missed him, regardless. Emotion tightened her throat, followed by a fierce wave of longing. The intensity of the attraction appalled her. Dispatched by the sisterhood to waylay his destiny, she had never expected to care, or pine for his erratic attention. His indifference cut her, surprisingly deep. Cheek laid against her suckling child, Vivet stifled her wrenching grief, unaware that her tender response was the puppeteer's pull of enthrallment . . .

. . . but Lirenda was party to all of the strings, trapped as the Matriarch's passive observer under the aegis of the master sigil. She felt the invasive, rippling chill, when Prime Selidie invoked her personal crystal and delved into the record of her private self. The rage and shame of her downfall rekindled, as the Matriarch's purpose tapped back into the primal longing once quickened by the Masterbard's empathy. Arithon's infallible artistry had illumined her spirit, pierced her heart, and ignited the blazing need for a love unimagined, and never experienced.

Selidie's ruthless manipulation threaded that wakened cascade through the other quartz point aligned to Elaira, then knotted the invasive thread through the genuine spark of her cherished regard for Prince Arithon. The diabolical fusion welded desperate, unrequited longing and intimate affection into a flame of torment. Last, Selidie strung the brew of potentized motivation through the link that enthralled the Daldari woman at Ettinmere.

Lirenda shuddered in sympathetic reaction, unable to whimper as the final cipher sealed the entrainment. She shared the shocked onslaught as Vivet awakened, wracked by a yearning to demolish reason and ravage the spirit. The Prime branded her with an inconsolable obsession to the Teir's'Ffalenn's essence.

For Vivet, the rip tide of spellcrafted desire inflicted a cruelty beyond surcease. Her already compromised peace of mind shattered, until the improbable hour her consort abandoned restraint and possessed her. Crushed by longing and abject despair, she buried her tears against Valien's dark head. Beyond her, under the adjacent oak, the mules switched flies as if naught were amiss. The merchants' drovers lounged in the dappled shade, chewing grass stems. Their gossip had drifted, as if no violation had tightened the intrigue that aimed to deflect the world's destiny.

For Lirenda, the visceral heart-ache let go, dissolved by the rush of dizzy relief as her thralled senses separated from Vivet's identity. Suppressed awareness resurged, restoring her to the stultified gloom of the canvas pavilion sited in Daon Ramon.

Her traumatized fury refocused in time to catch an insightful glimpse of Prime Selidie's satisfaction.

The fleeting expression was icily shrewd, proof of a rapt intelligence wielded in cold self-command. Appearances lied: the Matriarch's manic resolve never stemmed from erratic senility. Likely, she toyed with the ruse to mislead her enemies.

Lirenda's resharpened interest perhaps prompted the Prime's rare moment of confidence. "Did you presume my behaviour was irrational?" The low laughter that followed crackled like frost. "Then, for the import of our sisterhood's mission, pray the Fellowship Sorcerers agree. Let them trip on their overweening contempt and crash into the pitfall of misjudgement."

Although the day's conjury seemed an overt bid to breed a child candidate for the Prime succession, Arithon's perverse nature was disinclined to embrace Vivet's driven attempts at seduction. Recast as the feint for a radical thrust in another direction, the move foreshadowed a current of intrigue too murky for even the Warden of Althain to fathom.

Deathwatch

The invasion unleashed by the True Sect war host scoured the northwest barrens of Daon Ramon, the hopscotch pattern of their engagements and hit-and-miss spats of skirmish erratic as cricket fights swept by a scourge. Staged into the broad, rolling grasslands veined with seamed gullies and entangled briar, the campaign sought fixed roots, with each hill-top taken under a relentless, chess contest of wits. The Hatchet's foot companies seethed from their defensive positions by day in marched columns that furrowed dust off the trackless heath. Wave upon wave, the advance paused by night, while stealthy clan raids slipped through picketed sentries to set spring traps and cause surprise mayhem.

The stagnating heat and the flies by late summer should have exhausted the faithful. Yet none of the Light's officers caved in retreat despite their stale-mated frustration. Against ambush, veiled feints, and the pestilent seizures of misdirection sown by nefarious spellcraft, The Hatchet pressed the zealot weight of sheer numbers with his born genius for tactics. While the incessant casualties mounted, more than clan blood-lines suffered. The toll of carnage afflicted the flux. Unsanctioned trespass and traumatic death rippled discord through the lane currents, a lingering after-shock of malaise like a stain to mage-sighted awareness.

Cosach's charge to defend the free wilds demanded a response before dissonance marred the lyric chord sustaining the mysteries. To that end, Dakar suffered the needled assault of whining mosquitoes, tucked in a gulch down-hill from the scar of another garrisoned war camp. The latest and worst of The Hatchet's redoubts nestled behind palings atop a bald crag that commanded the landscape.

A moonless night's quiet infused the deep shadow, broken by the scuff of the night sentries' boots and the rasp of mail against weaponry. Stakes roped with twine marked off their beat, where daybreak would wake seething industry. A row of parked wagons loomed against the stacked lumber imported for out-buildings. Canvas tarps covered another dray, burdened with a camp forge, sand and quicklime in sacks, and the shovels, picks, and trowels stockpiled to carve the wild turf into fortifications. Ghostly under wan starlight, whitewash blazes splashed the boulders chosen to be prised from their beds, then shattered and dressed under the masons' mallets for permanent mortared embrasures.

On the surface, the scene appeared peaceful. The Mad Prophet wormed through the ink tangle of underbrush to the rim of the gully. Eyelids half-shut, for too long immersed in the altered awareness of mage-sense, he nursed his overstrung faculties. His vigil was altogether uneasy. Disconcertingly close to the lane's active focus sited at Caeth-al-Caen, and with midnight's tide crested two hours ago, the heightened surge of the flux taxed his endurance. Even the ebb current threatened to drown him. No surprise, that he wrestled the throes of exposure in the upshifted wake of Davien's meddling at Kathtairr.

Dakar's nerves were wont to leap at frissons like star-bursts, while his unstable focus in present time flinched, dazzled by the residual sheets of white fire left by the ancient echo of unicorns passing. He blotted his palms, rattled to the chaotic edge of insanity. Although Cosach's scouts dared not open their Sight in this place, a master spellbinder ought to be fit to withstand the proximal intensity.

Experience proved otherwise. But caution posed too costly a luxury. More than clan lives were endangered.

Dakar clamped his teeth, determined to stay anchored, while ecstasy rode him in shivering waves, at times fit to thrash him unconscious. Near blinded and deafened, he sounded the flood of exquisite sensation for the subsonic thrum of disharmony. That signal dissonance *had to be* present, hard by an enemy camp. The pitch of anxiety and rage cast at large by the True Sect invaders should gauge the strength of the nest Cosach's war band poised to attack. Action must rout the intrusion, before the defacement marred a resonant, grand junction vital to the free wilds.

Yet the only flare of ill temper in range needled Dakar at close quarters.

"Well?" rasped Cosach's whisper. "Have you finished the headcount?"

The Mad Prophet blinked. "Not yet." Stressed by the interruption, his ethereal vision shimmered through commonplace sight like a half-world unfurled out of dreams. The chieftain's gruff presence beside him crackled with impatience, torch-bright against a night landscape buckled into fluorescent haloes and electromagnetic distortion. Obliged to reknit his frayed concentration, Dakar dug back into immersive trance.

He acknowledged nothing: not the breathless scout just shoved in behind, nor the flurried responses raised by a report that rang like tapped glass in his sensitized ears.

". . . rampant idiocy, to use ox-drawn wagons before pack-mules."

"Wasteful," Cosach grumbled, equally taken by the stupidity. The Barrens wore summer's glory of forage, sweetened by adequate rain. "D'you wonder how many axles they broke? Or men's backs, when their wheels bogged down? Your patrol's off their mettle. Couldn't they hear the penned cattle at distance or smell the reek of manure on the breeze?"

"No. That's because someone's enterprise slaughtered the livestock. Maybe they've roasted the lot for a feast?" The scout flashed a weasel's grin. "Makes a quick task for our handful of archers. Luckless as gaffing frogs if those squatters are snoring, gut-stuffed with beef."

Cosach scraped at his tangled beard, less amused, though the drays offered cover to obscure their advance from the enemy sentries. "These are not priggish merchants we're raiding."

"Not like you to slink like a cur from a bone tainted by the whiff of uncertainty." A wry shrug, and the clan scout sobered. "So you're thinking we fire the tents and the tarps?" Easy enough to thin out the targets once they pelted into the open. "Drop the watchmen, then swoop on the tents to dispatch the startled survivors?"

"Right enough." Cosach fingered a talisman under his shirt. "Dawn won't wait. Send the word."

The scout slithered backwards, gone on silent feet while the chieftain elbowed Dakar's barrel ribs. "Forget the bungling reconaissance. We'll grow roots for your fussy delay."

Dakar surfaced, befuddled, until the dawning impact of the clansman's decision jabbed him to alarm. "Don't move on that camp!"

"What?" Cosach snapped.

"Break off the attack. Do it now!" His sweep of the lane current had fingered *nothing*, which suspect quiescence in hindsight screamed warning. No time to pursue the suspicion of mage works. "Those wagons conceal a laid trap!"

Coward or not, Dakar spoke as a prophet.

Cosach chose to fall back, hamstrung by the need to order the retreat in silence. His signal relay reacted, too late: the strike leading the war band's advance already had broken away from deep cover.

Pinprick flames bloomed on the overlook. Then a volley of arrows creased the jet sky. Wakeful all along, positioned for the sally, the True Sect bowmen stormed the clan engagement from the crest, spurred by the blast of an officer's horn.

Cosach's band reeled under the hostile fire. No help, knowing the intruder's camp was laid bait. More shafts shot from above pelted into the parked drays and stacked lumber. Both sheeted into an oil-fed blaze, while other flights scribing their high, crimson arcs rained with staccato retorts through tarred canvas. The encampment crowning the summit ignited. No sleep-fuddled dedicates fled the inferno in shouting panic. Ominous silence instead erupted to a hollow boom as the box cargo beds of the wagons dropped ramps from false bottoms and disgorged armoured men, steel drawn for slaughter.

Cosach yelled for his surprised war band to scatter. The command marked him out. A viperish hiss of enemy arrows slashed through the covert of stunted brush. Twice, the sickening whap of a broadhead punched into living flesh. Cosach's agonized grunts caught Dakar still immersed and wide open to mage-sight. He reeled, wrung helpless, while the clan chieftain recoiled in torment. Cosach's breaths sawed as though drawn through wet cloth, a ghastly refrain to the shock of mass bloodshed, spread over a widening stage of disaster.

The spellbinder wrung in the mangle wrestled to salvage his boundaries. Nausea folded him into a crouch, while subsequent volleys slashed into the thicket and snicked in rebound off the bank at his back. The flights kept on coming. Launched from the hill-top, the whickering deluge pelted like hail, the near misses close enough to part hair. Safe movement was impossible. Nothing might salvage the war band's pinned men, with who knew how many already cut down, dead or drastically wounded.

Dakar shivered, seized by morbid awareness the assault from above only staged a distraction for something worse.

Yet Cosach's straits trumped the prescient suspicion. Trapped in the breach, the Mad Prophet seized the felled chieftain's ankles and hauled him under the embankment. Through the slide of loose pebbles and the redoubled impacts of hostile bowfire, Dakar sensed the surge of wrought spellcraft convulsing the flux. He glanced up, aghast, just as flickered movement veered one of the air-borne shafts in mid-flight. Unnaturally turned, it whistled straight in under the influence of a sigil of homing.

Dakar swore murder. Too stout for heroics, he sprawled his pudding bulk to shield Cosach. Crude practice the only available recourse, the spellbinder bloodied his palm in the seep from the chieftain's pierced chest. His other hand, scrabbling, snatched up a dead stick. He smeared the bark, slapped a hasty seal over a counter-ward, and hurled the slap-dash construct away. The spelled arrow swerved in its final descent, struck the lure, and hammered the split wood to earth amid a kicked spray of dirt.

Dakar yelped, stung by the raw back-lash. "Fiends plague the hereafter!" he snarled in despair. For his stop-gap defence interfered with no less than the Order of the Koriathain. His outmatched resource would not spare the war band, or thwart who knew what nefarious partnership aimed to eradicate clanblood. Neither could he take stock or count losses, flattened like a cur in a gulch. Even if Cosach had been the sole quarry, The Hatchet's engagements always mopped up with a relentless rear-guard action. Those clansmen yet able to flee for their lives faced being outflanked.

Even Cosach grasped the bad odds. "Ath wept! I need you to shove off!" Teeth clenched against shudders of pain, he heaved under Dakar's planted weight.

The Mad Prophet granted his desperation no quarter. "Stay put!" Fastened like a lamprey on the chieftain's wrists, he bore down against manic struggle. "Damn all to your rock-head bravery! Stop causing havoc! Embedded with arrows, you won't get far, and breaking from cover can't help when you're tagged by a spelled attack latched to your blood-line."

Cosach renewed his furious argument. "All the better! I'll make good use. My run as a decoy buys us the time for you to spin a defence. Just get my survivors away."

"Be still!" Dakar snapped. "Show yourself, and those archers will stick you like a seamstress's pincushion." His rushed effort to raise a protection sheared off, sucked away as a sudden, subliminal shift opened a well of unnatural darkness. The surrounding brush crackled and sang, quickened sap seized by a cold fierce as death, silver dusted with glassine hoar-frost. The encompassing density of the event suffocated all access to mage talent.

One hand alone wielded the naked element with the power to suppress Rathain's lane current.

"Daelion avert, my vision's gone dark!" Cosach's outcry showed panic. "I cannot face the end. Not before I've seen my people out of here."

"You aren't blind," Dakar contradicted. "Nor are you chilled by the turn of Fate's Wheel." Though his foolish tongue perhaps spoke too soon: an arcane residue tainted the set arrows. Soft fingers more suited to toying with whores than the nuance of advanced healing, the Mad Prophet measured a damage fit to wreck hope. He was not Asandir: never innately skilled or adept enough to defy the grim course of a spell-driven fatality.

Cosach ground on, oblivious, "Ath forfend! This is an onset of Shadow? Then by every measure of worth, I have failed!"

Dakar's aplomb shattered. "That's blustering arrogance on top of self-punishment! All human nature is fallible. Even the almighty Fellowship Sorcerers can't steer his Grace clear of jeopardy." Yet platitudes only insulted a sacrifice that soon must cost everything honour held dear.

Nothing appeased Cosach's wild fury. "Blast that minikin bastard and his s'Ffalenn pride! Just snap off the shafts and help get me up. I must draw the archers! As much to stand shadow for Rathain's crown blood-line, as to give my war band their chance to win free."

"The minikin bastard in fact disagrees." Arrived in a furtive rustle of brush, the breathless speaker slid in beside the chieftain's doomed struggle.

"Fiends alive!" exclaimed Dakar, battered afresh by the fists of Cosach's refuelled outrage. "You always deliver, like salt in a sore, slap on the thorns of a crisis."

Through the rattle of bowfire, Arithon's dry irony, "You think I'm here for the feckless blood sport of baiting the bear?"

"What else?" Cosach ranted. "It's a useless task, nurse-maiding celibate royalty hell-bent on flitting into harm's way."

"Be still! For all your misguided s'Valerient courage, a suicide charge will spare no one. In fact, your clan war band has nowhere to run." Jostled as Dakar muscled back in to suppress the chieftain's crazed rebellion, Arithon finished his summary. "The Hatchet's placed his rear-guard in ambush. Your folk are set up for a massacre."

Cosach bulled onwards, shamed beyond embarrassment. "Dharkaron's Black Spear take your gadding cant, the Avenger's caprice could not let this happen. My outlying scouts were not slacking off! Never, while we stalked a Sunwheel encampment for a covert attack."

"The Light's pious," declared Arithon, "had arcane help." Then, directed across Cosach's stupefied rage, the blunt impact of accusation, "Which choice gossip your prophet already knew." To Dakar, gaffed speechless, the punch line stripped tact. "Did you plan to warn Cosach, before I breezed in?"

The Mad Prophet swallowed, indecently scrambling. "Is this a torturous duel of conscience? I should know, at first hand, how it feels to suffer an arrow impressed by enchantment." He twisted the knife-thrust. "If your recall's not faulty, you'd be remiss not to remember that you were the thwarted target."

The bite of s'Ffalenn temper responded. "You're citing the life debt you once held from Vastmark? Surely the back-stab of betrayal at Halwythwood cancelled that score."

"Your access to memory isn't complete!" Lamed in self-defence, Dakar paid dear for the loyalty that protected Elaira.

Arithon's rebuke demolished nicely. "Let the clan chieftain breathe. He's got no strength to waste."

Dakar woke to that cruelty and moved, just as Cosach's composure broke into an urgent shudder of agony. No skilled healer mistook the ominous signs. Fate's Wheel was already turning. A dying man's dignity deserved the truth. "The manipulative hand in the enemy's glove is the Prime Matriarch of the Koriathain."

"The victim's aware." Gentled as his ministrations mapped the severity of Cosach's injuries, Arithon added, "Liegeman, be still."

But a lifetime of service as the realm's steward rejected complacency. "Your Grace, must I beg to salvage my botched legacy? Take your wily talent and leave this place. Guide my war band to safety without me."

Rathain's cross-grained crown prince objected. "Dakar's able to shoulder that challenge. I stay at your side, beyond question."

The Mad Prophet smothered dismay, with cause afraid the Teir's'Ffalenn's adamance stemmed from a prior debacle, when his attendance at the ninth hour had eased the lethal wound of another steadfast liegeman. If Sidir's prodigal rise from extremity underlay today's insane choice, Arithon's restricted recall could not fathom Elaira's vital role in that miraculous recovery. Dakar tried again to unseat false conviction. "You realize your presence is tempting a move against you by the Koriani Matriarch?"

"Yes." The word rang like iron.

One recalled, in that moment, the massive accumulation of *iyats* collected that unpleasant morning on the Tiendarion. Epiphany dawned late, and with bruising anguish, that the obstreperous resistance hurled down then likely had been a feint.

Stunned to realize his crown prince had not been obstructive at whim but had diverted restraint from a strategic action, Cosach protested through gritted teeth, "Surely, your Grace, you're abetting the purposeful snare the Prime's laid to play you from the start!"

But attempted dissuasion only provoked the formal response of the crown prince faced by a liegeman's passage: "Be at peace. Leave the threat to the realm in my hands. *I'cuelan am-jiask edael i'tier*, Cosach," Which translated, *"your feal prince attends you."* Then came the grave promise last spoken to Sidir, downed by a lung wound as grievous. "All you fought for, my hand will put right."

Cosach arched, distressed.

"Go, Dakar," urged Arithon, working his craft as he spoke. "My plague storm of *iyats* will strike within minutes. You will take that opening. Break the lines of the enemy ambush and grant the High Earl his war band's deliverance." While Shadow impeded the archers' aim, he closed quickly, "You can't argue my rightful place here."

Dakar caved to exigency. He knew far too much. Noosed as he was by the volatile secrets buried in Arithon's history, straightforward cowardice relieved his quandary to keep the cruel facts safely buried.

The Mad Prophet wormed, swearing, into the gulch, eager to be quit of both battle-fields. "Given you got yourself in here unscathed, you're welcome to your own devices." He did not look back. And because he was rankled, his spurious talent for augury failed. Dakar never forecast the catastrophe sown in the wake of his slinking departure.

For Cosach, the terrible wait for release resharpened his leaden regrets. Some, he could do naught to assuage: his thirst for Jalienne's tender kiss, and the legacy owed to an infant child abandoned ahead of maturity. The fatherly pride and adult advice lost to his eldest son, Esfand, and two more daughters by an earlier marriage forsaken untimely. Smaller things carried an unforeseen sting. Experiences not to be savoured anew: the brisk gallops in snow under cobalt sky, or the fierce joy that tingled the nerves when the first blush of solstice sunrise crowned the ancient oak groves in Halwythwood.

Yet even those yearnings dwindled before the wronged crown prince, stationed in steadfast futility beside him. Breath drawn against the grate of the broadheads lodged into bone and viscera, Cosach argued, "Your Grace, you must leave! Since I never granted you my feal oath, in fact, you have no obligation. Don't burden me further by risking your neck to a True Sect offensive."

His liege chose not to answer; in fact never heard, immersed as a mage to finesse his elemental mastery of shadow. The pause hung, while the chilly breeze sieved through the brush carried fragments of horn-calls and distanced shouts. Throughout, the enemy arrows still flew. Between his hitched gasps, Cosach picked out the explosive crack of stressed wood, snap-frozen and shattered like glass. He realized, clenched against desperate tears, that far more than Dakar's escape had been covered.

Beyond view in the dark, the ambush was routed. The war band's survivors were well away, with his crown prince's adamant vigil as fixed as a boulder in hostile terrain.

"No more can be done, here," Cosach gasped, insistent. "Don't waste yourself for a stranger's useless recrimination." Bitter experience acknowledged the fact: blood loss must eventually finish him.

"I might lift the worst of the pain." A stir of leather and cloth, in the void, as Arithon settled for the duration. "By your leave?"

Seized in the throes of a terrible spasm, the clan chieftain bent to necessity rather than widen the disaster by flagging adverse attention. He shouldered the shame and let Arithon's deft handling ease his contorted body. Nothing assuaged his laceration of spirit. The fateful rejection on Thunder Ridge could not be reversed, any more than averting the harrowing grief he bequeathed to his absent family. But humility might appeal for forgiveness if a dying man dropped his towering pride and addressed his mistake.

Cosach fumbled, at a loss to begin. The presence beside him was too self-contained, a stranger schooled to high mastery, and dangerous, given his relentless command of darkness obscured every natural referent. Initiate power was not wont to speak first. A mage who honoured integrity volunteered nothing, unasked.

"However, Athera's Masterbard might," the Teir's'Ffalenn responded aloud to his liegeman's stricken uncertainty. The touch that ministered to Cosach's distress never faltered, while the trained voice resumed with sincerity, "You did not fail your charge to Rathain's crown lineage."

Remorse erupted like a burst boil. "Kharadmon's censure was unequivocal."

"Was it?" Under the pall of primordial night, that shrouded a desperately naked intimacy, Arithon's stifled laughter held astonishment. "Given that Fellowship Sorcerer's nature? I'd stake my life the ferocious rebuke was a lesson for Dakar."

"It wasn't. Don't crapshoot with fate out of misguided kindness." Cosach's wet cough carried scorching irony. "I was stripped of title. Were you not told? My son Esfand's been named for succession."

The prince trampled objection. "And have the Seven not made intervention before? History records, in the bleakest of times, they've used their designate authority to secure a significant lineage. I've lived to bear witness. Your forebear, Earl Jieret, endured the same. At infancy, his daughter Jeynsa was made heir apparent to stand shadow behind Rathain's throne."

Cosach grunted in derision. "A shell game of semantics did not land me in exile, banished from my family in Halwythwood."

"Exile?" Shock displaced bemusement, recoiled, and sharply attacked the assumption. "On the soil of Daon Ramon? How, when you bleed on the same turf where the Riathan Paravians once ran wild? And have you not fallen in defence of Cianor Sunlord's birthplace?" Charged to indignation, Arithon snapped, "Damn all to Kharadmon's wicked style! This matters: you haven't fought for a monument but to save Mankind's viable future. How have you forsaken your obligation by defending the clarity of the mysteries?"

"Would I know?" Cosach coughed again, a sodden paroxysm that set his head reeling for lack of air. Not long now, he hoped, while he floated, adrift as a wisp in the velvet dark. Scent acquired a preternatural clarity: of deer-hide and steel, blood and sweat and exertion, threaded by the headier fragrance of meadow grass silvered with dew. Wrenched by sorrow, he remembered the night he lay with his first wife, dead these long years of childbirth in a lean winter. He had been a strapping eighteen, filled with braggadocio and a rebellious desire for a scarlet shirt. "Given a choice in this world, I'd have begged to be town-born."

Resentment smouldered, for the harsh lifestyle that clan tradition scratched out in the wilds. His young bride, like so many, had perished in the cold, while women elsewhere enjoyed snug houses, bedecked in loomed cloth and bright silk. They went shod in slippers and raised daughters and sons with the luxuries of books and pens for their learning.

Rancour festered beneath the hard wisdom of years, and the fortunate bliss of Cosach's second marriage to Jalienne. "I'd have the truth, from the prince who's rejected his crown. Is the preservation of proscribed ground worth the toll in clan lives, or the toil and sacrifice needed to keep the free wilds untamed? There are days," Cosach fumed, "when I endure my heritage by rote. In our cups, we all wonder. Is our labour to uphold the compact a high-handed checkrein to grind Mankind down and repress the advantage of progress?"

Arithon shifted. The pause of his fingers against stricken flesh suggested the terrible question not broached: that access to shelter and specialized instruments may have bought reprieve for an injury, lethal out here on the field.

"Should I die," Cosach ranted, "for the sake of the ancient restrictions writ by Sorcerers for a moribund cause? If we hallow the land for a legend, why cling to a compact that stifles Mankind's intellectual prowess?"

"Sethvir answered that point, once," Rathain's crown prince admitted. "I had challenged his grounds for a coronation with—politely, let's say—a scathing remark on the evident tyranny of the kingdom charters."

Cosach's chuckle emerged as a wheeze. "Dakar's said you're the flaming stake in the arse of the Fellowship's policies."

The pause stretched, through an awkward rustle of cloth. Perhaps having shrugged in self-conscious embarrassment, Arithon qualified, seamlessly,

"Althain's Warden responded that Ath's creation has infinite facets. He argued further, humanity's endowment holds a raw possibility beyond the ingrained prejudice stifling the scope of our imagination. One avenue closed will open up an unlimited range of alternatives. Where reliance on mechanical industry is suppressed, creative solution must branch in other directions to compensate. The Sorcerers say Mankind's residence on Athera has started that change. They insist, as our senses become more refined, that our destiny leads to a break-through of stunning invention. A Fourth Age, when our species learns, as a whole, the expansive ability to tap and harness the flux. The virgin resource springs from the free wilds, and access will open to us through an increased expression of harmonic empathy. Our future could bestow a heightened expe-rience in cohabitation with Athera's Paravians. The gift of that legacy to our children's children is the shining promise behind compact law."

"Do you believe that?" Cosach whispered, his cynical doubt punched through ringing ears and sharp vertigo.

"I have known the presence of a living Paravian," Arithon stated with bed-rock simplicity.

Cosach hacked through his next laboured breath. "Which blessing I surely can't stay to experience."

From an eerie silence no longer creased by the whine of enemy bowfire, Arithon said, "Well, that does lie within my power to mend."

Which arrogant claim slammed into the teeth of Cosach's entrenched disaf-fection. "How, where the Fellowship Sorcerers themselves have failed beyond recourse?"

"We can't waste the time on theoretical debate," Rathain's prince pointed out. "Permission's required. Give me your hand and allow me the unreserved trust of an open heart."

Cosach made his apology, aware the dimness leaching his senses was not anymore the effect of wrought shadow. "Too late. My fingers are numb." He shivered, clutched by fear as the end overcame him.

Kindness supported him without stint. "You are not lost to the world's beauty, yet." Arithon's clasp cradled his slackened fingers. "I'm with you. Let go in release."

The act of surrender flushed Cosach's dulled nerves with tingling warmth. As a drowning man offered a sweet gulp of air, he embraced the plunge into rapport. The transition was not seamless or impersonal. Tumbled into a buffeting turbulence, aflame with reined-in emotion, he encountered a tender-ness beyond measure, vivid with the self-contained fury of Arithon's utter helplessness: *again* on the desolate soil of Daon Ramon, another downed liegeman could not be saved. Cosach saw his name graven beside other giants from heroic legend, his loss the fresh entry on a bitter list to be mourned alongside Earl Jieret and Caolle.

Then the marvel of fellowship was swept away as Arithon nestled a commonplace pebble into the chieftain's palm: and stone spoke, enlivened by the shared rapport of a sanctioned crown prince's attunement.

A pinprick spark danced across Cosach's innermind, igniting a flare that tightened his chest. He lost voice to protest or scream. Just shy of unbearable, the pressure burst. Failing vision shattered under a fountain-head dazzle of light.

Cosach gasped, whirled beyond the suffering of stricken flesh. He no longer noticed the bite of the lodged arrows, or felt the harsh ground, or heard the wind through the brush. Instead, he beheld a vista of meadow grass, fragrant under full sunlight. Over the downs that in living memory grew only sorrel and briar, he saw the shimmering glory of the Riathan Paravians. They came, golden horns lifted and polished coats gleaming: an ethereal presence as elusive in daylight as the silver shimmer of moonbeams. Joy seized him. Ecstasy bright as new morning uplifted him beyond all concept of mortal pain. Made witness to the unspoiled chord that sustained Ath's creation, Cosach yearned for completion as never before. The drive to encounter the fullness of his Name amid the grand arc of eternity parched him with insatiable desire. Infinite self-awareness glimmered just within reach, a riddle's answer no further away than a unicorn's breath on the fingers of his outstretched hand.

Then the vision darkened like a snuffed candle.

Cosach surfaced, weeping, eyes still dazzled with light, stretched too large for a body that cased his belaboured spirit like lead. A lifetime's aspirations had withered to ash, with earth-bound existence reduced to a cobweb that hindered his need to cast off old boundaries and soar.

Change had vaulted his human awareness too far. He no longer grieved. The outworn constraints he released lost all meaning, but for the single poignant regret that twisted his vitals.

"I never knew," he apologized to the crown prince beside him. "I paid lip service to my s'Valerient heritage, ignorant of the terrible stakes if our clan diligence slackened. I let you down, and much worse, my people, that morning on Thunder Ridge."

"Did your ancestors know any better?" Arithon responded without censure. "I've read Ciladis's appeal for the foundation of the clan lineages. At the conclave that wrote the compact's restraints, he said to your forebears, '*The select individuals called forward today have the potential to procreate talent. Given they're willing to commit their offspring, Mankind might shape a dream beyond reach of the species, born elsewhere. Ath's grace touched this world. That gifted heritage could enrich the human race, unilaterally, provided the mysteries that forestall the spiral of entropy on Athera continue to flourish. Embrace coexistence with Athera's Paravians, and the benefits of longer life and robust health will evolve an enhanced connection to heightened awareness. This potential would benefit more than your children. All people may inherit the chance to expand in ways unimagined.*'

"You did not fail," declared Arithon s'Ffalenn. "The legacy Ciladis envisioned lives yet. You've experienced the incontrovertible proof: the Mysteries endure, and a Paravian presence still exists in seclusion. Rathain's free wilds await their return, a restoration made possible through an unswerving trust, carried across generations."

Cosach shuddered, chest seized as his heart-beat faltered. While flooded lungs foundered, he broached the last words left unsaid. "My liege, listen well. You placed an artifact from your past under seal in a hidden cove in the Cascain Islands." The chieftain rammed onwards against ebbing strength. "You'll have to locate the site by your wits, near the same place you once cached the ship-wrights' tools salvaged from the yard at Merior."

Cosach spluttered through a gush of blood. Unable to feel the warm grasp that supported him, he finished his bequest. "My final wish! After your forgive-ness, I beg the requite of your royal promise. Don't abandon me as you were made to leave Caolle, at risk of usage by Koriathain. Don't let me languish like Jieret, as a crippled pawn in the hands of your enemies."

In extremis, Cosach sensed the flare of flash-point rage behind Arithon's patience. Fading, he interpreted the sharp silence, broken by steel-clad resolve. "The Prime Matriarch won't try extortion again, or set a bloodprice on my associates. After today, I'll be taking the challenge onto the sisterhood's turf."

At the end, in regret, life ebbed too fast. Cosach crossed the veil, the illu-mined grace of his fleeting glimpse of Athera's Paravians marred by a warning he never delivered: that his death in Daon Ramon surely had baited the snare meant to break Rathain's charter and destroy the compact.

Nexus

A trap had sprung under the night sky in the vales of Daon Ramon. Tarens awakened from vivid dreams whose grim fabric frayed to a fragment.

Somewhere an arrow had flown, drawing blood.

Yet his effort to recover the critical details slammed into vivid echoes of Arithon harried in close pursuit through the dark across the open heath. Perhaps his Grace was the stunned target of a hostile archer. Or maybe the nightmare stemmed from a phantom terror, born of the frustrated anguish endured since the emphatic severance atop Thunder Ridge. Tarens tossed, laced in sweat and haunted by formless anxiety. The glimmer of pre-dawn limned the loft's eastern window, grey back-drop to the lumped forms on the adjacent cots, still peacefully sleeping.

The bell to roust the hired field-hands would ring shortly. Tarens flung off his snarled bed-clothes. Dressed before the pink advent of sunrise, he crept out and fetched his tools from the shed, shaken enough to try to unseat his foreboding. Contract labour tied him to Backwater until autumn. Before chasing after directionless phantoms, he exhausted his shoulders, swinging the scythe. Let work sustain him through another rootless day, until he sorted a clear-cut course of action by which to make a sound choice.

The brute effort failed. His disquiet persisted. The sense of pending danger to Arithon stabbed gooseflesh across his skin, even in the glare of full sunlight and the distraction of human company. Not the figment of stressed nerves after all but a crisis prompted by the uncanny Sight of Earl Jieret's legacy.

Tarens dared not succumb. Not where suspect talent raised inquiry. Light-headed amid baking heat, his nose filled with the fragrance of timothy, he blotted his face on his sleeve and bent to the toil of raking the cured hay into windrows.

Noon brought him no respite. The blot of his shadow swam with incipient images, speared by the razed yellow stubble of sod. Solid earth underfoot seemed to shudder, threshed to powdered dust by distant ox-trains and the marching tramp of the Sunwheel war host. Surely activity too far away to threaten Arithon's interests: yet the creeping suspicion continued, that some other power at large plucked the threads of connected event.

Tarens shivered. Reason insisted he need not panic. A crofter's hire lent him the safety of anonymity. Or so he believed, when the bell clanged for the midday meal. He tossed his tool aside in the dirt. Flaxen head gleaming amid the sunburned straggle of field-hands, he joined their convivial tramp towards the open-air trestle stacked with wicker hampers.

Change visited, regardless. The aproned cook was not alone under the gaudy shade of her parasol. She broke off subdued speech with an angular, silver-haired stranger at the hireling's approach.

Eyebrows raised, her dumpling face furrowed with sympathy, she breasted the inbound press of the hungry and clasped Tarens's wrist. "You're free to go straightaway—for a death in the family, I'm sorry to hear. Of course, you're excused without obligation. Your outstanding wages have been paid in full to your kinsman."

Kinsman? Tarens's puzzled regard indignantly surveyed the brazen imposter. The seamed brow, gaunt nose, and cragged cheek-bones turned towards him were stern as quarried granite, set on a lean frame as imposing. The leathers on the long legs were briar-scraped, powdered with dust, and redolent of the saddle as the fellow's brisk-strided impatience advanced.

Ice-grey, eagle eyes fixed on his objective with urgency. "Iyat-thos Tarens?"

Earl Jieret's experience delivered the lightning-bolt recognition: come seeking him was a Fellowship Sorcerer, his demeanour as grim as disaster. The by-standing field-hands melted away. Whoever had died, the name would not concern the blood family abandoned in Erdane. Reflexive s'Valerient preroga-tive drove Tarens to meet the summary obligation head-on. He fell in with the Sorcerer's ground-eating pace without pause to retrieve his belongings.

Past earshot, unspeaking, the Sorcerer surrendered the wash-leather bag with his earnings.

Tarens's stiff reserve snapped. "Kingmaker, don't say you've come because Arithon's lost to an enemy arrow."

Asandir declined the grace of a direct answer. Blunt bronze, his fierce profile stayed trained ahead as he proceeded onto the rutted lane. "The death that brings me is Earl Cosach s'Valerient's, and the call for your support involves the kingdom at large." Then, through the crunch of desiccate grass, in a clipped string of consonants, "I've come to beg you to travel to Halwythwood and lend your service to Rathain's young *caithdein*."

"Esfand!" Tarens blurted, surprised. "Why, when my primary loyalty's owed to Prince Arithon? Has his Grace been wounded? Is he under pursuit?"

Asandir disregarded the impertinent questions, veered across the dirt lane, and rammed through the entangled scrub at the verge. Pressed down-slope towards the wind-break of trees at the stream bottom, he addressed his original topic. "I ask because Althain's Warden has foreseen your significant choices: to die at your liege's shoulder for naught. Or else to ride north at my bidding to Halwythwood and give the clans your advice as a war captain." The Sorcerer cast his piercing rebuttal across the chasm of poisonous doubt. "By my earnest word, your suspicion's unworthy! Our Fellowship's influence has not stifled the clarity of your Sight."

Tarens tripped over a hummock and swore, flustered as the Sorcerer continued apace.

"We can't help your liege's predicament, regardless. Aside from the Law of the Major Balance, Arithon's fate was cast outside our purview when my oath sealed the terms of our debt to the Koriathain."

Tarens's aghast recoil elicited no sympathy.

"The upshot is moot," Asandir snapped. "Whether you were informed of his Grace's straits, or if you knew where to seek him, your help could not change his lot for the better, hounded as he is by arcane interference. He must save himself at this pass."

Tarens seized the grim gist. "You don't think he can."

Asandir shrugged, fatalistic as iron. "More hangs in the balance than a crown prince's life." Before anguish whiplashed in rebellion, the Sorcerer qualified briskly. "I'm here because your free course of action is not resigned to futility! The Hatchet's recent brush with Shadow in Daon Ramon has redoubled the True Sect's armed fervour. The whole of the north will see reiving and slaughter. For the world's deep mysteries to stay viable, Rathain's clan bloodlines have to survive. They won't, without every tactical trick that Caolle taught to Earl Jieret. Your support, paired with Esfand, may serve hope for the future, where perhaps none may be salvaged."

The plunge from sunlight into dappled shade masked Tarens's hamstrung onslaught of grief. He could not in conscience refuse this appeal. Nor could Asandir afford to waste time with a coward's deliberation. Ahead, ink against the shagged boughs of the oaks, a black stud awaited, saddled and bridled, and equipped with bedroll and provisions.

"Ffiathli ot sanient, dasil am'n i'cuel'ien laere?" The stallion came at the Sorcerer's call, ears pricked through more rapid instructions in Paravian.

The horse stamped at the finish. Its noble head lifted and turned. Tarens found himself transfixed by the eerie, intelligent gaze of the creature's ghost eye. Anguish gripped the moment the field Sorcerer surrendered the bridle reins into his hand.

Gentleness softened Asandir's final word, which ripped away consolation. "My own mount will bear you at speed across Araethura."

"You don't need him, yourself?" Implied, Tarens's earnings could purchase a hack.

"No. Where I'm bound, flesh and blood cannot follow." Hands with prominent knuckles raised the saddle-flap and tightened the girth. "When you reach the notch at the Arwent ford, turn the horse loose. He can fend for himself. My instructions will have primed the scout relay. They'll provide your remount and a swift escort into Halwythwood."

Tarens accepted the leg up that flung him astride. "You realize Caolle's hardened sensibility will insist their clan lodge house must be put to the torch?"

"Lives rely on that wise lack of sentiment." Asandir shoved Tarens's foot home in the stirrup and slapped his calf to set him on his way. "Do as you must and take charge! Esfand's youth will resist uprooting the chieftains, and ruin will overtake them if they hesitate."

The black wheeled and clattered through the shoaled creek-bed on iron-shod hooves. Tarens faced north, sick at heart, for no memory in Jieret's store of experience matched the frayed exhaustion stamped into the Sorcerer's bearing. Whatever threat Arithon Teir's'Ffalenn faced, wider tragedy swung in the balance. Dread remained, that Cosach's bad call upon Thunder Ridge may have sprung the cascade to disrupt the compact.

"I should never have left my firm stance at my liege's back," Tarens lamented through the black mane whipped against his clenched teeth.

"No," rebuked Asandir's voice, arisen from empty air as the stallion splashed up the far bank. "Iyat-thos Tarens, you made the right choice! Had you stayed by Prince Arithon's side at Tiendarion, you would only have given the Ettinmere shamans the leverage they sought to control him."

On the hour Iyat-thos Tarens released the black stud at the gorge that rimmed the plateau, Arithon Teir's'Ffalenn nursed his stolen mount southward at a flagging trot. After days on the run through the glaring exposure of the open dales at his back, he still led the Light's dedicate pursuit away from the battered clan war band in Daon Ramon. Isolate terrain and the heightened flux lines of the free wilds had enabled the tenacious Sight of the True Sect cohort's talent diviner, an advantage first used to draw the chase on, until elite lancers cut off his clean escape route through Ithamon. With a second company closing on his shortened lead, Arithon bolted flat out, every subtle trick brought to bear before their spread net pinned him at bay against Daenfal Lake. The chaotic bustle surrounding the trade town posed his last chance to shake off their arcane tracker.

Which necessity turned him down the notched track through the narrows, where a creek tributary laced through a tight ravine adjacent to the frothed race of the Arwent Gorge. Above loomed the seamed crag overlooking the peaked roofs of Daenfal, site of the crumbled, Second Age amphitheatre, where bygone Paravians once mourned their departed. Rebuilt over the ruin, Mankind had nestled the layer-cake warren of a Third Age necropolis. The silhouettes of the spired memorials erected by wealthy merchants cluttered the monument first carved by the centaurs, dipped bronze against afternoon's egg-shell-blue haze. Shadow wrapped the grey cliff beneath, the dank gloom grave chill after the Barrens' parched heat.

The spent gelding stumbled beneath Arithon's injured weight. The bellows heave of its soaked flanks gusted through the percussive chink of shod hooves, and the echoed thunder of the river-course ahead, careening towards Daenfal's cove harbour.

Stay astride, and the game beast would founder. Arithon braced in one stirrup, teeth clenched, and swung his pierced leg over the cantle. The jolt to the stuck arrow as he dismounted ripped him to agony. Wrung faint against the gelding's steamed shoulder, he wrestled off his tattered boots.

The breathless pause snatched in recovery cost time, while the ambient noise funnelled up the ravine masked the sound of the on-coming lancers. Arithon worked fast by necessity. He wedged his footwear into the stirrups, tied the cuffs, then unfastened the bedroll strapped to the cantle and fashioned a scare-crow's torso. A lancer's stolen canteen topped the effigy, the uncorked neck propped on an empty scabbard, then hooded with the cerecloth rain-cloak filched from the gelding's kit. A convincing sham or a fatal mistake, if the rabid dedicates at his heels carried a seeing glass. Arithon lashed his contrivance to the saddle and hastily knotted the reins.

Dusk would not fall fast enough for the ruse to grant more than a handful of minutes. Arithon hazed the blown horse downhill. The poor beast might fall into the caring hands of a hostler if it reached the ferry. Past such respite himself, he checked the field bandage strapping the snapped arrow lodged in his thigh. The embedded broadhead sawed deeper with each movement. No saving the risk to the artery, as a horn blast sounded from the defile, behind.

The True Sect company pounded through the crooked bends, within sight in a matter of seconds. Run or bleed out, Arithon would find himself caught like a dog in the open.

He hobbled off the road and wedged into a seam in the rock, inadequate cover should the company officer dispatch men, searching on foot. But the cranny might be overlooked by his horsemen, driving at speed through deep shade with their attention directed ahead.

Arithon shut his eyes. Light-headed, in pain, he paced his breath, slowed his pulse, and shuttered his mind against the temple diviner. He withstood the relentless trial of nerves as the lance company poured into the notch, yelled, and spurred hell-bent after his decoy.

The column breezed past to the snap of lance pennons and jangling harness. Arithon shoved away from the cleft, reliant on luck, that no riders glanced back. He limped through the brush fanned by their swift passage and slunk, pressed against the scarp on the opposite side. His fresh bleeding redoubled, the makeshift bandage sodden before he reached the narrow foot stair that angled up the vertical cliff. He climbed barefoot, no matter that he blazed a trail for a tracker: horses could not follow, and a man dismounted in leather-soled boots risked a fall where seeped springs grew virid slicks of moss.

Already, the blare of the officer's horn wheeled the cavalcade. The rag ruse was unmasked, with the only path left for a fugitive the steep ascent to the necropolis. Hope hung on a thread, that the pride and the privilege of elite rank kept the dedicates astride when they drew rein in the roadway below.

Arithon drove upwards, run to the bitter edge of endurance. Behind, the Sunwheel officer's shout rebounded from the floor of the defile.

"Lancers! Split company! Left wing, form ranks and cordon the stair. Right wing, double file and fall in! We'll take the roundabout sweep up the carriage-way to contain and close in from above."

The access road looped behind the escarpment, a league's distance that finished, uphill. Winded horses would require pauses to breathe, which bought Arithon a tenuous respite but no grace. Emerged from shadow into the feverish warmth of daylight, he laboured upwards in desperate straits. The necropolis posed a problematical refuge, the maze threading the underground chambers without exit as a deterrent to grave robbers. Unless he acquired a stout length of rope, the hundred-yard leap from the face towards the Arwent dropped sheer, the boulder-snagged race underneath churned to white water fit to thrash a swimmer to pulp.

Against macabre death, the prospect of a live capture acquired a glimmer of merit: provided the climb did not defeat him beforehand, crumbled away to gapped risers in places that offered scant purchase. Arithon dragged his wounded leg, jaws clamped against whimpering outcry. Tenacity brought him to the crest on one knee, where an unexpectedly sturdy hand gripped his arm and hoisted him upright.

His surprise met a round, freckled face and an upturned nose flushed like a turnip, a fly-away coil of taupe braid, and a woman's muscular frame.

Yet the focused assessment that flicked upwards from his bare feet, to the grisly, stained linen wrapped over his breeches, then piercingly surveyed his strained face was too keen. Arithon acknowledged the shock of encounter that identified an adept talent.

"Arrow or steel?" she inquired of his wound, then remarked in withering interest, "Do True Sect dedicates often make a hunter's sport of their deserters?"

"The next broadhead's apt to cut short explanation," Arithon gasped. "If you're the attendant here, have I your leave?"

His urgent glance assessed the memorial stelae, behind her, then quartered the rotund walls of the mausoleum, with its pillars and plinths perched with statuary; the carved spires with their frozen ribbons of inscriptions, and stone wreaths swagged like fungus above the triple arched portal. No need to plead his desire for sanctuary. The smoked dust kicked up by the double file of horsemen already clouded the flank of the promontory. Their lathered charge up the switched-back approach scattered pedestrians, and pelted through a decorous procession of mourners, black veils flapping like startled birds.

"I'm not the overseer," the woman allowed, too comfortably imperturbed. "Be glad. That fellow would pauper you for a bribe, then fatten his dishonest purse on the bounty." Her alto note of mockery added, "Call me a nameless talent on hire to settle an unquiet shade in transition."

"And the unrequite living?" Arithon quipped. "Might they also merit the peace of an undeserved rest?"

Her laughter was silvery as a flute. "Well, the niches for the burial urns are useful only to nesting jackdaws, and the catacombs are searched thoroughly when petty thieves try seeking an illicit refuge. Are you squeamish?"

Arithon managed a breathless smile. "Not I."

Her lips threatened a sly smile. "Then you must recline like the dead."

Delight lit his blanched features. "A sarcophagus?"

"Quickly, I think." Her no-nonsense grip shifted. She draped his arm across her sturdy shoulders before his legs crumpled.

Arithon leaned on her pragmatic support. They proceeded, awkwardly paired as puppet-string dancers. She stooped to accommodate his shorter frame, bearing up his hopped strides. Down the windswept walkway, striped in shadows cast by the obelisks, they passed under the weathered span of an archway built by no human hand.

Inside, the mausoleum enveloped them in whispered echoes. Dusty light spilled from slit windows, faced west, with the feeble haloes of fluttering candles scattering flecks in the sepia gloom. A miasma of dank earth, bees-wax, grave oils, and incense clung like stifling velvet, where once, wide open to the night sky, a soaring ring of stepped stone had surrounded a plinth of white marble inlaid with jasper. Gone and forgotten were the spirit-lamps burned there in silent lament for departed Paravians.

Built and rebuilt on the original foundations, the Third Age jumble of mismatched memorials descended the concave depression to a stone catafalque, with pillars spanning a pit to contain the oiled pyres for cremation. The surrounding walls were cheese-holed with niches for funerary urns, with the dim portals leading into the warrens of tunnels burrowed out for the lesser tombs in the catacombs. Fashionable wealth had crowded the terraced tiers with free-standing sarcophagi, broad as tables, and wreathed like confection with house crests, ornate lilies, and supplicant bronze effigies. Blood-red sunset limned an imposing black edifice of stone, where his benefactress directed his halting step. A recumbent figure in tarnished silver languished atop a massive lid embellished with vine leaves.

Arithon measured the daunting tonnage that capped a refuge of frightening permanence. "Please reassure me. You've stashed a supply of old grave soot by chance?"

"Why? To blacken your face as the grieving servant, abased at the feet of the interred master?" Her rueful grin matched his morbid wit. "Oh dear. The invention's too pat. Besides, an artful lackey wears livery, not bloodied rags." Rushed by the racketing clatter outside as spurred horses crested the last switchback, she parked his sagging frame against the frigid curves of a matron sorrowfully bowed over a cherubic infant. "Try not to drip where the mess can be seen."

His interested glance followed as she slid back a mechanical latch, withdrew the crank key for a recessed lock, then engaged a hidden mechanism. The massive stone cover rotated to the clicked ratchet of a geared counter-weight.

"Marvel of marvels," remarked Arithon, entranced.

"Gaemar, in town, does the neat engineering. The Light's lancers, one hopes, aren't likely to fathom toy fancies enjoyed by the rich." Her distress smoothed by chatter, the helper whose kindness raised frightening questions boosted Arithon's racked torso into the vault. "The tomb's empty, you see? Its doddering claimant's still alive, cherished by a wife who fritters his fortune on gestures of appalling sentiment."

"Tell me her name, and I will sing her praises." Arithon grimaced, nursed his injured leg over the rim, and courageously settled, arms folded on his chest with satirical irony. "Do you weep for the fallen?"

"I redress their woes, first." Dead-pan, ruled by unknown intentions, she twisted the key in reverse just shy of disaster. The filtered clatter of hooves and commotion brought the lancers en masse into the outside courtyard. His rescuer's last warning whispered through the narrowing gap as the lid grated closed. "Lie easy, but don't fall asleep if you snore. Surely the dead are beyond any mortified officer's purview to question?"

"Perhaps," allowed Arithon, faintly bemused, "though I'd rather trust your knack for persuasion. Yon cur pack would maul the bleached bones of the saints. Muzzle their zeal, if you can, before their denned quarry perishes from suffocation."

"You've a quick and irreverent tongue," she admonished, given the evident fact he would have perceived the fresh draught through the well drilled to house the gears driving the chain. "Serve you right if you don't rest in peace!"

"Angel, whatever comes, I renounce my ungallant ingratitude." His last sight, rouged by the blush of day's afterglow, was the tense oval of her freckled face turned expectantly towards the entry. Then the massive lid of the vault thunked home and sealed him in darkness.

She stowed the key, while the Sunwheel horsemen regrouped at the archway. The officer's brusque command to dismount added the names of the men detailed to manage the horses. He split the rest into squads and dispatched them to quarter the necropolis. Before their invasion disturbed the mausoleum, the nameless initiate resumed her incomplete work and laid down a ritual circle in white sand. Again, cagey strategy prompted her choice to leave her service smock folded inside her satchel.

When The Hatchet's dedicates swarmed through the inner portal, they encountered a planted woman, clad in a nondescript linen shift without any badge of authority. "Dolts! Crass animals! Must you elbow and crowd? Creation is eternal! Respect paid to the departed is unseemly, acquitted in brutish haste."

The obstructed officer brandished his lance. "We're sworn dedicates to Divine Light, not civilian mourners come here for devotion. Step aside, woman! Your temple shelters a dangerous fugitive. We'll leave when he's bound into custody."

"Temple!" Female outrage raised hackles and bristled. "This is a shrine for the blameless dead, and no place for your armed threats!"

"By the Light of the Canon!" the balked captain swore. "Clear our path before you get hurt."

"I'll move for no man with steel in hand." Chin raised, the woman dug in her heels. "If you insist on a useless search, then disarm yourselves first. At least show the pretence of civilized manners."

Tossed that dubious compromise, the lance officer unstrapped his helm and scraped a scale gauntlet across his stubbled chin. "You swear you've seen nothing? No black-haired prowler on the run like a rat?"

"Do I look blind or foolish?" Scornful, she gestured, "If the crannies behind the funerary urns sheltered pests, we'd have scandalized relatives, and honest groundsmen turned off in shame!"

The harangued lancer waved off the argument. "You lot!" he barked to his craning men. "Get this forsaken mausoleum cordoned. Kill on sight if the wretch bolts from cover. The rest of you, drop your sword-belts and toss this bone-yard as ordered. Stay sharp! If the Spinner of Darkness is holed up here, he's cornered. Carelessness might see somebody killed, or worse, let the bastard escape."

While the grumbling search-party shucked their baldrics, the lance captain quibbled over the subject of belt-knives with the recalcitrant shrew in the doorway. "Surely your catacombs are infested with vermin."

"Beetles, too," she conceded, sardonic. "Defile their nests down there all you wish. You'll gratify a few spiders and hungry snakes before autumn's cold makes them torpid."

The disparaged company filed over the disputed threshold, those not unsettled by superstition choking their impious laughter behind buttoned lips. The diviner in his white vestment came last, a gaunt man whose match-stick shanks and minced strides propelled a skull face with a chinless jaw. His suspicious glare crossed the woman's cold regard and took pause.

"Inspect her satchel."

Exposed under the lancers' rifling hands, her grey cloth and white ribbons of charitable service stirred a satisfactory round of consternation: for no True Sect talent dared to run afoul of an initiate enchantress of the Koriathain.

"What's the bother?" a loutish pragmatist scoffed. "Isn't her order allied with our faith against the Master of Shadow?"

"That may be," the Canon's diviner allowed, stiffened by the encroachment of a rival practitioner. "But she's one of their wandering independents, not answerable to a sisterhouse."

When the unmasked enchantress said nothing to cool his scorching distrust, the unnerved officer upbraided his slackers before they shirked duty under the distraction. "I don't care who that witch is! We don't harken to her above captain's orders. No one's relieved until this place is searched."

The uneasy huddle broke up. Sidled past the bottle-neck, the men fanned out in determined formation. Aware of the enchantress watching their backs, they pried into crannies and corners, ungainly as they bashed into the flourished scrolls with their inscriptions and ran afoul of dolorous statues knelt in vigil over the epitaphs. Men quickly discovered their jokes rang too loud. Undue haste amid the raised tombs tripped them up on carved ivy and barked their shins on heraldic finials.

Progress faltered as the outdoor light failed, then resumed by the purloined store of the gravediggers' pine torches. Men clumped up the spiralled stairs to the belfries and swept swooping shadows across the louvered cupolas. They cursed the wisped cobwebs that garnished their helms as they scraped the low ceilings in the pillared catacombs down below. Their ransack poked into noisome dark crevices, until the chambered niches breathed wafted smoke, reverberated with the chinks of rowelled spurs, vacant scabbards, and mail shirts.

"The skeletons we disturb aren't missing their dinner," a harried lancer groused at due length. When complaints failed to move the relentless diviner, he pressed, "How far must we ride to make up for lost ground when we come up empty-handed?"

The temple's talent wagged a waspish finger. "Consummate evil would make the dead walk!"

"Well, nothing's down there beyond buttons and bones," quipped a cheerless dedicate, emerged from the stairwell.

The diviner's gimlet glower brushed past him and measured the vaults. "We've not checked the sealed tombs."

"Are you frothing mad?" The Koriani enchantress shoved to the fore. "That's desecration!"

The priesthood's official dismissed her outrage. "I will have the Spinner of Darkness flushed out! No one's blameless remains will be exhumed, provided you don't interfere."

"Uncivilized swine!" The enchantress presented her back, while six burly dedicates braced up for the onerous duty.

"East to west, buckos! Let's take the biggest ones first." Grunting with effort, they hefted a thick slab, burdened at each corner by the outstretched wings of marble angels, entwined and weeping. Stone shifted with a grate. A patter of dust sifted into the cracked vault.

Through grunts of gut-busting effort, a man's gritted gasp, "Where's the forsaken torch-bearer?"

A bystander's scuffed footstep, and wavering flame-light spilled into the dank darkness within. Etched against appalled silence, somebody gagged. Then the massive lid slipped from another man's nerveless grasp. The rest loosed their hold, and the stone lid dropped with a boom.

A man swallowed noisily. "Somebody else can open the rest." Then he gagged, clutched his middle, and spewed, while his revolted fellows leaped away, cursing.

"No blighted fugitive's holed up in there," remarked a disgusted companion. "Lie in with those worms, he'd go screaming insane. We'll all heave up our collops if we keep at this."

"You spurn the work of your salvation under the Light," the diviner retorted. "The Master of Shadow would lair up without qualm in the bosom of vile corruption."

"Well, he might, supposing the wee scoundrel could raise such a stone, never mind he's been wounded. Damn my sorry shade along with him if he's stuffed himself in a blighted coffin."

The rebellious man shrugged and looked to his superior, while his blanched companion wiped his fouled mouth and shoved past the insistent diviner. "The dead may rot on their own, and you with them, that's my last word on the matter!"

The officer gauged his sullen, exhausted company and chose not to pressure them further. He declared the search finished and retired to the courtyard, where his captain accepted the closure of his crisply delivered report.

The diviner lingered on amid the fallen gloom. "Don't assume for a moment that I've been deceived!" His insectile finger stabbed at the enchantress. "You've meddled here. Righteous men have been swayed from their path by your unwholesome influence. If you've harboured the Master of Shadow, I won't rest until your last sisterhouse burns under the Law of the Canon."

"You threaten the Order of the Koriathain?" she said, the chill in her presence no empty warning.

The horn call that signalled the company's withdrawal relieved the outfaced diviner. He stifled his fuming reply and took his thwarted fury into the noisy commotion outside, where the mounted company swept him into their ranks and formed up for immediate departure.

While their cavalcade clattered off down the carriage-way, the enchantress kept watch amid the reproachful silence of the carved monuments. Around her, the embers of the spent torches dimmed and winked out. Dewfall silvered the faces of glistening stone under a risen half-moon, and the eddied air within the mausoleum relinquished its freight of stirred dust. She roused only after the diviner's Sight had passed beyond range, and with shaking fingers, retrieved the crank key and released the lid of the sarcophagus.

She found her dangerous fugitive not only living but conscious. He stirred, a bit clumsy from prolonged chill and stiffened limbs. Tangled black hair emerged over the tomb's rim, then his face, disarmingly split by a debonair grin. "You worked a deception under the nose of a talent diviner. I'd give you a kiss if I didn't feel darned together through the pores of my skin."

He had beyond any doubt sensed her sigil, unleashed when the searchers scuffed through her sand circle.

His perilous saviour smiled regardless, unable to govern her sympathy. "The lancers actually did my work for me, helped on by a mirror spell folding their dread back upon them."

Arithon clambered out of the tomb, painfully nursing his leg, which had bled unchecked through his agonized, motionless waiting. "What of the Light's faithful who suspect your defection?" But his abstruse question regarding her motive lost impetus, the squelch of soaked cloth not quite masked by his breathlessly charming apology. "I'm afraid I've anointed death's door prematurely."

Swung downward, he gripped the tomb like a limpet, too light-headed to stand.

The enchantress supported his unsteady frame. "Did you plan to bleed yourself out like a pig?"

"Me?" Arithon's rejoinder quite failed to distance his helpless distress. "No. The brute with the chestnut beard and unshakeable aim with a longbow."

But the back of his shirt and his breeches were sodden. "Ath wept!" she snapped. "You don't have to pretend you're immortal!"

"The True Sect's conviction left you unconvinced?" Contrite apology fading, he swayed. "They insist I'm personified evil itself." Collapse overtook him. He slid to his knees, smearing a scarlet swath down the verses graven across the vault's pedestal.

"I'm sorry." The tears she could no longer stem striped her cheeks as she eased him down at her feet.

Arithon lost his adamant grip, still fighting defeat at the last.

Her conflicted regret chased his release into gentle unconsciousness. "Damn the self-righteous stupidity of blind faith! Had those pious fools not disclosed your identity, honesty might have let me free your spirit through credible ignorance."

Ramifications

Awakened to enervated weakness, captive under the adept ministrations of the Koriathain who binds him to life, Arithon answers her anguished apology lately addressed to him in extremis: "I don't hold you to blame for your choice of loyalty. The Light's Canon would have enforced my execution. My ambivalent hope prefers the gamble your Matriarch's purpose wants me alive . . ."

Deep into the night, Sethvir paces the library at Althain Tower, second by agonized second tracking the surge of unfolding event: while earth-sense shows Elaira's desperate move, outwitting a dedicate sentry to bolt northward into the mountains to Kewar; and the critical value Prime Selidie assigns to Arithon's survival dangles in the balance . . .

Rainy sunrise puddles the corpses of the dedicate lance company attached to the temple diviner, struck down, man and beast, on the Daenfal Road without any sign of trauma: and the constable's hysterical dispatch to The Hatchet, overseen by a True Sect priest, blames the unnatural slaughter on sorcery spun by the Master of Shadow . . .

VIII. Fifth Upset

A rithon Teir's'Ffalenn lay insensate for days, held submerged in dreamless oblivion by the Prime Matriarch's urgent directive. The same orders
moved him, against the indignant objection of the healer who removed
the arrow-point from his leg. Inert and strapped to a plank to prevent a relapse
into uncontrolled bleeding, he felt nothing throughout the transit that hefted
him into a waiting wagon. Tucked like a bolster beneath bales of broadcloth,
he was driven off, eastward, amid the stacked freight of an indebted guildsman.
Coin changed hands to appease the crooked exciseman, whose squint eye
assessed the haulage tax levied on the lake-shore causeway. For a cask of white
spirits, the tower guard winked and ignored what seemed a harmless caper
staged by petty smugglers.

The bribed officials never suspected their complacency stemmed from a spellcrafted influence. The lance company slaughtered to silence the Koriani collusion
atop the necropolis kept the temple's inquiry preoccupied elsewhere when the
laden wagon paused between post-stations. A brief rendezvous saw the comatose
Master of Shadow shrouded under blankets and tarpaulin, then installed in a
jouncing horse-litter. Under a sky clouded like pebbled iron, the guileful skills
of three Senior enchantresses spirited him into the wilds of Daon Ramon.

Their Matriarch's explicit instructions were met: to divert the scouring search
for his person driven by True Sect decree, and to wield every binding sigil at hand
to keep Arithon unconscious. The strategic cover of a bramble thicket let his escort
tighten their arcane stays. They proofed their scribed spells against spitting rain,
by then most concerned with ensuring their secured charge stayed disabled.

Haste and rough handling exacted a toll, and the set-back of recurrent bleeding. The leg wound fared poorly, damp weather followed by blistering sun compounding the complication of wound fever. But the sensible rest to let blood-vessels knit invited far greater peril, not least the Prime's signal displeasure. Delivered at speed as a dangerous liability to the remote field camp in the Barrens, Arithon breathed at the Matriarch's mercy, brought in due course under canvas and installed in the privacy of her pavilion.

The furore caused by his arrival escaped him, as the terrified boy wards directed to shift furnishings flinched under the proximal range of the ward sigils stitched through the carpet spread underfoot. The tingle of that arcane containment lanced into the depths of unconsciousness and stung the flicker of surfaced awareness. Bedevilled by pain, hazed under strong drugs, Arithon felt the bump as his bearers couched the plank on the trestles positioned to cradle his pithless infirmity.

Close air and trapped heat wore the rancid taint of summer-warm canvas, but no saffron tint filtered through his closed eyelids. His surrounds were curtained in gloom, with his wheeling dizziness and nausea derived from the back-lash of stayspells wrought by the Koriathain. Sickness weakened him further. Ambient sounds rang too loud, as though he was feverish.

He leashed rank impatience; tempered with caution his muddled fight to reorient his scattered focus. A furred tongue and dry lips bespoke the enervation of severe blood loss.

He lay bound hand and foot to a surgeon's plank. The animal reek of his person included the whiff of clotted linen and medicinal astringents, and worse. Humiliation encountered the helpless indignity veiled under a dusty blanket. Arithon quenched his explosive fury. His straits had not been victimized by neglect. The deep ache of his leg wound explained the necessity keeping him prostrate. Patience mapped the extent of the damage. The drawn arrow-head had breached the wall of the artery, the grazed vessel and torn muscle precariously closed by festering stitches. Straps immobilized him at chest and thigh, bound overtop of the dusty scout's leathers none had dared, or snatched time, to remove. Unattended, the injury would have been mortal: his right legging, sliced away at the hip, bared skin that recorded the expert support of a field bandage. More sigils placed there for regenerative healing rasped his inflamed nerves and played havoc with his effort to concentrate.

A life salvaged by enemy interests did not bode well. Arithon clung to the pretence of unconsciousness, sweating out his drugged torpor and striving to wring meaningful sense from the nearby activity.

A laden servant's deferent footfalls dispensed cool water freshened with citrus peel. Over the clink of porcelain, a derisive remark sliced the whispers of onlookers crowded to gawk. "For a creature as pitiful as a soaked cat, he's caused us a sack full of trouble."

"A fool's risk, to invite the sort of perilous trick that blindsided the Ettinmere shamans." Through an agitated sigh of fine silk, the dominant speaker insisted, "I say put the bastard to death straightaway and be quit of his mettlesome spirit."

"Execution has merit," rasped a gravid alto, a cool pace removed. "The blow would cripple Fellowship interests. Why fuss? The mute man-servant could drag in a barrel and drown him without drawing blood."

Seated to the sigh of squashed cushions, a wheezy colleague agreed. "The sorcerer's too viciously wily for our further use as a game-piece."

Another sister disparaged, "You seriously think he'd let himself be caged as a brazen tactic?"

"The chance can't be ignored," declaimed a different initiate's fluttery treble. "You'd think differently if you knew how often he's played my best scryers along like rank fools."

Arithon had foiled their most advanced workings: more than once, tagged wild hawks with his personal imprint. A misleading strand of hair noosed to a taloned leg, or a blood-stain set into a feather had caused errant chases down avian flight paths for weeks.

"Well," huffed the fatuous sister called down, "he can't provoke mayhem under restraint!"

Which vapid prattle met caustic silence. Too many Seniors had cringed under first-hand experience: Arithon's sleight-of-hand acts of incapacity always presaged his most vicious ripostes.

While collective debate caught its breath, the Prime's entry crushed further discussion. "Get out! Every one of you, leave."

Her command cleared the pavilion forthwith, to a brisk bustle of skirts. Arithon's dread swelled at the speed of the onlookers' departure. He was unfit to mount a defence. His senses swam under the harsh flare of daylight, snuffed into thick gloom and stagnant air as the curtain partition whisked shut.

A frantic attempt to manage his faculties crashed against spell-wrought barriers. Head spinning, he gasped for breath, while raced pulse and the punitive recoil of powerful sigils scraped his nerves to sparkling agony. Taxed vision recorded the oppressive blur of a female face hovering over him. Through the strained impression of bedazzling jewels and state dress, he grasped the heightened pallor of excitement and animosity, expertly obscured by cosmetics.

Selidie's presence itself thrust an icicle pall through the heat of broad daylight. No delusion to mage-sense: the pervasive chill stemmed from a clinging nimbus of darkness attached to her form. Something more than the spells that maintained her longevity dimmed the natural stream of the flux. When her clubbed forearm hooked the draped blanket away to examine her prize, Arithon shuddered from her touch with revulsion.

The Matriarch wrinkled her nose. Two days, perhaps more, of prostrate infirmity would tax even a slattern's lack of hygiene. Which caustic embarrassment wrung Arithon to a breathless laugh. "Behold, the creeping blight's sullied the rose-bed. Your healer neglected to detail the nicety? Intractable bleeding has always required restraint and prolonged immobility. Since I'm delivered from blissful unconsciousness, I'm expected to blush with embarrassment?"

Annoyed as the fumbled blanket slithered into a heap at her feet, the Prime snapped, "Don't waste undue gratitude!"

"And no thanks for the meddling favour, since I'm alive to voice the objection," jabbed Arithon.

Prime Selidie applauded. Gross deformity muffled by wraps of lace gauze satirized the indignity of his position. "The assumption, in your case, that surcease exists is delusional madness."

"Knowledge has limits. Imagination does not." Arithon turned a face white with strain. "Since when has your order done other than rot, suffocated beneath a secretive hierarchy that kills innovation?"

"Why chase the seduction of useless debate?" The ferocity behind the Prime's wide-lashed stare prickled chills over his clammy skin. "Did you honestly think I'd reward you with death?"

Mired in nightmare antagonism, the bound victim stared down stark defeat. "Hope does not surrender. Even for you."

Bluster saved nothing: his bluff would be called. The spelled templates blocking his access to Shadow were impenetrable, perfected during his prior captivity. Selidie's gesture dismissed toothless threats and summoned Lirenda's assistance. "Secure his tied wrists with the warded shackles."

Arithon flinched from the cipher-stamped chain. Spurred by visceral memories of horror, he thrashed as the cuffs of wrought copper and glass clasped his flesh. The blazing pain struck as the sigils took hold. Recoil wracked him to convulsions. The scream ripped from his throat choked off as the pins locked in place and demolished resistance.

Arithon lay, a puppet with clipped strings, hard-breathing and still, the flame of awareness crushed by the tailor-made spells that subdued him. He could not prevent the subduction of will, or marshal his body for useless fight.

His rage stumbled, mute, while his spinning descent into darkness echoed with Selidie's victory crow. "Imagination serves naught, in your case. The Fellowship Sorcerers forsook your royal blood-line and sealed my absolute claim on your destiny."

The dark thinned and broke to smeared light like grey cobweb, acid with the burn of clamped sigils whose grip disbarred access to talent. An attempt to swallow rasped Arithon's dry throat. His abused frame felt gelid as flotsam. Bound flat on a table, his arms ached with cramps, wrists painfully gouged by the anchoring tension of glass cuffs and warded chain. His oblivion had lasted just long enough to secure his captive survival. The regenerative spells on his leg had released, the scabbed-over weal closing naturally.

Which vital recovery saw his handlers setting the Prime's final plan into motion. Movement wafted the air at close quarters. An industrious sister's rustled silk breathed the musty scent of pressed rose-petals, cedar, and lavender, as she aligned a bronze tripod with a hooped rim above his brow.

Memory raised the spectre of the atrocity suffered when his consciousness was imprisoned in crystal.

The galvanic reflex to wrench himself free smashed against cruel restraint. Arithon seethed, seized immobile, while the hapless course of his fate moved apace, directed by the avid voice of the Prime Matriarch.

"No!" Charged with desire, Selidie qualified. "We stand to gain knowledge beyond precedent. Arithon's experience settling free wraiths has enabled him to unlock direct access to Athera's mysteries. I've witnessed proof. His Masterbard's gift, refined through his land-sanctioned royal attunement, can resurrect ancient patterns and fuse the old workings of Fellowship Sorcerers. More, he thwarted our invasion of Caithwood when he harnessed those forces in tandem with prior enchantments wrought by the Paravians."

"You claim he has wielded the primordial flux?" The seductive prospect raised covetous awe, an empowerment with an unparalleled edge to contest the Seven's omnipotence.

Eyes narrowed, Selidie embraced the risk of that priceless prize. "He stays living until I've extracted the methods by which he commanded the interface."

The sister fitting the tripod leaned forward. "He's coming around. Is letting him hear our intentions entirely wise?"

"No matter," snapped Selidie. "Forcing the mind scars and cripples the spirit. If he doesn't succumb to violent madness, he'll survive as a biddable idiot. In which case, Vivet can harvest the s'Ffalenn lineage without his temperamental objection."

Shock caught Arithon's breath. Speech failed him, as his muddled reason grasped just how brutally he had been played. Hindsight *indeed* raised bitter questions regarding his oath to sponsor a child at Ettinmere, the unmalleable ethic of royal compassion engaged through cold machination. Vivet's alleged assailant had died, consumed by a struggle to speak. Her knife-thrust in plaintive self-defence passed unquestioned, with no living witness to testify. The grotesque revelation overturned decency, that her violation had been brutally staged, with the *rapist* her enthralled victim.

As damning, the drugged aphrodisiac concocted during the aftermath. Gullible male sympathy *almost* had compromised Rathain's crown lineage. Arithon shuddered, galled incandescent. A criminal murder, appended to the birth of a child predisposed to be used as a game-piece ignited his accusation. "Here's another innocent's destiny maligned, if not cashiered for death under reckless endangerment! You've a heart better suited to a stone ornament, and not a drop of warm blood in your veins."

"You refer to Fionn Areth and Valien? What are they but dust motes in the storm?" The Prime shed culpability with venomless logic. "Two backwater

253

yokels of average endowment, weighed against stakes where the measure of any one life does not signify."

"For what greater good?" Seared wild by outrage, Arithon pressed, "What kind of principle stands on the high-handed sacrifice of autonomy? I shudder to picture the society moulded by your sisterhood's creed. After all, you Koriathain have no sense of humour, no quaint vulnerability, and ah, yes, let's not omit unassailable frigidity. How many young girls have been forged into passionless tools, suborned of their intellect and denied any standing to question?"

"You cannot possibly envision the scope of our order's commitment." Selidie's fixated regard never flickered. "Broad-scale issues lie in the balance that reduce this world to a cipher."

Wrists welled scarlet, Arithon strained against the glass fetters. "Pardon the sand grain crushed under your heel for protesting the insignificance!"

Selidie's cameo smile showed amusement. "You can't gall me into a stickling debate over points of philosophy. The option is mine to break you at will and silence your gad-fly insolence."

The threat was not empty. A lifetime's adept mastery slipped Arithon's grasp like water poured out of a jar. He fought restraint anyway, extended trained reflexes until agonized back-lash punished him senseless.

His vision went patchy, crossed by shadowed movement as another silent assistant placed a massive amethyst sphere in the tripod over his head. Arctic cold sliced through him, skin and bone. Terror melted his viscera. The jewel's rank presence weighted his chest as though he were drowning. His skull rang like a tapped bell. Out of time, lost to resource, he sank into a purple mist that flayed flesh and spirit like the cut of a thousand scalpels.

He battled the onslaught, beyond tears to weep, his pounding heartbeat pummelled towards the nadir of primal oblivion. The cascade of disasters unleashed if he failed threatened ruin beyond contemplation. Yet his desperation wrestled no reprieve from the onslaught.

Pain pulverized all resistance and fed the Waystone's vortex of power. Lashed by the animal need to cry out, Arithon arched against the restraints, tendons rigid beneath bloodied skin. Primal struggle gained nothing. Selidie up-stepped the force set against him, until the relentless torrent demolished his deepest defences. The last bastion guarding his mind breached and crumpled, stranding him beyond redress.

Caged in isolation, Arithon did not feel the distant thunder of Sethvir's step, pacing the library at Althain Tower. He knew nothing of the empathic despair that brought Elaira to her knees in the Mathorn heights.

Love endured with tied hands as the insufferable happened. A sanctioned crown prince fell to deadly enemies, cut adrift and flayed under the focal vortex of the Prime's most powerful crystal. Arithon Teir's'Ffalenn reeled, alone and stripped naked, while the brutal probe levelled to ransack his being rendered his adept mastery as vulnerable as air-bubbles shaken to the surface of a tapped glass.

While the avalanche of upset probabilities rocked the world on its axis, rain like spun glass swept in sheets across the cragged downs of Atainia. Run-off glossed the grim stone of Althain Tower and varnished the slate shingles lapped over the eaves. Droplets clung, trembling, to the tread of the Sorcerer who circled the library floor, then unravelled under the side-swiping gusts that shivered the leaded casements.

Althain's Warden did not bear his vigil alone. The glare that iced the barren table-top also stamped Asandir's seated form in granite and ebony. Eyes of sheared steel watched Sethvir pace. Hair still clubbed to ease yesterday's heat wore a tarnish of dust from the road, and anxiety chafed his lean flesh to bleak bone. As ruthlessly scored were the leathers abused from rushed travel on foot to bear witness. Speech failed in defeat, with the brutal course of two Ages of hope fast sliding towards ruin.

Naught could be done. Braced nerves must withstand the agonized wait, while Sethvir's earth-sense sifted the stream of event from moment to moment. Always, he stifled bad news behind silence, dread buried while the cresting wave of disaster built into a nexus of certainty. Asandir curbed his impatience until his tense colleague saw fit to declare himself.

The iron restraint that stemmed premature speech was no frivolous affectation. Even a single word carried weight amid the unfolding, charged course of destiny: all the more where ancient stone rang like a tuning-fork to the tidal surge of the Third Lane. Althain Tower's foundation straddled a grand convergence of ley lines. Here, mage-tuned senses already quivered and leaped to the pulse of concurrent activity. The whisper of Sethvir's restless tread echoed the marched tramp of armies: True Sect dedicates in Tysan hounding the clan fugitives under Saroic s'Gannley; counterpoint to The Hatchet's crack companies in Rathain besieging Halwythwood's warded ground. The heart bound to Athera's weal ached for the insufferable consequence. Esfand, as freshly invested *caithdein*, faced harsh choices fit to snuff the last embers of youth.

As dreadful to contemplate Elaira's plight, alone in the peaks of the Mathorns, a raw toll of anguish that paled, given the day's unravelling spiral might unseat the mysteries preserved through millennia.

Sethvir reached the west casement and stopped, a forlorn silhouette rimlit by the storm. Clenched knuckles planted on the sill, he seemed frail enough to snap under the grief piled upon his bowed shoulders.

Asandir shoved erect. Fast for his angular frame, he closed in a stride and latched a supportive grip on his colleague. The flesh under his hold was fever hot, the muscles beneath cranked as wire. "Should you drive yourself mad? If my oath did naught but defer Arithon's doom, your bravado won't even signify."

Sethvir shivered, drawn white. "His Grace hasn't lost his identity. Not yet." Steered to a chair, he sank into a heap, gaze averted. "Life's not lost, though Arithon's current state of awareness cannot be counted a mercy."

Asandir dropped the notion of pausing to brew tea. "Show me."

The pause hung, then stretched far too long. Asandir kicked aside the adjacent chair and drilled a stare at his colleague, full-face. Aquamarine eyes lifted, blank, the mighty awareness of the world's weave subsumed: not in sweet reverie, intoxicated by the liquid melody of a thrush's song, or the sonorous splendour of whales in the deep. Instead, the vast torrent encompassed by Sethvir's awareness lay shadowed into eclipse. Black pupils dilated by terror, the incarnate being entrusted to bear the span of Athera's earth-sense was flogged senseless on adrenaline fear.

Few things in creation could sap a Fellowship Sorcerer's courage. That *Sethvir's* grasp on the reins of broad-scale vision should flag dropped Asandir to his knees. "Cal, come back! Prince Arithon's anguish is not yours!" Powerful fingers urgently chafed the Warden's unresponsive wrist. "Our ranks cannot surmount this crisis without you."

A fierce, controlled shake raised a laboured breath. Sethvir blinked and stirred. His eyes refocused, welled up with tears.

Asandir spoke gently across fallen gloom. "Is his Grace lost entirely?"

Sethvir shuddered. "The mind is associative." Further detail emerged at a whisper. "Trauma has him reliving the moment he fell into prior captivity."

The field Sorcerer recalled that lamentable history: when, taken in duress to Whitehold over two centuries before, Arithon had languished in enchanted fetters at the mercy of the same adversary. Then, he had laughed into Prime Selidie's teeth, in combative charge of his faculties.

"What is my life worth? Do you imagine I'm cowed enough to forsake my integrity just to stay breathing?"

The withering thrust of Selidie's response, recorded by Sethvir's precise script in the Tower's archive: *"The Fellowship holds your blood pledge to survive, no matter the cost or the consequence."*

"Madam, you'll have nothing taken by force." Eyes shut as the blue fire of the Skyron aquamarine blazed into his shielding, Arithon wielded a master's command over mind and spirit. His defence had bent his agony into song. Beauty and decency had clothed his torment, no matter how vicious the pressure against him.

Selidie remarked she had heard wittier satire before up-stepping the power.

The duel had raged day and night, until the bard's sustained melody cracked and broke. Tenacious, Arithon had laboured onwards in verse, and for longer, the strict bulwark of cadence and metre upheld him.

The Prime reviled her victim's doomed triumph. Impatient, while a voice rasped ragged by stress continued in determined resistance, she snapped, "I will see you howl like a dog in despair . . ."

* * *

Even chained down under the flaying attack, Arithon still had noted the presence brought forward against him. Denied sight, reft of senses, the cry of his heart recognized his beloved's singular essence above all others. If his fury had towered before, today's vivid recall of his explosive rage smashed all boundaries—and then rushed away, without warning lost into a void impenetrably dark and deep . . .

Asandir expelled in a sharp breath, devastated by the pitfall unveiled behind Sethvir's distress. "Ath wept!" For Arithon lacked any context to realize that the sudden, blank pall of oblivion was not caused by Selidie's working against him.

"He's mired under the misguided assumption his beloved betrayed him," Althain's Warden confirmed.

Asandir swore again, beyond helpless to exonerate Elaira's innocence.

For the past threat of abuse to his cherished lady, turned as leverage, had been the crowning stroke that demolished Prince Arithon's adamant resistance, before. Disaster had forced his choice to embrace the only possible counter-move. His defiant riposte, spoken then, yet rolled a charged echo into the present: *"This extortionate act I can stop, and I will . . ."*

Beyond sorrow, the courageous rebuff the initiate master once shaped to salvage grace from the jaws of defeat: Arithon had truncated his cherished recollections of Elaira, a severance forged by self-mutilation. He had gathered the sum of her living memory, along with other, more dangerous knowledge his vital strength chose to keep sacrosanct. Every secret he guarded beyond life itself had been thrust intact beyond Selidie's reach, into the emerald signet of Rathain. The ring held as his pledge of royal troth, bestowed on Elaira, and safe as a vault since the kingdom's crown jewels were defended by Fellowship mandate.

Asandir locked anguished eyes with Sethvir, both Sorcerers wracked by relief that the desperate measure yet escaped Arithon's recall. "At least," he said, fraught, "we won't face the resurgence of Kralovir necromancy."

Thanks to Arithon's stringent foresight, the horrific rites from the Black Grimoires yet remained sealed beyond access.

But at such terrible cost: reduced, that past hour, to a gutted shell, Arithon's shattered cry in the aftermath still harrowed the fast silence of Althain Tower.

"Have done! Do your worst and be quick. I have nothing to lose, any more than a husk stripped of name and identity."

For mercy, then, the plunge into oblivion had ended his crippling anguish . . .

But not on this day. The on-going trial in Daon Ramon allowed no such forgetful reprieve. World-spanning stakes rode the compact's suppression of the sisterhood's archival heritage. To secure a successor with the raw talent to preserve that irreplaceable store of proscribed record, the Prime Matriarch harrowed up Arithon's massacred dead to pulverize his identity. The tactic assaulted an integrity already made vulnerable by the falsified evidence of Elaira's betrayal.

Sethvir sprang erect. He circled the library's confines again, a huddled stick puppet wadding the moth-eaten sleeves of his velvet robe.

Asandir looked on, hands ruthlessly laced. "Our crown prince is more than well-tempered to withstand even this vicious onslaught." Whoever meddled with Arithon's spirit provoked more than a scion of Torbrand's volatile lineage: the hardened survivor of Davien's maze commanded the tenacity to disarm the trap of futility. "Are you in fact certain his Grace has stopped fighting?"

"No," Sethvir snapped, ashen. Such relentless suffering, in Arithon's hands, indeed might lend him a perverse, adversarial advantage: the brute tactic could be strategically turned to unseat the Prime's fixed objective.

Asandir refigured the premise. "The mind is associative." Memories, bunched in graphic, hysterical storms might subvert the concerted assault through the Waystone. "The Matriarch's not emotionally equipped to withstand that grisly tactic of misdirection."

Sethvir turned, aghast himself under the barrage of Arithon's flashback relivings. "But methodical torment cannot buy time. Selidie has forsaken patience. Worse than hounding our crown prince to madness, she's seeking access, through triggers, to key his remembrance of a specific event. She's driving to access his mystical encounter with the Ilitharis guardian's spirit in Caithwood last winter."

Asandir stared, appalled. "Not the rarified vision that restored his self-awareness of absolution!"

"The same." Sethvir flinched from the price, that the innate expansion endowed by that contact had bestowed the intuitive access to flux imprints across two Ages of history. The intimate knowledge prised out of that moment would unlock a fearful array of specialized mastery: Arithon had aligned the templates of three disciplines, then wakened the lines of ancient magic which tapped the well-spring of Athera's mysteries. Those harnessed forces had sealed the forest verge against the Prime's spell-cast invasion.

"Tea," Asandir insisted, his gall hobbled to the gesture of a palliative. Draughts stirred by his movement reeked of ozone, the white flicker of near-to-limitless might chained in ruthless abeyance. He fetched kindling, tipped out the ash-pan, and sparked the brazier on the table-top. Moved ahead to the cupboard for restorative herbs, he sensed the break in the Warden's clipped strides. Warning spun him volte-face.

Sethvir buckled, wrists seized in collapse by the field Sorcerer's timely strength.

"Ath above, we are finished!" Asandir cried in anguish. "The murderous witch has broken through?"

"Not Selidie. Teylia," Sethvir gasped, then channelled the earth-sensed insight directly . . .

Across the bloody mire of relivings that damned soul and spirit, a fragment of recall resurfaced, branded in fire against urgent need. Arithon knew the old woman only as the nameless ally whose fierce intervention had freed him from his prior ordeal of imprisonment.

"You are not all they say! Truth has many facets. Where you have suffered all manner of grief, your inner heart cannot lie to you. But emotions can be manipulated to inflict an undue toll of cruelty . . ."

At Althain Tower, the field Sorcerer shook off his stark surprise, too canny to bank on the moment's fragile intervention. "Koriathain will never retire the contest." Though Teylia's foresighted seed of assurance might steady Arithon's besieged identity, Selidie's stolen youth only had deferred the untenable straits strangling her succession. No forthcoming talent met her pervasive need to secure her high office. The stake hanging on the outcome today would not relent anytime soon. Asandir chased down Sethvir's chipped pot, scrounged the crock of spring honey, then set about brewing peppermint tea, while the assault engaged in Daon Ramon continued apace, beyond let-up.

Selidie directed her will through the Waystone, the channelled power of seven ranked Seniors honed to a needle's point. Strike after strike, she pierced the veils of frayed memory guarding her victim's integrity. Time and pressure shredded Arithon's resistance. With his self-contained arrogance already crushed, the last bastion weakened, with the genius trove of his unequalled talent close as shredding the lock off a tattered book.

"I suggest we're in danger of killing him, first," interrupted the healer detailed to watch Arithon's life signs. Lips pursed, she measured the toll on taxed flesh: the sped pulse and sawed breathing; the fingers whose technique on the lyranthe were legend, clenched involuntarily rigid; the sweat-streaked skin drained to translucent pallor, and the green eyes dulled under slack lids. Gone, every vestige of dignity from the subject's wracked frame.

"Keep on," warned the healer, "stop his heart, and risk damage enough to fragment his cognizance beyond retrieval."

Selidie frowned, inconvenienced by the needful delay to change tactics. "Lirenda? Fetch the packet of diluted *tienelle* from my herb chest, along with the little brazier. A touch of smoke should speed my progress." The narcotic's effect would intensify her probe, with the bogging detritus of Arithon's remembrance dissolved like cobweb as the uplifting thrust of the herb punched open his refined faculties.

"See to the dosage," Selidie instructed the healer. "Under the influence, I'll resume the onslaught at strength and seize my objective directly."

A collective sigh swept the circle of Seniors, temporarily relieved of their entrained trance. The Prime stretched like a cat, then settled to steady herself ahead of the bracing expansion. The striker snapped. Flint sparked against steel and ignited the flame, thin as shot silk in the gloom. A silvery thread of smoke twined aloft, sharpened by the abrasive scent as the infused leaves caught and burned. The Prime netted the fumes in a hood of veiled silk and inhaled. Discipline harnessed the uprush that followed. The stifled atmosphere became gravid, every onlooker likewise affected, lungs steeped in the wafted haze.

The effect swept through Arithon in extremis like the blast of a gale-wind. Explosive intoxication whirled his deranged consciousness, already forcibly frayed to a thread. His frantic pulse slowed. His tortured breaths deceptively deepened. Relaxation eased his rigid frame, cramped sinews wrung pithless through the soaring lift as facile intuition unfolded.

Agony lessened, as his mind drifted free of his tormented flesh. The active Waystone loomed overhead, its proximal chill fit to sear naked skin and its depths vast enough to drown Sight. His expanded awareness had no other stimulus. The jewel's crystalline lattice dominated his proscribed existence, the fresh influx of sinister power shrilling like stroked glass as the Prime Circle's assault coursed through its focus.

Trained mastery responded. The surge of initiate reflex aligned Arithon's consciousness *towards* the hostile thrust ranged against him.

The reverse startled Selidie's quickened aptitude and caused her to overreact. She engaged, bent upon conquest with redoubled savagery.

Arithon spurned retreat. Goaded as the leopard touched by the whip, he launched his awareness into the jewel to grapple her hold at the source.

Selidie quit the contest. She relinquished control of the amethyst's matrix and emerged with a cry of triumph. "The ripened fruit falls into my hand." Flushed by the ease of her victory, she laughed. "He's doomed himself, truly. The Waystone's inherent malice will finish him. Lirenda? Extinguish the brazier. Have my servants bring in refreshments. We need do no more than stand idle watch until the Teir's'Ffalenn succumbs and dies."

The great jewel, by nature, would capture everything: all the brilliant nuance of his gifted talent. At leisure, the Matriarch could retrieve the imprinted record, and without hindrance explore the prized pattern left behind by his trapped consciousness.

Plunged deep within the Waystone's mineral lattice, Arithon sensed the abrupt dissolution of Selidie's aggressive presence. Direct opposition faded and vanished, with his disembodied identity left stranded inside. Self-aware, he surveyed the mighty vault of the amethyst, a structured geometry of facets that sheared outside light into purple tones rich as stained glass.

The bias of the jewel's power surrounded him, masterless, but still enabled: the piezoelectric properties of quartz, ferociously enhanced by a gem cutter's art, amplified and released captured energy. Arithon's past experience imprisoned in crystal called for preternatural caution. Since back-lash from every attempt to break free would recoil into punishing agony, he stilled his impulsive panic and invoked a bard's skilled proclivity for listening.

Unlike the clear stone that ensnared him before, the amethyst sphere was not silent. His practised perception of nuance disclosed the Waystone's extreme sensitivity, fine-tuned enough to be influenced by the surrounding environment. Arithon picked out the resonant hum raised by the day's ambient heat, then the flickered static as the slight friction of draughts raised back-drop fluctuations akin to weather.

More disturbing, the high-frequency spike introduced by his pensive quiet. The jewel's nexus quivered and surged to the naked flare of his living aware-ness. *Every* minuscule deflection aroused shimmering ripples of reactive charge, the matrix explosively poised to align to the least whisper of influence. Self-command held small purchase, caged inside of a gem engineered as a potent echo chamber. Any thought would trigger a response. Helplessness sparked the split second's desire to unleash that magnified force and dismember the sigils that ruled his confinement.

Arithon doused the reckless impulse, too late.

The focus engaged with preternatural speed and spun up a cataclysmic whirlwind. The storm trampled mastery. Arithon's tattered identity drowned under a tidal bore of hostility. He had no shields. Already stripped of his innate defences, he failed to centre before the Waystone's tempestuous ferocity pulver-ized his attempt to reinstate neutral quiet. Mage-Sighted awareness lost cohesion, torn piecemeal by the remnant cacophony of sundered lives and mass destruction. Long dead, not forgotten, the Great Waystone held the trauma of entire populations hurled like so much chaff across Fate's Wheel.

Its ancient, relict witness encompassed the ending of worlds, with the violent experience of entire cultures scoured to ashes and ruin. Arithon thrashed as a mote in the deluge, milled under the battering desolation raised by refugees doomed to exodus. He knew wrenching sorrow, and the sore desperation of war-weary survivors made wretched by epidemic disease and privation. The collective testament of human misery wracked him with the panic and pain of *unimaginable billions*. Men and women, children and babes, the Waystone's residue of the uncleansed misfortunate wailed for deliverance with deafening need.

Trampled under the flood, Arithon was flayed senseless. He lacked the refined concentration to winnow out every trapped figment and sing for their requite release.

He languished past respite until the tattered recall resurfaced: *in fact he had confronted the gist of this ghastly tableau once before.* The final test of his mettle incurred by the maze under Kewar had foreshadowed a facsimile of such large-scale crisis. Then, Arithon had unravelled the clamour through a reckless invocation of the primal ciphers of unbinding. Inside a guarded sanctum,

JANNY WURTS

contained under the seal of a Fellowship work of grand conjury, his shaped response had bordered upon stark insanity. The same remedy, attempted at the enabled lens of a major quartz focus, toyed with peril beyond all imagining.

Safer to sound for the resonant notes and try clearing the crystal's imprinted disharmony. Yet, when Arithon gathered himself to regroup, the amethyst's brew of trapped consciousness rose up in virulent retaliation. Not the clamorous echo of deranged ghosts: this vicious resistance was self-aware, launched by the order's prior, failed candidates, who had lost themselves during the initiate passage to claim the prime succession. The mineral lattice still harboured their tormented spirits, a host entrapped for countless millennia, and long since abandoned to hope. Extended captivity had stewed them into a maelstrom of ravening madness, fury distilled to insatiable might by the great amethyst's focus.

Unshielded before them, Arithon fled. The matrix offered no bolt-hole, no safe harbour in which to snatch rest. His demented attackers converged in pursuit, a storm of hatred inflamed by his utter defencelessness. Driven, he coursed through a thousandfold layers of compounded knowledge and catalogued history.

Images erupted around him like dreams, excited by the spark of his passage. Impressions fragmented as mirror shards, painted with scenes otherworldly and strange: of silver cities beneath carmine skies, and tropic seas foamed by breakers the colour of lime. He viewed engines blazing white streaks across starfields, and the translucent violet of a desert sky hung with alien moons of pearl and cabochon opal; elsewhere, steel spires melted in wreaths of blue fire, and teeming blocks of grey tenements toppled into crevasses torn asunder by shattering quakes. He saw inconceivable marvels as well: forests teeming with exotic life and cities that hovered in bubbles. Stacked buildings the size of mountains, agleam with windows like cloisonne enamel, and arched bridges suspended from towers, spanning vistas that smoked with spewed gouts of lava.

The Waystone cached more than outlandish history. The detritus of old conjuries burdened the matrix, with the frozen memories of the order's past Primes strung in veils like layered cobweb. Arithon brushed through libraries of foreign knowledge, each cache vast enough to overshadow the archives at Althain Tower. Twice, he floundered against guarded sectors, blocked like vaults from unauthorized access. He streaked past grimoires of dark practice and light, written in unrecognizable ciphers and translated into dead languages. The accreted trove encompassed more information than any one mind might access in the course of a lifetime.

The staggering size of the collection helped nothing. However Arithon twisted and turned, he ran blind, while the ravening shades stalked at will, unimpeded where the embedded sigils of ward imperilled his living integrity. They hounded his progress, pursued him into the murky depths, where the

262

amethyst's contorted inclusions abetted their manic chase. If safety existed within the labyrinth, the stone's entombed denizens thwarted his search.

They whittled down the range of his choices and narrowed his marginal lead. He could not outstrip the hunt, or evade defeat, only hazard what freedom remained to strike out before he was surrounded.

Arithon doubled back, a suicidal attempt to seize a surprise advantage. His tactic failed. The horde closed and pinned him. Trapped beyond quarter, he braced for a battle he lacked any resource to win.

Yet the lethal assault he expected did not commence. The Waystone's malevolent entities made no move to destroy him. Lost to all recourse, Arithon listened, hopeful his Masterbard's ear might discern a last avenue for resolution. If no other option existed, he might sound for the notes to abate the mass insanity ranged against him.

The Great Waystone itself answered his patient query with the shocking imprint of his own Name. Arithon weighed that astonishing overture, taken aback. If the confined shades—fallen cream of the most talented Koriathain—had indexed the jewel's vast archive, suggestion allowed they may have herded him to this particular junction for a purpose.

Arithon defied the sensible prickle of trepidation. For good or ill, against certain ruin, he surrendered himself to the riddle . . .

The imprinted reference bearing his signature unfolded a vision of darkness and candleflame: record of a closed audience amid a curtained, hammer-beam chamber. The scattered glitter of mother-of-pearl inlay and the jet lacquer of Vhalzein furnishings framed a disturbingly familiar setting. *The scene matched the transaction, encountered before, captured within the quartz sliver reclaimed from the cabin in the Storlain Mountains.* Arithon realized he viewed the fateful bargain sealed between the enchantress, once his most dearly beloved, and Selidie Prime. Except the Waystone's eidetic witness retained the intact event . . .

Called onto the carpet before her Matriarch, travel-worn and aching with weariness, the initiate, *whose name was yet lost to him,* declared herself without compromise: "I *will not betray Arithon.*" Although her refusal invited a swift downfall, she firmed her shaken resolve. "*If that's what you have brought me here to achieve, let me clear the least shadow of doubt. I'll cast off my vow of obedience, even welcome the punishment that makes final end of my love as your private weapon. Never again will I be the tool to gain leverage for Koriani politics.*"

Riveted, Arithon beheld the enchantress whose love had claimed the heart core of his being. The cherished features expunged from his memory were not hardened against him but etched by anguish and terrified turmoil as her omnipotent Prime laced a ruthless threat with the poisoned honey of back-hand persuasion . . .

* * *

"Did you know our great amethyst can record and enforce promises?"

The subordinate initiate shivered. The Matriarch before her was no green antagonist but a master player who countered her moves with frightening, cold-blooded intellect. *"Don't do this."*

"I require your trust," said the Prime, unequivocal. A freezing finger of cold stirred the air, then a ripple of malice clothed in stinging power, as the sisterhood's most perilous focus stone awakened to enact her will. *"For the record, in duration of my lifetime, bear witness to my words as Selidie Prime: initiate Elaira will never be forced to betray Arithon Teir's'Ffalenn in the interests of the Koriani Order."*

The re-echoed surge as the spoken vow engaged the amethyst rippled throughout the quartz matrix. Arithon had no chance to ponder the import. The re-enacted archive of the audience unreeled to finish with absolute clarity . . .

"You are given my sanction to wield the powers of the Koriani Order in the cause of Prince Arithon's life."

"Ath, of course!" The conflicted enchantress shot to her feet. *"With the usual condition, that he would owe us his personal oath of debt for our service. Even the Fellowship must honour that stricture, no matter if the price we demand should seal his final downfall."*

Selidie inclined her head. *"We have never granted exception for birth or any other privilege of rank."* A brittle smile bent her lips. *"The choice remains yours, whether or not to offer your prince the option of our help. You are, as you see, the initiate best suited to carry out this mission. The only direct command you will bear is to stay involved with Prince Arithon's affairs."*

"A feat far easier said than accomplished." The bronze-haired enchantress drew a steady breath and showed the unyielding mettle of her character. *"If I don't go, I suppose you'd send Lirenda?"*

"My ends can be served out of love, or from hatred," Selidie agreed with poisoned logic. *"Which emotion will sway Arithon's fate in the straits of his uncertain future . . . ?"*

The exposed truth delivered an exoneration, corroborated by recent proof: *the affray upon Thunder Ridge verified that* Dakar's *word under a mishandled* Fellowship *auspice had been what invoked the* crown's *outstanding debt to the order!* Not, Arithon realized, his personal bond bestowed under the far-more-sacrosanct trust. His beloved had never betrayed him. The sliver of crystal planted in the cabin had selectively painted a lie.

The manipulative deception lay at the feet of the Koriani Prime Matriarch. Arithon bent his regard upon Selidie, ablaze with a rage beyond caution. His determined intent to pierce the secretive darkness surrounding her person catalyzed yet another referent response from the Waystone.

Its pristine record delivered the orchestrated sequence of criminal conjury once invoked over a quartz vein in the Skyshiels. There, Morriel had engineered a catastrophic upset of Athera's lane forces to blindside the Fellowship's oversight when her act of necromancy had cheated death.

Arithon witnessed the horror, full bore, as mage-trained perception rent the dimmed veil and disclosed the hag's theft of a victimised woman's young body.

"Ath wept!" Pity unleashed in full measure the empathy of his crown heritage. His peal of anguish stirred through the captive shades who had driven him to a standstill, and reverberated in wild outrage across the crystal's aligned matrix. "Your Prime's *smothered a subordinate's birthborn right to autonomy and kept her suppressed consciousness buried alive?*" The cruelty trampled ethic and reason, an assault on free will beyond all human decency.

When Arithon's revenant antagonists made no aggressive move to protect their sisterhood's exposed infamy, the grim theory dawned: the jewel's pervasive hostility might not, after all, be directed against him. Perhaps instead, he confronted the chafed gall of rebellion, for millennia bound by intractable oaths, and helplessly yoked under the iron fist of a perverted, tyrannical mistress.

The Great Waystone itself may have turned its subjugate might as his ally. Arithon engaged his initiate mastery on that posited gamble. He weighed the measure of the abomination entitled to rule the Order of the Koriathain. Then he mustered the reach of his gifted talent, engaged artistry, and composed a Masterbard's song to lay down a harmonic unbinding.

Late Summer 5924

Breaking Point

The on-going vigil in the Koriani pavilion extended past nightfall under the flicker of candlelight. The ranked Senior Circle remained in attendance, retained by the command of their Prime. Most enchantresses dozed where they could, aged indignity slouched upon chairs, or reclined on spread cushions, wrapped in their mantles against the draughts that stirred through taut canvas and tapestry hangings. Outside activity in the encampment had long since quieted under a fair sky. Past midnight, the first chill of summer's end breathed through the dense heat. The Prime retired in curtained privacy, with a skilled healer entrusted to stand the death-watch at Prince Arithon's side.

The appointed sister was not remiss. Minute to minute, she tracked the prisoner's life signs as his condition deteriorated. His erratic pulse and shallow breathing suggested Rathain's royal lineage would be extinguished before dawn. Armoured against pity, the enchantress bestirred herself for another routine inspection. Her impersonal touch clasped the victim's chained wrist to affirm the inevitable onset of heart failure.

Yet this pass, the flaccid flesh under her touch showed a flush of revitalized warmth. The order's observer straightened, surprised. Her rapt survey revealed Arithon's respiration also had deepened and steadied. More, the strengthened beat in his vein indicated the flow of life energy quickened.

The sister repeated her detailed review, waited, then rechecked to confirm. Against expectation, the prisoner under her charge had upset the slide towards attrition. The enchantress arose. The improbable change, however minute, demanded an urgent report.

Yet her dutiful step to seek counsel already chased the turn of event. The Waystone cradled above Arithon's brow crackled with sudden static. Disturbed

266

vibration stuttered against the bronze tripod, then ranged into a buzz as the quartz sang aloud.

The Prime did not require an informant. Prodded awake, Selidie bashed through her privacy curtains, her pale hair wisped over her night-rail. She rushed across the pavilion, hindered by her huddled Seniors, aroused also, and stirred to alarmed inquiry.

"Douse the Waystone immediately!" the Matriarch shouted, while the crystal's piercing emission scaled upwards.

"Move aside! Clear my way!" The Prime lashed out, barefoot, and kicked a stool from her path. Deafened, her crippled hands tucked to her chest, she elbowed through her drowsy, disordered subordinates, slowed by their belated responses.

"We've already tried," despaired the seniormost talent in crisp response to the crisis. "The stone does not answer. More, the sigils constraining your captive are unravelling and nearly inert."

Shoved past the press, Selidie accosted the distraught healer. "Use your knife! Damn the excuses. Go and find one. Kill the prisoner, forthwith!"

Shock defied comprehension, that Arithon s'Ffalenn had achieved the impossible: subverted the great amethyst, a convolute feat far beyond the best of the order's Senior talent. An unimaginable coup, given the jewel's notorious attributes doomed most candidates groomed for the trial of ninth-rank initiation. "Curse the bastard's meddling cleverness!" swore the Matriarch in strangled rage. Crowded by her flustered adepts, she lunged for the bound form on the trestle to wrest back usurped charge of the Waystone.

Her command of the focus must be re-established straightaway. Selidie claimed the healer's vacated seat, frantic to salvage the remnant impression of Arithon's consciousness before the knife-thrust dispatched him. Her planned triumph was ashes, unless the Waystone yielded to her signal will before he died.

The Matriarch clasped the resonant jewel between her deformed palms. Determined to crush the reversal, she threaded the matrix and shaped the Prime's ciphers to harness the focus, each master sigil handed down peer to peer through the course of millennia. Assured of her supremacy, she enforced her due claim under her Named identity.

But the rite to subjugate the Waystone failed. Her bid for dominance floundered amid a cast net of harmonics. No rogue diversion, the working of a bard's tuned ear for sound: Arithon's lyrical invocation framed the unique pattern for *one* living spirit. Morriel's entrenched shade, knotted over the strangled spark of Selidie's self-awareness, sieved headlong through a razor-edged cry that winnowed seed kernel from chaff. The result ripped their entwined identities to instantaneous separation.

Wrenched back to split consciousness, the dominant matriarch recoiled too late. Her grasp on her host's enslaved flesh slipped momentarily beyond her control. Selidie's repressed spirit snapped free, while the sundered shade of

Morriel encountered her true Name, transfixed within the ruthless coil of the Waystone's compromised matrix.

"You will not survive the audacity," she snapped at the bard, set aback, inconvenienced, but unvanquished yet by the imprint of his feckless melody.

"I beg your pardon?" Arithon's retort was stripped of amusement. "For the black practice of necromancy, and the brutal enslavement of a young girl, on the sovereign soil of Rathain? There's a flagrant breach of charter law. Which criminal offence I am oath-bound to prosecute under a Fellowship mandate. Dare to leave the confines of the Waystone, and crown justice condemns you."

"I think not," Morriel's dispossessed essence rebutted. "Your cited authority has no jurisdiction over the affairs of the Koriathain."

"No? In your seat, I'd not care to test that assumption under the Sorcerers' scrutiny. A fussy point of conjecture in any case, since I've picked this fight for a different priority." Arithon quenched his crafted melody with a flourish of acidic irony. "Madam, by free-will preference, in trade for your bond on the actualized surety of Selidie's due liberation, I surrender Rathain's lawful claim on your life and cede your fate to the Waystone forthwith."

"I should stoop to a ludicrous bargain with beggars?" Rankled enough not to wait for the healer's blow to dispatch him, Morriel's thrust snapped his hold on the crystal's focus. Whether or not his threat carried weight, hesitation placed her at risk of imprisonment with the damned souls trapped within the great amethyst. Furthermore, she must recoup swift possession of the donor initiate's natal body. A ruinous exposure, if the girl rallied her browbeaten consciousness, cried foul, and demanded a summary impeachment for perverted practice by the Senior Circle. Exigency required swift action to gag that felonious secret.

Morriel attacked through the jewel's poised focus, hell-bent to expunge the bard's meddling influence. No remedy for the collateral loss, that her riposte would annihilate the snared identity of Rathain's precocious crown prince.

The blast of her strike should have expunged every tie to Arithon's mortal existence; and would have, had the crystal's enabled channel not rejected Morriel's entitled command. Instead, the destructive blow twisted against her.

Flayed by the fatal stroke of her own making, the ancient Prime registered fleeting dismay in the riptide before dissolution. Destroyed by one perfidious dealing too many, she met her end as the victim of the vow engaged through the Waystone itself.

Suborned tool of the order, the crystal unleashed the actualized penalty for the forsworn promise made to Elaira: *never to seize on her love as the tool to engineer Arithon's downfall.*

Consequence hit, lightning followed by thunderbolt.

A whining snap creased the stillness that riveted the enchantresses in the pavilion. Then a splitting, electrical crackle erupted, pierced by a shriek as the Waystone shattered. Raked in the throes of befuddled recovery, the traumatized spirit of Selidie recouped conscious awareness with a scream of agony. Static charges raced up her arms, laced her head, and rammed her erect.

Locked rigid as the Great Waystone's matrix unravelled, the pent forces layered throughout the course of millennia hurled the victimised woman bodily from her chair. Bloodied and limp, nerves seared beyond function, she tumbled face-down amid the glitter of crystal shards on the floor.

The shock wave of release raked across the attendant Prime Circle caught in proximity. Torn spirit from flesh in an instant, they crumpled like rags, heart-beat and breathing suspended. The impact hammered Lirenda unconscious and swept outward through the surrounding encampment. Every enchantress stationed within range buckled at the knees, knocked senseless under the surge through the corded ties of bound service.

Lirenda recovered awareness past daybreak, her first impression the rank reek of death trapped beneath sun-heated canvas. Swimming vision revealed the fringed hem of a tapestry a handspan from her opened eyes. The encampment outside the pavilion walls seemed deserted, the industrious churr of summer's cicadas eerily undisturbed by human activity. Inside, only flies buzzed in the gloom, disturbed to a gyrating, silvery cloud when she stirred and rolled over. They flew in manic circles and alighted on the filmed eyes of the corpse tumbled amid crumpled skirts an arm's length away. Others flitted like motes between the half-lit furnishings, pausing to feed on the noisome stains of gushed effluent soaking the carpet.

Gagged by the stench, and appalled by the toll of strewn casualties, Lirenda surveyed the butchered forms of her sisters, slumped in disarray against table legs, or fallen across upset chairs, or sprawled without dignity amid the crumple of red-banded mantles. Her stunned wits struggled to number the fallen, while horror reeled under the import of the disaster unfolded within the Prime's private quarters. A moment passed before the survivor recognized the profound change: the master sigil of the Koriathain no longer enslaved her free will.

Lirenda blinked through an uprush of tears. Her innate choice of expression and speech were released from duress after two hundred and forty four years.

At long last, the Matriarch's downfall had ended her imposed ordeal of punishment. Selidie's body lay grotesque in death, naked in the flayed shreds of her night-rail. The pearly perfection of youthful skin was despoiled, bloodied from the explosion that dusted her surrounds with pulverized crystal. Arisen amid the charnel-house quiet, Lirenda picked an unsteady path between the winnowed husks of her cohorts. Her hesitant footfalls on the warded carpet incurred no punitive censure. No voice of authority challenged her progress. She moved from one prone form to the next, and encountered cold flesh, limbs locked in rigor. *All of the Senior Circle lay dead.* None of the order's top-tier enchantresses had escaped the past night's debacle.

Triumph was absent. The wild exultation that should have uplifted this spurious victory dissolved as Lirenda grasped the extent of the order's most irreplaceable loss. The sharp fragments crunched underfoot were not glass but shards of deep purple: amethyst. She trod over the wreckage of the Great Waystone, by lengths the most powerful focus in Koriani possession. The atrocity of the sisterhood's murdered talent paled before the blow imposed by the jewel's destruction.

Eyes shut, teeth clenched in mute rage, Lirenda shuddered with suppressed nausea. Granted her coveted position as the ranking initiate, she cursed fate.

Always, she had intended to seize her due claim to the succession. But never amid her dark hope of revenge had she envisioned taking the Prime seat with the might of order's inheritance gutted.

Matriarch in fact, Lirenda became the sole party responsible for steering the sisterhood's future. Her task alone, to shape the response and redress today's ghastly atrocity. History would measure her fallen predecessor harshly: the bare plank, and the dangling, broken cuffs that remained of the enspelled restraints held no culpable prisoner. Arithon Teir's'Ffalenn had snatched his villainous advantage from the lap of opportune chance.

A cursory survey of the pavilion exposed the burst wards and smashed lock on the coffer that guarded the former Prime's paraphernalia. Lirenda trod through the wrack of the murdered dead. Deaf to the wakeful stir risen outside, as the encampment's uninvolved residents stirred from the seizure that had stunned them senseless, she knelt and surveyed the chest's rifled contents, relieved as she found most of the critical inventory left undisturbed.

Selidie's select cache of minerals still lay secure in their ties and silk wrappings. Except for the one crystal of choice significance to Rathain's prince, gone missing from the collection. No coincidence, that the stolen quartz pendant had served as Elaira's personal focus.

The flare of Lirenda's fury defied words. Never mind that Arithon's striking reverse had brought a corrupted Prime to her demise, his revenge at one strike had reduced the Koriathain to a minor power on the proscribed world of Athera.

Goaded beyond rage, Lirenda slammed down the coffer's lid. She shoved erect and vowed over the unshrouded bodies of her slaughtered sisters, "I will see you undone, Teir's'Ffalenn, and savour my satisfaction in full when the woman you love before any other gets cast down into witless misery."

Hardened by hatred kindled long before the blow dispatched on this day, Lirenda crossed to the wardrobe and appropriated the deceased Matriarch's costliest purple silk mantle. She shouldered the weight of all nine bands of office, retrieved the order's swan seal from the chain at Selidie's neck, and took brisk command when the first distressed sister parted the privacy curtain and called in frightened inquiry.

Lirenda shaped her first directive as the Koriani Prime Successor with granite resolve: to mete out devastation in equal measure, with every resource the order possessed aimed to bring down the renegade enchantress, Elaira.

Vexations

Morning gilded the tatters of cloud, while the droplets clinging from last night's rain winkled glints of citrine across the heath. Althain's Warden sat, oblivious to the view, a tucked silhouette in the ward-room's cushioned window-seat five floors below the draughty height of the tower library. He appeared to be drowsing. Only the crabbed grip on his tea-mug marred the tranquil illusion of sleep. Though the gruelling tension of Arithon's escape had resolved by up-ending the Koriani Prime succession, Sethvir refused to stand down. Against sense, he stayed upright, alert despite the bruised lines of exhaustion knifed into his cheeks.

No better rested, Asandir perched with folded legs on a hassock. Silver hair plaited behind his bent head, he whipped the last seam in the unfinished leathers hastily cut to his measure. The piece-work was Sethvir's: a pilferer's penance, done in contrition for the worn garment just filched to cut patches for the tower's rickety hand-pump.

No bath-water would become drawn tonight. The ancient contrivance lay stripped to loose parts, the failed gaskets not yet refurbished with the newly greased set of replacements.

The punch of the awl and the whisper of the field Sorcerer's stitches clocked the tense silence, while the after-shock storms of causation rippled across Daon Ramon, and the Warden's fixated attention mapped the hazards of Arithon's flight against the on-going momentum of probable event.

Sethvir's tears marked the moment of blessed relief when the crown prince took cover at last in a bramble-choked gulch in the Barrens. No hostile scryers hounded his trail. The bid to secure an unsanctioned accession anchored Lirenda's attention. The foreseeable future would keep her hands tied, reining in distant rivals while she firmed her grip on the order's affairs. Which pause granted a moment for additional insight.

"The wraiths released at large when the Waystone broke asunder?" Asandir asked with tart delicacy.

"All have crossed the veil," Sethvir confirmed. "Poor, sad creatures. No credit to us, their hideous torment is ended."

Asandir whipped a knot into the tail of his thread, each movement brisk with annoyance. "A sorry hour when we have to scrounge our accomplishments by default!"

His outburst dangled without further comment. Enough dire factors left in loose play might yet hurl the world's course to disaster.

When Sethvir's eyelids snapped open, Asandir's alarmed start just missed jabbing the awl through his finger. "What's afoot?"

"Kharadmon, inbound," Althain's Warden declared, nettled nerves evinced by his owlish stare. Then a cut rose dropped from clear air and bounced off his head. Tumbled to the floor, then snap-frozen to glass, the bloom shattered to fragments as quickly erased by a whirlwind of arctic displeasure.

"You kept him uninformed!" howled the Sorcerer's shade to Sethvir in a blast that shuddered the casement.

Althain's Warden sat up and blinked, discomposed as a badgered poet.

Before his dissembling fuddle absorbed the angst behind Kharadmon's tantrum, Asandir spoke, his challenge cold iron hurled into the tempest. "You reference the war host at large in Daon Ramon? My view is current in fact."

The self-contained wind devil raked across the chamber. Quill pens whisked air-borne. A loose parchment flurried. The sturdy clothes tree festooned with torn bridles tottered, snatched back into testy stability with a clashed chime of buckles and bit rings. The breeze ran on, riffled the linen on the spare cot and batted a miniature blizzard of eider-down from a moth hole in the pillow. A hamper of socks crashed against Asandir's saddle-bags. Thrown a steel glance for importunate insolence, the shade said in breezy retort, "You're dispatched to handle the war host, I see?" Sarcasm bleak enough to snap crystal huffed on into accusation. "We've inflated our brazen self-importance to nose-lead humanity's choices?"

Sethvir salvaged the hackled pause. "You've come to belabour our share of the blame for Davien's twisted forecast?" That tired debate, which claimed the compact reduced Mankind's free will, in practice, to the role of playthings and puppetry. "Asandir acted on that threat three weeks ago, while you raked muck with Verrain, nose deep in the black pools at Mirthlvain."

"I find breeding monsters and pestilence less twisted than two-legged sheep! The crankiest snakes strike for self-defence. Unlike human intelligence that sickens on fear, then turns rabid over a semantic difference in principle." Except Kharadmon's hyperbole was misplaced. He knew best of any: the suspension of Fellowship stewardship exposed more than humanity's short-sighted prospects to ruin. Deflated to grumbling, the Sorcerer's shade spiked tendrils of hoar-frost on the paned lamp. "In case you haven't checked, clan numbers may not withstand the massacre. The Hatchet's mandate from the temple includes a directive to derange Halwythwood's wardings. To that end, he's poised his dedicates at the verges for ravening slaughter."

"Our choices had to be weighed against back-lash," Asandir pointed out, the bitter, immediate losses in Rathain laid against the long-term reprisals incited by a True Sect recoil. "A strong intervention would pitch the fanatical cry for extermination worldwide."

"We'll grapple that anyhow," Kharadmon snarled, unappeased by dispassionate logic. "Has Sethvir mentioned Saroic s'Gannley's heroic evasion in Camris has fuelled the dismal strategy?"

"Asandir lent his escort to Traithe, leaving Morvain," Sethvir pointed out, oblique reference to the flotilla of galleys requisitioned for troop transport across Instrell Bay. Armed companies mustered for The Hatchet's attack: the reinforcements withdrawn from north Tysan had stressed passage through the port towns for a fortnight.

"A bolstered campaign, launched near the onset of winter called for a revival of Earl Jieret's crafty tactics. My counsel sent Tarens," Asandir confessed. Whether that gifted resource equipped Rathain's clans to deflect the brunt of The Hatchet's offensive, the broad-scale deployment certainly poisoned the last-minute prospect of peace. The Fellowship's field Sorcerer tied off the last lace, unfolded lean shanks, and stood. "Travel takes me through Rathain in fact, though my purposeful business lies elsewhere." A quicksilver glint nicked his glance as he belted on his new leathers and hefted his packs for departure. "By the roundabout route my black horse will rejoin me."

Kept too ferociously busy for doubts, The Hatchet's subordinates dug in for engagement, the gleam on their armour powdered by the trampled dust of the war camps. Their debates, thrashed over as tactics by lamp-light, launched by day the sweaty tours of reconnaissance. The scouts' sketched reports of the outlying terrain were poured over by a wispy man with a squint. Hounded by The Hatchet's astringent critiques, his tactile fingers recreated Daon Ramon's topography. The meticulous work in pinched clay engulfed the plank trestle, from the undulant furrows of the Barren's hill-crests, to each seamed vale, painted with the blue veins of the low-country rivulets. Where water was scarce, the wrinkled taupe hinterlands detailed the snaking course of dry gullies. Clumped horsehair, stiffened by dipped ink, represented the impassable thickets of black briar and hazel.

Strategy arranged the pin counters for troops, identified by toothpick silk standards, while other locations mapped in secret demanded the talent of the Temple diviners.

Outside, ordered in magnified counterpoint, The Hatchet pushed his outfitted companies to finesse his triumphant closure. He gamed the men's fractious morale in cold blood, his rank-and-file foot sent hither and yon on forced marches until they seethed under the lid of harsh discipline. Griped on boredom, billeted under stifling canvas and fed to the teeth, men chafed through the brutal grind of their assignments, explosively pitched for release.

Towards that steel-clad stew, and the massed sinew primed for engagement, a lone rider astride an uncanny black horse crossed a country-side stripped of its herdstock. The thin traffic abroad pursued martial demand, with the movement of goods likewise steered awry by the northern campaign.

The thirsty mule-train blocking access to the creek packed a tell-tale burden of reeking green hides. Amid the clamour of harness bells strung upon bridles and breast-straps, the caravan master southbound to Daenfal blotted his peeling forehead with apology. "Aye, we're noisy to put off the wolves, not just fiends. This stinking haul's consigned for the tanners. Light rest us, I'd beg to clap my ears deaf! Nobody sleeps, and my outriders are wall-eyed from chasing off predators, ever since the herds grazed in Daon Ramon Barrens have been drastically culled."

"Slaughtered to provision the True Sect war host?" Alerted by yips from the outriders, Tarens side-stepped as the watered mules spun, muzzles dripping, and surged en masse up the stream-bank.

The stocky master grunted, swung astride his lean nag to depart. "Just the game. The better horses were Sunwheel-branded for the dedicate war host." His parting glance measured the glossy black stud. "Yon's a quality mount. Wise to keep him close. Shadow's blight upon war-bond tithes, our best hacks were skinn't off us for piety, and no thanks for the robbery of requisition."

Tarens reined on his way, more concerned that the Sorcerer's loan might see him arraigned for a burning. His circumspect passage due northward from Backwater thinned the opportune chance for reliable gossip. Only one foot-loose tinker who plied a wheelwright's skills had encountered the task forces scouring the Barrens directly.

"The Hatchet's captain of archers has practised troop marksmanship by reaping the dun herds of deer."

Yet the chinless granddame who wound his waxed thread described other forays set after small game. "The outriders have teamed with the head-hunters' tracking dogs. Not just for coursing. They use beaters to flush and kill even the cotton-tail in the brakes."

Tarens surveyed their ramshackle stall, gagged by the reek of poorly cured leather. The collection of strap stock, priced by the penny, confirmed the excess that undercut values. The push to denude the Barrens aimed to pressure Halwythwood's clans by starvation. Foragers compelled to hunt farther afield increased their exposure to the True Sect bountymen.

More sinister still, the uneasy clan sentries at the Arwent Gorge reported smoke smudging the horizon towards Caith-al-Caen. "No blaze touched off by a storm," they explained as Tarens reined up. "Eastward, The Hatchet has reivers burning the coverts."

His farmer's origin regarded askance, despite Asandir's advance word, the scouts added snide comment that his heeled boots marked too vivid a trail for the trackers.

Tarens rebutted their scorn, convinced that his country trappings lent him an advantage.

"Well enough, perhaps, while you crossed Araethura," sniped a youngster, sighting the edge on his knife. "But in the free wilds? Mind you aren't shot in the back by one of our own."

"That's a moot concern, these days," a bearded companion dismissed, while the kindlier of the two veteran women shared her meal of mixed jerky and berries. No one broached the unsettling threat, that an enemy shaft placed any patrol sent abroad in the Barrens at hazard. While a dry wind rustled the trees, punch-cut against a copper sunset, the watch change stepped up and recapped the more troublesome news from the west.

"The Hatchet's set companies from Tysan along the trade-road by Instrell Bay. Armed patrols, with placed sentries in timber towers command the smuggler's coves. Standing orders are to cut off and destroy any fishing-smacks caught landing cargo. We've warned off our allies. Hard times and bad business, but we daren't jeopardize their livelihoods for a smuggler's haul of fresh cod."

Others belittled the blockade with shrugs. "The troops' pious attention's hell-bound to slack once cold weather sows discontent."

"Not this time," warned Tarens. "These companies are not posted to choke your supply but to cut off your people's escape."

Eyebrows lifted in stark disbelief.

"Are you mad?" The incredulous speaker spat in contempt. "Coward's talk says we can't hold our ground behind Fellowship wardings raised at full strength!"

"Don't gamble the blameless lives of your families," snapped Tarens. "Not while I bear Asandir's urgent charge to relocate your rooted presence. The caithdein's lodge and the heart of your settlement must look to Deshir before Halwythwood's defences falter."

While the hot-heads slapped incensed hands to their weapons, and galled outcries questioned the Seven's endorsement of Tarens's loyalty, the grizzled codger who tended their remounts commented from the side-lines.

"Have you all gone blind? The claim of Fellowship sanction is true! Or did you miss the uncanny ghost eye on the black horse yon crofter rode in on? The fey animal left," the man added, regretful. "Lit off on its own under arcane command the moment I stripped off Iyat-thos's bedroll and gear." Turned to the fair-haired envoy ringed about with jaundiced ill will, he declaimed, "Your crotchety goats are across the gorge. Best collect them before they get butchered."

All stares fixed on the town-bred's scarred face.

"*Goats?*" The watch captain's taciturn features flushed scarlet. "Whatever for? Did you imagine we'd fiddle with husbandry?"

"Not a bit." Behind Tarens's hayseed amusement, his blue eyes wore the sheared glint acquired from Rathain's legendary *caithdein*, Earl Jieret. "What town-bred foray in benighted country won't slack off stickling duty to chase down the windfall of grain-fattened meat?"

The Hatchet exuded anticipation. Fist clamped to his sheathed sword to save his clipped stride from entanglement, he strutted to meet the stopped wagon, just rolled in under a temple escort. The dedicates regarded his rapt approach, his short frame shadowed between two taller officers. His ferocious glance surveyed their road-weary ranks, the jerked plume on his helm wagged right and left like the tail on a swaggering rooster. He missed nothing. His hard mouth flexed, displeased by the sight of the white-and-gold vestments planted in their armoured midst.

"Don't I already have enough priests on my rolls to feed twoscore able soldiers?"

"Erdane has sent an additional cadre to serve your expanded campaign." The haughty worthy in charge stayed serene, unlike his train of underlings and diviners, who turned faces pinched pink with offence.

"Oversight, rather." The Hatchet's inspection raked the awkward scribe, whose arms were clutched to a wicker crate crammed full of quibbling pigeons.

The priest smiled amid the flare of gold braid. "Naturally. What did you expect? The mortal world is rife with corruption, and the High Temple must be kept informed." And would be, in detail, given the shocking expense underwritten to clean out Rathain's Shadow-ridden barbarians.

By now, avid spectators crowded the side-lines, drawn by sharp interest in the close-kept plan to finish the Halwythwood campaign. Yet The Hatchet's obstreperous scowl quashed the eavesdroppers' hopes before the first tarps were unlashed. The repulsed bystanders sauntered away, while the Temple's armed retinue shouldered the locked chests, each three spans long, and unwieldy enough to bend backs and raise grunts of effort.

This was not the usual cargo of oil casks and baled lint. Though the two wagons positioned behind hauled the expected arbalests mounted on timbers, coin laid on the rampant flurry of wagers suggested the forest was not slated to burn from the eastern flank.

The Light's First Commander's lips remained sealed as the seam on a walnut. He spun on his heel and ploughed a furrow through the priestly escort, reckless as a hammer swung on a string. The burdened bearers chased his spraddled gait, trailed by the scintillant flutter of Erdane's rebuffed delegation. The clerk scuttled crabwise behind, staggered under his hamper of messenger-birds.

The Hatchet stumped into the command tent, one mailed fist on his sword in plain sight, and the other clutching his tactical strategy close as the hair on his chest. He waited, impatient, until the trailing procession arrived under canvas.

"Let's have the lids off for my inspection," he snapped, as the sweating men lowered the ungainly boxes in the lamp-lit gloom.

The ranked priest swept forward and unkeyed the locks. His dedicate body-guard breached the wax seals, parted the silk shroud, and bared the priceless cargo of metal rods bundled inside. "Pure copper, blessed and founded by the Temple at Erdane. Sited as planned on the major flux points, they'll unravel the Fellowship's lines of protection without any casualties."

The Hatchet's beard split to the gleam of bared teeth. "Perfect!" His gravel bass ground into a glued silence, stirred by tentative murmurs, then sliced by his right-hand captain's bellowed astonishment. "You'll dare to harness the lightning?"

Laughter rumbled behind The Hatchet's breastplate. "What else?" The equinox storms packed the punch to destabilize spellcraft founded by electro-magnetics. "The shock will be glorious."

Repaired to the trestles spread over with Daon Ramon's miniaturized terrain, The Hatchet outlined his brazen strategy with an array of stabbed nails. "We'll ground the strikes here, and here, and along this line. Our diviners say stress brought to bear at these sites will unravel the Sorcerers' web." As excited talk swelled, he roared, "Clap your tongues! I'll gut any yapper whose brainless noise leaks a whisper outside this tent."

His forest-born prey must have no warning. He would have them penned like bunched sheep for ripe slaughter when the shield of protections came down.

The massive arbalests rolled into position that night under cover of darkness, each equipped with specialized quarrels, wood cladding sheathed over purified copper. The bare rods designated for Daon Ramon's free wilds were assigned to select lancers for placement. Those elite parties assembled by morning, horses fresh off the picket lines, and accoutrements dazzling as low sunlight rinsed the tableau dull red. Summer's last gasp sweltered over dry grass and baked earth, lidded in haze, while the breathless air shimmered above the reivers' swathes of scorched ground, and denuded gullies winkled with reflections sparked off the depleted creeks. Encamped on stripped country-side, twenty leagues wide, the Light's forces hemmed the green border of Halwythwood, backed to the south by the Arwent Gorge, with alternate egress thwarted by Athili and the shoreside garrisons at Daenfal Lake. Westward, more companies secured Instrell Bay and commandeered the Mathorn trade-road.

Heat wilted the standards and sweated The Hatchet's acrid impatience. He paced through the priests' ceremonial blessing. Tinged bilious under the tasselled canopy, the brosy clerk hovered with his lap desk and pen, a bagged pigeon at hand for the prompt release of the commemorative message. The inked lines were half-penned when a shouting disturbance burst through the line of poised lancers.

"Lord Commander!" Livid, the breathless master of horse let fly his howling grievance. "Blight puckle yer lot o' slack sentries who've been caught asleep at their posts."

The maligned watch captain, striding behind, bellowed his vigorous protest, "Powers of Darkness! Shut your lying yap. It's your layabout grooms we've caught snoozing."

The priest's blessing stumbled. The clerk blinked and snatched for a fresh sheet of parchment, pen nib scratching through The Hatchet's roar of annoyance.

"You bunglers got bested by a thieving wild stud?"

"The rank brute charged in black as death in broad daylight!" The captain's flustered retort entangled with the hostler's rant. "Stirred up randy havoc, the brute! The frenzied mares snapped their head-stalls and trampled over the staked picket lines." Through yammering rage and stable-yard language, the bad news emerged. "Yon rogue made off with every sound animal in the command post."

The priest stiffened. "If that's the hoofed demon with the ghost eye, this campaign is bedevilled. The same ill-starred harbinger fore-ran our defeat at Lithmarin."

"Shut your snivelling before I punch your front teeth through your nape!" The Hatchet wheeled with blood in his eye and detailed his mounted lancers. "Ride out. Now! You have your orders." Refocused upon his flustered watch captain, he added through a curled upper lip, "Send two companies. Quarter the country-side until they've recovered our forsaken horses. And get Arwi Unfrey! I want his head-hunters' dogs and best trackers to run down that stud and see him destroyed. Tell him to bring me the head and flayed hide. I'll have them nailed up with my trophies."

His granite glance noticed the diligent scribe. A lashed boot bashed the lap desk, to a black spray of ink. Servile scrabbling overset the pigeon bag. The panicked messenger-bird flapped aloft. Struck by its squirt of guano, The Hatchet cursed. "I'll also rip the wings off your tattling birds if you keep on spreading hysterical superstition!"

News of the horse theft blamed on his black stud reached Asandir on foot, as he crossed the dry gulch that once channelled the Severnir's headwaters. "Dakar's impetuous idiocy did *what*?"

Echoes of his dismay shattered off the rock-walls that hemmed the gorge on both sides. The stallion tagging his heels shied back, snorting. Reins and saddle-girth loose, hooves clattering over unstable boulders, the flesh-and-blood horse was a hundred leagues from the Light's disrupted encampment and nowhere near the dedicates' randy mares.

Asandir curbed his flash-point temper. A quelling touch on the animal's soaked neck, and a swift apology to the stomped rocks likely spared his mount from a broken foreleg.

Paused after his companion settled four-square, the field Sorcerer braced for the set-back behind Sethvir's cryptic sending: *"The Mad Prophet has wrecked our sage plan to reduce the worst of the Halwythwood clans' losses."*

"By that, I gather he chose not to wait. Or did the chieftains flinch from the sacrifice Tarens suggested to gain their families' safe passage from Halwythwood?"

Sethvir's sigh could almost be felt from his distant perch by Althain Tower's library casement. *"Dakar's erratic Sight failed to forecast the greater disaster beyond the handful of casualties. A short-fall not helped by Esfand's inexperience."*

Sethvir's earth-sense unreeled the summary havoc sown through The Hatchet's encampment by the spellbinder's precocious illusion. On another occasion, the field Sorcerer might have laughed as the rogue facsimile of his stallion flummoxed the True Sect's diviners and sent the war host's loose string into high-tailed stampede.

Yet on this day, the milled grist of malfortune sprang from the confusion stirred in the aftermath. *"A bold sally by the* caithdein's *scouts raided and killed an escort squad of temple lancers,"* Sethvir disclosed in disastrous summary. *"The young fools waylaid one of the copper grounding rods sent from the High Priesthood at Erdane."*

"Those scouts can't possibly hope to stave off the collapse of Halwythwood's wardings!" The dedicate force entrenched in Daon Ramon outstripped the clan war band's scant resource. Nor might the equinox squall lines be turned without back-lash, or the flux currents answer to Dakar's inept mastery, unless— epiphany dawned with a galvanic shock. Asandir swore, at odds with the tender handling that reined his black stud around in the dry river-bed. "Ath avert the affliction of jughead stupidity! Dakar hasn't dared put that forsaken rod to reckless use?"

"He surely has," lamented Sethvir. *"His crack-brained scheme's aimed to draw down the lightning at Caith-al-Caen."*

The repercussive cascade of mass consequence wrung Asandir to a cold sweat. "The idiot! Doesn't he realize the galvanic surge from that nexus will whiplash the entire Fourth Lane?" A flare on that scale would render Halwythwood too reactive for human habitation, and worse. "Chain Dakar to Sithaer's deepest pit for eternity, don't say his wilful genius overlooked the latitudinal bleed off!" The untoward burst would splash a storm of electro-magnetics clear across Daon Ramon Barrens, a spike potent enough to drive the Light's diviners insane and afflict The Hatchet's massed troops with raving hallucinations.

"You can't leave Althain Tower to stop this!" Asandir cracked, alarmed. "How near is the first squall line?"

"Too close." By lane or direct transfer, intervention posed a lethal prospect

at this pass. *"The flux charge in the vicinity is overburdened to peak instability. No sending I've tried carried through."* A discorporate colleague dispatched to warn Dakar put the messenger's unshielded spirit at risk of being ripped asunder.

A drawback already rejected as Sethvir's effort to ameliorate the upset continued apace. *"Traithe's sent to Lanshire at speed. He'll raise stop-gap stayspells to preserve Seshkrozchiel's hibernation."*

Asandir tracked the Warden's summary oversight, aware the drakes' restive turmoil beyond Northgate could erupt beyond salvage if the somnolent dragon aroused prematurely, stung livid with wrath. Other simmering crises would gain momentum long before the excess resonation dispersed. The incoming shock wave already tinged prescience with the spectre of ruin. Swept en masse by another flux-based disturbance, the fanatical priesthood at Erdane would cry foul and blame the fell works of Shadow and sorcery.

Sethvir crystallized the quandary forthwith. "Our guarded care not to inflame the religion is blown to ashes and dust."

"Defend Tarens from mayhem, I can't lend support," Asandir cried in anguish. Toppled priorities forced his immediate choice to douse the outbreak of worse fires, elsewhere. "Dispatch Kharadmon to Rockfell. I'll ride to join him straightaway." An incarnate Sorcerer must stand in partnership with the discorporate's presence *before* Dakar's miscalled strategy thrashed across latitude and destabilized the grand wards that incarcerated Desh-thiere. Miss that urgent rendezvous, and damage to Athera herself would outstrip war and chaos as the equinox squalls ignited the major nexus at Caeth-al-Caen.

Reassessments

Sequestered in the caverns that riddle the mountains at Skelseng's Gate, Arithon sounds the nuanced records harboured in the matrix of Elaira's crystal; and the knowledge found there defers his oath-bound support of Valien's upbringing at Ettinmere Settlement, and prioritizes his preference in favour of solving the riddle behind Cosach's death-bed legacy . . .

While the seasonal thunder-heads darken the sky above Daon Ramon, and one fateful lightning strike unleashes chaos through a copper rod planted at Caith-al-Caen, Lirenda closets herself with the Skyron aquamarine, immersed for days in an extensive search of the order's history, first to defend her succession from rivals, then to seek clues to the secretive agendas engaged by her murdered predecessor . . .

Abandoned to loneliness at Ettinmere with her bastard infant, ridden day and night by the strain of spellbound attraction, Vivet's bitter resentment of Arithon's absence fires her resolve to delve into the mystery behind his evasive identity . . .

IX. Secrets

When the True Sect campaign to purge the old blood-lines from Halwythwood finished in disaster, news of The Hatchet's disordered retreat at first eluded the scrutiny of Erdane's populace. The advance, cryptic messages carried by pigeon informed only the exalted High Priests. Their dismayed, hushed whispers rose and fell behind the pillared arches of the temple's innermost chambers, until the rumours leaked from the seaports outpaced the written reports from the field. Broken at last, the shredded decorum of secrecy sowed panic and stunned indignation. Talk in the streets and the wine-shops decried the plight of the war host gone barking mad in Daon Ramon Barrens.

If the long distance withdrawal let most of the dedicate companies regroup their shocked wits, none of the stricken diviners recovered. Despite the healers' diligence, the afflicted talents stayed intractable, unfit for service and forced to languish in sequestered confinement. The plucked note of hysteria by then tried far more than the armoured nerve of the Temple's faithful. A flock chafed restive by war tithes threatened a True Sect crisis of faith.

Not blind or deaf, as Lysaer's valet, Dace Marley tracked the course of outside events in the routine pursuit of his duty. Amid the cross chop of tension, he hauled his weekly allotment of linens up the staircase of the central arcade. No alternate route from the laundry allowed him to side-step the turmoil. The stone cell where the avatar lay in recovery had been a secluded chapel for offerings, converted into a private sick-room with no backstairs access for servants.

Mass upheaval made today's progress more difficult. Dace breasted the press, careful not to cross the prerogatives of his superiors. A crowd of officials overwhelmed his ascent just below the third landing. Dace shrank against the tapestried walls, his stacked basket turned to fend off a harried first-level examiner. The priests just behind tightened their ranks and broke off a heated discussion. Dace bowed deep, face pressed into the folded sheets in transparent pretence: a wise servant overheard nothing concerning his betters' affairs.

The glittering party swept by without pause. Dace started upwards, stopped again by a peremptory grip on his shoulder.

"You, there, are you deaf? I said, bring those linens along straightaway! They're required to settle our fallen diviners."

Dace stifled protest and bowed again. "I'm the avatar's valet," he demurred, hopeful the temple's hierarchy might deflect the demand.

"Nonsense, come along!" The insistent priest bore the badge of a senior healer. "Downstairs staff can replenish your basket, with the blessing of the Light's glory your due reward for the inconvenience."

Dace dared not venture a second excuse. Here, a s'Gannley descendant with Fellowship ties lived and breathed in the quicksands of jeopardy. Any hint he was not the devout lackey he seemed would invite the scrutiny of an examiner. Dace shrank to imagine Lysaer's lonely fate if the untoward gaffe unmasked him. He followed the healer priest up one more floor, past the rhythmic thump of the looms, where conscript craftsmen wove silk into vestments, and the chanting of the second-year novices choursed in recitation.

Dace turned where he was led, down a dim corridor faintly laced with the ammoniac whiff of slopped urine. A carpet padded with broom-straw dampened stray noise, to little effect. Moans, deranged screams, and hysterical laughter erupted from the incarcerates locked behind the stout doors.

The healer priest beckoned Dace down a cross corridor. Ahead, two attendants idled in plain livery, one bald-headed, and the other thatched with marigold ringlets.

"Can't you quiet them down?" the priest healer demanded. "This bedlam will unsettle the inbound arrivals from Daon Ramon."

"Perhaps your newcomers have our lot stirred up." Forehead burnished with sweat, the speaker shrugged his jaded dismissal. "The ravers react to any uncanny disturbance outside of reasoned awareness."

"Imbecile!" The healer shouted over the clamour of crazed fists beating at the walls hard enough to pulp flesh. "Quit prattling nonsense and care for your less fortunate brothers before they take further harm!"

The mop-haired attendant swanned off in compliance, while the other's pouched chin quivered above his starched collar. "The new rooms have been cleared. That way, on the right." His gesture denoted the bright swathe in the gloom, where several cell doors down the passage gaped open.

The priest healer's reprimand fastened on Dace. "Along with you, then. You're needed to furnish those pallets." To the remiss attendant, "Those beds should have been ready long since!"

The flushed malingerer shuffled off, grumbling. "Not my fault those slug-gardly junior initiates took their time moving out. It's a bootless assignment, not worth spit and polish. These lunatics wet themselves in a rage if you so much as look at them sideways."

No glance acknowledged the servant behind. Dull humility being the safest tactic, Dace crossed the threshold of the first cell.

As his dazzled eyesight adjusted, Dace confronted bare walls and a wash-stand with flaked paint, the rail under the ewer denuded of towels. Flooded in daylight beneath opened shutters, the pallet's stripped ticking lay empty.

"Are you lack-wit or lazy, you can't make up a bed?" the attendant lashed out in exasperation.

"Neither one, grant me forbearance." Dace thumped down his basket.

"Well, hurry along!" Above the racketing bellows and shrieks funnelled in from the corridor, the attendant added, "I won't abide laziness!"

"Light's will be done, always." Dace's unctuous bow lent the crass fellow the grace to clear out of his way. The allotment of sheets drawn for Lysaer obliged him to complete several pallets. Fast work must see him excused before the next lot of lunatics arrived. Aware as his arrogant betters were not, Dace feared his spirit-marked presence had triggered the outbreak of tantrums.

Delay thwarted his bid for escape. Two chattering flunkies sent to replace the mildewed mattress in the last room kept him under the eye of the critical attendant. He smoothed the final fold in the top sheet and stuffed the slip on the pillow, too late. Heavy footsteps approached. Four muscled men burdened with a litter manoeuvred through the narrow doorway. Dace clutched his basket, trapped where he stood.

The diviner they carried in strapped restraint muttered in agitation, then started to thrash with a violence that jostled the bearers off balance. They grunted and swore, while their prostrate charge bellowed through frothed lips.

"A minion of Shadow lurks in our midst!" Bound limbs strained against the leather cuffs, the mad talent turned a contorted face, rolled eyes fixed upon Dace with outraged accusation.

The attendant's appalled regard noted the servant, flattened against the wall with his wicker basket hugged to his chest.

"Burn him!" screeched the diviner. "Bone and sinew, throw his spirit-marked flesh to the flames! Let evil's corruption be cleansed!"

The unsettled healer yelled for a priest.

"Grace wept!" the lead bearer swore, fed up as the buck of the litter skinned his knuckles against the door-jamb. "This your first assignment? You'll learn, soon enough. The afflicted see Shadow in every dim corner!" Through the diviner's incensed yammer, he snapped, "Bedamned to this crackpot's noise. Servant! Have you got a cloth handy?"

Dace swallowed, shaken from paralysed fear. "None, by your will."

"Then hop to and find one!" The dedicate nodded to his harried partner, then deposited his end of the litter on the freshly made bed. Ears ringing from the racket, he laced into the dumb-struck attendant. "Gag the raver forthwith! He'll bite. Scratch, too, mind your eyes. Guard your bollocks as well, this one kicks like a horse whenever we loosen his straps."

The moment the towel was yanked from his grip, Dace bobbed a subservient gesture and squeezed past. He left the wrestling men to their duty and fled, head down, for the threshold. The pretence of decorum sustained his escape, while the unhinged diviner struggled in the maniacal frenzy behind, and the festering chorus of outcries chased him the length of the corridor. The burly priest healer who moved to waylay him spied his empty basket and waved him on. "Light save us! The ward will be rife with loose bowels. Tell the laundry to send up more linen at once!" Spun away, he yelled towards the dispensary. "A round of valerian possets, before every blighter we have fouls his bed."

While the furore up-ended the steamy routine of the cellar laundry, Dace made his noon meal the excuse to duck further requests for service. Returned late from the kitchen to replenish his basket, he waited as the chattering women wrung the sopped sheets from the vats, then collected them, dried and pressed. When at length he ascended to Lysaer's quarters, the cadence of song from the temple closed the late-afternoon devotions.

When Dace reached the sixth floor without incident, trouble met him on the side stair that accessed the avatar's tower apartment. Contentious voices reverberated behind the closed door above. Paused in the tight passage, Dace also heard whimpers of anguish, recognizably Lysaer's.

Anger trumped fear. Dace thumbed the latch, his laden basket braced against his hip. He found the lock turned and used his valet's key to gain entry.

Beyond the cracked panel, the plush horsehair chairs in the foyer loomed empty. Cold daylight spilled through from the bedchamber casement, flickered by the passing shadow of someone beyond the far doorway.

"You are not yet excused," snapped a testy authority. "Your charge to extract the current location of the Spinner of Darkness is not satisfied."

Dace slipped inside and eased the oak panel shut. The wool carpet silenced his step, while powerful men unaware of an eavesdropper locked horns in continued argument.

"And I've told you already! A forced reading is like trying to sound the mind of an animal! I've already split my skull with a headache. A search is impossible where no structure exists." Through a murmured objection, the tirade resumed. "Oh, by all means, seek a second opinion. Another examiner will tell you the same. That's if prying deeper does not shock the subject into a fatal seizure."

The rebuttal bristled with impatience. "Harmful risk is no option. The avatar may be a drooling imbecile, but the asset of a living figure-head still inspires the populace to renewed faith."

Alarmed beyond care for himself, Dace crept through the dusky, spice-scented air. He passed the pearl-inlaid altar atop the low dais, with its spooled rail and tasselled cushions where priests knelt to pray and burn incense. Pulse racing, he neared the far door, while Lysaer's distressed sobs under-ran the impersonal conversation.

"Indeed, a show of pageantry's needed after the failure in Daon Ramon," the first speaker continued. "A spectacle to instill awe and resharpen the upright fear of heresy would do best after nightfall. Staged with lensed mirrors and hidden candles, the impression of a divine aura might enhance the enthroned avatar."

"That's folly. Light save! Your puppet cannot stand up unassisted!" A sigh followed. "Let that weakness be seen, or if a slipped veil should disclose his marred eye, we'd wreck the illusion of credibility when we most need the masses' fervent devotion."

Higher authority killed the debate. "No more talk of frivolities when evil itself has just outfaced our troops on the field. Disaster looms if the corruption of Shadow casts the Canon's truth into question. Action must restore our demoralized host and bolster the garrison at Etarra. We need a sure target to offset a drained treasury and quell the unrest stirred up by the tithes."

Hesitation ensued, pressured by the silent resistance of the examiner.

"Lives have been lost, and sanity squandered." The decisive tread past the casement took pause. "I will risk no more dedicate talent without purpose. The Light's avatar was made incarnate to serve! He strayed, to his downfall. Spend his life against Shadow, he may find his redemption, and there, our duty commands you. Either ferret out news of the Spinner of Darkness, or show yourself apostate before witnesses."

"On your head the consequence," snapped the cornered talent, then added his resigned instructions to tighten the subject's restraints.

Lysaer's furious bellow rattled the sconces. Dace shouldered forward, scorched fearless by rage. He bashed into the bedchamber, basket clutched to his chest, when sound sense should have sapped his resolve at the threshold. His sally met a daunting wall of white vestments: no less than three High-Temple officials, the loftiest thrown into eclipse by the jewelled headdress of His Hallowed Eminence, the Light's Priest Supreme. The talent lately brow-beaten with threats bore the sunburst of the Exalted Examiner.

Shoved against the apex of the True Sect hierarchy, Dace gained sight of the bed, where Lysaer bucked against lashed wrists and ankles. The ripped sheets and pillow-case were flecked scarlet, testament to the coarse handling of the armoured dedicates ordered to gag him.

From battered features, the single blue eye blazed with imperial fury.

No mistaking the baleful malice of Desh-thiere's curse, raised by the ill-advised probe seeking knowledge of Arithon's affairs. Lysaer's prodded resistance had nearly failed: unbridled, incendiary violence lay only a heart-beat away. Dace embraced that peril, magnified twofold: for a valet to launch a direct intervention empowered by Fellowship artistry before the eyes of True Sect authority risked the exposure of his covert role.

Dace chose the innocent tactic and tripped. The cascade of unfolded linens masked the thrust that slammed his basket into the examiner's back. The disrupted talent pitched to his knees. Wrenched from invasive, trance-focused immersion, the severance of his deep probe wrung him dizzy. The after-shock caused Lysaer to throw up. The cadre of officials recoiled, aghast, not only concerned for their splashed clothes. A servant's witness of a gross violation, visited upon the divine person, threatened both the Canon's integrity and their devout reputation.

Dace responded in self-preservation. Prostrated amid the spilled laundry, he latched supplicant hands onto the nearest priest's ankle and cringed as though braced for a cuff. His stream of profuse apologies tangled with the man's bellowed annoyance.

The nudge of a disdainful toe only rattled him to panicked excuses. "Your Lordships, Exalted, forgive my lapse! I was side-tracked by the needs of your healers, and unable to be here in proper attendance. I beg you, leave this morbid unpleasantness to me. Care of the avatar's revolted nerves is unseemly for your higher office."

Kicked aside, Dace let go. Abased humility dared no glance upwards to know if the pathetic display had defused suspicion. Movement rustled beside the pallet. The disgruntled examiner righted himself and snatched one of the fallen sheets. He blotted his soiled vestments. While the Supreme High Priest ordered the dedicates to cut the bound avatar loose, his complicit entourage also seized their moment to recoup decorum.

Seconds passed. Awash in the sour stench of spilled bile, Dace trembled with unfeigned terror. He had no responsible avenue left if his servile pleas failed to evoke the impression of harmlessness.

"Oh, get up, fellow!" the Supreme High Priest exclaimed. "No fallible mortal can shoulder the blame for the avatar's sick-room distress. Stiffen your spine and clean up his mess. The Light's Canon demands our attention elsewhere."

Dace stalled, crushed against the wracked linens, as the haughty parade of silk slippers and vestments swished past him and crossed the ante-room threshold. When the shut door at length restored privacy, he stood and surveyed the damage.

Lysaer shivered amid his despoiled bed-clothes, clotted nose and bitten lip purpled with swelling. But the smouldering rage in his single blue eye was no longer curse driven. Dace confronted the ire of lordly affront: murderous offence for the dedicates' handling, further incensed by the demeaning shame of bodily failure. Dace approached with respect, his unruffled calm pitched to placate. "My Prince, your dignity's in no fit state. Allow me?"

The good eye snapped shut, a tacit permission less pathetic than the mangle of attempted speech. Lysaer's wounded mind had not spared the awareness of his damaged intelligence. The proud statesman grasped how drastically far he had fallen. Granted royal prerogative since birth, Lysaer suffered the excoriating self-contempt that he could not escape his own squalor without able assistance.

Dace unlaced and removed the soaked night-shirt. Practised tact knew where firm support was required, and understood without condescension when to let impaired function strive without coddling. Lysaer endured the staged labour that eased his frame off the stained sheets. Propped upright on fresh pillows, he tolerated the undignified touch that sponged him clean and reclothed his humiliated nakedness. While Dace mopped the floor and disposed of the soiled linens, Lysaer's laboured breaths eased. Rigid tension unwound. His overtaxed body ceased trembling.

Dace found a fresh towel, refilled the wash-basin, and set gently to work on Lysaer's battered face. Thankfully, the split lip had not torn through. The straight bones of his nose were unbroken. But the sculpted male beauty that once had stunned sight sagged yet from atrophied muscle. A full year since the wounding, the ravaged right eye socket dripped fluid down the caved cheek. The skull beneath wore flesh like melted wax where the major nerves remained severed. The internal brain tissue scarred by the arrow also left an arm and one leg nearly paralysed.

Day upon day, Dace marked the raw courage: as by naked will Lysaer refused the cowardly snatch for the shaving razor plied by his hand. Pity could not have reacted in time, had the determined grasp of the unimpaired fist turned the steel for a suicide. Functional cognizance was not intact; in painful, slow stages, the long convalescence was barely underway. Yet mindful courtesy was never absent.

Dace sensed the gratitude for his loyalty. He read the moments of lucid embarrassment, and longed amid heart-break to whisper a word of tacit reassurance. He would never forsake his guard over Lysaer's integrity.

Yet he dared not speak. High Priests came and went at all hours to pray at the altar in the shrine outside. The chance could not be risked, that he might be caught apostate inside the Light's holy sanctum. Reduced to the infantile language of touch, Dace extended his tender care to the wreck of the man in his keeping.

One day, given time, Lysaer would rise whole. Meanwhile, the steadfast valet kept his invalid master's volatile secrets. The Exalted Examiner had failed at this pass, not because the Light's Divine Prince did not track the affairs of the Spinner of Darkness. Lysaer's mind might be dimmed, and his tongue denied speech, but Desh-thiere's curse still branded its brutal directive into living flesh. Any night spent in the avatar's presence revealed where the source of his unrest walked abroad: just now, far south-eastward and moving, expressed by the whimpering outcries wrenched from Lysaer's wracked throat. Verified with a weathercock's clarity, Arithon Teir's'Ffalenn was bound straight cross-country towards Rockbay Harbour.

* * *

The Mathorn uplands were a miserable place for a lone traveller in late autumn, as the short days approached winter's edge. Clouds bleak as cold iron lidded the peaks. Frost sculpted the landscape beneath to a netherworld, black rock and sere ledges keened over by gusts. The bite of an on-coming blizzard knifed cold like a blade through the lungs. Elaira huddled into her cloak, her clouded breath shredded in the thin air. Seasoned by her reclusive years at high altitude, she recognized the urgent need to find shelter.

But the sealed entry to Davien's retreat presented a stark lack of options. A barren site, scarred by recent cataclysm, the surrounding slopes were scraped clean by rock-slides. The sheared cliffs wore cracks left by earthquakes, pocked by glassine scars where tumultuous forces had pummelled slagged stone into craters. Amid the colossal rubble, a sculpted gryphon mantled spread wings above a square opening, incised between the talons that flanked a stairwell's descent into darkness.

The monstrous statue was not ornamental. Carved eyes gleamed with the restive spark of a guardian spell. The boundary where its latent defences lay coiled in check chafed the nerves and raised gooseflesh. A coronal flare blazed if Elaira approached, a proximity warning that days of initiate survey had failed to disarm. Her knowledge fathomed no means to gain entry. Outmatched, with her supplies now exhausted, she relied on skilled hunting to forage. But pending bad weather drove the sparse game deep into sensible cover.

Hungry and tired, Elaira rejected a retreat to civilized shelter. The unwieldy mass of The Hatchet's balked war host clogged the Mathorn Road, an obstruction that narrowed her unsavoury choices: withdraw from Davien's lair and hunker down at the risk of starvation. Or else cross the ridge against worsening weather and seek the dread portal to Kewar's maze, seven leagues off as the crow flew over desolate, alpine terrain.

"Death and death!" she snapped, still wrung pithless by her memory of Arithon's harrowing experience.

The exasperated assessment found her near the end of her resources. Lowered clouds promised the oncoming storm would smother the peaks before nightfall. Elaira took bitter stock. She might try a brief, last attempt on the wards before hunkering down in the wilds. Her one, untried avenue at least required only a short invocation.

At the wardspell's edge, Elaira engaged her refined senses and assayed the sealed circle until she located the point of closure. There, she sketched an opening rune, attached a precise chain of ciphers, and probed as a locksmith might ply a wire by delicate touch through a keyhole. When she encountered resistance, a whispered charge breathed into a sigil enacted her query for access.

The wards woke in defence, interference struck down with Dharkaron Avenger's unrequited ferocity. Reamed through, up-ended, and slapped dizzy, Elaira discovered that Davien's protections were forearmed against even the mildest use of her third level artistry. Grounded awareness and discipline failed as the recoil hammered her senseless.

Her first moment of conscious recovery brought darkness. Shrouded in texture-less oblivion, Elaira grappled dismay. Patience changed nothing. Her featureless disorientation suggested Davien's working entrapped the primal essence of her being. Hunch also implied that she had been graced by fortune to have survived.

Davien the Betrayer had no mercy to spare for the Order of the Koriathain. Though a probable ally against the sisterhood's interests, Elaira's appeal for his help might be claimed through renouncement of her initiate's oath. Yet such a Fellowship grant of severance carried an interlinked consequence. Beyond her well-being, the fate of her personal quartz rested on the outcome. Its loyal service, gifted in trust, imposed a steadfast obligation. The Biedar crone's advice from Sanpashir had claimed such a quittance would shatter the crystal: "... *no more to shine as a beacon in darkness* ..."

A warning grown weighted with poignant significance, since the pendant had passed into Arithon's keeping: his sole access to unfiltered memories of her resided in the mineral's matrix. That precious, true record of her affection offered his life-line to heal the wrecked trust imposed by the sisterhood's meddling.

"*Should your Master of Shadows fail you, or you come to fail him, the result will call down disaster,*" Traithe once had cautioned, based upon Sethvir's earth-Sighted augury.

Elaira rejected the choice to cause harm as the price of her own salvation.

Resolve sealed her fate. The void that cocooned her dissolved, her released awareness jolted back into sensation and breathing flesh. Punishing cold shocked her fully awake. Sprawled in collapse, she was numbed to the bone and wretchedly shivering. Gale-force wind stripped away what little core warmth remained, broken by nothing but the drifted snowfall banked against her crumpled cloak. Through dulled shock and exposure, she recognized her narrow escape. A less subtle test of the Sorcerer's wards would have unravelled her body into a haze of primordial elements.

The storm kept her in jeopardy. Elaira fought the exhausted urge to surrender and sleep. Prolonged chill had sapped her. Locked muscles almost balked her effort to rise. Hunched on her knees, fingers numbed to dead wood, she reached for the last object in her possession that might best a Fellowship Sorcerer.

Elaira hooked the thong slung from her neck and clawed the flint knife from its deer-hide sheath. Biedar leave had been given. Allowed one boon in her own behalf, she resorted to the wild-card of their Eldest's cryptic promise.

Snow mired her ankles. Unbalanced, without ten steps left in her, Elaira shoved upright and staggered ahead until she felt the wards flare. Then she slashed the stone blade with the reckless intent to sever Davien's grand conjury.

The weave parted. Elaira overbalanced and crashed face-down. Too depleted to rise, she crawled under the gryphon's spread talons. The nine-yard marathon wheeled her dizzy. Finished off if she succumbed in the open, she wormed to the entry on her belly and stared down into fathomless darkness.

No way to discern how far down the shaft ran; descent of the stairs lay beyond her. Lost without shelter, she shoved over the brink and let gravity take her. The bruising tumble broke none of her bones but found a soft landing, caught by a pair of capable hands.

"By glory," Davien declared in dry welcome, "come this far, couldn't you wait to be decently met at my threshold?"

Elaira managed a breathless reply. "Does civil propriety honour a break-in?" Set back on her feet, her overtaxed sinews unravelled. Polite determination frayed like blown smoke and spiralled her into oblivion.

Recovered under the suspect kindness of Davien's hospitality, Elaira sat tucked in a cushioned nook, nestled under a vaulted ceiling upheld by enamelled posts. She was reclad in a laced jerkin, dark trousers, and a white shirt with tailored cuffs, likely cast-offs from Arithon's past residence. Her Sorcerer host lounged nearby, eating toast, his back braced against the arched door-jamb. His lion's mane of shoulder-length hair lay tamed at his nape with black cord.

His preference in colours stayed autumn and gold, no more the conjured whim of a shade but clothing a flesh-and-blood presence. The change was not settling. His inscrutable mantle of power in close quarters still rattled quick wits.

Davien's genius had been dangerous, always. But the creature made reincarnate by Seshkrozchiel exceeded the compass of arcane experience. As if the unruly flare of cobalt flame imbued by congress with a dragon might lick through his aura at the drop of a pin, each word with him carried a heft and weight, the collateral peril of light conversation more abstruse than ever before.

Courage restored by food and drink, Elaira broached the thin ice with impertinent inquiry. "You're not annoyed that I trespassed your wards?"

The Sorcerer stopped chewing and stared. "No ward is proof against the Biedar crone. As you saw, her will surpasses a force of nature."

Elaira rasped on through a throat dry with nerves, "You're not disturbed by my ties to Koriathain?"

Davien's eyebrows rose. "The old Matriarch of your order never learned when to keep her wise distance. If her successor sets foot on my turf, she'll receive her comeuppance as well. Do you fear her intrusive reprisal?"

Better sense fled. Elaira deflected the personal question and attacked her priority headlong. "Are you unconcerned for the implications of Asandir's standing oath?"

"Not to assist with Prince Arithon's survival?" Evasive, amused, Davien shoved off and paced. "But this is the crone's business, make no mistake. You realize her tribe's involvement precedes Athera's Second Age record?"

Still seated, unsinged, Elaira tried tact. "The Eldest informed me. Jessian's plight and her conflicted secret provoked the sisterhood's undercover society to coerce the Biedar for access to their ancestral knowledge."

Impatience spiked Davien's riposte. "Since that flint knife's history binds one of your own, you'll want to pursue the forbidden diaries inscribed by the former initiate you knew as Enithen Tuer."

Elaira gaped. "Erdane's ancient seer? She was Koriathain?"

"Much more." A vexed predator, the Sorcerer spun to a stop. "The renegade woman's account is shelved here because the better part of her heritage could not stay with the Paravian archive at Althain Tower." Black eyes bored back with a nettled gleam. "You aren't going to ask about Ettinmere's shamans, or the consequence of your beloved's breached promise?"

Barely, Elaira smothered her flinch. Rattled by the abrupt change of subject, she stiffened her guard, sorting her thoughts for response.

Davien thrust through her recoil, "The Fellowship were not your friend, or Arithon's, regarding the seduction assayed by Vivet."

"Stale news! You Seven desire a royal conception, almost at any cost." Flushed down to her collar, Elaira hit back. "Had the hussy wrangled her way with his Grace, don't posture. Your colleagues would have claimed her issue as Rathain's crown heir with scarcely a pause for permission."

Davien's salacious smile raked over her flaming discomfort and chastised, "Think again, worthy consort. You were a signal party to the burden of debt invoked under crisis at Athir."

Elaira tallied the fine points. "I had Dakar to swear in behalf of the crown to avoid the attachment to Arithon's person." The life restored to him by her healer's work *as the heir* slammed home the barbed summary. "Ath wept!" Sethvir's innuendo had implied the same. "Should the prince sire a natural child, *the term of the quittance sworn by Asandir becomes invalidated?*"

Not precisely; under Davien's fixed regard, Elaira dissected the question again with the scrutiny of a lawyer. "You're saying the runes laid in stone at Whitehold, that verify the Fellowship pact of nonintervention apply to Prince Arithon as Rathain's crown successor?" The conniving atrocity wrung her to shaking. "Then your Fellowship *could* condemn a royal-born infant to salvage his mastery of Shadow!"

Davien never blinked. "A moot speculation since no s'Ffalenn offspring exists."

Elaira glared at his impenetrable sang-froid, gripped by the effort to curb her runaway fury. "Your riddles annoy like the cockleburr," she snapped, ridden by the abrasive certainty Davien's comments *never* lacked purpose. Sketched between lines, crafted with artful subtlety, this was not a cloaked warning for her nor a caution aimed at any posited offspring begotten by her beloved. But perhaps—*oh, yes, surely!*—a sideward appeal made on behalf of the Sorcerers. The shift in topic was not a non sequitur. What had seemed two different conversations, in parallel, actually threaded one strand.

Elaira pounced. "You want the crippled remnant of the Order of the Koriathain broken forever!" Biedar interests and Fellowship need were the same: the crone's knife had cut through Davien's wardings, past doubt, *but only by his back-handed invitation.*

As though her dumb-struck conclusion had been spoken, Davien's grin lit with crocodilian delight. "You are my honoured guest by your own design, and Asandir's oath is inviolate."

Elaira knuckled her eyes, dragged the candle-lamp closer and worked the next line in the leather-bound diary into translation: *"Requiar, male adult of Lassiver's heritage, stood surety for Jessian's secret. Next generation, the offspring of Hasidii's lineage birthed the weak link that broke covenant."*

"Lineage would seem the predominant theme," she murmured, then blotted her quill before dried-up ink clogged the nib. Closeted with Enithen Tuer's proscribed library, she memorized the historical names, stretched a cramped shoulder, then pored over the next faded entry.

While the old seeress had a clear hand, the desert tribe's obscure language imposed the hardship of an encryption. Elaira sighed, dragged open a weightier tome to her left, the parchment pages musky with age and deckled by nibbling rodents. A sneeze watered her eyes as she referenced a new word, entered in crude characters that appeared to derive from symbols scratched upon rock. Plainly, penned records were not the Biedar's archival preference.

"Responsible charge to mend the breached integrity of the tribe therefore claimed both lines of descent, and laid the ancestral burden upon future progeny."

Elaira paused. Thumb marking the page, she flipped back to the inscription on the diary's fly-leaf. *"Written by Audua Sedjii an Teshua, last-born of Hasidii's heritage."*

Audua, who had answered to Enithen Tuer after Asandir freed her from oath-bound service as a Koriathain. Why the woman should have forsaken her creed in exchange for the sisterhood's rigid hierarchy seemed senseless! The Prime Matriarch was the Biedar's avowed enemy, a perverted practitioner of their sacred knowledge. Unless, mused Elaira, Audua's wayward intent aimed to redeem the ancient score against the Hasidii blood-line. Answers, if they existed, called for painstaking work.

"The flint knife was knapped, shaped in blood and fire, the soul mark of responsibility bonded in perpetuity to both lineages until the hour of reckoning." Elaira eyed the sheathed artifact beside her and exclaimed, "Do I take this to mean the disembodied spirits of *two* persons inhabit this blade? One Hasidii progenitor, and one Requiar?" Shuddered by revulsion, she added, "Wouldn't such practice involve necromancy?"

"Assuredly so," Davien confirmed from a stance behind her, "had a bonding ritual of dark coercion occurred."

Elaira started nearly out of her skin and swivelled her chair to face him. "While we're speaking of ghosts, did you have to creep up unannounced?"

The Sorcerer's mantle of sere black and silver wafted the outdoors scent of snow as he advanced. "May I?" He presented an inquiring, opened hand in request to receive the flint dagger.

Not quite reconciled to his lack of apology, Elaira hooked the deer-hide thong, and surrendered the heirloom flint dagger in trust.

Davien's clever fingers enclosed the laced grip. He unsheathed the ceremonial weapon halfway, stilled for an instant of piercing survey, then slid the blade home. "No unrequite shades are lodged here, either by willing consent or attachment. The Biedar tribe doesn't embrace dire artistry, far and long as anyone knows."

"Then they're unparalleled masters at forging talismans," Elaira mused, wise enough to be wary of the potent protections enacted against both the Grey Kralovir and Desh-thiere.

"You hold something more than a powerful token." Davien's precise touch returned the ancient stone knife to the table-top. "The tribes perfected consensual avenues to interact with their ancestry."

"By an impeccable standard of ethics?" Elaira digested that concept, now awed. "You imply this flint knife embodies such a key?"

Davien gestured towards the massive volume before her, whose dry pages preserved more than history. Two-thirds of the chapters mapped centuries-long columns of births, exhaustive genealogies predating the Biedar's residency on Athera. "That book was not sanctioned by the tribal elders. Its summary content derives from stolen knowledge, transcribed from an original record preserved in crystal. Koriathain versant with the antiquities understood that the Biedar disciplines were passed down by direct initiation, descended through kindred."

Elaira considered, raked over by chills as she measured that implication against the Eldest crone's interest in Arithon. "Perhaps I ought to be looking at the Third Age chronicles of the royal families as well."

Davien shrugged. "Those lineages are common knowledge. When you've exhausted Enithen Tuer, you'll find copies of the crown registers shelved in the east vault, beginning with s'Ahelas."

The piled weight of obscure familial heritage already warped a sag in the oak trestle. Promised the long-term ennui of a siege, Elaira jabbed ink-stained fingers through her wisped hair.

"Quite." Davien laughed. "Unless you prefer camping in blizzards to the provocation of my hospitality? Snowfall has buried the high Mathorns in drifts. Sethvir's last assay of near probabilities suggests the Koriathain won't pose a significant threat to Prince Arithon before he eludes their short reach altogether."

The sameness of days ran one into the next, and weeks became months. At first hand, Elaira came to appreciate Arithon's suppressed exasperation concerning his stay with Davien. The Sorcerer's wayward appearances and his duelist's style of debate tested both nerves and intellect. Sharp wit met his arid ripostes like crossed blades, with the sting of perspicacity gloved in slight comments and sudden humour. Challenged relentlessly through every sally, Elaira developed the opaque stare of the owl ruffled awake in broad daylight.

"I haven't an unranked patch of skin left," she confessed at the Sorcerer's latest inquiry after her comfort. Spread under her forearms, in dog-eared notes, lay the salient facts cobbled from the accounts of Enithen Tuer's long life.

Davien poised by the mantel, his ruddy, streaked hair underlit by the rebuilt blaze at his back. The delicate fragrance of birch cheered the room, further softened by tinselled silk cushions and tapestries. The bronze rods and candle stands gleamed, without tarnish, and exquisite Vhalzein lacquer-work furnishings shimmered with mother of pearl.

Elaira felt like a toad in a flower-bed, her mussed dressing-robe thrown over an indigo shift, and the plait untidied since morning twisted up with a haphazard pin. She could not recall when she had taken a meal not encumbered by musty, old books.

"Your translation's completed," the Sorcerer observed, black eyes wicked. "Have you connected the missing bit of the puzzle?"

Sparked to rueful annoyance, Elaira glanced up. "That's an opening play for your next blood-sport game of intellectual chess? I'm too tired. Unfit to challenge anything stiffer than yesterday's custard."

Time tended to blur in the sanctum of Kewar. Davien acknowledged her dark-circled eyes, aware she had been reading all night. "Does a breakfast of pastries and poached eggs sound better?"

Elaira waved off the kindly retreat. Undaunted, the Sorcerer unlatched a cabinet that surely before had held only books. He removed two clean goblets and a corked bottle of cider, chilled to sparkling beads of condensation. Where Asandir prepared meals like a peasant, Davien stocked his larder through mystical conjury, food and drink proffered with such nonchalance the uncanny process seemed natural.

Temptation triumphed. Elaira accepted the elegant, filled glass. She sipped tart perfection, long since grown accustomed to what seemed a feckless practice. The caustic ascetic in other ways, Davien's extravagant gestures might be an honest preference or another sly means to provoke. Or perhaps, in this case, the excuse for a tonic that banished her fog of fatigue.

Elaira saluted the subtlety of her defeat. "Point and match."

The Sorcerer's interest was not passive. Wraith-quiet, he claimed the seat opposite and savoured his share of the cider.

Elaira fortified herself with another swallow and shouldered the contest. "Audua was a birthborn tribal seer. If I've interpreted rightly, something prompted her to swipe a hallowed artifact from her Elders. She ran and joined the Koriathain, likely not seeking sanctuary from a theoretically awful reprisal."

Davien smiled. "Go on."

"Audua was Hasidii by direct lineage." Braced for ridicule, Elaira summarized the damning account handed down through generations. "That heritage bore the stigma of weakness. Whether some foreseen disaster motivated Audua's rift, or whether she meant to redeem the family's ancestral burden because Requiar's blood-line was ending—"

Davien levelled a glance past the rim of his goblet. "You would stake your life on the veracity of that translation?"

Elaira shivered, took pause, then corrected herself. "No." Precisely, the choice of phrase stated Requiar's lineage *'was gone from the world.'*

Which fine point the inscripted genealogies confirmed: among living Biedar, the blood-line that claimed surety for Jessian had dwindled to a single, feeble old man. Elaira laid her glass down before her trembling fingers created a spill. "The arcane properties attached to the flint dagger answer to only two lineages. Let's suppose Audua forecast the debacle unleashed by the True Sect religion. Maybe she feared the Light's examiners would target her tribe for extermination. Or else, in-breeding and low birth-rate might take their eventual toll. Afraid her family's debt might never resolve, perhaps she tried to take down the Koriathain from within the sworn ranks of the order."

The diaries' statements, sparse in detail, were unequivocal on the outcome. "She failed," said Elaira. "Audua might have misjudged the forceful hold the Prime's master sigil held over her. Or worse, she encountered a ward wrought at strength that the flint knife's endowment could not outmatch."

"The artifact's properties never fell short." Davien lifted the bottle and replenished Elaira's half-emptied goblet to ease her dry throat. "Audua's defeat was a matter of scope."

"Impossible to gain covert access, therefore, she could not destroy every defended cache of knowledge guarded by the sisterhood's administrative rank? That occurred to me." On her own account, Elaira had grappled that impediment to an effective subversion. "Audua's duplicity was discovered. She fled the order to evade punishment, and since Mother Dark's grace had been declared forfeit upon her defection from the Biedar, she pleaded for a Fellowship intercession. Asandir answered and severed the grip of her initiate's vow. Once the master sigil's hold became broken, the Prime Matriarch dared not attempt a reprisal. As Enithen Tuer, Audua settled in Erdane, likely because the town's policy is bitterly hostile to Koriathain."

Against silence dense enough to freeze air, Elaira carried the tale towards its lonely closure. "The dagger was not returned. Audua thought she alone possessed access, as the last living Hasidii, Requiar's lineage being absent. She engaged its power once to free two orphaned children from a binding wrought by the Kralovir. One act, done for pity, earned her that deadly sect's lifelong enmity. She kept the knife afterward for her own protection, justified by her certainty its properties would become useless after her death."

Steady as steel, now arrived at the crux, Elaira faced Davien and finished.

"The brave woman believed no harm had been done, that Hasidii was the only surviving lineage, until the day Asandir brought two princes under her roof, half brothers matrilineally related." The last riddle loomed too large for denial. "We know Lysaer s'Ilessid invoked the properties of that consecrated knife. Both by his own right, and in direct behalf, through an intervention certainly made on the let blood from his navel, by Sulfin Evend. Lastly, to me, the Biedar crone asserted the knife's purpose is destined for Arithon s'Ffalenn."

The circumstantial link remained to be verified. "Therefore," challenged Elaira, "exactly how did Requiar's line get entangled with the s'Ahelas descent? I'd hazard there's more to the record than a rote pursuit of the royal genealogy."

Davien laid down his cider, his upright form chiselled against the back-drop of an antique tapestry. "Have you the ironclad bravery to see?"

Elaira raised her goblet in irony, then tossed back the dregs. "I've accepted the charge of an artifact, what, a bit shy of nineteen *thousand* years old? Whether I lack the brass nerve is moot. I must shoulder the course, if only to resolve how to serve Arithon's better interest."

Straightforward as the task seemed, access to the Fellowship's documentation of s'Ahelas genealogy gave up no secrets. Elaira chased down every branch since Queen Cindra's accession in Third Age Year One. Nothing surfaced, until after the breaks in descent caused by massacre through the rebellion.

"Fiend's plague!" swore Elaira, irked enough to kick herself, or better, blister Davien in foul language for cryptic omission. "I ought to have chased the subject of royal issue backwards from the present day!"

For the notation inked amid the heraldic seals was obvious, when viewed in hindsight. *Only* one match in Atheran history had defied the strait-laced precepts of Fellowship policy. "Custom forbade *caithdeinen* from marriage into the royal families."

The unique exception being Meiglin s'Dieneval's conception of Princess Dari s'Ahelas. Left no other heir after the youthful death of the last sanctioned prince, the Seven had been without option. And from that cross, which surely did more than raise eyebrows, sprang the infamous, rogue talent for augury that made the mind-set of today's cursed descendants intractable.

When Elaira presented her belated request for the *caithdein*'s lineage of s'Dieneval, Davien never blinked. He tossed her the key to access the locked aumbrey beneath the s'Ahelas archive.

And there she uncovered the volatile connection: an outbred boy by a Biedar mother, couched in what first seemed a tragic account of forbidden love. One of Ath's white adepts had cared for the father, a young clansman stricken to madness during his trial of exposure to the Paravian presence. She had fallen from her exalted state into a carnal liaison, then relinquished her half-breed offspring to the Biedar for nurture. The boy-child never developed the requisite talent to integrate with the tribe. The Eldest crone banished him. As an exile, he became the progenitor of the *caithdein*'s line of s'Dieneval when the prior lineage ended by mishap. Centuries later, his sole, surviving descendant, in ignorance of her family heritage, had conceived to the royal lineage.

Meiglin's congress with Shand's sanctioned crown prince had birthed Dari s'Ahelas, trained at Althain Tower by Sethvir, and related in direct matrilineal descent to Prince Lysaer and Arithon.

A cross check with the ancient Biedar genealogy yielded the finalized proof: Rayar s'Dieneval, through his desert-blood mother, claimed a Requiar line of descent.

Elaira shut the antique volume with a thump. "Both half brothers share an ancestral claim to the key in that Biedar knife. Ath's glory, how much of that convolute history was planned?" Influenced, surely, by the Biedar crones, and quite likely abetted by Fellowship oversight. Fed up with research, Elaira chased down Davien and pitched him the searing question. "How much did Meiglin know, and did she ever grant her permission as an informed participant?"

This time the Sorcerer eschewed the sugared overture of refreshment. "Meiglin was a true s'Dieneval seeress. She offered herself unconditionally, in a statement three times repeated, to do all in her power to defeat the Mistwraith's incursion. Her appeal was heard and accepted in earnest by the last centaur guardian at Althain Tower."

Elaira digested that, weak at the knees. The daunting confluence of powers involved made her charge of the Biedar's flint knife seem a pittance.

"*I don't see how our lines cross,*" Prince Arithon once had insisted, adamant in deflection of the Biedar crone's claim on his destiny.

Under Davien's sharp gaze, Elaira acknowledged the persistent threads stitched through her beloved's fate. In him, and in Lysaer, the cross-braided currents of ancient history converged like the sheen on a blade layered under a ruthless forging. Past question, Enithen Tuer would have known whom she guested in the grey twilight of Desh-thiere's mist. Surely, Asandir had lodged his royal arrivals from Dascen Elur under her roof to present her with Requiar's living descendants.

The gravid, next question woke shattering heart-ache. "You imply the old crone in Sanpashir would have saved Arithon Teir's'Ffalenn from death by wasting, regardless of Dakar's or my intervention that gruelling night at Athir?"

"Perhaps," Davien allowed. "Or she may have reclaimed Requiar's lineage through Lysaer, or another s'Ahelas relation sequestered beyond the Worldsend Gate on Dascen Elur. The issue was never put to the test. If Sethvir knew the probable range of alternatives, I suggest you are best advised never to ask."

Elaira gave way, found a chair, and bowed her head to mask tears. "I have to decide where to go from this place."

The Sorcerer laid his hand on her shoulder, a comfort unsettling beyond his most wicked verbal assault. "No need to choose now. You can't leave in any case with the Mathorn passes buried under ice. As a balm for the troubled spirit, Arithon found delight in Ciladis's treatises on healing and natural conjury."

Islands

A miscreant sailhand in his right mind would suffer a flogging before shirking his duty in Rockbay Harbour. The treacherous waters drowned men in prime health when shipwreck cast them on the rocks. Survivors who escaped the murderous rip and the suck of the tidal eddies faced a desolate shore, ripe for misery and starvation. Both sides of the strait were free wilds, and no place for an unsanctioned trespass. From Vastmark's broken shingle and forbidding cliffs, the nearest inhabitants lay fifty leagues distant: hardy shepherds who grazed herds in the remote mountain vales with large dogs and tribal independence. Alive on sparse resource, they were disinclined to welcome a destitute stranger.

Off the perilous shoals in the straits, running east, the obstreperous little sailhand signed onto the *Wasp*'s crew at Spire became the feckless exception. Unwashed, ungroomed, his fox features nestled in matted beard up to the eyeballs, the fellow was an agile spider aloft. His seamanship shamed the mate, an embarrassment that overshadowed, at first, his penchant for rough-house pranks.

No one suspected him when a filched poke of pepper was sewed to the head-sail hanks, and canvas raised in a freshening breeze wafted the spice in a noxious cloud over the oar deck. The rowers lost their stroke, folded at the benches, helplessly sneezing. The coxswain's established beat went to shambles, while the quarter-deck officers fell over each other, strangled by hacking coughs. Croaked shouts prevailed over chaos. The beset galley recovered her way, righted course, and skinned by the shoaled narrows off the north spit of Myrkavia.

The off-watch crew smirked, until the *Wasp*'s night entry into Forthmark's reveted anchorage ran them afoul of a patch of lard, smeared on the fore-deck.

The hands dispatched to secure the downed head-sail skidded headlong into the rail. One tumbled overboard. His panicked yells, and the froth raised by back-watered oars at the harbour mouth, raised guffaws from the by-standing salts on the wharf. Later, the fights sown by ridicule pummelled the crew given shore leave. The *Wasp*'s captain paid up for their damages, fuming. Fines levied for breaking the peace brought the vitriol stew of complaint back aboard, along with the men nursing bruises. Arguments devolved to fisticuffs over whose misplaced joke was to blame.

Captain's orders saw the galley cast off to quash the tension caused by restive tempers. Underway to the rumbling beat of her oars, the *Wasp*'s sullen atmosphere smouldered into side-eyed accusations. More mistakes soured her passage south. A poorly flaked coil kinked a dock line at Shandor, causing a second botched landing that made the ship's master the butt of snide humour. None of the *Wasp*'s company laughed to his face; for hours, a man spoke at his peril. The purser's return from the excise shed brought two cancelled bills of lading, with a hefty portion of the consigned cargo transferred onto more trustworthy keels.

The galley embarked under a cloud, high on her marks and forced on short ledgers to finish her run down the strait. She made fair speed towards more hospitable waters, her board timber to be exchanged for wool bales at Ithish, and a roster of fresh oarsmen waiting. Her harried company itched to spend their pay on the pleasures found in the famed Innish brothels. Anticipation might have eclipsed the mishaps that plagued their seaward passage, had the hammocks not let go in the night and dumped the off-watch crew onto the forecastle deck. Crashed in heaps, their yells hurled the *Wasp* into mass pandemonium, while the sneak who had tied the criminal slip-knots remained at large.

Next morning, men bleary-eyed from short rest found the main sheets entangled. The meddler's fingers also had shortened the lead line, which malicious trick upset the soundings in an easterly, hard against Vastmark's treacherous lee shore. The captain wore a thunderous scowl, and the furious cook balked his duty, when his best pots were found, clanking, run up to the masthead.

The *Wasp* moved under oars, while the sail crew squirmed under the surly eye of the mate. "I will have the name of whoever's sown merry hell on this ship!" Hunched against the spatter off the main yard, he bored onwards, "If no one comes forward, the rum ration's cut. Then I'll flense bollocks with a dull knife until somebody rats out the culprit."

Nobody collared the saboteur. As if the mate's warning had teeth, no more mishaps occurred as the *Wasp* picked her way through the rocks off the peninsula. Rounding the Cascains towards milder waters, her hackled company mellowed into routine.

Then the captain awoke with bait-fish in his berth. His roar shot the corpulent cabin steward like a singed bear through the starboard companionway, where the nippy perpetrator cannoned straight into him. The steward closed meaty arms and clung, bellowing, until the mate topside dispatched two oarsmen to help. They manhandled the struggling culprit on deck, to barrages of thumps and inventive cursing.

The insolent captive displayed no remorse. Exposed before his victims, he shot off wisecracks. Determined rage crumbled. Muffled laughter unravelled decorum, until the deck officer cuffed the buffoon into silence. Still, the feckless creature remained uncowed. Teeth gleamed through his overgrown beard, bold as the pearls in an oyster.

Several hands smothered untoward amusement. Another guffawed. The pinned scoundrel exuded the scapegrace charm of the underdog baiting authority. The divided crew hung on his fate: half vindictively wanted him drowned, while the rest choked back mirth for the novel amusement. Their hilarity peaked as the captain emerged, dripping putrid fish, his furious stomp squelching as slimy fry slithered out of his hair and clothing.

Ludicrous play aside, the *Wasp*'s company had lost revenue by the effrontery. Singed pride made no case for a capital charge, lawful only for murder and mutiny, and subject to oversight by the magistrates seated at Ithish. By convenience, the desolate shores of the Cascains side-stepped the hindrance of a lawful trial for summary justice.

"Let's have the offender marooned," the captain decided forthwith.

Through crows of approval, the *Wasp*'s coxswain collared sailhands to sway out the skiff. They rowed the wee rat ashore and dumped him off with his sea chest, while the purser expunged his luckless name from the crew list with nary a pang of conscience.

Arithon s'Ffalenn hunkered down on the strand, elated to have achieved his desired landfall without leaving tell-tale tracks. Caution kept his impatience cloaked under the guise of morose dejection. Bearded chin propped on his fists, he waited until the *Wasp* weighed her anchor and rowed beyond view. No witness remained when at length he arose.

He kneaded the cramp from his scarred thigh, shoved dry feet into his sea-boots, and dragged his trunk into the brush. The look-out's glass on the next vessel, passing, must see nothing but the white stripes of barnacles on the barren rocks. Purposefully forgotten, Arithon took shelter out of the wind. He sharpened his knife, bathed, and shaved off the odious beard.

Then he strapped on his sword and followed the game trails to a natural spring. Muddy turf lined the verges, laced over with tangled scrub willow and hazel. He cut pliable saplings, dragged the bundled withies to firm ground, and began weaving the frame for a coracle. The plank tray from his sea chest made a seat, and stashed sail canvas covered the bottom. When nightfall shrouded the plume of smoke, he melted the tar-pot acquired from the chandlers and sealed his makeshift craft watertight.

Grey dawn found him fishing for breakfast under the wheeling dip of white gulls. Afterward, whistling, he scavenged for drift-wood and carved a paddle. The desolate wilderness soothed him, waves broken over into webbed foam to coy flashes of lucent emerald. The jagged terrain of the puzzle-cut coves wore the scents of wet shale and tidewrack in the looming shade of the cliffs— *he had been here, before.*

Vivid memory resurfaced, of a woman's face set like a jewel amid fair hair and the sparkle of sapphires. Never his lover, though her beauty had stolen his breath, and exchanges of repartee like flung knives had flaunted her quick intelligence.

When grey clouds rolled in bringing rainfall, the melodious trickle of run-off and the hissing gusts through the scrub carried a familiar refrain.

He *had* been here before: the forces of wind and tide framed a rhythm he understood as a mariner. Though he had no chart of the maze through the Cascains, the channels were narrow, and the coracle's weight light enough to be carried. Judicious use of the current would steer his tentative course.

The storm passed, and slack tide smoothed the water to a silvered mirror. Arithon launched his frail craft and sculled through the black reefs where few hardy souls ventured. For a fortnight, he heard no human voice. Only the piping cries of wild birds and the splashes of jumping fish. He waited out squalls beneath his egg-shell boat, while the waves thundered and crashed, unravelled to whipped spume. Slowly, the way unfolded before him, like images on a painted fan: this jutted point, and that remote cove, and the misty, notched profiles of certain, cragged ridges.

And the day finally came when he passed the tight narrows that twisted through slabs of dark rock, the coracle buffeted by the foam riffled off the submerged shoals. The keyhole notch resounded with echoes, cacophonous with the weave of flocked birds startled up by his presence. Then the close channel opened out into a protected bay. Calm water lapped at iron-grey cliffs, gripped in preternatural quiet. Ahead, egress between facing islets and the jutted spine of a point led him to the secluded inlet referenced by his late *caithdein.* Low swells lifted gently into the shallows and curled against a shingle of rounded stones.

Almost, Arithon heard the echoes of diligent mallets in the crescent cove. Raucous laughter rang behind silence, to hoots and coarse comment by yester-year's shipwrights, and the tart barbs of a blind splicer hired under his former employ. Arithon's throat tightened. The sudden edge of grief stopped his breath, for the friends dead and gone, and the distance in time that had plundered their vivid comradeship. The wood shack was gone, that once housed the haughty, spectacular beauty of Lysaer's cherished princess, tendered by note for her ransom. For a pensive moment, the coracle drifted beneath the cries of the gulls.

Then the tug of the tidal bore jostled Arithon from reverie. He gripped the oar and sculled forward, before the current endangered his cockle-shell craft.

Coasted landwards on a lisping breaker, he leaped barefoot into the foam and stepped ashore.

Almost, he still smelled the pine shavings scrolled off the planks being planed by the coopers.

The present showed no sign of habitation. The notched rim wall above raked the pied clouds, adrift in a fair-weather sky. Beached seaweed entangled no trace of human flotsam. The song of the flux and the nuance of mage-sight revealed the natural world in stately unison, until Arithon reached the west rim of the cove.

There, where the brackish eddies of a little inlet met the plumed falls unreeled from a cleft, a signal note quivered beneath the surface flow of the flux. Intuition prompted Arithon for his true Name, not spoken, but framed by the signature tones that defined his spirit.

A veil parted, stripped of the glamour that suggested a shallow brook. Revealed in its place, a deepwater channel let into a hidden anchorage. A little pleasure sloop rode on a chain cable, swathed in stayspells against time and rot. The preservative spellcraft was his own, sealed under the shadow-wrought bindings of a long-term concealment. The shock of the unforeseen revelation accessed his lost trove of a lifetime's trained mastery.

Arithon gasped as rich chapters of recall cascaded into remembrance. He knew the sprightly name embellished on the craft's stern: *Talliarthe*, called after a mythical sprite and built by his hands, from her keel to her cordage. The thrill raised a flush of delight and chased gooseflesh over his skin. Back-tracked at a sprint, he relaunched his coracle and sculled out to the boat's mooring. Her elegant bright work and varnished spars flooded his heart when he grasped her spooled railing and boarded. For the planks underfoot sang to him with the splendour of everything dear he had lost.

Wonder embraced the tangible proof of his most personal roots. He touched a taut shroud. Traced a finger-tip along her starboard pin-rail, then breathed the bracing aroma of tarred oakum, clean paint, and the tang of a hull sheathed in copper. The excellent craft remained seaworthy, awaiting his hand for more than two hundred and fifty years.

Displaced and alone ever since his escape from the Koriathain's incarceration, still hounded by murderous enemies, Arithon shivered under the impact of reintegration. Belowdecks, the crew locker promised him clothing, tailored to measure and fitting his taste. This moment's homecoming was not transient. Restored pride in a place all his own made him whole, and beholden to no one at last.

Talliarthe breasted the blue-water swell with a grace that calmed the spirit and bordered upon ecstasy. Arithon rested in his berth to savour the moment. Above deck, the tiller was lashed for self-steering. While the thrum of fair wind through taut canvas filled the hours, he reviewed the sweet, private fortnight spent mapping the records in Elaira's crystal. Her personal memories were not as his own. The fact that the matched portion of his experience stayed elusive suggested an act of deliberate tampering.

He would unearth the reason for the disparity, come whatever cost.

Meanwhile, the respite of unpressured solitude let him put his recovered sloop through her paces. He paged through the notations in her log-books, a jotted chronology of his affairs from the day of her launching at Merior. The lost joy of children's laughter and the renewed pain of adult friendships ended untimely annealed the rediscovery of who he had been, before Koriani imprisonment had robbed the foundation of his existence.

The sough of the sea rocked his circling thoughts into sleep. Arithon dreamed of his father, lost in blood and flame on a ship's deck, far offworld on Dascen Elur. Aroused, drenched in sweat, he recalled another nightmare captivity, written under drug-ridden anguish and marked by old scars on his wrists. He shoved upright, lit the gimballed lamp over the chart desk and flipped open the last volume of *Talliarthe*'s log.

The dated entries spanned the years from 5671 to 5674, and finished with the blank page whereupon *Talliarthe* became shrouded in spellcraft. Between, inked in his own words, Arithon perused the idyllic descriptions of moments spent aboard with Elaira. At long last, cherished proof stared back from the page: an intimate relationship *had* matured between them after the initiate sister's quartz pendant had left her keeping. Yet no matter how deeply he sounded the wellspring of his unconscious, his memory of her remained dark. No trace surfaced. No means recovered the empathic connection once shared between them.

Arithon lifted the sconce and pinched out the fluttering wick. In darkness, he smothered his dread, that the blank silence meant she might be dead. Without contrary evidence, hope clung to frail logic: the lock on his recall had no reason unless she still lived. Offshore, stocked with adequate provisions laid in at Ithish, Arithon suspended his driven pursuit for more answers in favour of healing his body and soul. He checked the trim of the sails and resettled, drifted off to the glimmer of stars above the cracked-open hatch.

He roused to the sharp heel of a freshened gust, then the thunder of changed wind against slackened sails. The air wore the ominous thickness of storm, under a sky torn ragged as spilled ink by the edge of a towering squall. On deck, wide-awake, he freed the tiller and swung the sloop head to wind. Fast as he dropped canvas and storm-reefed her main, the freshening breeze frothed the whitecaps and shrilled through the rigging. The wind reversed again and blew hard from the west, while the hammer-to-anvil crack of close lightning glittered through tinsel rainfall.

Then the battering torrent broke over the cockpit with the scream of a full-blown gale.

Talliarthe was a sound vessel, steered by his seasoned experience. Arithon had weathered many a rough bout, worried in the teeth of the blue-water tempests that whipped the far southern latitudes. He secured the hatch, seized the tiller, and whooped in exhilaration as his braced weight manned the buck of the rudder. The sloop slewed as though winged, scudded into a trampling downwind course that eased the strain on her timbers. Like a chip in a race, she pitched down the rollers, then breasted the troughs with a saucy dip. Spume crashed at her bowsprit, tossed at the crests like the manes of wild horses.

The squall spent by daybreak. Swollen cloud shredded and burned away to an enamel-blue sky. Arithon took a sun sight at noon, formulated his notes in the running log, and fixed *Talliarthe's* offshore position. The storm had blown her east of Scimlade Tip, under a fair breeze running westerly. Yet mariner's instinct whispered in the blood: the flawless blue dome, horizon to horizon, bespoke a fresh gale in the making. The Cildein could brew vile weather with a speed that walloped the headland like vengeance unleashed. Rather than bear northward and risk that lee shore, Arithon maintained a broad reach, south-east. If prudence might have beat for a safe harbour, he had a chafed head-sail to mend, and unfettered freedom. The thought of port-side humanity chafed, noise crammed between the incense-soaked dives, with harbour fees regaled in regulations and taxes. Shelter along the less populous coast invited an even less welcome encounter with the Biedar Tribe in Sanpashir.

Which blithe miscall overtook him before he restitched the sail that enabled the westward turn onto port tack. The gale raked down as a black cauldron of cloud, the change from steady breeze to flat calm freakish even for these changeable waters.

The storm struck before Arithon could hank on the trysail. *Talliarthe's* reinforced, reefed main blew to rags and left him with bare poles. He deployed the sea-anchor, poised at the aft bitt to make fast, while the water rose green and broke under the bowsprit. The pin-rail holding the head-sail halyard sheared into splinters and was carried away. The freed line lashed alee like a berserk whip until the endsplice jammed in the masthead sheave. The rough seas prevented him from going aloft to retrieve the bound tail, or rove through a replacement. No chance he could draw an *iyat* to answer with the sprites satiated on the wild charge of the elements. Combined set-backs crippled his choice to heave to, lash the tiller, and ride out the worst.

Talliarthe porpoised, her stern held to the following swell by the drag of the canvas drogue. She reeled by evening, as the onslaught intensified. The monstrous waves reared and crashed, white water broken at the crests boiling over her counter. Raw might raged in an ocean gone mad. Arithon roped himself into a cockpit sloshing like a spun cauldron. The gyrating compass vanished into the murk. Wind lashed up spindrift until air and sea were no longer separate, and the howling blast threatened drowning. Huddled with salt burning his eyes, Arithon wrestled the helm against forces fit to spring planks and tear out oak fastenings.

He had sailed through great storms on the Cildein before. Yet by dark, under savage conditions, the onslaught tested his hardy expertise. *Talliarthe* careened like flotsam in the brunt. Her swamped cockpit forbade opening the hatch to snatch respite below. Arithon slaked his thirst in the brackish deluge from his hair. He napped in bursts, doused awake by the punch as rogue crests rampaged over the stern-rail.

Night thick as felt yielded to a dim day like sopped flannel. Still, the storm flailed the face of the deep. *Talliarthe* thrashed over the massive seas, the wallow and roll of her sluggish recovery taking on water. Arithon blistered his palms on the pump, unable to sound where the caulking had sprung or assay the stressed planking for damage. Blinded amid the thundering gale, and deafened by its banshee shriek through frayed rigging, he endured, pummelled to bruised exhaustion.

Arithon hung on with grim fortitude. Conditions in due course must ease. Instead, the grim storm got worse. The seas steepened. *Talliarthe* battered upwards. Her bow plunged against the scud, lurched in hesitation, then bucked each crest, tilted, and walloped into slewed descent towards the troughs. Pitched again and again, the sloop fought to shed the green tonnage of water until her deep keel dragged her upright. Arithon wrestled a tiller that stripped swollen skin and pulled at his aching sinews like lead.

The shift, when the winds backed and turned, did not come, nor any sign of abatement. Instead, the enormous, peaked swells tore away, frayed into the mercury downpour. Day's end dropped like a sable wall, with the little sloop hammered like a toy through the howling elements.

Dawn on the third day brought the beaten fatigue of oblivion, a charcoal tableau of soaked misery that vanquished all memory of comfort. The winds crescendoed to a roar fit to shake apart flesh, bone, and timber.

Then, at a breath, the punishment abated. The lour of cloud thinned and broke port-side, and silvered the horizon with light. An azure circle of sky opened up, set like the gem in a bezel. Arithon shoved erect. He yanked free the knots that lashed him aboard. *Talliarthe* bobbed into the storm's eye, a brief respite before a redoubled onslaught. He had minutes to unfasten the hatch, nip below, and gather provisions: jerked meat and hard-tack, honey and water-jacks, fast secured under oilcloth in the stern locker. Midships, he tightened the dead-eyes that hardened the sloop's slackened stays. He cleared the snarled lines, then pumped the bilge, his raw palms wrapped in rag. Last precaution, he replaced the frayed tackle on the sea-anchor. Under the loom of catastrophe, he strapped himself into the cockpit again and wolfed down sustenance.

No time left, to grease his salt-water sores, or to pine for dry clothing and oilskins. Westward, the sky glowered, massed cloud streamered black as the manes of Dharkaron's Horses. The eye-wall of the storm scythed down like damnation, the sped winds of the cyclone worse on the far side. *Talliarthe* faced the trampling maelstrom with worked seams and tackle already harrowed. The calm passed like the blown flame in a lamp. One moment, Arithon breathed mild air, dazzled under clear sunshine. The next, the gale's shuttered darkness clapped down with unbridled vengeance. *Talliarthe* heeled sharply, rolled onto her side, the first brutal knock-down of many.

Arithon suffered the barrage on the open deck. Pounded and jounced, soaked to the skin, he hunkered in misery, while intelligent thought became thrashed beyond sense, and spirited courage was battered away before stoic survival. He lost count of the days and the hours, pummelled dizzy and sawed by the lashings that secured him through the violent pitch of each roll. Torrents inundated the cockpit repeatedly. He resurfaced, wretchedly choking. Whiplashed over the wave-crests, he rode out the fate of his sloop, while the boom, broken loose from the traveller blocks, flailed arcs that carved up spray in rooster tails.

Fatigue dulled him past stupor. Arithon sank into delirium from lack of sleep. The few moments he catnapped, he woke, nearly drowning. The burn of salt in his nostrils and lungs curled him, retching, until he blacked out. Other times, sunk into uncontrolled mage-sight, he viewed a vista fractured into rainbows that shimmered between solid existence and the ethereal realms past the veil.

Charge danced at the tumultuous maw of the void: Arithon beheld bouts of actinic lightning, near continuous strikes that seared coruscations through his clenched lids. One dazzling burst seemed to shred the fabric of the known world, as if a crack opened up in creation, with tortured water and wind seized into eerie suspension. Then the slamming crescendo of thunder rang like a mighty bell. Stinging vibrations chased through the frail wood of the vessel beneath him. Arithon held out. Glued to life by his white-knuckled grip on the whipstaff, he breathed air saturated with ozone, while the lurid glare of Saint Elmo's fire scribbled the wheeling masthead.

He tended the pump to the edge of his resource, the gale shrilling a hags' chorus over him. Almost, he made out the snarling words, when at last the horrendous wind slackened under broken cloud. He was too wrung to celebrate. Jellied to rags, he clung like a half-wit while *Talliarthe* slewed and slammed over the swells, waterlogged under the punch of the capricious gusts.

Collapsed finally, draped over the tiller, Arithon slept as though kicked unconscious. He did not dream. Sunk in black-out oblivion, he did not resurface for a night and half the next day.

He woke to the burning glare of noon sun. Around him, the polished, residual swell heaved and dropped, clumped with foam and clots of sargasso weed. *Talliarthe* wallowed. The bump of her floor-boards below decks meant her sprung seams had taken on water. The overrun bilges flooded the cabin.

Arithon scrubbed his crusted eyelids, stung by chafed skin and wincing at stiffened muscles. Fingers swollen, he picked out the seized knots in the safety line. Breath hissed through his teeth, he straightened and stood, heart pierced by the wreckage that met him. A ramshackle mess of torn lines draped the fore-deck. Frayed and overstretched rigging allowed slop in the mast. If his short-lived relief lay dashed against the toll exacted on his sloop, her strength had withstood the test.

Talliarthe floated still. Repairs could restore her trim enough to limp back to safe harbour. Arithon set to and pumped her dry. He patched the worst leaks with torn sailcloth, and wadded oakum into the worked planks. Then he cleared the fouled lines and cut away the tattered canvas.

His inspection of timbers and spars found a check in the mast deep enough to require a fish splice. Arithon went to work. The calm broke, as he laboured, the fitful breeze fore-running a freshening westerly. A mild set-back, given his fixed position: the storm had blown him far eastward and north. A hundred and eighty leagues off Orvandir, he had a stressed mast, able to bear tender use of the main, but too weakened to withstand the head-sails. The jury-rig would not beat to weather. The broad reach or the run he could manage required changed wind for a downwind course for return to the continent.

Meanwhile, the sloop drifted farther afield, held stern to by her sea-anchor. She would weather the added delay without hardship. Provisions were plentiful. Her fresh water and nonperishable stores in sealed casks had taken no damage. Arithon washed, aired his clothes, and buffed the rime off his marlin-spike. He was not discontent as he whipped a new end-splice on an unravelling sheetline. Maintenance of a sea-going ship was stock fare for a seasoned mariner.

Nightfall, under starlight, he strung his hammock on deck and settled to sleep, lulled by the lisp of the whitecaps and rocked to a stiffened westerly.

In the pre-dawn pallor, the boom of a comber ripped him awake. The hissed rush of current as the breaker receded chilled the blood in his veins. Ahead, the ragged line of a reef rimmed the dark mass of a looming coast-line. Wind drove his sloop hard against a lee shore, with naught but a sea-anchor holding her course, and no sail to grant vital steerage.

Arithon swore and raced to bend tattered canvas on the main boom. He had no jib to claw off, with the breeze dead astern and the swell in shoaling waters risen to peaks. His little craft breasted the chop and rushed forward, coasted into the clinch by each passing crest.

At risk, out of time, Arithon hoisted the weakened main and made fast the halyard. Then he threw the helm down, cut loose the drogue, and trusted his lot to Dame Fortune. The odds ran against him. *Talliarthe* lacked the sea-room to beat her way free. At best, Arithon sought a gap in the reefs to sneak through.

The thrash of surf and bursting spume starboard offered nothing, and the limited draw of the main heeled the sloop into a side-slip. She trounced, ungainly as a lugger, while Arithon fought her unbalanced helm. He wrestled her broadside approach, unable to point the bow higher. Louder, the crash of the waves walloped into shot spray. Through blown salt and the backwash seethe of thrashed foam, his searching eye found no entrance.

Talliarthe careened onwards, bucking her fate, while the orange tinge of on-coming dawn notched a forested shore-line. Tried spirit and sinew to maintain her course, Arithon remembered just one charted land-mass in the vast expanse of the Cildein. Los Lier's remote atoll lay distant from the coastal sea-routes, where the clockwise trade current nudged deep-water ships around the slack doldrums between. Location made the remote landfall difficult, useful only to refill casks in a pinch on extended voyages. Navigable access from the northwest spur had a sand bottom, too exposed for a secure anchorage. Nor had the archipelago he recalled ever extended this far to the south.

Whether through faulty navigation, or by dated maps in the locker, the landfall he faced matched nothing Arithon recognized.

Dire straits granted him no time to ponder. The weakened mainsail chose that moment to give. Bellied canvas parted with a coarse rip and spilled out her wind. *Talliarthe* bobbed upright and slowed, with the sucking seethe at the reef disastrously close to her quarter. Arithon threw down the helm. Swung stern to, as the following wave lifted, he caught the trampling curl of the breaker and let *Talliarthe* surf.

The sloop rushed ahead, barrelled down on the shoal with the comber still rising beneath her. Then her keel struck the coral head. Impact slammed her onto her beam ends. She crunched down and slewed, wallowed broadside and stricken, while water gushed through her bashed strakes. Then the next swell heaved her upwards and reeled her over the barrier into the jewel-toned shallows beyond. There, jetting bubbles, she settled and sank.

Arithon bobbed to the surface over her submerged cockpit, striped in the forlorn shadow of her canted topmast, which poked through the placid lagoon against the lemon glare of daybreak.

Small blessing, his craft had not hung on the seaward side, where the merciless sea would have smashed her to matchwood. At rest three fathoms deep in flat calm, at least he could dive for salvage. Arithon put heart-ache and losses aside. He ducked under, descended into the cabin and retrieved the black sword. A foray into the chart desk hooked the oilcloth bag protecting Elaira's quartz pendant. Out of breath, he resurfaced and swam through the opaline wavelets and stumbled ashore.

There, wrapped in the resinous fragrance of pine, the castaway encountered his most brutal loss. The packet's waxed seams had not withstood the immersion. Devastation dropped Arithon to his knees: salt water had soaked the silk wrapping inside and cleared the volatile quartz matrix. Emptied of its precious burden of record, now a sparkling blank, the crystal's dedicate service to his beloved was finished. Arithon bent his head, desolate, too shattered to weep. For every time he seized hold of his destiny, fate conspired and ripped the reins from his hands.

Presence

S hipwrecked on an unknown shore, Arithon drew in a shuddering breath. Personal grief once again must defer to the urgency of survival. The beach underneath his clenched fist showed no trace of habitation. The breeze wore the astringent accent of salt, pungent with evergreen resin. Rhythmic surf boomed on the outer reef, stitched by the refrain of lapped wavelets, and the lonely piping of birds that pecked morsels from the petticoats of receding foam.

Yet the site was not ordinary. The flux currents here wove a vibrant tapestry, their harmonic range too richly complex for a pristine wilderness. A bard's hearing caught a lyric cadence like melody, a *presence* that raised the ephemeral resonance into a confluent splendour. Arithon paused, captivated by the echo of surreal rapture. Pursuit of the essence eluded his reach. His trained sensitivity entangled and crashed, ripped apart as the pain of his loss overset the rarified strain of peace.

Arithon gripped his sword to ground his excess emotion. Centred and still, he imposed self-command through initiate discipline. Under the sudden surge of heightened senses, he settled in listening calm: and fell prey, seduced by a quietude that stormed his identity with irresistible strength. Hurt lost its edge, soothed as though by a lover's caress. Fingered by a thrill, sparked to abstruse joy, Arithon trembled. Then he gasped, overcome by bright ecstasy. *He was not alone!* The ripple of resharpened awareness seized hold, mighty enough to annihilate reason and shear through his flesh like a tonic.

Stress and fatigue fell away. Thought unravelled. Each indrawn breath recharged his spirit in waves. Arithon shuddered, rapt. Sheer joy drove the dance of his heart-beat. Self-image up-ended, until he wept for the beauty that flooded creation. Rocked by the effervescent, thunderous chord that sustained the world's teeming vitality, he laughed with the shimmer of wind on clear water, riven by a force to free him from the clay feet of mortality.

Tenderness beyond all imagining welcomed his Name as one point of light in the grand chord that sustained Athera. Sweet yearning like roses and honey unmoored him. Arithon lifted his head, whirled into expanded Sight. Dazzled in the deluge, hurled toward dissolution, he understood he need only let go. Give way, and sorrow's ache would transform, striving and care scoured out by the tide of infinite celebration.

Mage discipline teetered at the verge of the veil, where mortal perspective lost meaning. Pierced, heart and spirit, Arithon acknowledged the resonant shifts that unstrung the balance of cognizance. He had been uplifted in absolution by the touch of a guardian centaur; had sought and found healing, immersed in a Sunchild's music. But nothing prepared him for a living encounter with a wild unicorn.

She approached in a haze of light written on light, an impossible splendour of gossamer and star-shine that by rights should not have withstood the brazen blaze of full sunlight. Under her delicate hooves, the pearlescent sand shattered to rainbows. Her gold, spired horn rang with a vibration fit to pulverize flesh and bone. Grace reverberated when she reared rampant. The spear-sharp point aimed at Arithon's breast inspired no fear. Scalded under a torrent of rapture, wrung pithless by beauty that burned, he felt himself shred like tissue sublimated in raging flame.

No art he possessed could capture a music that soared beyond gifted talent. Inadequate, naked, imperfect, and shamed, he clenched his hand on Alithiel's unsheathed steel. A Fellowship Sorcerer's blood bond to survive was insufficient to keep him earth-bound. He tried anyhow, with his last strength raised the weapon to deflect the clarion call to abandon himself.

The sword screamed. The rune inlay fired the length of the blade as the force of the star spell unleashed. Explosively virulent as never before, the primal song that Named the winter stars blazed like an actinic torch and enveloped him. The redoubled assault outstripped what his overstrained senses could bear. Arithon crumpled. Unconscious, he measured his length, while the dire tip of the unicorn's horn scythed above, and a glory to unravel his being sliced through the air overhead.

The Riathan Paravian's charge swept past his felled form. She landed and spun, his sprawled body under her velvet shadow, and her delicate hooves planted four-square across him.

Asandir's frantic, long-distance sending from the wayside forge located in Radmoore reached Althain Tower hard after Alithiel's cry pierced the stream of Sethvir's earth-sense. *Ath wept! What just happened?*

Althain's Warden scrubbed soaked palms over his flash-blinded eyes, stupefied as though struck by lightning. He fought shaken wits, while the shattering ripple of unleashed event cascaded through his overwhelmed faculties.

Equilibrium wobbled. The flood whirled him adrift. He managed to translate the immediate vision: *of Arithon cast senseless in white sand on a perilous shore-line, his frame silver-lit by the raised wards of his sword, and* also *the luminous shimmer of flux, fluoresced by a living Riathan Paravian.*

Asandir's retort doused the flame of elation sparked by the lost race's presence. *"That fails to explain the active tie to the blood oath I demanded of his Grace at Athir!"*

Sethvir groped for cohesion amid wheeling upset, while the shades of probability rapidly shifted, then said terse, *"The unicorn challenged for trespass because Prince Arithon set foot where nothing born mortal had due leave to tread."*

Asandir's astounded silence vaulted over the clamour of questions, while his field-hardened reflex sorted the most urgent priorities. Insight into the Paravians' harrowing exodus, and what drove them to seal themselves into a haven beyond the Fellowship's auspice must wait. Crisis demanded the unicorn's motive. *"She'd uplift a sanctioned crown prince through transition against our stay of surety under the compact?"*

"She would have," Sethvir confirmed, past aggrieved. *"His Grace would be lost, had Alithiel's wards not engaged in his rightful defence."* Given the back-drop clangour of worked iron, his itinerant colleague continued resetting the shoes on his black stud. Through the hiss of the bellows worked by the smith's boy, Althain's Warden qualified precisely, *"Just cause was compelled by Arithon's attuned royal blood-line, irrefutably sealed by your charge to survive, and bonded by consent through your invocation."*

Asandir's rant emerged through the nails pinched between his taut lips. "Fiends take the day our Fellowship woke the fire of Kharadmon's slap-dash wisdom!" He finished his thought by covert sending, *"And Elaira? She's heart tied!"*

"Shielded! The lady's safe under Davien's exemplary wardings at Kewar." Eyes shut, without consolation to offer, Sethvir endured the cruel suspension, while far distant, the unicorn poised over Arithon's prone form stamped a hoof with imperious inquiry. Unspeakable grief tangled with heady joy, as the unresolved verdict on Arithon's fate seized the moment in petrified agony.

Asandir's undeflected acerbity pounced on the glaring discrepancy. *"Best explain how this impasse occurred before Kharadmon torches off in a temper."*

"Avert!" Sethvir gasped. *"Do, please, refrain from sword-rattling tantrums under that hornets' nest."* Kharadmon's provocations could be deferred, given his cantankerous spirit ranged underground in the Storlains, redressing the ignorance of four miners caught delving for contraband tin.

Althain's Warden pared down the facts for Asandir's stifled impatience. *"Our crown prince sailed through a freak gale that unleashed electromagnetic havoc.*

Sheer chance, enabled by virulent lightning, hurled him through an impervious ward, cast across time and space."

"*Dharkaron's Horses trample the hindmost! That's the scale of magnitude driving the power that cloaked the Paravians' retreat?*" Ferociously quick, Asandir seized the gist. "*Then Arithon's landfall has ignited the flash-point of an unsanctioned disclosure.*"

"*Yes. No matter that his damaged sloop was not seaworthy when she was wrecked, his misfortune has violated a hidden sanctuary.*" Paused through a shuddering breath, Sethvir reeled, earth-sense struck in reverberation by the note of a centaur guardian's horn.

Echoes shivered across the trackless deep, alive with subsonic vibration. Then movement unlocked the frozen tableau on the forbidden isle. The Riathan Paravian bent her proud head over the castaway sprawled at her feet. Golden light shimmered in deadly proximity, as the ethereal peril of her horn raked over him: not to touch, a contact lethal to mortal flesh. The scald of purified light passed him by, an uncertain reprieve as the unicorn withdrew the untenable grace of her presence.

Althain's Warden rested wet cheeks in his palms, unstrung by relief. "*The Riathan sentry's acknowledged him. Finally.*"

"*Too late, if her encounter has swept him too far past the veil.*" Asandir sighted the trim of the stallion's rear heel, too pragmatic for optimism. He hefted the next crescent shoe. His infused charm against lameness riveted several mop-headed apprentices, as the steel flared bright blue. Deaf to their gasps, the Sorcerer placed the spelled horseshoe. He plucked and slotted a nail, which he set by a mallet blow and clinched with a practised twist. "*Tell me,*" he flung back to Sethvir, his distress at grim odds with his capable labour, "*has our endebted concession to the Koriathain left his Grace with anything meaningful on this side to lose?*"

Sethvir winced. "*Only time will tell.*" Whether or not s'Ffalenn integrity, bound under blood oath, packed sufficient incentive to survive, free choice might not even signify. Not if the Paravians enforced their secretive retirement.

Whatever befell, Sethvir could not fathom the course of Arithon's plight. Once the piercing chord of Alithiel faded, the impenetrable warding that curtained the isle severed his earth-sensed access. Nor was he immune to the desolate wrench that followed the sharp separation. Fingers knotted, jaw clenched, the Warden did not cry out. While the agony lingered, he breathed in the fusty scent of his books, acrid with oak gall and varnish and ink. What felt like the desperate absence of hope plunged him into the abyss. He endured, as he must, bereft as the Paravian presence faded past reach.

Misery weighted the unflinching summary owed to the field Sorcerer directly afflicted. "*Worry more that our crown prince might recover, only to become detained.*" Concern suggested the Paravians might keep the Teir's'Ffalenn in exile to protect their seclusion. "*Fate has dealt us a hand without recourse, except to bide on the outcome.*"

If his Grace survived the shock of confrontation, he would bear a responsibility beyond any invested High King of old. The Fellowship's case rested on his voice as liaison to salvage the compact. Unknowing, alone, he shouldered the burden as Mankind's sole advocate.

Variables

Arithon Teir's'Ffalenn never feels the delicate touch of the Sunchild who arrives to tend him in collapse; senseless, he breathes, a hairbreadth from death, while the strength of a centaur guardian lifts his slackened frame and bears him to shelter, where the battle for his recovery rests on the resiliency of his own merits . . .

News of the surprise contact with the Paravians finds Traithe at Telmandir, placed as advisor to High Queen Ceftwinn's court; and dismay prompts his warning, sent to Sethvir: *"Better that the Koriathain should have murdered Rathain's prince, than to face the ruin if he falters. Has somebody else with hale faculties gone to stiffen my stop-gap protections and safeguard Seshkrozchiel's hibernation . . . ?"*

Blind to the perilous judgement shadowing Mankind's grant of leave to inhabit Athera, dedicate officers harden their troops at Etarra, while The Hatchet broods over his tactical maps, and fumes with impatience for the coming spring to resume his campaign to crush Rathain's displaced clans . . .

X. Riddle

Returned from the nadir of black-out after shocked perception collapsed, the glimmer of restored awareness cascaded into disorientation. The shear came too fast for the mind to assimilate, the grand chord of the infinite and the rarified octaves of singing joy smashed into fragmentation. Senses stretched too far past the veil stumbled, too abruptly crammed back into the range of animate, mortal experience.

Mage experience equipped Arithon s'Ffalenn to surmount the chaos of extreme derangement. Mauled in the storm, he curbed the first spike of terrorized panic. He endured, while flared nerves wracked his body to seizures. The hot sweats and chills of back-lash fever accompanied the shuddering onslaught of grief: loss of a depth to wring spirit from flesh always followed exposure to a Paravian. The punishing gamut had threshed him before: where the flash-point bursts of gifted Sight deluged intellect, and the cyclonic delirium of vivid dreams ebbed into ghastly depression. Adept mastery braced Arithon for the brutal course: an arduous passage survived by endurance, until forgetfulness blunted the explosive, first agony of separation.

But this re-emergence surpassed his experience. The recoil cut deeper. Untamed, unknowable, the glory evoked by a living Riathan stripped the soul naked and shattered integrity. As far as Arithon had plumbed the crystalline matrix of minerals, and as widely as an unbounded immersion had plunged him into the abstract surge of the planetary flux, the enthralment spun by the unicorn's challenge left him dazzled blind, pierced with longing, and mortally wounded. Earthly magnificence paled, a ghost shadow after the jewel-toned radiance that shimmered beyond reach of human identity. The ecstatic glamour inflamed him with a tormented desire that eclipsed every bodily need.

Arithon drifted, stupefied in the throes of withdrawal. Days might have passed, or unremarked minutes. Time's span was irrelevant. The unshielded blaze of the infinite seared the heart beyond care for all worldly reward. Crowned High Kings before had abandoned the intolerable burden of earthly penury. They had passed, clothed in glory, uplifted to bliss and fulfilment that never looked back. Selfless service by right bestowed the freedom of their unfettered passage. Arithon yearned towards the path of his ancestry, a golden ribbon that arched past the veil, and a cry in the blood that foretasted the pristine dawn of ultimate reunion. The clarion call thrummed through his pulse, too powerful to deny.

Yet the flight towards transcendent triumph jerked short, his unfolding awareness yanked backward as though collared and leashed. Recoil dissolved the resonant harmonics. Struck by the very mallet of discord, Arithon screamed.

Ripped from immersive ecstasy, he fought, though no effort availed him. Trapped as the caged bird, he battered bruised wings, flensed as the promise of radiance tarnished, then extinguished like a winnowed flame.

Arithon crashed, helpless under the visceral sting of defeat. Cold fury recognized he had been bound, tethered by an inviolate stay of self-sacrifice, granted in free will. Likely the working stemmed from his blood oath, when a knife's cut at Athir had sealed his intent to embrace unconditional survival.

Except that the unclean hold on him bore no mark of the Fellowship's immaculate conjury. In fact, Ettinmere's shamans had crafted this noose, a furtive knot slipped through his given consent to sponsor a fatherless child. *Valien's* life forged the shackle that strapped his fate to outside interests. An infant's survival posed the perfect bait, given his line-bred s'Ffalenn compassion could not stomach an innocent's death by exposure. Who else but Koriathain orchestrated the trap behind his self-blinded mistake? They had hidden their pitfall with murder, then blindsided him through distraction, as Vivet's irksome charms sought to snag his affection.

The bloodless effrontery abrogated every concept of mercy. Anchored to life, the mind schooled to mastery confronted a prolonged ordeal, fit to strand the spirit in the crucible of raving madness. Perhaps, at the end, a coil to deny a clean passage across Daelion's Wheel.

Blood scion of Torbrand's ancestry, Arithon committed to action instead. He would live to serve Ettinmere's shamans their reckoning, not just for the cruelty of their claim but for whatever twisted agenda had allied them with the Koriathain. He would strip their purpose bare in defeat. If, after Selidie's utter destruction, the sisterhood crossed him further, he would rout their meddling atrocities and crush their order to oblivion.

Arithon bent his ferocious will to the course of incarnate recovery.

Resolve grappled the agony that lacerated his focus. Self-command demanded the stabilization of his deranged faculties. Iron discipline must surmount the torment of body and mind. Eyes filmed, lips crusted by fever, Arithon battled muscles jellied with weakness. Vertigo shattered his effort to sit upright. Spun wretched with nausea, he barely stemmed the spiral back into unconsciousness.

Arithon panted for air, entangled in clammy sheets, and without recollection of his unknown benefactor. Determined not to befoul himself, he rolled off the mattress and crashed on the floor. There, the crisp scents of pine resin and bees-wax brutalized his unmoored senses. The assault smashed the last of his dignity. He retched, dry heaves that brought up only bile, until he lay limp with exhaustion.

His dry-cotton mouth warned of dehydration. He forced himself, reeling, and crawled to the nearby washstand for relief. Beaten weariness defeated his struggle to stand. By necessity, he upset the basin and lapped up the spill.

Sleep ambushed him there, and smothered him in a febrile unconsciousness trackless as the face of the deep.

Arithon knew nothing until scalding pain smashed through his insensate oblivion, waking him into the chaos of overextension. Drifted awareness delivered a welter of sensory stimulus. Experienced wisdom sought stillness, while patience breasted the battering influx. He breathed and waited, until scrambled perception encountered the pulse of his heart-beat. Arithon fixed on that rhythm. Inhale to exhale, he held on until bewilderment settled into a semblance of orientation.

Burning discomfort quieted to warmth on bare skin. The dazzle that tormented his eyes mellowed into a slant patch of sunlight, streamed through an unshuttered window. The deafening din in his ears resolved last, to the trickle of running water and bird-song. Errant breezes wafted the pungent fragrance of pitch pine. A borrowed shirt clung to his frame, crusted with unwashed sweat. Sleeve cuffs adorned with exquisite embroidery were rucked back from his skeletal wrists. He surveyed those details in supine detachment, ground to prostrate indifference under the trauma of sensory overload.

The oblate flare of sunlight narrowed and moved, glinting on chased enamel where the basin lay overturned. Softer highlights brushed the grape-vine motif carved into the toppled washstand, civilized refinements as abused as the wracked towels dumped over by his incapacity.

Desecration of someone's charitable hospitality pricked him to embarrassment. Galled from leaden apathy, Arithon groaned. He turned over. The effort narrowed the edges of vision. He lay heaving, skin clammy, his swimming sight fixed on the legs of the bedstead. The cap fittings were beautiful: verdigris bronze wrought into a lattice of intertwined dragon-flies.

Pervasive hush reigned. No footstep came to right the crumpled coverlet dragged off the mattress, its ivory linen patterned by a jacquard loom. The same elegant taste pillowed his cheek on a floor that required no carpet. The exposed grain of the wood suggested a preference that valued nuance above creature comfort. The glass panes in the latched-back sash had been bevelled, and snug, half-planked walls wore the egg-shell patina of whitewash.

Arithon shifted his head. The changed vantage revealed book-shelves. Cupboards with plate racks flanked the slate chimney above a clean-swept, cold hearth. Polished copper utensils and nested iron pots suggested a pantry kept plentifully stocked.

Thirst eclipsed the overdue need for food, with the gurgle of the streamlet outside his likeliest water source within reach. Apparently left to his own devices, Arithon dragged himself belly down towards the door. More than the chance to wet his dry throat, the creek offered him means to ease his condition. Immersion into a tumbling current would discharge his aura and stem the onslaught of sensory overload.

Since the resident owner never appeared, Arithon fielded the whiplash set-backs incurred by his severance from the Paravian presence alone. He knew what to expect. Each day's hard-won progress drowned in deep sleep, unravelled repeatedly in the transition back into waking consciousness. Weakness and recurrent fever brought relapses into oblivion. He muddled through the eerie, stretched moments when physical senses forsook him: stumbled into furniture his deranged eyesight failed to discern, and winced as though fractured, when sensitized hearing spiked amplified sound through raw nerves. The least wafted scent pummelled into the over-stressed tissue of consciousness. Step by visceral step, he surmounted the necessities: tidied his person and laundered his soiled bedding and clothes. He fetched wood for the grate, and rifled the jars of jerked meat and picked fruit in the pantry to rebuild his strength.

Nights passed the hardest, when the risen flux tides razed through his fissured awareness. The further he strayed into dreams, the worse the disorientation faced by morning, each onerous fight to quench rogue bursts of mage-sight wearing him down. Unlike a stress recoil incited by over-extended faculties, these after-shock surges of ephemeral perception were followed by corrosive grief. Recurrent flashbacks reopened the wound of heart-sore separation, until sorrow sapped his resilience and numbed his morale like cobweb soaked in camphor.

Few survived the duration. Dulled after the dazzling brilliance of the infinite, worldly passion dissolved into apathy. Brooding loss, and bouts of untenable longing evoked hallucinations, while reason lapsed into lassitude as fatal as narcotic poison. The morass opened the pitfall to suicide for the unwary. Arithon stared down the crippling odds. This pass, no liegeman as steadfast as Kyrialt guarded his unsteady steps. No brazen clan healer's remedies buffered his terrible anguish. By his own devices, Arithon walked the abyss under the cold-struck threat: that failure consigned his roped spirit to who knew what ill usage by Ettinmere's shamans.

Fury bolstered his drive to stay wakeful. Harrowed by disorientation, he latched back the casements and stood naked in the brisk spring air until shivering chill lashed him sober. He fussed over light meals, then paced on bare feet to escape the languor of repletion. Into the wee hours, he sang ballads until his voice cracked, then recited epic lays in rasped verse until concentration forsook him.

When the candleflame's flicker mesmerized reason, he snuffed the wick and quartered the darkened cottage night-long, the focus required to drive each step turned to harness the aimless drift into mage-sight.

At length, when he tired, the shelves lent relief. The small library included rare volumes in ancient Paravian, some dangerously scribed with the prepotent phrasing of actualized language. He read without light: original books penned in common characters, with no matching copies amid Davien's proscribed collection at Kewar. Select subjects here surpassed parts of the greater archive stored at Althain Tower. Arithon surveyed treatises on herbals and healing, and folk recipes compiled in scrap-books bound with tooled leather and yarn. Crisp labels identified boxed sheaves of field notes, catalogues of pressed flowers, ink drawings of fish, painted beetles, and wing feathers, annotated in elegant, familiar script.

Wonder stilled his finger-tip on the page at the prickle of recognition: *the elegant hand belonged to Ciladis!*

Giddy, Arithon leaned on a pine desk that quite likely belonged to the missing Sorcerer. When he steadied enough to pursue curiosity, he ran his palm over the silk finish of the cupboards and gently fingered the clam-shell drawer pulls, artfully pierced into filigree. The horn stand of quills, the ink flasks and river-stone paper-weights stood sentinel over the cushioned rattan chair, well-worn by use.

Dust coated nothing. Any intimate clutter and scrap-paper notes had been tidied away, as though the meticulous master had planned to vacate his personal quarters. Perhaps to succour a needy castaway, or not: the alternative sparked an unpleasant analysis.

If someone else tended the empty cottage, Ciladis's departure might not be recent, or prompted by the inclination for privacy preferred by an initiate power. The house wore silence like a shrine, the cherished craftsmanship of the carvings, the waxed floors, and the priceless books preserved through millennia.

Arithon paused, embarrassed. He dared not, any longer, shy from the predicament of his degraded condition. His stalwart passage brought too little progress. Doubt threatened to drown him in ice-water fear: that likely the Paravian refuge packed a resonant charge too potent for mortal recovery.

Arithon clenched his teeth. "I will not succumb. Not here and not now!" He pitched himself, reeling, into the chair, determined to combat the mire of insanity through the knowledge in Ciladis's books. If no other palliative existed, the greater reach of Fellowship wisdom might purge the bleak thickets of apathy.

He plunged into days of fixated study. From treatises on herbals, he perused the notations on which local plants brewed tisanes to stay wakeful. What listed poisons repressed mage-sight proved useless: anything potent enough to ground a beguiled awareness also damaged gifted talent. The volumes on refined healing offered no better solution. Arithon turned in stark desperation to Ciladis's surveys. He pored over sea-charts. Analysed the cycles of the local tides, and searched the intricate, silver-point maps that detailed the regional electromagnetics, adjusted for season and phase of the moon. But no haven existed where the bore of the flux current was less reactive.

The high resonance on the warded isle that guarded the Paravians in seclusion matched, or exceeded, the frequency of the proscribed free-wilds ground, where even the time-tested blood of the clans feared to tread.

Arithon fought despair. Concentration and mage-gifted Sight became his last weapons against the long nights. Furtive sleep ambushed his vigilance. When breaking dawn caught him unaware, he lost himself to the intoxicant flood of the natural world past the casements. The influence of the Paravians' proximity fevered his dreams, drugging him under the fecund fire that unfurled every quickening bud. The song of the elder races charged the earth and the air, until each breath heightened his undying desire to search for their hidden glens until he collapsed, faculties abandoned to the volatile bliss that graced their eternal existence.

Arithon resisted the honeyed temptation. Scourged by the siren call of the flux, he defused the dreams that plagued him to exhaustion by sprinting down forest game trails until he gasped, soaked in sweat. Once, he swam in an icy inlet until his pink skin turned white, and he panted through blue lips and chattering teeth.

Indifferent to hunger, he foraged by rote, hunting with the informed respect that took small game by ritual permission. He found viable seeds preserved in the pantry. But if the Sorcerer had kept a kitchen garden, his herbs had gone wild long since.

The unwelcome impression of abandonment nagged.

Arithon swerved from that painful thought. Lest pilfering reason should beggar hope, he fled until he ran out of land. At the isle's west shore-line, while afternoon waned, he waded and fished, lulled by the lucent turquoise shallows and the white thunder of surf on the reef.

Whipcord fitness returned. Innate balance steadied. In due course, the morning arrived when Arithon's venture outside to draw water did not upset his adamant discipline. Tiny leaves gilded the willows arched over the brook: the passage of days had slipped into the turn of the season. Anxiety ruffled his fragile calm. For last year's peril resurged with the spring. Dry roads on the mainland would wake True Sect fervour and unleash The Hatchet's campaign of conquest.

War and red slaughter would return to Rathain, fuelled by fanatical hatred.

Rogue far-sight shattered the veneer of tranquillity. Roughshod, the horrific blast of raw prescience trampled over hard-won equanimity.

Arithon gasped, collapsed to his knees by the rush of probable vision. Then the spun-glass bubble of his self-awareness burst altogether. Fists rammed in the dirt, he shuddered, while the stretched moment slowed time, and the ground underneath him dissolved into the primal shimmer of energies that knitted creation. He no longer recognized tangible form. The purl of the flux chafed his unshielded nerves, until the electromagnetic surge of the elements eroded his existence down to naked spirit.

He endured, as he must. No clean release from his quandary existed until he broke the power of the Ettinmere shamans. Barraged by re-amplified sound and cast adrift in tormented distraction, Arithon grappled the slip-stream of displaced sensation, all of his precarious footing unstrung by one careless, abstract thought. Breathing too fast, he marshalled himself, the unravelled span of his attention refocused strand by laborious strand, until he re-established the boundaries of human perception.

The set-back cost dearly.

That evening, he mapped his cautious steps with a staff to affirm the solidity of the floor under him. He latched the storm shutters against the full moon, lest his tenuous focus should stray, mesmerized by the silvered reflections glanced off the swirling brook. He met the gad-fly demands of clothing and meals by grim rote, then retired to the worn rattan chair and thumbed through Ciladis's field journals.

Arithon read the collection in order and paused at the one left unfinished. Inchoate dread fed his reluctance to examine the final entry. He already knew the last leaves were blank though the faded slip-case of stamped leather was older than the completed volumes numerically titled. The flocked parchment was yellowed with years, suggesting an incomplete body of knowledge, pursued over an extended time.

Ciladis's known passions were healing and harmony. His signature style had breath-taking elegance, shaped by an intellect of adamant gentleness. Hope was loath to pry into the intimate mystery behind his private retreat. Arithon hesitated, afraid to broach something more ominous than a reclusive desire for sanctuary among the Paravians.

The Seven's affairs were no man's to fathom, all the more at the risk of unbearable grief. The opened book might seal the terrible proof: loss of a spirit whose keenly felt absence already diminished the Seven.

Yet the stakes riding Arithon's crisis were desperate, with the on-coming horror of the True Sect war stacked against the integrity of his survival. No master accepted defeat under compromise. He would not cede his autonomy to the Ettinmere shamans or permit the meddling link to the former Prime Matriarch's collaboration.

Regret lost validity, commandeered by the mandate of a Fellowship oath to survive *no matter the means or the consequence.*

Arithon lifted the journal from the shelf. If Ciladis lived, he might never forgive the personal trespass. But if Mankind's turmoil darkened the mysteries, and discord drove a downwards spiral towards entropy, the enduring grace of the Paravians might forsake the world altogether.

Arithon unlatched the stained cover. The calligraphy of the fly-leaf's inscription matched no Atheran language, except for the Third Age runes underneath, which recorded the date of Desh-thiere's incursion. He turned the page, crestfallen, as the first entry upset his assumption. Ciladis had not written a verbal account of the Mistwraith's invasive conquest.

Instead, Traithe's portrait stared out of the page, a deft rendering that captured life's essence. The black, brimmed hat with the silver band was doffed, the bare shock of the Sorcerer's fly-away hair wisped as though teased by a wind sprite. Strong-boned features radiated amusement. The mirthful glint in his dark eyes promised laughter, beneath wide-lashed lids not yet hooded by the ache of chronic debility. The set of the mouth showed light-hearted whimsy, unlined by the brackets of sorrow Arithon remembered. The vivid image revealed Traithe as he had been, before the crippling damage incurred by his heroic closure of South Gate.

More drawings followed, wistful views of places and children, some done in fine ink, and others more spontaneously shaded with charcoal. Landscapes from Daon Ramon radiated an emotion delicate enough to wring tears. Ethereal silver-point depicted Riathan amid the spring wildflowers that once had flourished before the great dam diverted the River Severnir, and the lush meadows parched into scrub thicket and thorn.

Discovery illumined each subsequent page. Cianor Moonlord's shining nobility haphazardly faced the breath-taking chiaroscuro of towering flame that ignited a living drake's aura. The intricate detail that revealed a snowflake's fragility also had traced the latticed emanation of crystals. Each subject reflected a ferocious tenderness, all the rapt wit of the Sorcerer's vision unveiled to initiate insight.

More intimate than a diary, Ciladis's memoire contrasted his cherished remembrance with the calamitous harm wrought by Desh-thiere's invasion.

The tone of the entries darkened with time, as the erosive impacts compounded. As though frenetic acts of creativity had striven to defy an insidious melancholy, Arithon viewed alphabets of intertwined capitals formed out of beasts and curled vines: prototypes for the illuminated volumes sequestered in Davien's library. A grumpy cartoon of Luhaine caught the huffed breath that preceded his lectures. Another showed a debonair Kharadmon, eyes half-lidded in the snide sidewise glance that fore-ran his needlesome smile.

Recipes improving the degraded dyes that afflicted the artistry of the Narms craftsmen were scrawled between poetry that trailed off into the hen-scratches of a quill nib scraped dry of ink. Arithon recognized fragments of verses, later evolved into ballads passed down through Athera's Masterbards.

As prolific as these idle fancies, he encountered the ruled drawings of spells, many encoded in the refined geometry preferred by the Fellowship Sorcerers. Arithon marvelled over the original ciphers that empowered Ciladis's Sunloop, a working that defied entropic attrition. Stored at Althain Tower, the shining artifact still performed its embedded office. The tuned invocation to track the return of the sunlight at the Mistwraith's defeat yet reflected the daily advent of dawn across the world's compass.

The next entries were sombre, exact drawings of fungi and wilt, then shrivelled leaves powdered with must, the decay arisen from prolonged damp and extended winters. Ciladis's study mapped the dark veins in the auras of plants afflicted by the pall of Desh-thiere. Sketched vistas unveiled what appeared as swirled fog, until closer survey discerned subtle smears that resolved into distorted faces. Long since, Ciladis had unravelled the cankerous presence of the embedded wraiths; centuries ahead of his Fellowship peers, he recorded the deadly phenomenon certainly shared by Athera's Paravians. The horror, perhaps, had been too great to bear, given the historical omission. While the wraiths' maligned state thwarted scrying, no hope of reprieve existed beyond the riddle of Dakar's West Gate Prophecy.

As though the untenable pain poisoned quietude, Arithon encountered pictures of deformed trees, a botanist's catalogue of maples, and oaks, willow, white birch, and spear-straight stands of ash. Yet on each page, opposite, their familiar forms had been reworked, the energies of individual species reclad in a different aspect. Arithon beheld growth that seemed taller, more stately, more achingly serene, nature's symmetry imbued with a beauty beyond worldly vision. He took pause, a thumb hooked to mark his place in a book gently closed for further contemplation.

Davien once had asserted that Mankind's perception shaped Athera's flora and fauna into conformity with racial memory. Paravians interpreted the same electromagnetic signatures differently. Arithon's venture down the forbidden pathways linked to the King's Glade in Selkwood had explored the perilous interface, where bodily senses and mage-sight unravelled. The light and sound underlay shifted patterns, and form rippled: like a rotated kaleidoscope, the known face of reality altered. A similar transience infused the sanctuaries maintained by Ath's white adepts, and surely, also, created the uncanny phenomenon found at the borders of Athili. The Second Age focus circles that synchronized the lanes with the flux tides and enabled the dissolute transfer across distance were also empowered by resonant memory. Davien wielded an engineer's grasp of the principle, and archival history described Sethvir's ability as a shape-shifter.

Yet no Sorcerer in Arithon's hearing ever mentioned which gateway had enabled the old races' exodus from the continent.

Extant record suggested Ciladis had not embarked on his search for their passage by boat. A sea-crossing would have encountered the wards, impenetrable to Sethvir's earth-sense. Whether the journal decoded the structure, the next sequence of configured diagrams proved too dense to decipher. Arithon studied their dazzling symmetry in vain, incomplete learning unable to fathom the dragon-sourced mastery possessed by the Seven. He admired the beauty, silenced by awe, and thralled by ephemeral tingles as he traced over the inscribed parchment.

Then the occult notation gave rise to more portraits drafted after Ciladis's retreat. Sunchildren danced within circles of flame, their delicate faces like petalled flowers or strung pearls rendered against satin-black darkness. Stately centaurs posed, mantled in spindled light, the magnificence graven in bearing and features infused with the patience of ages. Hope blazed eternal in the forms of Riathan, trailing silvery torrents of excited flux, with the sparkle of *iyats* crowding their wake, blurred under shrouding mist.

The sketches embodied much more than aesthetic exuberance. Arithon encountered sequential images of unbudded willow fronds, paired with phrases of notated melody. His Masterbard's gift grasped the purpose written in primal harmonics. Here lay the inspired idea for the completed work on the shelf, that explored tonal means to transform through refiguring sound. Ciladis had evolved a method by which the crystalline flutes of the Athlien singers might offset Desh-thiere's blight on the landscape.

Which refined application still acted in force: bardic talent detected the remnant echoes, found stamped into stones and ancient trees, and wound through the chord of the flux. The imprints bespoke the work done to maintain the land's shining health across the dismal centuries enshrouded in fog. Perhaps the last verse of the Sorcerer's remarkable legacy: few marked pages remained before the blank signatures bound in the unfinished memoire.

Arithon turned over the next leaf, and gasped. For the structure Ciladis had scripted raised light, a silver sheen that confounded vision, and flared mage-sight into conflagration. Momentarily blinded, Arithon shielded his face, shut the book, and breathed until his pulse steadied. He shied off from conclusion, refused the uneasy dread that had stalked his thoughts all along.

Yet the persistent sorrow could not be dismissed. Ciladis had been recording Paravian consciousness in full glory, unshielded by limiting flesh. Strung out between an incarnate existence and the upscaled vibration of unclothed spirit, the Sorcerer may have lost himself to beguilement.

Rather than dwell on fearful supposition, Arithon steeled his weak nerve. He thumbed forward into the section left blank, then flipped backwards to the final entry. The drawings unveiled did not dazzle him witless. The left-hand leaf showed an inked rendering of an outcrop, seamed diagonally by a stepped ledge that descended into the shadowed mouth of a cave. The right-facing page recorded a mighty working, the strength of the geometry also not rendered in actualized form. Arithon recognized the rune for elemental light embedded into the Fellowship's complex style of shorthand. The interlocked figures were patterned for perpetuity, similar to the artful array on the Sunloop, but greater in execution and magnitude.

Arithon pondered the heart-breaking conundrum until daybreak speckled rose light through the boughs past the casements. Ciladis might have achieved his completion with the resonant working to salvage the viability of the Paravian refuge. Sunk into despondency by his complete knowledge of Desh-thiere's malevolence, he may have surrendered to the grace of an ethereal release. If so, the last pair of drawings shaped a cryptic epitaph.

Or, Arithon mused through the flutter of dread, determined hope had defied grief. The diary's contents affirmed the bent of that steadfast purpose. The Sorcerer's diary expressed more than wistful sentiment. His persistent articulation of vibrant beauty, offset by the poignancy of fading loss, mapped the visceral gap between discord and symmetry. The contrast might aim to spark meaningful insight, silent testament of an obdurate pursuit of constructive ideas. From the smallest imbalance to large scale disharmony, each entry had been followed with an exacting remedy formulated in the numbered field manuals.

The outcrop depicted offered a clue to the riddle of Ciladis's disappearance. If the site lay within the warded refuge, and provided the diagrammed spell-craft on the next page was interlinked, the local flux tides ought to reflect the traces of its active presence. Arithon resolved to risk chasing the theory, although the decision was dangerous. While the accurate charts in the cottage mapped the uplands to direct his search, proximity to the Paravian presence posed him a consummate peril. Since his unstable condition disallowed a direct contact to ask for guided permission, the reckless alternative forced his reliance on immersive mage-sight.

Arithon set off rested and fed, precautions that fortified mortal flesh, but no anchor at all against the frayed state of his spirit. The filled flask, the short bow, and the oiled cloak bundled over rolled blankets required his mindful focus, no use if strayed wits overtook him in the open.

Which storm assaulted his unsheathed nerves before he turned inland, away from known country. The chance glitter of sunbeams on dew, the searing peridot flames of new leaves, and the liquid warble of bird-song snared his wayward attention. Spring's bewitching cascade flooded him with the tonic of fecund rebirth, until his drugged senses strayed into the numinous vista of waking dreams.

Entranced perception plagued his human steps, both as pitfall and warning. Where confluent wells of high resonance exceeded the threshold of tolerance, seductive beauty blazed brightest. The heady scent of the passing breeze scattered his purposeful reason. There, he must turn aside. Or like the moth drawn to flame, he could succumb to the fatal allure of Athera's mysteries.

Wrung dizzy, Arithon stumbled upon a pebbled lake-shore too wide to swim. He circled the verge with blindfolded eyes, his hesitant progress achieved by touch to avoid the scald of pure light off the opalescent riffle of water. Against the siren's song of wet stones underfoot, he stripped off his shirt, until the crisp bite of the wind lost efficacy as a last measure to jab him alert. Wooed into reverie, he tripped. The fall shocked him back to awareness. Spared, he could not guess how far he had strayed, warnings missed as he veered into jeopardy.

Pain stymied his resource, while he shuddered and retched, then slipped the muffling cloth from his face to stanch the gash in his banged forehead.

Cleared vision revealed that the boulder that caught his toe had been recently carved, the fresh chips from the mason's chisel scattered nearby. The incised characters were familiar: directional symbols used by centaur guardians of old to demark hallowed ground on the mainland. Arithon blinked, sobered. Evidently, the reclusive Paravians had placed a sign-post to steer him towards safer ground.

He had no time to dwell. Sundown fired the lake to a shimmer of salmon and gold, frisked by the prank breezes that freshened at dusk. Fallen under the indigo shadow of night, with the star-song re-amplified by water, the allure of this place would be deadly. Arithon drove himself upright. His whispered gratitude acknowledged the gift of exalted assistance as he pressed forward. If solving the puzzle of Ciladis's fate outmatched his ability, at least he had not been called out for trespass.

His progress blurred through the following days. From twilight until the first blush of dawn, he battled his drifted senses. What fitful catnaps he snatched in duress spun him into bouts of delirium. Arithon traversed a dazzling land-scape, half-stunned. Jewel-toned rainbows fractured his mage-sight to a distraction that sapped him of purpose. He trod forests of patriarch trees that soared upwards, their broad trunks and massive, arched crowns a marvel on an isle exposed to the Cildein's rampaging gales.

He splashed across brooks with clear pools, rimmed in velvet moss and teeming with trout. The meander of willow-stitched banks woke amazement, burst into glory without warning where roaring falls jetted off the stepped ledges. He traversed shaded grottoes and hidden glens, charged with the oil-sheen glimmer of the unbearably heightened flux. The deer and the wildcat matched his moon-struck stare, fearless. He stumbled and fell time and again, hurled into mage-trance by the chance-met brush of bare flesh against leaves, or else bashed his shins, shocked out of his senses where vistas of scintillant light painted over the architecture of eternity.

Arithon grappled the spiralling plunge towards insanity as his birthborn talent intensified. Refined awareness unmoored him, until his least movement rang like bronze bells through his altered perception. The flux currents danced, gold, to the sigh of the breeze, energetically reactive to his thoughts and apt to flower into illusory bouts of nightmare. A lifetime's discipline fought to curb panic, while the heady, lush fragrance that rushed every breath wrung him to trembling ecstasy.

Yet the flow of one day to the next, measured by the changing lane tides, was not timeless. Outside the seduction of paradise, the surge and bustle of activity elsewhere spun the grim thread of disaster. Idyllic reverie too often convulsed into farsighted visions of terror and blood, shuddered by the drum-beat of war and the wing-flaps of gravid birds settled on carrion. Thaw on the continent would be drying the trade-road under the Mathorn foot-hills. Cleared passes would unmuzzle the fury of the Light's war host across Rathain.

Arithon shivered, crossed from the syrup of noon sunlight into dense shade under a stand of pines. Gooseflesh pebbled his arms, perhaps from misted damp: somewhere ahead, a tumbling waterfall wafted the scent of dank stone. Or not, he mused, chilled by felted gloom that smothered clear daylight. The evergreens nestled against a sheer cliff, the vertical face entangled in vines, and streaked virid where seeped springs dripped from the clefts. Arithon shoved through the needled branches, drawn by the glimmer of uncanny rays, spun like cobweb through the gloaming ahead.

The silver light flared from a marker stone, hoary with lichen and fallen twigs. Arithon braced for the resonant surge unleashed by Paravian workmanship. But no such upset unmoored him. The emanation that met his approach sang to a different register. Thrust under the encroaching greenery, Arithon cleared the detritus and found the star glyph of the Fellowship Sorcerers.

He stared upwards, astonished. Above, inked in shadow, a sloped seam notched the cliff wall. Ferns scalloped the aperture, laddered in creepers, likely the site of Ciladis's sketch, before overgrowth blocked the view.

Thrill raked Rathain's prince, spiked by trepidation. The muffled air wore the weight of the ages beneath the drooped boughs, hanging breezeless. Against the dulled roar of the falls, a near-desolate hush suppressed even the small, furtive rustles of wildlife.

Respect called for due care. Though if the setting harboured a tomb, the unkempt stone lacked the dignity of a monument. Unlike the cottage, lovingly preserved, this site had been abandoned to nature. Mystery or memorial, the marker bore no other inscription. Hope died, that a ready key had been left to decipher its codified purpose.

Arithon crouched. He laid his trembling palm flat on the earth. Without safer means, ill-prepared for the perilous assay, he murmured a request, begged forgiveness, then opened his already overwrought senses.

He had only the embedded imprints in the flux by which to chart Ciladis's active intent.

The dreaded plunge into the range of raised frequency did not shred Arithon's precarious balance. Instead, he settled into replete peace, soft as cotton. A soporific spiral of calm eddied the dynamic current of the natural flow, apparently to preserve a static field in sealed isolation. Mage-trained perception could not pierce the veil. Arithon drew a slow breath and took pause.

To collapse the stay outright would expose the unknown construct to the reactive swirl of the lane tide. No means existed to gauge the consequence. His sole measure to grapple that fathomless peril was to spiritwalk: forfeit his grounded attachment to flesh, then surrender his consciousness to the spell and trace its coil backwards to centre. That rash prospect flushed Arithon to cold sweat. An unshielded immersion, in his fractured state, risked shearing the tenuous foothold that anchored his being. Supposing he threaded the gamut intact, the resonance of the engaged working might overwhelm him.

Already, the resinous air spun his senses. Arithon gripped a branch for stability, the bite of rough bark insufficient to ground him. Indecision saved nothing. On-coming nightfall would hasten his plunge into seductive entrancement. Whether he perished quickly through meddling folly or dwindled slowly into terminal dissolution, defeat finished him either way.

Arithon gritted his teeth and battled his swimming dizziness. Before the irrevocable choice to commit, he cautiously sampled the flux currents again to determine the stay's point of origin. The spare elegance of Fellowship handiwork was elusive by nature. Yet here, the exception sprang stark to the eye and took Arithon by surprise. The inaugural configuration aligned with his birth gift! Shadow, woven from the element functioned as a direct trigger, with the stasis of the mighty construct sustained by the covering shade of the evergreens.

Even a glancing exposure to sunlight would touch off a volatile unbinding.

"Daelion Fatemaster wept!" whispered Arithon.

For the entrained configuration was strikingly similar to the Sunloop, a specialized artifact created to herald the Mistwraith's defeat. Logic's breath-taking leap suggested the greater array in place here should have captured the first shaft of untrammelled dawn, and unravelled in spontaneous release.

A banishment meant to occur long before, had a stand of pines not taken chance root and thwarted the cue for dispersal. Which meant Ciladis had never sequestered himself by wilful abdication. Instead, hopeful oversight had misjudged the pervasive endurance of Desh-thiere's blight.

Arithon knelt on the mat of shed needles. Two hundred and eighty eight years too late, he dispelled the pinned wisp of shadow that stabilized the Sorcerer's last work.

The flash-point collapse of the ward was past visible, a clap of reverberation beneath mortal hearing. Yet the tremor that shivered the earth shook the trees and flared in recoil through the local flux. Arithon shuddered at the brink of unconsciousness, fighting to stabilize his beleaguered senses. Whatever his impulsive act had unleashed, the slip-stream of displacement shocked home. A diverted pocket in time and space reintegrated with the present.

When the queasy blur of the interface settled, Arithon stood. He reoriented himself amid the blue gloaming filtered through the dense pines. At first, nothing seemed changed. Then a scatter of loosened rock from above bounced and clattered through the meshed vines. His startled glance upward beheld a lone figure, emerged from the gloom of the cleft.

"Ciladis?" he murmured in hoarse amazement.

A bright flicker of movement: the silvered head turned, roused from a bemused survey of the encroaching trees. The ebon face that peered downwards was clean-shaved, and gaunt as pinched clay. A crooked nose and fleece eyebrows jutted over flat cheek-bones. Deep-set eyes the colour of ale resharpened to fixated interest.

Arithon staggered, stripped naked under that searching regard. Unstrung, he beheld himself mirrored: from the ingrained grime in his rolled cuffs, to black, tangled hair and stubbled chin, to the festered scab on his forehead. Yet his unkempt state did not scald him to self-conscious humiliation. Rather, he felt cherished by the tender kindness of total acceptance. His instinctive recoil softened to trust as, eased beyond turmoil, uplifted in spirit, Arithon was embraced by a pure compassion that pierced the core of his being. The paralysis of stressed uncertainty lifted and melted him to his knees. Defenceless awareness lost breath and wits, dazzled by the grace of a rapport lit by the blaze of the infinite. His tears welled, unabashed, while the might of the myriad world seemed to spin on its axis around him.

The adept shielded himself before Arithon crumpled. Shuttered, his power folded inward and left an earthy old man, clothed in a dusky grey mantle snagged with a jackdaw's cache of small twigs. The saffron eyes creased in gentle inquiry.

"These trees," the Fellowship Sorcerer mused, his mellow baritone husked in the grain as aged whiskey. "They are over five hundred years old. How long has the Mistwraith been vanquished?"

"Not defeated completely," remarked Arithon, discomfited by his borrowed clothes, which surely belonged to the speaker. "The fog-bound wraiths were fought to confinement, then sealed within Rockfell Peak." Mage perception would verify the fraught truth behind his shocking answer. "By Third Age reckoning, the year in question was 5638."

Ciladis's smile banished dismay. "For that long, Dakar's West Gate Prophecy has achieved closure!" The exclamation digressed to a further deduction of intimate accuracy. "Then you would be Dari s'Ahelas's mage-trained descendant, and by twice-royal lineage, acknowledged by Asandir's mark as Crown Prince of Rathain. Your Grace, I'm indebted to you for deliverance from the pitfall of my own enchantment."

Release

The squall line that rampaged in after sundown tapered off to light rainfall that pattered like mercury off the soaked pine boughs. The sheltered seam in the cliff-face stayed dry. Aromatic smoke twined off a neat bed of birch coals, wafted in the dank gusts through the run-off, splashed from the moss ledge above. Arithon sat cross-legged on the rammed-earth floor, an unfastened cloak draped over his shoulders. He did not flinch at sounds or cringe when the lightning flashed. But the mug of restorative tea cradled in unsteady fingers betrayed his facade of unruffled discipline.

Across the embers, as if naught lay amiss, the Sorcerer most beloved of the Seven knelt beside the forked sticks of an improvised spit. Flame-light carved lean features that seemed suited more to a veteran warrior, while hands that once penned the finest tracts on healing proved equally facile with noose snares and a skinning knife. Respect marked each movement. Tenderly, though his catch was no longer alive, Ciladis skinned and jointed the hare taken for supper. Where time and moths left frayed holes in his shirt, the Sorcerer himself seemed unimpaired by the centuries spent in stasis.

Sidewise glance warm as amber, his concern expressed by cheerful domesticity, Ciladis laid the cleaned meat on the scraped hide and answered Arithon's turbulent thought. "Our Fellowship does not succumb to the rapture arisen from Paravian exposure. Not because we are privileged, mind, but because of the binding bestowed upon us by the dragons." The pearl-handled knife better suited for pen nibs was quite sharp enough to point a green stick. With their frugal meal spitted to roast, Ciladis rinsed his smeared fingers and qualified. "The drakes' initiation expanded our range of perception in ways that transcend mortality. A drastic trial by fire, and an irrevocable change beyond your imagining. A gentler stay is effective through resonance."

Arithon stirred, his applied will a palpable force as he battled exhaustion. "The stone in this place has been spun down to a slower vibration. Your touch, I presume?"

"Indeed." Ciladis stood. His rag-picker's shadow swooped in the fire-light as he approached the cliff rim, still talking. "Proximity reduces the flux charge and eases excessive strain on the senses." He flung the befouled water into the rain, then hooked his hide bucket under the drizzle to refill. "I fashioned the working to buffer a long-term sleep without dreams. The residual echo won't fade straightaway, a benefit to your relief. I'd urge you to rest if you care to listen." Which subtlety side-stepped an outright command to stop fighting the soporific.

Rathain's prince disregarded the mild remonstrance. Though the strong tisane weighted his eyelids, relentless interest still fired his febrile attention. "The warding you raised here does not explain the uncanny recognition exchanged between us upon our first encounter."

"Ah! That." Ciladis smiled. "You never explored the particulars of your ancestry in the archive at Althain Tower?" His direct gaze flared yellow as a wyvern's eye as he crouched and poked up the coals. "Each of the royal lineages was selected by one of us Seven. Davien bowed out, acrimoniously opposed. Luhaine deliberated for weeks, undecided between several candidates. Asandir's arbitration favoured the perception inherent in Iamine s'Gannley, who declined, which elevated Halduin s'Ilessid. Traithe named Rondeil s'Ellestrion, and Kharadmon appointed Cindra s'Ahelas. Sethvir played his selection close to the vest, then put forward Bwin Evoc s'Lornmein for Havish."

The ancestor left unstated flicked Arithon to wary surprise. "Then you stood behind Torbrand s'Ffalenn? The surly grain of the family temperament seems ill-matched."

"Do you think so?" Ciladis's mahogany face crinkled with merriment. "Each of us responded to a quality inherent in our own characters. Torbrand's provocative disposition stemmed from an empathy vulnerable enough to require protection."

"You don't share that defence," Rathain's Prince fired back, sharp enough to imply accusation.

Ciladis tipped his head in acknowledgement. Then he settled, unruffled, back braced to the wall, with the dead branch employed as a poker bridged across his tucked-up knees. "The bleeding distress can be tempered through solitude." His mild glance dispelled any sting. "Does the subject jab too close to the bone?"

Arithon shivered, shook off drowsiness, and rejected sympathy. "Torbrand surely measured the pertinent facts before he gave his consent."

"Whereas his hapless heirs were born victimized, infelicitously ignorant.

Very well." Primed for the descendant's nettlesome intelligence, Ciladis faced the barb unoffended. "Each candidate's raw affinity granted our sponsorship a needful point of foundation. We branded those partnered virtues into your heritable blood-lines. The imprinted traits were brought to actualized potency through the sympathy of conjoined resonance."

Arithon sucked a breath through his teeth, the fingers on his mug tensed to blanched knuckles.

"You encountered, in me, the mirrored endowment bequeathed through your ancestry." The sizzle of fat dripped onto the embers sheared through a brittle silence. Ciladis watched Arithon shelter his face with one hand. Further words offered nothing but tawdry noise; the least human touch would humiliate. The constancy of the Sorcerer's care was a fathomless flame, gifted freely enough to dismantle the barriers of personal privacy.

"You never forsook your colleagues," ventured Arithon, steadied when at length he accepted his portion of the toasted meat. "You encountered the truth behind Desh-thiere's bound wraiths, which drove you to seek the Paravian refuge. I've admired the scholarship in your journals. Without stint, you applied your healer's knowledge to spare the old races from lethal despair."

Ciladis stretched out his legs, ankles crossed, his quiet relentless until his inquisitive guest started eating. Then he said, "Mortality fosters irrational hope, and brief life-span inspires an extraordinary tenacity. Mankind by nature was better suited to endure the Mistwraith's incursion. One of the Seven had to shoulder the task of raising the localized flux currents before the Paravians lost their vitality. Afterward, the sealed wards shielding this sanctuary could not come down, which committed me for the duration."

Green eyes met and locked with the Sorcerer's, over a half-consumed meal. "The old races value their secrets," agreed Arithon.

A ferocious understatement from a man who had quartered the seas throughout decades of search, with repeated landfalls to replenish his water casks at the guarded islet's north anchorage. An initiate talent's acuity had never detected the displacement ward, wrought dense enough to blindside even the broad-scale vision of Althain's Warden.

Which was no play on mild irony at all, but a frontal assault at the core of a subject Ciladis preferred not to broach.

The bucket set under the run-off overflowed. Fortuitous accident, or tactical evasion, the Sorcerer arose. His distorted shadow swept the far wall as he fetched the full vessel and replenished his pot, then tossed in foraged herbs to heat an infusion. His unhurried activity rebuilt the low fire. Then he sat, a dark silhouette with an ancient dignity tucked up like a peasant in rumpled cloth. Without speaking, he finished his meat. Yet his reticent calm bespoke a shrewd vigilance: he waited, while the spelled rock did its work, hastened by the fragrant steam released from his boiling infusion. He did not miss the moment when Arithon's eyelids slid closed. His timely move rescued the tilt of the mug, sliding from slackened fingers.

Then Ciladis caught Rathain's prince as he toppled, and as tenderly as he had skinned a killed hare, eased him down beside the spent fire. Then he spread his borrowed mantle over shoulders grown sorrowfully thin.

Through an interval while the rain sluiced outside, he measured the form in repose at his feet, emptied of the raw fire of will in oblivious sleep. Dirt-rimmed broken finger-nails, far removed from the mastery that plied exquisite art on the lyranthe string. The drawn features seemed too frail to have survived Davien's maze; too pithless to have surmounted the spiritual mauling that brought down the vile practice of the Grey Kralovir.

Ciladis read far more into the man than the shared stamp of compassion. His insight traced back to the first breath at birth and weighed up the aggregate sum of experience. He perceived the vow that had salvaged a child, and grasped the immensity of the risk, when dire need once in the past had called for the salvage of the damaged wardings at Rockfell. Livid as a brand, he interpreted the consequence imposed by Davien's seal of longevity, which, times over, rewrote the natural course of mortality during the captive years spent settling Marak's unleashed horde of free wraiths.

At rest, recorded in skin pale as candle wax, and in the deep tremors that clenched muscle to bone, the Sorcerer mapped the cost of the endurance that yet sustained spirit and flesh.

Weariness had extracted its toll. Within days, perhaps less, Arithon's initiate strengths would collapse. Mankind was not endowed to survive the charged resonance inside the Paravian refuge. Regret did not dwell on the impacts of Arithon's adamant resistance. The relentless intimacy which stripped the heart and bared the most intimate secrets was the attribute of all Fellowship Sorcerers.

Ciladis's pity stemmed instead from the trials thrust upon the resiliency of sterling character. "Rue the day Asandir sealed your blood bond for cold surety," he murmured with vibrant remorse. "The Seven have meddled with you above every design envisioned by Torbrand as line-bearer." For the tragic betrayal by friends at Athir and the appalling cascade of consequences sprung from Dakar's mistake, even farsighted wisdom lost words. "I will have your answers," the Sorcerer vowed. "You have not lived, or suffered, or sacrificed only to waste in an exile that leads to your death."

Determined to speak in the crown prince's behalf, Ciladis shrugged on his holed cloak with its tarnished damascene thread. He drew up the hood lined in pale saffron silk. Then he soundlessly left the sheltered crevice and strode away through the pounding rain.

Darkness swallowed the Sorcerer's path through the pines, and wind buffeted his crossing of the puddled meadow beyond. Where Arithon's course approached from the southwest, Ciladis went north and eastward, where the flux charge far exceeded mortal capacity. The open land in due course became wooded, with secluded glades carpeted in moss and grasses. Here, the living trees wore the glory bestowed by Paravian habitation. Mighty trunks soared aloft, crowns leafed with a majesty that whispered and roared in the gusts that chased off the storm. Serenity cloaked the remote hollows. The Sorcerer stepped softly where the melodic drip of slackened rainfall gleamed like fallen crystal and diamond, and the silver braid of small streamlets trickled over round stones. The greenwood retained its fair aspect here. All forests elsewhere had faded since the Paravians abandoned the mainland. Even where Mankind's trespass was forbidden, deep inside the free wilds where the mysteries still flourished, the magnificence of Athera's life web had diminished under the long shadow cast by Desh-thiere.

Which bitter spiral Ciladis aimed to reverse, before loss eroded the grand arc of renewal.

Night bled into dawn underneath tattered cloud. The Sorcerer picked his way in descent, sheltered under the ridge, which narrowed to a fissured cliff, then plunged like a giant's spilled dominoes into the sea. Daybreak rinsed the tableau in coral and rose, the glassine rollers polished to aquamarine under the cleared zenith. Then the risen sun struck the air gold, rays airy as harp-strings strung across a crescent cove, encased by ramparts of rock. Springs plumed down the face, threaded by swooping swallows, and winnowed spray fired scintillant rainbows above the nestled emerald of a shoreside meadow. Pristine calm ruled the early hour, with the vista yet pleated in purple shadow.

Splendour quickened Ciladis's spirit. A being would be blind and deaf, not to be overtaken with awe. Pressed onward, the Sorcerer picked his way over slippery stone, shaken by the roar where the spring-waters leaped in cascades off the brinks. Spangled in damp, he reached the sea's edge. Raucous gulls dipped and weaved overhead. Ever quick to delight in his presence, the sand-pipers that scuttled at the petticoat hems of the breakers took wing in his wake like a streamered scarf.

Flux sheen haloed everything under the influence of the intensified lane currents. The exuberance of heightened resonance caused the sand grains underfoot to whisper and sing. Lapped in that wild melody, the Sorcerer turned down a path folded into the rolling meadow. Ahead, vision dazzled, he moved into a blaze as intense as an undying star. His escort of shore-birds sheared away, replaced by chirping finches and the thistle-down flit of field-sparrows. Ciladis walked, wreathed in birds, towards the ethereal source, shivered bone deep by harmonics as ringingly pure as glass chimes. Presently, he encountered the veil where the senses dissolved, and mage-sight opened to wonders.

Crossing that threshold exceeded the flesh: yet Fellowship Sorcerers wielded the powers bestowed by Athera's dragons. The shift in vibration unfolded, for them, an alternate view of creation. Ciladis trod upon ground where plants and meadow flowers shattered into prismatic motes, their colours also expressed as toned sound. He perceived the fluoresced lattices within rocks, while around him, the commonplace birds became *different*, reclothed in fair semblances otherworldly and strange.

Ciladis moved amongst thistle-down beings, airy as drifted light, while up-shifted awareness perceived a far country beyond the range of mortal experience.

Adept enough not to be mesmerized, Ciladis reforged his incarnate identity. As Arithon had once done, unwitting through music, to resolve the last riddle in Davien's maze, the Sorcerer imposed his core pattern of being upon the reactive energy. Shape solidified under his focused awareness. Between steps, the exotic unknown reconfigured to match the primal existence of his human origin. Rewoven to that familiar template, Ciladis trod an earthly landscape again but heightened to the brilliance of gossamer silk. The sunlight in the sheltered meadow ahead softened to pearlescent haze. Embedded within, the shimmer of an embodied consciousness ignited the flux charge to streamered, white flame.

The experienced eye beheld the wild glory unfurled by the unicorns, dancing: the thrust and passage of exquisite, dipped horns, and the spring of cloven hooves, lifted. Sight became seared by the ripple and blaze of manes and flagged tails, and the burnished glimmer of translucent coats. Ciladis caught his breath, as anyone must, who entered the living presence. The unbridled joy of Ath's hallows embraced him, celebrating the absolute fullness of Name. The Sorcerer received welcome for all that he was, and all that he ever would become in the arc of eternity.

He bowed his head, overcome by a terrible beauty. Nothing aware, not even the Seven, encountered the Riathans unmoved. Might and strength availed nothing, nor seasoned experience. Ciladis masked his face, shattered by sweet rapture. He quaked, pierced by sorrow for such harmony lost to the outside world. Also, he wept for the trials left to his abandoned colleagues. No matter, that his careful labour in exile had stabilized Paravian survival. How nearly he had buried himself alive, while crucial events wracked affairs on the continent during his extended absence.

But to mourn the omission became self-indulgence before the Riathan Paravians, whose nature embodied the conscious bridge linked to Ath Creator's unbounded glory. Moment to moment, their ethereal pavane encompassed the requite past and the unfulfilled future. All things, born and unborn, lay unveiled in reflection. Everything, since the concussive spark of divine consciousness unfolded the grand chord across the black deep and shaped form, until the implosion of time at the ending of Ages. Their motion illumined the sweep of the infinite. The ancient smokes as Cathukodarr's drakefire laid waste to Kathtairr mingled with the later cataclysm, when the Arch at Tolgrath crumbled before the desperate wrath of the centaur, Havkiel Haltfoot. Layer on recent layer, the True Sect burning of talent overlaid the black conflagration when Alestron's sea-gate became breached by the zeal of Alliance besiegers.

Shadow and light, from bleak death to exquisite exultation, the dance encompassed events large and small, even seemingly insignificant. Patience might count the separate jewels of dewdrops strung upon spiders' filaments, or splash with the snow-melt at dawn's light, when Cianor Sunlord was crowned. The bygone flourish of the guardians' horns still resounded, pierced by the whistles of rapacious Khadrim knifing the frigid heights above Teal's Gap. Princess Vicienna's tears at the break of the cordon restraining Desh-thiere melted into the cinder-grey rain fallen on her steadfast dead; or the silent snow drifted over the slain at Taerlin Waters, where earth mourned yet for Riathan slaughtered in frenzy by drake spawn.

Morbid peril stalked the illumined awareness. Lured to blinding ecstasy, or immersed in the throes of past grief, trained consciousness risked confounding itself in the multidimensional weave. The unwary witness might linger too long, bedazzled by the fabled wonders of Ithamon's Second Age ascendance. Perception might delve too deep, perhaps to snap in the after-shock reverberation, when the fast citadel crowning sea-girdled Corith became cast down into ruin.

A Fellowship Sorcerer did not court the gyre of enthralment. Ciladis stayed anchored by the raw power unleashed by the drake's dream of summoning: still ringing in force, the cry that had drawn the Seven in meteoric descent to their destiny at Crater Lake. As the rock parting the currents of history, he viewed the actualized present before him. The Riathans' spiral swirled widdershins, a stately wheel ruled by the spring stars. This daybreak, near the pending equinox, no Athlien singers accompanied. The absence of their crystalline flutes meant the festival of renewal would be underway in the hidden glens. The nocturnal feasts extended for a sevenday, illumined by the burning of the grass dwellings which sheltered their kind through the winter.

The warp threads of new leaf and budded flower laced a weft weave of sorrow: no young had been begotten at solstice. Nor had any live birth increased the host of the blessed. The dearth begun by Desh-thiere's invasion yet saw no fecund change. Such felicity remained unlikely while conflict convulsed Mankind's affairs in the mainland.

Ciladis had sampled that bitter current, and others, embedded in Arithon's consciousness.

And yet no Paravian sequestered in sanctuary had foundered beneath a morass of despair. None wasted, aggrieved, a failure deferred by Davien's farsighted action at Kathtairr. The resonance sustaining the mysteries held, still, a beacon in the shadows of misguided turmoil, mayhem, and bloodshed. If the dark threads did not, yet, disorder the fair, a Paravian return could never withstand the outbreak of war.

Cut off from Sethvir by the ward curtain, beyond access to outside counsel,

Ciladis weighed the immediate quandary. Any plea ventured in Prince Arithon's behalf invoked peril, against prudent sense and diplomacy. Even a cautious query would impact the Riathan dance. If interpretive augury tipped the frail balance, Arithon's exile might become permanent. Yet not to advocate for his strengths disenfranchised his initiate mastery and the tenacity of royal character.

The Sorcerer silenced his inner debate as a sudden shadow raked over him, untrammelled sunlight replaced by the radiance of a Paravian presence. A tingle razed his skin like a tonic and displaced his acclimatized senses.

"You cannot speak for his Grace of Rathain," the Ilitharis arrival rebuked. His voice echoed, a sonorous bass that struck music across the full spectrum.

Ciladis steadied his demeanour and arose. "Tehaval Warden! Your counsel is honoured." He bowed, forearms crossed with respectful apology. "Have you come to say Arithon's fate is determined?" Up-stepped yet again, Sighted vision pierced the blinding coruscation and unveiled the guardian's form: the same being whose service at Althain Tower had been passed to Sethvir when the Mistwraith smothered the continent.

Tehaval's majesty towered, enriched by the history of ages. Massive as oak, nine spans high at the shoulder, he was vast power and terrible love, leashed into a balance that whispered. His hide gleamed as honed steel sheathing muscle and bone, spattered over with coin-silver dapples. Mane, bannered tail, and his feathered fetlocks glistened white as thistle-down. A black harness belted his torso, opalescent with mother of pearl, and his breastplate and bracers were midnight-blue lacquer embossed with nine stars surrounding a moonburst.

Overwhelming as Tehaval's magnificence seemed, a fierce glory imposed at close quarters, the mightier stature of Cianor Reborn would have cast him into eclipse.

Ciladis waited, wise enough to quell urgency. Presently, the antlered head inclined towards him, broad brow bound with a circlet adorned with twelve heirloom moonstones, and a rainbow obsidian cut by Imarn Adaer's peerless artisans.

"The doom of Rathain's crown prince is not ours to steer, even by a counsel fiat," Tehaval declared. "The binding constraint on his destiny springs instead from your Fellowship colleagues."

Ciladis stared upwards at the centaur, aghast. "That I should live to endure such a wrong!" A fair morning suddenly seemed less than bright, while the paean danced by the Riathan became all the more vulnerable. "What caused my colleagues to forsake their profound obligation?"

Tehaval yet commanded his earth-link to Athera. Sympathy moved his heart for an anguish fit to sow savage despair. He extended his massive wrist, horned head bent, and invited Ciladis's clasp: not to offer support but to engage willing contact for a full disclosure.

For the direct touch of Paravian consciousness imperilled a being enfleshed, an expansive impact not to be trifled with, even by a Fellowship Sorcerer.

Sunlight streamed down, while the huge clasp of the guardian enveloped the smaller hand, once born human. Time seemingly paused. A punch-cut hole in existence divided the notes of spring bird-song. Ciladis stayed upright, apparently frail as spun smoke under Tehaval's shadow. The centaur's knowledge opened to him as a cascade of golden motes sown through his aura. The flecks waxed into sparks, then ignited and blazed, shearing across sensate awareness.

Shattered by the barrage, Ciladis received parallel threads of experience compressed into a fractal moment. The surge shocked his cognizance nigh unto breaking. The Sorcerer stretched to assimilate what Sethvir's faculties sorted in an eyeblink, unmoored until the torrential onslaught released him.

Whiplash left him reeling. Staggered a step, he fought air into paralysed lungs and braced to recover his balance. The blast of simultaneous events confounded the plod of sequential reasoning. The Sorcerer begged Tehaval's patience. He sat on a nearby boulder. Discipline let him tap the stone's assets and stabilize his equilibrium. Then he grappled the relevant referents to the Fellowship's primary directive. When Ciladis married the viewpoint garnered from Arithon's memory into its wider context, the import of Tehaval's warning took shape.

A subversion of charter law had broken precedent, sprung from the Mad Prophet's pithless mistake. *At one stroke, Rathain's crown succession and the vital key to the Mistwraith's defeat were left subject to Koriathain.* Ciladis weighed the import of Asandir's formal oath, witnessed in force by the runes laid in stone at the Whitehold sisterhouse.

"Father and mother of chaos!" Pummelled under the after-shock headache, the Sorcerer snapped, "We are caught in a dice throw for life-and-death stakes!"

"Dice don't premeditate malice," Tehaval amended, distressed by the gravity of the predicament. "For better or worse, your Teir's'Ffalenn has received our leave to depart without hindrance."

"A frail cipher upon which to hang the hard sacrifice of three Ages." A grue chased down Ciladis's spine. "Though few spirits alive carry his depth of integrity, his Grace's resilience is frayed by deep loss and bitter defeats. How long before he snaps under the strain?"

Tehaval's regal head turned. "Even my breadth of vision cannot part the mists." The great mysteries could stand or fail by the havoc hung on the tenacity of one mortal thread. "Your Fellowship's surety steers the course of Mankind's ultimate destiny."

Ciladis fielded the punch of inexpressible grief. Whether or not a failure of the compact called the Seven to account, and compelled the demise of humanity, the captive status of Desh-thiere's blight burdened the scales of the current dilemma. "Let the Teir's'Ffalenn leave, and the shielding veil here can no longer mitigate the risk to Paravian well-being."

The hidden knowledge of the Paravian refuge would accompany Arithon's return to the continent.

Tehaval extended a broad hand to the Sorcerer, this time to raise him to his feet. "Your crown prince does not lack for advocates, truly. Alithiel's chord woke for him, which clinched the support of Ffereton s'Darian. Several more revered elders expressed steadfast faith in him. Elshian the luthier decried shame for cowardice if we let a bard of such stature fade from the world. Kadarion spoke also, as Kadierach's last living brother. His adamance won Avileffin's support, and with that, willing help from his shipbuilding kin."

Ciladis glanced up, astonished. His joy caused a passing thrush to alight on his shoulder. Transferred, fluffed, to his extended finger, its cheerful song burst through his exclamation. "You suggest the Ilitharis will raise Arithon's foundered sloop from the shallows?"

"We've done more." Tehaval's pleasure rippled the surrounding flux to shimmering gold. "The vessel's sprung planks are restored, and her broken tackle, refitted. She's afloat in the quay, seaworthy and fully provisioned."

The thrush took wing. Her shadow flickered across Ciladis, his ebony profile torn by regret. "Safest, I think, that I don't meet his Grace before he sets sail."

Moonstones flared in the brilliance of morning as Tehaval dipped his antlers in rare homage. "Most brave!" he declared. "Such strength humbles our pithless concern that your heart might have wavered. We removed your temptation. Already, Tieriendieriel Merevalia is speeding his Grace's passage away. Above all Athlien, she claimed the burden of easing the contact. While nothing is certain, her singers recognized Arithon's quality when he braved the King's Grove in Shand for deliverance."

Ciladis accepted the choice with conflicted gratitude. He would have traded the sun and the moon for the chance to bestow a kindly last word upon Rathain's prince: to assure that his handfast beloved still lived, and to seek her solace before everything. His Grace's upcoming trial should have merited a timely warning, that the score against Ettinmere's shamans was an ill-starred pursuit better off abandoned.

For disaster awaited Arithon in the Storlains, beyond his worst imagining.

Yet Asandir's binding vow to the Koriathain forbade the decency of a farewell. Ciladis's night departure must finish in thankless abandonment; while Tehaval's apt intervention spared the default of the Fellowship's closure of crown debt.

Forced to keep his wise distance, Ciladis applied his aggrieved thoughts to the present. "Sethvir will need my support to redress our affairs on the continent."

"But not on this day!" Tehaval stamped a fore-hoof. "Let such woes unfold as they may, unburdened by premature sorrow! The felicity of your release will be taken amiss by the blessed should you forsake tonight's feast."

"Arithon Teir's'Ffalenn!" The imperative cry stabbed through the half-world of dream, true Name invoked with a tenderness to align the sleeper's awareness.

Arithon beheld a Sunchild's features that his past obligation compelled him to recognize.

She was as he remembered: midnight hair, hazed by radiance as bright as the sheen on a pearl, and skin burnished like poured moonlight. Her presence an ephemeral visitation to shield his over-stressed nerves, the song-bird's feathers worn for her adornment did not flutter with her spritely bearing. Yet even her sending excited the flux, a prismatic shimmer surrounding her grace in translucent splendour.

Assailed by rapture that scalded, Arithon scraped up a ragged apology. "Compromised as I am by meddling shamans, your exalted summons is wasted."

The arch of her brows inflected a frown. "I've not come to ease your passage across the veil!" Her jade glance reproached as she added, "My kind did not sing your deliverance from Desh-thiere's curse only to see your life's purpose abandoned, nor does crown service grant you the leave to languish and die here."

"I'm not quite fordone," chided Arithon, his gallant's reproof without heat. "Though I cannot access my forbears' exalted transit by way of the mysteries, decency might point out the shortest path to the sea."

Her laughter rang like musical chimes. "That you might swim offshore with the out-bound tide and spare Ciladis the bother of your final rites? As if no favour should honour the courage that brought his deliverance!"

Dreaming, Arithon did not feel her touch on his person. Light as a thought adrift on a breeze, he lacked the bodily awareness to know whether he walked somnolent, or if he was borne on a litter, or if the song of her crystalline flute wrapped his being in ribbons of light and towed him like a wisp through the ether. Through sheeting brilliance, he beheld wonders endowed by a beauty that flayed like edged glass. Palaces of translucent stone speared upwards, buttressed by a lace-worked confection of arches. The tiered hill-side beneath lay honeycombed with dwellings, walls and roofs braided of flowering vines and walled by entwined, living evergreens. Paravians built with unparalleled harmony: structures that embraced the needs of small animals, with niches and spires for nesting birds, and shaded arbours bejewelled with iridescent insects. Butterflies flitted on the intoxicant breeze, scented by salt spray wafted inland.

Whether the jumbled impressions were phantoms distilled from hallucination or wistful fantasies spun between moments of black-out delirium, Arithon never determined. Strung over the abyss of disintegration, he tracked the susurrant rush of white surf, then the beat and splash of what sounded like oars rocked him over jewel-toned swells. The astounding view of a tiered ship with patterned sails that netted the wind melted into a vision of high-flying clouds, and the lullaby creak of silk cordage.

The flute's song dwindled somewhere in the course of his disjointed journey. He wept for the hot roar of blood through his veins, and flinched from the thundering drum of his heart-beat. Tumbled in the maelstrom, his consciousness floundered as torrential sensation swallowed him, utterly. Drowning, the weight of the air in his lungs as heavy as liquid glass, he heard the Sunchild's parting echo through his deranged awareness. "Beware of which faction most stands to gain if you should surrender your birthright and abdicate."

But long since, the meaning of words had forsaken him. Arithon reeled into the desolate dark, either to fight for the rags of his life or to abandon the struggle for worldly existence.

Spring 5925

Policies

The shifted dynamic sprung by the Paravians' disrupted seclusion splashed across the world's weave and vanished, sunk into a poised silence. The ripple passed unnoticed, outside the rare few. The Rei-yaj Seeress plumbed the motionless depths, staring sunwards from her tower eyrie. The secrets behind her opaque, marble eyes stayed inscrutable as her pact with the tribes at Sanpashir, who remained a force unto themselves, with interests outside the compact that served Athera's great mysteries. Ath's Adepts owned the requisite vision, past question. But their sentinels at the world's etheric portals guarded only the volatile hush at the heart-core of their hostels, held sacred by their stricture of nonintervention.

Unlike their renegade fallen, who jealously hoarded the residual power coiled in the old vortex at Ettinmere: of the shamans' staked interest, no echo sparked through the erratic flux in the Storlain Mountains. Unflinching as basilisks, Roaco's enclave rebuffed the piercing regard of Sethvir.

Althain's Warden preferred not to heckle that wasps' nest. Elsewhere, his watch saw the lightning-burst flare of event subside into latent absence. No faction's curiosity rippled in hindsight. The True Sect's high talent stayed buried in blinkered complacency under the Light of their Canon. No gifted clanborn scryer alive owned the experience to note the fleeting radiance of the Paravian presence. Day on day, undisturbed, Mankind's contentious trade and belligerence chased their entrenched pursuits on the continent. Lawful sufferance under the compact granted the townsmen's activity free rein: which peril plucked at the quivering string, tensioned for the unsounded note that threatened humanity's future.

Fate dangled upon the unravelling question: how the old races might choose

344

to respond to their accidental disclosure. The uncertainty made Asandir hair-trigger cross. Sethvir gave his annoyance the wary stare of a discomposed cat, unable to measure the outcome, given Tehaval Warden himself had spun the strategic gaps in his earth-sense.

"From a nuisance akin to being nibbled by ducks, we're like cripples dodging loose knives in a fiend storm," Kharadmon grumbled in passing. "All we need is a green Matriarch's fork in the broth to spike the last hope held between us."

Sethvir poured fresh tea in scalded offence. "Avert!" His greater awareness already grappled that cup of fermenting poison. The upset accession to the Prime seat elevated a creature smelted in the crucible of an excessively cruel punishment. Lirenda was a dark-horse entity, re-emerged from centuries of oblivion. The restive seethe of her displaced opposition lent a juggernaut spin to the jackstraw toss of grim industry bent upon war.

On the hour she chose to exert supreme power, her brazen demand for a mandated summons jerked the snarls of dissent and stripped every single established sisterhouse of its administrative authority. The stroke dropped with no warning, served upon her ranked peeresses by a crystal transmission, thrust into the message relay.

Which dissonant shock, punched through offworld quartz, grazed Sethvir's skittish awareness at Althain Tower. His startled cough sprayed a mouthful of tea across a leaf of new manuscript.

"Fiends plague!" Arrested by stark fascination, he ignored the marred parchment, instead riveted on the blistering recoil, as one hundred and eighty Senior enchantresses snapped short under their upstart Matriarch's leash.

Loudest, the appalled dismay of those farthest from Whitehold, who confronted the harsh inconvenience of travel when winter's last snowpack choked the high passes. Low country, melt frothed the fords in full spate. While thaw softened the trade-roads to sucking quagmires, traffic with urgency moved by the southcoast galleys, with scarce passage sold dear at peak season.

"Clever timing, Lirenda," Sethvir murmured, disarmingly vacuous as his broad-scale awareness mapped her bold strategy: isolated by distance, from all points, and hobbled by adverse conditions, the dissatisfied peeresses and their Senior entourages would be disunited for months, with no chance given to regroup.

"Outclassed ahead of the party, my dears." Beard split by a barracuda flash of bared teeth, the Sorcerer ruminated, "Though I'd pillow my head on a sack full of scorpions before taking a step in Lirenda's shoes."

The succession's end-play must unfold in due course. Immersed in the dicey present, meantime, Sethvir framed a contrite request, then swept his quill feather across the spoiled parchment. Marred ink realigned like snapped ribbon under the splattered tea, which obligingly dried without stain. Althain's Warden scribed his next line. The measured scratch of his pen resumed in sunlight, and continued under the wan moon, while the ebb and flood of the tide marked its measure, and Mankind's affairs on the continent implacably darkened towards bloodshed.

War's prelude fired the oratory of the priests and clattered to the painted-bone dice, cast by the mustered dedicates packed into the seamy ale-houses. Pending violence rode the clogged indoor air, in the sour redolence of unwashed wool, wet leather, and rust, with the reek of goose greased steel welted through the fecund tang of fresh buttermilk. Against the vigorous splash of spring rain, tension shrilled through the wharf-side exchange, where brokers moving the bids for supply haggled over last year's grain stores.

While True Sect tacticians bent their eyes north, with pin counters arrayed on The Hatchet's maps of the Plain of Araithe, the clans withdrawn to Strakewood braced for invasion. Sethvir tracked the tension in their council circles. He tasted their despair in the night, as the harried scouts reported off watch, and grim women plaited green hide for the spring traps. No plan offered a clear course of action. The seers' talent needed to thwart ghastly odds raised no visions, only formless menace and dread.

Foresight of the assault remained veiled, even to Siantra's exceptional gift. Amid fear like rasped flint, her youthful inexperience failed to recognize the gravid pause seizing the flux.

Sethvir's earth-sense grasped the awful, pent hush, the storm's eye where possibility locked before an on-coming nexus. Momentum converged, as unstoppable forces cascaded into alignment. Althain's Warden listened for the snapped twig at the forefront, ruffled to gooseflesh in the twilight draught spilled through his opened casement. By nights, he tended his seedling herbs. Daily, he tracked the melancholy honks of north-flying geese, chorused against the crack of calved glaciers and the browsing of gravid deer. Nothing else spoke in the natural world. Whatever arose to deflect the world's course, the catalyst stayed elusive.

A fortnight crept past. Late-falling sleet tapped the pillars at Northgate, where scoured rock wore leaden puddles. Southward, rain sheeted through the Mathorns, roaring in runnels down the ravines that hampered The Hatchet's deployment. Teams hauling supply to Etarra splashed at a crawl up the trade-road, goaded by swearing teamsters. Draught animals threw shoes, and huddled, heads lowered, while dismounted outriders laboured to shift laden wagons bogged to the axles. Dedicates on cut rations scoured rust from their mail, miserable and raked by disease from encampments wallowed to a standstill.

Throughout, like stranded pearls in the burlap of workaday commerce, came the Koriathain summoned to Whitehold. Clustered in their red-and-violet mantles, they endured the packed inns, purses flattened by premium rates. They dickered with tight-fisted galley-men for deck space, or shared quarters within a cramped cabin, nerves flayed by quartz-amplified talent. From the eastshore, they braved the rough passage by ship. Overland, from the west, sisters traversed Araethura on mule-back to the Backwater ferry, then boarded the flat barges at Daenfal with the caravans bound on to Shipsport.

When the first arrivals from Highscarp straggled into the Whitehold sister-house, the pique ignited by the uprooted peeress's reception snagged Althain's Warden's attention. In simultaneous pursuit of a sink-hole through time, opened by the doings of dragons, he glanced up in the darkness fallen over his tower seat in Atainia. . .

"Stars above! Lirenda has no justifiable cause! A talent sounding, demanded of us?" The sister's dismay railed against the invasive assay customarily applied to rank novices. "The imposition's a criminal insult!"

"None are exempt." The initiate minding the gatehouse qualified without sympathy. "Your Prime has her purpose, which demands your unquestioned obedience." Or else hazard the inflexible penalty for oath breaking . . .

Sethvir tracked the stew of road-wearied outrage, denied due relief to clean off clinging mud, seek a meal, or exchange closet gossip. Quarantined instead, Highscarp's arrivals seethed in isolation, while their peeress received summons, alone. The Prime's choice to conduct her sessions in private brushed fore-warning across Sethvir's faculties.

For the Whitehold peeress was established in power, not wont to be cowed by a pretender one step above her own station. Particularly when a subservient testing invited a contest to seize brute control: a pitched duel of folly against the order's only eighth-level initiate, a former First Senior herself, groomed lifelong for the Prime succession. The subordinate sister's downfall gave Lirenda legitimate cause to prosecute her rival for disobedience. Sethvir witnessed the summary reprisal, brutalized by the burn as the Prime's master sigil excised the rebellious defector. The condemned peeress survived as a vacant puppet, useful for menial chores and rote service with no spark of conscious intelligence.

"To Sithaer's darkest pit with your order's unnatural practice!" fumed Althain's Warden, the reach of his hands tied twice over. Whitehold lay under town law, subject to Melhalla's crown justice; and the charter that underpinned royal authority rested on the compact's tenet of free choice. He could not save an initiate sister oathsworn under crystal unless she placed a direct appeal to the Seven for help to reclaim her autonomy.

Without recourse, the Sorcerer banged a fist on the table in acid frustration. "Dharkaron, Angel of Vengeance! If I believed in sordid redress, I would cast the fabled black Spear and have done with the order. Rue the day, until the violation allows us the due process for a swift destruction."

Until then, the Fellowship's might stayed constrained. Sethvir did nothing, *nothing at all*, except bear cold witness as the peeress's subordinate was called, next in line. Today's horror would repeat, as the ordeal screened the ranked seniors one by one. No sister raised to red rank was exempt. Those who harboured dissent would be culled, crushed, or cowed, before their resistance fermented.

"The vicious price of a disputed succession," Sethvir remarked, unimpressed by a sovereignty forged under tyranny. The claimant to the Prime seat was no longer an obvious creature, wedded to ambition. Punishment had annealed Lirenda's spirit and throttled her natural emotions. Her controlled intent barely inflected the probable future, a concern that taxed Sethvir's nerves.

He sharpened his nib with fussy precision, while his broad-scale awareness sifted Mankind's doings and measured their impacts, all the way down to the pebbles ground under the boots of The Hatchet's dedicate troops. He knew what disrupted the high-flying swallows and the nestled colonies of roosting bats. From the stir of the currents in the black deeps, alive with the flicker of schooling fish to the rumbling purr of a khetienn with kittens, to the roar of white magma far belowground, the living trace of Arithon Teir's'Ffalenn as yet eluded his grasp.

"Dharkaron's Five Horses trample the hindmost!" Althain's Warden hurled his pen. The quill shrieked through the air and struck with quivering distress, nib impaled in the granite wall. Too galling, the stalemated consolation, that the impasse stymied the new Prime Matriarch's aggressive interests as well . . .

Lirenda swept into Whitehold's main hall, her step swallowed by cavernous emptiness. The purple fall of her over-robe whispered echoes across gleaming marble, icy under the morning light spilled through the harbourfront casements. The rumble of barrels rolled by the wharf's industrious stevedores thrummed through her hollow chest. Behind the plate armour of discipline, fear frazzled her nerves.

For the truth gutted pretence. Selidie's upset left a yawning breach. Lirenda mounted the dais to the Prime seat as the rightful claimant, her grasp firm on the reins of the Matriarch's absolute power. Show doubt, and her subordinate Seniors would tear her apart like starved jackals.

She was the last eighth rank and fittest to rule. Yet the core purpose that steered the Koriathain had died with her predecessor, the historic, first gap in a heritage unbroken for countless millennia.

Aristocrat to the bone, Lirenda came steeled for the challenge. Gold combs pinned up her sable hair. The diadem on her brow glittered like twilight's frost with amethysts and diamonds. Her accomplished deportment salved nothing. The Fellowship runes impressed below her raised chair mocked her toothless authority. More than proof of an oath kept intact, Asandir's handiwork served up the constant reminder of Selidie's miscalculation.

The sisterhood's future hung in the balance. Trip over the dangerous holes in her knowledge, and the True Sect's zeal for burning talent might turn on the order. Their priesthood must be held in check, as the brush-fire expansion of Canon writ also suppressed the outbred offshoots of talent Koriathain required to restore their pruned ranks.

Noxious thoughts, as the bossed doors opened. A pair of trustworthy sisters, grey-clad and marked by the white ribbons of charitable service escorted two more docile figures, bovine stares and slack features vacant. These were followed by lackeys, who arranged eleven carved chairs in a half circle before the dais.

Then Whitehold's summoned Seniors arrived for their joint audience. They bent their stiff knees in obeisance, until their new Prime's flicked fingers bestowed leave to rise. Erect in discomfort, not permitted to sit, they faced dread and intimidation. Their former peeress, and the sisterhouse's subordinate senior, now being prodded to kneel like cud-chewing cattle, both rendered witless for use at their Matriarch's beck and call.

Morriel, before, kept two pretty, matched boy wards to fetch and carry for her convenience. After her, Selidie had enslaved Lirenda for menial service. Yet this brazen display of their fallen superiors shocked the breath from the Seniors just released from isolation.

Lirenda sealed her ascendance before the stunned gathering. "Behold the forsworn, disclosed by trial and swiftly condemned for insurrection. Witness their demise! I will tolerate no secret dissent! Sisters who toy with conspiracy will be stripped without quarter." Dead-pan, Lirenda breathed in the taint of her subordinates' acrid sweat. Cold patience learned under oppression let her extend their petrified expectation.

Amid the appalled silence, she broached her agenda. "Koriathain, you are the marrow of an order whose influence has spanned millennia. Our origin predates this world, and all you know of human history. I have no mercy for offenders because on your shoulders, and in my hands rests a guarded repository of human knowledge beyond our collective experience. Everything that we are, and the sum of our sisterhood's tireless work for Mankind's betterment has been thrown into jeopardy. This critical hour sets our founders' purpose under siege as never before. Surmount adversity, or founder in ruin, our deeds at this cross-roads will define us."

Before stopped expectation, a shimmer of jewels as Lirenda stood before her raised chair. Eyes the flat brass of the lioness raked over her following, formless as wax to be shaped by her mould. "The murderous strike at my predecessor also destroyed priceless assets. Along with the lives of our best Senior Circle, we have lost an irreplaceable focus stone and its store of encoded records. This disaster has weakened our vital strength, and I tell you now: we may never reckon the damage inflicted by Prince Arithon on that bitter night in Daon Ramon Barrens."

One outraged sister exclaimed, "Retribution is long overdue for that rogue sorcerer's crimes."

Lirenda's raised hand quelled the outburst. "Yes! But the order's recovery takes priority while we pick up the pieces." Her salvo of orders was brutal and brief. "At the threshold of war, time is urgent. You'll return to the Highscarp sisterhouse forthwith. The husks of the condemned go with your company, tasked under my thralled directive. They will catalogue the library. You'll surrender every book, every scroll, every journal and folio of correspondence, and also the imprinted contents encoded in crystal. Throughout, your mindless sisters will work under lock and key, sequestered until I've reviewed the compiled index in person and detailed the list for initiate access."

Against stunned speculation, Lirenda rammed through her next point. "You Seniors, meantime, will conduct an assay of our underling talent. Determine which sisters are fit for promotion and submit them for a prompt investiture. Any endowed with augmented seer's talent will be transferred from charitable service immediately and reassigned to the lane watch."

The new Prime trampled over murmured consternation. "An onerous tour of duty, I realize! But by stark necessity, our order must rally! Enact my commands with unquestioned diligence."

Lirenda courted no illusions. She had to strengthen the sisterhood's defences, and where overt power was lacking, fresh resource must seek the levers for extortionate pressure against outside threats.

"I'll receive the summary transmissions twice daily, with the following topics marked for imperative report. Any change in Lysaer's status at Erdane; also all forecasts made by Dakar the Mad Prophet. I want instant word of the forsworn third-rank initiate, Elaira, whose sanctuary under Davien's protection thwarts her sentence for treasonous liaisons. Last and not least, if Arithon Teir's'Ffalenn should return to the continent, I'll be told where he sets foot ashore. No more holding him hostage as a captive resource. For Selidie's death, and for the vicious blow dealt to our order, I declare his life forfeit. Do whatever's required to corner him."

That ringing closure flickered probable shadows, formless as smoke reeled off a snuffed flame.

Sethvir whumped his book shut in vexation. The ephemeral harbinger fore-ran yet *another* on-coming nexus, with humanity's fate already treading the ghastly precipice of reprisal. The new Prime failed to grasp the harsh scope of the stakes, or the blood-bath a mis-step could unleash if reaction compelled a Fellowship response. For Lirenda's blind directive to sift through the layered sediment of history thrust the proverbial poker into the white-hot coals of disaster.

Chills broke Sethvir to a cold sweat: for sooner or later, the witless sisters appointed to scour the Koriani library would disclose the forgotten annals of an event far more wisely left to obscurity.

Late Spring 5925

Unveilings

Granted a gentle recovery at sea, guarded under the Ilitharis shipwrights' unrivalled protections, Arithon sails into the Salt Fens of West Shand, leaves Alithiel in concealment with his anchored sloop, and knowing the auric flare sown by his Paravian exposure fires the Fourth Lane like a beacon, drives onward through Falwood towards the south spur of the Storlains to bring reckoning to his enemies . . .

Lysaer's fit of curse-driven rage shreds the night quiet at Erdane's High Temple, alerting a wakeful priest at his prayers, and by dawn, a dozen messenger pigeons take wing to the east bearing word of the Master of Shadow's return to the continent . . .

The first spark of the on-coming fire-storm sends diligent lane watchers to their Prime Matriarch with the prioritized news: "The gambit to reel in your quarry's in play. His Grace of Rathain has deferred his pursuit of Elaira in favour of closing his feud with the Ettinmere shamans . . ."

XI. Black Dawn

W hile Sethvir paced in his tower eyrie, stymied by the absence of divergent portents, and Asandir in the field looked askance at the inexplicable calm fallen over Northgate's restive dragons, the Hatchet's reorganized campaign in Strakewood readied its assault against Rathain's entrenched war band. The oppressive dark prior to dawn cloaked its assembled position, the signal to advance awaiting first light.

Dakar sensed the imminent clash of engagement, overset by a horrific vision of bloodshed, splashed over virid, crushed moss. He kicked free of his blankets, swiped down the rooster tails of tangled hair at his nape, and struggled to dress. Shaky hands snarled his points and laces. He snagged toes as he clawed on his boots and swayed as he stood on the crumpled-down heels.

"Dharkaron Avenger's almighty bollocks!" He staggered outside, blundering at a sprint across the deep-woods clan outpost: too late to do aught to defray the attack but to spare what he might through scant warning.

Unchecked bursts of augury trampled his sight. He ploughed, clattering, through a rack of stretched hides and reeled into a hung bucket. Doused blind, he smashed into a cross-bar notched for javelins, woke someone's baby to wailing complaint, then folded across a target sack, left by children for archery practice.

"Fiends alive!" Back upright, shedding straw and blunt arrows, he griped, "Why not draw The Hatchet's charge here for the nuisance? We'd have dedicates toppled like ninepins."

The comment earned him an urchin's shied rock, which struck with a game

353

hunter's accuracy. The sentry at the encampment's perimeter used insults, but Dakar owned no scrap of attention to spare for his injured feelings.

His distraught haste located Deshir's council seers, sequestered in their secluded lodge beneath the inked canopy of ancient trees. The best and most resolute plied their talent, still, against odds seeking last-minute guidance.

Yet their most persistent courage was ashes, all hope of a pre-emptive action too late. Dakar barged ahead to sound the alarm, shocked again by the roil of imminent slaughter. He blundered into a guy string. Jerked tent canvas billowed. Entangled and cursing, he measured his length, while someone within broke away from the circle and pushed through the flap to investigate.

"Dakar?" Siantra's spidery grip caught his elbow, the brush of her braid a ghost figment against his flushed cheek. "You're unwell?"

The Mad Prophet scarcely heard her suggestion to seek refuge ahead of the onslaught.

"You should go, yourself," he entreated, against rising nausea.

"In due time." Her bravura was feigned.

Dakar's fraught talent pierced her reserve, tracking the stifled anxiety bound to the talisman threads on her wrist. She had linked her awareness to the family signatures of Esfand, Khadrien, and Laithen s'Idir, and other Names alongside of those she held dearest.

"You can't stay for them," Dakar entreated.

Siantra shook her head, voiceless. True-Sighted since Athili, she had been forced to recognize the locked nexus that fixed a course of event. A dissociate trance could no longer outpace the raw ripple of on-coming trauma. Wise counsel, caught blinkered, must split the clan lineages, some to fly southward into the Mathorn peaks, while others risked summer's pestilent fevers in refuge amid the fenlands to the north.

"Start the exodus. Now!" Dakar pleaded, sick at heart for the wakeful babe, likely doomed.

Siantra sighed, shaken. "Esfand issued the order. Some families refused. Khadrien's with the rear-guard, as protection. But truthfully, nobody's fooled."

Fear shrouded the encampment's flux currents like cobweb. Bogged in the miasma, Dakar fought to breathe, wrung clammy with feverish sweat.

Siantra took pity. "You can't linger. You'll go mad. I'll find you an escort."

"No." Dakar pushed her away, before the forewarning tingle of his errant vision disclosed the ghastly scope of the catastrophe. Sorrow would come, though by grace not beforetime under his inept handling.

No flight could outstrip what descended on Strakewood. The Hatchet's onslaught was an invasive swarm, by foot troops alone pitched thirty to one against Rathain's furtive defenders. When sunrise blazed red through green leaves, the waiting hush shattered, bird-song fled before strident horn-calls. The front ranks advanced to a cloudless day's thunder of hoof-beats and drums, rent by the screams of the first dedicate casualties. Others followed in a breaking wave. Fallen shuddered like mangled dolls in the fern-brakes, impaled upon pit stakes dug into the ground. More were punched down by bunched arrows as they avoided other men dropped in writhing agony by spring traps, or horses, collapsed, threshing in disembowelled heaps. Where Arwi Unfrey's trackers ran their mute hounds, the dogs perished before they flushed out clan prey, convulsed without sound, noosed and strangled in snares. Over the sodden, torn ground with its wrack of butchered flesh, the second companies closed in tight wedges. Numbers told, over time. Steel blessed for the Light of the Canon and glory swept the routed resistance ever deeper into the forest.

Brightening day saw the third and fourth assaults surge in, relentless as tide, each enemy onslaught trampling over the savaged ground scoured by the last. The shock recoiled through the free-wilds flux and riffled the gyres spun off the forbidden glades, the ancient well-springs of the mysteries besieged as red chaos enveloped the heart-wood. Dakar flinched and wept in dread of the consequence. The percussive knell would rattle Althain Tower, if violation upset those sacrosanct sites. Failure was unforgiving, should Strakewood's lane currents become harrowed to dissonance that tipped the spiral towards entropy. The Sorcerers had not intervened, which grave absence lent weight to the stark dearth of auguries. If Rathain's clans lost sovereignty, defeat weighed the grant that permitted Mankind's cohabitation. The harsh reckoning loomed, however valiant the stand taken by the day's feal defenders.

Dakar careened down a bank, lashed by spruce boughs, too heartsick to grapple the reason behind the Seven's delinquent presence. He splashed through a stream, skidded on mossy rocks, and plunged waist deep into the swift eddies. He veered up the far bank, away from the falls that frothed in stepped descent towards the grottoes. Sodden hose blistered his heels as he clambered for handholds in scrambling ascent.

Arrived at the ragged rim of the ravine, misted by the flung spray thrashed off the River Tal Quorin, the Mad Prophet collapsed to his knees. Distance from the battle-front brought little relief. He shuddered with dry heaves, while the mangling press of clashed steel and the sucker-punch shock of fatalities pummelled him helpless. He clung, curled in spasms, while dislodged pebbles bounced off the brink, rattled down the cliff-face, and flicked through the sun-motes that dappled the canyon below. Bird-song trilled overhead, a live counterpoint to the past resonance of a Masterbard's paean of release: mage-sense still captured the residual echo, ghosted through the ravine. Dakar wept for the remnant of Arithon's inspired healing, which had settled the slain in a historic conflict as bitter as this one.

Mercy on today's vivid fallen, who would receive no such requite peace in the aftermath. Their on-going, agonized passage brutalized the Mad Prophet near witless with ungoverned empathy.

"Twice brainless and ten times the fool," the miserable spellbinder groaned through his teeth.

Wisdom had better sense. The carnage at Lithmarin had established his uselessness, mired under the misery of a battle-field. Hands clutched to his reeling head, Dakar rocked in sick wretchedness, addled as a skin full of jelly.

The nearby, rhythmic stroke of a knife carving wood at length penetrated his shattered attention. Surprised to find he was not alone, Dakar glanced sideward and discovered Iyat-thos Tarens worked almost on top of him.

"You didn't appear to want company, either." The laconic apology masked bitter rage: despite a renowned war captain's experience, he was not bearing arms alongside Strakewood's defenders. The exclusion hit hard, given that his harsh counsel to relocate the clans had not lifted the threat of extermination.

"I've always shirked the glory of sacrifice." Dakar sat, sweaty hands clasped over his knees. "My equally ostracized vantage suggests no moral need to explain yourself."

"No," Tarens agreed. "But were Arithon here, he would seek to buy time for the children and mothers in flight."

"Not in that way!" Dakar objected, appalled by what Tarens crafted. Old injustice fuelled the vicious calm, busy shaving a pointed stake. The knife flashed, angled for the expert, last cut, which split the green wood with the wicked, hooked back-slash. The flexible barb would open on recoil, sunk deep into dedicate flesh.

Dakar jammed his palms over his mouth before his roiled guts revolted. Too readily, the bumpkin drawl sugared over the fiendish precision of Jieret's touch with a spring trap.

Misapprised by Rathain's clansmen himself, Dakar grumbled, "You'd think these backwoods ferals might credit an ally, given you skewered a Canon examiner under the lances of an arrest squad."

"Well red-handed murder wasn't my birthright," Tarens remarked, his snarl forced past teeth clamped on the peg for the trigger latch, "until the unnatural creature threatened my family."

For him, as for Jieret, hatred of the fanatics carried the septic sting of experience. The last host to storm Strakewood had visited atrocities upon women, children, and elders: a legacy never more poignant than here in the verdigris gloom above the grottoes, where a mother and four innocent younger sisters once had passed over Fate's Wheel in an unparalleled act of atrocity.

Dakar had not witnessed that ugly debacle. But he had Seen Jieret's array of brute tactics savage a campaign march staged through the narrows at Valleygap. That memory raised chills, despite the felt blanket of summer humidity. The burden of that uncanny influence more than hardened the kindly, straight grain of the crofter's character. Strakewood's war woke a cold-cast ferocity better off left buried and sleeping. Rightfully, Jieret Red-beard had been feared for the ruin visited upon his enemies.

The laugh lines weathered into tanned flesh at the plough underscored the wolf's gleam in the eyes. As though the flash-marked vista was not centuries gone, where Lysaer's levin-bolt strike had immolated a tent refuge to carbon, the large, farmer's hands worked with terrible steadiness, lashing the trigger string onto a sapling, toothed with vicious spikes. No generosity softened the set of the jaw beneath the crooked nose. On this day, ruthlessness re-birthed the cycle of murderous slaughter.

Or maybe not: Dakar realized the crofter expected to die here, haplessly bound to the iron resolve of a *caithdein*'s responsibility. Dread sparked by the gift of the seer held in common, he blurted, "What do you See?"

Deft fingers looped the trigger noose. A deliberate foot lifted, tenderly, off the arched wood until the bend stabilized under tension. A killer's preternatural concentration suggested Dakar's question would dangle, unanswered.

But then, Tarens said, "That no trespasser lives to desecrate this place. I promised Esfand." Which statement blew like a cold wind from the past, rejecting anew the untenable agony of a generation fallen to butchery. For Tarens, who mourned two nephews taken by fever, the sorrows of untimely death bit too deep. "I met The Hatchet's measure at Torwent. He is the High Priest's rogue mastiff, an outcast raised without nurture, then baited to ravening madness."

Slaughter would not stain Tal Quorin's banks uncontested, nor would reiving troops run amok without penalty on the savage license of victory. Jieret's legacy and Tarens's tender pity rewrote yester-year's script, and riddled the sunken ravine with a diabolical gamut of snares.

Rushed by the tingle of battle-charged prescience, Dakar bit his tongue, expecting to silence the grisly barrage of this moment's lethal handiwork. Pain failed to curb the onslaught of vision. Instead, the coppery tang of fresh blood unsealed his runaway faculties. Vertigo pitched him onto his face. Reeled limp, he howled until his lungs emptied. Then starless darkness swallowed his fit and dropped him, witless, into prophecy.

Dakar woke to the thump of his nape on a rock. A stick slapped his ear. Then stiff stands of bracken whipped his cheek under a fluttering fringe of bent fronds. He moaned, sneezing spores, knotted helpless with dry heaves. His feeble attempt to fend off the abuse trounced him over a rotten log. Split lids dealt him the punishing dazzle of sunlight, speared through a spinning view of the tree-tops. He hung upside down. Someone's barbaric grip on his ankles dragged him headlong through the forest.

His garbled attempt at a protest half-choked him on an inhaled leaf.

Movement stopped. The merciless hold let him down. Tarens's chalk features swam into his revolving sight.

"Fatemaster's mercy," the crofter admonished, voice blurred under ringing overtones. "Thank me later. Your thrashing fit almost carried you over the cliff."

Dakar spat out bile and grit, and husked through a percussive headache,

"What did I say?" Always, his unconscious bouts were true augury, fated with inexorable certainty. Fear spurred his alarm. *What did I say?*

Tarens averted his glance in discomfort. "Enough not to wait out your puking back-lash."

"Don't imagine you'll keep the impact to yourself." Dakar wrestled distressed equilibrium and propped himself onto one elbow. Near movement showed him the crofter, back turned, knife busy disarming a spring trap. "Tarens! What are you doing?"

"Saving your hide from my miserable work." The snick of the blade severed a laid string. The arched-over sapling whipped straight in release, spiked stake whistling in harmless recoil.

Dakar mewled, "You're leaving?"

Tarens's reply rang on the ear like clashed chimes. "Southward! At speed! Before Strakewood's verge is surrounded."

Cramped double by sickness, Dakar ground out, "Forget the traps. We can't outrun the slaughter! When Deshir falls, and The Hatchet's conquest defiles the forbidden glens, Mankind's tenancy will be revoked by the terms of the Fellowship's compact."

Tarens ignored sense and plunged on, "Don't descend by Split Rock, there's a pitfall with stakes. The scouts' markers will show you the safe trail across the Tal Quorin."

The spellbinder argued, unable to tell whether his plea had been heard or if his jangled hearing fore-ran a relapse into tranced prescience. "Barking donkey! Earl Jieret might argue your final stand should serve the clan's covenant to safeguard the mysteries."

"No! The late High Earl's spirit forces my choice." Floated back through the rush of the falls, the crofter's anguished, last words spiked Dakar to terror: "The compact won't fall into jeopardy here! Nor will Deshir's heart-wood be threatened. Fellowship help will not arrive, *because your blind prophecy spelled warning at Ettin and Daenfal!*"

The Light's advance into Strakewood, meantime, showed no sign of let-up. Midafternoon cooked the jaundiced gloom under canvas where The Hatchet maintained his tactical headquarters on open ground to the east. Despite tied-back flaps, the air was stifling. Staffers and field officers streamed anxious sweat, in wait for requests and instructions from the helmeted conclave bent over the chart trestle. The engagement's press reeked of blood and exertion, pierced from outside by screams from the surgeons' camp, and the quick-marched tread of relief squads called up for swift reinforcement. Jammed at the centre, a squat caricature in glittering chain-mail, The Hatchet peered up at the third company's runner, who wheezed through another report. "The enemy war band's boxed on three sides, taking heavier losses. We'll have their backs when they run out of arrows."

"You say!" The Hatchet's crow split his nutcracker jaw, like filed iron with several days' stubble. "By dusk, we'll finish them!" His elated fist thumped on the tactical map. The doomed jumble of enemy counters bounced helter-skelter off the breastplates of his officers, then rolled underfoot, mashed with relish under his boot-heel. "Light's glory, we'll gut the resistance right here. Where's fourth company's runner?"

Enthused, in his element, The Hatchet leaned over the map. "By now, our skirmish lines should have swept the low ground. Once their relay confirms, I'll close our flanks like a pincer. Rout the rats up Tal Quorin's ravine, where our fifth will meet them at the head-water. Crossbowmen stationed on the rim can mop up the rear-guard survivors, neat as shooting trapped fish in a barrel."

A stir shuffled the bystanders at the entry. Impatient, The Hatchet waved the messenger off and barked orders at the sallow captain beyond. "Ready your foot to march out. Full armour. I want axemen and pikers with bill-hooks. Chew through the infested coverts, and drop any varmints that bolt."

"Fourth company's runner has yet to report," the Light's message officer cautioned.

The crest on The Hatchet's helm whipped left. One jaundiced eye fixed on the splotched smock of the battle surgeon. "Why are you here? If there's a supply problem, damn well collar my quartermaster!" Without stopping, he snapped, "Where in Shadow's black arsehole is Arwi Unfrey? His runner's late, too. I need him with trackers and dogs straight away to run point for the task force dispatched to clear out the canyon."

No witness rushed forward to break the bad news: the clever league head-hunter had died, messily, sawn nearly in half by a noose snare. The uneasy pause wore, filled by the metallic scrape of shifted accoutrement. Then the outside upheaval, gaining momentum, brought raised voices. Discord clashed through the clangour of arms as the pressured sentinels braced for a barricade.

"Fiends plague! What's that dastardly racket?" The Hatchet craned his bull neck. View obscured by his staff officers, he rammed forward, elbows raked up like a mantled fighting cock. Counters crunched under his hobnailed soles. Petitioners wedged in his way jumped like lackeys, treading on toes. An equerry bearing a tray dodged aside, spilling his pitcher. Thrust past him, dripping, The Hatchet stamped through the air-borne flutter of napkins.

No overdue messenger fielded his wrath. Instead, a ceremonial procession inundated his active command post. A tinkling nuisance of bell-ringers and hooded penitents with brass cymbals escorted three palanquins crammed with priests in jewelled regalia. The outrageous parade stonewalled his out-bound runners. More, against shouted threats, several acolytes with mirrored lamps borne on wands jostled the stance of his posted guards.

The Hatchet jammed short, just shy of a collision. Choked by a billow of incense smoke, he ducked a lit censer. The back-swing clanged against his armoured nape and stuttered the bell-ringers' rhythm. Pelted by sparks, he snuffed his singed horsehair crest with a murderous clap of his gauntlet.

Through a hacked cough, he exploded, "Which lick-spittle chump do I hang by the bollocks?" His swipe broke the golden chain of the censer. "We already suffered devotions at sunrise. That puppet-show wafted blessings enough to gag a maggot at forty paces!" His throw pitched the bauble in a fuming arc, which quenched with a hiss of steam in a horse trough. "I'm conducting a war! I'll not have your faithful die unsupported while my chain of command gets bogged down by posturing mummery."

Shocked silence descended. The officers crowded within the command tent stared, stunned, while the High Priest at the forefront unfurled his stiff finery. Emerged from his tasselled palanquin, chalky with offence, he extended a ringed hand with a scroll.

"I'm asked to bestow a clerk's scribble on *this?*" Confronted by supercilious frost, The Hatchet tipped his chin, brows bunched as the boss on a bull flagged to gore.

"No endorsement's required." Wax seals glinted, ribboned in state formality. "A direct mandate from the Light's blessed avatar demands your compliance. Immediately."

The Hatchet snatched the document. His violent irritation shattered the seals and batted away the burst ribbons. He snapped open the roll, the sparse contents read at a glance.

His face purpled. Reflections juddered over his armour as he snapped the divine edict over his shoulder. A gasp confirmed his tense subordinate's receipt of the content: affixed to cream parchment, verified by the seal of Erdane's temple council, a thin strip of rice paper carried by bird bore the light-burned impression of a thumb print. Beneath, the gilt ink of divine effrontery ordered the withdrawal of the Light's forces from Strakewood.

"Pull back, you say? *Disengage with all speed and quick march my war host two hundred leagues to the south?*" The Hatchet's galled tirade gained pitch. "Abandon my victory and disown the sacrifice of my fallen? Over my bloodied carcass! I'll rend Strakewood's clan menace to carrion, first."

"The barbarians can be broken another day," The priest dismissed with superior sang-froid. "Our avatar is the will of the godhead, personified. Bow to Lord Lysaer's sacred directive or be damned for apostasy. Decree says the Spinner of Darkness has set foot in West Shand. Refuse to destroy the tap-root of evil, and Canon Law condemns you as Shadow's collaborator, to be pierced by the sword for the fire. Embrace destiny, before higher wisdom sets a more devoted man in your place. Sound the retreat. The invasion stops. Now."

The Hatchet fumed, butted up to the Sunwheel blazon on the High Priest's chest. "I'll cede the day on command. But when the Master of Shadow is taken, no trial and no quarter! I'll drive the blade through his black heart myself, and torch his remains on the scaffold."

* * *

The war host's abrupt disengagement from Deshir began with a trickle. Messengers dispatched at a lathered gallop to reorder the supply lines stitched dust across the Plain of Araithe, where spring's lush growth leached to pale yellow, and the breeze fore-running the dry blaze of summer waved tasselled seed-heads. As though the outriders carved the path for a flood, the pebbled helms of ranked dedicates followed. First the mounted divisions, their white-and-gold banners flanked by the snap of the emblazoned company standards.

After, splashed like foam over newly chopped turf, came the resplendent dazzle of the vested priests, foot ranks surrounding the gilt-fringed palanquins heralded by braying horns, and cowled acolytes singing adoration. At their heels, the teams of cream oxen plodded with capped horns and caparisoned harness, hauling the temple drays laden with hampers of incense, and folded pavilions, and chests of holy paraphernalia.

The glissades of trumpets gave way, in turn, to the throb of the drums, matching the tramp of the dedicate infantry. The host milled ochre dust from the beaten earth, its flood thinned to a mud-coloured draggle of camp-followers: the cooks' and the smiths' wagons, the laundresses and the harness menders, trailed by the sentenced labourers and the officers' equerries. Last came the rear-guard, felted in dust, its arrowed formations of outriders chivvying stragglers and the ragged jetsam of feral children.

The massed passage roiled the natural flux, a disturbance compounded as, wave upon wave, the host trampled the bank of the upper Liffsey and splashed the churned ford to billowing silt.

The flare of upheaval ranged south on the lane tide, striking the sensitive leys beneath Kewar into dissonance. Elaira's talent affinity through water suffered the relentless barrage, no matter how fiercely she focused upon the research pursued by necessity. The distraction compounded her galling frustration as the exigent knowledge eluded her.

"Needles in haystacks at least would respond to a cantrip aligned to draw steel!" The enchantress huffed fallen hair from her eyes, and piled up the books that held nothing.

Extended hours by candlelight, and days spent rummaging through cupboards and mining the stacks atop lofty shelves had produced a sore neck and rife irritation. Reliable facts on the Biedar culture proved sparse, even in Davien's proscribed collection. "A sweet word of guidance would help, damn all to the blistering honour of Fellowship oaths!"

Her host could lend no assistance since the heirloom knife involved Arithon's fate. Worse, a culture whose eldritch lore evoked etheric discourse with their deceased ancestry had made written knowledge superfluous.

"Blight take the nuisance!" Discouraged, Elaira returned the borrowed tomes back to the shelves. "Can't the elders' finicky ties to their ghosts raise some benighted assistance?" For their mouldered cause, she had spent fruitless weeks, poring over generations' worth of crabbed script on fusty scrolls and flocked pages. She had nothing to show except eye-strain.

A frisson shuddered over her skin, dismissed as she flung open an aumbry and sequestered the final volume. The book slid into its place and hung up. Its flaked-leather spine jammed the door.

Grumbling, Elaira fished into the cranny and removed the obstruction: a thin treatise in an ancient cipher, apparently pushed out of place.

Sharper gooseflesh flicked her flesh in reproach. "I'm so sorry!" she gasped. "Entirely mine, the ignorant oversight." Too immersed, she had never imagined to ask; or else better sense shied from the unnatural peril. Since an unseen power fit to cross Davien's defences might take who *knew* what advantage of a free-will invitation, Elaira accepted the uncanny windfall with cautious humility.

The old script required three more scholarly texts on ancient languages, followed by a closer study of obscure dialect to grasp the content. Elaira rubbed ink smears from a wan cheek, as under her hand, the laborious notes in translation disclosed the properties bound into the Biedar knife. The arcana exceeded her minimal vocabulary and involved concepts beyond her depth. Yet *how* the blade's working outstripped the temporal bounds of perception did not matter. The purpose was clear. She guarded a talisman fashioned for striking magical bindings asunder.

That hard-won discovery roused her to inchoate dread, before triumph.

Elaira fretted through three idle days, still rudderless after months of intensive study. The constant disturbance of the outside flux skewed her attempts to scry Arithon's activity. Anxiety drove her to seek quiet refuge: not in the library, with its perilous secrets sequestered in parchment and ink, but in the ruined, parabolic chamber where the only fresh air could be found within Kewar's seclusion.

Her solitude did not last long before Davien remarked out of turn, from behind, "A True Sect company in an ordered retreat would not break due south towards Daon Ramon as the crow flies."

Resigned to the Sorcerer's inquisitive appearances, Elaira did not startle out of reverie. "This is your sideways jab to alarm me? In fact, the main war host bound for Etarra has split off a dedicate strike force?"

"A division of light horse just received a packet of urgent orders." Davien's word detailed the fore-running quiver of probability she had sensed through the flux. A treble note like tapped brass, the deflected tremor in the current arrowed towards the western horns of the Mathorns, on direct course down the lane sited through the Sorcerer's private retreat.

Elaira arose from her seat by the spring, which welled out of the deeps from a girdle of rock. The broken rim still showed the fragments of elaborate carving, sundered by a dragon's explosive emergence from her stone chrysalis of hibernation. Collected, the enchantress regarded Davien, poised like a lynx in a burned-orange doublet beaded with onyx. Immaculate without Kharadmon's rakish extravagance, he wore his hair loose, the frosted tumble of russet ice lit by a shaft through the holed dome overhead.

Elaira quashed her impulse to cringe. "To rout out the dread scourge of Shadow. I'd guessed. These days, the draw of Desh-thiere's curse seems a more reliable compass than my heart-linked affiliation."

Davien fielded her barb, complacent as mercury balanced on glass. "If you knew where your beloved has been, and what exalted company hosted his presence, the considerate ally makes no apology for Kewar's defensive shielding."

Elaira stabbed back, acerbic, "Without even the token pretence of free will?"

"Guest rights handed me the entitlement." Stone re-echoed the Sorcerer's tart astonishment. "The wards here forestalled a breach of *my* integrity." Watching her sidelong, Davien added with delicacy, "You'd prefer the brute ethic that permits harm to visit you under my roof?"

Unresigned to a disadvantaged defeat, Elaira held her ground before the deep pool, fathomless under the mirrored sheen of sky-caught reflection. "I resent being nurtured like a mushroom, planted neck deep in the dark!"

The Sorcerer's rapt silence forced the enchantress to outline the obvious. "My conjecture says his Grace has holed up in the Storlains, where the unstable flux lends the tactical edge to blind hostile scryers. But even there, my repeated failures outstrip credibility. I'm practised at nuanced evasion enough to see more than chaotic electromagnetics at work."

Davien hesitated, his gaze apparently fixed on a cloud drifted across the chink overhead. His reticence ceded Elaira no option except to pursue the lopsided discussion.

"The only time I've known Arithon to languish, his equilibrium had been frayed into grief by interaction with a Paravian." A hitched pause ensued, consumed by startled thought.

"Go on!" snapped Davien, his unnerving impatience reaffixed upon her as though welded.

Stunned, Elaira sat on the lip of the spring, numb to the chill as water wicked into the dipped drape of her skirt. "A back-lash caused by a Paravian visitation?" Rage catapulted her to accusation. *"For how long have you interfered with my awareness?"*

This time, Davien answered. "Only through the duration of proximal contact. Your extended blindness in the aftermath was not caused by my shielding."

Accustomed to the abstruse guidance dispensed by Fellowship Sorcerers, Elaira tackled the terrifying conundrum. "Which implies my beloved made landfall under a protection wrought by the old races themselves!"

Davien's opaque regard remained comfortless as a freeze out of season.

Which blunt absence of denial spurred Elaira's scathing conclusion. "If Arithon needed no refuge, he's hell-bound through the Storlains for some other purpose." Which point suggested the frightening reverse: surges through the region's destabilized flux would degrade even an exemplary working's efficacy. "His Grace plans to challenge the Ettinmere shamans over the lapsed terms of his oath?" That frightening truth fit. Character would drive Arithon to break their binding to a child, hooked into a sworn obligation whose breach afflicted his birthborn autonomy.

Elaira snatched a desperate breath. "Ath wept! Does Arithon have any grasp of the stakes?" Discipline brazened through logic to finish. "Unless he knows the roots of the enclave's power, he can't guess. His opponents will see him coming."

No brave front could thwart the invested perception of a Fellowship Sorcerer.

"I cannot abet your desire to warn him." Davien quashed the transparent leap of her hope. "Not only would your departure from Kewar throw you naked to your Prime's vengeance, I cannot sanction the choice." Not without the disaster of breaking Asandir's oath.

"I would be too late to intervene, anyway," Elaira declared, courageously conversational. The riddle spun by her late scrying was solved. Prince Arithon's activity explained why Dakar and Tarens had fled Strakewood as though hounded by Sithaer's furies.

If Davien appeared to receive her anguish in velvet-gloved quiet, she was not disarmed beyond sense. Her subtle analysis swept his bearing and read anxiety in the black wells of his pupils. The Fellowship Sorcerer was afraid.

Which dread discovery screamed risk. Reason flinched from the prospect of playing the reach of such fathomless power. And yet: the tremulous flicker of Davien's citrine ring spoke of intimate tenderness, behind his clenched fist.

Gestalt epiphany suggested a vulnerability deep as her own. "You love him, too," Elaira blurted, before thought. "After your own fashion." Embarrassed for her presumption, she blushed. "If you cannot break an untenable pledge, his Grace has powerful friends." The tribal elders at Sanpashir owned the main strength to stand as his ally.

"You have met the Matriarch of the Biedar." Davien need not elaborate, given the dagger bequeathed in conflict with her Koriani obligation: tribal interests did not rescue human fallibility. Nor were the desert-folk subject to the compact that secured mankind's leave to inhabit Athera.

Davien's gaze bored into Elaira. Intense as an artisan measuring clock-works, he watched her absorb disappointment. No intervention would come from Sanpashir. Biedar reckoning had acknowledged the Teir's'Ffalenn as a descendant of s'Ahelas ancestry. But he was not the last living scion of Requiar's blood lineage.

"I am not complacent," Elaira declared. "More, I have gathered the specific knowledge I came for."

That challenge snapped Davien's adamant silence. "Then press your free will and cross mine at your peril! A fool would presume to fathom my intentions, or worse, spurn the privilege of my hospitality. Be sure, Elaira, when the moment arrives, *if the opening presents,* my colleagues must act in behalf of your crown prince without hesitation."

"I don't know your directives," Elaira agreed, outmatched and outfaced as small prey gripped in the jaws of a predator. "Since the fool lacks your vision, what's left beyond a supplicant's plea of forbearance? Forgive the effrontery of short-sighted pain. I fear I might find scant cause to rejoice in the outcome arranged by your Fellowship!"

Davien laughed, his mercurial joy a reprieve against suffocating uncertainty. "My dear, your loyal heart is a treasure! Let's call an amicable truce and retire. I'd rather delight your sharp tongue with fine wine since the mess of stacked odds at the moment don't favour anyone's hope of felicity."

On last year's journey to Thunder Ridge, Iyat-thos Tarens and Cosach between them had dragged the Mad Prophet along by the scruff. Not protesting his misery as dead weight, at this pass, the fat spellbinder pushed through his slack endurance by arcane sorcery. Day upon day, streaming sweat in the heat, his choppy jog flanked Tarens's longer strides in a race against certain disaster. Panting exertion disallowed speech. Spirit acted, regardless, and wasted no breath on the sensible choice to stand down.

The chance to turn back became forfeit, regardless, as the hostile war host coalesced in withdrawal and ravaged the country behind them. Harried by The Hatchet's armed outriders, Tarens threw off pursuit. His inherited grasp of Rathain's terrain knew where the gulches softened to bogs, and which windswept hill-tops lacked cover. The rivers dividing the lowlands swirled past their first spate, still swift where the current buffeted, chest high. Forced to swim, the chilled travellers sunned themselves dry. They foraged for berries and milkweed shoots, and stalked game, until the open country made cookfires risky. When their reduced rations gave out, they pushed on and went hungry.

Two dozen leagues brought them to the stony track leading into the Mathorn foot-hills. There, they smoked speared fish over charcoal, nestled in the steep vales with their rucked blanket of fir, spangled white between the top branches where the looming summits wore late-season ice. Higher, they clambered over the treacherous rubble of a winter avalanche, splashed by the frigid, tumbling falls that rushed toward the placid, skeined streams in the dales far below.

Neither man mentioned reducing the pace. They snatched rest in catnaps and ate smaller game caught in the loop snares set at twilight.

Dakar tightened his belt, the slack paunch of his jerkin gathered like frills on a bolster. Privation raised none of his usual complaint. Nose and cheeks peeled the raw hue of blood sausage, he pumped upwards upon drumstick legs until breathlessness dropped him prostrate.

"Grace forsaken!" Tarens exclaimed. Forearms crossed upon his bent knee, he waited, while Dakar whooped, prone in the shade of an outcrop. "You'll serve no one's cause if you perish."

"Longevity training," the Mad Prophet gasped. "How many sweethearts did you wish you'd kissed? I'll rally ahead of the short count, for those who'd have slapped you in protest."

Tarens mopped his brow and raised sceptical eyebrows. "Aren't you a marvel for slippery deception! If Cosach would skin you from beyond the grave, I'll corner your pledge of unlimited beer for the fact you're a lying wastrel."

Dakar rolled onto his back, eyes pinched shut to escape spinning vision. "If I can't rise, we're dead. Or hasn't your access to Jieret's awareness checked on our back trail?"

There were hoof-beats, in fact, drummed through the ground and rapidly closing. Tarens swore. "League scalpers?"

"No. Worse," Dakar rasped. "We've got the Light's best troop of horse at our heels. They're not scouring the foot-hills for clansfolk. Canon mandate's dispatched them over the Mathorns for the same reason we're running south."

"They aim to take Arithon?" Tarens offered a hand, hauled Dakar to his feet, and towed his reeling frame uphill. "Then we'll have to outpace them. Or else become a trophy hunt for their trackers."

Jieret's wily evasion took them up the precarious trails through the ledges, over trapped ground that might slaughter or save them. There, the mountains buckled into sheer cliffs, and rock slides left treacherous heaps of debris jumbled into surprise bottle-necks. If frost and erosion had not fractured the scarp, a narrow foot track wound into the notches, impassable to mounted riders.

The climb blurred into a misery of windy nights and days of scant food, stitched by the bellows ache of short breath in the frigid, thin air. Between the gales that struck without warning, the cry of the kite split the lucent sky, while the groaning complaint of pressed ice underfoot foreran the grinding thunder when melt split the glacier into crevasses. Always cold, the travellers picked their way where a slipped step threatened a tumbling fall into the abyss.

Even Tarens's robust strength wore down to gaunt hollows, his scarred nose burned livid above cracking lips, and his eyes glazed to bloodshot exhaustion. Paused to soak blistered feet in a spring, he waited out Dakar's immersive trance, engaged to sound for the proximity of their pursuit.

"We will reach the divide ahead of the horsemen," the Mad Prophet confirmed, voice husked to a croak. The Light's mounted dedicates wound through the deep vales, where milder elevation gave access to fodder. "If we don't snag the interest of their diviner, we'll make the clan outpost above Leynsgap before they overtake us."

One threat less, against the greater concern, that with each passing day since the war host's withdrawal, The Hatchet's revised orders sent by advance messengers would be staging Etarra's reserves to the south. The ranks of the faithful would swell further as the temple's dovecotes sent off carrier birds, and town garrisons on the Eltair coast answered the imperative call to take arms. Daon Ramon would be swarming with troops, bound to Daenfal and Backwater for the Temple's muster against Shadow.

Tarens crammed his sore feet back into snagged hose and laced his torn boots without comment. Denial alone dulled the agonized knowledge that their race to thwart a predestined event was a gesture flung against futility.

A day's travel beyond the Mathorn divide, fogged in cloud where the stripped scarps combed the wind past the timberline, Tarens remarked on the lack of vigilant clan scouts. "They have not challenged our presence. Do we have to build a string clapper and signal them?"

"Be quiet!" snapped Dakar. Bearded and raffish, one ripped sole swathed in rags, he jerked to a stop between steps.

Tarens halted before slamming into him. "What's amiss? Did we stray?" Jieret's recall of the back route to Leynsgap was changeable, where seasonal ice savaged the rough terrain, and the dry-wall bridges over the chasms had to be rebuilt every year. His gesture encompassed a site scoured bare of stone markers, customarily stacked to blaze the trail during summer. "I don't know this place. All broken scree, and no lichen, as if we tread over the aftermath of a cataclysm."

"You feel unsettled?" Dakar rounded, eyes rolled to the whites. "Wise fellow, you should. We've attracted the Sight of an uncanny watcher."

Tarens scraped at his stubbled chin, his affable nature turned thoughtful as he plumbed the location from Earl Jieret's perspective. "Might your jeebies have something to do with the fact we're tramping down the back side of Kewar?"

Dakar smacked his forehead. "The devil!" He cat-footed forward. "Avert the cross-grained eye of Dame Fortune! Please, let's not reap the whirlwind of Davien's attention."

"Too late." Tarens yanked the spellbinder short by the collar. "We already have."

A tear in the mist unveiled an immense stone gryphon, carved in detail enough to seem living. The baleful, slant eye above the raptor's beak glowed ruby with warning.

Dakar shook off restraint. Shoulders squared beneath tattered clothes, he crept onwards through the chinking slag. "That forsaken thing's one of Davien's guardians, spellcrafted to repel trespassers. It's aware. Very dangerous. Keep a wide berth, show no disrespect, and beg for the forbearance that we'll be allowed leave to pass."

Something stirred in the sullen gloom beneath the statue's mantled wings. Presently, a slight person in a traveller's mantle emerged, hauling two lumpish packs. The unhooded features were not ascetic, or male, and the long, auburn braid belonged to no Fellowship Sorcerer.

Sight of her froze the Mad Prophet as though a storm crow had fluttered to roost.

"She's not armed," Tarens observed, "though she settles the flux as she moves like a clan scout. You believe she's a threat?"

"That's Arithon's Koriani enchantress! Worse than a case of the plague, and forbye, she shouldn't be here." The Mad Prophet stiffened, his pudding jaw jutted for a knock-down confrontation.

Tarens regarded the inbound peril with keen interest: an elfin figure with a determined air, not a whit discomposed by her overstuffed satchels. As she neared, he received her intense survey, in turn. Eyes the pristine tint of a dawn sky dominated fine features and the inquisitive, arched brows of an acerbic intelligence.

Dakar cleared his throat, riled pink with embarrassment. "Elaira. You can't—"

The enchantress breezed past. Ignored him, while the worry that tightened her mouth melted into a welcoming smile directed at the crofter behind him. "Tarens? I am grateful! For the loyal friendship shown to my beloved, now and forever, my help is yours."

Caught off guard by her grace, Tarens regarded a spirit annealed under sorrow to a tempered courage that left him speechless.

While he floundered, she rescued him with an arid humour that snuffed any trace of self-pity. "I've bear-baited Davien with threats to his books until he caved in and released me. I'm free on blind faith, with two parcels of cake, a blanket, and a fly swatter."

Tarens grinned outright and offered a hand to relieve her of the larger pack. Surprised when the burden tested his balance, he realized she carried trail gear as well as provisions. "My dear, for your wit, you'll cross Sithaer itself, even if I have to carry you." Struggling, he hid his dismay; refused by bare-knuckled strength to acknowledge the wretched fact that her mission was hopeless.

Both men were aware: Dakar's immutable prophecy already forecast Arithon's downfall. Elaira might believe she slipped Davien's protection through her own initiative. But by strict adherence to Asandir's oath, no Fellowship Sorcerer dared to grant her liberty if aught in the world suggested she might upset his Grace's doomed fate.

As though Tarens's gloom was transparent, Elaira swore with exasperation, "Don't think to batten my anguish in cotton! Davien has allowed me to go because Ettinmere's shamans have already triumphed."

"What?" Dakar stared, gut-punched. "Then you know the worst? That Arithon's going to be taken?"

Shocked first by the crofter's stunned gasp, Elaira glared at the fat prophet, angry enough to rip him to the viscera. "You failed to tell Tarens?" Before anyone answered, she broke her shocking news. "His Grace walked into the trap the shamans had set for him. Sethvir's confirmed. They sealed his captivity, hours ago." Then, "Damn you to Sithaer!" she accosted Dakar. "Is there no limit to your shrinking cowardice?"

For a mercy, Tarens kept a level head. He curbed his impulse to broaden her short-term awareness. For as he and the spellbinder were acutely aware, the crisis at this pass presaged a far more grievous disaster. One that, all along, pushed their desperate rush—not to serve a lost cause—but to spare Mankind's demise under the greater reckoning sprung from the Fellowship's compact.

Dakar also stood firm before Elaira's bravery, as much from distrust of her order as to dodge the failures that poisoned his mishandled life. "You realize you've leaped into a cauldron of intrigue stewed up for explosive revenge?"

"A pot stirred to the boil by the Prime Matriarch's long spoon? I know." The enchantress stopped short of pulling her hair in exasperation. "We might as well give the True Sect diviners a threefold incentive to try for canonical fame."

Ambush

The false step that brought Arithon's plunging fall into black-out oblivion had not been caused by a slip in his treacherous ascent of the Issing Ravine. Nor did his disrupted awareness spring from a resurgent back-lash, when the trauma that followed Paravian exposure relapsed into the grief of profound separation.

Instead, Arithon recouped his first glimmer of consciousness in a smothered state of suspension. Mage training failed to define what had triggered his disorientation. Mazed senses encountered no obvious symptoms: not the after-shock sting of grazed skin or the ache of snapped bones that attended an injury. Darkened sight did not clear. Recall yielded nothing beyond his last view, of a slice of night sky strewn with stars, spanning the narrow seam of the river course, with its ladders of flindered trunks, wedged amid the scraped scars of old rock-slides.

In fact, his numbed awareness gleaned nothing. Not the whisper of breath or the rhythmic thump of his heart-beat. The void swallowed all tactile sensation. Trained use of his initiate talent grappled what seemed a pocket of utter oblivion. Even his mastery of shadow failed to harness the featureless dark.

Unable to seize the initiative, Arithon measured the scope of his error in judgement.

He had not tumbled to his demise, broken at the verge of a natural death. Instead, he had succumbed to a snare wrought to paralyse intellect and disable him. Unlike his confinement by the Koriathain, crafted of mirrored light, matrixed in crystal, or the sigils imposed through their Waystone, this working stranded him in isolation, amid a null state of emptiness.

Not a Fellowship construct, laid down in accord with free will, or the seamlessly omniscient weavings of Sanpashir's tribesfolk. The binding on him matched nothing familiar, which forced the default conclusion: he had been over-confident, and ten times a fool, to have misappraised Ettinmere's shamans.

Crushed under their aegis, stripped naked of everything but self-awareness, Arithon retained no measure of time. Cocooned, he received no stimulus on which to anchor his human identity. Dread gave rise to whispered despair. As an insensate trophy, he might become subjected to worse than public display and humiliation. Under Ettinmere's archaic code, council judgement could hang the condemned on a meat-hook, with the living flesh drawn as food for the shamans' carrion birds. Fear inflated the horror, that his execution may have happened already, with his dismembered consciousness hung at the turn of Daelion's Wheel.

The fraught terror followed, that he might drift until he went mad, suspended without surcease forever.

Which grotesque nightmare *had not occurred, yet!* The spiral of irrational panic broke finally, crushed down by stark courage. Arithon rallied his pulverized discipline and sorted the likely facts. His predicament would be a cold-blooded strategy, engineered by the shamans to break him. As a tactical play to destroy his morale, hysteria sprung from the scars of his past surely would strike a blow fit to smash his integrity. If he lost himself to insanity, he might spill his core secrets in raving bewilderment. A lifetime's initiate knowledge might fall into wrong hands, and be turned to who knew what evil purpose.

Arithon forced himself to shift focus before that peril spurred runaway thoughts. In command of nothing but his active mind, he grappled his prior experience with the onset of total derangement. Disorientation had to be tempered to survive the boundless abyss. Ordeals before this had forged the means to refurnish his threatened identity from naught. If not through the gifted use of his talent, then by bare-knuckled invention.

His command of shadow had not prevailed. The skilled music that had triumphed over the last challenge in Davien's maze also gave him no purchase, which eliminated an exploratory assay through tone to sound out the trap's structure by resonance. Denied the method by which he had tamed the lane flux in Rathain during Kharadmon's crisis at Rockfell, Arithon groped, adrift, tacitly seeking. He encountered no trace of past malice; no unrequite echo upon which to seize the toe-hold for active resistance. If, like the Great Waystone, past spirits had suffered this torment of incarceration before him, their misery left no residual echo.

The miring darkness was untextured velvet, silent as the primordial void. Arithon's efforts exerted no influence, no matter which angle he tried. The sealed stasis retained no imprint of its maker, which left him no lead to pursue. Naught remained but to resift his predicament with yet more exhaustive precision. A force *must* exist that negated his influence. *Something* stabilized his confinement against erosive decay.

Arithon abandoned all preconceived thought and listened with a Masterbard's ear for nuance. Mage-senses extended, he stretched his perception across frequencies, from the lowest register into the highest, above the extreme range of human hearing. Ettinmere's cabal did not know his history. Surely, the shamans might fail to fathom the reach of his seasoned expertise. He owned an initiate's talent enhanced by the practice of centuries, settling hostile free wraiths. More, his blood-line's resilient attributes had been tested anew by the rarified influence of the Paravians.

Iron will built upon those core strengths a state of absolute stillness that mirrored the vacuous emptiness. Then, Arithon dissolved his active defences. He blended himself into oblivion and let the pervasive absence of pattern absorb his quiescent identity.

He drifted, unfurled, for a timeless age, or perhaps for one magnified instant, unbounded as a raindrop melded into the greater expanse of the ocean. Existence dissolved, until death itself promised the blessed relief of a reawakening. And still, he held, beyond count of endurance.

Spontaneously, without forewarning, an inversion flipped his perception.

Enervated anaesthesia burst into a dizzy explosion of colour and sound. The transition did not restore the full range of orientation. Arithon regained the awareness of breath, but no heart-beat. As he recouped the displaced thread of his mage-sense, the eerie suspension of mortal flesh and bone opened into the more familiar sensation induced by a spiritwalk. A lush glen surrounded by forest embraced him, pewter with dew under starlight. But the terrain that cushioned his barefoot step was *other*, born of an eldritch loveliness beyond the natural world.

Caution froze him in place. As if careless movement might rend the veil of a fragile illusion, he surveyed the preternatural terrain around him with resharpened focus. Meadow grass licked his ankles, glass cool. Each blade was formed with surreal perfection, just as his skin seemed remade without scars, reborn into glowing health. Tiny wildflowers scattered the turf like dropped snowflakes, shivered by the delicate wing-beats of moths, iridescently pale green and azure. Taken by wonder, Arithon stared at a silver wolf, curled in unruffled repose. Other wild creatures sheltered nearby, unconcerned by the predator's proximity.

Arithon counted the browsing form of a tined buck, then three does, undisturbed by the black-and-gold leopard draped on a limb overhead. The wild cat's fixated gaze held no threat, despite an intelligence, fiercely aware and unfathomable.

Beneath the cat's perch, a spring burbled over the stones of a pool, sheened like moonstone in the gloaming. A black-barred owl glided over a foraging mouse, while a hare and a tortoise grazed, just as peacefully oblivious. The fragrant breeze fingered Arithon's hair, rich with the resin of pine, and green oak, and pungent with flowering witch hazel.

Yet solid appearances here were deceptive. Like the altered signature of a grimward, Arithon knew he walked through a vision derived from a singular consciousness. The interface was similarly reactive, in form and feature subject to change by the influence of a thought.

However, this waking state of volatile subjectivity did not spring from the mind of a dragon, living or dead. Whatever drove the transient reality, the sweeping prickle raised by another presence suggested that Arithon was no longer alone.

A striking woman emerged from the wood. She was dark, her lean flesh moulded on bone like the Biedar, but without their rough-spun, goat-hair garments. Clad in flowing white, and hazed in the pale gold of an exalted aura, she was ally, not enemy: joy infused her presence, pristine as the water welling from the spring.

The purity of her aspect demanded a master's respect. Arithon bowed his head in startled homage, distrust refigured by courtesy. "Forgive me. If I've inadvertently trespassed, is it permissible to ask ignorant questions?"

Her smile charged him to delight. "I am here for that purpose. Nor have you imposed." Her narrow hand gestured. "You behold the reflection of your true self, the manifest analogue spun in symbol and form from the deepest core of your being." Flawless in composure, she seated herself on a stone, materialized in the grass at his feet.

Arithon knelt. Gently testing, he ruffled the silky fur of the wolf. When the animal leaned into his brazen caress, he regarded the woman, eyes level. "You suggest I'm hallucinating?"

Her amusement danced with the tumbling water. "No. You have not lost your way, or abandoned yourself to indiscipline. Quite the contrary."

The wolf yawned and rolled over, content to be stroked on its belly. Arithon sat on the greensward and obliged, the taut muscle under his touch proof enough its quiescence was dangerous. "Explain, if you will. I was trapped. Apparently beyond recourse, until the aspect confining me shifted. You suggest I've driven my consciousness inward?"

The lady's brown eyes regarded him, tender. Her raised finger acknowledged the diamonds, sprung from nowhere, like a diadem of glittering stars netted over her ebony hair. "Your gallantry adorns me?"

Arithon laughed. "Indulge my presumption, that comes empty-handed. I've been stranded adrift for too long."

"But not powerless," the adept admonished. "In fact, you were imprisoned in formlessness, enforced by a wrongful use of the creative force derived from the mysteries. You did not suffocate, or go mad, because you embraced absolute quietude. That perfected intent matched the bias of the ward, which surrounded you with a locked field of inertia. When you blended at one with that featureless state, the nexus of your true awareness bled into the barrier and slipped through. You have accessed the living web of our sanctuary, virgin power streamed intact from the everlasting by Ath's adepts."

Arithon took signal pause to reflect. "You are not," he said presently, "allied with the shamans of Ettinmere Settlement."

"They are descended from our sorrowfully fallen." Her bitter-sweet sadness underscored the bright, minor trill of a nightjar. "What power they wield in corruption is finite, severed from the prime source."

"Yet their forceful reach apparently still commands strength enough to ensnare me," Arithon mused. "What else?"

The adept answered directly. "The resonant peace of the hostel, before this, once quelled the lane currents driving the volatile flux in the Storlains. A reservoir mighty enough, then and now, to stabilize the region's fractured fault-lines."

The sprawled wolf sprang erect, bristled in reflected response to Arithon's temper. He muzzled his flared outrage. The animal settled short of a snarl, ruff soothed in response. More carefully, Rathain's prince pursued his deferent inquiry. "White adepts don't interfere with the world's ways. They deny freedom to nothing living. Without imposition on your moral code, what are my ethical choices?"

The adept's reserve shattered into a smile. "Fate's forger, you are, and beautifully taught, with the generous heart of your forebears. By your measure this moment, two paths lie before you. The first, and the safest, invites you to step into the pool. The act will immerse your being in the prime chord. A passage of total surrender will then uplift you to dissolution. Subject to the greater law of Ath's mercy, every binding the shamans laid on you releases. Claim divine transformation, and I may lend you my escort, either to an exalted crossing beyond the veil, or through one of several etheric gateways that intersects with Athera. The nearest hostel kept under our aegis is located at Spire."

Arithon regarded her shimmering calm, deceptive strength and fathomless wisdom tempered by the harmony of the infinite. "If I commit myself, what becomes of my mortal form, left at large with the Ettinmere shamans?"

"They would find themselves empty-handed, bequeathed a dead husk." Her lifted finger stayed premature speech. "Or," she qualified, "the light of the prime source would transmute everything that you are. Your subsequent preferences then must be honoured, whether or not to return incarnate. You might emerge whole, both spirit and flesh reintegrated at Spire's hostel. Therein lies no surety. For none who pass through the crucible remain of the body, unchanged."

"I'd win free of the Ettinmere cabal, either way," Arithon summarized. "But by implication, their renegade practice of violation through usurped power stays unchecked. Your adepts receive no due redress."

She inclined her head.

Which aggrieved gesture clenched Arithon's fists. The silver wolf rumbled a growl, as he said, "Then give me the passage that's not guaranteed. My way takes the path to defeat the cabal's warped domination."

"You would serve the balance at risk to yourself?" The adept arose like poured moonlight, her luminous aura studded by the flitter of displaced moths. "Then take my hand. Release thought and emotion until your awareness is emptied, and this construct collapses back into the void. If you recross the barrier whence you came, my presence, through yours, can enable a restored connection to the prime chord. A balance shall be re-established thereby, that no wayward faction may tame."

Arithon stood also, his clasp laced through hers with anticipation. "Then by all means, let's raise mayhem and convulse the Ettinmere cabal with seizures."

"They'll suffer no harm," the adept amended in response to his sardonic humour. "Though if your sacrifice allows our adepts to reclaim their stolen sanctuary, be warned. By the restored tenets of Ath's order, all constraints would be forfeit. Anything binding the body and every etheric stay on the spirit disbands in our presence forthwith. You will be awakened, set free on your merits. But we may not intercede between you and your enemies or act in your personal defence."

Arithon smiled, all teeth. "For sweet satisfaction, leave that part to me."

A sunburst blast of light and gusty wind restored Arithon's natural senses. His reflexive move to shield flash-blinded eyes wrenched his bound wrists, currently roped over his head and abraded to weeping sores. He dangled in darkness, stretched against a stout post. Hard upon that unpleasant assessment, his restraints succumbed to the dominion reasserted by Ath's adepts. Shredded knots pattered over his naked skin. Dropped onto jellied legs in abrupt release, Arithon buckled to his knees. Agony seized the mauled muscles held cranked under strain for too long. Desperation spurred his fight to regroup.

Resinous smoke from an extinguished torch swirled on the cross-draught, tainted by human sweat and the rancid cloy of clay body paint. Surprised disarray gripped the shamans surrounding him, fanned by the whumping beat of panicked wings. Distraught handlers blundered to recapture their birds, cut loose inside a wicker enclosure.

Stars gleamed through the chinks. The hour neared midnight. Terror needed no talent to grasp the ritual setting for a ceremonial dismemberment. Galvanic rage drove Arithon erect. How narrowly he had escaped the horror of having his eyes plucked by buzzards!

A shadow lunged for him. Steel flashed. He ducked the cleaver swiped at his neck, and followed up with a knee to the belly that folded his Ettin assailant. He stamped on the man's wrist, kicked away the dropped blade, then charged through the clouting gamut of distempered vultures. Human hands snatched at him. He clubbed off their fumbling, chopped away other fingers that seized his hair. A knife licked at his side and cleanly missed. Arithon parried the next thrust, caught the wielder's forearm and savagely twisted before the reverse slash eviscerated him. Rammed onwards through battering chaos, he realized:

the cabal was not just disempowered, but blinded, utterly stripped of their mage talent. Before they sorted out their confusion, or someone struck a spark to a torch, Arithon lashed punches at all that moved. Ploughed into the flimsy wall of the enclosure, he rammed the dry palings and shouldered through, raked by splintered basketry.

Fresh air bathed his face. The moonless glimmer of summer starlight unveiled the setting, a barren, volcanic mound centred inside the rimmed bowl of a dormant caldera. Evergreens clothed the slope beyond the outer rim. Their saw-toothed tops notched the seamed crevice of a vast, sheer-sided ravine, cleft through the central Storlains. The icy flanks of the peaks framed the site in a vista of jagged foil and rock. Majesty stole Arithon's breath, beyond regard for his urgent straits.

Nor was he alone. Twelve adepts in pearlescent robes surrounded the shamans' enclave. The crude structure of board palings and woven osiers was roofed in stretched canvas, painted over with eldritch symbols. Black bindings and spellcraft laced the hard-scrabble ground of chipped lava, where trapped power coiled beneath reverberated with a potency fit to club Arithon prostrate.

A containment already tearing asunder, he realized, shuddered by the crackling dissonance as Ath's adepts reclaimed their usurped sovereignty. Forces chained into stasis strained towards explosive release, the unravelling stays a wisped net billowed over the titanic seethe of a geyser.

The eruption shook the air and the earth, as the pressurized flow of pooled power burst from the reservoir sealed beneath Ettin. Light blazed, the unbridled blast of chaos caught short, then tamed, rejoined to the prime source after stagnant centuries of severance.

The shift afflicted more than the deposed cabal. Freed current rushed through the ground underfoot, reconnected to a gold pillar of etheric light. The reunion unfurled a cry of sweet harmony that knifed Arithon through, bone and viscera.

He faltered, undone. The scalding flood unstrung the fight in him and vaulted his spirit to ecstatic surrender. He could shed no enemy's blood in this place: not in defilement of absolute purity, no matter whether survival relied upon self-defence. More than a fire to cauterize aggression, the upscaled change in frequency roared through his sensory perception and altered his close surroundings.

A spring gushed and burbled out of dry rock, where no watercourse had been in evidence. What seemed a murky encroachment of shadows thickened and leafed into a forest, massive trees wound with flowering vines, and soaring crowns pinpricked with starlight. The mystical transformation unfolded apace, the grace of the infinite respinning the original sanctuary's volatile matrix. Arithon fought crippling vertigo and moved. A step ahead of pursuit by the cabal, he had to escape the thundering torrent before he lost himself into beguilement.

The ground underfoot shuddered. Arithon cried out and stumbled, caught and steadied by the presence of a pale wolf. Braced short of a fall, he pleaded for guidance. From the manifest circle of Ath's adepts, the female initiate who had spoken within the etheric glade inclined her head in homage. Through the shimmering deluge of energy and past the iconic blaze of her aura, Arithon perceived the stubs of two posts, once the uprights for a pillared archway carved with Paravian ciphers. His path lay that way, given trust in her counsel.

Her whisper sped his flight with encouragement. "Run far and fast, blessed! Take with you always the gift of Ath's peace for what you've done for our white brotherhood."

Tanuay intercepted his sister's return from the meadow briar patch. He hounded her heels across the summer settlement, his clipped tread up her cottage stair the drummed chorus to his badgering argument.

Vivet turned a deaf ear. Valien's slack weight braced astride her right hip, she juggled a crockery bowl of wild strawberries in her crooked elbow, left hand freed for the string latch. Twilight shadowed her tight-lipped irritation, as she bashed the door inward.

"Grief break your rock-headed stubbornness, you're not listening!" Embittered past fury, her brother's tirade cracked like a rooster's crow. "Your excuses are finished. The shamans have Arin. Condemned for unlawful desertion, by now he's three days' dead, cut and drawn for exposure as buzzard meat."

Exasperation exploded, Vivet spun, burdened, upon her dark threshold. "How by Teeah's ever bounteous milk will Herthov's suit better my lot?" Trampling over his retort, she ranted, "He's a clinch poop and a leering swine, with a reek to his promises like unwashed laundry. Valien's better off growing up fatherless than curdling under that man's sour influence."

Tanuay jammed his foot in the door-panel her shove tried to slam in his face. "You risk a future of menial labour for the rest of your barren life."

Vivet laughed. "I've sunk that low, long since. Lower, if that puckered bollocks sack imagines I'd give my consent." Tried as the fretful squirm her toddler threatened to upset her balance, she squashed the debate. "No. The day Arin's picked bones are thrown to the dogs, curse your whining disgrace, I'll be going."

"What's happened to you?" Tanuay's distress switched back to appeal. "Is there nothing left of the common ground binding our ties of blood kinship?"

Vivet had no words. Beneath his stiff neck and traditional clothes, she regarded the weathered, flaxen-haired stranger her older brother had become. Hardened by disappointment, his critical, lined eyes held little trace of the cherubic lad with skinned knees who had led childhood escapades to the creek. Vivet groped for the words to soften necessity.

"Leave again, and your kin have no choice," Tanuay threatened, mistaking her hesitation for weakness. "They'll take Valien from you. Strike your name from the family. No reprieve, once that happens. You'll seal your own exile."

"Then good riddance!" Patience broke under stress. "There's a world outside of this miserable settlement, and more kindness shown towards me and Valien by the wives of the summer traders." Vivet kicked out her kinsman's obstructive toe. "Unless you're minded to help stir my jam? I'll thank you for taking yourself elsewhere."

The freed door thumped shut. The latch plinked. Vivet leaned against the stout plank, eyes clamped against tears. The ambitious folly that had once lured her as a runaway brought her to this bitter turning.

Tanuay, of them all, had fixed the leaks in her shingles. His passionate care brought the portions of meat, flour, and eggs, when she lost flesh from nursing her infant. If his easy laughter had gone with maturity, Ettin's suffocating rigidity never seemed to choke his contentment. He could not comprehend: would not dream of the price she paid now, entrapped by the absolute terms of an outside order's deadly obligation.

If anything, Arin's demise freed the bind that shredded her conscience. Morning would bring final proof of his end. Exhausted from dawn-to-dusk toil, and scalded by lye soap and boiled linens, Vivet faced her priorities. The ungainly crock tilted, dragged awry by Valien's weight, plump legs and dirty toes dangling. Nonetheless, she held out, until Tanuay's stomping retreat passed beyond earshot.

"Here, Valien." She eased the drowsy child onto his feet. "Soon we'll have jam and cakes." Small fingers seized her kirtled-up skirt, which gave way, tugged loose by his wobbly balance. Chortling, pleased, he sat with a thump and sucked on his sticky knuckles. Vivet ached for that innocent happiness. Knotted back straightened, she secured the filled bowl and moved on to brighten the lamp by the open window.

"I'm not waiting for curs to scrap over my bones," said a ghost's velvet voice from the darkness.

"Arin!" Vivet dropped the crock. Raked by the smashed fragments, she back-stepped and snatched her son clear of harm's way. Through his startled wail, she exclaimed, "You abandoned us! Spurned your sworn obligation to Valien the day after his birth." Offered no answer, far less explanation, she vented her stymied annoyance. "Arin! I waited for over a year without word. Where under sky have you been?"

"Where I truly belonged. Rest your case. I have more pressing questions." Always, his tread was unnervingly silent. When the shutter snapped shut at his hand, Vivet flinched.

Stung by the disadvantage, she hushed Valien and plunked him on the braided rug by the settle. Then she fumbled the striker off the bent nail and snapped a spark to the hanging lantern. The wick flamed and caught. Fitful light exposed Arin, retired to the cedar chest next to her bed. Discoloured scabs mottled his desperate nakedness, covered hastily by a snatched blanket.

"If you'll wash first, I have button trousers and a smock shirt in the armoire." Vivet had not traded the clothing his trapper's coin bought, made to measure.

"I sluiced off at the falls, first." He sported spectacular bruises, not dirt. Pain hitched his movement as he padded around the bedstead and laid claim to her surprise offering. He dressed quickly, his adamant privacy shielded behind the armoire's gapped door. The raw rope burns on his ankles unavoidably stayed within view. Nor might he bear proper weight on slashed soles, infected and angry with swelling.

Vivet's heart twisted with unwanted sympathy. "You'll need salve for those wounds if you plan to run." She ruffled Valien's hair, more for her own comfort as she admitted, "I cannot shelter you from a death sentence." No one survived the shamans' retribution, far less escaped as a fugitive.

Arin answered her note of alarm. "The ghouls with the cleavers are beating the brush everywhere else but inside the settlement." He stepped out, engrossed with lacing his cuff points, and there, bared to light, lay the welted scar burned into his forearm by the Light's holy avatar. Talking still, misapprehending her flash-point fear, he ran on with disarming gentleness, "Are you coming or staying? You have time to pack. Roaco's not apt to rush the colossal shame of exposing his toothless embarrassment."

"The cabal will kill you!" Proof of his secret identity spiked Vivet's fraught protest. "Valien and I will suffer as well if I stir a finger to help you."

He looked up. "Your association with me taints your name, regardless." Preternaturally calm, he measured her jagged terror, unflinching. "At least in my company you'd have to be caught, first. The cabal might gang up against us with clubs, or maybe pitch stones from a distance."

Which blistering confidence wrenched Vivet up short. "*What?* Are you addled?" She grabbed her straw broom and attacked the lesser vexation of cleaning up shards and squashed fruit. "Every forsaken bird in their mews will be hunting you down!"

"Well, they would," Arin admitted, bemused, "provided the sentries still steered their familiars through spellcraft."

Her palliative clatter filled the stiff pause while Arin perched on the bed. He steadied Valien's tipsy bid to stand upright, and admitted, "I've defanged Roaco's conclave of serpents. Their poisonous power is broken."

Vivet's sweeping stopped with a jerk. "Then you've made me a sitting target!"

Arin inclined his head. "Only if you renounce my obligation to Valien. I returned to see both of you settled and safe. But not here. Agree to leave Ettin tonight, and I'll do all I can to support your son's well-being until his maturity."

The assurance just spoken reflected the dread resources of his true heritage. Born to royal authority, also Master of Shadow, the man under her roof never once had displayed the full range of his arcane talent. Not until his defeat of the Ettinmere cabal. Slight in build, unassuming in manner, he seemed deceptively ordinary with his thumbs taken captive by Valien's unbalanced grip. Always, he had avoided the indulgences that might impair his free movement. Vivet noted the striking change and realized such relaxed self-possession meant her glamour of beguilement no longer affected him. Which set-back ground hurtful salt in the wound since her fate stayed embroiled with his beyond quarter.

Vivet dropped pretence. No choice, in fact, remained to be made. She had ever been a slave to her duty, resigned to play through the terrible end game. "I'll be packing, then, as soon as Valien's had something to eat. I gather there's no time to sleep? Then you might as well shred my bed-linens for dressings and care for your injured feet."

Knife's Edge

Sethvir watched all that moved in Athera, distanced in glass-eyed reverie amid tipsy piles of books in his library eyrie at Althain Tower. Again forced to defer a perilous sojourn into the Radmoore grimward to wrest information from Haspastion's shade, he straightened at the percussive, first note of The Hatchet's advance into Daon Ramon Barrens. Prelude to an onrushing disaster, the quick-marched columns cut a swathe of bruised vegetation beneath the enamel sky of midsummer. False comfort, the brief reprieve bought for the besieged mysteries in Deshir's free wilds: the True Sect host's abrupt turnabout unleashed a more dreadful array of priorities. Sethvir stared into the eye of a crisis far beyond the scope of the clan losses spent to hold Strakewood's defence.

For the nexus forecast by the Mad Prophet's augury strung Mankind's future above the abyss.

One moment, inevitable, turned destiny's card like the bell stroke that shattered all hope; or else, like the phoenix birthed from immolation, a spark struck in bright, helpless pain might salvage the cold course of destiny. No way to tell which ahead of the crux where possibility ended, and probability dimmed to opacity. The veiled outcome had been graven in time since the perilous hour Asandir marked his oath to the Koriani Prime by stone's witness.

Reckoning begat consequence: deferred only, the promised debt at last became rendered due.

The freshly trimmed quill in Sethvir's hand splayed and snapped. Fingers stippled with sprayed ink, he watched a stain jagged as despair mar his penned line of manuscript.

"Fatemaster's grief, we're pinched by our short hairs!" Shaken, he tossed the spoiled nib aside, then pushed back his carved chair, and rose.

The barrage of the earth-link thrummed on, the flicker of heat lightning become distant thunder as he padded barefoot to the north wall. There, the antique aumbry of Vhalzein lacquer held a cluttered cache of stray oddments. The Sorcerer dug his ceramic pot from the jumble of spooled thread, dried ink-wells, and an herbwitch's charm circlet of mouse skulls. He refilled his mug with raspberry tea, steeped acrid and long since gone tepid.

Althain's Warden sipped the bitter brew, while the wrens cheeped in their thatched nests under the outside eaves. Around him, statement of obdurate endurance, the tower's warded stonewalls baked and sweltered, while summer's ascendant sun shimmered the powder-blue haze of Atainia's horizon. Sethvir abandoned the barren view, while, from broad-scale trends to minutiae, the bleak pattern tightened.

Air gave him the flights of the temple messenger-birds, winging the thread-tied cylinders with their cryptic reports between High Priests. Movement answered, ponderous, inexorable, as The Hatchet's orders provoked a deeper reverberation, and writs of alarm mustered the garrisoned men out of Jaelot and Tharidor. Day on day, the dissonance mounted, as jammed roadways hampered the trade caravans west-bound over the Skyshiel peaks. From the notch, down the switch-backed descent to the Paravian marker where the dry course of the Severnir met Daenfal Lake, Sethvir sensed the panic, as pressured supply sowed scarcity in the town markets. Through the forge fires' tang and the reek of smoked fish, he heard the hungry poor, and in silenced tears, the whisper of Dace Marley's recrimination: that one choice, enacted, had allowed Lysaer's edict to turn the Light's war host southward. Countless lives had been spared in Deshir. But at what dire penalty, sown elsewhere?

"Ah, my dear, may you never bear the harsh brunt," Sethvir murmured in anguish.

Others, predestined, would not escape the blind grace of moral ambiguity. While portents dimmed the flux like a storm front, the next signal ripple flickered through water: Dakar, Tarens, and Elaira forded the shallows of the Aiyenne by the gleam of a cloud-mottled moon. In their company, Sethvir noted the point of polarized, green fire, and another frigid as black ice. Bound into the gyre, the enchantress still carried the royal signet of Rathain and Mother Dark's fearful token of ending, fused into the Biedar's flint dagger.

Althain's Warden shuddered with a nascent chill. While his earth-sense, unerring, soared with the revitalized lane forces singing in restored balance through Ettin, his spidery hands started clearing the books and loose manuscripts from the library's obsidian table. Although Arithon's spectacular reverse had broken Roaco's cabal and delivered a triumph to Ath's white adepts, that victory fell into eclipse as a crystal transmission from the Koriani lane watch informed the Prime Matriarch at Whitehold . . .

* * *

"Your coveted news is confirmed. Rathain's crown prince has taken flight. While the shamans are vanquished, Ettin's council rules yet. Their pursuit from the settlement has driven him north. As you hoped, he has chosen to game with live fire: he's taken the woman and child along under his free-will protection . . ."

Althain's Warden paused, aggrieved, as the terrible, incoming torrent interlaced, warp through weft, with the steel thread of his Grace's fatal determination . . .

. . . under cover of night, Iyat-thos Tarens nestled joints of wrapped meat in the embers of a furtive cookfire in Daon Ramon Barrens.

"Why ever would Arithon protect that woman? Her child is not his blood offspring." The crofter prodded hot coals overtop of the meal just settled for baking. "Further, he knows she's hostile, steered by a Koriani directive."

Huddled in misery, her auburn plait wisped with neglect, Elaira jabbed her sticky skinning knife clean in the loamy soil. "He gave his oath of safe-guard, for one thing. Compassion won't let him abandon an innocent babe to the witches."

"There's more." Tarens shied his charred stick in frustration, while Dakar watched, a tucked owl in his tatty cloak. "Fatemaster's deathless mercy, what else?"

Her eyes brimmed then, from the sorrow endured since Dakar's oath of debt had cast her beloved to the Prime's mercy. "You can't guess? Arithon hopes to gain the information our proscribed straits cannot give him."

She paused, face averted, while Tarens fumbled to frame a contrite apology.

Dakar intervened to spare her the agony of the conclusion. "His Grace does not know if Elaira is dead or alive, or whether she's still bound to the order." The ghastly pause stretched, filled by the rustle of grass in the breeze and the whistling cry of a night-hawk. "I'd hazard the guess that Arithon taunts the appalling risk to find out. He'll be staking the sympathy of his bard's gift, first to win trust from the child, then to wrest Vivet's loyalty free of the sisterhood's influence."

While Elaira arose sharply and left to escape unwanted pity, Tarens regarded Dakar as though sight could flense skin from bone and exact a poisonous reckoning. "You didn't forewarn her!" he accused, low voiced. "Her poor, steadfast heart's not fully aware that our mission is useless."

Dakar hissed through his teeth. "You tell her, then! I can't slaughter her hope." Armoured against biting sorrow, he added, "Be most careful if you think to shield her. She's an initiate Koriani enchantress, and Arithon's match for pigheaded temperament. Ten silvers against a handful of broom-straws, the lady goes forward unflinching regardless, with both eyes wide open . . ."

. . . Sethvir gripped the stone table at Althain Tower, by white-knuckled control curbing an endowed power sufficient to slag the world's bed-rock. With the s'Ffalenn scion moved outside of his ethical provenance, naught remained to deflect the Mad Prophet's dire augury. Like Elaira, he must abide the untenable. For Lirenda Prime's response to the Daenfal sisterhouse set the fatal sequence in motion.

Sethvir ignited the central brazier with the confluent powers of the Third Lane. Hard blue, the reflection sparked in his eyes as he sent urgent summons to Asandir, on the far side of the planet in the alkali flats of Kathtairr, *"Don't look now. The crux laid out by your sealed oath at Whitehold builds towards the final crisis."*

"Davien's released Elaira," the field Sorcerer surmised, a cough suppressed behind his sinewed wrist as he beat acrid dust from his leathers. Gaze fixed on the gelid pool where something viciously suspect raised ripples, he concluded on a taxed breath, "Naturally, she'll be headed for the maw of disaster. I'm wanted on station at Whitehold?"

"Straightaway, once you've dispatched that ill-spawned anomaly. I've witnessed Prime Lirenda's unpleasant instructions to the sisterhouse peeress at Daenfal." Sethvir paused, while the thousandfold threads of cross-woven connection resounded through the world's weave. *"Our margin grows short. You have roughly a fortnight, unless you rush your passage by way of a grimward."*

Davien's errant stance stayed beneath mention, just as pointless as raw speculation over Ciladis's continued absence. Asandir's clipped nod showed the lines in his face scored by more than Kathtairr's noon glare. Strategy for the end game lay beyond even his capable grasp. Against despair, his steadfast part must be carried through without flinching.

While the midnight stars ruled the zenith at Althain, Sethvir laced his veined hands on the cold, obsidian table. A second call, spoken to water, sped through the ocean deeps in the abyss west of Corith.

Kharadmon swirled alert, a frigid jet of agitation amid the black pressure at the sea-floor. *"Ath wept! We are clearing the decks for the bloodbath?"*

"Perhaps," Sethvir poised for the discorporate's blistering recrimination. None came: for no long-sighted vision yet discerned the scope of the on-coming recoil.

The Rei-yaj Seeress, who might have revealed more, faced skywards in her gimballed chair, enigmatically silent; and the Biedar Crone in Sanpashir divulged nothing, stilled as the bones of the earth in her lair.

And another dawn came, loud with bird-song over the scrub downs of Atainia. In the library, etched by the azure flare of the lane current ignited in the bronze brazier, Sethvir abided the moments as droplets fused into a torrent, and unfolding event underwrote the momentous page of full reckoning.

Farther south, amid pre-dawn gloom, the Light's advance muster converged for Lirenda's crowning play at Daenfal; while silent as the arrow shot from the bow, the Teir's'Ffalenn led a woman and her dependent child in covert flight towards freedom . . .

* * *

Arithon's bid to shed Ettin's pursuit was not lunacy. Unlike old blood clan scouts, the folk hounding his trail lacked the refined skill to interpret the flux patterns. Without their bird familiars, a blind chase on foot lost them vital ground in the back-country beyond their closed borders. Rathain's prince led the hunt northward into the crags, where naked rock thwarted the trackers. Coverless on the slopes past the timberline, he moved through the angled, low sunlight that dazzled observers and slanted shadow over the crevices, or where drifted cloud concealed the high ramparts, blinding the long-sighted archers.

Sound carried at distance with dangerous clarity, a hazard with a toddler testing his first, determined autonomy. Arithon used diversions learned from the clans, when pouty noise risked them to head-hunters. Beneath bent black heads, an unstrung cuff lace with elaborate knots fell apart to Valien's inquisitive tug. Amid searing noon silence, their game counted the hawks soaring upon the high thermals, then turned to fascination with insects, or finding stray pebbles with holes. Arithon's tireless contrivance fashioned puzzles from withies and reed, and made a sailor's tell-tales of thread to snag the boy's fractious attention.

"What happens if your invention runs dry?" Vivet prodded, tucked up to untangle her red hair in the cranny where they holed up.

Arithon's smile was sweetness and light, over Valien's engrossed contentment. "Does imagination or joy come with limits?" He crouched on his heels, shod in uncured hide and perversely unfazed by the stink. "The wide world births wonders beyond mortal measure. One has to be soured, or taught, to retreat into narrow-minded rigidity. When did disappointment shrivel your outlook?"

"Come from Ettin?" Vivet shrugged. "There's stubborn tradition enough to throttle anyone's frivolous fancies."

"That's why we're leaving," Arithon reminded, and gently quick, intercepted a chubby fist before Valien ingested a twig. A Masterbard's nuance stalled the infantile wail of displeasure, the disputed morsel placed at the child's feet with a flourish. "See here! Let's build a sentinel's tower with a bird, and an archer fashioned from lichen paste. Which stick comes next?"

Valien pointed, to Arithon's mock horror. "Not one that's round! Let's finish the construction. *Then* you'll knock it down."

Indignant tantrum, or delighted shrieks, Arithon kept the overtaxed child amused, then consigned him, drowsy, to Vivet while he sought the ridge-top to scout.

Returned as the mist thickened, against stiffening breeze, he signalled the urgent need to move on. "Storm's coming. We'll need shelter. The east rim of Baffiel's Cauldron is a rugged climb into the summer snowpack, but the steam vents will keep Valien warm."

Vivet strapped on the bundled blankets and supply, while Arithon perched the fretful child on his shoulders. When overexhaustion made the boy squirm, he resorted to song, lulled the mite into a comatose sleep, then bore him slung limp in a cloak.

Against icy wind that watered her eyes, Vivet weighed the motive behind the man's flawless consideration. He was a sorcerer, well-fitted to expose her covert connections. Sly distrust, perhaps, masqueraded as kindness: his attention to Valien's welfare conflicted her hostile directive against him. A mother scarcely would provoke harm that might place her child at risk.

When buffeting flurries greyed out visibility, he kept close: caught her wrist, when she stumbled, and slackened his pace as her breathing grew laboured. His cagey gallantry revealed nothing. No behaviour suggested the concealed knowledge, that he walked the knife's edge in defiance of her suspect standing. Whether he planned the demise of a string puppet played by Koriani intent, or if innocent, uninformed altruism moved him to shepherd her conflicted spirit to freedom, Ettin's pursuit over rugged terrain bound their fates into brittle alliance.

Vivet fought for emotional distance. His soaked clothes and waif's build were quick to wring sympathy. Fine hands reddened with chill, and piercing concern for her welfare too readily chafed at the directive stayspells enacted to break him. Vivet hardened her heart, while the cruel snow thickened, and pelting wind taxed the strength prodigiously spent to shield Valien. Forget at her peril: he was Master of Shadow, and dangerous, and inhuman centuries older than his appearance.

Vivet endured, masked behind hollow eyes. Huddled in her damp mantle, she gasped in the thin air and weathered the pinched hunger from days of scant rations. Fatigue played havoc with her perceptions, until the keening gale seemed to endlessly shriek her brother's recriminations. She breathed in snow and coughed, her throat raw, while each step battled the endless, white maelstrom.

Nightfall hurled them into charcoal oblivion, ripped to further misery by jagged outcrops of lava that shredded boot-soles and clothing. Fingers ached and went numb. Exposed cheeks chapped and stung. Arithon limped on feet swathed in blood-stained tatters, when at last they scraped through the zigzagged, slit access into a ravine that sheltered their backs from the blasting gusts. The rock-walls narrowed, clad in ice by the steam risen off a hot spring farther below. Cumulative freezing had roofed the cleft, with sufficient space to snatch refuge.

Valien was wakeful and crying past remedy. Vivet shivered, hobbled by her sodden skirts. While she sought in vain to comfort her son, Arithon gathered their soaked cloaks, then requested the use of her shawl. He wadded the cloth at the entry to block off the frigid draught. When trapped heat from below fogged the cavern in warmth, he stripped his jerkin and shirt, and fashioned a nest for the traumatized child. "He'll settle once he's had something to eat."

Vivet dug into the supply pack, found a dry heel of bread, and broke off a crust. "Here, Valien." The boy took the morsel two-handed, stopped wailing, and gnawed, softened into contentment.

Arin withdrew the cloth-wrapped support of his hand. "I can soak the smoked meat in snow-melt, and cook millet in the pannikin, given a nearby blow-hole to boil the water." His oversight while she shook crusted snow from her skirt made Vivet feel like a stalked bird. Prolonged absence had changed the dynamic between them. Despite the prepotent glamour laid on her, his gaze no longer held sexual interest.

"What are we to you?" Vivet dropped her wrung hems, afraid of him as never before. "Why shoulder an obligation to us you never desired in the first place?"

The blizzard's shriek outside sufficient to risk conversation, he countered, "What made you leave your Ettin kinfolk before this? I think the honest beginning starts there."

But that question broached the vulnerable opening for an interrogation. Vivet bent her head, worrying the soaked cord knotting her bodice. Averted sight scarcely blunted her awareness of him, heightened by the pernicious effect of the spellcraft engaged in close quarters. Dim light through the curtaining fabric defined the elegant musculature sculpted over neat bone, the fine skin mottled with bruises and scabbed from the shamans' mishandling.

Terrified of the way she had come to be used, Vivet deflected the subject. "You can't very well traipse about over pumice before tending your feet."

"I'd not planned on walking." Arin tossed aside his damp shirt, his amused glance spiked in sudden reflection as something flashed on his left hand. Not jewellery: Vivet knew he wore nothing for personal vanity. While he had avoided conjury in her presence, he had backed Roaco's cabal down to a standstill, then had broken them by a method beyond her ken. Vivet fought to steady her breath, defencelessly out of her depth.

Arin removed the bright rings and tucked them inside his clenched fist. Then he cast away what seemed to be emptiness, until a stiff breeze whined past Vivet's ear, lashed her hair and prickled her nape.

"*Iyats!*" she gasped.

"Yes. I culled them from the storm. If you'll fill the pannikin with clean snow? They'll return engorged and discharge thermal heat." Arin's brief smile failed as a reassurance. "After I've dressed my feet, I might snag a few more. If they can be wrangled, an experiment with refined possession might dry our clothes."

Vivet shuddered. "That's Sithaer's unnatural work, bidding fiends. Tanuay's said more than once, you're a demon."

She braced for the flaying retort her brother would have received, but Arin only leaned forward. His mild reach hooked the supply pack. He fished out the pannikin, then braved the outside chill with bare arms and returned with a dollop scooped from a nearby drift. While his uncanny method prepared an unremarkable supper, he said, "Have you never risked all for something you loved? My lunatic artistry was contrived in a pinch to spare friends from a hostile attack. Sithaer's influence, you are quick to accuse. An unholy blaze, to fight fire with fire, except your small son can't withstand more exposure. Which earthly ethic means more to you?"

She had relaxed too soon. Waylaid by reason that carved altogether too close to the bone, Vivet dared not answer, cornered as she was by inflexible straits. One mistake, and Valien's welfare might become as expendable as the trapper's. Shame burned her cheeks. Unable to meet Arin's level regard, she discovered that Valien slept, the chewed bread-crust gone soggy in his slackened hand.

The storm raged with a fury to pen them for days, a strain wont to try any man with a known aversion to intimate company. Vivet stood on her guard, edgy as never before with the secret of her duplicity. Pretended innocence could not salvage the stakes sprung upon her by Arin's undeclared identity. Like the fool who groped to cage a stray mouse and encountered a den full of weasels, she had no retreat from the back-stab of justified vengeance, or the frightful prospect of fielding his verbal dissection. Much too late, Vivet wished she had not birthed an innocent to the hapless role of a game-piece.

Yet if Rathain's prince planned a scathing riposte, or whether he toyed with a cornered victim's distress, he deferred his reprisal, while nightfall leaded the niche in mute tension. Vivet watched, without recourse, the fine, chilblained fingers fill and light her little clay oil-lamp. The hellish, fluttering flame exposed the effort applied to the comforts of shelter and food. In due course, Valien slept in her lap, warm and properly fed for the first time in days. Vivet fought her own heavy lids. She watched Arin scour the pannikin, still wakeful when he surrendered to exhaustion. Denied the tinder for her distrust, at due length, she also succumbed and sank into dreamless sleep.

The next morning, the storm howled outside with no sign of abatement. Handed breakfast upon waking, Vivet amused her son, while the dread Spinner of Darkness methodically soaked his festered soles in hot compresses dipped in the mineral spring's salts. She suffered through the sulphurous fumes, then the bandaging, thoroughly done. Her attempt to provoke, using sarcasm, became drowned by the shriek when Valien tripped, and skinned his knee.

Song, then a story, spun for the boy's ear, led to a game with loose threads that finished with Valien tucked up for a nap. Then the renegade sorcerer, done with looking raffish, proceeded to shave. Afternoon came and dragged on into tedium. Vivet sat, while with expert stitches, her maddening companion mended his clothes. When he settled, eyes shut, with no courteous overture made to invite conversation, her frayed patience snapped.

Voice raised over the snarling tempest, she prodded, "I know who you are."

That opened both eyes. Pinned under a considering gaze that blistered for its bland indifference, she stiffened.

"Do you, in fact?" said the man who *was* Arithon Teir's'Ffalenn, beyond question. Bored lids fell and shuttered his unkind dismissal. "By the second hand taint of public opinion, no doubt, and in the dearth of my confidence."

The sally struck home; and owned up to nothing. Stung, Vivet attacked. "And is your bard's gift of sincerity false? I have heard you sing for Valien's comfort."

A smile of irony bent the hard mouth. Then Arithon said, "Valien wants to be care-free from pain." The lean body, reclined against cruel stone, stayed sapless, while his comment thrust for the viscera. "Since when have you given me any glimpse of sincerity from which to work a true note?"

Weather enforced their confinement throughout the night and relentlessly, all of the next day. By the time the gale spent its fury and tranquil weather returned, clear and cold, Vivet faced defeat, having exhausted, by every means, her directive to crack his facade. The bite of his worldly wit outmatched her. His patience outlasted her relentless efforts to pry. Where her badgering only lulled him to sleep, he could infuriate her with a word, then dissolve her affront with the weapon of Valien's laughter. But then, her task always had been unfair, doomed as she was under a yoked obligation, with her child the chip cast into a harsh bargain, sealed by her regrettable ignorance.

When the bitter dark brightened to a sparkling dawn, she broached the more mundane pitfall. "We'll need to restock our provisions."

Which announcement unexpectedly sparked his virile temper. Quick fingers, perhaps guilty of sorcerous murder, hooked the pack's lashings from her: as though her slack rationing might have leveraged the dearth of supply to create the unforeseen delay.

Vivet stated the painfully obvious. "I can't quiet Valien's crying if he becomes pinched with hunger."

Her target glanced up, dulcet humour restored. "Alas, freedom comes at a price. Coin for the toll, we'll take the troll's slog through the bog, and not the promenade into the sunset."

The terrain lay against them. The vertical ridge to the west blocked quick access to the forested glens, where a set snare could bag game. The milder path from the barren heights turned downwards into the vales, a stepped descent leading into the flatlands of West Halla. Once below the timberline, they could not return to the direct route, at altitude, before Ettin's archers seized the high-ground advantage. Ambush at the notch through the Storlain divide barred safe access to sanctuary in Elkforest.

Which finished Arithon's plan to secure High Queen Ceftwinn's justice, under charter rights, at the border of Havish. Pressed eastward instead, birthborn claim to free will relied upon ground where the old law ruled, crownless, by accredited stewardship. Flight to reach Melhalla's *caithdein* in Atwood must cross a hundred leagues of wide-open plain, under armed interdict by the Light's Canon, and then run the gamut of trade traffic moved by road and by river to Shipsport and Pellain.

Displacements

At dawn in Daon Ramon Barrens, Dakar the Mad Prophet and Iyat-thos Tarens share dismay for the set-back unveiled by Elaira's tranced scrying: "As we feared, Arithon's been driven east," which raises the prospect of crossing The Hatchet's dedicate war host, and forces her drastic suggestion, "I see only one way for us to proceed . . ."

An invisible presence on posted watch over the affairs of Lirenda Prime, Kharadmon fumes over the message, just relayed to the peeress at the Daenfal sisterhouse: "The storm deflected over the Storlains has won our desired result, with the key pieces in motion to avenge our Prime Circle's criminal destruction . . ."

Southbound at the vanguard of the Light's war host, The Hatchet receives a dispatch from a horse courier's hand, cracks a ruby seal with a swan cartouche, and reads with a satisfied crow, "Fetch the Lord High Examiner and his diviners! Our chase to hound the Spinner of Darkness will run him to ground in Daenfal . . ."

XII. Exigencies

The quarry marked for Prime Lirenda's retribution crossed the Tiendarion with his entourage of woman and child, driven before the persistent fury of the Ettinmen's vengeful pursuit. Loss of the settlement's bound raptors had not impaired their skilled archers. A flight loosed from the high ground would kill at extreme range without discrimination. Running targets, the vulnerable boy or the mother might fall prey, even an innocent life declared forfeit over the shame bestowed on a scandalized family.

Arithon laughed in the teeth of the threat, eyes sparked to baleful hilarity. "Sithaer take the hindmost, we still own the initiative. Roaco's pack-dogs have no recourse left but to tail-chase our lead and trip over the consequence."

"You say!" Vivet bristled, her russet braid a snaked tangle, and one harassed fist twined in Valien's shirt to curb his fixated poke at a scuttling millipede. "Given we have no bows on our side to retaliate, the trackers against us won't face fatal stakes."

"Don't they?" Arithon lashed in rebuke.

The implications posed by his identity by far too dire to broach, Vivet recoiled, exasperated. "You haven't a weapon to carry the fight if we're harried into close quarters." They had only the kitchen knife snatched from her hearthstone, a short blade with a wood handle better suited for jointing a chicken. "We've the means to whittle a sharpened stick! Nothing to shield us against bodkin points aimed with a downhill advantage."

"Well, by glory, tipped odds haven't murdered us yet. Only the cast-iron fool believes lethal force is the only option." Manner irreverent and black hair dishevelled, the s'Ffalenn bastard dismissed her fear. "Imagination exceeds limitation. I'll deliver the proof. Stylish invention can outmanoeuvre the mob strategy of superior numbers."

"Black craft-work and devil's tricks!" Vivet retorted, caution abandoned. "You'd set the dark arts against innocent men, some of whom are my cousins?"

"No." Arithon sobered, his wicked glance bleak. "I should think child's play better suits your kinfolk's cold-hearted sentiment."

Valien whimpered under restraint. While he filled his lungs for an ear-splitting howl, the sorcerer half the world wanted dead scooped him up and nestled a whisper into his ear. "I need round pebbles. Lots of them. Can you find enough to stuff both of your jerkin pockets?"

Vivet cut across the frivolous distraction. "What unnatural cruelty will you contrive? Are blameless men to be gutted in those dreadful traps used by the forest barbarians?"

"How delightful that murdering curs keep your sympathy," countered Arithon. "You've a cake of tallow soap in that pack?" Her furious nod woke a grin like a shark. "No ravening slaughter, by your express wish. Though if I cede my claim to a nasty revenge, we'll attach formal terms to the contest. You'll owe me an answer to my chosen question as forfeit if nobody dies."

"You have nothing to lose," Vivet retorted, flouncing the fir needles out of her skirt. "If you fail, and my countrymen perish, what paltry sop rewards me at the outcome?"

Smiling, Arithon surged to his feet. "The point's moot, for my part, since I'd be dead also. You'd be sadly left to console the survivors and cash out the Light's bounty on Valien's behalf."

Argument crushed, he set a cracking pace, shepherding his dependents under a close rein that took no chances. Noon came and went through Vivet's clammed stand-off. The toddler napped, borne on Arithon's back, cheeks striped in the shadows sieved through the scrub, with its chorus of chattering birdsong. Overhead, clouds sailed across a lapis sky, whisked by a breeze baked amid the sun-beaten rock of the heights. Sound carried, at altitude, magnified where freak echoes bounced off the slopes. Vivet walked with her skirt kirtled up, entreated by gestures to duck the low branches and by-pass the deadfalls without snapping sticks.

Yet efficiently as their small party travelled, the encumbrance of Valien slowed them. Ettin's pursuit outmatched all exemplary effort. Snatches of conversation drifted through the ear-splitting buzz of cicadas, cut by the sharp cracks of pebbles, dislodged and bouncing down-slope as the enemy trackers steadily closed.

Vivet ached. Her tired feet blistered. Dusk's purpled shadow crept across the creased vale and at length snuffed the flame of the afterglow. She sank, grateful, onto a wayside boulder, snatched short of rest by Arithon's unsympathetic grip on her elbow.

"Not here, not yet," he murmured, steering her into the next switched-back, dizzy descent.

She endured, muscles trembling, while nightfall clapped down like the lid on a pot, sugared by profligate stars. Pressed onwards by touch through the warm velvet dark, they inhaled the verdant breath of the mists, lapped like cotton batts over the low country. Flight maintained under an urgent silence, they broke past the crabbed stands of dwarf evergreen and climbed down, like stairs, the roots of the stunted hardwoods. The dappled trail became licked by the late rise of the yellow, half-moon. Vivet carried on in a daze, splashed wakeful by the cold springs that gushed, leaping, from ledge to ledge, and plunged swirling into a rock-pool. Arithon followed the tumbling freshet, a jagged seam carved into the face of the mountain, broken where they forded the smoothed-granite basins, lapped in icy foam to the knees.

"Not far now," he murmured, aware of Valien's whimpers under the splash of the falls.

Vivet offered a twist of meat jerky and stroked the child's tousled head. He quieted, sucking on the tidbit, a stop-gap distraction at best. "I can't quiet his complaints for much longer," she warned, her own stamina long since spent.

Steps mechanical, arms and back in strung knots, she pressed onwards in chilled exhaustion, her wet hem dragged against her shins and ankles as the little stream swelled, and tugged every footstep with gathering force. The ground shook to the roar where the confluence of a second, larger cascade jetted over the brink. The falls thrashed the humid air into gusts, whipped to frothing lace where the spray sheeted into a glassine pool far below.

"Don't slip," cautioned Arithon through the barrage.

Moss slicked the wet stone. Vivet clambered downwards, teeth chattering, relieved to bestow Valien into Arithon's charge. The night sky hung deep as a caul overhead, pocked with the haloed glimmer of strewn constellations. The thunder of the cataract diminished behind before the weary party gained respite.

"Here," whispered Arithon. His touch guided Vivet ahead through the mist, and then doubled back. Several stumbling steps brought her into a grotto, hidden beneath a sloped ledge. Water sang and dripped, fed by overshot moisture from the falls above, and guttered down the seamed face. Inside, the leaf-lined cleft remained dry. If wolves had whelped here, the den was unoccupied.

Vivet folded, without care for the cobwebs, and reclaimed Valien's squirming distemper. His plaintive wail cut like a blade, risen to beet-faced rage. Savaged by his tantrum, she scarcely heard Arithon's hurried instructions.

"Get yourselves settled and fed. Then sleep if you can. I'm off meanwhile to set a few snares." His regard raked her with an acuity that belied his mild remark upon parting. "Relief is at hand. If my plan delivers, the journey won't stress you as sorely hereforward."

Alarmed, Vivet rallied to ask if his traps were to be laid for animals. Before speech, he was gone, melted into the night. Valien had outworn the impulse to cry. His boneless weight in her lap sapped the will to arise. Whether she might forewarn the Ettinmen set at risk, the lead seized under pressure had widened too far, with her resiliency spent. If the falls did not drown her shout, a perfidious outcry might tip her hand and upset the directive laid on her. Neither could Valien stay on his own through a search likely foredoomed to failure. Arithon's skill in the wilds was legend. Too often, and with bitter oaths, Roaco's trackers had been balked by his wily experience.

Compelled to abide, Vivet tucked up with Valien, asleep from the moment she laid down her head.

Vivet woke to the morning light in her eyes. Daybreak had passed, the sun risen to flood the east-facing cranny. Arithon was already alert, slouched like a feral tomcat with one elbow braced at the brink. Protected between, Valien sat on his rump, poking his cache of smooth pebbles into straggly rows.

The indolent atmosphere of camaraderie ignited Vivet's short temper. "We might have slacked off last night's pace, it would seem." She was all-over stiff and welted from biting insects. Beyond aching muscles and abused joints, her heels stung, crusted with burst blisters. Her next breath for carping complaint met a cobra-fast finger, pressed to her lips. Then Arithon released his high-handed censure and without apology pointed upwards.

Scraps of aggravated conversation floated down-slope through the din of the cataract, peppered by the inflections of Ettin dialect.

The insolent quarry appeared undisturbed by the hunters' proximity. Quite the contrary, his gaze through disordered black hair gleamed with intrigued speculation. "How many," he murmured, "do you suppose Roaco's sent for the blood-bath?"

Vivet shrugged, surly and unwilling to rise to his goading. Border patrols always worked in pairs, expanded by squads of six. Under his quizzing regard, she flicked off the obvious sum on disdainful fingers.

Arithon's lips flexed with joyful irony. "You've underrated our criminal value, my dear. I've sorted twelve individual voices." Expectantly paused, his attention unwavering under her reticent silence, he said cheerfully, "My count when their heads broke the sky-line at dawn confirmed an even fourteen."

Nothing suggested this fact was news; long since, he must have ascertained the strength of the opposition. Vivet disregarded the provocation, relieved when his interest deserted her for a whispered exchange with Valien.

The boy nodded, forehead puckered with concentration. His small, grubby fingers selected the best of his collected pebbles. After earnest thought, he added two more, then bestowed the gifts into the man's open palm, grinning in sly conspiracy.

"*Anli,*" Arithon murmured, the diminutive spoken in Paravian. "Very good. Now we play for the prize."

While Vivet suffered tugged heart-strings, the fey creature who claimed her son's trust uncoiled with animal grace. Head cocked, he listened, as if a recognizable language patterned the random air-currents that traced over his skin.

Vivet noticed, then only: Arithon had stripped to rolled shirtsleeves, the older scars on his bruised wrists and forearm exposed against his habitual reticence. Further, his discarded jerkin and cloak were not in the sheltered cleft.

The moment stretched, turned suddenly perilous. Oblivious yet, the snapped speech of the Ettinmen flickered nearer. Through the sussurant hiss of the falls, a snapped stick silenced the bird-song. Nerveless, intent, Arithon's fixated eyes wore the sheared reflection of summer's foliage. Against the lucent back-drop of sky, *he was the purposeful predator, poised for an ambush on familiar ground.*

"You've been here before," Vivet blurted, before sense.

His head turned, with a testy glance fit to peel skin. "By glory, did you imagine I could toss jackstraws with your child's life? If you ever thought I would court danger at fortune's caprice, what earthly reason gave your consent to rely on my guardianship?"

Vivet reeled, stung breathless. Pinned beyond hope of a sensible answer, she endured in discomfort a survey more scouring than a Koriathain's.

Let the s'Ffalenn sorcerer never discern the tap-root of her secret terror. Whether Arithon suspected a convenient recapture by Ettin's pursuit might buy her release, he must never fathom the price rendered due if his bid for escape should succeed. "My child's no son of yours." Before she blurted the more fatal confession, she attacked to deflect him. "Why should a nameless, dead stranger's by-blow matter to you?"

Not heartless stone, the motive behind Arithon's inscrutable purpose: impatience, contempt, or perhaps a flashed glimpse of exasperated endurance slipped through before he quashed his startled emotion. "Valien is himself, and innocent of his begetting. Take care you don't mar his joy with your bitterness, in or out of my presence."

As nothing else could, his defence of her son made Vivet choke back a scream for his folly. Better sense—*in harsh fact any claim to wisdom at all*—should have warned him to jettison her plight outright. Honey and poison, the ceaseless inner turmoil that defeated her wit to express: for she was the made tool of his enemies. Her weakness netted his insidious strength, relentless as bait on the hook. He would buy her deliverance, come whatever cost, no matter that his accursed tenacity sealed her fate without quarter.

Her blank anguish drowned horror. If she could not bear his cold-blooded slaughter by arrows before the eyes of her child, self-interest flinched also from withering fear: a brazen betrayal to force the quick end might waken the monster and unleash the black arts of the Master of Shadow. Vivet froze at the crux, a trapped pawn seized by the merciless claim on her destiny.

Through Valien's sing-song burble of pleasure, and the liquid trill of a thrush, the inflection of the human voices closed through the thrash of white water. Like echo, Arithon's bearing transformed. Become the blade unsheathed, he unhooked from his belt a sling fashioned from rag and knotted sinew: the sort used by small boys to bag game for the supper pot. Loaded with Valien's cache of smooth pebbles, a man's strength whirled a lethal weapon. Yet Arithon did not launch the missiles upslope but arced his stones in a bunch above the tree-tops beneath. The impacts cracked harmlessly into the adjacent, buttressed outcrop. But the rattle of their falling trajectory woke the Ettin archers to shouting alarm.

Arithon's wicked smile accompanied the dust puffs kicked up by the scattershot ricochets. Vivet back-traced their pinging descent to a sunlit niche on the far slope, strategically occupied by a stuffed effigy made from the missing jerkin and cloak.

"Now, Valien!" the tactician encouraged with unnatural, infectious glee. "We get to count the prize haul of big splashes."

The enemy fervour unfolded, disordered, to a warning, deep grate of rock. The monolithic rasp triggered off the squirted, wasp hum of multiple arrows, loosed raggedly wide of the mark as the bowmen were rocked off balance. More shouts erupted, spiked by a fresh hail of kicked stones, which smacked downwards, shredding thrashed leaves off the overhead branches. Then dismay cranked the oaths a shrill octave higher. Chaos gathered momentum: Ettin's best archers windmilled, teetered as their footing gave way. The convenient flat outcrop, by no chance at all, had presented the opportune stance to rain fletched death upon the cloth decoy.

Hindsight recalled the seamed ledge, sited at the brink of the falls. Stable enough under Arithon's weight the past night, while he stretched to refill a flask from the spray: until his subsequent visit had doctored a layered fracture for purposeful sabotage.

The sprung trap delivered its engineered malice, as, grinding protest, the shifted slab slid. Gravity's inexorable pull loosened the snap and ping of the pebbles speeding its ponderous skid. Then the massive stone toppled. Its titanic descent sledded down-slope to the thunderous whoosh of its splash in the basin. Treble yells from the air-borne men, trailing, piled into glissades of wet impacts, while the backwash of sloshed water rained down amid spluttering expletives.

"Seven," murmured Arithon, his comment pocked by yet another immersion. "Ha! There's eight." Eyes crinkled with hilarity, he tallied the separate cries, pleased as the child beside him over each outburst of jabbering rage.

"You've only inflamed their murderous cause," Vivet cautioned, while the Ettin hunters who remained unscathed swarmed to rescue their floundering comrades.

"Well, yes. It's a lame, slapstick comedy. Enter, sopped dignity, charging to patch the savaged decorum of a deadly man-hunt." Arithon grinned. "Behold, and applaud the finale."

More noise erupted on cue, embellished by shrieks of ear-splitting fury.

Clutching his ribs, Arithon gasped, "That would be the effect of your soap, slathered to grease the descent."

Overcome, he folded in helpless mirth, while another resounded barrage of ripe thumps thrashed, tumbling, through abused greenery, and more hapless bodies met their demise in a glottal explosion of splashes.

The joke unleashed Valien's giggles, and Arithon's mangled epilogue. "Felled to the last man, boots . . . sinew . . . and weapons."

Cocky before Vivet's appalled silence, he surmised, "There won't be a functional marksman among them. Not only are their laminate recurves prone to warp, soaked-gut bow-strings will stretch under tension for days. I suggest we'd be wise to bolt like hares across the next ridge."

Arithon set a brutal pace. Valien straddled his shoulders, fists clutched in his black hair. Dragged at his heels, out of sorts on a sour stomach and broken sleep, Vivet still noticed the measuring glances the sorcerer cast over his shoulder.

"You're not gloating," she jabbed. "Why haven't you claimed the self-styled prize for your ill-gotten victory?"

"Brava. You imply I might have sufficient integrity to honour fair terms?" Arrived at a streamlet, left hand clasped to Valien's ankle to free his grip to assist her across, Arithon tendered a sheepish apology. "If honesty matters, I plan to cheat while your countrymen strip to dry out their clothing."

Vivet stared, her unease redoubled as the humour left his expression. "Devil's tricks for the curtain-call," he admitted. "I have no better means, beyond plaguing *iyats*, by which to relieve your drenched countrymen of their breeches."

"What?" Vivet exclaimed. "Clothes only? Not weapons?"

"Pity the fellows if you were in charge," Arithon chided, remorseless. "No blades and no bows, bare-arsed in these wilds? The predicament would be an unnatural cruelty. The chase takes us into the foot-hills by nightfall. A tracker stripped down to his tender skin becomes meat for the biting insects, with added punishment from the thorn patches lacing the scrub. Our valiant pursuit won't press their chase, naked. By the time the wretches can trap for green hides to redress their miserable modesty, our trail will lose them in Silvermarsh."

Night fled over the open heath of Daon Ramon, with midsummer's air blood-warm and breezeless around the small, furtive party southbound. Dakar perched atop the stacked rocks used to bake the past evening's meal, jabbing a stick into the powdered ash in the fire pit. Tarens awoke to the arrhythmic sound. He turned over, alert, since the nervous habit signalled upcoming trouble. The Mad Prophet's lumped form notched the pre-dawn gloom, unkempt as an abandoned tinker's sack.

"Where's Elaira?" For the hollow in the brush covert was empty, her dusty blanket removed as well.

"You let her go off alone!" he accused, rattled onto his feet.

Dakar dropped the stick with a start. Eyes rolled sidewards and his pouched expression morose, he allowed, "I'm impressed you believe that I might have stopped her."

"Damn your slacking hide." Disgusted, Tarens snagged up his baldric, cinched the buckle, and adjusted the hang of his daggers. "When did she leave?"

"Too long ago. You'll chase your own tail, pelting after her." Yet Dakar's evasive stab at the embers engendered suspicion rather than sympathy.

Tarens snatched the offensive stick. "Damned if you didn't nod off through your watch!"

Dakar winced. "I did not sleep a wink, fiends plague the sharp stones and the roots." Balled into a clench, his untrustworthy features sparked by sly interest, he added, "Has it never crossed your yokel's mind that some women prefer not to drag along a defender?"

Incredulous, Tarens bent to the task of obliterating the fire pit. "Don't feed me that idiocy. Not with The Hatchet's picketed scouts swarming the country like an infestation."

Dakar watched, unblinking, a brown toad in his tatty ruckle of loosened clothing. "You're speaking of Rathain's handfast crown consort, who scarcely requires my leave, or anyone's. She'll travel this kingdom's sovereign territory just as she pleases."

The next moment, with scarcely a rustle, something riffled the air behind Tarens's back. He spun, alarmed, into a white billow of fabric that enveloped his face, and entangled his reach for his dagger. He clawed off the obstruction, then snarled a curse as he noted the gleam of a recruit's Sunwheel surcoat. The garment was foisted on him by Elaira, arrived back with cat-footed stealth.

"Wear that!" she snapped, freezing his impulse to fling down the offensive cloth. "It's genuine issue, brought fresh from the encampment's laundress by a bargain neither of you could repeat. Sully the outfit, and you'll shame the veteran who's agreed to mentor your orientation."

"We're infiltrating the ranks?" Tarens surmised, aghast. "I tried that once in Arithon's company. The tactic sent us Sithaer's way to ruin. I'm condemned under seal by the Canon, what's more. Whoever you've cozened to cover my tracks, I'm a bone to be tossed for a rich reward to the True Sect examiners."

"No. You'll see." Elaira's peeling glare transferred to the Mad Prophet.

"I'm moving already!" he groused, before she kicked his arse.

She talked on through the lumbering thrust that heaved his bulk upright. "I've located prior acquaintances who know me as a harness mender. That's my plausible story, already arranged. Dakar, are you good for a tinker's work in the forge? That will do. You'll pose as my drunken assistant, and Tarens, a green conscript signed on from his former post as a caravan guard. We'll pass, provided none of us ruffles the flux in a manner that broadcasts trained talent. I have only one officer's tent to avoid. The main host's encampment is sprawling enough and chaotic from the recent musters. Provided we slip through at the dawn change of watch, our presence won't attract questions."

Tarens griped, aghast, his calloused hands tugging the hateful surcoat over his shoulders. "Your Sunwheel henchman will expose my bumpkin's ignorance inside of an hour."

Elaira thumped a pair of waxed boots at his feet, followed by a rucksack packed with a foot soldier's gear. "He'll accept you, no question. Get dressed."

"You pinched that kit out of somebody's tent?" Dakar's eyebrows buckled with awe. "Slick move! Until that soldier wakes up and gets hopping furious in his bare feet. What's to spare our trusty crofter from the whipping post for petty theft?"

Elaira served the spellbinder with a contempt to clip bollocks. "Learn how to have friends," she retorted. "Or stay here on your merits. Daybreak won't wait, and I've had enough of your gutless objections."

The sky wore the hazy colour of ash, scribbled over with smoke from the cook-shacks and the chimneys that hooded the forge-fires. Beneath spread the vista of Sunwheel tents, rows of peaked canvas tinged rose with the advent of dawn. The enchantress's party of three sauntered towards an atmosphere of seething bustle, pocked by harried shouts and blared horns as the Light's war camp stirred awake. Committed past recourse, Tarens trailed Elaira's lead, pursued by Dakar's wheezy complaints. The air fore-promised broiling heat, summer's haze thickened by the ammoniac reek of picketed livestock and trampled manure. They skirted the perimeter sentries' overlook through a hollow, crossed a shallow creek, and made their bold entry, shadowed against the thornbrake behind the horse-lines. The returned patrols had already dismounted, steaming animals being stripped of their tack and led to water by bleary-faced grooms. The riders out-bound, amid saddling up, jostled into restive formation. Others milled, cursing the slackers, who stalled, grumbling, over the draw that assigned their current mounts.

Elaira plunged undaunted into the press. "Mending!" Her cry pierced through the hubbub. "Bring me your harness, broken or worn!"

A frantic page dashed past a cluster of officers, burdened with a torn girth. At his heels came a freckled squire, trailing a set of broken reins. Elaira foisted their strap goods on Dakar, and, passing, hooked up a bridle with gold bosses left unattended. She thrust the flash tack upon Tarens, forthwith. "That belongs to your mentor, returned from repair. Behave like you own it, and don't look back."

"Mending!" she shrilled, momentarily paused to burrow into her satchel. "A stitch in time spares an unlucky spill!" While she strung tags with the owners' identities onto the leather-work, Dakar groaned, now yoked under a damaged chariot collar, winking with brass terrets. Tarens bided, uneasy, until a kick in the shin focused him on the label the enchantress slapped into his palm. "Knot that onto the bit ring! Quickly!"

Tarens complied. He ploughed after her wake, dodging a fractious war-horse, then warned away from the heels of the next by a switch-bearing, pimple-faced groom.

Dakar waddled, by then, weighted further by worn traces, a fringed horse-cloth with a ripped hem, and a saddle in need of restuffing.

Someone's ribald query chaffed Elaira over the prowess of her paunch-bellied pack-mule.

She laughed and hollered a cheerful retort. "Can you studs not imagine a use for yourselves past a laggard's roll in the blankets?" A prod at the spell-binder's stiffened back wrangled his offended tread onwards. "Caught out, gutfull with a contraband flask? This pathetic fellow's damned grateful I snatched him away from a justified whipping."

More grooms bustled up, each with a fresh offering. Elaira walked jingling, shoulders regaled with bridles, and Tarens, conscripted, acquired a rowelled spur with a broken strap, two holed boots, and a baldric with a cracked buckle. The marginal advantage, that he went armed, became moot under the encumbrance.

He followed, knees whacked by the swing of the officer's shanked bit, while Elaira threaded her way through the bedlam of lackeys and runners, flushed idlers, and cranky men fixated on breakfast. Under the dazzling flare of the sunrise, through an armourer's industrious clangour, Tarens realized Elaira was speaking.

"You've scarcely an hour before this camp's set on the march. Your mentor will steer you through your assignments. He's already aware of the history he's shielding. Find me with Liess the laundress, if needed. Any plausible errand will cover your visit."

She paused, divested Tarens of his load, then elbowed him towards a petty officer's tent more dingy and weathered than most. "Take the bridle inside. You're expected." Then she nodded to steady his pulverized nerves and abandoned him to her arrangement.

Tarens wrestled reluctance. Cursed out of the path of a hustling equerry, he firmed his step, clamped his delivery in clammy fingers, then bent his fair head and ducked through the flap entry.

Gloom enveloped him, tainted by mildewed canvas and the martial reek of rancid grease, rusted metal, and sweat-clogged fleeces. He paused, made aware through the prickle of goose bumps, of someone seated to his right.

Movement stirred. A sturdy man shoved off a creaking camp stool. "Light deliver!" he gasped, shaken gruff. "That snip of a mender spoke true!"

Tarens snatched the impression of height, spiked with short, greying hair. Then the outside light revealed a weathered face whose bearded, blunt features haunted him for an aged resemblance to his brother, Efflin. The next instant, the clasp of two massive arms crushed the stunned breath from his chest.

"Father?" he gasped, shaken by disbelief as the fierce embrace released his rocked balance.

Astonished, he surveyed a familiar grin, grown uneven with two broken teeth. Eyes as blue as his own crinkled with joy, spilling tears down leathery cheeks gouged crosswise by a battle scar. "You're called Tethos, I'm told? A fine name from good family. Now, let's pack down this tent. We'll eat on the march if you're hungry."

While dust raised by The Hatchet's southbound war host silted the arid downs of Daon Ramon, summer's white haze lidded the low country and steamed off the scummed bogs and sinkpools that patched Silvermarsh like liquid glass splashed off a smelter's rod. Beyond the thornbrakes that defeated the Ettinmen's unbreached pursuit, the flat mire unrolled, clotted by tangles of hazel and bull grass, and stamped with crowned thickets of marsh maple. By night the air reeked like a sodden sponge, and by day, the welter of heavy humidity rippled like fumes off a vat.

Biting insects shimmered in swarms. Every patch of uncovered skin became welted to itching misery. Arithon kindled smudge torches only between dawn and dark to avoid visibility. What broken rest could be snatched after nightfall relied upon beds of cut bracken, tented under the stifling linen of Vivet's tattered shift.

No recourse availed when Valien's fussing exploded to cantankerous tears. Cajoling him from his tantrums demanded a near-to-mystical patience and all of a Masterbard's artful skill. Vivet battled the exhausted urge to abandon her bitter objective. Over and over, she stiffened her purpose with the cold-hearted reminder: the man striving beside her was not what he seemed, a mere criminal on the run, but a sorcerer steered by an inscrutable purpose. Altruism alone did not sustain such devotion under the hardship of their east-bound flight.

"What on this forsaken earth do you want from me?" Vivet demanded, knee deep in reeking muck, her scalp itching under a filthy kerchief.

Arithon turned in his tracks and regarded her, his tangled black hair clenched in Valien's fists, and lean cheek-bones clamped between the boy's grubby, skinned knees. Through the maddened drum of bare heels on his chest, he said, injured, "I thought I'd ceded the victor's claimed forfeit."

Vivet scrubbed her streaming brow, palms sliced raw from grasping at saw-grass tufts in slimy footing. "From the start, we've been a thankless burden. What incentive do you have to keep us?"

His smile split a face as worn as her own. "Not everyone styles their motive for gain. Tell me, what were you running away from when you left Deal?"

A slip off a tussock spared her reply. Vivet spat a splashed mouthful of grit, mauled by a suicidal urge to unburden. Whatever else the man might suspect, surely he guessed she had knifed the trapper before the luckless fellow refuted the falsehood that framed his assault.

Vivet sloshed through the sink-hole, swearing over the perilous bent of her candid self-examination.

Yet Arithon addressed only the obvious facet of her frustration. "You've been a game traveller. Perhaps a day more, and the marshes recede. The dry plain beyond will see us the rest of the way through West Halla."

Vivet suppressed her alarm. His uncanny guidance had far outstripped her best estimate of their progress. Almost too late, she grasped the dilemma, that she must react quickly to slow him down.

"Story, story, *story*!" yelled Valien, bored by their conversation.

Arithon laughed. "Lad, have mercy! Stop drubbing me to a pulp, and I'll surrender and spin you a tale."

The boy quieted, lulled by the cadence of exquisite speech, while the sun sweltered down, scalding reflections off the stirred ripples. Vivet trudged, steps measured by the wet plop of frogs and the squawking flight of startled herons. Shoes hung by tied laces around her neck, and with the runnelled sweat stinging her eyes, she hiked her muddy skirt over her wrist. Bunched cloth masked her furtive snatch for the cooking knife sheathed at her waist. The blade left her hand with scarcely a splash, lost at once in the turbid mire.

Hours passed, and the low sun snuffed early, swallowed by flannel-grey cloud that chased icy gusts through the pale stands of marsh reed. Caught in the open when the squall struck, Arithon bundled Valien under his wet shirt, his own body the boy's shelter from the frigid rain, and the pea-sized hail that pinged down and scourged exposed flesh. Thunder slammed through the battening murk, sizzled with actinic spears of close lightning. Valien keened with fear, unconsolable, his hiccuping sobs exhausted to whimpers as the maelstrom subsided to vertical rainfall. The aftermath melted into fallen dusk, gloomy under thinned drizzle that tapered off into steamy mist.

"Valien's chilled," Arithon observed through the patter of droplets off sodden reeds. "We have to risk a small fire to warm him."

The need to shave sticks for dry kindling disclosed her disastrous loss of the knife. After a glance at Vivet's aghast face, Arithon withheld comment, even to remark on her untoward shiver. "We won't go hungry," he ventured through the discomfortable pause. "I'll rake for snails and mussels while the light lasts. Afterward, with cat-tails for torches, we can scoop for crawdads with the pannikin."

So the evening went, the drilling whine of mosquitoes momentarily suppressed by the violent weather. The small flame kindled to ease the child also boiled their noisome catch, the rubbery morsels picked from the shells with stems of plucked sedge. Valien raised objection to the clammy taste, until tearful fury wore him down, and he slept despite the pinch of his hollow belly.

Vivet chewed through her share, her guilty apology smothered, while Arithon sat wakeful to watch. Between them lay silence like an accusation, while the frogs croaked in deafening chorus, and the humid night clung like spilled ink.

He spoke at last, while Vivet tossed, chafed to restlessness by wet clothes, upon ground that squelched to each movement.

"What were you promised if you brought me down?"

Fist jammed against her clamped teeth, Vivet shrank, feigning sleep to avoid a confession. For the consequence of her sabotage once again had unravelled Arithon's plan. Without steel, he could not skin snared game in the wild, or provide for a small child's comfort. Confronted by two more fortnights of hard-scrabble foraging, he knew, exactly as she had: Valien's welfare demanded a turn northward in pursuit of civilized amenities.

The set-back this time was not faced with complacency. Though he might have, Arithon did not wield sorcerous arts, or sing to melt her into pliant surrender. His bardic voice nuanced only by compassion, he appealed to evoke her free will.

"I know that your father was a kindly man who indulged you, among two other daughters. He sickened when you were eight, injured by a blow to the head while felling timber. Your mother nursed his infirmity for five terrible years, traumatized by his fits of irrational screaming. Tanuay and your brothers struggled to cope, forced to seek work while underage to sustain your family."

Eyes shut, arms hugged to her breast while tears leaked through shut eyelids, Vivet dared not drown his recitation by muffling her ears. To move was to break, unstrung by sympathy fit to seal her destruction. Paralysed by threat, and stark fear for survival, she endured, while his onslaught continued.

"Your elder sisters married early to relieve the stress on the household. Older men wed them, a practical choice made to ease the additional obligations imposed by marital kinship. Duty forbade the girls their youthful sweethearts, since a husband not yet established risked the burden of further dependence. You were resented for keeping your freedom. No matter, to them, that you were alone, a child overfaced by an adult's share of the household chores. You watched your mother suffer the brunt of your father's violent insanity. Too small, you were helpless to do aught but cower, while she became battered and bruised."

Vivet shivered, while the gentle delivery exposed the nightmare gist with pitiless clarity: of the terrified hours, spent huddled inside the chicken coop through her father's bellowing rages; of sweeping up broken crockery, and washing the clothes caked with spilled food and excrement amid her mother's listless depression. Vivet still flinched at shouts, marked deep by the trauma as arguments flared from her brothers' frayed tempers; she ached still from the poisonous loneliness of her sisters' sullen detachment.

Sobs stifled, Vivet relived the bad memories, while Arithon concluded her sorry history with eviscerating kindness.

"The day came when your father pinned you against the chopping block. Your mother doused him with boiling soup, almost scalding him blind to keep him from killing you. He died that night in his bed, perhaps by a desperate act of suffocation. Your mother was shunned for suspected murder, without a witness to claim otherwise. In harsh consequence, you were declared eligible, to be made handfast at fourteen years of age for the betterment of your lot."

Vivet held, strangled breathless, but the sordid account cut off short of full closure. No reference was made of her flight from the settlement; no weighted conjecture implied the bargain struck with Koriathain for shelter when she had reached Deal, scared and starving.

"You alone must decide where your destiny leads," Arithon finished. He never mentioned Valien's fate, sharpest weapon of all in the battle between them.

The last of the night passed in brutal silence. Arithon kept his wakeful vigil, until dawn lit the world grey as misted pearl, and they broke their squalid camp to turn north. When sunrise flared like spilled blood from a wound, Arithon shared out their belongings as usual, but lashed the pannikin to his own belt for safekeeping.

Two days more brought them out of the swamp to the pebbled shore of Daenfal Lake. Valien by then was pinched sallow with hunger, his shrieks loud enough to startle the wading birds and perhaps, flag a passing trade barge bound downstream for Shipsport. Fortune's back-handed favour instead gave their party a fishing boat, beached in the aftermath of the freak storm. She lay canted for repair on the strand, her sunburned crew sitting idle on casks, three dicing to quips of caustic humour, while a fourth with a squint toasted skewered bread and cheese over a drift-wood fire. Long since, they had patched her breached hull with sail canvas. A fished spar mended the split mast. They had lingered only because one of the crew languished in a sling with a broken collar-bone.

Arithon's effort to barter his healer's skills for a rigging knife became stonewalled by their bandy-legged captain.

Crumpled features crested with a game-cock's cow-lick, the fellow sized up the destitute woman and child, then measured Arithon's able build with a gimlet stare. "You'll pull an oar well enough to get by. Sail's in tatters, and this tub needs four at the benches to limp back into Daenfal." Terms declared, he puckered and spat, striking a gull into squalling flight. "It's passage for your three selves across. Else go your own way, and bedamned. Coin's paid for fair labour after we dock, and you'll find knives aplenty for sale in the market." Against Arithon's cornered reluctance, he added with unforeseen kindness, "Get us launched straightaway, and I'll throw in your board, if only to shut that wean's pitiful noise."

Daenfal

The lake-side trade port piled against the gorge at the mouth of the Arwent carved a notched silhouette against the pellucid sky of imminent dawn. On approach, the crumbled necropolis promontory reared to the east, toothed by its skeletal spine of memorial spires. The town nestled beneath, buttressed by a crenellated sandstone wall, dusted in blown mist from the falls that reeled off the cliff rim of the Arwent Plateau. The pen-stroke of the rope ferry's cables sliced across the roiling outflow beneath. Crammed between, peaked slate roofs and corniced abutments lay jammed in serried disorder, flagged with the banners streamed from the guild-halls and the turquoise pennant of the mayor.

Noise racketed off the busy wharf, the boom and rumble of rolling barrels sliced by the vendors' tremolo patter. Down the steep, narrow alleys where night's shadow lingered, lit windows and torches still glimmered orange, nicked like sequins between the mica-flash glitter, where glazed casements caught the flare of first sunrise.

Bells tolled. A flock of white shore-birds winged over the ripple of chop. Valien pointed and laughed, perched in Vivet's embrace at the fishing-craft's rail. She minded her child with protective dread, while the oars drove the prow through the gap in the breakwater. Arithon laboured with the crew at the bench, the current rib-splitting joke shared among them diverting his notice of her apprehension.

Long overdue and beyond turning back, her cold reckoning waited ashore.

Two men shipped their sweeps. One raced to the bow to hook the float mooring, while the other guided the tillerman's course through a crowded anchorage scattered with buoys. Idle vessels bobbed like schooled fish, nosed to windward with furled sails. The captain's barked orders saw his damaged craft shackled, and her tender launched from the transom. First away, the mate went to schedule repair and buy replacement tackle at the chandler's. The remaining crew stowed the lines and swabbed decks, while the return pass delivered the injured man home to his family.

Too soon, Arithon arrived smiling at Vivet's elbow, a faded waterman's kerchief tied over his midnight hair. He took charge of Valien's excitable bulk, nodded aft, and said gently, "Time we were away."

His escort delivered her into the boat, with her fearless toddler passed into her arms by the sailhand remaining aboard. Then Arithon shouldered the oars with the captain. Their tandem strokes skimmed the craft to the wharf, where, unladen amid the water-front bustle, the vessel's master clasped Arithon's blistered palm and squared up his debt.

"Might be soft as a lubber, lad, but I ken the work of a blue-water rigger." He bestowed a wash-leather bag, a generous twelve coinweight heftier than promised. "I'm still a man short. Once we're refitted, be welcome aboard if yer wantin' a berth."

"That's kindly," said Arithon, his flushed pleasure sincere. "I'll remember your name though the plight of the child and his mother comes first."

The pair parted ways with genial regret, the captain to chase down the mate tasked with the list for the chandler's, and Arithon to pursue resupply and a quality blade at the market.

Vivet all but flinched when his gaze focused on her, mindful as an intimate touch.

"You look tired." Her evident strain explained by the rough passage and restless sleep, he steered a firm course down the dock, speaking through the boom of a caulker's mallet and the jostling, bare-chested labour of the steve-dores. "Let's find lodging for you and the boy, with a meal. Take your ease for the day while I seek arrangements with an east-bound caravan. With luck, we'll be on the road before nightfall."

Vivet gestured her limp acquiescence. The bustle and noise forgave her reluctance to speak, and the warped boards underfoot excused her downcast glance. She wound through the mounds of wet fish-nets and stacked crates, the gunny-sacks and the roped barrels, while the hubbub of Daenfal's trade crowded the ramped gangways. The taints of tarred hemp, strewn sawdust, and gutted fish aggravated her queasy nerves. A low stair connected the timber wharf with the barge ferry's buttressed stone landing. There, Arithon's panther stride checked beside her.

She looked up, shocked by the bloodless pallor of his set features. "Are you ill?"

"No." His green eyes snapped to meet hers. Ice-cold, the fingers that guided her steps up the risers. Shadowed by the massive, chafed bollard that anchored the barge ferry's cable, he snatched a second to right his discomposure. She lacked the means to fathom his upset: that, until now, their lake passage had buffered the graphic disclosure riffled through the land-bound flux currents:

The Hatchet's war host commanded the northerly plain. A hostile encampment surrounded Daenfal's landward access and restricted his ease of movement.

He said only, "This town always has been unlucky for me."

Worse than the presence of Sunwheel might, the entrenched imprint of active Koriathain infused the stonework, both past and present. Up the ancient causeway, drenched in mist from the falls, his made double once had wrestled a balky pony and matched sword-play with a burly watch officer under the squat arch of the river gate.

Steeled for trouble, Arithon faced his latest, ill-starred entanglement. "Vivet. From you, I want nothing but this: tell me what hold the Koriathain have over you. Trust my word, their binding can be safely broken. Granted the freedom to reclaim your fate, you must be aware: the glamour their seniors settled upon you was an imprint, stolen from a woman I cherish. Tell me, does Elaira still live? And if not, might you know what befell her?"

Vivet recoiled. Her palpable fear met his nailing regard, as her secretive past caught up with her present. She dared not speak. Her directive permitted no recourse: *bear his natural child or else see him dead.* Failure to deliver the first sealed her ruin unless he abandoned her to save himself.

A horn brayed on the water. The winch cable thrummed to the ferry's approach, and a surly bargeman shouted, "Move along!"

And the dazed moment fled, another chance to unburden passed over for self-preservation. Arithon fielded her rudderless stress without censure and recovered his purposeful stride towards the shoreside taverns. "I will provide the room and the meal, as I've promised. Perhaps you'll regain the presence to think while I'm away at the market."

The room he selected was quiet, located in a north-facing wing, away from the racketing crush of the landing. The third floor dormer overlooked a narrow alley, puddled with the overflowed suds from a laundress's vats. A gangling adolescent with a piled hand-cart pinned up the rinsed shirts, then collected the dried breeches and sheets flapping in the breeze funnelled between the brick-and-timber tenements. Vivet used the view to evade conversation, watching a brown tabby stalk small prey holed up in a drain-pipe. She endured the slow minutes, dreading the meal arranged during their rapid pass through the downstairs tap-room.

Yet Arithon did not linger to eat. He stayed only to see Valien settled. At the door with intent to depart straightaway, she received his clipped instructions. "Pin the latch when I've gone. Don't venture out. Once the girl brings the tray, admit no one. I'll come back with supplies before dusk, and I plead, choose for the sake of your child's future, if not for your own."

Vivet returned no word. Before she turned from the casement, the door swung soundlessly shut at his heels.

* * *

The delegation Vivet expected followed the simple meal, settled savourless into a cankered stomach. Footsteps crowded the hallway without, a paralysed moment's scant notice that her dread obligation came due. No polite knock lent the pretence of privacy for a meeting she was powerless to refuse. No courtesy call, peremptory authority flung open the unlocked door.

Koriathain invaded the room. A tall woman with pinned hair and a violet mantle, banded with scarlet ribbons: Daenfal's peeress, close followed by four other ranked Seniors, then two more hooded sisters from the local sisterhouse. The circle of seven, arrived in grim force, were not a surprise. But the white-robed figures trailing behind them flushed Vivet to clammy anxiety. The enchantresses accompanied a True Sect examiner, regaled in his gold robes of office.

Crowded at his heels, quick as rat-hunting ferrets, a pair of Sunwheel diviners crammed inside before the door closed. Servants of the Canon, they surveyed the chamber with the riveted focus of their occult faculties.

The jittery one with the frown remarked first. "Your prize quarry appears to have fled."

The peeress gave the comment short shrift. "Of course! Wily bastard, he's Darkness itself. No one leashes the Teir's'Ffalenn without leverage." Glance fallen on Valien, her brisk order followed. "Take charge of the boy, straightaway."

"No!" Vivet's shocked instinct reacted, too late.

Someone's strong arm checked her outraged rush. Protests availed nothing. The avid diviner swooped past and scooped her drowsy toddler off the bed. Wakened by the rude grip of a stranger, Valien's terrified wail cut across the enchantress's warning. "Vivet! Take command of yourself! Resist our directive, and I'll see your oath of service enforced, and your by-blow destroyed." Disgusted by the child's kicking tantrum, she urged the diviner, "Get the brat away and secure him. He's the Master of Shadow's accessible weakness and our guarantee of the mother's compliance."

The examiner's surgical stare marked the child's dark hair with suspicion. "That mite's the demon's natural offspring?"

"His name is Valien!" Vivet cried, shaking. "Let me comfort him! He is innocent."

None heeded her plea. Examiner and Senior Koriathain locked stares, the former self-righteously bristling, while the door whisked open behind them. The harried diviner hastened away, muffling his bundled captive's hysterical screams. While the toddler's wails retreated through the outside hallway and dwindled down the stair, the peeress denounced the examiner with piercing contempt. "If black hair hackles your sanctimonious principles, by all means! Sound the miserable creature for talent and prove his forgettable paternity to suit yourself."

Vivet succumbed to her jellied knees. Released from duress, she sank against the edge of the bed. Too late at this pass, to lament her failed initiative: she had squandered every available moment to provoke the Master of Shadow's demise on her own. Valien had been thrown to the wolves for her weakness. Cheeks soaked with distraught tears, she cowered under the peeress's questions. "When will the conniving sorcerer return? Don't hedge your answer! He's embraced insane risks for your bantling, already. The drive of his blood-line, and murderous pride, won't let him change his priorities now."

"He intended to get us away before dusk," Vivet said, defeated. "Please! I beg you! I will see this through. Only promise you won't harm my child!"

"The whelp's fate belongs to the Koriathain, and don't dare forget yourself. More than your personal future rides on the probity of your commitment." Maternal anguish dismissed, the peeress commanded her Seniors. "Carry on with your tasks. No mistakes! We are matching wits against the mind of a fiend. You'll have no second chance with the s'Ffalenn bastard's volatile strategies."

Ruby pins flared like spilled blood in coiled hair as Koriani prerogative faced down the examiner's fatuous scepticism. "You want True Sect credit for winning the day? Then trust my Prime's long-term experience to arrange the defeat of your criminal target."

The temple official pursed fleshy lips, his rosy hands laced in his cuffs. "As you claim, sister. Perhaps. I've seen no firm evidence. Nothing here verifies the vile presence of Darkness Himself."

The peeress brushed the quibble aside. "Not being a fool, the Master of Shadow will do nothing to draw unwanted attention. He's a secretive man, with unique susceptibilities that our plot will use to advantage."

The examiner inclined his groomed head. "Nothing lost, nothing gained, beyond wasted time if you've overstepped." His unimpressed gaze tracked the diligent Seniors, one of whom unreeled a spool of fine copper chain from a silk bag. Two others fastened the glimmering strand with gloved hands and wood mallets, fixing its length with bronze tacks to the inside window frame. They joined the ends under the jut of the sill and sealed their work with an incantation. Then they crossed the room and treated the doorway and its board threshold the same.

The remaining diviner ventured his stuffy opinion on the particulars. "Nothing, your Eminence. If that strand carries spellcraft for an entrapment, I detect no shed ripple of resonance."

"Naturally not!" snapped the peeress, amused. "How else would you blindside a clever adept with initiate mastery?" Galled by her Prime's unwanted alliance, she lectured the True Sect upstart with brittle exasperation. "The ciphers were forged in warded secrecy elsewhere. They are currently dormant. No quiver of warning must deflect the flux before the pre-set catalyst triggers our snare."

While the temple examiner received the assurance without satisfaction, the peeress was disinclined to reveal any further details. Her Seniors completed their task in brisk order, received their due leave, and departed. The True Sect delegation stayed only to witness the peeress's last word to Vivet. "You will remain here. When your promised escort comes to collect you, do nothing. His downfall will unfold in due course."

To the haughty examiner in his glittering jewels, she added with minimal courtesy, "Take your party down the backstairs, exactly the same way we came. I must clear the traces of energetic residue from this inn, and follow up with a sweep of the street." Unwithered by his supercilious scowl, she ushered him over the threshold, still talking. "No one with talent remains for the capture. *None of yours, or mine, linger in the vicinity!* Never forget! We stalk a master sorcerer with a crown prince's attunement, treading upon his sovereign ground in Rathain. He will be on the alert for any arcane interference. Light save you, I'll hound any meddler to Sithaer who crosses my prearranged plan."

The room emptied, and the breached door closed at length, the plink of the latch final as the last nail driven home in a coffin lid.

Vivet passed the unendurable day in wretched misery. She breathed in dread of a light-footed step on the stair, and sobbed by turns, shredded over the plight of her child in the bitter event the arrival she feared never came. Tension destroyed her peace. She paced and fidgeted, her stomach clenched, while the outside heat baked the slate roof, and the dingy room went from claustrophobic to stifling.

Vivet wrung herself dry of tears, while the workaday noise from the alley racketed through the long shadows of afternoon. She huddled, dulled by exhaustion when the subdued murmur of folk homeward bound drifted through the open window. Quiet fell as commerce slowed and the lake-side wharf settled at eventide.

The Master of Shadow had not returned when the bells tolled at sunset, nor by twilight's grey pall, filtered through the mullioned casement. Vivet fretted in a cold sweat, distraught. Surely he had come to his logical senses and taken off on his own, unencumbered. She wept, cursing his name for her faint-hearted trust. *Almost,* she had come to believe his false promise, that he held the power to free her. Darkness at due length erased the last light. Deaf to the laughter and raucous shouts filtered up from the water-front tap-room, Vivet lay prostrate, reduced to despair. She dared not save herself. Ruin awaited if she left her post without the sisterhood's formal permission. No matter that the trap laid by the Koriathain had failed through no fault of her own, until Arithon's capture, both she and her child as hostage confronted the terrible consequence.

Arithon expected the inevitable enemy bid, aware Vivet's straits cast the net to ensnare him. Therefore, he had given the inn a wide berth on his timely return from the market. His cautious watch over the occupied room from a distance extended into the quiet past midnight. Keen senses detected no dubious figures on covert guard. No talent lurked at the tap-room door, and none of the rowdy crowd, coming or going, had shown any signs of suspect behaviour. His exhaustive survey with mage-sight exposed no markers for arcane talent, even after a pilfered rope from the water-front let him scale the inn wall for a better vantage from the peaked roof.

The lack of threatening activity did not slacken his guard. On the contrary, the tavern contained a set trap, masked under concealment during his absence.

Arithon maintained his close observation for another hour, prone on the cool slate with his arms crossed. Breeze off the lake stirred his hair and slapped rhythmic wavelets against the pier's weedy pilings below. A heavy door slammed, and a dog barked. The town-watch on the water-front beat paused to forestall a burgeoning fight. Amid shouting complaint, several men-at-arms hauled two roaring drunks through a catcalling cluster of onlookers. More muscular men from the tap-room stopped stacking the empty beer casks, and pitched in to disperse the unruly crowd. Soon after, the tavern's tousled potboy slouched into the street and clapped shut the dock-side shutters. A last, ousted gaggle of patrons ambled away, singing off key.

The mule-drawn slop cart clopped past, flanked by two skinny teens wielding pitchforks, then the garrulous rag-pickers crew collected the baskets of fish waste to be stewed for bait in the trap shacks. Dockside, the lamps burned low and flickered, fuzzed by a scrim of mist off the lake, when moonset at last cloaked the puddled back alley into black-velvet gloom.

The dank air thickened. Nothing stirred near at hand but the fishmonger's cat, skulking after rats in the gutter. Arithon moved then, careful to cast no furtive silhouette against the night sky. Slung from the rope anchored to the stone chimney, he lowered himself down the tavern's back wall, primed for trouble, and on heightened alert for any untoward disturbance. Silent as shadow, he poised beneath the jutted overhang where the lightless square of the latched-back casement marked the hired room's dormer window. Nothing stirred. Stilled with the crosswise rope digging into his shoulder, Arithon listened.

Sound gave him the whisper of Vivet's breathing. Beside her anxious tension, the hollow quiet suggested her child lay asleep. Which tenuous evidence supported the likely conclusion she was not being held in duress.

Arithon dared not probe any further for surety. While the building appeared not to harbour any latent trace of enchantment, to broach a threshold or sill, even by the use of his subtle faculties, invited all manner of risk. Instead, he scooped a handful of rock salt from his pocket and tossed the coarse grains into the sash.

The whispered patter of impact raised movement, then the wooden clunk caused by a stumbled collision with the interior furniture. Vivet's startled response brought her to the window, distraught and frightened. Hope and terror charged her appeal as she registered his late arrival. "A Sunwheel examiner has taken Valien!"

Unforeseen, the development stunned him. Arithon reeled in dismay, momentarily rocked off balance. The dangling rope shifted. He flung out a hand to check the mild spin, missed the tavern's whitewashed wall, and grazed the wood frame of the casement instead. The glancing contact with his bare skin launched the spellcraft fashioned against him.

Sultry light flared and burned. Sprung from the embedded copper inside, the enchantment noosed his careless finger-tip. He was not caught outright. His readied defences expected an ambush, forearmed by a master initiate's ability to repel a hostile assault.

Except the strike tailored against him came barbed with a melody. Recognition of his own composition snagged his startled attention. That split second's instinctive sympathy loosened his guard. The lyric measure from his high art once had challenged Lirenda on a bleak winter night, long ago, when his successful deflection had championed another innocent's escape from an execution in Jaelot.

But on this vengeful hour, the coiled chain of dark sigils flicked through Arithon's core defences.

Paralysis lanced into him faster than a snake-bite. Numbness seized his hand to the wrist, then raced up his arm and devoured the left side of his body. His tenuous grip on the rope succumbed next. Right palm burning to brake his uncontrolled fall, Arithon slid, scrabbling, down the stone building. He crashed onto the cobbles, undone, bruised, and breathless, crumpled in a limp sprawl.

He battled the brutal incapacity that swept him. The desperate fight to uproot the entanglement drove his aware focus deep inward. Plunged towards unconsciousness, he heard nearby footsteps through Vivet's terrified scream.

Posted watchers converged who were not Koriathain. Arithon's fading faculties noted their talentless auras. Control of his flaccid body escaped him. He could not fend off their invasive restraint, or feel the harsh bite of the cords used to bind his slack wrists and ankles. The brisk handling that loaded him into the laundress's hand-cart overset his patched vision and wrung him dizzy. The surge broke his last resistence as his nameless captors pushed the rattling conveyance down the night street and snuffed his adamant awareness.

Cognizance flickered, briefly, an unknown interval later. His unfocused view of a woman's face swam in the candle-lit murk above him. Not Vivet's uncanny likeness to Elaira: Arithon snatched the familiar impression of taupe hair, and freckles scattered across a pink nose set into round features. The glower boring into him like honed teak belonged to the independent Koriani healer, recalled from his disastrous affray at Daenfal's necropolis.

His effort to speak met the flat of her hand. Breath hissed from his lungs, unresisting. His helpless tongue stayed unresponsive.

"Curse the day," the witch chided, annoyed. "You're twice the born fool to have returned to Daenfal. The bait piece from Ettin was not worth your measure! What under sky drove you to increase my burden of sorry regret?"

He heard, but felt nothing. Struggled and failed to wrest back the voice to protest when her shaking hand cut his bindings. She lifted his wrist. Deadened nerves recorded no sting as her surgeon's blade opened his vein. He lay powerless as the hot gush of his blood spun him down into black-out unconsciousness.

Impact

Tarens roused to a toe in his back, jabbed through the side of his tent. Stiff muscles unravelled by yesterday's drill complained as he stirred and rolled over. He groaned, eyes opened to black, with dawn's filtered gloom nowhere in evidence. "I'm not on the night roster, curse you!"

"Tethos!" The urgent whisper was Dakar's. "Move your bumpkin's hide, damn you! Get up!"

The following kick snagged only canvas, while the false name attached to his current position caught up with his laggard faculties. Tarens shoved to his knees, grumbling. Any day, in the misery of war-bond service, he felt worse than the times he had drawn the short straw for milking. Earl Jieret's fickle gift of instant alertness deserted him, utterly, unless he slept under the stars. Stumbled upright, head bent beneath the low ridge-pole, he yawned and scratched at yesterday's bruise on his chest.

Dakar's urgency nattered on without respite. "Tethos, you need to let us in, *now*!"

For of course, the entry was laced shut, a deterrent against the camp's pilfering thieves with his father assigned on patrol. Tarens fumbled through the stifling darkness, and clumsily untied the knots.

Dakar shoved inside with a second, slight figure braced upright against his shoulder. "Don't brighten a light," he snapped, puffing. "I've come for shelter in a crisis."

The flare of someone's passing torch cut off as the canvas slapped shut at the Mad Prophet's heels. Snapped fully alert, the big crofter noticed the stricken figure Dakar supported was female.

"Elaira? She's hurt!" Shocked, Tarens cleared the pair's blundering passage

416

past his vacated cot in cramped quarters. Wise precaution, the spellbinder chose to move blind before use of mage-sight that might flag the temple's diviners.

"She's unharmed," Dakar qualified, groping until he bashed into the camp chair. "It's the straits of Arithon's capture afflicting her."

"They are bleeding him," gasped Elaira in hoarse distress, embarrassed her weakness required male strength to assist her into the seat.

"What?" Tarens clasped her clammy hands, horrified. "Why inflict such a cruelty?"

Dakar found the filled pitcher beside the wash-basin, soaked his cuff, and knelt to bathe Elaira's forehead. "The filthy tactic is practised by necromancers to weaken initiate mage talent."

Steadied by the cool water, Elaira stiffened her boundaries and recouped the presence to qualify. "In this case, Koriathain are wielding the knife to deplete him before he's surrendered for execution. Prime Lirenda's afraid of him." Shocked by a shudder from head to foot, Elaira mustered the rags of her courage. "As Matriarch, she won't jeopardize the order's resources or burden herself with the risk of putting his Grace to death under the order's aegis. Her dark bargain's been struck with the True Sect priests in trade for Arithon's person. His formal demise as the Spinner of Darkness wins the Light's sanctioned blessing for the sisterhood and grants the High Temple's endorsement to practise arcana under the Law of the Canon."

The bitter pause stretched, laced by the rancid taint of greased mail, and the pungent bite of the lye soap used to kill lice on campaign. While the kindly crofter choked back futile anguish, the fat, worldly spellbinder strangled his grief and made a lame stab at diplomacy.

"What can we achieve at this pass, pinned under surveillance by temple diviners?" Too wise to lie outright, Dakar wielded reason to dodge the admission they faced a lost cause. "Surrounded by dedicates three thousand strong, in the clinch of The Hatchet's armed war host, an intervention gets all of us killed without saving your best beloved."

The camp chair creaked to Elaira's stiffened affront. "You speak as if you think Arithon's helpless, no matter how often you've witnessed his ferocious tenacity." Angry enough to spit nails, she continued, "Doomed or not, he doesn't cave in to defeat! Against a dire set-back, even drained white by the Grey Kralovir, you'll remember, he kept on fighting. The point's never been about what we might do. I came here to follow his opening move and back up his wild-card strategy."

Merciful darkness hid Dakar's shamed flush and Tarens's stricken dismay. Language did not exist, then or anywhere, to soften the impact of abject despair. Amid staring disaster, the enchantress's refined intuition had yet to grasp the vile scope of the new Prime Matriarch's crowning play. The double-blind coup of a True Sect execution made Arithon's plight the irresistible bait for Elaira to reveal herself. The diabolical stroke freed the Koriathain for their vengeful move to enforce Elaira's defiance of her sworn oath.

"The Fellowship Sorcerers can't move to defend you, or any of us, given our stake in Arithon's interests." The Mad Prophet braced for her blistering argument, no matter the hour was past to plead for sensible precautions.

Debate was useless, in any case. The blared fanfare of the temple's horns split the night, proof that the True Sect's coveted prize was delivered alive for Canon retribution.

Torchlight flared without, to more shouting commotion as the war camp seethed awake. Dedicates rousted out of their blankets raised cheers, electrified by the announcement that the Master of Shadow was taken into True Sect custody. Someone jangled the cook-shack bell, surrounded by whooping companions. Chorused voices chanted pious slogans, while the priests gathered for the pre-dawn devotion burst into ecstatic song.

Dakar shut his eyes, devastated. The clammy chill of prophetic foresight confirmed what he already knew: the Light's triumphant, staged slaughter was going to happen at noon.

Mail scraped against a sheathed weapon, without. Then a flared torch cast a man's grotesque shadow across the tent canvas. Too quick for response, the loose flap swept open. Tarens's father shouldered inside, returned early from scheduled patrol. The disastrous influx of light from behind caught the irregular visitors in huddled conspiracy.

Dakar's dissembling wits seized charge first. He clapped his hands over his middle and folded with a soulful moan.

"Bad food," quipped Elaira, snatching his lead. Her gaze lifted in touching distress, she appealed to the family penchant for kindness. "Poor fellow. His billet lies next to the armoury. The constant clangour would drive a man mad who wasn't doubled with gripe. Would you mind? If he might stay here in peaceful quiet, I'll do my part looking after him."

"By all means." The bemused veteran raised his eyebrows, then winked, satisfied the flimsy story would pass amid the massive upheaval. "Belike he'll get over his ailment the quicker without the camp healer's putrid decoctions."

His son received a less sympathetic appraisal under a keen eye that missed nothing. "Get dressed. Morning field drills are cancelled. That leaves you a little time with your friends before being called up for duty. The Hatchet's dispatched the bursars under priority to appropriate timber. Haulage from the sawyers will demand at least eight pairs of oxen and a sober teamster to yoke them in harness. We're tasked with erecting a scaffold before midday's execution, but the work can't begin until after the lumber's delivered."

Outside, the deep bray of horns resounded, drowning the drums sprung up in the tumult. Deafening noise seized the trembling air, split by the bugle of the parade trumpets and shrill blasts from the officers' whistles, blaring for order. Conversation defeated, the battle-worn father wrapped his burly son in a crushing embrace. He delivered his last exhortation into Tarens's ear. "Whatever frightful subversion you're planning, Light's grace, I beg you, don't get yourselves caught! I'll cover for your friends' presence. Abet your desertion, if you must flee. Just don't make me bear your ruin by Canon writ at the hands of the Sunwheel priests."

The blast of the temple horns at Daenfal called the faithful to witness the imminent demise of the Spinner of Darkness. The ominous, deep note resounded four times every hour. Which desolate thrum of vibration set an ache to the bone, even in the stone cell below-ground where Arithon lay incarcerated.

There also, Vivet languished in duress, slumped behind a locked door in the bare, vaulted ward-room tucked under the magistrate's hall. Several tallow candles burned in the fixed metal wall sconces, caged in mesh against sabotage. The bench underneath her being too heavy to lift, she possessed nothing to ignite, beyond her own clothing.

The perfidious sisterhood had cast her off, and bound her fate over to temple authority at the High Examiner's demand. The act was a charade, played on the groundless pretext of sating the priesthood's suspicion of Valien's paternity.

"Do as you wish with the mother, meantime. Our order won't question your judgement." The summary dismissal carried down the outside corridor as the Koriani peeress departed, her conclusion faded to echoes beyond the iron-strapped door. "Her child's your surety of compliance. We ask only that you keep them separate until the day's business is settled."

Vivet swallowed, afraid. Too late, beyond salvage, she sweated over the unforeseen quandary that the order's interests had discarded her service. As though she posed a venal embarrassment, her anguished pleas on Valien's behalf had received stonewalled silence and furtive glances. Reference to her future confounded by broken-off snatches of hushed conversation, she found herself shackled under Canon Law for ice-blooded, tidy convenience.

The High Examiner's unnerving trial must be endured as a matter of form. A daunting formality, but surely no threat. Due process would prove her boy's blameless birth. The truth lay beyond question. Valien was not Arithon's issue.

Yet no justified line of consolation restored Vivet's quietude. Empathy frayed the illusion of comfort, immured within sight of the prisoner who languished insensate behind a barred grille.

Arithon lay sprawled, cuffed in chains, his limp form grimed with the suds from the gutter, wicked into his clothing and hair. Blood seeped with sullen persistence through the sodden bandage dressing his wrist. The right palm and fingers scraped raw from his uncontrolled slide down the rope seemed too frail, lifelessly robbed of the vibrant dexterity that had wrought artful melody on the lyranthe. The slack features of witless unconsciousness decried the charge of criminal sorcery. Dread haunted Vivet with vengeful persistence, that the man who had sacrificed all to stand by her might not recoup his wily awareness. Surely not in time to forestall his demise on the scaffold. His turned head exposed his watered-milk pallor, the parted lashes of his bruised lids still as death over dulled, vacant eyes.

"Arithon. Please! You need to wake up!"

If he heard, her appeal aroused no response. Only the use of his actual name forced the bitter acknowledgement of his integrity.

Regret hitched Vivet's breath. Ripped to the quick by his shocking helplessness, she beheld the gravity of her mistake. Arithon's treatment of her belied every evil ascribed to him by the religion. She had blinded herself in denial for years, only to stare down the ruin engendered by her betrayal. Escape at this pass lay beyond reach, an irreversible defeat under her dearth of resources.

Vivet shut her eyes upon welling tears, wrenched by sobs that threatened to tear her in pieces. "By Teeah's fair covenant, what have I *done*?"

Grated footsteps in the outer corridor interrupted her pang of conscience. Startled to her feet, Vivet whirled as the key sprung the lock and the door moaned open on strapped-iron hinges. Four armed dedicates entered, followed by a robed priest with pink skin and gentle blue eyes. He regarded her with kindly concern written across his scrubbed features.

"My dear, for your own sake, mind your careless tongue. The supplicant in your situation ought not to denounce our true faith. In particular, under the unwise presumption that nobody else might be listening."

Vivet sat on the bench, the starch pummelled out of her. Chilled fingers clamped in her skirt to disguise her trembling, she said carefully, "Teeah's covenant underwrites the elders' law, by which every village in Ettin is governed. The archive predates the blessed avatar who founded your Canon. How does a code that serves justice threaten your upright practice of the Light's principles?"

The priest sighed. "That point begs the question, certainly, yes? Fires, they say, never burn without smoke. After all, your debased little shamans' nest came to harbour the Spinner of Darkness. Mercy on you, I'm sorry. Prepare yourself."

His regretful gesture signalled the dedicates, who closed in and seized her. "My daughter, you need not fear the presence of grace. For the sake of your unsullied salvation, your case calls for the High Examiner's scrutiny."

The panicked fight in her crushed by main strength, the men dragged Vivet bodily upright. They secured her ankles with a leather strap. Buckled cuffs on her wrists, and threaded an overhead rope, then strung her on tiptoe from an iron ring-bolt, as if she were a dangerous criminal.

Vivet's frightened cries shattered off the close stone. Tearful pleading evoked only the priest's passive sympathy. Whether Arithon registered her hoarse distress, his own plight forestalled chance of rescue. If the dedicates cared, their dutiful poise stayed unmoved.

The examiner swept in as the knots were made fast. The men finished their task and melted from his path as though his snowy vestments packed a lethal poison. The priest stood aside also, hands clasped in his sleeves, posted for the duration.

Vivet's terror redoubled. Dread jerked her backwards against the restraints like an animal ear-marked for slaughter. Pent breath left her lungs in a reflexive scream as she thrashed in panic to evade the ringed hands reaching to frame her face.

"Hold still!" The examiner fisted two handfuls of her auburn hair, his remorseless hold pinning her struggle until his clamped grip boxed her temples.

His fixed gaze trapped hers. Powerless as a mesmerized hare, she could not blink to break his locked stare. One split second, her scalp felt licked by the burning agony of molten flame. Then his honed talent bored into her forehead, trampled down privacy, and rifled the seated core of her consciousness.

Her life store of experience was winnowed and flayed, every personal intimacy plundered. Ruthless talent dissected the content and discarded the pulverized dregs. The violation raised indescribable pain, the emotion and motives of her innermost being pierced by a coercion that raped mercy. Undone, shredded piecemeal, Vivet sensed the unholy blaze of excitement sparked off by the memory the True Sect fanatic expected to find: her passionate instant of congress with Arithon, inflamed by the proscribed use of enspelled aphrodisiacs.

"Light save the innocent, what have we here?" The Examiner's feverish zeal overwrote any pretence of detachment. He analysed none of the subtle details; disdained the fair course of an inclusive review, that would have affirmed a partial encounter cut short ahead of consummate completion. Instead, he dropped his invasive probe with a jolt that shocked nerves the length of his subject's strapped body.

Vivet sagged, wrung pithless. Savaged by a throbbing headache, she heard the True Sect verdict declared through the buzz in her ears.

"The child's parentage is tainted, begotten in sexual congress with Shadow Himself. As the Spawn of Darkness, I pronounce Valien condemned by the Light. Let him die on the scaffold alongside his father, consigned to damnation by fire and sword."

"No! Look again!" Vivet shuddered, still pleading, "My son's paternity sprang from common stock. I swear, soul and spirit, he's innocent! Test my word through a second trial, or at least grant a humane stay of clemency until the sisterhouse record confirms the boy's town-bred lineage."

The Lord Examiner chided her, his brusque manner saddened by pity. "Your order acceded to the temple's claim to enact the sacred duty of your prosecution. Why under the blessed Law of the Canon should I profane my faculties, wallowing in the wanton filth of a heretic's perverted lies?"

Vivet recoiled as though doused in ice. Her disbelief raked the immaculate priest with a hatred that left her shaking. "May Dharkaron strike down your blinded devotion to a hollow faith."

"Woman, beware!" the examiner warned. "Such blasphemy revokes your right to forgiveness under the everlasting Light."

"Grace hallows my cause!" Vivet bristled with rage. "You miscall your practice of betrayal and murder to foster divine enlightenment?" She tossed back snarled hair and shouted defiance. "The poor wretch you have caged is a mortal man, and my son, a child born harmless. You priests may gild your warped creed in pomp ritual to cozen the masses. But the merciful truth strips your scripture as fraud and condemns your false justice as slaughter."

The High Examiner flicked his ringed fingers towards the by-standing dedicates. "Still her tongue. Now! Before she revokes her remaining chance for redemption."

Senseless in desperation, Vivet spat in his face. "I rue the day I met Arithon Teir's'Ffalenn, thrust into his destiny as the used instrument of Koriathain. But more than any sordid act in my life, I regret that my weakness has mired my son in his downfall."

The High Examiner dabbed off her spittle, the sparkle of his embroidered sleeve scarlet under the grease-fed flicker of flame-light. "You have declared yourself in alliance with evil. Renounce your wicked outburst at once. Would you spurn the glory of the Light's compassion and darken your immortal spirit forever?"

"Your doctrine is heartless," Vivet retorted. "Decency does not sentence a child to a vicious spectacle of ritual slaughter."

"Decay must be expunged, even by amputation," the examiner corrected. "Purity of conviction alone minds the lamp that keeps Shadow's corruption at bay." A harsh pause ensued, while his reverent fingers caressed his Sunwheel pendant of office. "I serve the highest good. For humanity's sake, could I let the reckless seed of a black sorcerer survive to poison the next generation?"

Run dry of tears, shattered beyond hope, Vivet met defeat in the zealot's enraptured eyes. She said, "Moral posturing may have misled me once. But not any longer." At the anguished end of her strength, with naught left to protect, she discovered her courage. "Don't spout your adulterated theology, or justify sanctimonious treason to me! Not after I've given over to you the two lives in this world I hold dearest. If Valien and Arithon die by the sword under your accursed Canon, their murder has already besmirched my name on the rolls of the Fatemaster's judgement."

"You have sealed your damnation beyond all reprieve," the examiner snapped, out of patience. "Receive your just deserts." His strike followed, quick as a venomous snake. He clapped his palm on the crown of Vivet's head and snuffed out her life like a candle.

He prayed briefly over the pathetic remains, slack flesh hung like a gutted fish in the aftermath of his handiwork. Then he turned his back and strode away, clipped orders tossed over his shoulder. "Burn the carcass, Light brighten the day. Our beleaguered world supports one less minion of Shadow."

Triple Jeopardy

Immobilized in the spelled grip of paralysis, Arithon bears aware witness, eyes sparked to savage fury by Vivet's demise; and responsible charge of her tragic legacy drives his unwavering focus: to salvage her bereft, orphaned child from a sorcerer's death on the scaffold . . .

At Althain Tower, the stressed pitch of Athera's electromagnetics stirs the unquiet spectre of Shehane Althain's dread presence, while agonized suspense rides Sethvir's leashed strength for a Fellowship given no ethical option, and Mankind's survival swings on the cruel thread of Arithon's choice of reaction . . .

Astride his black stallion and streaming the sullen wind of a passage wrought through the chambered drake's skull in the Kathtairr grimward, the field Sorcerer, Asandir, reaches the Paravian focus circle at Old Tirans, and stretching the fabric of time itself, speeds north towards Whitehold to play through the bitter closure of his long-term strategy . . .

XIII. Expedient

rithon sprawled, paralysed, behind the locked grille. All but unmoored, at the edge of a black-out faint, he clung to awareness throughout the horror as the True Sect guardsmen cut Vivet down. The scrape of their boots rang too loud in his ears. Their unsavoury jokes ripped his helpless spirit to anguish. He could not turn his head or close his glazed eyes. His tormented sight absorbed the callous handling that dropped her corpse with a thump on the floor. He endured the sniggers and obscene innuendo spewed by the men's idle boredom, while a litter was fetched from the armoury. None of their crude conversation escaped him. When their interest changed subject, he heard the grotesque details of his forthcoming demise embroidered by salacious speculation.

He made no effort to shut out their speech. His distorted perception of sound warned how narrowly close he lay to unconsciousness. He must not react to his futile emotion, or let anxiety mire him in circling dread. Peril imposed the brutal priority: he must stay awake at all costs.

Even that basic effort evaded his grasp. Sucking dizziness stripped concentration. Minutes passed before his hazed faculties connected his affliction with blood loss induced by the knife. He had suffered the ugly practice before. Grey Kralovir's necromancers once had sapped his vitality to unstring his resources and keep him passive. Yet unlike that prior ordeal, he felt nothing of his chilled extremities. The desecration inflicted on him by Koriathain brought no attendant with honeyed water to relieve dehydration, or the salted mash needed to nurse his continued survival.

Which patent neglect confirmed the grim bent of the dedicates' gossip. His prize value, alive, amounted to nothing past the staged exhibit of a temple spectacle. Night was almost spent. Though flame-light illuminated the windowless cell, changeless between dark and dawn, his crown prince's attunement marked the lane tide's cresting surge and measured the passage of time. He had only the fleeting hours before noon to recoup his plundered autonomy.

Arithon engaged what sparse resource remained to rally his impaired mastery. Suspended, spinning, between past and present, he recalled his grandfather's brusque remonstrance when he had been ten years of age . . .

"No. Try again! You must be able to function clear-headed, even while holding your breath through a slow count of three hundred. Why is this necessary?"

Perched on the rock rim of a tide-pool, sodden clothing plastered to his wiry frame, Arithon reasoned the purpose behind the arduous exercise. "For defence and protection? Because invasive spellcraft cannot be imposed against the alignment of a stronger will."

"Yes, and also for improved performance under adverse stress. A master cannot afford a mistake! All the more when you're caught solitary. You'll have no one else to catch you short by the scruff if you stumble and fall to a back-lash under high stakes." The high mage encouraged, impatient to resume, "Practice must heighten your intact awareness and extend the boundary of unconsciousness . . ."

Self-command sprang first from impeccable focus. Light-headed, Arithon laboured to deepen his breathing and relieve the fluttered heart-beat of a sapped body starving for air. Discipline gradually steadied his vertigo. Slowly, he recouped the fragile semblance of grounded control.

The grisly activity outside the grille subsided also in due course. Coarse laughter and complaints dwindled as the detailed dedicates bore Vivet's body away. The strapped door to the corridor slammed shut in their wake, while the fortunate pair who had drawn the long straws kept the layabout's post, standing watch. Sentries' protocol silenced all frivolous speech. Amid fallen quiet, Arithon engaged the requisite self-survey, comparing what *should be* to what *was not*.

Beside sight and hearing, the fust of dank stone and the sour odour of his clammy sweat affirmed his unimpaired sense of smell. He could not swallow. His tongue and throat remained numb. In horrific fact, he felt nothing at all: not the chill floor underneath his slack body or the bite of the steel manacles on his chained limbs. Every nerve that enabled touch and voluntary movement stayed deadened in disconnection.

His painstaking search for the cause found no underlying trace of narcotic. Instead, Arithon encountered the signature whine of the sigils locking him under paralysis. No simple construct, imposed from without, this ugly impairment was tailored to match the pattern of his Name. The interface was not perfect. The signature template for the entrapment had been imprinted before his transformative encounter with the Paravians upon their warded isle.

A small loop-hole, sufficient to enact an unbinding, had Arithon been in prime shape. But his flawed concentration marred the integrity needed to challenge the invasive ciphers. He could not dissolve their grip at one stroke or indirectly negate their effect using counterpoint resonance. His sorry state disallowed intact recourse, still less where the temple diviners' hostile oversight might detect a concerted attempt to change his condition. He would have to worry at the enchainment. Wear down by persistent rebuttal the mismatched points where the spellcraft was weakest, until each flawed seal fractured under attrition. The course proved onerous, like fraying a triple-stitched seam with a needle, thread by resistant thread.

His labour received no peace and no privacy. Priests came and went, chanting prayers and fanning noxious fumes from lit censers. Guards were added, then changed, their numbers redoubled, the latest replacements bedecked in plumed helms and the dazzle of ceremonial parade armour. What measured progress Arithon managed was slight. An hour passed before he regained the muscular control to shut his stinging eyes, a paltry relief too quickly offset by the torment of his unslaked thirst. He walled off the distraction of his dry mouth. Against noise and discomfort, he turned all of his attention inward to worry at the ciphers that hampered him.

Reward came at last. One linked chain of spellcraft gave way. Barely, Arithon suppressed the tremor of recoil as command of his elemental mastery resurged. Small gain, and no victory: he lacked the finesse to harness his inborn power of shadow. Denied the refined touch to apply the effects, he feared he might trigger a reaction that would wreak havoc upon Daenfal's blameless populace, or much worse, destabilize the lane current that underpinned the volatile border of Athili. The explosive reach of his rogue far-sight crushed the vicious temptation to sow rampant fear in the country-side. At all cost, Arithon refused to provide impetus to spur the True Sect religion. He would not gift Koriathain with more fertile chaos as leverage to up-end the compact.

Valien's safety rooted his intent.

Stilled as the coiled adder, gripped by granite patience, Arithon subdued a fresh rush of vertigo and tackled the next layer of sigils. Acute tingling surged through his extremities, followed by the ache of cramped muscles and the excruciate agony where steel cuffs had cut into his inert flesh. He regained slight movement in fingers and toes. Then the turnkey arrived and unlocked the grille. Several more dedicates crowded inside, under orders to ready the Spinner of Darkness for his appointed fate on the scaffold. These brought a white-robed diviner in tow, a trained talent primed to sound warning at the least suspect stir of arcane practice.

"He's too small to seem dangerous," one man remarked, his nervous contempt gritted at each step by the scrape of hobnailed boots.

"Shut the loose talk! Pay attention!" cracked the captain in charge by the door. "You stand in the undilute presence of evil, endangered as you've never been in your sorry lives. Shoulder the task and escape in one piece. The quicker we finish, the better."

Arithon felt the diviner's obscene talent comb through his aura. He stilled all subtle activity, granting the probe no reaction to read as the dedicates bent to their work. He stayed limp, inert, even as his partially restored sensation delivered the bite of cold steel where their mailed grip manhandled his person. They cut off his shirt. Aware feeling delivered the jolt to seized limbs, as the pins that fastened the chain to his manacled wrists were jerked free. A shove rolled his prone body over. Pinned flat on his back, he forced the endurance to withstand the pain, breaths kept even and his abused flesh held flaccid as though still devoid of nervous sensation. The dedicates yanked his arms to the front. They shackled his wrists back into restraint.

"Light above!" one man swore. "You see the murderous hate in his eyes? Fair loosens the bowels and gives me the shakes."

"Don't look," warned the sentry stationed by the grille. "Are you daft? Belike he'll remember your face if he can. Noose a sorcerer's curse on you, body and mind, fit to ride you to grief and destruction."

The acting captain quashed the untoward comment before unease ignited hysteria. "Pack it up! The Koriathain have bled the wretch nearly dry. Damned certain they left him too weakened to put up much fight."

"Yes, but what if the sisterhood's stayspell gives way?" The jittery official jangled his keys, quick to snap the lock shut once the last anxious man cleared the cell. "Torwent burned, don't forget! And our town saw a brave squad of lancers slaughtered, cursed to their demise without a mark on them after they tried to corner the demonic creature on the necropolis."

"No bother, today," the officer dismissed, talking fast, as his men formed up for departure. "Dark talent or not, he's leached to the point where he'll probably faint when the executioner's escort hauls him upright." His parting conclusion cast echoes behind as he hastened his squad from the ward-room. "Forbye, when the criminal's led to his reckoning, the Lord Examiner's arts will hold him in check until ritual death flings him to black oblivion."

Asandir strode into the grand hall at the Whitehold sisterhouse, his booted step brisk on the white-marble floor, and his gaunt shadow thrown before him, distorted by flame-light. He did not wear the stark splendour of his formal robe, indigo as a moonless midnight, starred bright at collar and cuff with silver braid. This sombre errand saw him clothed in his trail leathers, flecked with foamed horse sweat from the saddle, and pungent with the reek of volcanic sulphur and the lightning-struck taint of fresh ozone.

Twelve Senior-ranked Koriathain had gathered ahead of him. The Prime's most trustworthy circle sat enthroned on the canopied dais, their carved, high-backed chairs tasselled with gold and cushioned in scarlet velvet. The deep amethyst brocades of their state dress clustered like funeral lilies, they surrounded a tranced scryer with a crystal sphere, tuned into a long-distance engagement. Her focus tracked the momentous event yet unfolding in the packed plaza sited at Daenfal.

Asandir knew what transpired there in his own right, in tacit touch with one discorporate colleague and kept tightly apprised by the Warden at Althain Tower. Leashed power itself, the Fellowship's emissary passed the wide harbour windows, sunlit on this day as the hour advanced towards noon. Beneath vaulted stone, his approach scattered echoes, fallen to whispered reverberation when he stopped at his appointed place. Graven at his feet like an epitaph, the lines of runes inscribed by the potentized force of his given word.

The Matriarch acknowledged him from the Prime seat. Black hair, tawny eyes, the woman who bore the mantle of office was a sharp change from Morriel's tempered poise and Selidie's coquettish innuendo. Altered beyond recognition by the impact of cruel enslavement and the stigma of her irregular succession, Lirenda spoke with the punctilious snap of the born aristocrat.

"You've cut your timing extremely fine. Provided, under your sovereign oath, you're here to verify the completion of our debt held against the Crown of Rathain. If you have a speech, make it quick. Your royal heir is already bound for the scaffold."

"I am here for full closure, exactly on schedule." Asandir's mild correction belied the steel in his bearing. In fact, he had staged his moment. "Could an early arrival have made any difference?"

"No." Lirenda watched like the mouse playing the cat. The frigid distrust in her narrowed eyes expected some disingenuous wile behind the Fellowship Sorcerer's claim of good faith. "I would not have succumbed to elaborate pleas. You'll be granted no stay or revision of terms."

"Why not?" Asandir said, for distraction.

Lirenda returned a smouldering glare. "Because this is my overdue victory, and the last bequest of my murdered predecessor. I hold firm today to honour Selidie's legacy and discharge a just recompense for her requital."

Palliative words, not the actual truth, Asandir perceived, lent the Warden's perspective. Lirenda's past meddling once had spoiled the finest of Morriel's impeccable strategies. The sore set-back to the order's interests caused by that ambitious error of judgement had withered Lirenda's career, while Arithon walked free without scathe. Against natural reason, the repeat mistake would not happen today at Daenfal.

"You do not wear mourning," Lirenda attacked, while the vulture stares of her attendant Seniors dissected the Sorcerer's carriage.

Asandir faced their gamut, every nerve under glacial control. "Should I? My dear, you have overstepped. The Crown Prince of Rathain is still living."

"You cling to an empty hope!" Gemstones shimmered as Lirenda gripped the curved necks of the swans fashioned into the arms of her chair. "Which offensive notion proves I shouldn't trust you, or Sethvir, given his sneak penchant for a cheater's tricks up his sleeve."

Which remark cracked the lid on Asandir's annoyance. "I stand on my oath of nonintervention." Almost, his frame flickered with bursting, white light. "The Teir's'Ffalenn's fate continues to rely strictly upon his own merits."

"If any such opening exists at this pass." The gloss shifted on the coiled ebony of Lirenda's braid as she tilted her head towards her dutiful scryer. "Our seer's quartz shows the True Sect officials in place for the ritual execution."

Whether or not his Grace could save himself, only minutes remained before he faced his reckoning. Asandir need not consult the engaged crystal's reflection: Sethvir's stricken silence informed him the margin for action was slipping away.

Lirenda rubbed abrasive salt in the wound. "Do you suppose Elaira will manage to withstand the unbearable trauma?"

Asandir did not rise to the bait though awareness of the enchantress's danger brutalized his concern. Handfast to Rathain's prince, she could not be defended under his Fellowship's auspices. Her perilous case rested with Tarens and Dakar, reliant upon the precarious foothold of their better sense. Kharadmon lurked on station, unknown to them, and constrained as a passive observer.

Linked contact with his discorporate colleague delivered the frightful moment when the gathered crowd at Daenfal sighted the prisoner's escort. Their atavistic roar flared the flux, to the cry of Kharadmon's seething frustration. *"His Grace damned well left his move in the Kralovir crisis bitterly late!"*

Shared resonance spiked a response from Sethvir. *"That was Davien's irregular influence, a perilous asset we cannot afford."* The remark sparked an earth-sensed glimpse of the scaffold, a raw lumber platform etched under sunlight, packed with the scintillant white-and-gold panoply of the temple priests. Beneath surged the ravenous crowd: a shifting, restless sea rammed against The Hatchet's dedicate cordon, a veteran company gleaming in full arms and stationed in files of twenty ranks deep.

"As if the Betrayer would stir his arse to brake the hard fall to disaster," Kharadmon opined in disgust. *"He can cosset himself in relentless seclusion, but that does not excuse his refusal to bring the rest of us into his confidence."*

A gloomy quibble, belatedly raised, that the estranged Sorcerer had yet to leave Kewar, or contact Sethvir. Granted the renegade's presence or absence, the Fellowship Sorcerers could do nothing to shift the pending stroke of harsh consequence.

Asandir held the drawn line with the rest of his colleagues, pinned under

Lirenda's rapt expectation. He moved not a muscle, while mankind's right to inhabit Athera swung in the balance, suspended, fast tipping towards the harrowing moment a True Sect sword fell and murdered the future.

The roar raised by thousands of throats slammed the air to endless thunder when the dedicate escort dragged Arithon before the multitude craning to view his demise. He felt the hammering wall of vibration drum through him, skin, bone, and viscera. Blood loss whirled his senses to vertigo and ripped unsteady vision through patches of black-out. He felt pummelled to rags, all strength and vitality sapped hollow by weakness. He could not support his own weight. Armoured dedicates braced him at both shoulders. More men behind prodded his lagging step with pole weapons, while four abreast led him, dragging the chains cuffed at his wrists and ankles.

Deafening in the maelstrom, Arithon beheld the scalding dazzle of gold, shattered off by noon sun striking the phalanx of temple dedicates who hemmed his path on both sides. The palings of the plank scaffold loomed above their plumed helms, packed by a snow-drift array of robed priests, the Exalted Examiner stationed among them. The stair upwards swam in the sweltering heat, a scant dozen yards ahead.

The sword and the burning were nigh upon him. He could not save himself. Even to salvage survival at all costs, he lacked the stamina to engage a broad-scale use of shadow. Only Valien's plight might be bought on the gambled stake of a loophole contingency. Arithon mustered the dregs of his resource. Eyes half-lidded to mask the gleam of fierce purpose, he commanded the limited range of free will wrested back through subversive persistence. He expended that hoarded reserve at one stroke, and severed the contiguous symmetry of the healer's sigil staunching the vein in his wrist.

Heat raced up his arm as the stay let go. He felt the spurt of fresh blood gush and run, soaking the layed bandage. A bright stream leaked through and dribbled from his hand, to shouted alarm from his keepers. Their rough grip pinioned him. Other mailed fists caught his arm. Direct pressure staunched the reopened wound, while someone called for a bystander's handkerchief.

The contrived tourniquet lessened the stream, twisted tight until the flood ceased. But not before spattered droplets struck earth on the sovereign soil of Rathain.

Arithon languished amid the furore. Unresponsive to the epithets of the annoyed men, scarcely conscious of the brutal shoves keeping him upright, he spoke aloud under the crowd's pandemonium with a tongue wrestled free of paralysis. His murmured phrases were short and succinct: a threefold summons, invoking Sethvir of the Fellowship, under his Crown Prince's right. "I declare Valien as the next heir to Rathain, with full rights to royal legacy bestowed in trust, sealed by my word in sound mind, and confirmed by my blood and through invocation of my true Name."

The charged response he relied on surged back, mercifully swift.

"Done and done!" sent the Warden of Althain. *"Your testament as crown prince is granted, star-stamped and sealed into record."*

Tarens, Elaira, and Dakar that moment lurked inside the dedicates' cordon, crouched in perilous refuge beneath the enclosed struts of the scaffold. In hiding there since the chaotic construction had hastened the structure to completion, they waited out the event, hunkered down amid the shaded gloom directly below the board platform that seated the temple's officials in state. The Mad Prophet crouched in the gap between beams, fists rammed with deliberation against the brick pavement. His contact detected the shimmer as the flux responded to a Named crown prince's appeal. The bold overture signalled Arithon's bid to salvage his compromised fate. Grief born of foresight wrenched Dakar's heart. His bent for immutable prescience exacted its cruel price: whatever move followed, the remedial effort was destined to fail.

The prophet suffered in redoubled agony for his rash lack of foresight at Athir. His choice to swear the Crown of Rathain into debt to the Koriathain bound the Seven in force, which diabolical stricture anchored the tranced augury lately unveiled in Deshir. Marked and measured, tragedy already roosted upon this day's building calamity.

Nothing could change. The nexus point of the vision approached as the minutes raced forward.

Dakar sweated in paralysed dread. Before him, the blaze of cloudless noon sliced the square opening, sawn through the scaffold floor. There, the massive, set post stacked with faggots awaited the prisoner's reckoning, the tang of fresh sawdust tinged by the fumes of volatile oil and turpentine. The taint poisoned the air, adding the light-headed roil of faintness to his nauseous tension.

Movement flicked, to his right. Elaira grabbed Tarens in sudden support, rendered weak at the knees by fraught horror.

Roused from torpor, Dakar thrust forward. He knelt by the woman handfast to Arithon and exhorted with low-voiced urgency. "Elaira! I'm sorry, my focus has slipped. What just happened?"

Shaking, she scrubbed fallen hair from her face. Tarens gathered her into his staunch embrace as, chin lifted, she mustered shocked wits. "His Grace has formally declared Vivet's boy, Valien, as royal heir to Rathain."

"And Sethvir accepted?" Dakar lost his breath. "Ath wept!" His chest felt strapped in lead. "As you promised, your crown prince has taken action."

Elaira stared back, stricken, while the crescendo of human clamour pounded into the platform above. Dust fell, loosened by the appalling din as the crowd's howling passion redoubled. Then armoured steps shuddered the outside stair, chased by the plinking rattle of chain as the Spinner of Darkness mounted the scaffold.

"My beloved seeks to spare Valien's life," Elaira explained in tormented despair. "He doesn't know the Seven are hobbled! Nor can he imagine the intractable fact that a crown prince's right to protection lies forfeit! Koriathain won't flinch. They'll seize their claim of damage in full and demand the sacrifice of the child."

Dakar swallowed. Aghast, he interpreted Elaira's tears, for the pain such a loss would inflict upon Arithon. The Mad Prophet had no shred of comfort to offer. Words died before the full scope of the impact unveiled by his unruly talent. For he knew: the upcoming settlement presaged far worse.

"What do you See?" Elaira demanded, alarmed by the disastrous pause. Amid the hateful, incessant noise, she yanked away from Tarens's support, scalded to wildcat fury. "Don't imagine you can spare me!"

Dakar bowed his head. Fright sucked him pithless as he snatched Elaira's clenched hands and entreated, "My brave lady, through everything, you must hold firm!"

Spellbinder, seer, and master initiate, the shrinking spirit wrapped in human flesh perceived the raw quandary tossed onto the Fellowship's shoulders. Dakar grasped their ruthless directive, none better. Which true purpose wracked him with the cruel choice: to crumple in failure again, or to stiffen his spine for unbearable stakes and hold the unconscionable line at the Sorcerers' back.

Unstrung by sorrow, the spellbinder stared down the horror birthed by his fatal error at Athir. Hard-fought maturity gauged the terrible price, strung on a thread through the narrowest margin, by which the cost of his mis-step might be redeemed.

The enchantress deserved no false encouragement. "Tarens!" Dakar cracked. "Save us all, every one of us has to stand fast!"

The blond crofter turned his head as though trapped in a nightmare, his pummelled wits apparently dulled to the urgency driving Dakar's appeal. Shock followed, as the Mad Prophet also shared the view that haunted his loyal heart. The same dread vision had visited him one past night at Kathtairr, birthed amid the gestalt trance of a *tienelle* scrying: he, too, had Seen the Sunwheel cloth spread over the altar visible through the opening above. Placed opposite to the upright post, there, the shining sword rested, etched in glare, ready for the gloved fist of the Light's executioner.

"I know this moment," Tarens muttered, appalled, while the pealing barrage of raw tumult stormed against the timbered bulwark. "Earl Jieret's Sighted talent has seen this!"

"Yes! That's why you'll say nothing." Dakar stifled the crofter's outcry by ruthless necessity. "Trust me, I know! We cannot, *we dare not!* upset the course of Prince Arithon's finished transaction."

Nothing must disrupt the sequence in motion.

"Help steady Elaira!" the Mad Prophet pleaded. "At all cost, we cannot break down and react." Not before the Prime Matriarch's hold on the Crown of Rathain achieved closure.

The frenzied roar of the crowd swelled to a pitch to crack nerves when Arithon reached the top stair of the scaffold. Towed forward in chains, shoved by dedicate zeal from behind, he stumbled onto the level platform, dazed stupid and pulped beyond strength.

A jostling intrusion shouldered past his armed handlers. Through vision rinsed by bouts of black-out faintness, he confronted the furious glare of the True Sect's Exalted Examiner, attended by several agitated diviners.

Their hostile interrogation thrust against the tissue-thin barrier of his scarcely mended defences. "What Lightless coil of spellcraft did you just unleash?"

No hapless victim, but an initiate master care-worn to the bitter edge, Arithon dredged up a mocking smile. Lashes raised, he matched the Examiner's stare, secure in his fearless belief that the Fellowship's obligate commitment to the crown would uphold his purpose and defeat the priesthood.

"Kiel'd'maeranient," he challenged in succinct Paravian. "Anathema! Find out. Or else spare the child and leave without scathe."

A mailed fist in the belly silenced his insolence. Stunned momentarily, Arithon felt the electrical stab of the Examiner's resharpened probe. He resisted, though driven nearly unconscious. Whatever the temple Canon asserted, the True Sect priesthood's tame talents were outmatched by the training bestowed by Rauven's s'Ahelas mages.

Blurred awareness recorded the flurried recoil, embedded amid the concussive noise. Then came the Examiner's rattled shout, commanding the dedicates to haste before harm befell the Light's faithful. "Have the rite over and done! No one's safe, or delivered from evil until this black sorcerer's pierced carcass has smouldered to ashes."

Jostled forward, then dragged, bludgeoned by vengeful fists, Arithon reeled past the seated conclave of priests. Ahead loomed the post, spiked with the wrought-iron hook for his shackles. Beneath yawned the square-cut pit, greased fuel stacked for the pyre, with access off the raised platform bridged by a narrow plank. Too spent for more than a token resistance, Arithon endured the battering passage across. Limp weakness reclaimed him as the armoured escort manhandled his half-stripped person and strung him up for the spectacle.

Throats many thousands strong shrieked at the sight of him, thirsty for the thrill of a barbaric slaughter. Pulverized under the ravenous sound, Arithon scarcely felt the excruciate bite as the cuffs took his hapless weight. His searching glance by-passed the gleaming sword, dimmed under a cloud of incense smoke as two priests approached, swinging censers to sanctify the altar. Instead, his spinning gaze found and locked upon Vivet's terrified, dark-haired child.

Cord lashed the toddler's forearms to his waist. A second rope tether affixed his ankles to a ring stapled into the platform. Armoured dedicates shadowed him at each flank, while another High Priest in sparkling regalia poised behind with raised hands, his prayer exhorting deliverance from Darkness over-whelmed by the shattering din. High as a bird's cry, the boy wailed with fear. Roughly handled by strangers and forsaken by kin, he rolled tearful eyes and located the only familiar face on the scaffold.

"Arin!" he shrieked in heart-stopping appeal. While the priest seized his shoulder and shouted for silence, his panic burst into hysteria.

"Spare the child," begged Arithon through whitened lips. Since no Fellowship intercession could happen before he exhausted all recourse, he twisted his head in fraught appeal to the Exalted Examiner. "My own end is nothing. I cast no blame. Only spare the boy. He is harmless."

The temple official glared back, unmoved, into green eyes stripped of all artifice. The unnerving sorrow and compassion laid bare wrenched him short, a threat to shake a lifetime of devotion. He flinched away before his conviction wavered, and base human frailty fell prey to corruption.

"The risk shall not be sanctioned lest the spawn of evil should survive in this world." Fist raised before his howling flock, he signalled the executioner. "If the boy springs from innocent stock, let a higher authority reward his purity. The stainless child's spirit will never perish but be welcomed into the Light everlasting."

A figure in scalding white armour strode forward, his short stature at first beyond notice amid the seated rows of cowled priests. A crested helm topped the aggressive jut of a lantern-jawed face. Steel-rivet eyes glittered through a sweeping glance that exuded vengeful triumph. The Hatchet advanced to the altar with the jaunted strut of a spurred cockerel. He laid claim to the weapon blessed by the priests. Blade raised in exultant salute, he basked in the crowd's screaming approval. Then he pivoted smartly to render his service under the Law of the Canon.

The child cried out at the sight of the sword. The point swept downwards in a fiery arc. No Fellowship Sorcerer arrived. No living power arose to bestow a timely intervention. Arithon gasped and strained at the post, stranded by the aghast recognition his move had been ruthlessly taken and used for an expedient sacrifice. Chained over the pit, drained near bloodless and swim-mingly faint, he drove himself to react through shocked horror. He gathered the desperate shreds of his awareness and threw all he had left into voice, true pitch informed by a Masterbard's artistry.

"Valien!" *Almost*, he achieved his desired intent. Very nearly, his call struck the actualized power of Name, forged in harmony with the untarnished grace of the grand chord that sustained creation.

But not quite. Flawed enough to fall short, just shy of the clear resonation Asandir's might had achieved—the peal of infinite tenderness that once had summoned a lost spirit intact from torment by the Shadows of Mearth—Arithon's shout still turned Valien's head. The boy's tearful green eyes met the man's, of sheared emerald: and held there, diverted through the brute thrust of the sword that pierced his small, racing heart.

Valien's choked-off cry of stunned agony crystallized Arithon's features. Failure armoured his vulnerability. Struck dumb, he watched the little boy's chest flutter and spasm, the bloom of seeped blood a ruby flower that opened and gushed. Master of Shadow, raised by Rauven's stern code, he endured, graven by the godless savagery of his anguish. He bore witness as The Hatchet's fist yanked the fouled blade free. He saw, in the speechless, blank fury born of an unimaginable betrayal, the slight form of the child become wracked head to feet by a shudder. Then young flesh barely past helpless infancy crumpled, a discarded rag shrouded in stillness and rope, in a widening puddle of scarlet.

Neither did Arithon Teir's'Ffalenn respond as the clotted blade angled to take him in turn. The Exalted Examiner's decree announcing his doom fell more empty than wind on deaf ears.

"Go to your eternal torment!" The True Sect official raised his arms and shouted against the crowd's insatiable uproar, "May Light's justice speed the righteous steel that frees us from the Spinner of Darkness!"

Arithon dangled from taut wrists on the post, ribs strained as he laboured to breathe. He engaged no blanketing shadow; wrought no recoiling blast of destructive retaliation. Staring down The Hatchet's gloating spite, the talent decried as the root of black evil made no sound at all as the stained blade plunged deep, quenching the luminous, bitter rage and draining the last stubborn spark of awareness from his fixated eyes.

The execution accomplished at Daenfal pealed a shock wave down the Fifth Lane. Ripples of recoil roiled the flux length and breadth of Athera's inhabited continent. In the solitude of Althain Tower's top floor, Sethvir slumped at the library table with his head bowed against his clenched hands, weeping for the inexcusable cruelty imposed under dire necessity.

The sorrowful tragedy outweighed all tears: for the child's riven spirit yet delayed from clean passage into the peace of the infinite. Slaughtered in violence, Valien's being had not been transformed by joyful ecstasy, raised beyond mortal pain. The Masterbard's consummate artistry had faltered, that could have sped the departed innocent in seamless transition across the veil.

The boy's sundered consciousness lingered in distress, wrenched separate from flesh and trailing the dismembered streamers of animal magnetism. He drifted at the cusp of Fate's Wheel, as the world's balance shuddered. The irreplaceable seconds flowed onwards, a poised future rocked by uncertainty, while the drastic, untenable price paid in full to complete the Koriani oath of debt against Rathain's crown approached final closure.

Asandir poised at the Whitehold sisterhouse, vised in suspension while the incised runes that sealed his dread oath stayed intact. Beyond compromise, the fibre that held him unflinching before the inimical eyes of the Prime's Senior

Circle gave away nothing: not the magnitude of his tearing grief nor a trace of his anguished regret.

Lirenda watched his stilled frame as the tiger marked prey, awaiting the first sign of weakness. "How does it feel to have your power bound, while all you have built goes to ruin? Morriel Prime should have lived for this hour! When, at long last, the tyranny of your great compact is smashed, and our order reclaims the unfettered span of humanity's destiny."

Denial required no wasted words. The scryer's quartz showed precisely what occurred amid the packed square at Daenfal.

Asandir bowed his head, his forearms relaxed under his threadbare, grimed cuffs, beneath which his strong hands stayed motionless. A stance whose mild aspect deceived: acquiescence clothed in a dangerous quietude, as the honed sword nestled in the sheath, while westward, the grisly cascade of consequence begat by Canon Law careened forward . . .

Beneath the board scaffold, harrowed to desolation, Elaira shouldered past Dakar's stunned bulk and cast her appeal to roust Tarens from paralysed despair. "We must act straightaway! Don't you see? The blade must be drawn and the flames quenched before the priests kindle the pyre. Else my beloved will perish beyond the last reach of recovery."

"No, Elaira!" Dakar bulled forward and seized her arm. "Stand firm! You must!" As her frantic jerk tested his planted feet, the Mad Prophet locked his grip, and pleaded, "The moment you came for has already happened! Let the wheels of destiny unleashed by Arithon's choice stay in motion."

"Then why is the Fellowship not here in force?" Through the rampaging noise of the multitude, and the dust sifted down by the footsteps shaking the planks overhead, she despaired, "Why haven't the Sorcerers acted?"

A cogent question and a point Dakar might have conceded. Yet astute explanation cost further delay, unthinkable amid a crisis past tipping point, fast sliding into a chartless arena beyond a mere spellbinder's purview.

"You dithering lackwit! I don't need protecting!" Elaira fought against sane restraint, the need in her shattered past quietude. "Why else under Ath's sky are we here?"

Her insane desperation dragged Dakar, stumbling, towards the post, while her protests shrilled into panic. "If we do nothing, Davien's imprint of longevity cannot salvage Prince Arithon's life."

"You can't throw yourself into the fray with a True Sect Examiner!" Dakar had no margin to stall her with reason, or to broach the weightier impacts of large-scale responsibility. Elaira carried the Biedar knife, as well as sole guardianship of the attributes that endowed Rathain's royal signet: a tribal talisman and a powerful crown jewel that must not be surrendered at all costs. Sethvir had set a *star stamp* on Prince Arithon's bequest, an indelible, sealed record with profound implication, evoked for a purpose past compromise. Dakar's savaged conscience acknowledged the irony. He wrestled the same vicious crux as Davien, who once had knocked him senseless to curb his free-will intervention, for Arithon's sake at Etarra: *also to safeguard a terrible course and play through an entrained sequence of horrific probabilities.* Elaira's crazed sentiment must be curbed by regrettable force if she failed to desist.

"Gutless coward!" Half-possessed and snarling oaths, she raked the Mad Prophet's wrist. Her frantic kick drubbed his knee-cap, buckled his leg, and displaced the blow aimed to drop her.

"Tarens!" yelped Dakar. "Help me contain the confounded enchantress before she exposes her presence. Koriathain ply her bereavement as leverage to reap the windfalls of disaster!" Fenced within of a cordon of dedicates, no possible recourse she owned might prevail. Not pitched against a pack of diviners, an examiner, and a temple conclave of True Sect priests. "If Elaira's not stopped, we risk losing her also, against Arithon's heart-felt bequest."

No response answered. Dakar turned his head. Through scouring pitch smoke, and the nauseous reek of spilled oil, he discovered that Tarens ditched sense. Baldric tossed aside, surcoat stripped, the blond crofter lunged forward. Not to hobble the endangered enchantress, but to smother the fluttering torch flung downwards to ignite the pyre.

Elaira snatched the diversion and stamped on the fat spellbinder's instep. "Put out the fire before we all burn!" She wrenched free and hurled herself toward the piled faggots, intent on clambering upwards to reach the slaughtered flesh of her beloved. Tears sheened Dakar's eyes. He was no Fellowship Sorcerer, fitted to shoulder the relentless far-sight of ages. Caved in to humane weakness at the last, he embraced the flawed character that forged his disgrace: he engaged the cipher to cancel flame, before the confounded woman and her loyal crofter became immolated in front of him.

Tarens never snatched pause to ascertain the lethal spark had extinguished. Unaware, or uncaring, as Dakar's active working blazed into the flux and alerted the temple's diviners, he bent with his hands laced into a stirrup. "Here, lady!" He caught Elaira's foot and boosted her weight. Her grip caught on the blood-slicked catwalk spanning the gap to the post overhead.

Through the True Sect watch-dogs' yells of alarm, The Hatchet reacted soonest. He seized the hilt sunk in Arithon's torso and jerked the embedded blade clear. Elaira's yank on his ankle unseated his balance, just as he spun. His counterstroke went wild, sliced through air, and bit wood, binding the weapon's edge as he staggered. His cat-quick recovery met Tarens's flung log, which struck his crested helm with a thunk, and up-ended him into the pit.

"To Sithaer yourself, you murderous runt!" Dakar kicked the fallen Lord High Commander under his gilt-blazoned breastplate. To his curled enemy, gasping for wind, he finished in bleak benediction, "May the day never come that you take up a sword to butcher the helpless again!" At the last, the Mad

Prophet used his bulk weight. He stomped on The Hatchet's gloved fingers and crunched the bones inside to splinters.

Tarens shouldered him off. Rammed past, he stretched his tall frame and snatched the grip of the stuck sword overhead. Borne onwards by Jieret's agile prowess, he scrambled up the stacked pyre, roaring challenge, to mount a *caithdein's* defence and repel the True Sect foes at Elaira's back.

The enchantress dared not pause to acknowledge his bravery. Hurled full length against Arithon's limp form, she engaged every skill she possessed to stem the fast-fading wisp of vitality. "My love, hold on! I'm with you at last." Hands drenched scarlet, she worked to reverse the tide's ebb, all of her healer's awareness engaged by the precepts taught by Ath's adepts. Heart and will, she plumbed Arithon's frayed aura, binding together the tissue-thin shreds as she searched for the seal of longevity embedded by Davien's Five Centuries' Fountain. The tenuous spark of her love's being still flickered. But the powerful seal to secure his spirit had not fired into renewal. The intact cipher stayed latent, inactive, where it ought to have blazed incandescent.

Dread revelation stunned Elaira to stopped breath. The Fellowship's binding of nonintervention *also* enforced this drastic stay of prevention. Her dearest beloved was lost past her reach without that crucial support.

"No. Arithon, no!" She fed the guttering flame of his spirit with her own hand, come what may, and wept without thought for the battle that viciously raged to cut her lone champion from his stance on the catwalk behind.

A man with a sword might stave off, for a time, the invasive might of a True Sect examiner. Yet no matter how skilled, despite the practised ability to bend flux derived from a forest scout's heritage, Tarens faced the fervour of a conclave of priests, surrounded and backed by a dedicate war host over three thousand strong. His courageous sally must fail, unlikely to hold long enough for Dakar to drive his walrus girth up the log pyre, far less finish his wheezing effort to gain the platform. Worse, the lethal mill of crossed steel at close quarters, as Tarens repelled his attackers, would haplessly carve him to collops.

Dakar seized the low ground. Too fat to run, and too shamed to hide, he retreated beneath the plank scaffold. Where he lacked the main strength to defeat the fury of the True Sect cabal, he might raise a swift warding and buy a delay, no matter how hopeless the outcome.

The Mad Prophet engaged his trained skill in the gloom. Settled cross-legged on the bruised turf, ears closed to the belling din of lethal steel and the hammering din from the rioting crowd that shocked vibrations through air and earth. He ignored The Hatchet's ineffectual whimpering, and immersed his honed awareness into the flux to sift out the signature Names of his threatened companions. Elaira's love wore the steadfast blaze of the stars; Tarens, the bonfire of a loyalty equal to Earl Jieret's bequest; and glimmering, weak as blown phosphor in a gale, the stream of the Teir's'Ffalenn's shattered vitality. Dakar swallowed remorse for what could not be changed. He wrestled back torn concentration. While focused on spinning a hurried confection of utterly futile grand conjury, his refined mage-sight unveiled the subtle anomaly: an etheric shimmer of spirit light drifting unmoored, luminous as a blown seed of thistle-down snagged in the torrid clench of raw combat.

Revelation struck like a blow to the chest. Belatedly late, the spellbinder unlocked Elaira's anguished conundrum. He *knew* beyond question why Fellowship interest had failed to support their urgent need in the breach.

Lirenda arose from the Prime seat at Whitehold. Before her, the scryer's engaged crystal disclosed the futile last stand on Daenfal's scaffold. The inevitable stroke of her victory loomed, a scant second away. Tarens's hard-fought defence at the catwalk pressed him another step backwards. He would die on the swords of the veteran dedicates or be thrown off his footing into the pit. Elaira's frail tie to Arithon's life-force rapidly waned. Since her inevitable fall into True Sect custody risked a disastrous disclosure of the order's privileged knowledge, her demise by the aegis of the master cipher must be swift. An end far more merciful than a sister condemned as a renegade deserved, but a casualty demanded by circumstance that would sting the Seven in punitive recoil.

Tawny eyes cold with astonishment regarded the submissive Fellowship Sorcerer, shackled to inaction by the runes incised in the marble floor. Bold enough to seize her rightful triumph, but without the scalded insolence of her late predecessor, Lirenda declared, "I never expected your word to stay sacrosanct. You may extend my ruthless admiration and condolence to the Warden at Althain Tower."

The titled Prime Matriarch moved to claim the match. Unrivalled at last, she swept forward. Breeze fanned by her formal mantle stirred the white hair on Asandir's head, where he bore silent witness as the supplicant beneath her dais. Lirenda assumed the ruler's position before her arc of poised Seniors, back turned towards the Sorcerer's presence to deliver her low-voiced command.

Asandir need not eavesdrop to interpret the eerie, prickling surge as the Koriathain melded their engaged powers into a collective trance.

Sethvir's earth-sensed perception supplied the unspoken thrust of the Prime's directive. *"She's raising the master sigil of command in force through her attendant Seniors."*

Lirenda's snapped fingers summoned a veiled sister forward with the coffer housing the Skyron aquamarine. She unlocked the clasp and unwrapped the cold jewel nestled within. Chill laced summer's warmth and infused the sealed chamber as she charged the latent stone's focus. "Mark and wait for my word!"

Asandir shut his eyes. Inner vision stretched to scintillant strain, he forced his locked hands to stay still. Through the harrowed, split second, he sensed the footfalls of Sethvir's fraught pacing; and he burned to the checked smoulder of Kharadmon's rage, equally unable to do aught but listen and bear the course of event.

Lirenda aligned her entrained sigil against the embedded record of Elaira's oath. Her touch was deliberate but not yet fluid. Acceded to Prime rank through a broken succession, she required meticulous care to enable a murder her predecessors could have achieved with one stroke.

Time slowed. The world's pulse hung suspended, strung on the order's pending engagement, and three gossamer threads that served hope. Against ruin, unsupported: one man's loyal steel, wielded by the intrepid endowment of a *caithdein's* heritage; the steadfast devotion of a woman's love; and on a weeping spellbinder's rattled attempt to refigure a fading, imperfect harmonic: the remnant chord left unfinished by Arithon's failure, all but drowned under the roil of blood slaughter and the thunderous roar of mass hatred.

Lirenda's next order smashed the seized quiet inside the great hall at Whitehold. "Now! Open the enabled quartz sphere to me."

Ceded the scryer's live channel as conduit, the Prime forged the connection to impress the Skyron aquamarine's amplified transmission into the flux stream at Daenfal. Unerring, she followed with the enchained sequence for activation. Then she unleashed the master sigil to strip Elaira of her conscious faculties.

Power surged down the link, building resonance, while from the hidden cranny on site underneath of Daenfal's scaffold, Dakar's local working leaped the split-second gap. Sobbing, undone, he engaged his wrought effort to restrike the pure intonation that Athera's Masterbard had narrowly missed: the true Name to call Valien's disturbed spirit into transition across the veil.

The flux flare responded. Sethvir's spontaneous outcry at Althain confirmed the completion of the child's passage. Instantaneous synchronicity erased the etched runes from the marble at Asandir's feet.

"Alt!" The field Sorcerer's shout at Whitehold resounded through the crystal spheres held aligned by Lirenda's directive. His authority snapped off the transmission, and stifled them into quiescence.

"The outstanding business between us is finished." His crisp declaration snuffed Lirenda's wild anger and silenced her colleagues' whiplashed outrage. "Rathain's oath of debt to Koriathain is fulfilled by the death of the crown's sanctioned heir. Valien Teir's'Ffalenn met his fate alone, without Fellowship intervention. He died by your order's ratified terms, and may Ath forgive us for the criminal cruelty of his unwarranted suffering."

No further moment was wasted for audience. Need demanded the Fellowship's resources elsewhere. Freed at last to respond in full, Asandir meshed with Kharadmon's distant presence, lurking at the locale of Daenfal's scaffold. "Reach!"

Effortless power enabled the transfer. Before dazzled vision cleared from the burst, the sisterhouse floor at Whitehold gleamed empty, unblemished in reflected sunlight.

Lirenda retreated to the Prime seat. She perched, a disgruntled, hungry hawk in the ruffled folds of her mantle. Empty-handed before her stunned circle of Seniors, and denied the satisfaction of just redress, she realized her order's interests were not crushed entirely by the facile trick. "Our bid to defeat the Fellowship has not collapsed into a total failure." Surely, her summary word to her sisters also stung Sethvir's rapt ears. "The Seven's exigent betrayal of a child surely will provoke their reinstated s'Ffalenn scion into a vehement estrangement."

Summer 5925

Reprieve

The same moment the Fellowship's impenetrable light bloomed in the packed square at Daenfal, dazzling the onlookers' sight of the scaffold, at Erdane's High Temple in Tysan the last line of the devotional song chant settled into the whisper-thick calm of late morning. Dace moved through air hazy with incense smoke, burdened under the extravagant drape of gold-crusted, white-satin vestments. For whatever reason, the True Sect High Priests had ordered lavish, formal raiment for Lysaer. Charged with the weighty delivery, the avatar's valet mounted the central stair, gut hollowed by sudden foreboding. The purpose behind the ceremonial clothing was unlikely to be innocuous. The stitched-bullion facings, gemmed buttons and seed-pearl embroidery surpassed ornate, a profligate outlay of temple tithes that might have uplifted the district's poor families for decades.

More, the pervasive hush on the subject squashed rumour. Whatever unpre-cedented occasion demanded the disruption of his liege's sequestered convalescence for a staged spectacle, not even the couriers' grooms gleaned a whisper. Such uneasy secrecy certainly stemmed from the temple's innermost ranks. Dace rounded the square landing, his thoughtful expression pinched into a frown by an echoing crash from above. Official indignation gave tongue, while a howl to bristle the hair at the nape resounded from the avatar's suite.

Lysaer! Dace bolted up the last flight, hampered by trailing silk. He dumped his armload of garments, swerved right, and breathlessly sprinted the narrower stair towards the ante-room door.

His rush collided with three flustered priests, then a pasty-faced acolyte, all routed from reverent prayer by their divine idol's corrosive displeasure. Dace thrashed his way upwards against the stampede. He extricated himself from

443

another shocked worthy in hell-bent retreat, grey head turned in a panicked glance backwards. A candlestick flew out the doorway and clanged, end over end down the marble risers. A white-silk pillow sailed after, gold tassels pin-wheeling through a leaked blizzard of feathers. Dace charged through the storm, ducking chaff as a hail of incense sticks clattered around him.

The cry rose again, a desolate note that poured chills down the spine.

The last shaken priest hiked up his vestments, fled the suite, and jammed into Dace at the threshold. "Light defend and protect! Go in at your peril. Divine presence has ridden the avatar mad as a dog at full moon."

Knocked against the pillared door-jamb by the coward's frantic haste to depart, Dace righted himself and stepped through. Two porcelain offering bowls whizzed past his ear. Grazed by showering coins and a splatter of holy water, he dodged aside, seized the massive, strapped panel, and slammed the outer door shut. The last offering bowl struck the studded wood and smashed into egg-shell slivers.

"We are private!" Dace cried into the roaring fit that gripped Lysaer, who vented his hell-bent fury, back turned, behind the splintered prayer rail. Already air-borne, the gilded kiosk that enclosed the Canon's scrolled writ hammered into the floor. The metallic crash rang loud enough to daze hearing within the closed chamber.

But Lysaer had heard. Fists ploughed into the ruckled cloth draping the desecrated altar, he went still. The last candle left burning tottered and drunkenly stood, guttered under the bellows gusts of his panting. Dace watched his master's heaving, tense back, well warned to keep his silent distance. If ever the man needed space for composure, this moment outstripped the scale of every previous outburst.

A minute passed; two. Disordered hair shimmered like submerged gold in the wrack. Lysaer locked his throat, his next outcry stifled by trembling force. Dace had a split second to measure the courage required, before the Light's avatar shoved upright and turned.

The livid face exposed to his scrutiny was not contorted by livid insanity. Instead, Dace stared into the agonized horror of self-damning shame. Not kindly madness, he realized, stricken, but the impact of a ruthless awakening brought by the absence of Desh-thiere's curse.

"He's dead," Lysaer whispered. The phrase slurred by damaged nerves was stunned hoarse by a strain unimaginable. "My half brother . . . has passed . . . the Wheel."

Dace swallowed, cast too far out of his depth. He had withstood Lysaer's testy rages before, from aristocratic fury at being handled, deformed, to the ferocious blaze of righteous ire that challenged the helpless ground down by iniquity. Never this edge of caged desperation, born out of gut-wracked exposure: not the lacerating hurt birthed by recognized guilt or the visceral wound of a spirit strayed past the moral compass of experience. Here stood the stricken champion, seared awake by the soul-deep acknowledgement of reprehensible acts beyond human accountability.

"How will Daelion Fatemaster judge me?" Lysaer laboured ahead in torment. "How would I judge myself if due terms of redress were mine to decree from the seat of crown justice?"

Dace smothered tears, bled by hindsighted recall of the merciless sentence once pronounced on a corrupted True Sect examiner, when, as Daliana, she had been the defendant wrongfully tried at Etarra.

This hour's criminal burden of wrongs outstripped any measure of equity. The s'Ilessid royal gift most perniciously whetted the thorns of embedded remorse and deepened the abyss of self-revilement without any bridge to forgiveness.

The tensioned shift in Lysaer's carriage gave scarcely a split second's warning.

Dace flattened his body against the shut door, distressed all the more by the warped twist of fortune: that his liege's disastrously weakened left side lent the cruelty of an advantage. "You are not going out to disenfranchise the Canon! The High Priest will have you killed outright if you try to tear down the True Sect doctrine without a plan!" Against mettlesome anger, he augured on, "No way will I let you give way to suicide!"

Lysaer made a choked sound. His reaction back-handed the remaining candle with his unimpaired forearm. Battened in sudden gloom, head bent, while the knocked taper tumbled onto the carpet, perhaps he wept in balked frustration. If so, the sculpted nobility left on his undamaged profile showed no sign, rimlit with the purity of a cameo against the bedchamber casement.

Dace filled his strapped lungs, speech forced through brutal quiet. "You are alive, yet, and not subject to Daelion's scales in the flesh. Culpability does not permit you the coward's right to abandon yourself! Or grant the excuse to leave True Sect fanaticism to its uncontested devices. A man with your history does not shrug off the responsible charge of his legacy."

A blurred movement, as Lysaer ducked into shadow and crumpled against the intact span of the altar rail.

Dace shut his eyes. Addressing a tortured hurt past imagining, he added, "Nor will I leave you. Not while you still breathe! No matter what you have done, or might cause in the unwritten future, you don't go on alone. Never, before the hour you stand upright and learn to temper your ethic with mercy."

Too careful, the halted words that emerged as though from behind muffled fingers. "You were not one of those widowed—or orphaned—or Ath forbid, torn by grievous loss as a parent bereft of a grown son untimely."

Dace fought the tightness strapping his chest. "No. But I was saved from the gutter by kindness." Impelled by instinct, he surged forward, picking his way through the scattered debris towards the huddled figure. "I was not struck down by an arrow, or scarred to infirmity for the upstanding denouncement of a corrupt doctrine. Your straits are not beyond salvage. Even under the grip of the curse, you never fulfilled the Mistwraith's primary directive."

Lysaer's hoarse response rejected sympathy. "If my hand did not strike my half brother down, direct influence still finds me culpable."

Dace offered the tenderness of ambiguity. "We don't know for certain the Law of the Canon has determined Arithon's fate."

"No." Lysaer seized a sawn breath. "Unless his body was burned in the aftermath, the priests' account may endorse a premature conclusion." The longevity endowed by the Five Centuries Fountain enabled that possibility. This moment's self-poisoned freedom of mind in harsh fact might be only fleeting. "The risk is quite real," Lysaer ground on, "I might survive to redouble the toll of mass slaughter laid at my feet."

The shudder met by his tentative touch dropped Dace to his knees amid the gutted wrack of kicked cushions. "A way forward exists to dispel the nightmare." Terrified to torch off the volatile struggle with self-condemnation in the tormented figure before him, he soothed, "Impatience won't find that elusive path. If you fall by surrender, you'll have given your flaws the fool's license to trample your innate goodness."

"How many more misguided dupes stand at risk to be sacrificed?" Lysaer agonized, stumbling onwards.

Dace winced at the store of anguish left unbroached. If the ruinous lists of past dead in their thousands could never be reconciled, how much worse, amid the untenable cost, that not every life lost was a stranger's? For Talith, for Ellaine, for Diegan and not least, for the loyal sacrifice rendered by Sulfin Evend, the steadfast heart now must not succumb to pity. "All," Dace declared, blunt. "There will come no end to the slaughter if you leave the True Sect Canon its undisputed sway over the next generations. Or else some might be spared if you rise to the task and apply every resource you own to founder the Sunwheel behemoth."

Silence gripped the following pause in an alcove too dim to map Lysaer's expression. Dace waited. Through the anxious pound of raced pulse, he sustained the pressured uncertainty; held out, unsure whether his aggressive honesty had led Lysaer towards sane redemption or tipped him to broken defeat. Under covert identity and for aching, undeclared love, he listened, while the shuddering rasp of his master's harrowed breaths resumed, jerked one into the next through clenched teeth. Dace suffered as well through each paralysed second of cruel indecision, while the damaged creak of spooled wood translated the shuddering tremors raked through the clenched body before him.

As the lowly valet, Dace hesitated to try contact again. He feared to move, even speak, lest another presumptuous intervention should unleash the pent tempest.

Then hard fingers reached out and gripped his poised wrist. A fierce tug rocked his braced balance. Dace blinked back his welled tears. For the battle on-going was not defeat, after all, but the struggle of mortal flesh and dogged pride, wrestling the short-falls of infirmity.

Dace shouldered the burden of Lysaer's crippled weight and boosted him upright. Neither spoke through the laboured, erratic steps required to cross the wrecked ante-room. No haven amid the True Sect's den of adders, their retreat reached the stonewalled confinement of the sick-room bedchamber.

There, Dace assisted his master's collapse. He slid the cool sheets aside, noted grazed knuckles in need of salve, and with tender hands straightened the ungainly sprawl of atrophied limbs. Although by slow increments healing had begun to reduce the scope of Lysaer's debilities, his one-sided body remained drastically weak. Daylight's flood through the barred casement exposed his wretched state. Unflinching honesty also laid bare the long odds of this moment's tenuous triumph.

Nor was Lysaer s'Ilessid the fool, to misappraise the lethal extent of his peril. The cavernous, blind eye sunk like a pit in the sag of paralysis did not impair his clear-sighted reason. Invalid, he lay in the innermost sanctum of the True Sect High Temple, a game pawn ruthlessly held at the dogmatic sufferance of powerful enemies.

Dace recoiled from the stacked probability in favour of full-scale disaster. Instead, he counted the formidable measure of his liege's character. Lysaer s'Ilessid still possessed iron will, and the magnetic force of imperial sovereignty. Born and bred to the challenge of royal authority, he would not flinch before the daunting obstacles. The unaffected side of his face showed his iron determination. Dace watched the chiselled mouth flex with distaste, then firm, while the lucent gaze of the alert blue eye tracked his tactful ministrations.

Neither master nor servant cared to belabour the frightening prospect: that ahead, unutterably dreary and dangerous, their strategy of deceptive intrigue must withstand hostile scrutiny under close quarters. Years might pass before Lysaer s'Ilessid regained the hale fitness to exert himself at full strength.

When his marred speech resumed, the magisterial inflection did not emerge without humour. "You'll have some—difficult—explaining ahead."

"Oh, yes," Dace responded, patiently oblique. "Starting off with the costly new vestment I dumped like a rag in the course of your tantrum."

"Light forfend!" One golden eyebrow rose, spangled in sweat against Lysaer's pasty forehead. "Here I thought I'd prompted the temple's most faithful to blaspheme by tossing them out on their arses."

Dace stifled a smile. "You don't want the worshipful lot at your threshold droning through tedious prayers? Then we'll need to contrive a plausible way to abolish the ante-room shrine."

A snort, from the pillows, perhaps prelude to a wicked burst of stifled laughter. "Certainly, that. Provided my heap of emphatic wreckage hasn't reamed that point home already." Then in sobered afterthought, as his confidante rose and delved into the remedy cabinet, "Please, I don't want the posset.

Since I cannot muster the spine to stand upright, surely I'm able to fake the convincing semblance of limpid prostration?"

"Perhaps." Dace set about mixing a tonic instead, then added a salve and clean gauze to bind up his liege's skinned knuckles. "Though you might regret the petty indignity. First of all, for your ill-tempered sins, I'm stuck with extracting your nasty collection of glass shards and splinters."

Last Vigil

Shielded within the impenetrable dazzle cast by the Fellowship's warding, few eyes observed what occurred at the post on the scaffold in Daenfal's main square. Asandir supported Arithon's weight in his arms. With smoking impatience, he waited: while Dakar hauled his corpulent, dazed bulk from the pit, pushed erect, and struck off the offensive shackles.

Sword abandoned, no enemies left to withstand, Tarens shed his mail gauntlets. His ready strength joined the on-going labour that eased the crown prince's maimed body down. They laid Arithon face-up on the spattered scaffold. Sight flinched to contemplate the gaping wound in his chest where the executioner's sword had struck home. Dakar scuffed the puddled planks with his feet, while Tarens wrestled the savage outrage bequeathed by a *caithdein* three-centuries dead. None of them dared to broach their worst fear: the streaked body on the boards stayed unbreathing, while the steady calm of Asandir's instruction asked Elaira to straighten her beloved's inert limbs.

Healer's touch shaking, near blinded by grief, she cried out through her ministrations. "His pulse has been stopped for too long! Is he lost?"

Kharadmon's discarnate presence surrounded her urgent distress like a blanket. *"Not just yet. Don't let up!"* His cool reason lent bracing support. *"Davien's seal of longevity grips your prince's body in stasis to stem the gush of arterial bleeding."*

On his knees with Arithon's head in cupped hands, Asandir added terse, "Elaira? Mend the wound where you can. Start with the torn heart and work outwards. Kharadmon will assist you, given permission. We hold lawful claim here through sovereign prerogative."

Amid gristly, unspeakable carnage, even the corpse of a sacrificed child for necessity must be set aside. Steadied by the immersive skill of her calling,

449

Elaira placed her hands on Arithon's stilled flesh and yielded her faculties to the relief of unerring Fellowship oversight. "The sword-thrust also mangled his Grace's spine."

"My dear, we're aware." The surge of Kharadmon's wisdom flowed into her, faultlessly poised to refine, augment, and, if needed, correct any gaps in her knowledge. *"Once the spirit has stabilized from the shock, and after we've redressed the acute loss of blood, rest assured Asandir will attend that concern."*

In fact, the field Sorcerer's directive to Tarens and Dakar pursued the exigency. "I'll need a litter fashioned to move him." Against a quiet as dense as balled cotton, words bit with preternatural clarity. "Scavenge whatever you can for the purpose. You won't be harmed by our conjured protection. Though heed my warning, the extant defences serve life! Be careful not to touch any steel that's been forged to inflict purposeful injury."

Tarens shed the skinning knife sheathed in his boot. The cuts and contusions from his recent stand hitched his agility as he straightened. He set after Dakar's shambling lead, not without qualms as he stepped into the unearthly blaze of the ward-field. Yet the daunting intensity of the active spell raised no trace of sensation.

Startlement provoked his surprised exclamation.

"That's the fearsome mark of a Fellowship working," Dakar grumbled under his breath. "Enough might to sunder the earth underfoot, transacted with scarcely a whisper. Don't be misled. The cross-grained kick of fell consequence if you violate the directive doesn't forgive. Makes Dharkaron's Black Spear damned near toothless as a virgin's kiss of forgiveness."

Whether or not the Mad Prophet's complaint stemmed from unhappy experience, the vista unveiled past the curtain of radiance showed the staggering scale of the Sorcerers' power. The True Sect officials caught at close quarters on the dais had been hurled from their cushioned seats and flung prostrate. They appeared unbreathing, plumes and jewels wrenched still, as though time itself stood snap-frozen. Beyond the scaffold, the dedicate cordon appeared to be shedding their arms in arrested, slow motion. The fall of dropped swords and halberds seemed suspended in viscous glue, while the clangour of metal striking the brick pavement resounded in distorted, stretched echoes. The riotous throng of the faithful assembled for Arithon's execution no longer stood upright. Stripped naked of hate by the clarion force of unbridled compassion, man, woman, and child, they cowered on their knees, heads bowed under the clean fall of sunlight. All had covered their faces in shame, while tears welled and spilled through their hands.

Beyond the packed square, Daenfal's slate roofs shimmered untouched. Farther distant, the natural breeze stirred the banners atop the peaked guild-halls. Sails carved the course of on-going trade through the indigo chop in the harbour. The water-front ferry crept shoreward on its cable, while the eerie, spaced toll of the noon carillons shivered deep, dopplered notes through the stunned air.

"Ath wept," Tarens murmured in awe.

"Fair strikes the wind from your chest," agreed Dakar, having withstood his share of Fellowship stays that cast slip-streams across time and space. "You don't ever get used to the upset, forbye. Tosses your guts inside out through the final course of the unbinding release."

Fat as a fluffed partridge, the Mad Prophet tacked a course through the threshed sprawl of dignitaries. His eye sized up their resplendent finery and seized on the gilt hem of the mantle draping the loftiest temple official. "Bad cess to the fact," he grunted, and pulled, "there's no cloth at hand that's not blighted with a forsaken Sunwheel blazon. And curse the True Sect's foul doctrine to Sithaer," he blasphemed as the unfrocked priest tumbled clear of the garment.

Tarens attended his assigned charge without comment, absorbed by the caution of picking his steps through a hazardous maze of dropped swords and halberds. The flag staves affixed to the platform's outside rail provided a ready selection of harmless poles. Momentarily, he regretted his abandoned knife. But when he set out to untie the flag halyards, the knots slid free with uncanny ease under his battle-sore fingers. He ripped off the banners, cast their gaudy silk into the stunned muddle of guards, where the bullion fringe perhaps might recompense the underpaid rank and file. Then he retraced his steps.

Dakar waited in a cleared space on the boards, seated amid a glittering hoard of pillaged state brooches. "Pins," he explained, his smug smile flecked with the sun-scattered highlights flung off by faceted citrines and diamonds. "Rightful booty, since we need these to secure the sling. And besides, the Fellowship owes us. Here's a decade's stashed consolation of beer coin for sticking our necks on the block for their crown prince."

"If you say so." Tarens chuckled, then bent to the task of creating the litter to bear a living prize far more precious.

Twilight's deep shadow mantled Daenfal when the party bearing the Spinner of Darkness descended the scaffold at last. Behind them, just stirring, the prostrate officials began to recover their disgruntled wits. The stupefied cordon of dedicates who permitted the procession to pass raised no protest. Scarcely an eddy of turbulence flanked their path through the spell-bound onlookers who had gathered that morning to witness the demise of evil. Past the waning influence of the Fellowship's ward, the quartet with its scarlet-stained parcel emerged at the south edge of the square in plain view of the workaday populace. Though the darkening streets beyond remained crowded with celebrants, none of the bystanders could have said how, or from where, the uncanny foursome had come.

The tall Sorcerer in the lead wore stained leathers, the silver spill of his hair in tangles over straight shoulders. The townsfolk who stared with wide-open eyes later argued whether or not his frame shimmered with a golden radiance.

The face they remembered without error: carved by deep sorrow and an ageless care that saw past pretention and scoured the spirit to tears of release.

Tongues fell silent before the mercy reflected in his mirror-bright glance. Even the most raucous revellers melted clear of his stride. Vendors stopped hawking their meat-pies and cheap trinkets, while the scrapping dogs and barefoot children ceased their boisterous play in the gutters. Silence fell in his wake like the well of flood-tide and settled, leaving the cries of the scavenging gulls flocking to roost overhead.

At the Sorcerer's back, the scarred, blond defender in bloodied mail carried no weaponry. He bore the poles at the front of the litter, partnered behind by a shorter man, plump as a bolster, with tired, hound's eyes and a tousled white beard streaked with cinnamon. He puffed, red-faced, although the load he supported was not onerous, his stumpy gait forced to hustle to match his longer-strided companions.

Yet after the Sorcerer's imposing presence, the fourth person overshadowed the rest. A spare, fine-boned woman flanked the bearers, russet hair bound into a braid worse for wear, and her eyes, pale as dawn, welled with tears. She walked with her hand on the sodden bandage wrapping the breast of the Master of Shadow. He breathed under her touch, the cut angles of his comatose features wax-pale amid sullied black hair. Enthralled during the aftermath, the onlooking witnesses later argued over the flaws in the True Sect doctrine. The creature the Light's dedicates had dragged to the scaffold had not unleashed baneful harm or dark practice. No Shadow had snuffed the sun at high noon. None had seen harm for the offence of harsh handling, even under the sword-thrust enacted to finish a murderous ritual. Nor had brutal vengeance been visited on the faithful for the slaughter of a blameless child.

In sobering fact, Arithon Teir's'Ffalenn in the flesh did not match the monster vilified by the Light's Canon. The injured form cradled in besmirched white silk seemed too slight to be a demonic criminal; too small for the enormity of the crimes that condemned him to death on the scaffold; too frail in extremity to be any less than mortal and sorrowfully human.

The wounded grief on the woman's grimed features stayed etched into the collective memory.

No voice arose to cite scripture in empty justification. None prayed, or sketched the Sunwheel sign to ward away evil as Prince Arithon of Rathain was borne onwards through the water-front gate and down the ancient, raised causeway. At the edge of the lake, on the stone stair at the landing erected by the art of Paravian masons, the four figures and the unconscious crown prince they carried disappeared into thin air.

No one screamed. There arose no hysteria. Peace gripped Daenfal like a gloved fist. While the lucent sky deepened into starry night, the chastened drunks and the glut of dazed revellers drifted apart and went quietly home-wards.

Coda

The temple chronicler of The Hatchet's campaign in Rathain, finished in Glory by the Ritual Death of the Master of Shadow in Third Age 5925, sequesters the signal passage from all but the most incorruptible eyes: that every devout witness to the execution turned apostate and thereafter abandoned the True Sect Canon, and neither priest, nor examiner, nor the Divine Light could restore the bulwark of their riven faith . . .

A familiar step reaches the top-floor landing at Althain Tower and crosses the library threshold softly as a breath of spring air; and Sethvir drops a book on his toe, his joyful crow like a thunder-clap under the bemused regard of Ciladis, who says, "I've two sacks of original manuscripts for your shelves, besides the fact you'll need help with the storm on the hour Prince Arithon wakens . . ."

Among the True Sect dedicates discharged into retirement after two decades of honourable, armed service, one weary, scarred veteran turns westward for home, and upon his midwinter arrival at Kelsing, reunites with his brown-haired eldest son and his daughter in the loft of her seamstress's shop, and through a night of laughter and tears, the family shares his astonishing tale of their fugitive brother's survival . . .

Glossary

AIYENNE—river located in Daon Ramon, Rathain, rising from an underground spring in the Mathorn Mountains, and coming above ground south of the Mathorn Road. Site of the ruinous battle between Earl Jieret's war band and the Alliance war host under Sulfin Evend, which enabled Arithon's escape to the north in Third Age 5670.

pronounced: eye-an

root meaning: *ai'an* – hidden one

ALESTRON—city located in Midhalla, Melhalla. Paravian built with warded defences. Once ruled by s'Brydion, placed under entailment by the Fellowship Sorcerers after the siege in Third Age 5672.

pronounced: ah-less-tron

root meaning: *alesstair* – stubborn; *an* – one

ALITHIEL—one of twelve Blades of Isaer, forged by centaur Ffereton s'Darian from metal taken from a meteorite, and inlaid by the Athlien with an arcane endowment for transcendent change, then infused with the tonal chord that Named the winter stars by the Riathan, which powers will only ignite if the cause of the wielder is just. Passed through Paravian possession, acquired the secondary name Dael-Farenn, or Kingmaker, since its owners tended to succeed the end of a royal line. Eventually was awarded to Kamridian s'Ffalenn for his valour in defence of the princess Taliennse, early Third Age, and held in the heritage of the s'Ffalenn royal line.

pronounced: ah-lith-ee-el

root meaning: *alith* – star; *iel* – light/ray

ALT—Paravian word for last, or finish, and used as closure for spells.

pronounced: alt

root meaning: *alt* – last

ALTHAIN TOWER—spire built at the edge of the Bittern Desert, beginning of the Second Age, to house records of Paravian histories. Third Age, became repository for the archives of all five royal houses of men after rebellion, overseen by the Fellowship Sorcerer, Sethvir, named Warden of Althain since Third Age Year 5100. Warded by the Ilitharis Paravian spirit of Shehane Althain.

pronounced: all-thay-in

root meaning: *alt* – last; *thein* – tower, sanctuary

original Paravian pronunciation: alt-thein

ANGLEFEN—swampland located in Deshir, Rathain.

pronounced: angle-fen

ANLI—exalted one, or special one, a diminutive applied to very small children.

pronounced: an-lee

root meaning: *an* – one; *li* – exalted

ARAETHURA—grass plains in southwest Rathain; principality of the same name in that location. Largely inhabited by Riathan Paravians in the Second Age. Third Age, used as pasture land by widely scattered nomadic shepherds.

pronounced: ar-eye-thoo-rah

root meaning: *araeth* – grass; *era* – place, land

ARAITHE—plain north of the trade city of Etarra, in the principality of Fallowmere, Rathain.

pronounced: a-ray-th-e, the final e being nearly subliminal

root meaning: *araithe* – to disperse, or send/properties of standing stones that temper the lane currents that once flowed unimpaired before Mankind settled the notch at Etarra

ARIN—abbreviated diminutive for Arithon, originally taken from his faulty recall.

pronounced: ah-rin

ARITHON—son of Avar, Prince of Rathain, 1,504th Teir's'Ffalenn after founder of the line, Torbrand in Third Age Year One. Also Master of Shadow, the Bane of Desh-thiere, and Halliron Masterbard's successor. First among Mankind to tap the transcendent powers of the sword, Alithiel, and also responsible for the final defeat of the Grey Kralovir necromancers. Held captive by Koriathain from Third Age 5674 until his escape in 5922, condemned to death under a crown oath of debt, with a stay on his life bought by Fellowship intercession for the purpose of utilizing his Masterbard's title to subdue the free wraiths from Marak, and left to survive on his own merits under Asandir's oath of nonintervention.

pronounced: ar-i-thon

root meaning: *arithon* – fate-forger; one who is visionary

ARWENT—river in Araethura, Rathain, that flows from Daenfal Lake through Halwythwood to empty in Instrell Bay.

pronounced: are-went

root meaning: *arwient* – swiftest

ARWI UNFREY—a head-hunter tracker who serves under The Hatchet.

pronounced: ar-wee uhn-free

root meaning: shortened from *maesiad* – to slide or skid; *arwen unfri* – novice racer

ASANDIR—Fellowship Sorcerer. Secondary name, Kingmaker, since his hand crowned every High King of Men to rule in the Age of Men (Third Age). After the Mistwraith's conquest, he acted as field agent for the Seven. Also called Fiend-quencher, for his reputation for quelling *iyats*; Storm-breaker and Change-bringer for his past actions when humanity first arrived upon Athera.

pronounced: ah-san-deer

root meaning: *asan* – heart; *dir* – stone "heart rock"

ATAINIA—north-eastern principality of Tysan.

pronounced: ah-tay-nee-ah

root meaning: *itain* – the third; *ia* – suffix for "third domain" original Paravian, *itainia*

ATH CREATOR—prime vibration, force behind all life.
  pronounced: ath
  root meaning: *ath* – prime, first (as opposed to an, one)
ATHERA—name for the world which holds the Five High Kingdoms; four
  Worldsend Gates; formerly inhabited by dragons, and current home of the
  Paravian races.
  pronounced: ath-air-ah
  root meaning: *ath* – prime force; *era* – place "Ath's world"
ATHILI—proscribed region located at the border of Havish and Rathain,
  between the principalities of Lanshire and Araethura, which bounds the
  grand portal created by Ath Creator when the Paravian presence was made
  manifest in the world.
  Pronounced: ah-ill-lee
  Root meaning: *ath* – prime force; *i'li* – a state of self-aware exaltation
ATHIR—Second Age ruin of a Paravian stronghold, located in Ithilt, Rathain.
  Site of a seventh lane power focus; also where Arithon Teir's'Ffalenn swore
  his blood oath to survive to the Fellowship Sorcerer, Asandir. Also the location of Teylia's conception and Dakar's swearing Oath of Debt in behalf of
  Rathain's crown, to Koriathain under Fellowship auspices in Third Age 5671.
  pronounced: ath-ear
  root meaning: *ath* – prime; *i'er* – the line, or edge
ATHLIEN PARAVIANS—sunchildren, dancers of the crystal flutes. Small race
  of semi-mortals, pixie-like, but possessed of great wisdom/keepers of the
  grand mystery.
  pronounced: ath-lee-en
  root meaning: *ath* – prime force; *lien* – to love "Ath-beloved"
AUDUA SEDJII AN TESHUA—Biedar birth name for the seeress Enithen Tuer,
  deceased in Third Age 5670.
  pronounced: ow-doo-ah sed-jee en tesh-oo-ah
  root meaning: lineage name from the Biedar tribes' dialect
AVENOR—Second Age ruin of a Paravian stronghold. Traditional seat of the
  s'Ilessid High Kings. Restored to habitation in Third Age 5644. Became the
  ruling seat of the Alliance of Light in Third Age 5648. Located in Korias,
  Tysan. Destroyed by the wrath of Seshkrozchiel's drakefire for misuse of
  hatchling skulls in Third Age 5671.
  pronounced: ah-ven-or
  root meaning: *avie* – stag; *norh* – grove
AVILEFFIN—Ilitharis Paravian, greatest of the Second Age master shipwrights.
  pronounced: av-ill-eff-fin
  root meaning: *avie* – stag; *lieffen* – pale yellow hair

BACKWATER—trade town located at the western end of Daenfal Lake in the
  principality of Araethura, best known for furs, spun yarn, and textiles.

BAFFIEL'S CAULDRON—a hot mineral spring located in the Storlain Mountains in Havish.
  pronounced: baff-ee-el
  root meaning: *baffi* – pot; *iel* – light
BARACH—former Earl of the North, second son of Jieret s'Valerient and older brother of Jeynsa; presided over the trial of Eriegal for betrayal; brokered a lawful peace treaty with Mayor Lysaer s'Ilessid in 5688; died Third Age 5712; forebear of Cosach s'Valerient and Esfand.
  pronounced: bar-ack
  root meaning: *baraich* – linchpin
BEKTISHA—a matron from Ettinmere Settlement.
  pronounced: beck-tee-shaa
  root meaning: *bektiashe* – a fuss pot
BIEDAR—desert tribe living in Sanpashir, Shand. Also known as the Keepers of the Prophecy. Their sacred weaving at the well produced the conception of Dari s'Ahelas, which crossed the old *caithdein*'s lineage of s'Dieneval with the royal line of s'Ahelas, combining the gifts of prophetic clairvoyance with the Fellowship-endowed penchant for far-sight.
  pronounced: bee-dar
  root meaning: *biehdahrr* – ancient desert dialect for "lore keepers"
BITTERN DESERT—waste located in Atainia, Tysan, north of Althain Tower. Site of a First Age battle between the great drakes and the Seardluin, permanently destroyed by dragon fire.
  pronounced: bittern
  root meaning: *bityern* – to sear or char
BLACKSHEAR ISLAND—isle located in Instrell Bay, east of Tysan.
BWIN EVOC s'LORNMEIN—founder of the royal lineage of Havish in Third Age Year One, bearing the gifted attribute of temperance.
  pronounced: bwin-ee-vok slorn-main
  root meaning: *bwin* – firm; *evoc* – choice; *liernmein* – to bring into balance
BRAGGEN—one of the Fourteen Companions who were the only child survivors of the massacre at Tal Quorin in Third Age 5638. Stood proxy for Jeynsa s'Valerient's absence upon High Earl Barach's oath swearing to Prince Arithon in 5671, which obligated him to execute Eriegal for crown treason in 5674.
  pronounced: brag-en
  root meaning: *briocen* – surly

CAINFORD—town located in Taerlin, Tysan.
  pronounced: cane-ford
  root meaning: *caen* – vale
CAITH-AL-CAEN—vale at a major intersection of lane and flux currents, where Riathan Paravians celebrated equinox and solstice to renew the *athael*, or

life-destiny of the world, and where the Paravians Named the winter stars by encompassing their vibrational essence into actualized language. Birthplace of Cianor Sunlord.

pronounced: cay-ith-all-cay-in

root meaning: *caith* – shadow; *al* – over; *caen* – vale, or vale of shadow

CAITHDEIN—(alternate spelling *caith'd'ein*, plural form *caithdeinen*) Paravian name for a High King's first counsellor; also, the one who would stand as regent, or steward, in the absence of the crowned ruler. By heritage, the office also bears responsibility for oversight of crown royalty's fitness to rule.

pronounced: kay-ith-day-in

root meaning: *caith* – shadow; *d'ein* – behind the chair "shadow behind the throne"

CAITHWOOD—free-wilds forest located in Taerlin, south-east principality of Tysan.

pronounced: kay-ith-wood

root meaning: *caith* – shadow – shadowed wood

CAMRIS—north-central principality of Tysan. Original ruling seat was the city of Erdane.

pronounced: cam-ris

root meaning: *caim* – cross; *ris* – way "cross-road"

CANON LAW—established doctrine of the True Sect, a following of the Religion of Light that split off from the Alliance at the Great Schism in Third Age Year 5673, when Lysaer abandoned the High Temple at Miralt and transferred his residence to the mayor's seat at Etarra.

CAOLLE—past war-captain of the clans of Deshir, Rathain. First raised, and then served under, Lord Steiven, Earl of the North and *Caithdein* of Rathain. Planned the campaign at Vastmark and Dier Kenton Vale for the Master of Shadow. Served Jieret Red-beard, and was feal liegeman of Arithon of Rathain; died of complications from a wound received from his prince while breaking a Koriani attempt to trap his liege in Third Age 5653.

pronounced: kay-all-eh, with the "e" nearly subliminal

root meaning: *caille* – stubborn

CASCAIN ISLANDS—rugged chain of islets off the coast of Vastmark, Shand. Temporary refuge for Arithon's shipwrights after they fled Merior in Third Age 5647.

pronounced: cass-canes

root meaning: *kesh kain* – shark's teeth

CASTLE POINT—trade port located on the west shore of Instrell Bay in Atainia, Tysan.

CATHUKODARR—Great Drake whose wrathful fire laid waste to the continent of Kathtairr during the Age of Dragons.

pronounced: cath-oo-kuh-dar

root meaning: grinder of rock

CEFTWINN s'LORNMEIN—Princess of Havish in Third Age 5923, her accession to crown rank confirmed by Asandir following her brother Gestry's death in the Battle of Lithmarin, which defeated True Sect invasion under command of The Hatchet.

pronounced: kef-twin slorn-main

root meaning: *kef* – jasper; *tuinne* – rose; *liernmein* – to centre or bring into balance

CENTAUR GUARDIANS—Ilitharis Paravians who were guardians, and anchors for, high-resonance sites on Athera. They were ritually bound to the land, a connection that transcended time and space, and thereafter, their names carried the suffix *erach*, denoting their root to that place.

CHAIMISTARIZOG—Elder dragon standing as Guardian of Northgate.

pronounced: shay-mist-tar-ee-zog

root meaning: *chaimistarizog* – Drakish for fire gatekeeper

CHIA—Ettin dialect for beloved mate.

pronounced: chee-yah

root meaning: *cian* – spark, corrupted from original Paravian

CIANOR SUNLORD/CIANOR MOONLORD—born at Caith-al-Caen, First Age Year 615. Crowned High King of Athera in Second Age Year 2545, until his death by Khadrim in Second Age 3651. He is the only Paravian in history to have a namesake, more properly termed a *tiendar'shayn'd* or "reborn." Cianor Moonlord was birthed at the darkest hour of the Second Age. He was present in Third Age Year One when the Fellowship Sorcerers wrote the compact that enabled Mankind to take sanctuary. His hand bestowed the sword Alithiel on Kamridian s'Ffalenn for valour.

CILADIS THE LOST—Fellowship Sorcerer who left the continent in Third Age 5462 in search of the Paravian races after their disappearance following the rebellion.

pronounced: kill-ah-dis

root meaning: *cael* – leaf; *adeis* – whisper, compound; *cael'adeis*, "gentleness that abides"

CILDEIN OCEAN—body of water located off the east coast of the continent of Paravia.

pronounced: kill-dine

root meaning: *cailde* – salty; *an* – one

CINDRA s'AHELAS—founder of the s'Ahelas royal line appointed by the Fellowship Sorcerers in Third Age Year One, gifted with far-sight.

pronounced: sin-dra sa-hell-as

root meaning: *cian* – spark; *diere* – life; *ahelas* – mage-gifted

CORDAYA s'VALERIENT—infant daughter of High Earl Cosach and Jalienne, born Third Age 5923. Sister of Esfand.

pronounced: kor-day-aa sval-er-ee-ent

root meaning: *kordi-a* – newborn; *val* – straight; *erient* – spear

CORITH—ruin on the isle of Caincyr in the Westland Sea, site of a drake lair and a First Age ruin. Here the council of the Paravians met during siege by drake spawn, and at their behest the Dragons dreamed the summoning of the Fellowship Sorcerers. First site to see sunlight upon Desh-thiere's defeat.
pronounced: core-ith
root meaning: *cori* – ships, vessels; *itha* – five, for the five harbours

COSACH s'VALERIENT—current Earl of the North and *Caithdein* of Rathain, husband of Jalienne, father of Esfand and Cordaya.
pronounced: co-sack s-val-er-ee-ent
root meaning: *cosak* – bluster; *val* – straight; *erient* – spear

DACE MARLEY—name of a valet in service to Lysaer s'Ilessid.
pronounced: days mar-lee
root meaning: *dace* – two; *marle* – quartz rock

DAELION FATEMASTER—"entity" formed by set of mortal beliefs, which determine the fate of the spirit after death. If Ath is the prime vibration, or life-force, Daelion is what governs the manifestation of free will.
pronounced: day-el-ee-on
root meaning: *dael* – king, or lord; *i'on* – of fate

DAELION'S WHEEL—cycle of life and the crossing point that is the transition into death.
pronounced: day-el-ee-on
root meaning: *dael* – king or lord; *i'on* – of fate

DAENFAL—town located on the northern lake-shore that bounds the southern edge of Daon Ramon Barrens in Rathain. Site of Arwent ferry, and also the ancient necropolis where Paravians once honoured their dead.
pronounced: dye-en-fall
root meaning: *daen* – clay; *fal* – red

DAENFAL LAKE—lake that bounds the southern edge of Daon Ramon Barrens in Rathain.
pronounced: dye-en-fall
root meaning: *daen* – clay; *fal* – red

DAKAR THE MAD PROPHET—formerly an apprentice to Fellowship Sorcerer, Asandir, during the Third Age following the Conquest of the Mistwraith. Given to spurious prophecies, it was Dakar who forecast the fall of the Kings of Havish in time for the Fellowship to save the heir. He made the Prophecy of West Gate, which forecast the Mistwraith's bane, and also, the Black Rose Prophecy, which called for reunification of the Fellowship.
pronounced: dah-kar
root meaning: *dakiar* – clumsy

DALDARI—surname of an Ettin family.
pronounced: doll-dar-ee
root meaning: *dal* – fair; *diere* – life

DALIANA sen EVEND—descendant of Sulfin Evend chosen by Asandir to stand heir to the lineage.

pronounced: dah-lee-ahn-a sen-ev-and

root meaning: *dal* – fair; *lien* – harmony; *a* – feminine diminutive; *sen* – descended of; *eiavend* – diamond

DAON RAMON BARRENS—central principality of Rathain, where Riathan Paravians (unicorns) once bred and raised their young. Barrens was not appended to the name until the years following the Mistwraith's conquest, when the River Severnir was diverted at the source by a task force under Etarran jurisdiction. Site where a combined Sunwheel war host led by Lysaer sought to corner the Master of Shadow, and met defeat against clan war bands under Jieret s'Valerient in Third Age 5670.

pronounced: day-on-rah-mon

root meaning: *daon* – gold; *ramon* – hills/downs

DARI s'AHELAS—crown heir of Shand who was sent to safety through West Gate to preserve the royal lineage. Born following the death of the last Crown Prince of Shand, subsequently raised and taught by Sethvir to manage the rogue talent of a dual inheritance. Her mother was Meiglin s'Dieneval, last survivor of the old *caithdein*'s lineage of Melhalla, which was widely believed to have perished during the massacre at Tirans. However, the pregnant widow of Egan s'Dieneval had escaped the uprising and survived under a false name in a Durn brothel.

pronounced: dar-ee sa-hell-as

root meaning: *daer* – to cut; *ahelas* – mage-gifted

DASCEN ELUR—splinter world beyond the western Worldsend Gate, connected to Mearth; primarily ocean with scattered archipelagos, including kingdoms of Amroth, Rauven, and Karthan, birthplace of Lysaer s'Ilessid and Arithon s'Ffalenn.

pronounced: dass-sen ell-ur

root meaning: *dacsen* – ocean; *e'lier* – small land

DAVIEN THE BETRAYER—Fellowship Sorcerer responsible for provoking the great uprising in Third Age Year 5018, that resulted in the fall of the High Kings after Desh-thiere's conquest. Rendered discorporate by Shehane Althain's defences in Third Age 5129. Exiled since, by personal choice. Davien's works included the Five Centuries Fountain near Mearth on the splinter world of the Red Desert through West Gate; the shaft at Rockfell Peak, used by the Sorcerers to imprison harmful entities; the Stair on Rockfell Peak; and also, Kewar Tunnel in the Mathorn Mountains. Restored as a corporate being through Asandir's interaction with the Great Drake, Seshkrozchiel in the banishment of the Scarpdale grimward in Third Age 5671. Bound into the dragon's service until Luhaine took his place when the drake hibernated in Third Age 5923.

pronounced: dah-vee-en

root meaning: *dahvi* – fool; *an* – one "mistaken one"

DEAL—trade town known for lumber, located in Gent, Havish.
   pronounced: deal
   root meaning: *dayal* –moss grown

DESHIR—north-western principality of Rathain.
   pronounced: desh-eer
   root meaning: *deshir* – misty

DESH-THIERE—Mistwraith that invaded Athera from the splinter worlds
   through South Gate in Third Age 4993. Access cut off by Fellowship Sorcerer,
   Traithe. Battled and contained in West Shand for twenty-five years, until the
   rebellion splintered the peace, and the High Kings were forced to withdraw
   from the defence lines to attend their disrupted kingdoms. Confined through
   the combined powers of Lysaer s'Ilessid's gift of light and Arithon s'Ffalenn's
   gift of shadow. Currently imprisoned in a warded flask in Rockfell Pit.
   pronounced: desh-thee-air-e (last "e" mostly subliminal)
   root meaning: *desh* – mist; *thiere* – ghost or wraith

DHARKARON AVENGER—called Ath's Avenging Angel in legend. Drives a
   chariot drawn by five horses to convey the guilty to Sithaer. Dharkaron as
   defined by the adepts of Ath's Brotherhood is that dark thread mortal men
   weave with Ath, the prime vibration, that creates self-punishment, or the
   root of guilt.
   pronounced dark-air-on
   root meaning: *dhar* – evil; *khiaron* – one who stands in judgement

DIEGAN—born an Etarran dandy, brother of Princess Talith, commanded
   Lysaer s'Ilessid's war host, responsible for the deaths of Arithon's witnesses
   after the debacle in the harbour at Werpoint, and again, with the mass
   slaughter of the twenty-five picked survivors from the Havens, died regretful
   of his drastic miscalculation on the field at the Battle of Dier Kenton Vale
   in Third Age 5647.
   pronounced: dee-gan
   root meaning: *diegan* – a dandy's ornament, or trinket

DOLCIE—kitchen scullion in a gentleman's house in East Bransing.
   pronounced: doll-see

DURN—trade town located in Orvandir, Shand. Birthplace of Meiglin s'Dieneval.
   pronounced: dern
   root meaning: *diern* – a flat plain

DYSHENT—trade port known for timber on the coast of Instrell Bay, Tysan.
   pronounced: dye-shent
   root meaning: *dyshient* – cedar

EAST BRANSING—town located on the coast of Instrell Bay in Tysan.
   pronounced: bran-sing
   root meaning: *brienseng* – at the base, at the bottom

EFFLIN—formerly a croft holder near Kelsing, and older brother of Tarens and Kerelie.

pronounced: eff-lin

root meaning: *e* – prefix for small; *ffael* – dark; *en* – suffix for "more"; *effaelin* – a dark mood

ELAIRA—initiate enchantress of the Koriathain, currently serving the order as a wandering independent. Originally a street child, claimed in Morvain for Koriani rearing. Arithon's beloved, became handfast to Rathain in Third Age 5672.

pronounced: ee-layer-ah

root meaning: *e* – prefix, diminutive for small; *laere* – grace

ELKFOREST—free-wilds forest located in Gent, Havish. Site of the Queen's Glade.

ELLAINE—daughter of the Lord Mayor of Erdane, once Princess of Avenor by marriage to Lysaer s'Ilessid, and mother of Kevor s'Ilessid, who became an adept of Ath's Brotherhood.

pronounced: el-lane

ELSHIAN—Athlien Paravian bard and master luthier whose prized instrument is held by Athera's titled Masterbard.

pronounced: el-shee-an

root meaning: *e'alshian* – small wonder, or miracle

ELTAIR BAY—body of water on the eastshore of Rathain.

pronounced: el-tay-er

root meaning: *dascen al'tieri* – ocean of steel

ENITHEN TUER—sister of the Koriathain, released by Asandir of the Fellowship, seeress who resided in Erdane and hosted the s'Ilessid and s'Ffalenn princes after their arrival in Third Age Year 5637. Provided the Biedar knife that Sulfin Evend used to free Lysaer s'Ilessid from the influence of necromancy in Third Age 5670, deceased.

pronounced: en-ith-en too-er

root meaning: *en-wethen* – far-sighted; *tuer* – crone

ERDANE—originally a Paravian town given over to Mankind's rule; became the seat of the old Princes of Camris and the s'Gannley blood-line until the uprising that followed Desh-thiere's conquest in Third Age 5015. Became an iniquitous nest of necromancy in the years following, then the site of the True Sect High Temple of the Light since the Great Schism in 5683, and where the conclave of priests signed the doctrine into the *First Book of Canon Law* in 5691.

pronounced: er-day-na with the last syllable almost subliminal

root meaning: *er'deinia* – long walls

ERIEGAL—second youngest of the fourteen child survivors of the Tal Quorin massacre known as Jieret's Companions. Renowned as a shrewd tactician, he was ordered to serve Jieret's son Barach as war-captain in the Halwythwood camp rather than fight Lysaer's war host in Daon Ramon Barrens in Third

Age 5670. Tried and executed for crown treason in 5674.

pronounced: air-ee-gall

root meaning: *eriegal* – snake

ESFAND s'VALERIENT—*Caithdein* of Rathain's heir designate in Third Age 5922, son of Cosach s'Valerient and Jalienne and brother of Cordaya.

pronounced: es-fand s'val-er-ee-ent

root meaning: *esfan* – iron; *'d* – suffix for behind; *val* – straight; *erient* – spear

ETARRA—trade city built across the Mathorn Pass by townsfolk after the revolt that cast down Ithamon and the High Kings of Rathain. Nest of corruption and intrigue, and policy-maker for the North. Lysaer s'Ilessid was ratified as mayor upon Morfett's death in Third Age 5667. Site where Arithon defeated the Kralovir necromancers in Third Age Year 5671. Also the seat of the Alliance armed forces. Ruled by Lysaer s'Ilessid, in residence since the Great Schism in Third Age 5683, until the mayor's authority was usurped by the True Sect priests in Third Age 5923.

pronounced: ee-tar-ah

root meaning: *e* – prefix for small; *taria* – knots

ETTINMERE SETTLEMENT—insular village located in the Storlain Mountains in Gent, Havish.

pronounced: et-tin-meer

root meaning: *etennd'miere* – a place that parted ways, slowed down and went separate

ETTINVALE—vale that holds Ettinmere Settlement.

pronounced: et-tin vale

root meaning: *e'tennd* – slow down, be lazy

FAECHAA—Ettin dialect for lying cad.

pronounced: fay-chaa

root meaning: *ffaecha* – inconstant lover, cad

FALGAIRE—trade port famed for glass-ware, located on the west shore of Instrell Bay, Tysan.

pronounced: fall-gay-er

root meaning: *fal'miere* – to sparkle or glitter

FALWOOD—free-wilds forest located in West Shand.

pronounced: fall-wood

root meaning: *fal* – tree

FATE'S WHEEL—see Daelion's Wheel.

FELLOWSHIP OF SEVEN—sorcerers bound to Athera by the summoning dream of the dragons and charged to secure the mysteries that enable Paravian survival. Achieved their redemption from Cianor Sunlord, under the Law of the Major Balance in Second Age Year One. Originators and keepers of the covenant of the compact, made with the Paravian races, to allow Mankind's settlement on Athera in Third Age Year One. Their authority backs charter law, upheld by crown justice and clan oversight of the free wilds.

FFERETON s'DARIAN—centaur armourer who forged the twelve Blades of Isaer, including Alithiel, carried by the s'Ffalenn heirs.
pronounced: fer-et-on s'dar-ee-on
root meaning: *ffereton*—craftsman, maker; *s'darian*—

FFIATHLI OT SANIENT, DASIL AM'N I'CUEL'IEN LAIRE—Asandir's call in Paravian to summon his stallion. "True light in darkness, lend me the grace of your choice."
pronounced: fee-ath-li ot san-ee-ent day-seel am'n i-kew-el-ee-en layer-e
root meaning: *fiathli* – true light; *ot* – in; *sanient* – darkness, emphatic form; *dasil* – lend; *am'n* –one's/me; *i'cuel'ien* – yours/your actualized form; *laire* - grace

FIADUWYNNE—site of a Second Age focus circle, and a vast complex of healer's gardens and telir orchards, located in south Lanshire, Havish at the banks of the River Lithwater.
pronounced: fee-ah-dew-win-e – with the last syllable nearly subliminal
root meaning: *ffiadu* – to make whole; *wynne* – orchard

FIONN ARETH CAID'AN—born in Araethura in Third Age 5647, shape-changed as Arithon's double by Koriathain as bait for an entrapment, rescued from execution for Arithon's crimes in Jaelot 5660-70, died fighting in the Siege of Alestron in Third Age 5671.
pronounced: fee-on ar-reth cay-dan
root meaning: *fionne arith caid an* – one who brings choice

FIVE CENTURIES FOUNTAIN—a well in the Red Desert of Rasinne Pasy built and endowed by Davien, as a test of Mankind's wisdom, specifically to determine whether men were fitted for long-term rule, its properties bestow five hundred years of longevity upon anyone who partakes of the water.

FORTHMARK—city in Vastmark, Shand. Once the site of a hostel of Ath's Brotherhood. By Third Age 5320, the site was abandoned and taken over by the Koriani Order as a healers' hospice.

GAEMAR—craftsman from Daenfal, employed by the rich to engineer clever fancies.
pronounced: gay-mar

GALLEY-MEN'S REST—a disreputable port dive on Instrell Bay in East Bransing, Tysan.

GESTRY s'LORNMEIN—heir designate of Havish, crowned High King of Havish in Third Age 5922. Died on the field at Lithmarin, wielding the crown jewels in defence of the kingdom during The Hatchet's invasion in Third Age 5923.
pronounced: guess-tree slorn-main
root meaning: *geies* – obligated duty; *tieri* – steel; *liernmein* – to centre or bring into balance

GLENDIEN—a Shandian clanswoman, wife to Kyrialt s'Taleyn, formerly the

heir designate of the High Earl of Alland; mother to Arithon's bastard daughter, Teylia, conceived in the confluence at Athir in Third Age 5672.
pronounced: glen-dee-en
root meaning: *glyen* – sultry; *dien* – object of beauty
GREY KRALOVIR—see Kralovir.
GREAT WAYSTONE—see entry for Waystone.
GRIMWARD—a circle of Paravian spells that seal and isolate the dire dreams of dragon haunts, a force with the potential for mass destruction. Since disappearance of the old races, the defences are maintained by embodied Sorcerers of the Fellowship of Seven. Of seventeen separate sites listed at Althain Tower, thirteen are still active.

HALDUIN s'ILESSID—founder of the s'Ilessid royal lineage in First Age Year One, bearing the attribute of justice.
pronounced: hal-dwin sill-ess-id
root meaning: *hal* – white; *duinne* – hand; *liessiad* – balance
HALWYTHWOOD—forest located in Araethura, Rathain. Current clan lodge of High Earl Cosach's band.
pronounced: hall-with-wood
root meaning: *hal* – white; *wythe* – vista
HANATHA—a matron from Ettinmere Settlement.
pronounced: ha-nay-tha
root meaning: *hani-atha* – busybody
HANSHIRE—port town on the Westland Sea, Tysan; birthplace of Sulfin Evend; mayors historically opposed to royal rule made it a hotbed of unrest in the rebellion, in an ancient alliance with the Koriathain.
pronounced: han-sheer
root meaning: *hansh* – sand; *era* – place
HASPASTION—ghost of the dragon contained in the grimward in Radmoore.
pronounced: has-pass-tee-on
root meaning: *hashpashdion* – Drakish for black thunder
HASIDII—ancient lineage of the Biedar tribes.
pronounced: has-sid-ee
root meaning: *hai shidi* – stigma, Biedar dialect
HAVISH—one of the Five High Kingdoms of Athera as defined by the charters of the Fellowship of Seven. Ruled by a queen apparent, after the death of Gestry s'Lornmein. Crown heritage: temperance. Device: gold hawk on red field.
pronounced: hav-ish
root meaning: *havieshe* – hawk
HAVKIEL HALTFOOT—Ilitharis Paravian mason whose wrath threw down the Arch of Tolgrath in the First Age, when Seardluin invaded from the east and attacked and killed his kin in Lithmere.

pronounced: have-kee-el

root meaning: *hav* – centre; *kiel* – pity

HERTHOV—Vivet's ugly suitor, from Ettinmere.

pronounced: herth-off

root meaning: *hierthov* – toad

HIGHSCARP—city sited near the stone quarries on the coast of the Bay of Eltair, located in Daon Ramon, Rathain. Also contains a sisterhouse of the Koriani Order.

IAMINE s'GANNLEY—woman who founded the *caithdein*'s lineage for Tysan.

pronounced: ee-ahm-meen-e sgan-lee

root meaning: *iamine* – amethyst; *gaen* – guide; *li* – exalted or in harmony

ICUELAN AM-JIASK EDAEL I'TIER—your feal prince attends you.

pronounced: ee-kway-lan am-jee-ask ee-dah-el it-ee-er

root meaning: *i'cuelan* – your, with prefix for "light"/focused intent; *am-jiask* – state of being bound by faith; *edael* – prince; *i'itier* – one who holds the light, attends

ILITHARIS PARAVIANS—centaurs, one of three semi-mortal old races; disappeared after the Mistwraith's conquest, the last known departure by Third Age 5100. They were the guardians of the earth's mysteries.

pronounced: i-li-thar-is

root meaning: *i'lith'earis* – the keeper/preserver of mystery

IMARN ADAER—Paravian master gem cutters from the city of Mearth, creators of the crown jewels for the Five Kingdoms of Athera, which are attuned to the land's flux and lane forces.

pronounced: i-marn a-day-er

root meaning: *imarn* – crystal; *e'daer* – to cut smaller

INNISH—city located on the southcoast of Shand at the delta of the River Ippash. Formerly known as "the Jewel of Shand", this was the site of the High King's winter court, prior to the time of the uprising.

pronounced: in-ish

root meaning: *inniesh* – a jewel with a pastel tint

INSTRELL BAY—waters off the Gulf of Stormwell between Atainia, Tysan and Deshir, Rathain.

pronounced: in-strell

root meaning: *arin'streal* – strong wind

ISAER—power focus built in the First Age in Atainia, Tysan, by the Ilitharis Paravians, to source the defence works of the Paravian keep of the same name.

pronounced: i-say-er

root meaning: *i'saer* – the circle

ISSING—river and ravine, located in Havistock, Havish, arises in the Storlain Mountains and flows south to Redburn at Rockbay Harbour.

pronounced: i-sing

root meaning: *yssing* – spindrift

ITHAMON—royal seat of the s'Ffalenn High Kings, built at an intersection of flux lines on the Fifth Lane in Daon Ramon Barrens. Originally a Paravian keep, site of the Compass Point Towers, or Sun Towers. Site of the Mistwraith's defeat by Lysaer s'Ilessid and Arithon s'Ffalenn in Third Age 5638.

pronounced: ith-a-mon

root meaning: *itha* – five; *mon* – needle, spire

ITHISH—city located at the edge of the principality of Vastmark, on the south-coast of Shand. Where the Vastmark shepherds ship their wool fleeces.

pronounced: ith-ish

root meaning: *ithish* – fleece or fluffy

IYAT—energy sprite, and minor drake spawn inhabiting Athera, not visible to the eye, manifests in a poltergeist fashion by taking temporary possession of objects. Feeds upon natural energy sources: fire, breaking waves, lightning, and excess emotion where humans gather.

pronounced: ee-at

root meaning: *iyat* – to break

IYAT-THOS—clan dialect name for Tarens.

pronounced: ee-at thoss

root meaning: *iyat* – broken; *thos* – nose

JAELOT—city located on the coast of Eltair Bay at the southern border of the Kingdom of Rathain. Once a Second Age power site, with a focus circle. Now a merchant city renowned for extreme snobbery and bad taste. Also the site where Arithon s'Ffalenn played his eulogy for Halliron Masterbard, which raised the powers of the Paravian focus circle beneath the mayor's palace. The forces of the mysteries and resonant harmonics caused damage to city buildings, watch keeps, and walls, which has since been repaired.

pronounced: jay-lot

root meaning: *jielot* – affectation

JALIENNE—wife of Cosach s'Valerient, *Caithdein* of Rathain. Mother of Esfand and Cordaya.

pronounced: jah-lee-en

root meaning: *jia* – binding, tie together, intertwine; *lien* – to love

JESSIAN OATHKEEPER—historical sister of the Koriathain, prior to settlement on Athera, when the order was a secret society, sent to the planet Scathac to treat with the Biedar, and witnessed the tribal rite that preserved the planet from Calum Kincaid's Great Weapon. Subsequently came to trial and imprisonment when she kept her sworn promise to the Biedar matriarch never to reveal what she had seen. Her secret was kept until she was executed, but her silence launched the Koriani Order on a search that resulted in coercive disclosure and theft of the ancient Biedar knowledge.

pronounced: jess-ee-an

JEYNSA s'VALERIENT—daughter of Jieret s'Valerient and Feithan, born Third Age 5653; appointed successor for her father's title, *Caithdein* of Rathain. Married Sevrand s'Brydion, and Khadrien's forebear.

pronounced: jay-in-sa

root meaning: *jieyensa* – garnet

JIERET s'VALERIENT—former Earl of the North, clan chief of Deshir; *Caithdein* of Rathain, sworn liegeman of Prince Arithon s'Ffalenn. Also son and heir of Lord Steiven. Blood pacted to Arithon by sorcerer's oath prior to the battle of Strakewood Forest, and known by head-hunters as Jieret Red-beard. Father of Jeynsa and Barach. Husband to Feithan. Died by Lysaer s'Ilessid's hand in Daon Ramon Barrens, Third Age 5670. Bequeathed his memories to Iyat-thos Tarens in 5923.

pronounced: jeer-et sval-er-ee-ent

root meaning: *jieret* – thorn; *val* – straight; *erient* – spear

KADARION—Ilitharis Paravian, or centaur guardian, living brother of Kadierach.

pronounced: kad-ar-ee-on

root meaning: *kad'i'ria'en* – to quicken etherically, to blossom under the masterful touch of refined awareness

KADIERACH—Ilitharis Paravian, or centaur guardian who was called forward by High Earl Jieret's transcendence. Also appeared to Arithon s'Ffalenn during his passage through Kewar's Maze in Third Age 5670.

pronounced: kad-ee-er-ack

root meaning: *kad'i* – to quicken etherically, or bring to blossom through refined awareness; *era* – place; *ch* – suffix for attached to or rooted to a site

KAMRIDIAN s'FFALENN—crowned High King of Rathain, first bearer of the Paravian sword Alithiel, tragically died from the effects of his conscience in Davien's Maze in Kewar Tunnel.

pronounced: kam-rid-ee-en sfall-en

root meaning: *kaim'riadien* – thread cut short; *ffael* – dark, *an* – one

KARMAK—plain located in Camris, Tysan.

pronounced: car-mack

root meaning: *karmak* – wolf

KATHTAIRR—barren land-mass in the southern ocean, across the world from Paravia.

pronounced: kath-tear

root meaning: *kait-th'era* – empty place

KELSING—town located south of Erdane on the trade-road in Camris, Tysan.

pronounced: kel-sing

root meaning: *kel* – hidden; *seng* – cave

KEWAR TUNNEL—cavern built beneath the Mathorn Mountains by Davien the Betrayer; contains the maze of conscience, which caused High King Kamridian s'Ffalenn's death. Arithon Teir's'Ffalenn successfully completed the challenge in Third Age 5670.

pronounced: key-wahr

root meaning: *kewiar* – a weighing of conscience

KHADRIEN s'VALERIENT—clanborn second cousin to Esfand s'Valerient, friend of Siantra s'Idir, descendant of Jeynsa s'Valerient and Sevrand s'Brydion.

pronounced: cad-ree-en sval-er-ee-ent

root meaning: *khadrien* – mercurial; *val* – straight; *erient* – spear

KHADRIM—flying, fire-breathing drake spawn, intelligent, vicious, and a scourge that slaughtered Paravians. By the Third Age, confined to a warded preserve in the volcanic mountains near Teal's Gap in north Tysan.

pronounced: kaa-drim

root meaning: *khadrim* – dragon

KHARADMON—Sorcerer of the Fellowship of Seven; discorporate since rise of Khadrim and Seardluin levelled the Paravian stronghold at Ithamon in Second Age 3651. It was by Kharadmon's intervention that survivors of the attack were sent to safety by means of transfer from the Fifth Lane power focus.

pronounced: kah-rad-mun

root meaning: *kar'riad en mon* – phrase translates to mean "twisted thread on the needle" or colloquialism for "a knot in the works"

KHETIENN—spotted wildcat found in the wilds of Rathain, also on the High King's blazon.

pronounced: ket-yen

root meaning: *kietienn* – small leopard

KIEL'D'MAERANIENT—Paravian word for anathema.

pronounced: keld-may-er-an-ee-ent

root meaning: *kiel'd'maeranient* – to be without pity, raised to the emphatic form

KORIANI—possessive and singular form of the word "Koriathain"; see entry.

pronounced: kor-ee-ah-nee

KORIATHAIN—order of enchantresses ruled by a circle of Seniors, under the power of one Prime Enchantress. They draw their talent from the orphaned children they raise, or from daughters dedicated to service by their parents. Initiation rite involves a vow of consent that ties the spirit to a power crystal keyed to the Prime's control.

pronounced: kor-ee-ah-thain – to rhyme with "main"

root meaning: *koriath* – order; *ain* – belonging to

KRALOVIR—term for a sect of necromancers, also called the grey cult, destroyed by Arithon s'Ffalenn in Third Age 5671.

pronounced: kray-low-veer

root meaning: *krial* – name for the rune of crossing; *oveir* – abomination

KYRIALT s'TALEYN—once heir apparent to the Lord Erlien, *caithdein* of Shand, his service awarded to Arithon s'Ffalenn to balance a slight of honour in Third Age 5671, stood as liegeman when Arithon ventured the King's Grove to break Desh-thiere's curse, served until his valiant death in defence of Parrien s'Brydion's treachery.

pronounced: key-ree-alt stall-ayne

root meaning: *kyrialt* – word for the rune of crossing with the suffix for "last," which is the name of the rune of ending. *Tal* – branch; *an* – one/ first of the branch

LAITHEN s'IDIR—clanborn woman from Fallowmere, descended from Sidir's lineage, mother of Siantra s'Idir.

pronounced: lay-then see-deer

root meaning: *laere* – grace; *thein* – tower; *laerethien* – pillar of grace; *s'* – of the lineage; *i'id'ier* – almost lost

LANSHIRE—northernmost principality in the Kingdom of Havish. Name taken from the wastes at Scarpdale, site of First Age battles with Seardluin that blasted the soil to slag.

pronounced: lahn-sheer-e

root meaning: *lan'hansh'era* – place of hot sands

LASSIVER—ancient Biedar lineage, from the time before their settlement on Athera.

pronounced: lass-ee-ver

root meaning: *lassiver* – from Biedar language, honour

LAW OF THE MAJOR BALANCE—founding order of the powers of the Fellowship of Seven, as taught by the Paravians. The primary tenet is that no force of nature should be used without consent, or against the will of another consciousness.

LEYNSGAP—narrow pass in the Mathorn Mountains, Rathain, famed site of Braggen's stand, where the clan Companion single-handedly fought and held off a troop of Sunwheel soldiers in pursuit of Arithon Teir's'Ffalenn.

pronounced: lay-ens-gap

root meaning: *liyond* – corridor

LIESS—laundress in The Hatchet's war host.

pronounced: liss

root meaning: *lios* – to write

LIFFSEY RIVER—flows from the Plain of Araithe to the northern coast of Rathain.

pronounced: liff-see

root meaning: *lieffesi* – to laugh

LIRENDA—former First Senior Enchantress to the Prime, Koriani Order; failed in her assignment to capture Arithon s'Ffalenn for the sisterhood's purposes. Held as a passive servant under the Prime Matriarch's sentence of punishment since Third Age 5670.

pronounced: leer-end-ah

root meaning: *lyron* – singer; *di-ia* – a dissonance – the hyphen denotes a glottal stop

LITHMARIN—glacial lake located between Lanshire and Gent in Havish.

pronounced: lith-mar-in

root meaning: *lieth* – flow; *mieren* – mirror

LORN—town on the northcoast of Atainia, Tysan.

pronounced: lorn

root meaning: *loern* – an Atheran fish.

LOS LIER—archipelago in the Cildein Ocean

pronounced: loss lee-er

root meaning: *lios* – to designate, scribe or write *l'iera* – exalted place

LUHAINE—Sorcerer of the Fellowship of Seven—discorporate since the fall of Telmandir in Third Age 5018. Luhaine's body was pulled down by the mob while he was in ward trance, covering the escape of the royal heir to Havish.

pronounced: loo-hay-ne

root meaning: *luirhainon* – defender

LYRANTHE—instrument played by the bards of Athera. Strung with fourteen strings, tuned to seven tones (doubled). Two courses are "drone strings" set to octaves. Five are melody strings, the lower three courses being octaves, the upper two, in unison.

pronounced: leer-anth-e (last "e" being nearly subliminal)

root meaning: *lyr* – song, *anthe* – box

LYSAER s'ILESSID—prince of Tysan, 1497th in succession after Halduin, founder of the line in Third Age Year One. Gifted at birth with control of Light, and Bane of Desh-thiere. Also known as Blessed Prince since he declared himself avatar for the following known as the Alliance of Light. Elected Mayor of Etarra in 5667. Declared apostate to the Light at the Great Schism in 5683; retired to his seat at Etarra, signed Treaty of Law with Rathain's clans in 5688.

pronounced: lie-say-er sill-ess-id

root meaning: *lia* – blond, yellow or light, *saer* – circle; *liessiad* – balance

MADRAEGA—woman from the Ettin cabal, overseer of tasks.

pronounced: mad-ray-ga

root meaning: *madri* – firm; *raetga* – buzzard

MANDA—kitchen scullion from East Bransing.

pronounced: man-daa

MARAK—splinter world, cut off beyond South Gate, left lifeless after creation of the Mistwraith. The original inhabitants were men exiled by the Fellowship from Athera for practices that were incompatible with the compact sworn between the Sorcerers and the Paravian races, which permitted human settlement on Athera. Source of the Mistwraith, Desh-thiere, and the free wraiths that threaten Athera.

pronounced: maer-ak

root meaning: *m'era'ki* — a place held separate

MATHORN MOUNTAINS—range that bisects the Kingdom of Rathain east to west.

pronounced: math-orn

root meaning: *mathien* – massive

MATHORN ROAD— trade-road running just south of the Mathorn Mountains.

pronounced: math-orn

root meaning: *mathien* – massive

MEARTH—ruin in the Red Desert, world of Rasinne Pasy, beyond the west Worldsend Gate. Destroyed when Davien was rendered discorporate, which caused the elemental working that protected his Five Centuries Fountain to escape from containment. Called the Shadows of Mearth, they continue to haunt the site, inflicting a geas upon the mind on encounter, which continuously repeats the worst experience held in memory until the victim surmounts the challenge of achieving release or succumbs to madness.

pronounced: me-arth

root meaning: *mearth* – empty

MEIGLIN s'DIENEVAL—the legitimate daughter born to the widow of Egan s'Dieneval in Third Age 5019, just after his death in the slaughter of the rebellion. Heart's love of the last High King of Shand for one night, just prior to his demise while fighting the Mistwraith. A weaving by the Biedar of Sanpashir, done at the behest of the last centaur guardian, ensured the union would bring conception, and the birth of Dari s'Ahelas. Also named Anshlien'ya in desert dialect, as the dawn of hope.

pronounced: mee-glin s-dee-in-ee-vahl

root meaning: *meiglin* – passion; *dien* – large; *eval* – endowment, gifted talent

MELHALLA—High Kingdom once ruled by s'Ellestrion lineage, held by the steward's line of s'Callient after the last of the royal line perished in the Red Desert past Westgate.

pronounced: mel-hal-la

root meaning: *maelhallia* – grand meadows, or open space.

MERIOR—fishing village located on Scimlade Tip in Alland, Shand, site of Arithon's temporary shipworks in Third Age 5644.

pronounced: mare-ee-or

root meaning: *merioren* – cottages

MIRALT—port town located at Miralt Head, on the north shore of Camris, Tysan. Revered by the True Sect as the site where the Light's Avatar first unveiled his divine nature in Third Age 5652.

pronounced: meer-alt

root meaning: *m'ier* –shore; *alt* – last

MIRTHLVAIN—bog with an ancient Paravian stronghold, located in Midhalla, Melhalla; infested with methurien, or Meth Spawn, dangerous cross-breeds of drake spawn, guarded and watched by the Master Spellbinder, Verrain.

pronounced: mirth-el-vain

root meaning: *myrthl* – noxious; *vain* – bog

MISTWRAITH—see Desh-thiere.

MORRIEL—Prime Matriarch of the Koriathain, invested in Third Age 4212. Upset the planetary electromagnetic lanes to conceal her covert possession of novice initiate Selidie's body in 5667; the death of her flesh created an irregular succession.

pronounced: more-real

root meaning: *moar* – greed; *riel* – silver

MORVAIN—city located in the principality of Araethura, Rathain, on the west coast of Instrell Bay. Elaira's birthplace.

pronounced: mor-vain

root meaning: *morvain* – swindler's market

MYRKAVIA—southcoastal island located in Rockbay Harbour, south of Havistock, Havish.

pronounced: meer-kay-vee-a

root meaning: *miere* – reflection; *kavia* – spruce tree

NARMS—city on the coast of Instrell Bay, built as a craft centre by Men in the early Third Age. Best known for dye works.

pronounced: narms

root meaning: *narms* – colour

NORTHGATE—Worldsend gate located above the Ruins of Penstair in Deshir, Rathain, leads to the world designated as the domain of the dragons who did not agree to the abdication of Athera to the Paravians, Chaimistarizog is the Gatekeeper.

OLD TIRANS—site of a Paravian focus circle, and Second Age ruin in East Halla, Melhalla; crown seat of the s'Ellestrion High Kings until it was sacked in the rebellion, Third Age 5018.

pronounced: tee-rans

root meaning: *tier* – to hold fast, to keep

ORLAN—pass in the Thaldein Mountains in Tysan where the clan seat has a hidden outpost.

pronounced: or-lan

root meaning: *irlan* – ledge

ORVANDIR—principality located in north-eastern Shand.

pronounced: or-van-deer

root meaning: *orvein* – crumbled; *dir* – stone

PARAVIA—name for the continent inhabited by the Paravians, and locale of the Five Kingdoms.

pronounced: par-ay-vee-ah

root meaning: *para* – great; *i'a* – suffix denoting entityship, and raised to the feminine aspect, which translates as "place inclusive of, or holding the aspect for greatness"

PARAVIAN—name for the three old races that inhabited Athera before Mankind. Including the centaurs, the sunchildren, and the unicorns, these races never die unless mishap befalls them; they are the world's channel, or direct connection, to Ath Creator.

pronounced: par-ai-vee-ans

root meaning: *para* – great; *i'on* – fate or great mystery

PELLAIN—trade town between East and West Halla, Melhalla.

pronounced: pell-ayn

root meaning: *peil* – odd; *ai'an* – hidden one

PRIME MATRIARCH—ruler of the Order of the Koriathain, acceded through a ninth-rank initiation.

QUINCE—serving boy in a gentleman's house in East Bransing.

pronounced: quinse

RADMOORE DOWNS—meadowland located in Midhalla, Melhalla.

pronounced: rad-more

root meaning: *riad* – thread; *mour* – carpet, rug

RATHAIN—one of the five High Kingdoms of Athera ruled by descendants of Torbrand s'Ffalenn since Third Age Year One. Device: black-and-silver leopard on green field. Arithon Teir's'Ffalenn is sanctioned crown prince, by the hand of Asandir of the Fellowship, in Third Age 5638 at Etarra.

pronounced: rath-ayn

root meaning: *roth* – brother; *thein* – tower, sanctuary

RAUVEN TOWER—residence of the s'Ahelas mages, on the ocean world of Dascen Elur, through Westgate. Where Arithon was trained to initiate mastery.

pronounced: raw-ven

root meaning: *rauven* – invocation

RAYAR s'DIENEVAL—founder of the s'Dieneval lineage of seers, and *caithdein*'s lineage of Melhalla, when the old line failed in the High King's service; forebear of Meiglin s'Dieneval, mother of Princess Dari s'Ahelas.

pronounced: ray-ar s'dee-in-e-val

root meaning: *ria'ar* – touch-cord, or link; *dien* – large; *eval* – endowment, gifted talent

REI-YAJ SEERESS—title for the Seeress sequestered in a tower in Shand, near Ithish. Her oracular visions stem from meditative communion with the energy gateway marked and measured by Athera's sun. Born sighted, but practice of her art brings blindness. The origin of her tradition derives from the mystical practices of the Biedar tribe in the Sanpashir desert.
pronounced: ree-yahj
root meaning: *ria'ieajn* – to touch the forbidden

REQUIAR—Biedar tribesman of Lassiver's heritage, who swore surety for Jessian Oathkeeper's integrity.
pronounced: reck-wee-ar
root meaning: *requiar* – a binding commitment, Biedar dialect

RIATHAN PARAVIANS—unicorns, the purest, most direct connection to Ath Creator; the prime vibration channels directly through the horn.
pronounced: ree-ah-than
root meaning: *ria* – to touch; *ath* – prime life-force; *an* – one; *ri'athon* – one who touches divinity

ROACO—head shaman at Ettinmere Settlement.
pronounced: row-ah-co

ROCKBAY HARBOUR—body of water located on the southcoast, between Shand and West Shand.

ROCKFELL PEAK—mountain containing Rockfell Pit, used to imprison harmful entities throughout all three Ages. Located in West Halla, Melhalla; became the warded prison for Desh-thiere.
pronounced: rock-fell

ROCKFELL PIT—shaft built by the Sorcerer Davien in Rockfell Peak to contain harmful entities; currently sequesters the Mistwraith, Desh-thiere.

RONDEIL S'ELESTRION—founder of the s'Elestrion royal lineage, until the last scion of the blood died in the course of the uprising in Third Age 5018; gifted with wisdom.
pronounced: ron-day-ee-el
root meaning: *roind* – cycle, season; iel – light; eliestrion – inspiration

s'AHELAS—family name for the royal line appointed by the Fellowship Sorcerers in Third Age Year One to rule the High Kingdom of Shand. Gifted geas: far-sight. Also the lineage that carries the latent potential for the rogue talent for far-sight and prophecy, introduced when the *caithdein*'s heritage of s'Dieneval became crossed with the royal descent in Third Age 5036, resulting in Dari's birth in winter, 5037.
pronounced: s'ah-hell-as
root meaning: *ahelas* – mage-gifted

SAIEDA—young female cousin to Sarioic s'Gannley.
pronounced: say-ee-dah
root meaning: *saieda* – winter

SANPASHIR—desert waste on the southcoast of Shand. Home to the desert tribes called Biedar.

pronounced: sahn-pash-eer

root meaning: *san* – black or dark; *pash'era* – place of grit or gravel

SAROIC s'GANNLEY—made heir designate of the *Caithdein* of Tysan by Asandir in Third Age 5922.

pronounced: sa-row-ic

root meaning: *sae* – circle; *roic* – to finish, or complete; *gaen* – guide; *li* – exalted, in harmony

SCARPDALE—waste in Lanshire, Havish, created by a First Age war with Seardluin. Once the site of the Scarpdale grimward, banished by Seshkrozchiel in Third Age 5671.

pronounced: scarp-dale

SCIMLADE TIP—peninsula in Alland, Shand.

pronounced: skim-laid

root meaning: *scimlait* – scythe

s'DIENEVAL—lost lineage of the *caithdeinen* of Melhalla, the last to carry the title being Egan, who died at the side of his High King in the battle to subdue the Mistwraith. The blood-line carried strong talent for prophecy and was decimated during the sack of Tirans in the uprising in Third Age 5018, with Egan's pregnant wife the sole survivor. Her daughter, Meiglin, was mother of Dari s'Ahelas, crown heir of Shand.

pronounced: s-dee-in-ee-vahl

root meaning: *dien* – large; *eval* – endowment, gifted talent

SECOND AGE—Marked by the arrival of the Fellowship of Seven at Crater Lake, their called purpose to fight the drake spawn.

SELIDIE—young woman initiate appointed by Morriel Prime as a candidate in training for succession. Succeeded to the office of Prime Matriarch after Morriel's death on winter solstice in Third Age 5670, at which time an unprincipled act of possession by Morriel usurped the young woman's body.

pronounced: sell-ih-dee

root meaning: *selyadi* – air sprite

SELKWOOD—forest located in Alland, Shand.

pronounced: selk-wood

root meaning: *selk* – pattern

SESHKROZCHIEL—name for the female dragon mated to Haspastion. Forged a bargain with Davien, who borrowed on her powers while she was in hibernation in exchange for his term of service, for however long she required it. Her wakening in Third Age 5671 incurred the debt, still on-going, assumed by Luhaine when she went into hibernation in 5923.

pronounced: sesh-crows-chee-ell

root meaning: *seshkrozchiel* – Drakish for blue lightning

SETHVIR—Sorcerer of the Fellowship of Seven, also trained to serve as Warden of Althain since Third Age 5100, when the last centaur guardian departed after the Mistwraith's conquest.

pronounced: seth-veer

root meaning: *seth* – fact; *vaer* – keep

SEVERNIR RIVER—dry river-bed located in Daon Ramon, Rathain, dammed and diverted at the source after the Mistwraith's conquest to empty into the Bay of Eltair.

pronounced: sev-er-neer

root meaning: *sevaer* – to travel; *nir* – south

SEVRAND s'BRYDION—son of Duke Bransian s'Brydion, heir designate until Alestron was entailed by the Fellowship Sorcerers in Third Age 5671; married Jeynsa s'Valerient.

pronounced: sev-rand sbry-dee-on

root meaning: *sevaer'an'd* – one who travels behind, a follower; *baridien* – tenacity

s'FFALENN—family name for the royal line appointed by the Fellowship Sorcerers in Third Age Year One to rule the High Kingdom of Rathain. Gifted geas: compassion/empathy.

pronounced: s-fal-en

root meaning: *ffael* – dark; *an* – one

s'GANNLEY—lineage of the Earls of the West, once the Camris princes, now bearing the heritage of *Caithdein* of Tysan. Iamine s'Gannley was the woman founder.

pronounced: sgan-lee

root meaning: *gaen* – guide; *li* – exalted or in harmony

SHADOWS OF MEARTH—elemental working of Davien's, see Five Centuries Fountain.

SHAND—one of the Five High Kingdoms of Athera, located on the south-east corner of the Paravian continent, originally ruled by the line of s'Ahelas. Current device, purple-and-gold chevrons, since the adjunct kingdom of West Shand came under high crown rule. The old device was a falcon on a crescent moon, sometimes still displayed, depicted against the more recent purple-and-gold chevrons.

pronounced: shand—as in "hand"

root meaning: *shayne* or *shiand* – two/pair

SHANDOR—port trade town on the west shore of South Strait/Rockbay Harbour, West Shand.

pronounced: shan-door

root meaning: *cianor* – to shine

SHEHANE ALTHAIN—Ilitharis Paravian who dedicated his spirit as defender and guardian of Althain Tower. The power that rendered Davien discorporate in Third Age 5129.

pronounced: shee-hayne all-thayn

root meaning: *shiehai'en* – to give for the greatest good; *alt* – last; *thain* – tower

SHIPSPORT—port trade town located on the shore of Eltair Bay in West Halla, Melhalla.

SIANTRA s'IDIR—clanborn daughter of Laithen s'Idir, of Sidir's lineage. A talent seer whose gift was enhanced by an encounter with the forces of Athili in Third 5923.

pronounced: see-an-tra see-deer

root meaning: *sian* – spark; *tier* – to hold fast; *a* – feminine diminutive; *i'sid'i'er* – one who has stood at the verge of being lost

SIDIR—one of the Companions, who were the fourteen boys to survive the massacre at Tal Quorin in Third Age 5638. Served Arithon at the Battle of Dier Kenton Vale the Havens in 5647, and at the siege of Alestron in 5671. Second in command of Earl Jieret's war band. Married Jieret's widow, Feithan in 5672. Founder of the lineage of s'Idir, descendants derived from a youthful liaison with a clanswoman from Fallowmere.

pronounced: see-deer

root meaning: *i'sid'i'er* – one who has stood at the verge of being lost

s'ILESSID—family name for the royal line appointed by the Fellowship Sorcerers in Third Age Year One to rule the High Kingdom of Tysan. Gifted geas: justice.

pronounced: s-ill-ess-id

root meaning: *liessiad* – balance

SILVERMARSH—large bog located south of Daenfal Lake, in West Halla, Melhalla.

SITHAER—mythological equivalent of hell, halls of Dharkaron Avenger's judgement; according to Ath's adepts, that state of being where the prime vibration is not recognized.

pronounced: sith-air

root meaning: *sid* – lost; *thiere* – wraith/spirit

SKELSENG'S GATE—a chain of caverns in the Skyshiel Mountains, Daon Ramon, Rathain.

pronounced: skell-sing

root meaning: *skel* – many; *seng* – cave

SKYRON FOCUS—large aquamarine focus stone, used by the Koriani Senior Circle for their major magic after the loss of the Great Waystone during the rebellion.

pronounced: sky-run

root meaning: *skyron* – colloquialism for shackle; *s'kyr'i'on* – literally "sorrowful fate"

SKYSHIEL MOUNTAINS—range running north and south along the eastern coast of Rathain.

pronounced: sky-shee-ell

root meaning: *skyshia* – to pierce through; *iel* – ray

s'LORNMEIN—royal lineage of Havish, founded by Bwin Evoc s'Lornmein in Third Age Year One. Gifted geas: temperance
pronounced: slorn-main
root meaning: *liernmein* – to centre, restrain, bring into balance

SOUTHSHIRE—town on the southcoast of Alland, Shand, known for ship-building.
pronounced: south-shire

SOUTH STRAIT—body of water and passage from Rockbay Harbour into South Sea.

STORLAIN MOUNTAINS—range running north and south, dividing the Kingdom of Havish.
pronounced: store-lane
root meaning: *storlient* – largest summit, highest divide

STRAKEWOOD—forest located in Deshir, Rathain, and free-wilds seat of the *caithdein*.
pronounced: strayk-wood
root meaning: *streik* – to quicken, to seed

SULFIN EVEND—son of the Mayor of Hanshire who held the post of Alliance Lord Commander under Lysaer s'Ilessid. Spared Lysaer from his dark binding to the Kralovir necromancers, and in the course of that awakened the talent of his outbred clan lineage: of s'Gannley descent, through Diarin s'Gannley, who was abducted and forced to marry his great-grandsire. Bound to the land in Third Age 5670 when he swore a *caithdein*'s oath at Althain Tower as part of his bargain with Enithen Tuer, who in turn imparted the ceremonial knowledge and the Biedar knife used to sever the etheric cords the cult used to enslave victims. Named the Heretic Betrayer by the True Sect in the belief he corrupted the avatar, Lysaer. Ancestor of Daliana sen Evend.
pronounced: sool-finn ev-end
root meaning: *suilfinn eiavend* – colloquialism, diamond mind "one who is persistent"

SUNCHILDREN—common name for Athlien Paravians, see entry.

SUNLOOP—magical device created by Fellowship Sorcerer, Ciladis, to reveal the return of the sun.

SUNWHEEL—heraldic symbol adopted by the religion of Light, and the device of the True Sect.

s'VALERIENT—family name for the Earls of the North, regents and *caithdeinen* for the High Kings of Rathain.
pronounced: val-er-ee-ent
root meaning: *val* – straight; *erient* – spear

TAERLIN WATERS—a lake in the southern spur of Tornir Peaks, and a ballad recounting the First Age slaughter of unicorn herd by Khadrim.

pronounced: tay-er-lin

root meaning: *taer* – calm; *lien* – to love

TAL QUORIN—river formed by the confluence of watershed on the southern side of Strakewood, principality of Deshir, Rathain, where traps were laid for Etarra's army in the battle of Strakewood Forest, and where the rape and massacre of Deshir's clanswomen and children occurred under Lysaer and head-hunters under Pesquil's command in Third Age 5638.

pronounced: tal quar-in

root meaning: *tal* – branch; *quorin* – canyons

TALITH—Etarran princess; former wife of Lysaer s'Ilessid, estranged from him and incarcerated on charges of consorting with the Master of Shadow. Eventually murdered by a conspiracy of Avenor's crown council, when an arranged accident caused her fall from Avenor's tower of state in Third Age 5653.

pronounced: tal-ith – to rhyme with "gal with"

root meaning: *tal* – branch; *lith* – to keep/nurture

TALLIARTHE—pleasure sloop, built by Arithon s'Ffalenn in Third Age 5644. Named for the mythic Paravian sea sprite who spirits away maidens who stray too near the tide-mark at twilight.

Pronounced: tal-ee-arth-e

Root meaning: *tal* branch; *li* – exalted; *araithe* – to disperse or to send

TANUAY DALDARI—brother of Vivet Daldari, from Ettinmere Settlement.

pronounced: tan-oo-way

root meaning: *tanuin* – swift or swallow; *ay* – past; *dal* – fair; *diere* – life

TARENS—town-born crofter from Kelsing, brother of Efflin and Kerelie. Liegeman to Prince Arithon when he inherited *Caithdein*, High Earl Jieret's memories in Third Age 5923, also named Iyat-thos Tarens by the clans.

pronounced: tar-ens

root meaning: tirans – *tier'ain* - protect

TEEAH—goddess revered by residents of Ettinmere Settlement.

pronounced: tee-ah

root meaning: Ettin dialect corruption of old Paravian *tien* – spirit; *ai'an* – hidden one

TEHAVAL WARDEN—last centaur guardian to leave the continent when the Paravians withdrew, Keeper of the Records and Warden of Althain Tower, transferred his post and bestowed the gift of earth-link upon Sethvir in Third Age 5100.

pronounced: tay-have-all

root meaning: *tehav* – tell, speak; *val* – straight

TEIR—masculine form of a title fixed to a name denoting heirship.

pronounced: tayer

root meaning: *teir's* – successor to power

TELMANDIR—seat of the High Kings of Havish in Lithmere, Havish. Ruined during the uprising in Third Age Year 5018, rebuilt by High King Eldir s'Lornmein after his coronation in 5643.

pronounced: tel-man-deer

root meaning: *telman'en* – leaning; *dir* – rock

TETHOS—alias given to Iyat-thos Tarens while he impersonated a recruit in The Hatchet's war host.

pronounced: teth-oss

root meaning: *tet-thios* – a fresh recruit

TEYLIA—a *tiendar'shayn'd,* ancestral soul of Biedar tribal origin, reincarnated as the bastard daughter of Arithon Teir's'Ffalenn and Glendien, widow of Kyrialt, born in Third Age 5672, sworn into the Order of the Koriathain by her own will at three years of age. Remained with the sisterhood to guard the course of Arithon's incarceration, until the last free wraith from Marak was released. Died foiling the death spell wrought by the Koriani Prime Matriarch to destroy Arithon, just after she assisted, then secured his escape from Koriani captivity in 5922.

pronounced: tay-lee-ah

root meaning: *tien* – dream; *lie* – note struck in harmony; *a* – female diminutive

THALDEIN MOUNTAINS—range bordering Camris in Tysan, site of the Camris clans' main outpost.

pronounced: thall-dayn

root meaning: *thal* – head; *dein* – bird

THE HATCHET—commander of the True Sect war host, defeated by High King Gestry in the Battle of Lithmarin in Third Age 5923.

THUNDER RIDGE—see Tiendarion.

TIENDARION—Paravian name for Thunder Ridge, a subduction ridge that forms the backbone of the Storlain Mountains in Gent, Havish.

pronounced: tee-end-are-ee-on

root meaning: etheric connection between sky and earth: *tiend* – spirit; *darion* – tie, with suffix for the emphatic

TIENELLE—high-altitude herb valued by mages for its mind-expanding properties. Highly toxic. No antidote. The leaves, dried and smoked, are most potent. To weaken its powerful side effects and allow safer access to its vision, Koriani enchantresses boil the flowers, then soak tobacco leaves with the brew.

pronounced: tee-an-ell-e ("e" mostly subliminal)

root meaning: *tien* – dream; *iel* – light/ray

TIERIENDIERIEL MEREVALIA—Sunchild who granted Arithon Teir's'Ffalenn's request to be freed of Desh-thiere's Curse in Third Age 5671.

pronounced: tee-er-ee-en-dee-er-el mer-e-vah-lee-a

root meaning: *tierien* – female successor to power; *dieriel* – queen; *miere* –

reflection; *val* – straight; *ia* – suffix for "the third domain" (three octaves of vibration)

TOLGRATH—mighty span built by Ilitharis Paravian masons, that crossed the strait between Havistock and Lithmere, thrown down in the First Age by Havkiel Haltfoot's wrath when Seardluin invaded from the east and destroyed all of his kin living in Lithmere. A standing stone marks the site.
pronounced: toll-grath
root meaning: *tolgrath* – arch

TORBRAND s'FFALENN—founder of the s'Ffalenn line appointed by the Fellowship of Seven to rule the High Kingdom of Rathain in Third Age Year One.
pronounced: tor-brand sfall-en
root meaning: *tor* – sharp, keen; *brand* – temper; *ffael* – dark; *an* – one

TORWENT—fishing town and smuggler's haven located on the coast of Lanshire, Havish, just south of the border. Descendants of many outbred clan lineages live there since the exodus to escape persecution under Lysaer s'Ilessid the pretender in Third Age 5653.
pronounced: tore-went
root meaning: *tor* – sharp; *wient* – bend

TRAITHE—Sorcerer of the Fellowship of Seven. Solely responsible for the closing of South Gate to deny further entry to the Mistwraith. Traithe lost most of his faculties in the process and was left with a limp. Since it is not known whether he can make the transfer into discorporate existence with his powers impaired, he has retained his physical body.
pronounced: tray-the
root meaning: *traithe* – gentleness

TRUE SECT—offshoot branch faith of the Religion of Light formed after the Great Schism, when the avatar turned apostate to the doctrine in Third Age 5683.

TUORAM—Ettin code of responsibility that assigns privilege through honour.
pronounced: too-ar-um
root meaning: *tuoram* – ladder

TYSAN—one of the Five High Kingdoms of Athera as defined by the charters of the Fellowship of Seven. Ruled by the s'Ilessid royal line. Device: gold star on blue field.
pronounced: tie-san
root meaning: *tiasen* – rich

VALENDALE RIVER—located in South Tysan, emptying into Mainmere Bay.
pronounced: va-len
root meaning: *valen* - braided

VALENFORD—town located in south Tysan, on the barge route at the River Valendale.

pronounced: va-len

root meaning: *valen* - braided

VALIEN—Vivet Daldari's son, born at Ettinmere Settlement in Third Age 5924.

pronounced: val-ee-en

root meaning: *val* – straight; *lien* – to love

VALLEYGAP—a narrow vale where the trade-road between Etarra and Werpoint notches the north end of the Skyshiel Mountains, and the site of Pesquil's death in Jieret Red-beard's devastating ambush when the Light's forces marched on campaign in Third Age 5645.

VASTMARK—principality located in south-western Shand. Highly mountainous and not served by trade-roads. Its coasts are renowned for shipwrecks. Inhabited by nomadic shepherds and wyverns, non-fire-breathing, smaller relatives of Khadrim. Site of the grand massacre of Lysaer's war host in Third Age 5647.

pronounced: vast-mark

root meaning: *vhast* – bare; *mheark* – valley

VERRAIN—master spellbinder, trained by Luhaine; stood as Guardian of Mirthlvain when the Fellowship of Seven was left short-handed after the conquest of the Mistwraith.

pronounced: ver-rain

root meaning: *ver* – keep; *ria* – touch; *an* – one original Paravian: *verria'an*

VHALZEIN—town located in West Shand, shore of Rockbay Harbour, near the border of Havish, famed for black lacquer and mother-of-pearl-inlaid furniture.

pronounced: val-zeen

root meaning: from Drakish, *vhchalzckeen* – white sands

VICIENNA—Princess of West Shand, wept for the fallen when the first cordon restraining Desh-thiere was broken in West Shand.

Pronounced: vee-see-an-a

Root meaning: *vie* – tame; *cian* – spark; *a* – female diminutive

VIVET DALDARI—a young woman from Ettinmere Settlement who ran away from home at the age of fourteen years, seeking her fortune and the opportunity to learn to read.

pronounced: vee-vet dahl-dar-ee

root meaning: *vivet* – bait; *dal* – fair; *diere* – life

WASP—a trade galleass, chartered for moving cargo on the southcoast.

WARDEN OF ALTHAIN—alternative title for the Fellowship Sorcerer, Sethvir, who received custody of Althain Tower and the powers of the earth-link from the last centaur guardian to leave the continent of Paravia in Third Age 5100. Prior to then, the titled post was held by a Paravian.

WAYSTONE—spherical-cut amethyst used by the Koriathain to channel the full power of all enchantresses in their order, lost during the great rebellion that threw down the rule of the High Kings, and recovered from Fellowship custody by Lirenda in Third Age 5647. Cleared and re-mapped, after Arithon's arranged sabotage, which infiltrated a stray *iyat* into the stone's matrix in 5671.

WEST HALLA—principality located in Melhalla.

Pronounced: hall-ah

Root meaning: *hal'lia* – white light

WESTLANDS—originally a term for the western kingdoms of Tysan, Havish, and West Shand. Evolved to mean a specific set of mannered customs mostly practised in Tysan after the great uprising that threw down the High Kings in Third Age 5015.

WEST SHAND—An adjunct territory including the free wilds of Falwood, once left exclusively to the Paravians in the Third Age, and protected from Mankind's encroachment by Shand's Heir Apparent. Annexed to the High Kingship of Shand, after the old races formally abdicated in Third Age 5100. pronounced: rhymes with "hand"

root meaning: *shayn* or *shiand* – pair or partner

WHITEHAVEN—hostel of Ath's Adepts, located in the Skyshiel Mountains, near Eastwall, Rathain, where Elaira received advanced training as a healer, outside of Koriani precepts.

WHITEHOLD—city located on the shore of Eltair Bay in East Halla, Melhalla.

WILLOWBROOK—A small stream located in Halwythwood, Rathain, site of Arithon and Elaira's tryst that incited a grand confluence in Third Age 5671.

WORLDSEND GATES—four energetic portals leading offworld, located on the continent of Paravia, one at each compass point. Constructed by the Fellowship Sorcerers early in the Third Age, functionally tied into establishment of the Compact.